A SALUTE A

RED PHOENIX

"The warfare is realistic and complete, covering the fighting on the ground, in the air and at sea."

—*Milwaukee Sentinel*

* * *

"Bond clearly understands the politics on the Korean subcontinent, and in the precincts of official Washington."

—*Baltimore Sun*

* * *

"A rip-roaring, modern war story."

—*Denver Rocky Mountain News*

* * *

"From its first pages to its surprise ending, *Red Phoenix* advances an alarming, frighteningly real story.... Making his solo debut, he sets a new standard for the techno-thriller."

—*Orlando Sentinel*

* * *

"*Red Phoenix* is fast-paced, action-packed and a terrific read.... Bond is not overly enamored with high-tech, and the weapons that fight the war are current front-line weapons, giving the story a sense of realism."

—*Journal*, Flint, Michigan

* * *

"Tightly plotted...well-conceived.... *Red Phoenix* should be atop your reading list."

—*Arkansas Democrat*

RED PHOENIX

A NOVEL

LARRY BOND

WARNER BOOKS

A Warner Communications Company

WARNER BOOKS EDITION

Copyright © 1989 by Larry Bond and Patrick Larkin

Cover design by Jackie Merri Meyer
Cover art by Peter Thorpe

Warner Books, Inc.
666 Fifth Avenue
New York, N.Y. 10103

 A Warner Communications Company

Printed in the United States of America

This book was originally published in hardcover by Warner Books.
First Printed in Paperback: May, 1990

10 9 8 7 6 5 4 3 2 1

ACKNOWLEDGMENTS

We would like to thank John Austin, Jim Baker, Sam Baker, Russ and Jano Blanchard, Jay Borland, Chris Carlson, Jackie Conlon, Dwinn Craig, Tom Fagedes, John Goetke, Jim De Goey, John Gresham, Jason Hunter, Louis Lambros, Daphne Marselas, Frances Mills, Gary "Mo" Morgan, Alan Morris, Bill Paley, Penny Peak, Tim Peckinpaugh, Jeff Pluhar, Pat Slocomb, Thomas T. Thomas, Chris Williams, Paula Bessex and Joy Schumack of the Solano County Bookmobile Service, the staff at *Fighter Weapons Review,* Digital Illusions and their game Falcon, and the 68th Tactical Fighter Squadron at Moody AFB.

All of them made the book better.

AUTHOR'S NOTE

They say collaboration is the hardest form of writing. Trying to get two people to agree on everything for the year it takes to produce a manuscript should be next to impossible. Happily, it is not only possible, but fun.

Patrick Larkin and I wrote this book together, working side by side over the phone and by computer—all despite being physically separated by 2,500 miles. He not only produced his share of the story but offered counsel and advice in my portions as well.

Together, Pat and I pulled this book forward from the faint glimmerings of a rough idea and a possible plot, and I cannot conceive of tackling this work without him. It is his book as much as mine, and he deserves at least as much credit.

Korean cosmology assigns a separate season and divinity to each of the four cardinal points of the compass:

The **East** is associated with Spring and the Azure Dragon,

The **North** with Winter and the Divine Warriors,

The **West** with Autumn and the White Tiger,

And the **South** with Summer and the Red Phoenix.

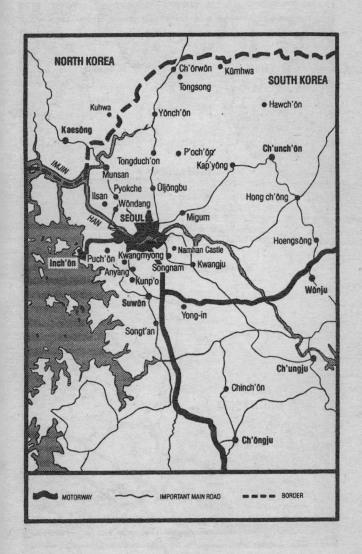

NORTH KOREA

SOUTH KOREA

Ch'ŏrwŏn

Kŭmhwa

Tongsong

Kuhwa

Yŏnch'ŏn

Hawch'ŏn

Kaesŏng

IMJIN

Tongduch'on

P'och'ŏn

Ch'unch'ŏn

Munsan

Kap'yŏng

Ilsan

Pyokche

Ŭijŏngbu

Hong ch'ŏng

Wŏndang

HAN

SEOUL

Migum

Hoengsŏng

Inch'ŏn

Puch'ŏn

Kwangmyong

Namhan Castle

Anyang

Songnam

Kwangju

Wŏnju

Kunp'o

Suwŏn

Yong-in

Songt'an

Ch'ungju

Chinch'ŏn

Ch'ŏngju

— MOTORWAY   — IMPORTANT MAIN ROAD   - - - - BORDER

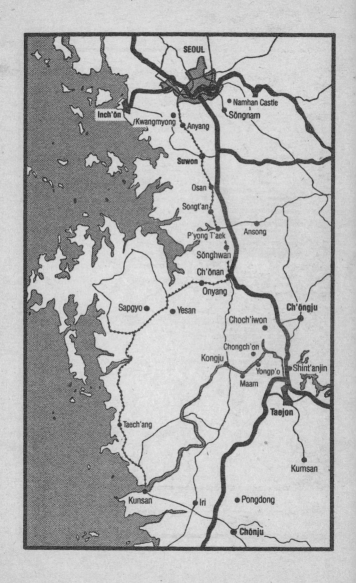

DRAMATIS PERSONAE

AMERICANS:

Paul Bannerman—The U.S. secretary of state.

Congressman Ben Barnes—Democrat of Michigan, chairman of the House Subcommittee on Trade.

Admiral Thomas Aldrige Brown—Commander of Task Force 71, the U.S. Navy's senior officer in the Korean theater.

Captain Marc Chadwick—A U.S. Army intelligence officer stationed in South Korea.

Captain Tony "Saint" Christopher—An Air Force F-16 pilot assigned to the 35th Tactical Fighter Squadron, 8th Tactical Fighter Wing, based at Kunsan, South Korea.

Major Colin Donaldson—Executive officer, 1st Battalion of the 39th Infantry Regiment, 3rd Brigade, 2nd Infantry Division. Stationed at Camp Howze, near Tongduch'on, South Korea.

Dr. Blake Fowler—A staffer on the National Security Council, Washington, D.C.

First Lieutenant John "Hooter" Gresham—An Air Force pilot assigned to the 35th Tactical Fighter Squadron, 8th Tactical Fighter Wing, based at Kunsan, South Korea. He is Captain Tony Christopher's wingman.

Captain Doug Hansen—Military aide to General McLaren.

Captain J. F. Hutchins—Administrative assistant to 2nd Division civil affairs officer, assigned to command a provisional infantry company.

Anne Larson—An Army civilian employee and computer expert working as supervisor of the logistics programming section at the U.S. Army's Yongsan Base in Seoul, South Korea.

Captain Richard Levi, USN—Commander of the Spruance-class destroyer USS *O'Brien*.

Second Lieutenant Kevin Little—An ROTC graduate assigned to South Korea. Platoon leader of 2nd Platoon, A Company, 1st Infantry Battalion of the 39th Infantry Regiment.

General John Duncan McLaren—Commander Combined Forces, Korea. Commands all U.S. and South Korean forces.

Captain Matuchek—Commanding officer, A Company, 1st Battalion of the 39th Infantry Regiment.

Jeremy Mitchell—Administrative assistant to Congressman Ben Barnes.

Corporal Jaime Montoya—Radioman assigned to the provisional company commanded by Second Lieutenant Kevin Little.

Sergeant Harry Pierce—Platoon sergeant, 2nd Platoon, A Company, 1st Battalion of the 39th Infantry Regiment.

George Putnam—The President's National Security Adviser.

Admiral Philip Simpson—Chairman of the U.S. Joint Chiefs of Staff.

SOUTH KOREANS:

General Chang Jae-Kyu—A South Korean Army officer commanding the 4th Infantry Division.

Major Chon Sang-Du—An A-10 pilot in the South Korean Air Force.

Captain Lee—A South Korean combat engineering officer.

General Park—Chairman of the South Korean Joint Chiefs of Staff.

Second Lieutenant Rhee Han-Gil—A South Korean Army officer assigned as liaison officer to 2nd Platoon, A Company, 1st Battalion of the 39th Infantry Regiment.

NORTH KOREANS:

Captain Chae Ku-Ho—1st Company, II Battalion, 91st Infantry Regiment.

Lieutenant General Cho Hyun-Jae—Originally assigned as commander of the North Korean II Corps, later promoted to Colonel General and command of the First Shock Army.

Senior Captain Chun Chae-Yun—The captain of DPRK *Great Leader*, a North Korean Kilo-class diesel submarine.

Major General Chyong Dal-Joong—Cho's deputy commander, later promoted to Lieutenant General and command of the II Corps.

Lieutenant Sohn—Platoon Leader, Assault Group 2, 1st Battalion, 27th Infantry Regiment.

Kim Il-Sung—General Secretary of the Korean Workers Party, President of the Democratic People's Republic of Korea, commander in chief of the armed forces. Called the Great Leader, Kim Il-Sung is the aging and infirm absolute ruler of North Korea.

Kim Jong-Il—Called the Dear Leader, Kim Jong-Il is the son and heir apparent to Kim Il-Sung, the Great Leader.

RUSSIANS:

Colonel Sergei Ivanovitch Borodin—A Soviet MiG-29 pilot heading up a training team in North Korea.

Captain Nikolai Mikhailovitch Markov—Captain of the Soviet Tango-class submarine *Konstantin Dribinov.*

Andrei Ivanovich Rychagov—Member of the Soviet Politburo and defense minister.

PROLOGUE

AUGUST 19—SOUTH OF THE DMZ NEAR HAKKOK, SOUTH KOREA

They found the North Korean tunnel shortly before dawn.

The two men—one an American intelligence officer, the other a South Korean combat engineer—stood regarding a three-inch-wide borehole as they might an ancient oracle, one that had given them good news.

Captain Marc Chadwick knelt and ran his fingertips around the edge of hole Five-A, feeling the damp, smooth rock. "Look at that pattern. Almost circular. We're right over the bastards."

His Korean counterpart, Captain Lee, nodded. "Almost certainly. Five-B and Five-D also indicate this location."

Both men smiled, feeling the excitement of a long hunt now nearing the kill.

Hole Five-A didn't look like much. Just a water-filled hole that went straight down through ten meters of solid rock. But it served as a detector for underground vibrations, like the ones made by North Korean engineers blasting tunnels under the Demilitarized Zone—the DMZ—and into South Korea. Explosive charges laid to carve out a new tunnel sent shock waves rippling through the rock—shock waves that slopped water out of the closest boreholes. Not much. Usually not more than an inch or two. But a good engineer could tell a lot from that, and Captain Lee was a good engineer.

Lee turned and looked north toward a small rise that blocked their view of the DMZ less than a kilometer away. He shook his head. The North Koreans had pushed this tunnel more than two kilometers from their side of the line before they'd been detected. It passed right under the Allied fortifications built along the DMZ, and the North Koreans could have used it to infiltrate spies and raiding parties into the South, or perhaps even for large-scale troop movements should war break out. Lee scowled. The communists were getting too good at this game for his taste.

He glanced east. The sun was coming up, spilling light over a brown, barren landscape blasted by summer heat and dry weather. The South Korean engineer mentally ran over the amount of work that would be required, pursed his lips, and said, "If I have my men start now, we should be able to break in by midday."

The American nodded and the two men studied the borehole in silence for a moment longer before turning away back down the valley toward their waiting jeep.

Captain Lee's estimates were, like everything else about him, precise.

Chadwick noticed the silence first. For six hours since daybreak the valley had been filled with a high-pitched, grinding whine as South Korean drills ripped their way into the ground, opening a path for the explosives that would break through into the suspected North Korean tunnel. He'd watched avidly for a time, but his interest had waned as the sun rose higher and the temperature climbed, and he'd finally retreated to a shadowed truck cab.

Now the drills had stopped. Chadwick sat up suddenly and pulled the latest issue of *Stars and Stripes* off his face. He stared through the windshield as combat engineers unreeled thin detonator wire from the enlarged borehole to a sheltered spot near where the trucks were parked. After a moment Lee stood and gave him a thumbs-up signal. The charges were in place and wired to go. He clambered out of the truck cab and ambled over to where Lee lay waiting with his noncoms.

The Korean grinned up at him and gestured to the plunger. "Care to try your hand?"

"Nope. You blow things up. I just take pictures of 'em. Before and after."

Lee chuckled, motioned him to the ground, and then pushed the plunger. Borehole Five-A erupted in a fiery pillar of smoke and thrown rock debris. A muffled roar rumbled through the valley and shook the earth.

Lee and his troops were up and running toward the hole before the dust even settled. Their explosives had torn open a jagged crater, three feet across at its narrowest point. Most importantly, it did not seem to have a bottom. Shining a powerful light straight down revealed only a circle of darkness. They were in.

Lee took an old Korean War–vintage M3 submachine gun—a "grease gun"—from his sergeant and slung it across his back. He looked at Chadwick. "I'm claiming the honor of going down first. Care to accompany me?"

The sweat stains under Chadwick's arms suddenly felt ice cold, but he shrugged and asked, "Do we get to use a rope?"

Lee grinned. "Naturally. Only Marines are forbidden to use ropes, Captain."

"Terrific." Chadwick checked the clip on his regulation-issue 9mm pistol. He didn't like this commando stuff. What if the bad guys were waiting down there for the first flies to drop into their parlor? Desk jockeys like him were supposed to analyze North Korea's tunnels, not invade them. But he couldn't think of any graceful way to back out, and he'd be damned if he'd let Lee see that he was scared. He and the engineer had been partners now for months and they'd made a good team. Chadwick didn't think that would stay true if he chickened out now.

He watched while Lee stepped to the edge of the hole, clipped a line onto his belt, and signaled his men to lower away. The South Korean dangled momentarily and then disappeared through the narrow opening, looking intently downward.

Moments later, Lee called up for them to stop. The end of the line came back up, and Chadwick stepped to the edge.

They lowered him slowly past the jagged sides of the hole that kept threatening to snag his battle dress and then on down into the darkness. He swallowed hard and tried to concentrate on mentally recording what he was seeing. It was the best way he knew to push away the fears his subconscious kept raising.

For the first fifteen meters the hole was nearly circular, but then the walls spread away, opening up like the lower half of an hourglass, and he was swinging in the air. Chadwick realized that the blasting must have caved in the roof of the tunnel. He looked down. Ten meters' worth of rock littered the floor below him.

He touched down on the uncertain footing and scrambled for a moment to get his balance. Something grabbed his arm and he jumped, feeling the adrenaline rush pulsing through his system. It was Lee, steadying him.

"Jesus Christ!" he whispered. "You scared the crap out of me."

"Sorry."

Lee let go and stepped back, swinging his light around in an arc to cover the tunnel in front of them. They had broken through the roof near the end of the tunnel, but well over to one side. The passageway itself ran north-south and was at least thirteen meters wide, big enough for a three-lane road. Away from the area currently under construction, the floors, walls, and ceiling had all been smoothed. There were lamps mounted overhead. They weren't lit though, and only Lee's flashlight and the sunlight pouring down through the explosives-torn shaft provided illumination—looking much like eerie spotlights in the dusty air.

More men were swarming down the ropes now, some carrying weapons and others demolition gear. Chadwick whistled softly as he saw crate after crate of explosives being stockpiled off to the side. "How much will it take to destroy this underground freeway?"

Lee cocked his head, studying what he could make out of the tunnel through the darkness and still-swirling dust. "Perhaps as much as a thousand kilos of C4. It will take us most of the day to wire the charges. This could be the second largest 'freeway' we have ever found." He smiled wolfishly and shrugged. "Who knows? If we time it right, we may be able to catch the communists as they return to their work this evening."

While Lee's men lowered their equipment through the narrow opening to the surface, the two captains moved off down the tunnel, accompanied by seven M16-toting enlisted men. The engineers needed security while they worked, and Chadwick wanted to get a good look at everything before it was too late.

His nervousness had evaporated with the absence of opposition. Now he had a job to do.

"What's that on the wall?" The American stopped as his flashlight hit a painted line of Hangul characters.

Lee stepped closer. "It says that this is the 'Socialist Awareness' tunnel." The South Korean sounded both amused and disgusted at the same time.

"Well, it's the 'Socialist Awareness' tunnel for about six more hours. Then it's going to be the 'Socialist Collapsed Hole in the Ground.'" Chadwick raised his camera and snapped a picture of the nameplate.

They'd already come three hundred meters from the entrance without seeing much of anything. Just the smooth rock walls and floors, an occasional ventilation shaft, and now this painted sign. It looked peaceful, but every step brought them closer to North Korean territory.

A few meters farther on their flashlights picked out a row of dark, boxy forms blocking the passage in the distance. Heavy construction equipment? That didn't make sense. You didn't use bulldozers to build tunnels.

They picked up the pace a little, closing on the shapes. They walked another twenty steps or so and then Chadwick pulled up short. In a very soft voice he said, "Oh, shit. Captain Lee, tell me those aren't what I know they are."

His flashlight pointed up and outlined the rounded form of a tank turret, and another one next to it, and another one next to that. Three tanks, with their turrets pointed aft, in travel position, were parked abreast in the tunnel.

Lee whirled and shouted something to a private, who took off running. Chadwick understood just enough Korean to understand "colonel" and "more men." Smart move. Get the brass and get reinforcements. Nobody had ever found any equipment parked in a tunnel before. Son of a bitch. Excitedly he ran over to the left. He shined his flashlight down the passage between the tank and wall. Yep. There was another tank past this one, and one past that, and on until the light was lost in the darkness.

Chadwick stood and stared, drinking in every detail. A long-barreled 115mm main gun. One 7.62mm coaxial machine gun. A heavy machine gun mounted on the turret for use against aircraft and helicopters. An infrared searchlight mounted near the main gun. There couldn't be any doubt about it.

These were Soviet-model T-62A main battle tanks. And here they were sitting in a North Korean tunnel, inside South Korean territory.

A wild feeling of exultation swept over him. This was an intelligence officer's dream. He wanted to do a hundred things immediately and couldn't decide which to do first.

Steady, Marc, old boy. Deep breath. He inhaled and exhaled slowly, then looked at Lee. "Any chance we can open up that hole and get some of these guys out?"

"I am going to ask my colonel for permission to do that when he arrives. If we work fast, we should be able to make it. Some of the men in my company are qualified tracked vehicle crewmen."

Chadwick leapt up onto the vehicle deck and looked for the gas filler cap. He opened it, delighting in the action the way a child might delight in working a new toy. "Empty, naturally."

"We can have diesel fuel here in about forty-five minutes," Lee said. "Don't worry, Captain. It will take us several hours to drill and blast a ramp."

Chadwick was climbing all over one of the tanks, opening its hatches and peering inside, when two colonels—one an American and the other South Korean—arrived, followed by a panting squad of heavily laden riflemen. The opportunity was just too good to pass up, so he stood at attention on the deck, saluted, and grinned at the two senior officers. "It followed me home, sir. Can I keep it?"

The senior American liaison officer with the South Korean combat engineers, Colonel Miller, just shook his head. "Report, Captain." But Chadwick could see the ghost of a smile flit across Miller's face.

Chadwick jumped down and saluted again. "Sir, there's at least a battalion of armor parked in the tunnel. All T-62 tanks, parked three abreast. Standing up on the deck there, you can see them going back until the light runs out. They aren't fueled, but they do have main gun ammunition."

"All right. Get the men checking out the vehicles for documents and other portable intelligence. Don't forget external markings. I understand we may be able to recover some of these?"

"The engineers think so, sir," Chadwick said, nodding to

Lee. The Korean was heavily engaged with his colonel, who was nodding and smiling.

"Then let's get on with it. You and Captain Lee take your party down the tunnel and see what else is there. Take lots of pictures. Proceed no further than one-half klick, starting from this point. Consider this the line of departure, but don't start a war, Captain." The warning in the colonel's voice was real.

"Yessir." Chadwick waved over to Lee, who had just saluted his own departing colonel. It was the first time he'd ever seen a Korean field-grade officer move at anything except a dignified walk.

They moved forward slowly, an officer in front on each side, followed by three heavily armed enlisted men.

Chadwick looked at his watch. It was just two-thirty in the afternoon. Topside it was ninety-five degrees and climbing, but the tunnel was as cool as his basement back home. Their handheld flashlights provided the only source of light. The tunnel had taken many slight bends since they had entered, and more since the start of the equipment. Probably done to avoid difficult rock formations and to confuse anyone trying to plot the progress of the tunnel from above. In any event, no light would reach from either end, so he got into the habit of calling out "Photo" before he took a picture. That gave everyone a chance to cover their eyes and avoid the painful flash.

Lee concentrated on the tunnel itself, doing a hasty survey of distances and directions.

Chadwick counted tanks. There were thirty-one, the book strength of an armored battalion. Behind were trucks, jeeps, and all the other hardware. Someone with an orderly mind had put this stuff in here. He could almost predict what would come next.

What the hell was all this stuff doing down here in the first place? There'd always been speculation that the North Koreans intended some of their tunnels as more than just infiltration routes into the South. But this kind of confirmation was spectacular and completely unexpected. It did make a twisted kind of military sense, though. Stockpiling gear like this in advance would cut down the preparation time needed to launch a major attack across, or under, the DMZ, and it would lower the warning time available to U.S. and South Korean forces along the line. But how could the North Koreans have possibly thought this kind of gear could just lie here undetected, year in and year out, until it was needed? He filed the question away for further consideration later. There was just too much to do right now.

After the tanks the vehicles were only parked two abreast, leaving one lane open. Chadwick guessed that the fueling trucks were next, and he was rewarded by the sight of large, fat-bodied tankers designed to carry the diesel that T-62 tanks guzzled by the gallon. They marched along through the trucks, passed a row of towed 122mm field guns, and suddenly came out into just empty blackness. They stood facing north, looking into the tunnel, regarding the dark and wondering what else was there.

Lee spoke first. "I think we should continue on, Captain. We should find out what else is down here."

"How far have we come so far?"

"Only about five hundred meters more. It is at least another five hundred meters until we are under the border."

Chadwick felt his excitement fading a bit, allowing a dose of reality to creep back in. "Yeah, but we're under the DMZ now. Come on, Captain, we've captured a communist armored battalion without a shot being fired. Let's quit while we're ahead."

Torn between his orders, common sense, and curiosity, Lee stood still for a moment and then shrugged in resignation, "All right. Should we survey this equipment then?"

"Yeah. I'd like to have Corporal Rhee assign men to copying license plates and markings and stuff. You and I can start looking for the command tank. It's probably back toward the—"

A tremendous *BOOM* rolled down the tunnel followed by a *CLANG* from one of the nearby vehicles. For one microsecond Chadwick thought they had started blasting up the tunnel, but the clang didn't fit. Then the pieces fell together: a shot echoing from ahead of them and a bullet ricocheting off metal.

His hindbrain had his body moving even while he shouted, "Hostiles! Cover!" He dropped back behind the bulky tires of one of the towed artillery pieces. Without thinking, one hand switched the flashlight off, and the other drew his pistol. He didn't even know it was out until he tried to work the slide while still holding the flashlight.

Stay cool. Chadwick took a short breath, held it, and crouched back farther behind the tire. All the lights were out, except for one that had been dropped and had rolled into the open center of the tunnel, throwing strange, distorted shadows onto the smooth rock walls. Chadwick could still hear the echoes of that first shot bouncing down the tunnel.

Before it faded away entirely, a new burst of fire struck around the dropped flashlight. Bullets spanged off the floor and ricocheted into vehicles and the walls. One slammed a South Korean private onto his back in a widening pool of red-black blood. Another threw a man forward, his hands clutching vainly at a face that wasn't there anymore. The sixth or seventh shot hit the light and shattered it.

The tunnel plunged suddenly into an eerie, half-lit darkness. And in the silence Chadwick heard voices echoing from ahead. North Korean voices.

Flames stabbed out of the darkness, muzzle flashes growing larger as the North Koreans charged forward. They were firing from the hip, spraying rounds across the tunnel. Lee's men shot back, aiming at the flashes, and Chadwick saw bodies tossed crumpled to the rock floor as bullets caught them. But the attackers were still coming.

He flattened as a point-blank burst tore rubber fragments off the tire above him and whipcracked overhead. Jesus! The North Koreans were too damned close, and there were too damned many of them. He felt the fear clutching his guts, urging him to stand up and run. He fought the temptation. Running was the quickest way to get killed.

Something heavy thumped against the tire and Chadwick rolled away to the side. Still rolling, he saw a strange combat boot and looked up. A North Korean crouched there, bringing his AK-47 assault rifle up and around to fire. Oh, God. Chadwick's finger tightened convulsively on the trigger of his pistol. It roared once and then again and again as he squeezed off rounds without thinking.

Four. Five. No more, his brain screamed. Chadwick took his finger off the trigger and he looked at the twitching ruin his bullets had made. Two rounds had ripped into the North

Korean's stomach, eviscerating him. The third and fourth, climbing higher as the pistol bucked upward, had torn through the man's chest. The fifth and final round had blown a gaping hole in the North Korean's throat.

Chadwick felt his own stomach lurch and he swallowed hard against the sour taste of vomit. He'd never killed a man before and didn't like the feeling. He wormed backward behind another tire, away from the corpse.

Safe in cover again, he stared wide-eyed at the scene around him. Bodies littered the tunnel floor, some lying in twisted, bloodied heaps, others splayed against vehicles. None were moving. Chadwick felt his self-control returning.

His hearing was coming back, too. It was hard to tell, but the gunfire seemed quieter somehow. He shook his head, trying to clear the ringing in his ears, and listened more carefully. Then he risked a quick look around the tire and saw Lee on the other side of the tunnel, backlit by the muzzle flashes from his submachine gun. Nobody was shooting back.

Chadwick waited for a few seconds more to make sure and then bellycrawled over to where Lee crouched, staying low and hoping that the surviving South Koreans weren't firing completely blind.

He tugged on Lee's belt and pointed down the tunnel, yelling, "That's it! They're all dead or bugged out!" He had to repeat it twice to make himself understood above the din.

The South Korean engineer nodded, pulled a whistle out from around his neck, and blew three short blasts. Cease fire. Cease fire. The shooting died away and their hand-held flashlights came back on.

Lee shouted orders in Korean and walked warily with his men out into the open. M16s at the ready, they moved among the motionless bodies, checking for wounded. There weren't any. Four South Koreans were dead and nine North Koreans lay sprawled beside them. Blood trails showed where others had been dragged back into the pitch-dark tunnel.

Chadwick moved over to Lee, his pistol still in hand. He felt oddly calm, as if the firefight had happened to an entirely different person. "Captain, you and I both know that was just a patrol. But you can bet they'll be back any minute with the whole goddamned army."

"I agree. We must mine this equipment in place and destroy it. I'll send for thermite and explosives. We can wire everything in five minutes once it arrives."

Chadwick looked at the bullet holes ripped through one of the fuel trucks and then shook his head wearily. "Shit, I hope we've got that long."

Men started to pour down the sides of the tunnel from behind them. Three troopers came clattering up carrying a machine gun and ammunition. They flopped down to the floor about ten meters past the vehicles and started setting up. The machine gun had a large tube on top that Chadwick suddenly realized must be a night-sight. Jim-dandy. If the North Koreans came back, at least the MG would get the first shot.

He watched the engineers at work, marveling at the way they disregarded safety instructions and normal procedures. Cases of C4 were placed on the back of each vehicle and simultaneously wired. Thermite charges were scattered around, and a large number of cases were simply piled on the floor.

They worked as quietly as they could, but they had to use lights, and Chadwick knew what kind of target they must make.

They were still working when a sound like tearing canvas echoed down the tunnel. The machine gun team had opened up. Lee shouted something and the men started working even faster, not placing any new charges but wiring all the existing stuff to a single cord and running down the tunnel with it, back toward the opening. The machine gun's fire was being answered now, with single shots and short bursts of automatic fire.

Chadwick saw a round shape roll out of the blackness and dove for cover behind an empty, bullet-shredded fuel truck.

WHUMMP. The floor rocked as the North Korean grenade exploded, spraying fragments through the machine gun crew. The gunner screamed once and fell back dead. His two loaders lay badly wounded beside him, and the machine gun itself was a twisted wreck.

Then the carnage disappeared from view, cloaked by a wall of acrid, lung-searing smoke that now filled the tunnel— cutting visibility to just a few meters. Hundreds of rounds buzzed past and tumbled bouncing off the walls. It seemed impossible to move without being shot. Both sides were firing blind as fast as they could reload.

More South Korean troops arrived, hurdling the prone combat engineers still frantically placing and wiring charges. Several were hit in midstride and collapsed in a tangle of equipment. The rest flopped down behind whatever cover they could find—truck tires, empty explosives crates, or bodies— and opened up.

Chadwick stayed where he was and looked for Lee. The engineer squatted nearby, his face a mask of concentration as he wrapped wire around a lead. Lee finished tightening it and glanced up. He flashed a thumbs-up signal in Chadwick's direction and reached for another charge.

Something blared sharp above the gunfire, and Chadwick's mind rocked. A bugle. My God, he thought, the North Koreans are still using bugles. Suddenly he felt very close to his father, who'd told him about the human-wave attacks launched during the Korean War.

He clutched his pistol tighter.

WHUMMP! WHUMMP! WHUMMP! More grenades went off in rapid succession, thundering down the tunnel, showering the defenders with deadly fragments. More dust and smoke followed, turning everything into a hazy nightmare.

A squad of North Korean soldiers charged out of the smoke, urged on by their bugler. They were cut down by concentrated rifle fire, but there were others close behind them and the bugle kept blaring.

Chadwick heard screams and yells of defiance rising from the men around him. A burly South Korean sergeant rose from behind a truck, stood braced against the recoil, and emptied his M16's magazine into the oncoming North Koreans. Four of them were knocked backward, their bodies, faces, and limbs disintegrating as the bullets slammed home. But then the sergeant was down, chopped nearly in half by an AK burst.

Time blurred as the fighting moved to close quarters.

Chadwick saw a North Korean run past, helmeted head down, pounding straight toward the engineers still working. He aimed quickly and fired twice. The soldier staggered and then slid dead to the tunnel floor.

He spun round as another came from the side, assault rifle

swinging high to smash his skull. Chadwick dodged right and felt the rifle butt hammer his left arm. He gasped at the pain and fired once into the man's stomach. The North Korean folded in on himself in agony and collapsed.

Chadwick sank to his knees cradling his left arm. It felt on fire.

"Captain Chadwick!"

He looked up in a daze. There were bodies everywhere in sight, sprawled like torn rag dolls across the tunnel. Lee motioned to him again. They were leaving. Several soldiers were still firing into the haze, trying to pin the North Koreans down, but the others were backing away—hauling their wounded with them and staying low.

Chadwick scuttled over to the South Korean engineer. "You done?" The smoke hanging in the air burned his throat.

Lee nodded vigorously. "Everything is wired." He jerked a thumb south toward the exit. "I suggest that we get out of here while we still can!"

The bugle shrilled again from down the tunnel.

Shit. The harsh rattle of AK-47 fire grew louder, and new shapes appeared out of the haze. Another North Korean attack. One of Lee's men turned to yell a warning and pitched backward, shot directly between the eyes.

Chadwick grabbed the dead man's M16 and fired a burst down the tunnel, wincing as the recoil jarred his left arm. One of the North Koreans dropped in a spray of blood. The others scattered, seeking cover.

"Come on, Captain! This is no time for heroics!" Lee put a hand on his shoulder and pulled him away. A bullet cracked past his face, bringing him back to his senses. The engineer was right. It was past time to leave.

Together with the other rearguard troops, they turned and headed down the tunnel—moving as fast as they could without unnecessarily exposing themselves to enemy fire. The bugle continued to sound behind them.

They reached the first row of T-62s before the North Koreans realized they were going. Rounds started to slam into the vehicles and the rock around them. Jesus. Chadwick and the others all broke into a flat-out run. Something tugged at his sleeve and he saw the man running in front of him fall, a stain spreading across his battle dress.

He reached down and grabbed the South Korean's arm, trying to drag him to his feet. He couldn't do it.

"Leave him! He's finished!" Lee screamed in his ear over the gunfire and pulled him onward. Chadwick obeyed.

They ran on, letting the fear they were feeling flow into their legs.

Harsh cries and the slap of running feet echoed down the tunnel from behind them.

Panting, they rounded the last bend and saw sunlight from the opening in the roof along with something even more welcome—two rope ladders dangling, waiting for them. Chadwick didn't even break stride. He hit the ladder four feet up and started climbing. The pain in his arm suddenly didn't matter at all. The troops waiting above exhorted them on, while Lee's sergeant marked their progress from a detonator box.

As soon as their shoulders cleared the opening, they were grabbed by a man on each side and half-dragged away from the hole. When they were well away, the sergeant screamed a warning in Korean and pressed the plunger.

It wasn't a very neat explosion. First, only a small, muffled boom, then a thundering roar, then a series of several teeth-rattling *THUDS*. The rippling lasted for a few seconds, and then a shock wave too loud to be called a sound slammed them into the ground. Flame, smoke, and shattered rock toppled away from the hole in slow motion as the ground subsided into a shallow, crooked gully leading north. The tunnel had collapsed.

Chadwick decided he really didn't need to get up right away, and he looked over at the rest of the men, who were in various stages of befuddlement. Lee shook his head like a punch-drunk prizefighter and lay panting on the ground.

After a while Chadwick levered himself to his feet and walked over to stare at the man-made gully that had become the graveyard of an entire North Korean armored battalion and its security detachment. He stayed motionless for several minutes and only gradually became aware that Captain Lee had joined him.

Lee smiled wanly through the dust that caked his face and

uniform. "You see, we were able to catch those communists after all."

Chadwick looked at him for a moment and then turned back toward the collapsed tunnel. "Yeah. We caught 'em all right." Then he swung around to stare into the Korean engineer's eyes. "But doing what?"

He looked down at the ground, as if he could read the enemy's intentions by scrutinizing the bare, weathered rocks and the sun-browned grass. But any answers they held were buried as deeply as the crushed remains of the North Korean tanks.

What the hell was going on?

C H A P T E R
1
Ignition

The anchorman looked earnestly into the cameras, seemingly wide-awake despite the early morning hour.

"In North Korea's first official reaction to the US/South Korean discovery of a tunnel filled with military hardware, radio Pyongyang today dismissed the find as, quote, an absurd forgery, a despicable and desperate lie fomented by the militarist clique occupying Seoul, end quote."

The anchorman, his unruly shock of brown hair, Italian-made suit, and the gleaming, high-tech anchor desk in Atlanta all vanished, replaced by stock-footage shots of the barbed-wire tangle and barren hills marking the DMZ.

"And at this morning's meeting at Panmunjom, the North flatly rejected the UN Armistice Commission's demand for both an explanation and reparations for the South Korean soldiers killed or wounded in the border clash. UN negotiators said they were prepared to press their claims against the North for as long as necessary."

The camera cut away to footage from Seoul showing streets around the National University filled with chanting students, impassive riot police, lobbed gasoline bombs, and tear gas volleys.

"In other news from Korea, radical students opened a new protest season against the government by hurling rocks and firebombs at police. They were met with tear gas and water cannon. More than ten demonstrators and police were injured in the two-hour clash. Student leaders vowed to continue their

17

pressure on the government until South Korea's National Assembly met their demand for a new presidential election and meaningful moves toward peaceful reunification with the North.''

The images of street violence dissolved back to a close-up of the anchorman in Atlanta.

"Meanwhile, here at home, police in California announced they were close to cracking the mysterious string of murders attributed to the so-called Bayside Butcher . . ."

AUGUST 25—PYONGYANG, NORTH KOREA

One hundred and fifty kilometers north of the DMZ, the capital of the communist Democratic People's Republic of Korea lay sweltering under a merciless afternoon sun. Like all artificial creations, Pyongyang's every aspect reflected its builders' innermost beliefs and priorities.

The city was an amalgamation of endless rows of drab, look-alike apartment towers, broad but empty boulevards, idealized, larger-than-life statuary, and massive, colonnaded government buildings. Propaganda banners flew from every gray, slab-sided building, exhorting passersby to "Strive Harder for the Fatherland," reminding them that "Work Is the Sacred Duty and Honor of Citizens," and calling them to "Self-reliance Through Collective Action." Loudspeakers at every major intersection repeated an unending, mind-numbing litany of praise for the North's Great Leader, Kim Il-Sung, and his son, Kim Jong-Il, the Dear Leader. In its dismal entirety, Pyongyang sat between its twin rivers as a reinforced concrete monument to the insignificance of the individual and the overwhelming power of the State.

Those few men and women outside braving the heat were sober and serious in dress and in demeanor. Only the required pin or button bearing Kim Il-Sung's portrait added any touch of bright color to their garb. Despite the glaring sun, they moved briskly from place to place, careful never to show undue curiosity and never to seem idle. The Democratic People's Republic was a workers' state and its people were expected to work. There were reeducation and labor camps aplenty for those who could not or would not learn that.

The nerve center of this sterile, humorless city sat at the end of a wide, empty avenue—a towering edifice of gray stone and grayer concrete, more a fortress than an office building. Squads of fully armed security troops stood at rigid attention to either side of the main entrance. They seemed antlike below sixty-meter-high banners bearing the likenesses of Kim Il-Sung and Kim Jong-Il.

Inside, the thousands of clerks, petty Party functionaries, and uniformed security officers who inhabited the complex moved quietly about their daily routines. Telephones were answered, documents were typed, reports were filed—all in an unearthly hush. There were good reasons for that. Open displays of emotion were regarded as unproductive and suspect, and supposed friends could easily become bitter rivals, always on the prowl for an indiscretion, a traitorous whisper, or the slightest sign of disloyalty to the State and its Great Leader. Silence was often the key to survival in the echoing, labyrinthine corridors of the headquarters of the Korean Workers Party.

Only one man of all those thousands could speak freely and without fear.

AUGUST 25—PARTY HEADQUARTERS, PYONGYANG, NORTH KOREA

Kim Jong-Il, the son of North Korea's supreme ruler, glowered at the thin, gray-haired army officer standing rigidly at attention before him. Light from a small desktop lamp bounced off Kim's thick, black-frame glasses and highlighted small droplets of sweat beading the officer's forehead.

"I hold you personally responsible for this fiasco," Kim continued, pausing to emphasize each damning word. "Your stupidity led you to stockpile important equipment in the tunnel too soon. Your incompetence allowed the imperialists to find it. And your cowardice allowed them to seize it."

The man started to gabble something, but Kim cut him off. "Silence!" He wiped a trace of spittle off his lips. "You have failed the State and endangered our historic plan. I will not listen to your excuses."

He leaned forward over his desk. "You came into this room as a colonel, comrade. You will leave it as a lieutenant. A lieutenant in charge of a penal platoon."

Kim smiled thinly as the officer's face crumpled. He had just destroyed a thirty-year career. "You are dismissed. Now get out of my sight."

He watched silently as his bodyguards led the man out of his office. Truly, no drug could possibly match the exhilaration that swept through him whenever he used his power as the Great Leader's son and designated heir.

But slowly, very slowly, the exhilaration slipped away, replaced by a growing sense of frustration. The tunnel the Americans had stumbled across was only one of many that were being dug at his orders, but its discovery would make them more alert, more careful. As a result, work on the other tunnels would have to be stopped—at least until the Americans and their South Korean puppets had again been lulled into a false sense of security. Kim Jong-Il could feel his carefully laid plans slipping once more into the distant future, and that was something he was unwilling to contemplate. He had always been impatient.

History was slipping away from him—out of his grasp. Every passing day made the South stronger militarily and economically. Every day increased the growing gap between the two halves of Korea. Every day brought with it the chance that his father might die without securing Kim's succession to the leadership.

Kim gripped the arms of his chair. He knew only too well that there were many in North Korea's government who would cast him aside if they could. Some were jealous of his power. Some called themselves "true communists" and claimed they opposed a dynastic succession. Others held grudges for imagined wrongs.

But so long as Kim Il-Sung lived, his son's enemies were powerless to move against him. More than forty years of absolute rule had enabled the elder Kim to build a nation shaped in his own image and governed by his slightest whim. Kim Jong-Il knew that kind of power could not be inherited, it could only be earned—forged over time his enemies would not give him, or forged in the fires of a war, a common struggle against the hated American enemy.

His own enemies inside the government had already tried to move against him once. Kim felt a small chill as he remembered the bomb planted aboard his father's personal train. A bomb planted by officers loyal to General Oh Chin-U, the then defense minister and leader of the pro-Chinese faction inside North Korea. The assassination attempt had failed, and the known conspirators were either filling unmarked graves outside Pyongyang or slaving away in special camps. Its aftershocks, however, were still rippling through the Party, the Army, and the Foreign Ministry.

Kim Jong-Il smiled thinly to himself. Not all the effects had been bad. He'd used China's suspected involvement in the bomb plot to persuade his father to side more closely with the Soviets. That had been an essential move. Only the Soviets had the kind of advanced weapons the People's Army needed to match the Americans and their Southern puppets. But Kim held no illusions about the motives of his Russian backers—they didn't believe in charity. They believed in power.

And every high-tech weapons system the Soviet Union gave or sold the North increased its hold over Pyongyang. At some point it would be too late to go back. He and his father would have sold their precious self-reliance for radar-guided missiles, modern battle tanks, and advanced submarines.

Kim Jong-Il shook his head. He knew the risks well. After all, what was life but a succession of risks—some greater and some smaller? Better to view the game as a race. A race between Soviet domination and military strength. A race between his plans for the war that would secure his position and an assassin's bullet or his father's failing health.

And now one incompetent officer had threatened all the preparations for that war. The fool. He should have had the man shot. Kim twisted uncomfortably in his chair.

There had to be something he could use to distract the attention of the imperialists. Something that would cause trouble for their lackeys in Seoul. Something that would drive a wedge between them.

He picked up his phone and started calling for files. He would work until he found what he was looking for.

It was well past dawn before he found it.

AUGUST 29—PARTY HEADQUARTERS, PYONGYANG, NORTH KOREA

Kang Hyun-chan sat carefully in the high-backed leather chair, bald head erect and deep black eyes fixed rigidly on an unseen point in space. The long, curiously effeminate fingers of his age-spotted hands rested unmoving on gray, peasant-style cotton trousers. Beneath his fingertips Kang could feel the damning evidence of his seventy years—his stick-thin, withered legs. Legs that had once been strong and wiry enough to carry him up and down Manchuria's rugged hills during his days as an anti-Japanese guerrilla. He smiled wryly. He'd fought for the Party all his adult life, first as a soldier, then as a spy, and finally, as a master of spies. And none of that mattered. Not now. Not here.

He had been ushered into this immaculately furnished office by an unsmiling bodyguard, ordered to sit down, and left waiting for nearly half an hour. He could hear water running in the small, adjoining washroom.

Kang recognized the game that was being played. He'd played it often enough himself during forty-odd years of service as a member of the Central Committee's Research Department. The silence, the uncertainty, the long, gnawing wait. All designed to unnerve the subordinate on whom disfavor had fallen, or was about to fall.

His predecessor as director of the Southern Operations Section must have had a similar meeting before he'd been "retired" to special work farm. For a moment Kang felt a surge of anger at the unfairness of it all. His predecessor had blundered badly, and his blunders had embarrassed the State. But he had done nothing wrong. He'd heard the rumors of Kim's rage over the tunnel catastrophe, but that wasn't in his area of responsibility. Why this meeting then?

With difficulty he pushed the anger away. It wouldn't help him in the next few minutes, and it might make things worse. Kang had always been something of a fatalist. The position he'd attained carried great rewards, and with great rewards came commensurate risks. It was the way of things, and no amount of carping or whining would change it.

"My dear Kang, how good it is to see you! And looking so well!" Kim Jong-Il, the plump, cherub-faced son of the Great Leader, Kim Il-Sung, bustled out of the washroom smiling from ear to ear.

Kang was astonished. This pleasant greeting was not at all what he had expected. He stood hastily and bowed to the man known throughout North Korea as the Dear Leader.

Kim moved around his desk and waved Kang down into his chair. "Sit! Sit! My dear Kang, this is no time for formality. This is a working meeting. A meeting of two old friends and comrades who've worked hard to preserve our Revolution, eh?"

Kang sat slowly, thinking fast. What did the man want? Aloud he said carefully, "Dear Leader, I am honored by your kind welcome."

Kim settled himself ponderously in his own chair. He'd inherited his father's stocky build, but unlike his father, he'd never been forced by trying circumstances to forgo the delicacies that could add pounds.

Kang found the contrast between the North's wiry, undernourished farmers and this bloated man who would one day rule them interesting. But he was careful to leave the thought there. Irony could be a swift road to oblivion in the Democratic People's Republic of Korea—especially for a man in Kang's position.

"Tell me, Comrade Kang, you've been following recent events in the South?"

"Yes, Dear Leader." What did the man think that he did all day? Read film magazines?

"Excellent. Then tell me, Comrade, how you would analyze these events. Specifically, these massive student protests in Seoul." Kim folded his hands over his stomach and rocked back in his chair.

Kang couldn't read anything in the man's expression. He took refuge in the time-worn language used in official propaganda and shrugged. "It is the old story, Dear Leader. The summer Olympics and orchestrated elections bought the Seoul regime a small measure of peace, but the progressive elements are once again trying to pressure the imperialist-controlled puppet government for significant reforms."

"And their chances of success?"

Kang shook his head. "Nonexistent. Uncoordinated street

protests are of little use against an entrenched fascist occupation." What was the man driving at?

Kim Jong-Il sat forward in his chair. "Why then are we not doing more to assist these progressives in their cause? Surely you see these demonstrations as an opportunity. As a chance to bring these students into a united front against the American oppressors and their lackeys."

Oh, oh. Kang wondered which of his rivals had been filling Kim's head with such nonsense. Too many carefully placed agents had already been "blown" in futile, wasted efforts to control South Korea's seasonal student protests. He'd better squelch this dangerous line of thought while he had the chance. "Naturally such a development would be welcome indeed. Unfortunately, most of these students have not reached the proper level of revolutionary consciousness. They want reunification with us, but they've been unwilling to accept the discipline needed to make that happen. As a result, several of our best networks were compromised during the last round of demonstrations. The benefits do not yet outweigh the costs, Dear Leader."

Kim's smile faded into an impassive, unreadable expression, and Kang thought it best to temporize. "Naturally, we continue to reevaluate each opportunity as it arises."

Kim's smile came back. "I am delighted to hear that, comrade. I have always known you to be a man of great sense." He gestured airily. "But of course I shall accept your advice on this matter as the last word. We'll leave these Southern students to their own devices."

Kang dipped his head in gratitude. It was a rare thing to be able to so easily persuade the Dear Leader to abandon a pet proposal—even one so cautiously advanced.

"Tell me, how is the Scorpion Project proceeding?"

For a moment the rapid change of subject took Kang by surprise. He looked at Kim carefully. This must be what he had really been summoned to discuss. The talk of aiding South Korea's rioting students had been a blind, a way to ease into something much more important to Kang and to the Research Department—the Scorpion Project.

In a way the Scorpion Project was Kang's special pride and

joy. It had occupied him for most of his career, and in fact, it had carried him to the upper echelons of the Research Department.

Scorpion was an agent—a deep-cover agent planted in South Korea in 1950, during the confusion caused by the North Korean invasion. Beria, Stalin's feared KGB chieftain, had first suggested it to Kim Il-Sung as an insurance policy against military failure. He believed that it should prove comparatively simple to build an airtight "legend" or cover for such an agent amid the ongoing devastation, slaughter, and chaos.

He had been right. The man known by the code name Scorpion had been recruited, carefully trained and indoctrinated, and then sent south through the enemy lines—armed only with the identity of an anticommunist long since dead in a North Korean prison camp. Surviving members of the real man's family had been rounded up and liquidated to ensure absolute security. No one was left alive to dispute Scorpion's authenticity.

In the nearly forty years since, the agent Scorpion had risen steadily through the ranks of South Korea's bureaucracy. And Kang had been his controller since the 1960s.

"Scorpion goes well, Dear Leader. Our man has attained a high position in the fascist internal security force."

Kim interrupted him. "Excellent, Comrade Kang. Perfect in fact. Then he is ideally placed to carry out the task I have in mind."

SEPTEMBER 6—THE MINISTRY OF HOME AFFAIRS, SEOUL, SOUTH KOREA

The man known as Scorpion in North Korea stood by his office window. From there he could see faint, whitish-gray wisps of tear gas rising above the city skyline. Another student protest that had turned into a riot. Good. It would make things easier. But not any safer—not for him at least.

He thought over the emergency signal that had arrived from the North. What possessed those fools? Had they lost all ability to reason? He'd spent years worming his way into this position, and now they wanted to risk it all on a single throw of the dice. He turned away from the window.

Should he refuse to carry out the order? The thought tempted him, but he dismissed it. That would be viewed as disloyalty and Pyongyang had a long arm. Better to risk detection by his colleagues in the South Korean security service than to risk death at the hands of his comrades in the North's Research Department.

Besides, there was a certain charming subtlety to the mission he'd been ordered to carry out. A careful word here. A thoughtful suggestion there. And all of them would be in character. He'd established his credentials as a hardline anticommunist with years of dedicated service and fierce talk. No one would be surprised by investigation that would certainly ensue if he was successful.

He stopped pacing by his desk. So be it. He'd evaded South Korea's counterespionage probes for four decades. Let them try again and he would outwit them yet again.

The man called Scorpion picked up the phone. "Get me the minister."

He would light the fuse.

C H A P T E R

2

Opening Round

SEPTEMBER 8—NEAR THE AMERICAN EMBASSY, SEOUL, SOUTH KOREA

General Jack McLaren leaned forward and rapped sharply on the divider. "Stop the car right here, Harmon. I want to see what the hell's going on up ahead."

His driver grinned back over his shoulder. "Anything you say, General. This is about the end of the line anyways. Looks like a doggone parking lot up there."

McLaren snorted and popped the car door open—and started to sweat as Seoul's hot, sticky summer air rolled into the air-conditioned limo. It was worse out on the pavement. Heat waves shimmered and danced along the mass of stalled cars now backed up all along Sejong-Ro—Sejong Street—the wide, multilane boulevard cutting north to south through Seoul.

McLaren shoved his heavy uniform cap squarely on his head and leaned back in through the open door. "Doug, you'd better get on the horn to their high-and-mightinesses and tell 'em I'll be late . . . but do it diplomatically, of course."

His aide nodded and reached for the command phone on the seat beside him.

McLaren turned away and began working his way up the street through the crowds. He frowned. Street vendors along the sidewalks were hastily packing away their goods, and department store clerks swarmed alongside them hurriedly unrolling steel mesh screens to cover display windows showing the latest Western fashions. Other drivers had gotten out of their cars and stood trying to see what had caused the tie-up.

By the time he'd gone just a couple of hundred yards, the reason for the traffic jam was obvious. Several hundred helmeted South Korean riot police had blocked off the whole multilane boulevard. Some were putting up crowd control barricades while others started waving cars off onto some of the smaller east-west roads feeding into Sejong-Ro. Bulky armored cars mounting water cannon and tear gas grenade launchers were parked behind the police line. McLaren could see the walled U.S. embassy compound several hundred feet past the barricades.

It's like damned clockwork, he thought. It's September in Seoul, so it must be time for another friggin' student demonstration. Another few months of tear gas, rocks, and a bunch of puppydog kids yelling their heads off for "democracy" and "economic rights"—things they had heard about but didn't really understand. There had been three already, all in the week since classes started. Each had been large and well organized, and each had been bigger than the one before.

He squinted up into the dazzling noontime sky. Seoul's

skyscrapers cast giant, gloomy shadows across Sejong Street, but wherever they left an opening, the sun seemed murderously hot. Bad time for a demonstration—"mob weather" they called it. The time when hot, muggy weather and harsh sunlight could drive people crazy, could make them snap without the slightest warning.

McLaren kept walking toward the police line. An officer—a lieutenant by his bars—braced and saluted him. McLaren returned the salute. The officer, of course, knew him on sight.

The lieutenant smiled. "Good morning, General McLaren. How can I be of service?" His English was pretty good, almost accentless.

"Well, for one thing, I'd appreciate it if some of your men here could get my staff car out of that mess back there and through your barricades. I've got a meeting with your President and Joint Chiefs up at the Blue House in just a few minutes."

The lieutenant snapped to attention. "At once, sir." He turned and snapped a string of orders in Korean that sent two of his troopers jog-trotting down the street toward McLaren's car. Then he turned back to McLaren. "We will have your vehicle through this obstruction shortly. And, if I might suggest, sir, it would be a good thing to leave this place as soon as possible. We are expecting a . . . how do you say . . . a 'spot of trouble' presently."

McLaren looked up the street. "Yeah. I heard there was supposed to be a demonstration today, but my liaison officer told me it was expected further southeast, near the cathedral."

"It did start there, sir, but the rioters have broken past our barriers and they are marching in this direction. We are most concerned about this disturbance. Several Combat Police have already been injured. One group was isolated, surrounded, stripped of their equipment, and badly beaten."

McLaren frowned. And how many kids have you guys put in hospitals, today? But it wouldn't be a good idea to ask that question aloud. Instead he just nodded. "Sounds bad, all right."

The South Korean officer kept smiling, but his smile seemed a little too fixed, and he kept swallowing. McLaren couldn't figure out if the officer was more rattled by the presence of Commander Combined Forces–Korea so near a demonstration, or by the demonstration itself.

He eyed the men along the police line carefully. Christ, what a bunch of green kids. They all had their helmet visors up, but their uniforms were soaking up the heat. They hadn't formed ranks yet. They were just standing around in small groups, talking, and although he couldn't understand much Korean, their voices made one thing damned clear. These kids were as nervous as a preacher waiting in line at a cathouse.

Then he saw the kicker. The thing he should have seen right away. Half these Combat Police conscripts weren't carrying their usual riot shields, nightsticks, and tear gas guns. They had very real M16s slung over their shoulders. And friggin' bayonets, too.

McLaren's face tightened and he leaned forward to stare right into the police officer's eyes. He kept his voice low and hard. "Jesus Christ, Lieutenant. Just what the hell is going on here?" He stabbed a finger toward the fully armed troopers. "Riot troops with rifles? What stupid bastard ordered that?"

The Korean stared at McLaren. At an inch over six feet, the broad-shouldered, barrel-chested American general towered over him. Ice-cold gray eyes glared down above a bent, often-broken nose and below the close-cropped white bristles of a regulation military crew cut. The general's face was the face of a man who'd soldiered in half a dozen of the world's most godforsaken climates—sun-browned, leathery, square-jawed, and lean. It was the face of a man born to command.

Nervously, the lieutenant licked his lips. "I have my orders, sir. Radicals and communists are marching here from the Myongdong Cathedral. They have declared their intent to assault the Blue House and depose our president."

"Hell," said McLaren, "they always say that."

"Sir, we cannot take such threats lightly. The disturbances have grown more violent each day, and this one has been most difficult to control. These criminals may think they can actually reach the palace. But they will not get through this line. It is all planned, sir. My men will fire a volley over their heads to force them back—if the tear gas doesn't work."

The lieutenant straightened up. "Those are my instructions, sir. And my men and I will carry them out. We cannot allow these terrorists to cause trouble this close to the Blue House— or this close to your embassy for that matter.

"In any event, General, this is an internal matter. And I am not under your command." The Combat Police lieutenant seemed slightly more at ease now that he had remembered that. He saluted sharply and moved back to his men.

McLaren stared after him—working hard not to explode in rage. The trouble was, the little son of a bitch was right. As the overall commander of all the regular military forces in South Korea, McLaren could control the movements of more than six hundred thousand South Korean and American troops. But he didn't have any authority over the country's internal security and paramilitary units, and so he could not issue orders to this one half-assed Combat Police junior officer. There wasn't any way around that—not in time for it to matter anyway.

His long, black staff car, paced by two sweating policemen, pulled up beside him, and Corporal Harmon stuck his head out the window. "Hey, General, sir. We're out and ready to roll."

McLaren climbed into the backseat and slammed the car door shut. "Did you get through to the Blue House, Doug?"

"They've canceled today's meeting, sir. Something about this upcoming demonstration 'requiring immediate attention.'" His aide laughed. "Whatever that means."

McLaren jerked a thumb out the window as they passed through the rifle-armed Combat Police. "Well, I'll tell you. It sure as hell doesn't mean anything good. Let's head up to the embassy to check in."

They sat back in silence as the car moved toward the gates of the American embassy compound. But as the Marine sentries at the entrance came to attention, McLaren leaned forward again. "Hold it, Harmon. I'm getting out here."

He turned to his aide. "Doug, you go on into the embassy and report in to HQ. Get a status report on the demonstration and try to find out if the CIA has any idea why the South Koreans are so goddamned spooked. Meantime, I'm going to go back and eyeball this one—I don't like the feeling I'm getting about all of this."

McLaren noticed his aide and driver exchanging rueful looks as he got out of the car. Well, let them. He knew they didn't approve of his gallivanting off into a "situation," but they'd also learned the hard way not to try to stop him. He just didn't see the point in holing up with the ambassador while something explosive was happening just outside the embassy's gates.

It really was none of his business. After all, student protests often seemed like a national sport in South Korea. The season ran from the time school opened in September until winter set in during November—and then it reopened in the spring until the summer monsoon closed it down in June. At times the protestors and the Combat Police—the ROK's internal security force—acted as though they were simply carrying out some age-old ritual. But then somebody would get killed—hit in the head by a tear gas grenade, torched by a homemade, paint-spray flamethrower, or beaten to death in a wild street melee. When that happened, it wasn't a game, and everybody damned well knew it.

Combat police did not carry rifles. Whoever gave that order was scared of something. He wanted to find out what, before the kimchee really hit the fan.

He moved back down Sejong-Ro and stood on the sidewalk watching as the streets emptied of civilian traffic and filled up with truckload after truckload of green-jacketed riot police. It was very quiet now and growing hotter as the sun climbed directly overhead.

Then he heard it. Softly at first, but growing louder with every passing second. A rhythmic sound that seemed to echo off the tall buildings around him. Then he recognized it. It was the sound of thousands of voices chanting, yelling the same phrase over and over: *"Tokchae Tado! Tokchae Tado!* Down with the dictatorship! Down with the dictatorship!"

The Combat Police at the barricades heard it too. McLaren saw their officers—including that s.o.b. lieutenant—cursing and kicking them into formed ranks. The engines of the armored cars behind them caught and roared into life. The turrets with the water cannon and tear gas launchers turned to point down the empty street.

McLaren was tall enough to see over most of the riot police, and he could just begin to catch glimpses of the front rank of the crowd marching up the boulevard. He whistled softly to himself. There were a damned lot of them—thousands at least. And their shouts were even louder now that they'd seen the police line.

Most of them didn't look like the longhairs who'd taken to the streets in the States while he was in Nam. They wore clean clothes and neatly cropped hair. But they were also wearing handkerchiefs and surgical masks over their faces to block out tear gas. And there was something unnerving about their relentless approach.

Despite the heat McLaren felt a chill run up his spine. This felt a lot like combat, but it was too mechanical, too predictable. It was like watching some kind of animated physics diagram—high-velocity mass meets immovable object. McLaren knew what bothered him most about it all. He wasn't in charge and he couldn't do a single thing to change the outcome.

Suddenly he tensed. Someone was behind him. It was the same feeling he'd had just before that damned Cong sniper put an AK round into his right leg back in Nam. Without turning around, McLaren stepped into the shelter of a store doorway and chanced a look back down the street. He started and had to stop himself from laughing out loud. It wasn't a rifle scope that he'd sensed. It was the big lens on a TV camera.

But he ducked back into the doorway all the same as the CNN cameraman and his assistant jogged past toward the barricade line. It wouldn't do at all for the folks back home to see an American officer in full uniform standing around in the middle of a South Korean protest. That'd be just the sort of thing that would give the nervous Nellies in the Pentagon PR office the fits.

Twenty yards down the street the cameraman clambered onto the hood of a parked car to get a better shot of the demonstrators surging toward the police barricades.

"*Tokchae Tado! Tokchae Tado! Tokchae Tado!*" The chant was even louder now, and growing more guttural, more threatening. McLaren couldn't hear the orders being yelled to the Combat Police, but suddenly the front two ranks brought their Plexiglas shields up and drew their nightsticks.

The demonstrators closed to within fifty yards, then forty, thirty, twenty. Bricks and bottles started clattering off the riot troopers' raised shields. McLaren snarled. What the hell were they waiting for?

Now. A grenade launcher on one of the armored cars

coughed. Others followed suit, and McLaren saw a white mist of tear gas billowing above the crowd, drifting downwind south along the street. He waited for the water cannon to open up. But the damned idiots had parked them too far back. The armored cars were rolling forward, but it was too late. The protestors were too close.

They smashed into the front ranks of the riot police—shoving barricades aside, wrenching at plastic shields or kicking under them, and still screaming, *"Tokchae Tado!"* The police fought back, clubbing students with their nightsticks and slamming shields into their faces. McLaren saw demonstrators going down with blood streaming from cut foreheads or broken noses. It wasn't enough.

The barricades were down, and the police line was beginning to give. There were Combat Police on the ground now, lying curled up as demonstrators kicked them savagely. Others were being pulled into the crowd or shoved sprawling back into their ranks. The students sensed victory, and more and more of them fought their way forward through the press to get at the police. McLaren saw an officer stagger back, his face smashed by a thrown brick. The stupid bastard hadn't had his visor down.

McLaren stepped out of the doorway. It was just about time to go. When the police broke and ran, it was going to be every uniform for itself.

But he stopped. The rear ranks of the Combat Police had unslung their rifles and were stepping forward—bringing them up and aiming over the crowd. And there was that damned lieutenant, getting ready to drop his hand to signal a volley like he was on some parade ground.

Then it happened. McLaren couldn't see what caused it—a thrown rock or bottle, an accidental elbow in the side, or just plain gutless stupidity—but somebody's M16 went off on full automatic, spraying twenty steel-jacketed rounds moving at 3,250 feet per second into the struggling crowd of protestors and Combat Policemen.

Everything seemed to slide into slow motion for a moment. Bodies were thrown everywhere inside the deadly arc described by the assault rifle's bullets. A spectacled student's face exploded as a round caught him in the right eye. A

Combat Policeman fell to his knees and then onto his face—a widening, red stain welling from the bullet holes in his back. A pretty girl stared in horror at the place where her hand had been. Others staggered back or fell over to lie crumpled on the pavement.

Then things snapped back into focus. The people in the front of the crowd were screaming and trying to run—trying to force their way away from the carnage around them. But the thousands of protestors pouring north along Sejong Street couldn't see or hear what had happened ahead, and they kept pressing forward—shoving the screaming men and women in front ahead of them.

Oh, shit, McLaren thought. That did it. The other young policemen had been staring in shock at the bloody tangle of bodies at their feet. But now, as the mob surged closer, they panicked. First one, and then the rest, started firing into the crowd at point-blank range.

Dozens of protestors were cut down in a matter of seconds—smashed to the pavement in a hail of automatic weapons fire. As they fell in writhing, blood-soaked heaps, the crowd finally began breaking, with hundreds, then thousands, of people screaming, turning, and trying to run.

But the Combat Police were now completely out of control. They began moving forward, still firing. And McLaren could see some of them fumbling for new magazines. Goddamnit, some of those bastards were even reloading!

Without thinking about it he left the doorway and started to run toward them. Maybe he could kick some sense into those frigging morons. But it was probably too late for that.

They were already chasing after the screaming crowds scattering back down Sejong Street. Some were still shooting, firing from the hip as they ran. Others contented themselves with clubbing any student within reach.

McLaren saw one trooper pause, aim, and send a long burst into a small group of pleading men and women cowering in front of a department store display window. They were thrown back in among the bullet-riddled mannequins.

He kept running down the street, but a muffled cry following a sharp groan brought him skidding to a stop. He turned. There, not ten feet away, was a crazy-eyed Combat

Policeman trying to tear the TV camera out of the hands of the CNN cameraman he'd seen earlier. The soundman sat slumped against a car door, hands pressed to his face with blood running out between them.

That, by God, was too damned much. McLaren didn't much care for most reporters, but these guys were Americans, after all. He charged in, pulled the riot trooper around by his combat webbing, and sent a right cross smashing into the man's face. The Korean staggered back, and McLaren followed up with a left into his stomach. The trooper grunted and fell over gasping for air. McLaren felt himself grinning despite himself. Not bad for a man in his fifties.

He turned to the cameraman kneeling by his partner. "Can he walk?"

The reporter nodded. "Yeah. I think so. But we're gonna have to help him along." He slung his equipment across his back. Then, for the first time, he took a close look at McLaren. "Jesus, man. I don't think I've ever been rescued by a real, live U.S. cavalryman before." He stuck a hand out. "Thanks. Thanks a lot."

McLaren shook hands. "No problem." He bent down to take one of the dazed soundman's arms. "Right now, though, I think it's time to get the hell out of Dodge."

With the wounded man stumbling between them, they lurched up the street toward the American embassy. Behind them, McLaren could hear the rattle of automatic weapons still echoing throughout Seoul's city center. It sounded like all hell was breaking loose back there. It might spread across all of South Korea. And if it did, he and his troops were going to get caught right in the middle.

CHAPTER
3
The
Washington
Waltz

The televisions are always on in a Congressional office.

"Good morning. I'm Amanda Hayes and this is a CNN special report—The Massacre in Seoul."

Jeremy Mitchell looked up into the TV screen perched precariously on his bookcase. One hand reached for his tortoise-shell glasses while the other shoved the latest draft press release on National Frozen Food Week off his notepad. Without taking his eyes off the small screen, he waved the nearest intern over, a short, pudgy University of Michigan junior who was spending his fall semester learning the business of government while duplicating constituent mail for a congressman. Mitchell ignored the discontented frown on the kid's face. Endless hours of gofer work—stapling, filing, duplicating—those were the dues you paid to get more meaningful work later on.

Mitchell had paid his own dues in full. Summers as an unpaid campaign volunteer. University terms spent crawling as an unpaid, overworked congressional intern. Two years after school as a poorly paid legislative correspondent, locked away for sixty-hour weeks drafting and redrafting answers to letters written by constituents. By then he'd seen how the system worked. You climbed over the still-warm bodies of those who'd thought they were your friends and coworkers. He'd used that knowledge to win a succession of promotions—first to handling domestic issues as a legislative assistant and later to committee staffer. A lot of people who'd trusted Jeremy Mitchell's sincere smiles, open-featured good looks, twinkling blue eyes, and firm handshake had long since come to regret trusting first impressions.

Now, ten years and a pile of broken friendships later, he held the top-dog slot in any congressional office: he was the administrative assistant—the AA. And that meant he ran everything and everyone in the office, including the representative, if the man or woman was malleable enough.

Mitchell smiled thinly to himself. Ben Barnes was so malleable that he often reminded people of the Playdough little kids loved to squeeze and squash. He darted a glance at the intern impatiently waiting. "Phil, go get the congressman. He's going to want to see this."

The intern nodded grumpily and went, threading his way through the crowded maze of desks, cubicles, bookcases, filing cabinets, and stacks of newly printed newsletters that marked any House-side congressional office. Senators and their staffs usually had more room, but House members and their people worked under conditions that would have made a sweatshop seem spacious. A single suite of two rooms usually held twelve to fifteen harried staffers, their phones, files, and personal computers.

Congressman Ben Barnes appeared out of his inner office moments later, looking rumpled with wisps of his thinning, ash-blond hair sticking up at all angles. A wrinkled red silk tie hung loosely from his open shirt collar, and his eyes were puffy and bloodshot. Mitchell took it all in and made a mental note to never again let the congressman attend an auto industry luncheon unaccompanied. Thank God there hadn't been any unfriendly press there. Barnes never seemed able to resist an open bar unless there was somebody around to pull him away.

The congressman smiled uncertainly and blearily at his AA. "What's up, Jer?"

Mitchell pointed at the screen.

"*. . . as this tape from a CNN camera team shows, armed troops began firing on the students—apparently without warning.*

"Reports are sketchy and the South Korean government has imposed a news blackout, but it appears that at least several hundred people have been killed. Sources in one Seoul hospital report treating dozens of gunshot wounds and emergency rooms all across the city are said to be overflowing with the critically injured. There are even unconfirmed reports that several American or European tourists have been killed.

"For now, Seoul remains under strict curfew. And South Korea's security forces have warned that violators will be shot on sight. That's a threat they seem all too willing to enforce. This is Amanda Hayes. We'll have more news from Seoul on the half-hour."

Mitchell reached up and turned the volume down—shutting out an ad for hay fever medicine. He spun around in his chair to face the congressman.

Barnes seemed puzzled. "Very interesting, Jer. But couldn't you have just put together a memo for me? I've got a million things to do before the committee meets this afternoon."

"But don't you see . . ." Mitchell stopped. Yelling at your boss was not recommended for Capitol Hill survival. He tried again. "Ben, this is the kind of break we've been waiting for. This Seoul massacre thing gives us the leverage we need to put an imports bill on the legislative fast track."

"That's great. That's really wonderful." Barnes still looked a little lost—an expression he was careful never to wear in front of TV cameras or constituent groups.

Mitchell decided to lay it all out. "South Korea makes those cheap Hyundai cars and other products that have the unions back home all hot and bothered. They want some more tariffs and import restrictions to even things up, but we haven't been able to move anything worthwhile through both the House and Senate."

Barnes seemed to be following along, so he threw in the clincher. "Right now these news reports are being shown all across the country—in every district—so I don't think South Korea's going to have too much public support by nightfall. They've been getting bad press for some time now, and this should really fan the flames. If we got a tough trade bill moving, we just might be able to ram it through before all the 'free traders' know what's hit them. And that would make the autoworkers back home very happy."

"And I'm going to need the autoworkers next year when I

run for the Senate." Barnes finished the sentence for him. He grinned. "That's great thinking, Jer. Let's do it. Draft up a real solid bill for me, something that'll pull in a big coalition and get me a lot of press. I'll take a look at it later this afternoon. Okay?"

Mitchell nodded and Barnes left humming happily. Mitchell spun back around to his keyboard and opened a new file, Korea-Bash. He smiled to himself. That was going to be a pretty accurate title.

Now, he thought, let's see just what kind of a packaging deal I can come up with. Packaging was everything on the Hill, and if you wanted to pass a bill, you had to be sure it had a little something in it for every important interest group. That was part of the fun.

Mitchell started making a list.

The first section had to be a strong condemnation of South Korea's human rights abuses and a tough set of required democratic reforms, with a short-term time limit for their implementation. Church groups and the other liberal lobbying organizations would really lap that stuff up.

Then came the sanctions the U.S. would impose if the Koreans didn't put the reforms in place before the deadline.

The most obvious were new tariffs on Korean imports coming into the country. That would give the union bosses their bone, and they, in turn, would give a lot for Barnes come the next election.

Mitchell paused, his hands held over the keyboard while he thought. Yeah, the U.S. had troops in South Korea. Well, we wouldn't want to prop up a corrupt, tyrannical regime, would we? He typed in "Withdrawal all U.S. forces if reforms not made." That would piss off the conservatives, but it would win solid backing from the liberals in the party caucus. Maybe they could make sure that any troops pulled out of South Korea were sent to bases in Texas. That would make the Speaker happy. And making the Speaker happy was a crucial part of getting any bill through the House of Representatives.

Now he needed something to help break up the conservative opposition. "Cut off all military aid to South Korea and use the money to reduce the deficit." Mitchell smiled. That would pick up a few votes. And it would give some of the Southern Democrats a conservative fig leaf to hide behind if they voted for the bill.

That should do it. Mitchell knew that the committee's legislative counsel could turn his rough notes into a polished piece of legal language in a matter of hours. He could concentrate on putting together all the background material they'd need—"Dear Colleague" letters soliciting support from other congressmen, fact sheets, and most importantly, press releases. Given two or three days and some good staff support, and he could flood the Hill and the airwaves with talk about Representative Barnes's new South Korean sanctions bill.

Then he frowned at the outline taking shape on his screen. Any bill drawn up along those lines should be a real votegetter. The trouble was it touched on everything from trade and taxes to defense and foreign affairs. And that opened the door for practically every major committee in both the House and Senate to demand a piece of the action.

Mitchell wasn't sure who had first called committees "God's gift to procrastination, sloth, and delay," but it could be a completely accurate picture at times. With only a few weeks left until the Congress was scheduled to adjourn, there just wasn't time to waste while every committee held hearings, tossed in its own favorite amendments, and issued its own thousand-page report. He was going to have to get Barnes to cut enough deals with the other committee chairmen to win expedited consideration for the bill. Even worse, he was going to need a senator to do the same thing over on the other side of the Hill.

Okay, it wasn't going to be easy—but it could be done. And if he could pull this off, his reputation as a top-notch legislative strategist would be made forever. That was something worth working for. He just hoped that the South Koreans didn't get smart and stop killing each other before they could get the bill through.

Mitchell turned away from his computer screen and started flipping through his Rolodex. It was time to start calling in a few favors. For years he'd made sure that Barnes carried water for liberal political action groups and for the unions. Now he was going to cash in. Besides, they'd all probably jump at the chance.

He pulled a card out of his Rolodex and started dialing. It had begun.

SEPTEMBER 11—THE CBS EVENING NEWS

The reporter stood framed against the Capitol dome.

"This is Phil Smith, reporting from Capitol Hill. Just three days after the Seoul massacre, Congress has begun moving against the South Korean government.

"In a press conference held this afternoon, Representative Ben Barnes of Michigan, chairman of the House Subcommittee on Trade, and Senate Foreign Relations Committee Chairman James Farell of New York, announced the introduction of a stiff sanctions bill aimed at South Korea. More than one hundred congressmen and thirty senators have already announced their support for the measure.

"The bill calls on the South Korean government to institute major political reforms. Among other things, it demands an end to press censorship, freedom for all political prisoners, and the immediate reform of the entire South Korean security force.

"It also seeks the complete removal of all trade barriers aimed at U.S. exports to Korea, and a significant reduction in Korea's trade surplus with the United States.

"If these conditions aren't met within ninety days after the bill is signed into law by the President, the measure would automatically impose tariffs on almost all South Korean products coming into this country, end Korea's most-favored-nation trade status, and cut U.S. military assistance. And in a move guaranteed to outrage congressional conservatives, it would also require the complete withdrawal of all U.S. forces now stationed in South Korea."

The picture cut to footage of Ben Barnes speaking earnestly into the camera.

"We have no quarrel with the people of South Korea. Nor do we seek trade protectionism for its own sake. But we also know that America cannot be seen to side with oppression, tyranny, and ruthless terror. The South Korean government must learn that its brutality will not go unpunished. America will not condone cold-blooded murder. And the Congress cannot stand idly by while democratic reform is crushed underfoot in South Korea."

The videotape of Barnes ended, cutting back to the *CBS Evening News* anchorman in New York.

"In other congressional news today, the House Foreign Affairs Committee continued its work on legislation aimed at improved Soviet-American relations by defeating an amendment that would have linked U.S.-Soviet ties with Soviet actions in Afghanistan."

SEPTEMBER 12—THE OLD EXECUTIVE OFFICE BUILDING, WASHINGTON, D.C.

Blake Fowler finished reading the telex from Seoul before tossing it onto the pile of papers on his desk. He leaned back, took his wire-frame glasses off, and rubbed his eyes. God, he was getting too old to stay up reading fine print all night. What you could do at twenty in college didn't seem at all possible at thirty-five.

Fowler let his head drop onto his chest and closed his eyes. Maybe he could get away with a short in-office nap. People had to make allowances for you when you'd been up for almost twenty-four hours straight, didn't they?

He already knew the answer to that question. National Security Council staffers were expected to be awake and alert for days on end, to brief politicians in a split second, to keep rival intelligence agencies from going to war against each other—and to leap tall buildings in a single bound for that matter. Just the kind of thing that getting a Ph.D. in Asian and Pacific Affairs prepared you for. Fowler squirmed, trying to get more comfortable. His damned desk chair must have been designed especially by the Spanish Inquisition.

"Good morning, Sleeping Beauty. Can I wake you with a kiss?" Fowler warily opened an eye to find his secretary hovering over him with a cup of coffee. She looked as tired as he felt. That wasn't really surprising—she'd been working all night, too.

He sat upright. "Sure, Princess Charming. You can kiss me. But then you have to save me from my wife."

Katie Morgan smiled. "No thanks, Beaut. I'd really rather go hunt a dragon for you. Have some coffee instead." She set the cup on his desk, carefully avoiding the stack of documents still waiting to be read, and dropped an interoffice memo on top.

"And speaking of reptiles, Putnam wants to see you in his chambers at oh nine fifteen sharp." She looked at her watch. "Which is in ten minutes. He wants to know what happened to the world while he slept, or attended the congressional prayer breakfast, or something."

"Ah, sh . . . darn, I mean." Fowler started leafing through the papers on his desk. "Katie, I'm going to need the latest Agency analysis and those NSA intercepts. Putnam probably won't understand them, but they look impressive." He stood up, stretching and yawning. This was a hell of a way to start the new day.

Walking outside over to the White House made him feel a lot better. He could have taken the tunnel over, but the crisp, cool morning air woke him up more than coffee ever could. A gentle breeze ruffled his straight, brown hair. It was getting long, he thought, and he'd have to try to find time to get it cut.

As Fowler strolled across Executive Drive, the early-morning sunlight threw his image against the windshield of a parked Volvo. He turned his head slightly while passing to study himself. And grinned when he became aware of the unconscious habit. Although he never changed much between glimpses, he could never quite break himself of the mannerism.

At only a tad over six feet, Fowler wasn't any taller than the average man his age, it was just that he was slender enough to make himself seem taller. His wife, Mandy, called him lean and rangy, but she was prejudiced. The tight fit of the khaki slacks around his waist made him realize that some of that youthful slenderness was starting to disappear—the victim of too much desk work, too many wolfed-down junk-food meals, and an aversion to most forms of exercise. For the thousandth time, he made a mental note to start swimming laps again, and for the thousandth time he dismissed it from his mind.

At least his face didn't show any immediate signs of falling apart on him. But not even Mandy would call it handsome. Instead, a long, thin nose, large green eyes, and mobile, arching eyebrows gave him a faintly professorial look— the quizzical, distracted air of someone always looking for more than the obvious.

He reached the White House, flashed his security badge to the Marine guard and Secret Serviceman on duty at the side door, and went in.

As the national security adviser, Putnam had an office just down the hall from the Oval Office itself—a fact that he was always careful to mention at cocktail parties. And Fowler noticed that he'd managed to get an even larger nameplate, GEORGE PUTNAM—NATIONAL SECURITY ADVISER, plastered all over his door.

Putnam's secretary looked up as he walked in. She smiled sympathetically. "Long night?"

He nodded, rubbing his chin and realizing he'd forgotten to shave again.

She looked apologetic. "His Excellency has asked that you take a seat for a few minutes. He's on a very important call with one of his old Hill cronies."

Fowler looked at his watch: 9:15 A.M. on the dot. That bastard Putnam. He seemed to think that you showed people how important and busy you were by keeping them waiting outside your office door.

Fowler thought that George Putnam, erstwhile national security adviser and full-time asshole, was a good example of the truism that when the pendulum swung, it usually swung too far.

Several of Putnam's predecessors had been highly professional career soldiers who'd somehow managed to get both themselves and the president they served in hot water. There'd been an outcry in the press and on Capitol Hill, and a whole slew of foreign policy pundits had come forward arguing that the next president should find someone who could work more easily within the constraints imposed by Congress and by domestic politics.

Well, that was advice the new president had taken—and Fowler thought he'd probably live to regret it. Putnam had been some kind of a staff bigwig on the Hill before the election, and then he'd wormed his way into a transition team slot with the incoming administration. After that, he'd managed to surprise everyone outside the Hill establishment by parlaying his temporary position into a nomination for the national security adviser's job.

Fowler had to admit that Putnam knew how to operate. That didn't make him any less of a jerk, but it did make him the jerk responsible for keeping the President up-to-date on national security issues.

Putnam kept him on ice for nearly fifteen minutes this time. And when Fowler walked in, he didn't even look up from the notes he was scribbling. Instead he waved vaguely toward a chair. "I'll be right with you, Blake. No rest for the righteous, eh?"

Fowler sat, trying manfully to conceal his disdain for his nominal superior. Putnam was still a young man, barely into his forties, but he looked older somehow. Not older and wiser. Just older. The national security adviser's fleshy, freckled face and petulant, thin-lipped mouth made him look like an aging schoolboy, like the bully who'd never been beaten up.

After a moment Putnam laid his pen down carefully, flexed his fingers, and sat back looking smug. He brushed a wisp of graying, reddish-brown, curly hair back into place. "Always pays to keep your ear to the ground, Blake. Got some really hot stuff from the Hill this morning."

Fowler knew that Putnam's "really hot stuff" was probably the latest dirt on some senator's love life, so he kept quiet.

Putnam looked a little exasperated that his subordinate hadn't begged him to share the latest gossip. "Ah, well. Can't expect you 'professionals' to care much about the way things really get done in this town, now can I?"

Putnam shook his head. "Someday, Blake, you'll realize that this town doesn't move on facts—it moves on perceptions. On rumors. On whispers."

He leaned forward across his desk. "And the granddaddy rumor mill of them all is right over there." He pointed off in the rough direction of the Hill. "That's where the action's at.

"Without the Congress, the President's agenda is dead in the water. So we've got to keep on our toes. We've got to know who's up and who's down—who the Speaker or majority leader like and who they don't. And we have to keep them happy. This administration has to have a sort of symbiotic relationship with the Congress. You know, 'you scratch my back, I'll scratch yours.' Do you see what I mean?"

Fowler could name quite a few presidents who'd been at their best when they opposed congressional idiocy, but it seemed a little too early in the morning for another pointless political debate. Instead he reached into his folder and pulled out a sheaf of papers. "Well, George, I'm afraid I'll have to leave the American political theory to you. I have a tough enough time keeping up with South Korean politics these days."

Putnam frowned. "Oh, yes. South Korea. That's what I wanted to talk to you about." He tapped a finger on his bare desk blotter. "Now look, Blake, we've got some real trouble brewing on the Hill over Korea. And the President needs to know just what the hell is going on over there."

Fowler handed him the latest CIA analysis, a stapled selection of National Security Agency signals intercepts, and a telexed report from the general commanding U.S. forces in Korea.

"Jesus Christ, Blake, I don't have time to read all this crap! That's what I've got you for. Did you bother to put together a one-pager for my signature—or was that too much trouble for you?"

Control. Control, Fowler told himself. Don't let him see that he's managed to piss you off. He held out the single-page summary he'd written at around four in the morning.

But Putnam waved it away. "Just give me the gist for now. I'll read it for details later."

Fowler tried hard to keep his voice level. "Essentially, our most recent reports show some improvement in the situation. Seoul and the other major cities are still under a nighttime curfew, but there are signs that the government will lift it sometime in the next three days. There have been some minor incidents outside Seoul—small demonstrations, a few rocks thrown at police, that kind of stuff—but nothing really dangerous. The National University is still crawling with security troops, of course, but there hasn't been any further trouble. The students still seem to be in shock.

"And so far the North Koreans haven't tried anything funny. We've gotten the usual propaganda blasts, but we haven't yet picked up evidence of anything worse in the works."

Putnam interrupted. "What about the massacre? Do we have any idea who was responsible? That's the kind of thing we're going to get asked by the press."

"Well, the government over there is probably going to lay the blame on some junior police officer—undoubtedly one of the ones who got himself killed. But that general of ours who saw the start of the whole thing argues the real culprit is whoever ordered the police to meet that demonstration with real guns in their hands.'' Fowler shook his head. "And that had to have been someone pretty high up—probably at the cabinet level."

Putnam snorted, "Stupid bastards." For once Fowler was inclined to agree with his boss.

"Yeah. We're still not sure just why whoever it was thought it was necessary. But we do know that the government's been under a lot of pressure from the heads of some of the South Korean industrial conglomerates, the *chaebol*, to keep things under tighter control this fall. The last round of unrest wound up costing them a lot in labor concessions, and that cut into South Korean's competitive edge. They didn't sell enough autos and computer parts last year to cut their international debt as much as they wanted to. But I don't think a full-fledged massacre is what they had in mind." Fowler slid the heavily underlined summary on top of the rest of the documents he suspected Putnam would never read.

Putnam looked across the desk at him. "So what's the bottom line? Can the President tell the press and the Hill this was just a one-time screwup that won't happen again? Or can we expect more of this?"

Fowler shrugged. "There's really no way to tell. After the 1980 bloodbath in Kwangju, things were quiet for six or seven years. But this happened right on worldwide TV and it happened in Seoul. And Seoul is the heart of South Korea—it's the capital, the population center, business center, cultural center, you name it. We just don't have enough information yet to make an accurate prediction."

"Now see here, Dr. Fowler. I've got to give the Man more than that. He can't just go out there in front of the cameras and say, 'Gosh, fellas, there's really no way to tell if Korea's gonna come unwrapped faster than you can say Iran.'" Putnam's attempt to imitate the President's voice fell flat, but the anger in it was real enough.

"And it's not just the press," Putnam continued. "We've got to deal with the House and Senate as well. You know about this Barnes sanctions bill that got dropped in the hopper yesterday?''

Fowler nodded. "I read the summary Legislative Affairs put out last night. Frankly, I can't think of when I last saw such a piece of dangerous stupidity—''

Putnam cut him off. "I don't give a great big goddamn for your uninformed opinions on legislation, Blake." He made a visible effort to control himself. "The point is, the bill's not going to go anywhere, but we have to form an administration position on it. And for once I want a single administration position."

Putnam looked over at his desk clock. "So what I want you to do, Dr. Fowler, is put together a top-notch, interagency working group to analyze the potential effects of the Barnes bill. Get all the key players involved—State, Defense, Commerce, CIA, and all the rest. Do it ASAP and make sure that all the documents flow through me, okay? I want a final report on my desk inside of two weeks from now."

Fowler mentally wrote off two weeks' worth of dinners at home with his family, his daughter's school play, and a lot of domestic tranquility. "You know that either State or Defense will fight like hell to chair this thing. And they'll want to route through their respective bosses first."

Putnam smirked. "I know. So what you do is this. Put me on the group as chairman, and then I'll just have you fill in for me. Got it?"

Fowler nodded his understanding. Putnam might be a slimy son of a bitch and he might not know squat about foreign affairs, but he did know how to play the bureaucracy game. The Korean situation involved everything from foreign policy and military strategy to questions of international trade and domestic politics. And all of that made the President's national security adviser the logical choice to head up an interagency group on South Korea. That gave Putnam power, because only the designated chairman of an interagency group had the right to present the group's final report to the President.

"Okay, Blake, I'm sure you've got work to do, so I won't keep you any longer." Putnam's eyes flicked over to the clock again. "Besides, I've got an important meeting right now."

Fowler stood, took his folder off Putnam's desk, and

walked to the door. He opened it, but Putnam's voice stopped him with his hand still on the knob. "By the way, Blake, try not to come in looking like a refugee all the time. I expect my senior staff to set the right tone for this shop, all right?"

Fowler didn't say anything. He just fought down the urge to go back and kick his boss in the nuts and went out—brushing past the man waiting in Putnam's outer office. Behind him, he heard Putnam trying out his best "one of the guys" tone of voice: "Hey, Jer! Good to see you! Come right on in."

C H A P T E R

4

In the Shadows

SEPTEMBER 13—PYONGYANG-EAST AIRBASE

The "Internationale" sounded odd to Colonel Sergei Ivanovitch Borodin. Its harsh, blaring refrain rebounded off the concrete-reinforced granite walls of the hangar—echoes chasing one another with nowhere to go. After a while Borodin swore he could have closed his eyes and heard the same series of notes three times over.

It was distracting, and he didn't need the distraction. There were too many things he needed to watch carefully, too many things to remember. This mission was as much a diplomatic gesture as it was a military assignment. Of itself that held no great concern for Borodin. He'd served the State in a similar capacity across half the globe. But this place was so—he searched for the right word—so confined, so suffocating. Nothing at all like the vast, open deserts beyond Tripoli or the rolling grasslands around Harare.

This feeling of walking a tightrope over a deep pit had first come over him as he'd waited to fly out of Moscow's Domodedovo Airport.

"Be careful, Sergei. Be watchful." General Petrov, deputy commander in chief for air combat training, had whispered in his ear as they stood together looking out the departure lounge window into the late-night darkness. The old man had chuckled at Borodin's alarmed expression, but his words had been blunt—a rare thing for the short, stout, white-haired friend of his father.

"These North Koreans are slant-eyes, yes, Sergei. But they are clever slant-eyes. They've played us off against the Chinese for decades, and only now does it seem that we're pulling them into our nets. But"—the old man had waggled a finger in his face—"only just. They could easily slip outside. We can't afford that, Sergei Ivanovitch. You understand? So you must not offend them. You must not disparage this personality cult nonsense—this godhead—they've built up around the old man Kim and his son."

Petrov had dropped his voice and laid an arm around Borodin's shoulders. "So, a word to the wise, eh? Walk softly in North Korea, there are powerful eyes watching. Politburo eyes, Sergei. You don't want to count trees or dig for gold, you understand? Walk soft."

Borodin shivered slightly as he remembered those last words. This might well be the season of glasnost, but the icy forests of Siberia and the man-killing mines of the Kolyma were still there—they'd just been pushed into the shadows a bit.

His memory moved on, through the long, high-altitude journey eastward across the Soviet Union, then lower above the rugged peaks of the Taeback Mountains, and finally south across the narrow plains toward Pyongyang. Into this cavernous hangar carved out of a mountainside east of the capital.

The "Dear Leader," Kim Jong-Il, son of North Korea's absolute ruler, had met the plane personally. No surprises there. Neither Borodin nor his political officer, Major Yepishev, had expected the Great Leader himself, Kim Il-Sung, to make an appearance. According to both the GRU and the KGB, the old man's health was increasingly fragile, and they'd arrived on a hard, gray day, heavy with cold rain driven by the wind.

There wasn't much trace of the rotten weather in here, though, Borodin thought, surveying the high-vaulted hangar that held not only his Ilyushin airliner, an Il-18, but also several other, smaller transports, a reviewing stand, and a uniformed crowd of North Korean dignitaries. The size of the place made a mockery of perspective and dwarfed its human occupants—stretching for several hundred meters from tunnels cut deeper into the rock out to a set of thickly armored main hangar doors. Lighting, ventilation, and fire suppression systems turned the ceiling into a nightmarish tangle of shafts, cabling, and piping.

The Soviet colonel couldn't even begin to imagine the amount of labor it had taken to carve all of this out of solid rock. It surpassed even the massive engineering works carried out by his own country's Civil Defense Force. He cast a sidelong glance at the row of impassive Korean faces on either side of him. What was going on inside those heads?

The silence alerted him. The band had stopped playing, and now Kim Jong-Il stood ready to speak at the podium.

Borodin found the man's appearance unsettling. On the surface the "Dear Leader" seemed soft, pudgy—a stark contrast to the colonel, who'd always prided himself on his trim, flat stomach and narrow, high-cheeked features. But the eyes, the eyes were dangerous—cold and hard behind those thick glasses. They were eyes that suited a man who now controlled his nation's entire internal security and military apparatus.

Kim's voice was soft, commanding attention by necessity more than by bluster. "Socialist brothers, we welcome your presence here. We hope that your gracious visit will permit a useful exchange of information between our two great peoples..."

"Exchange." Now there was an amusing word, Borodin thought. He and his men—some of the Soviet Union's top pilots and aircraft mechanics—were a training team. Their very presence here chipped away at Kim Il-Sung's so-called self-reliance doctrine.

It was all a nice little ballet. His team had to maintain the fiction that they were here to examine North Korean air tactics, and not just to show the Koreans how to fly the shiny new toys they'd been shipped from the Soviet Union. North Korean air tactics, what nonsense. These people thought the MiG-21 was a first-line aircraft.

At the same time, his briefings at the Defense and Foreign ministries in Moscow had emphasized how much the Soviet Union needed Kim Il-Sung's friendship and cooperation. The colonel knew that Kim's dynastic communism was anathema to his superiors, but the North Koreans were at least nominal socialists, and they were opposed to the West. More importantly, the country occupied a crucial geostrategic position—it was the fulcrum between the Soviet Union, China, and Japan.

The "fulcrum." The word described the Kremlin's view of North Korea with precision. The Politburo saw it as the vital agent through which force could be exerted against either the Chinese or the Japanese. Borodin smiled inwardly despite his concerns. Considering his mission here, that was even a clever word play, one worthy of *Crokodil*, the humor magazine.

And if his country didn't help Kim, the Chinese would be only too happy to oblige. That was something his country could not risk.

Borodin knew that firsthand. He had been stationed in the Far East early in his career. You couldn't fly out of Vladivostok and remain unaware of the Chinese threat.

Their planes were old, antique relics for the most part. Their tanks and artillery were laughable by modern standards. And their men were underequipped. But there were so many of them and they were close to the Trans-Siberian Railway, the lifeline between European Russia and its Far Eastern possessions.

Everyone knew that the Chinese were just waiting for the right moment to stab the motherland in the back. Hadn't those yellow-skinned, "pseudocommunists" spent years sucking up to the West, begging for technology and trade? Didn't they insist on setting an independent, often anti-Soviet, foreign policy?

Yes, Borodin thought, the Politburo was wise to worry about North Korea's leanings. The State didn't need any more enemies in this part of the world—it needed friends and allies. Puppets. It was vital to give North Korea's Great Leader as much help as he deserved, at the highest price he was willing to pay. The Koreans had already agreed to allow overflights by

Soviet aircraft. Next, port visits by Soviet warships would be expanded into a basing agreement. The new aircraft he and his team would teach the North Koreans to fly were the first token of Soviet reciprocity. Others would soon follow.

His mission was to smooth the way for the diplomats and their treaties by showing these Asiatics just how valuable Soviet assistance could be.

He focused his attention back on Kim Jong-Il, the Dear Leader, still mouthing sanctimonious phrases about their "historic friendship" and the "common struggle against imperialism." By all accounts the younger Kim should prove an ally in this quest for great Soviet influence, even if an unwitting one. His thirst for advanced military technology was well documented, and it was a thirst the Chinese could do little to satisfy.

Borodin came back to full consciousness of his surroundings as he realized that Kim's speech was finishing, winding up with what must be a standard invocation. "And so we are confident that the colonel and his men will gain a greater understanding of the international socialist struggle and the dynamic contribution made to it by the Korean people under the guidance of our Great Leader."

Kim stepped back from the podium to thunderous applause supplied by the phalanx of officers and enlisted men drawn up in the open area of the hangar. Borodin clapped along with them, meeting Kim's eyes steadily and with a diplomatic smile stuck on his face. The North Korean dipped his head slightly toward the podium.

That was Borodin's cue. As briefed, he bowed to Kim and the other dignitaries and felt carefully for the prepared speech scripted by the Foreign Ministry.

"The people of the Union of Soviet Socialist Republics send their greetings..." Borodin read the hackneyed phrases aloud almost without thinking about them. He had read the same kind of stilted nonsense a dozen times before in a dozen different countries. These ceremonies were unimportant. The real work would come later, behind closed doors and in the cockpits of jet fighter aircraft. He was growing impatient to get on with it. The sooner they began, the sooner he and his men could get out of this bleak, Asiatic fortress-state.

GRU SECURE SECTION, SOVIET EMBASSY, PYONGYANG

"... The sophistication and extent of the underground installations is impressive, as is the level of training ..."

Borodin laid down his pen and rubbed his eyes. The harsh, bright fluorescent lights of the GRU office were painful this late at night. He looked up from the paper, trying to get his eyes to focus on something farther than a few centimeters away. Not that there was much to see. A few old, battered wooden desks, paint scraps peeling off the walls, two clocks, one on Moscow time, the other set for Pyongyang, some filing cabinets, and the obligatory portrait of the General Secretary. Functional, but not esthetic. Borodin savored that last word. That was the kind of word only those who were really *kulturny*, cultured, could remember when they were on their last legs.

Little Mother, but he was tired. It was absurd to fly across eight time zones, spend a full day, and then spend the night hours trying to write a coherent arrival report. But his instructions from Moscow were clear. Complete, accurate, and timely reports were to be written, encoded, and transmitted by the mission commander, by him, each and every day. North Korea was clearly now a high priority for the staff bigwigs at Defense Ministry HQ.

He looked at what he had just written and nodded to himself. Certainly that was accurate enough. The North Korean air installations and crews were impressive. More than impressive in fact.

After the speech-making mercifully ended, the younger Kim had taken him in tow for a thorough tour of the Pyongyang-East Airbase. Borodin shook his head at the memory of it all. The vast transport plane hangar had just been the start. Behind it and above it lay a whole connected series of tunnels, barracks, offices, quarters, control centers, maintenance shops, and fuel storage tanks. The base radar installations were constructed in elevator shafts so that they could "pop up" and "pop down" for protection against enemy air attack. SA-2 Guideline surface-to-air missile batteries and radar-controlled antiaircraft gun positions dotted the mountain slopes—ready to turn any strike aircraft attacking the few above-ground installations into piles of flaming wreckage.

Even the logistics facilities and train yards were hardened to prevent resupply trains from being caught at their most vulnerable point.

Naturally the North Koreans had saved the best for last.

A hangar even larger than the first, crammed with sleek, delta-winged interceptors, Jian-7s—Chinese-model MiG-21F derivatives. They'd allowed him to move freely throughout the hangar, inspecting everything at close range. For Borodin it had been like diving nearly thirty years back into his own past. The MiG-21 had been the first real combat aircraft he'd ever flown.

So many years ago. He and his wife, Tania, had still been a happy couple then. Borodin shook his head. Those were unprofitable memories. It was more important to concentrate on the task he faced here and now.

The colonel narrowed his eyes, trying to recall as much as possible of Kim's last little speech, delivered near the wingtip of one of the camouflaged fighters. What had the man said? "We are confident of our ability to resist an imperialist attack and deliver a crushing blow in return. There are bases like this all over the People's Republic, and they make the aggressor's task impossible."

Borodin tapped his pen thoughtfully against his chin. There had been something else. Something that had struck him as even more bombastic, more dangerous somehow. Ah, yes. "Four more bases like this one were recently completed near the present Demilitarized Zone. From them we will be able to launch our final drive for the liberation of the South. Our troops are well trained and can use our equipment at its maximum effectiveness."

Borodin hadn't liked the sound of that. "Final drive for the liberation of the South." From anyone else he would have dismissed it as the standard propaganda line. But there had been a tone of inevitability or certainty in Kim's voice that sent chills up his spine. Should he highlight that statement and his impression of it for Moscow's attention?

No, perhaps not. You're tired, Sergei Ivanovitch, he told himself. You're dreaming. Putting strange interpretations on things you heard hours ago. Stick to what you know—air combat—and let the diplomats worry about the other things going on around this place.

He leaned closer to the paper, shutting away the uncertainties by remembering the show they'd put on for him.

Kim had no sooner finished speaking when he'd turned and nodded to a nearby North Korean Air Force colonel, who'd simply raised his hand overhead and shown a clenched fist.

A klaxon had blared from the hangar roof high overhead and Borodin had jumped. He'd had to stifle the urge to run for an aircraft—the old reflexes were still there from his days in the air defense forces, *Voyska PVO*. Instead he'd turned to watch men pour from doors in the walls. He'd picked one man in a flight suit out of the mass and tracked him as he ran over to a MiG—no a Jian-7, he corrected himself, not quite the same thing.

The North Korean pilot had bounded up the ladder like a gazelle as ground crew circled the aircraft, moving equipment and performing last-minute checks. Then a howling roar as the first jet engine fired up. The noise had bounced off the walls and hurt Borodin's ears.

He'd felt air moving and looked up to see huge ventilation fans pumping fresh air into the hangar. More noise. The pilot he'd been concentrating on had just started his engine. Most of the exhaust seemed to be directed into a vent or pipe directly behind the aircraft. More tunnels in the rock, Borodin thought. Mother of God, these people were like moles.

As the first interceptor rolled off its chocks toward the main hangar doors, a North Korean Air Force colonel had pointed wordlessly to a huge clock directly over them. Obviously started the moment the alert began, it had shown just a little more than two and a half minutes elapsed time. Even considering the simpler systems and controls on the MiG-21/Jian-7, that was still a good time, well within Soviet training norms.

The exit doors, however, had still been closed. For a moment Borodin had half-wondered if they planned to show him an interceptor smashing head-on into reinforced steel. But then, as the Jian-7's nose wheel crossed a yellow line painted on the floor, he'd heard a loud, ringing alarm above the howling jet engines and watched in amazement as the hangar doors snapped open, tons of metal moving in seconds. The jet had shot through, followed by another and another, until the entire battalion of aircraft had been scrambled. The entire exercise had taken nine minutes and fifteen seconds.

Borodin thought that was a damned good time. Even assuming that he'd been shown a hand-picked group of pilots and ground staff, it was clear that the weekly practice alerts carried out by the North Koreans paid off in professionalism and speed.

The colonel nodded to himself. Yes, mix the pilots he'd seen today with the newer MiG-23s he knew were operating out of other bases, add the even more advanced planes his country was shipping soon, and you'd have a damned good air force. An air force capable of handling almost any mission it was given.

Borodin remembered Kim Jong-Il's cold, challenging stare. The final liberation he had said. Could he have been serious? What was it General Petrov had said about the North Koreans? Something about Pyongyang being almost inside the Soviet Union's nets. Borodin began to wonder if it might not be more accurate to turn that phrase around.

C H A P T E R

5

Night Flyers

SEPTEMBER 9—KUNSAN AIR FORCE BASE, SOUTH KOREA

Captain Tony Christopher, USAF, stood outside the squadron building watching the sun set beyond the flight line. One hand held his gray helmet and oxygen mask. The other held a thick stack of papers—flight plans, bomb range restrictions, maps, and divert fields—all the stuff that training missions are made of. He wished again that the F-16 had a bigger cockpit. He always had a tough time squeezing his six-foot frame plus assorted paperwork into the plane.

He squinted into the bright, orangish-red light thrown off by sun as it dipped toward the Yellow Sea. Where in God's name was his wingman?

Suddenly hands landed heavily on either shoulder. Tony started a bit but kept his voice calm. "Hi, Hooter."

"Shit, Saint, you're no fun. I did that to you yesterday and you jumped three feet." His wingman, First Lieutenant John "Hooter" Gresham, came around to stand beside him.

"Yeah, well my nerves are all worn-out and I need what's left for this mission. You've got four ninety-four."

"I know." Hooter looked smug. "As your friendly training records officer, I make it a point to keep fully informed." Every pilot in the 35th Tactical Fighter Squadron did more than just play fighter jock full-time. Each also wore another "hat," doing all the other administrative work needed to keep the squadron flying and combat-ready. Hooter's second hat kept him busy making sure that every pilot complied with the rigorous training schedule set down by Air Force regulations.

Hooter snapped his fingers. "Say, that reminds me. Speaking in my official capacity, I need to know when you want to schedule your next chemical warfare flight."

Tony groaned. "C'mon, Hooter. Cut me some slack. I just did it a couple of months ago!"

Hooter grinned. "Nice try, revered boss and flight leader. But you and I both know that a new period started July first. And you've gotta fill in the square once every six months."

Every pilot Tony knew hated chemical warfare training. Trying to fly a plane while wearing the special protective gear it required was like wrestling a giant octopus in a Turkish steam bath.

"Okay, okay. But can I at least wait till it cools off some? That rubber suit is hell. Just let me worry about this hop for right now."

"You got it."

This was going to be a night ground-attack training mission, and although the F-16 can fly and fight at night, it does not have sophisticated sensors like the Air Force's dedicated attack aircraft. To see their target, Tony and Hooter were going to have to coordinate their efforts: one plane would drop flares while the other made the attack run. Simple, until you remembered that each pilot would be flying at four hundred knots, so close to the ground that an unintentional twitch could turn both F-16s and their highly educated pilots into a short-lived fireball and a shallow crater.

They needed teamwork to fly and teamwork to fight. Tony studied his sandy-haired wingman out of the corner of his eye. When you wear the same clothes, have the same job, and talk about the same things, you do not lose your individuality. Differences become more apparent; not less. And there were differences. It was as if somebody in the Air Force personnel office had decided to try teaming opposites as an experiment.

Tony was the quieter of the two. There is no such thing as an introverted fighter pilot, but his unhurried movements and restrained speech contrasted sharply with Hooter's ebullient manner. Anyone watching the two of them together would notice the wingman in almost constant motion, his boundless energy seemingly uncontainable.

Tony was vastly more experienced than Hooter, which may have explained some of the difference. After the Air Force Academy, Tony had moved directly into the F-16 and had been with the aircraft from the beginning. After his initial tour he had attended Fighter Weapons School, at Nellis Air Force Base in Nevada. Unlike Red Flag, which teaches air combat, Fighter Weapons School teaches how to employ effectively all types of ordnance. Only the best pilots qualify for admission.

The men who graduate from that difficult course teach the rest of their squadrons what they know, which is how to best apply the Falcon's impressive firepower against any kind of target. Additionally, it was an important ticket to be punched on the way to higher rank and more important assignments.

After the school, Tony had continued to assimilate everything he could find, not only to stay current, but because he knew it might make the difference someday. He was definitely the squadron's, and maybe the wing's, best expert on how to blow up things with airplanes. He had been in Korea for over half a year.

Hooter, in contrast, was still in his first tour, fresh from ROTC, and had only been in Korea a few months. He was still discovering the Falcon's good and bad points. Every flight was an adventure, an experience to be remembered.

Tony welcomed Hooter's almost constant stream of jokes and tricks, knowing that he applied the same energy to his ground duties and his flying.

Also to his after-hours activities. They were only a few years apart in age, but Tony had to work hard to keep up with his younger companion.

Though he'd never have admitted it out loud, Tony knew he couldn't consider himself the best flier God had ever made. He was good, damned good, but he wasn't the best. Instead, he'd found his edge in air-to-air combat with an ingrained ability to look at an adversary's maneuvers, plan a step ahead, and force the other guy all over the sky. He'd overheard Hooter talking about him in the O-Club one night.

"Now the Saint doesn't fly the best plane in the sky," his monumentally inebriated wingman had said, "but he does fly confounded tactical."

Hooter, on the other hand, was a natural shot and a demon flier, but he lacked experience and sometimes he lacked good judgment. His abilities and aggressiveness could usually get him out of the tight spots he landed in. In Tony's book, though, "usually" wasn't good enough. He'd been working Hooter hard to get him to understand the difference between "acceptable risk" and "frigging stupid." Still, they'd been flying together for months now, and Tony had to admit that they made a damned good team. Their very different personalities and flying styles made a winning combination in the air.

There were differences on the physical side, too. Hooter was shorter by four inches, which meant a lot more room in the cockpit. That was just as well because Tony knew that his wingman had trouble keeping still anywhere. He smiled to himself. Even now he could see Hooter shifting from foot to foot while they waited to get a jeep ride out to the aircraft shelters.

He came out of his thoughts as the jeep they'd been waiting for came careening around the squadron building and slowed down to a crawl in front of them.

Hooter was already in motion. "Hey, Saint! Shake a leg. Daddy's come to take us to the prom!"

Tony grinned and clambered aboard. They sped off across the tarmac toward the aircraft shelters.

Their planes for the night's mission, side numbers 492 and 494, were parked in shelters G and H. These were reinforced concrete arches, strong enough to take anything up to a one-thousand pound bomb hit and protect the airplane inside. The armored blast doors in front and back were massive, but perfectly balanced, so that if the power drive for the door failed, they could be pushed open by hand. They could also be sealed against poison gas.

Crew Chief Baines was already in shelter G waiting for him. Sergeant Baines was assigned to tail number 492 full-time. The same pilot did not fly this plane all the time, but Baines was always its crew chief. As far as he was concerned, it really belonged to him, and the pilots just "rented" it for occasional hops.

The shelter was big enough to hold a twin-engine F-15 or a larger aircraft, so the single-engine F-16 "Electric Jet" looked small, almost lost. It was surrounded by the paraphernalia needed to get a Falcon in the air: a ladder, starting cart, and fire extinguisher.

Tony started his preflight. It wasn't that he didn't trust the crew chief, but Baines was human. You were only allowed one error in a jet aircraft, and Tony hadn't made it yet. There were pilots who made such a great show of trusting the crew chief that the only thing they checked was the side number, to make sure they were getting in the right aircraft. Tony remembered the time that Crew Chief Baines and his cohorts had pulled a fast one and parked a plane without an engine in the arch. The hapless aviator assigned to fly it hadn't caught on until he hit the starter for the third time.

Okay, then. The load: first a cigar-shaped centerline drop tank, carrying an extra three hundred gallons of fuel. The Sidewinders on the wingtips were mandatory. This was an air-to-ground mission, but you always had to be ready for air-to-air. Besides, the rails wouldn't carry anything but the missiles. The plane's port inboard rack held a flare dispenser and the starboard held a cluster of practice bombs. Each bomb weighed about twenty-five pounds and had a small gunpowder charge. Just large enough to make a satisfying bang and a mark large enough to judge exactly where it had landed. Pretty harmless stuff compared to the one-ton monsters filled with Minol that the F-16 would carry on a real ground-attack mission. Finally, the cannon was "hot." The drum held 20-millimeter ammo for the strafing runs they would practice later.

Next he checked to make sure all the arming tags were removed from the ordnance and the racks. If the pins weren't taken out, the practice bombs and flares wouldn't drop when he pressed the release. Tony walked all the way around the plane, looking at the skin, the fueling points, the exhaust, following a mental routine he had performed almost a thousand times. He ended up by the ladder and signed the form Baines offered. It was now "his" airplane, at least until it was wheels down again.

He climbed in and strapped himself to the seat. If he had to eject, the straps would ensure that he stayed with the ejection seat as it pulled him from the plane. Connect oxygen, g-suit umbilical, microphone lead. Tony looked at his watch: 1955. Not bad, five minutes to engine start and all he had to do was light off the INS.

He turned on the Falcon's master power and started the inertial navigation system. It took the gyros three minutes to spin up, more time than it took to start the engine. While it did, he performed the rest of his cockpit checks. When he finished, he called his wingman on the ground frequency. "Hooter, you ready?"

"Rog, Saint, on your call."

From this point on they would use their nickname call signs exclusively. They were easier to remember than "Echo Zulu three," and less confusing than "John" or "Tony." There might be more than one pilot named John on a frequency, but the Wing's call sign committee made sure there was only one Hooter and one Saint.

Tony looked at his watch again. It was exactly 2000 hours. He said, "Go."

He signaled Baines, who hit the button to open the shelter's blast doors. Tony simultaneously hit the starter and listened as the F-16's engine spooled up. First a whine, a sound like a vacuum cleaner, then the teeth-rattling roar as he throttled to sixty-five percent power. Enough to start the ship moving.

Tony called on the ground frequency, "Bluejay flight on the North Loop ready to taxi."

A disembodied voice answered in his helmet, "Bluejays, you are clear."

Time to release the wheel brakes. He started rolling and came out into the night.

He looked to the left and saw Hooter leaving his arch. Tony switched to the tower frequency. "Bluejay flight rolling."

"Roger, Bluejay, you are number three for takeoff. Wind is one five zero at ten."

Rolling side by side, they reached the North Loop taxiway and turned right. The 35th had its shelters dispersed around a circular asphalt taxiway as wide as a two-lane road called the North Loop. The 80th had a similar "South Loop."

As they approached the runway, they heard a two-ship formation of fighters like them take off. They rounded the last corner and saw a C-141 cargo plane lining up for its run. He heard the tower give it clearance and it started rolling. Tony called the controllers again: "Tower, Bluejay flight 'number one' for the active."

"Roger, Bluejays. Stand by, you're next."

The Starlifter cleared the runway, lumbering into the night sky. His earphones crackled with another transmission from the tower: "Bluejay cleared for takeoff."

Tony called, "Request permission for combat departure."

A short silence. "Granted."

Hooter had been monitoring the circuit, and as soon as they had permission, they rolled the planes onto the end of the runway and lined up.

Tony glanced over at his wingman and called, "Go."

They both hit the throttle, first going to one hundred percent normal power and then to afterburner, which pushed them into their seats and threw the planes down the runway.

Both F-16s quickly reached flying speed, about 100 knots. Tony held it on the runway for a few more seconds and it built up to 150. Okay. "Rotate."

He pulled up into the sky and looked over to see Hooter's nose coming up at the same time. They raised their landing gear and flaps, and by this time they were at five hundred feet and clearing the end of the runway.

Tony said, "Now." And chopped the throttle back to military power, killing the afterburner. The noise level dropped and he banked the aircraft hard left. He also thumbed a button on the stick, sending a string of small flares trailing out behind him. Hooter followed his movements.

Turning, killing the afterburner, and dropping flares would confuse any heat-seeking missiles launched by an enemy. Combat departure takeoffs were supposed to be practiced frequently because the "simulated" enemy could turn out to be very real: North Korean commandos landed by sea with shoulder-fired SA-7 missiles.

Having successfully gotten away from the airfield without being shot at, they climbed to five thousand feet and turned to the southeast. The range was about fifteen minutes away—not worth climbing to a higher, more fuel-efficient altitude. The sun had set, allowing the ground to cool and reducing the turbulence.

Tony started to relax. Unlike the States or Europe, there were few restrictions on where or how to fly. Few complaints were received about supersonic flight at treetop level. The bad guys were too close.

As they approached the bombing range, Tony rocked his wings to signal Hooter and changed his Heads-Up Display—the HUD—to air-to-ground mode. He armed his practice ordnance, then descended to five hundred feet. This was the minimum peacetime altitude allowed for nighttime flight. In wartime they would fly as low as the light and terrain allowed, one hundred feet or even less. From here on, they would use wartime procedures.

The target range was in a small plain, with several north-south valleys leading down to it. The two F-16s dropped into one of them, relying on the valley walls to mask their approach from enemy radars that weren't there now, but that would be if this were the real thing.

They had arranged for Hooter to make the first attack. Tony rocked his wings again and they accelerated, changing formation. Hooter held back, allowing Tony to take the lead. He selected "Flare" on his weapons panel.

The two jets screamed out onto the plain at four hundred knots. As they cleared the valley, Tony pulled up and hit the weapons release. Behind him a million-candlepower flare lit up the plain with white magnesium light. Tony imagined all the attention he would be getting right now and practiced evasive maneuvering, popping chaff and flares to decoy any missiles that might have been fired at him. The wild maneuvering alternately pushed him into his seat, then pulled him out of it. If he hadn't been strapped in, his head would have been thrown against the canopy.

Hooter pulled up behind Tony, too, but only until he could see the target—a ten-meter-wide paint mark on the ground. Then he nosed over into a shallow dive. He steadied up and pressed his stick's "pickle switch," locking the F-16's weapons computer onto the target's location. The HUD changed, showing lines leading to the target and the range. As soon as he was happy with the lock, he increased throttle to full military power and closed on the aim point at over five hundred knots.

The light from the flare was starting to fade, and shadows flickered on and off the target. The landscape streamed by, flashing past almost too fast to consciously see, and Hooter concentrated on lining his nose up exactly with the target line on the HUD. The word RELEASE flashed in the corner and he pressed the release button on the stick, simultaneously twisting it hard to the right. He grunted hard, tensing his muscles as his weight suddenly quintupled. The practice bomb flew off the rack, literally thrown toward the target as the plane turned away.

They both turned south and headed out on a prearranged bearing. Hooter called, "Good timing on the flare, Saint. Any earlier and I wouldn't have locked on in time."

Tony looked over to pinpoint his wingman's plane against the dark night sky. "Your run looked good, Hooter. My turn now, watch the interval on approach."

They reversed roles and prepared for another run on the target. In wartime, making a second run on a now-alerted enemy was a good way to suddenly lose an airplane. But this was training, and each aircraft had enough bombs for three attack runs.

Tony's first run on the target was good, but Hooter's evasive maneuvers were pretty limp. They switched again and Tony told John to keep one eye on him as he threw the ship around. On the next attack run, Hooter's flare didn't ignite so they bugged out of the target area and reformed. As they turned back south for Hooter's final go at the much-abused paint spot, Tony shifted in his seat. He was starting to get tired and he had a few runs left to go. He frowned and settled in to concentrate on the oncoming target.

As Tony pulled up and hit the flare release, he heard a *beep-beep-beep* sound in his earphones. He spared one glance at his threat display, then pushed the ship over into a six-g turn to the left. At the same time he called, "Hooter! Scrub the run and join on me! Inbounds."

His mask pressed into his face, and he tensed his body to fight the g forces.

Hooter's voice was excited. "Roger, you have the lead. I'll come up on your right."

As he heard his wingman's voice in his helmet, Tony thumbed a button on his throttle. The radar display changed to air mode, the pattern on the HUD display shifted, and the word CANNON appeared in the lower left corner. Although the bombs and Sidewinders were practice versions, the 20-millimeter ammo in his M61 gun was live. The weapons computer automatically selected cannon when he pressed the dogfight button.

As his nose swung around, the radar picked up two contacts about twenty miles out. Both showed positive IFF. They were friendlies. Whew. He turned the radar off, to avoid revealing his position.

Easing up on the turn so that Hooter could join up quicker, he looked over his right shoulder. His wingman was on burner, pulling into position about a mile to the right and back. "Hooter, they're friendlies. Safety out your ordnance and we'll play."

"Arming phasers, Kyptin."

Tony was unimpressed. "I'm going for a nine-lima slew, then we're going vertical." As he said this, he put the aircraft in a gentle dive since a lower altitude made them harder to spot or lock on to. Hooter followed him down automatically.

"Rog. It's showtime."

The range had closed to about ten miles. Still nothing visible in the night sky ahead. Tony turned the radar back on and put it in SLEW mode. A new circle appeared on his HUD marking the spot where the radar "saw" the lead bogey closing at five hundred knots. Tony used a small control to move it over to the left, well off his line of flight. This was going to be a difficult shot, but he was the squadron's weapons officer. He had to teach it to everybody else.

Suddenly a small box appeared around the circle—he was locked on. He selected the AIM-9L Sidewinder on the left wingtip and was rewarded with a growl in his headphones. The IR seeker on the missile had its target in view and was telling him with an audible signal. SHOOT appeared on the HUD and he pulled the trigger.

The missiles were practice rounds without propellant or warheads, so nothing left the rail. But if it had been real, his target would be dead. Tony grinned under his oxygen mask. The video recorder would display all the data on the HUD as proof back at debrief.

The two oncoming planes were just visible now, rushing toward him out of the starlit darkness. They were F-16s.

Tony came up on the wing frequency. "Lead Falcon heading south over Range Alpha, this is Bluejay One. Gotcha." The missile's growl was audible on the circuit.

There was no answer, but their two opponents broke hard left, turning toward them. Tony saw it and called, "Burner." He shoved his throttle all the way forward. As the engine responded with a satisfying roar, he pulled back sharply on the stick.

The F-16 Falcon is one of the most agile aircraft in the world. Among its other sterling qualities is an engine that puts out more thrust than the aircraft weighs. This means that it can do very interesting things, like accelerate while going straight up.

They climbed, quickly passing the altitude where their two opponents were still turning left. Tony did a rapid calculation in his head and rolled the aircraft to the right, still climbing, so that he was "facing" their adversaries, who were now behind and beneath him. Hooter kept with him, hanging on to his wing as if he were glued there.

Still pulling on the stick, Tony passed over the top and saw a dark horizon, the ground, climb up the back of his canopy. He searched quickly "over" his head and was rewarded with two bright points of light—the two "enemy" F-16s had also gone to burner, but it was too late. They were still turning left.

Diving on full burner, he pressed the cannon select button on his stick. As the radar shifted he called, "Hooter, I'm going for a gun on the aft ship." He heard Hooter click his mike switch twice in answer.

The radar locked up immediately and he adjusted his dive slightly to put the "death dot" aiming reticle over the target. He forced himself to count "one potato, two potato" so the gyros could catch up with all his hard maneuvering. The SHOOT prompt came on again and he pulled the trigger. "Aft ship, this is Bluejay One. You're a mort."

Hooter's excited voice came over his phones. "Beautiful, Saint. I wonder if we can frame a videotape?"

Without a word the two "enemy" planes pulled up and rocketed off for points unknown, and the Bluejays turned for base. Two blasts of afterburner had significantly reduced their fuel.

"Saint, who were they? I didn't see any other Falcons scheduled in our area tonight."

"Probably some Juvets from the 80th ordered to surprise us. I heard a rumor the wing commander was going to try something like this."

Hooter chuckled, "Well, they can surprise us like that anytime they want."

"I'll pass. They might have been real gomers. Thank God we dropped enough ordnance to mark off the box. If they had interrupted us sooner, we'd have had to repeat the mission."

"Yeah, then you wouldn't have safetied out the cannon."

Ten minutes later they were back at base, and it took just five minutes more to taxi to the arch. Tony climbed out of his cockpit feeling like he'd been there for a year. Pulling five to seven g's wears you out. It was 2130 and he and Hooter still had an hour of debrief left before they could sleep. But there were two poor bastards in the 80th who'd be up late, too, and they wouldn't have much fun watching their after-action videotape.

CHAPTER
6
Uncertain Welcome

SEPTEMBER 14—KIMPO INTERNATIONAL AIRPORT, SOUTH KOREA

Second Lieutenant Kevin Little was more than a little worried. So far, at least, on his first real day of active duty as an Army officer, nothing—absolutely nothing—had gone right.

It had started with his flight into Kimpo International Airport that morning. Bad weather in Seattle had kept him from making his KAL connection in Anchorage, and he'd had to wait for the next plane. That had turned a planned fourteen-hour trip into a full twenty-four-hour nightmare. That would have been bad enough. But then he hadn't been able to get through to the battalion travel office at Camp Howze to let them know that he'd been delayed.

So now that he had finally gotten into Kimpo, his transport to the battalion had been and gone. And the Eighth Army captain in charge of ground transportation at the airport was making it crystal clear that sympathy was in short supply in South Korea.

"Listen, Lieutenant whatever-your-name-is, I don't give a raggedy rat's ass about your missing ride. We've just come off a six-day alert and I've got better things to do than to spend time rounding up a car and driver for every woeful, wayward, green-as-grass replacement wandering around in Korea. Like getting some sleep, for example. Got it?'' The captain kept his voice low, but Kevin could swear that every lowly PFC and clerk in the room had heard every word.

Cripes, now what? His first, miserable day in ROTC basic training flashed back to him. The captain had asked a question to which there was only one permissible answer.

Kevin drew himself to attention. ''Sir, yes sir.'' He almost stopped—why was the captain's face turning bright red? Hurriedly he carried on, ''Could the captain please direct me to the nearest cab stand or bus station, then?''

''Oh, shit, boy . . .'' The man seemed to be trying hard not to laugh, ''Don't you know Americans aren't real popular around this country right now? You might be able to get a cab, but you'd be just as likely to end up way down in Pusan as at Camp Howze.''

The captain turned to bellow at one of his sergeants standing just a few feet away. ''Fergie! See what we can do for this little lost lamb! I guess we're playing nursemaid today.''

He looked back at Kevin. ''Don't expect too much or anything too fancy. General McLaren, the Big Boss here in Korea, doesn't like seeing officers spending their time riding around like some kind of foreign potentates.'' The captain's Alabama drawl stretched the word ''potentates'' into something that sounded vaguely obscene.

The captain yawned. ''You're lucky I'm in a merciful mood, Lieutenant. And now that I've put your case in Sergeant Ferguson's capable hands, I've done all that I can.'' He yawned again. ''If you'll excuse me, I've got some important paperwork to clear up.'' With that, the captain sauntered into his office and closed the door.

Sergeant Ferguson, a wiry, little man, motioned Kevin over to a chair. ''Better take a pew, Lieutenant. This might take awhile. Not a whole lot going up toward the Z today. Should be able to get you something though.'' He started flipping through a huge stack of papers on one of the desks.

Kevin sank into the chair. Jesus, here he was. Stuck in Korea. Stuck in the hands of a bunch of Army clerks. His new battalion commander had probably already listed him as AWOL, absent without leave. He could just see writing to his parents: "Dear Mom and Dad, arriving back from Korea tonight. Please write care of Leavenworth Army Prison." He leaned his head back against the office partition in misery and then sat bolt upright.

The captain snored.

ALONG ROUTE 3, SOUTH KOREA

Two hours later Ferguson came through and Kevin found himself in the cab of an Army supply truck trundling north toward the DMZ. Jet lag was starting to catch up with him; he was tired, sore, and more than a little nauseous, and the truck driver, a shifty-looking corporal, seemed to delight in making hairpin turns, sudden lane changes, and ear-splitting gear shifts.

The driver hadn't even saluted him when he'd climbed aboard back at Kimpo Airport, and Kevin wasn't sure if he should report the man for insolence or just ignore it. Maybe they kept discipline pretty casual here in Korea—he just didn't know.

He looked out the window to hide his discomfort. They'd driven right along the Han River through Seoul before turning north. And Seoul, at least, seemed pretty interesting. Tall, modern skyscrapers and huge freeways all built right next to delicate, tile-roofed palaces and narrow, winding streets. The place was huge, too—a lot bigger than Spokane or even Seattle. It must have been nearly an hour before they left the city's sprawling suburbs behind.

The countryside wasn't like anything Kevin had ever seen back in the States either—flat, green, water-logged rice paddies reaching out all the way toward rocky, knife-edged ridges running along both sides of the highway. The tiny villages they passed looked like something out of *National Geographic* with brown-painted cottages topped with curving orange, green, blue, and turquoise roofs. Narrow country roads bordered by tall poplars and gently swaying willow trees bordered the highway. Kevin began to feel a bit better. Then the odor hit him. Charcoal smoke and unleaded gasoline and thick humidity rolled up into a foreign smell that seemed to magnify the strangeness of the place.

The corporal chuckled a bit when he saw Kevin wrinkling his nose. "You won't notice the smell by tomorrow morning, sir.

"If you think that's strange, they got that homemade napalm relish they call kimchee. They don't eat nothin' without it. Take a bunch of red peppers, cabbage, cucumbers, radishes, and stuff, mash it all up, and let it ferment for months. You can smell kimchee all the way to Honolulu if the wind's right.

"Course, it ain't so bad right now. You oughta smell it in July and August when the heat really comes on." That was just about the last complete sentence Kevin could get out of him all the rest of the way to Camp Howze.

CAMP HOWZE, NEAR TONGDUCH'ON, SOUTH KOREA

Camp Howze looked like an Army camp. The rows of whitewashed barracks, supply warehouses, and office buildings were all laid out with straight-edged, military precision. There was a big difference, though, from the stateside bases Kevin had seen. The camp was surrounded by barbed wired and cleared fields of fire, and he could see camouflaged bunkers guarding the main gate.

A large sign declared that Camp Howze was "HQ 1st Battalion, 39th Infantry Regiment—3rd Brigade, 2nd Infantry Division."

The driver let him off right in front of the main entrance and watched while Kevin hauled his bags out of the back of the truck. Then, without a word, the corporal wheeled his truck around and drove off back west toward the highway.

A sergeant walked down from the gate to meet him. "Reporting in, sir?"

Kevin nodded, fumbling in his jacket pocket for his travel orders. "My plane was late. I was supposed to be here last night."

The sergeant glanced through his orders. "Yes, sir. Battalion left word that you're to report to Major Donaldson, the XO, as soon as you arrive."

Kevin looked down at the pile of baggage at his feet and

was acutely aware that he desperately needed a shower and shave to look, feel, and smell human.

The sergeant smiled. "I think you could interpret that order a little loosely, Lieutenant. I don't think we'll be able to log you in here at the gate for another half-hour. In the meantime, we'll get you up to the BOQ."

The sergeant broke off to yell up at the two privates watching from the gate. "Malloy, Brunner! Move your lazy asses down here and help the lieutenant with his bags." He turned back to Kevin. "Welcome to Camp Howze, sir."

A quick shower at the BOQ—the bachelor officers' quarters— left him feeling a lot better, but Kevin still had knots in his stomach when he knocked on Major Donaldson's door.

"Come."

He opened the door, stepped inside, marched toward Donaldson's desk, and came to attention. "Reporting in as ordered, sir." Damn, why did his voice have to break every time he tried to sound properly military?

Major Colin Donaldson, a short, square-jawed man, looked Kevin over carefully for a brief moment, with all the studied disinterest of a man eyeing a horse he might want to buy someday. The major's gaze made Kevin feel as though he were being x-rayed. He wondered what Donaldson saw.

He knew he wasn't tall—barely average in fact. And though ROTC exercises and training marches had kept him in good shape, with a trim, flat stomach and muscular arms and legs, Kevin also knew he'd inherited his father's stocky build along with the older man's straw-colored hair and pale blue eyes. His father only kept his weight down by working from sunup to sundown on the family's Eastern Washington ranch. The Littles didn't have much choice, Kevin thought. It was either sweat or grow fat.

Feeling self-conscious under Donaldson's gaze, Kevin held his shoulders back and head rigid, resisting the temptation to scope out the maps and personal mementos scattered throughout the major's office. He had the feeling this wasn't the right time to give his innate curiosity full rein. Not by a long shot. In fact, if he'd learned anything in the ROTC, it was that there was always a time to just play dumb. A succession of increasingly irritable instructors had made that painfully clear to him over three summers of basic and advanced training. It had been a difficult lesson to learn.

Curiosity, brains, and the itch for adventure were a large part of why Kevin wasn't back home herding beef cattle from one sun-baked hill to the other. If he'd been the average kid in Ellensburg, Washington, he'd never have wanted to go to college. And if he hadn't wanted to go to college, he'd never have signed up with the ROTC to pay for it. And now his service obligations to the U.S. Army had landed him smack dab in the middle of this camp just south of the DMZ.

Part of him was still pissed off. South Korea hadn't been what he'd bargained for, and his orders to report there had come as both a shock and a disappointment. But another part of him was excited. This posting was sure to be a lot more interesting than the godforsaken spots in Texas, Tennessee, and Georgia that most of his classmates had been shipped off to.

After what seemed like an eternity, Donaldson pushed his chair back and came around the desk with his hand held out. "At ease, Lieutenant. I ain't going to bite your head off."

He shook Kevin's hand, waved him into a chair, and then perched himself on the corner of his desk.

Kevin thought he should explain why he was late. "Sir, I'm sorry I didn't get here on schedule, but you see, my plane was—"

Donaldson interrupted. "Don't worry about it, Lieutenant. We don't expect our officers to control the weather, or even the airlines. Eighth Army phoned this morning to let us know what happened to you." He paused for a moment. "But don't get the idea you can be late from now on. I'm going to expect your platoon to be ready to move when I say 'move' and to jump when I give the word. Clear?"

Kevin nodded.

"Good. That's settled then." Donaldson pulled a file off his desk and started leafing through it. There didn't seem to be much in it.

"Now, I see from your service record that you've had some language training. That was in Korean, I hope."

Kevin couldn't quite keep the bitterness out of his voice. "No, sir. I took four years of German in college—I never expected to . . ." He decided it might not be a good idea to finish the sentence.

Donaldson looked over at him, amusement clearly showing in his eyes. "You never expected to get sent to Korea, Lieutenant?"

"Well, sir, no. No, I didn't. I applied for an Army Intelligence posting in West Germany."

Donaldson shook his head. "Let me get this straight. You took years of German, probably studied their politics and culture and all that stuff real hard, and then you expected the Army to send you to Germany?"

The major tossed the personnel file back on the desk. "Welcome to the real U.S. Army, Mr. Little. Let me clue you in on a well-known secret. The Army moves in mysterious ways. It doesn't send you where you want to go, or even where you're best suited to go. It sends you where you're needed."

Donaldson stood suddenly, walked over to a map of South Korea, and jabbed it with a finger. "And that's right here, Lieutenant. It just so happens that we're short a platoon leader in this battalion. That's going to be your job for the next twelve months. You read me, Lieutenant?"

Kevin remembered the Eighth Army captain's laughter at his cadet salute, so he simply nodded. "Yes, sir. I'll do my best."

Donaldson smiled again. "Good. I know you will. Now let me bring you up to speed on your assignment."

He walked back over to his desk. "I'm giving you the Second Platoon in A Company. That's Captain Matuchek's mob. Matuchek's a damned good officer, so you live up to his standards and you'll go far. You'll also stay clear of trouble and off my shit list—which is exactly where you want to stay."

The major handed him a thick folder. "Here are the personnel records for your troops. Get to know them. Get to know which ones you can depend on and which you've got to watch. But remember, those records are just paper. They don't tell the whole story. You get to know the real men—the ones behind the paper—and you'll do all right."

Kevin didn't know what to say to that, so he just nodded again—feeling a bit like one of those little bouncing dogs some people stick on their car's dashboard.

He looked up as Donaldson asked, "Now tell me, who's the one man you can rely on to set you straight, spoon-feed you the info you need, and generally make sure you look and act like a proper young lieutenant?"

This sounded like some kind of test, but it seemed straightforward enough. "Captain Matuchek, sir."

"No. No, Lieutenant, it ain't Captain Matuchek. He's got a lot better things to do than try to keep you in line. No, the man you'd better rely on pretty damn heavily is your platoon sergeant. He's the one with the experience and the motivation to keep you from screwing up too badly."

Donaldson looked down at him. "And that's where you're a lucky man, Lieutenant. Your platoon sergeant, Sergeant Pierce, is a fine soldier—one of the best. He's a combat vet. Did two tours in Nam. So you listen up real close when Sergeant Pierce 'suggests' something. It just may save your platoon in a shooting situation. May even save your life, too."

The major stood. "Okay, Lieutenant. I've jawed at you enough." He looked at his watch. "It's eleven twenty-five hours now. Your troops won't get back from the firing range till fifteen hundred. So get some lunch, study those records, and then go over and get acquainted with your men. Any questions?"

Kevin did, but this didn't seem like the right time to ask about transfer application procedures. He shook his head, stuffed the platoon personnel files under his arm, and saluted.

Donaldson returned his salute lazily and turned to some of the paperwork piled up on his desk. But as Kevin headed for the door, Donaldson's voice stopped him. "One more thing, Lieutenant. Forget most of the crap they drummed into you in ROTC." He pronounced it "*Rot*-see." "It ain't going to help you worth a damn in dealing with real soldiers."

2nd PLATOON BARRACKS—CAMP HOWZE

Excluding the commanding officer, a full-strength U.S. "leg" infantry rifle platoon contains forty-five men, and all forty-five of them were lined up and waiting for Kevin Little when he came in the door of the whitewashed building housing the 2nd Platoon, A Company, 1st Battalion, 39th Infantry Regiment.

"Attention!" A loud, bull-like roar brought the troops up

straight and nearly gave Kevin a case of premature cardiac arrest. He'd hoped to come in quietly and talk to the platoon sergeant before officially assuming command. Scratch Plan A. Too bad he didn't have any Plan B.

A big man wearing sergeant's stripes stepped out of the ranks and saluted him. "Welcome to Second Platoon, sir. I'm Sergeant Harry Pierce." Pierce was even taller than Kevin and probably outweighed him by at least fifty pounds—all of it in muscle. He wore his graying hair in a crew cut so short it was almost invisible.

Kevin knew he couldn't just stand there gaping like some kind of idiot. He cleared his throat. "Thank you, Sergeant. Ah . . ." Cripes, now what was he supposed to do, make a speech or something?

Pierce cut in. "Would you care to inspect the platoon, sir?" His tone made it clear that this was one of those "suggestions" that Donaldson had talked about, and Kevin felt grateful. The sergeant seemed to be doing his best to keep him from looking too stupid.

Kevin nodded, trying to act as if taking over a platoon was just an everyday occurrence for him. "Yes, Sergeant. I certainly would." Jeez, that sounded pretty pompous. Well, he'd just have to drive on.

Pierce led him along the row of soldiers lined up by their bunks. Names and faces flashed by Kevin so fast that he knew he'd never remember more than a tenth of them. PFC Donnelly, 1st Squad Leader Corporal Kostowitz, PFC Simpson, his radioman, Corporal Jones, Weapons Squad Leader Corporal Ramos, and on and on.

The equipment he saw looked in pretty good shape, although Kevin knew he'd have had trouble telling the difference between a really well-cared for weapon and one that had just been "prettied-up" for inspection. But Sergeant Pierce obviously knew his business, and he hadn't taken any names—so everything must have been A-okay.

There was just one thing left out of the inspection, and when they reached the end of the line, Kevin turned to Pierce. "I'd like to take a look at the APCs, too, Sergeant. I assume they're parked over at the motor pool?"

Kevin heard a muffled chuckle, or maybe it was just a

cough, from somewhere in his new platoon. He reddened. Now what?

Pierce flashed a warning glance into the ranks and kept his voice low. "We don't have any armored personnel carriers, Lieutenant. The battalions in the Second and Third Brigades here in Korea are pure foot soldiers. We've got trucks to get us up to the Z and back again. But anywhere else we want to go, we walk—just like the old days."

Oh, shit. He should have remembered that from the briefing paper they'd given him back in the States. It had just slipped out of his brain somewhere along the way.

"Right. I suppose that's because we'll be fighting from bunkers and the other fortifications up at the DMZ—if it ever comes to that." Jesus, that sounded professorial as all hell.

Pierce eyed him calmly. "Yes, sir. That's about the size of it. Plus the fact that mechanized stuff doesn't do too well plowing through rice paddies or trying to climb the bastard-steep hills they've got around here."

Kevin nodded as if Pierce was just confirming everything he'd known all along. He had the uncomfortable feeling, though, that he hadn't fooled anyone—and certainly not the platoon sergeant.

He'd better get out of here before he said anything else that was laughably ignorant. He clasped his hands behind his back. "Well, Sergeant, the platoon looks fine. Carry on with today's schedule. See me in my quarters after chow tonight, and we'll go over the plans for the rest of this week. Okay?"

Pierce saluted. "Yes, sir." The sergeant wheeled to face the troops still standing in ranks. "All right, you heard the lieutenant. You know what you're supposed to be doing. Now, move." The troops broke ranks—the polished image of unity and order vanishing in a split second, changing instead into a milling crowd of individuals who just happened to be wearing the same clothes.

Kevin looked around him, trying hard to conceal his uncertainty. He wasn't ready for this. By rights he should be sitting at a desk on a base near some little German village, evaluating the latest intelligence reports coming in from across the Iron Curtain. Korea hadn't been in his plans at all.

Damn it, it just wasn't fair. He'd joined the ROTC to help

pay for college and to see the world. But not to wind up making an ass out of himself in front of a bunch of tough, professional soldiers. And he had a sinking feeling that was precisely what he was doing so far.

Pierce's deep voice broke into Kevin's thoughts. "Don't worry, Lieutenant. It isn't really as difficult as it might seem. You've got a good group of troops here. I've worked 'em hard and they're ready for just about anything." Kevin nodded. The men of his new command might be ready. But he sure as hell wasn't.

C H A P T E R

7

Reports

SEPTEMBER 19—WASHINGTON, D.C.

Cigarette smoke fogged the small, wood-paneled conference room, and Blake Fowler, his eyes watering, wondered why so many people in the intelligence community still smoked. Was it nerves or just the desire to look tough?

He could barely make out the wall clock through the haze. It was just after five in the evening. Outside the Old Executive Office Building's Victorian walls and gables, Washington's streets were filling up as tens of thousands of career government workers headed home—fighting their way through traffic that seemed to get worse with every passing day. Fowler laughed inwardly. At least this job kept him from sitting behind the wheel of an immobile car.

He looked around the crowded conference table. Almost everyone in the Korean Interagency Working Group had arrived. First, Mike Dolan from the CIA, a middling-tall, pug-nosed Boston Irishman with hair as black as night and an infectious devil-may-care grin. Fowler had always thought Dolan looked more like a middleweight boxer than a spy, and he had the feeling that was how the CIA agent wanted it. In contrast, plump, smooth-featured, pipe-smoking Alan Voorhees looked exactly like what he was, an academic turned Department of Commerce bureaucrat—complete with stylish Adam Smith tie and expensive leather briefcase.

Voorhees was deep in conversation with a tall, ramrod-straight black man who would never be mistaken for a mere bureaucrat. Even in a pin-striped, double-breasted suit, Brigadier General Dennis Scott looked as though he belonged in uniform. Fowler knew the Defense Intelligence Agency representative was nearing fifty, but only the gray speckled through his hair provided the slightest clue to his age. Scott still left younger opponents gasping for air on the squash courts near his Falls Church home.

Waspish little Carleton Pickering of the National Security Agency was barely visible beyond the general. Pickering's keen eyes, thick, bushy eyebrows, and fussy, precise voice had been a Washington intelligence community fixture for years. The tiny, fox-faced analyst had an uncanny ability to turn the tiniest fragments of raw intelligence into a polished and plausible picture of enemy intentions, activities, and capabilities.

The door suddenly slammed shut behind the Pentagon's representative, a bluff, hearty Navy captain named Ted Carlson. He swaggered to the corner coatrack, shrugged off his damp overcoat, and then whipped off his plastic-covered uniform cap. Water droplets cascaded from the cap onto the carpet. Carlson grinned at his startled colleagues and took an empty chair near Fowler.

One man wasn't there. Tolliver, the prep school kid from the State Department, was late again—as usual. Fowler had called State to find out where he was, only to be told by Tolliver's secretary that he was in another meeting and that she wasn't sure when, or even if, he could get there. Well, Tolliver could play catch-up on his own time.

Fowler rapped gently on the table, breaking through a hum of quiet shoptalk. "We've got a fair amount of material to cover this evening, gentlemen. So let's get the show on the road. I, for one, would like to get home before midnight."

General Scott smiled. "Not going to wait for our little friend from Foggy Bottom?" He didn't seem too upset by the prospect.

Pickering leaned forward, a slight smile on his narrow face. "I don't think Tolliver is likely to get here anytime soon. I hear the Secretary's given him a new job—he's working on the American desk these days."

Fowler and the others chuckled softly. It was an old joke but just true enough to stay funny. State Department "desks" were charged with keeping track of the issues and interests of particular countries. And the other agencies and departments with foreign policy responsibilities often wished that State had a similar organization to protect American interests—interests they sometimes felt were overlooked by the striped-pants diplomats in Foggy Bottom.

As the laughter died down, Fowler looked over at the CIA's representative on the Working Group. "Mike, why don't you kick things off tonight." When they'd first assembled the group, he'd asked Dolan to keep them up to speed on current events behind the scenes in Seoul. It had been a natural assignment. All the men sitting around the table had some measure of expertise in Asian political and military affairs, but the CIA had the best collection of sources in the region.

Dolan stubbed his cigarette out in an ashtray. "Yeah, okay." He pushed the ashtray away. "I got a telex from our people just before I came here tonight.

"Things are still fairly quiet in the streets. But that won't last long. NSP says the students are planning more demonstrations. And our people over there confirm that. The government's tried making police sweeps of Seoul National University, but the leaders they need to grab have all gone underground." Dolan handed the multipage telex he'd summarized over to Fowler.

"What about the official report they promised on the massacre?" Voorhees looked as though he really believed it might solve their Korean problem.

Dolan snorted. "Our sources say it's going to be released tomorrow. But it sure as hell isn't going to improve the situation."

He waved a hand toward Fowler. "You called that one

right, Blake. It looks like they're going to try to blame some lowly police officer for the order to fire. And he very conveniently got himself killed in the riot."

Grim laughter from the other members of the Working Group interrupted him.

"And just in case no one buys that, they're going to announce the simultaneous resignation of the Home Affairs minister. Apparently, he's been chosen to play the part of the sacrificial lamb."

General Scott cleared his throat. "Goddamnit, that's not going to settle anything. I've met the man's deputy and he's even more of a hard case than his boss. The bastard's probably the one who really gave the police orders to meet that demonstration with force."

Dolan nodded. "You've got it right, Denny. What's more, the students and opposition leaders know that as well as we do—probably better. The trouble is, nothing short of a complete government surrender will satisfy them now. And the government isn't going to hang out the white flags anytime soon."

Fowler and the others around the table knew what that meant. More demonstrations, more riots, and probably, more blood in South Korea's streets.

Fowler sighed. "Okay, all of that makes our analysis of the Barnes bill even more important. Legislative Affairs still says the bill won't make it to the floor, but it's already getting more press attention than they'd predicted."

He looked down at his notes. "Plus, I just got word this afternoon that the House Foreign Affairs Committee is planning to mark it up tomorrow morning."

The others sat up a little more sharply. A bill markup was the action stage for a congressional committee. Hearings weren't really important—markups were where the real work got done.

"Jesus, they're moving pretty damned fast, aren't they?" Captain Carlson sounded worried.

"C'mon, Ted. You know what the Foreign Affairs Committee's like. If those guys bent any more to the left, they'd fall right over on their asses." Scott's contemptuous assessment won agreeing murmurs from around the table.

The general continued, "And everybody knows that Barnes

and that son-of-a-bitch Dugan are like that." He held up two crossed fingers to represent the Trade subcommittee chairman and the chairman of the Foreign Affairs Committee.

Fowler and the others nodded. Barnes and Dugan were both from the same wing of their political party, and they'd been allies for years. They could be expected to trade favors. And the same could be expected from their counterparts in the Senate. Fortunately, though, the bill still had to run the gauntlet of the Armed Services committees on both sides of the Hill—and those committees, though less conservative than in past years, still leaned more to the right than the left.

Which was nice to know, but it didn't move them any closer to putting out a single, consistent administration policy paper on the legislation.

Fowler tapped his typed agenda. "Okay, next item. The trade sanctions provisions our friend Mr. Barnes has in his bill. We've already agreed on language spelling out just what they would do to importers and exporters in this country. The key question is, will the sanctions work?" He glanced around the table.

Voorhees took the pipe out of his mouth. "You mean, will they force the South Korean government to reform?" The Commerce Department representative sat back further in his chair. "No. I don't know about the rest of you, but I just don't see it. The Koreans are too proud. Giving in to Barnes would seem as bad to them as surrendering in a war."

Dolan backed him up—something that was probably a first. "Hell, the South Koreans are even more stubborn than the fucking South Africans. They aren't going to do diddly damned all just because the U.S. Congress threatens them."

Fowler stared down at his notes as the discussion rose and fell around him. Everything he'd seen during his year of postgraduate work in Seoul and everything the other Working Group members said tended to confirm Dolan's offhanded assessment. And that raised an ugly scenario. If the Barnes bill somehow made it through the congressional gauntlet, the South Koreans wouldn't meekly buckle under before its threatened sanctions went into place. They'd try to tough it out—at a potentially catastrophic cost to their own economy.

Over the last several years the South Koreans had run up a

forty-plus billion dollar foreign debt to modernize their country. They'd produced an economic miracle with the money—building superhighways, ultramodern factories, universities, all the infrastructure of a powerful industrial state. But it was an economic miracle that rested on a single, somewhat shaky base: exports. Back in 1984 fully a third of South Korea's gross national product had come from its sales overseas. To pay its foreign debts, South Korea had to run large trade surpluses with the rest of the world in each and every year.

If the Barnes trade sanctions went into effect, South Korea would lose most, if not all, of its single largest market almost overnight. And Fowler knew that the Europeans and Japanese would probably be close behind the United States in imposing protectionist tariffs on Korean products. They faced the same kinds of domestic political pressure groups as the U.S. Congress, and they'd already shown an even greater willingness to surrender to them.

And unlike South Africa, Iran, or Libya, where trade sanctions had failed miserably, South Korea didn't produce any irreplaceable products. Its companies had prospered by being able to manufacture cars, computers, and ships more cheaply than their competitors. But nobody's economy would collapse without access to Samsung TVs or Hyundai cars.

Fowler frowned. The economic risks for South Korea were clear. What would happen to a country whose whole economy rested on exports if the rest of the world suddenly turned off the cash flow? Whatever it was, it wouldn't be anything good.

He flipped to the next page of his notes, taking a discreet look at his watch while he did it. These meetings went pretty smoothly without having to listen to interminable speeches from the State Department's Tolliver. Maybe he could have Katie "forget" to notify Tolliver about the next session. It was a tempting thought and he knew he'd have to work hard to resist it.

He studied the other men around the table. "We've all seen Ted's paper analyzing the provisions in the Barnes bill that would force us to withdraw American troops from South Korea. He argues that the timetables for withdrawal would be difficult, if not impossible, to meet. Anyone have any questions or comments?"

The others shook their heads, but Carlson wanted to supplement his earlier written report. "Don't forget that it'd be godawful expensive, too. You're talking about shipping three squadrons of fighters, six artillery battalions, SAM batteries, helicopters, and a whole damned infantry division all the way across the Pacific."

Scott whistled. "Son of a bitch. That'd tie up a pretty big percentage of our strategic sea- and airlift assets."

Carlson nodded. "I've got my staff running studies now. We should have some hard numbers in a couple of days or so."

Fowler scribbled a reminder to himself to follow up on that. "Okay. So we'd have trouble implementing the withdrawal provisions on time and they'd cost an arm and a leg. Plus, providing the ships and planes to move our troops would eat into our ability to respond quickly to crises in other parts of the world."

He looked up. "Is that a fair summary?"

Mike Dolan answered for everyone. "Heap big white man from NSC speakum truth." The others around the conference table laughed.

Fowler grinned. Trust Dolan to keep him from getting too comfortable in the chairman's chair. He put his pen down. "That's settled then. But do my Indian brothers have anything to say about the military effects of pulling the Great White Father's soldiers out of Korea?"

That sobered them up.

General Scott spoke up first. "It'd be a damned big mistake—no ifs, ands, or buts about it."

"I don't see it, Denny." Voorhees shook his head. "We've got, what, maybe forty thousand men over there. Okay, that sounds like a lot. But the South Koreans have more than six hundred thousand troops. They don't need us to keep the peace anymore."

"Bullshit." Scott obviously didn't believe in mincing his words. "Sure the South Korean military is tough. Hell, they're very tough. But those bastards on the other side of the DMZ are just as tough and they stay put for one damned good reason." Scott held up a single finger. "Because the last time they tried invading, we kicked their butts all the way back across the thirty-eighth parallel."

Blake agreed with the general, but knew that he'd skipped over a few things—like the fact that it had taken three years of hard fighting and more than fifty thousand American dead to win the uneasy truce along the Korean Demilitarized Zone. Voorhees looked unconvinced.

Dolan broke in. "Look, Alan, the trouble is that the military threat South Korea faces has been growing dramatically over the last few years. There's a lot going on up there in Pyongyang that we need to be worried about."

"Like what? And don't give me some kind of 'need to know' runaround. I've got Code Word clearance just like the rest of you."

Dolan eyed Voorhees calmly. "Okay. Like the fact that the Soviets have been supplying the North Koreans with first-line combat aircraft. Like the fact that Kim Il-Sung and his boys are getting advanced tanks, artillery, and surface-to-surface rockets for the first time ever. Like the fact that North Korea's resident chief lunatic Kim has given the Soviets overflight rights and access to his naval bases—something that he's refused to do for more than thirty years."

"Oh, come on, guys." Voorhees laughed, a bit nervously. "You can't tell me you're going to try feeding everyone the old 'the Russians are coming, the Russians are coming' bullshit. No one's going to buy it. What kind of confirmation do you have? I mean, couldn't this stuff just be rumors spread around by the NSP to keep us backing the South Korean government?"

Fowler decided it was time to intervene. "Some of it may be. But not all of it. Our satellites have caught glimpses of new equipment being fed into the North, and we've spotted increasing numbers of Soviet warships and planes in and around North Korea."

He paused for a moment. "So we know for sure that North Korea's engaged in a sizable military buildup. What we can't get is solid data on what they plan to do with all that hardware. And in a way, that makes the situation we face worse. We can estimate the North's capabilities but we can't guess their intentions. That means we've got to plan for the worst case."

He looked over at Dolan. "Your people haven't been able to get anyone inside North Korea, have they?"

Dolan shook his head. "No. We don't have a single agent on the ground up there. The damned place is too regimented, too paranoid to infiltrate. We've worked with the NSP for decades to try to plant somebody. It never works. They go in . . . and they don't ever, ever come out."

Scott agreed. "Yeah. The only human intel we can get from inside Pyongyang comes from some of the Japanese companies that do business there. And we can't confirm much of that."

Time to bring it home. Fowler looked straight into Voorhees's eyes. "So what we've got, Alan, is a country that's already militarized beyond all reason. A country that's certainly acquiring even more weaponry. And a country that has a forty-year-old track record of aggression, assassination, and terrorism. Just how do you suggest we should interpret those facts?"

Fowler studied Voorhees's face carefully. He looked less sure of himself than he'd been before. Good. They had to convince him that there could be an increased military threat if the Barnes troop withdrawal provisions went into effect. If they didn't, Voorhees might talk his boss, the Secretary of Commerce, into disapproving the Working Group's report. That wouldn't please George Putnam one little bit. More importantly, it would set the stage for still another disjointed administration response to half-baked congressional legislation.

Fowler caught Dolan's eye. "Maybe you could let Alan take a look at your latest assessment of North Korea's military capabilities."

Dolan nodded back slowly, a barely perceptible smile on his face. "Sure thing." He turned to Voorhees. "I'd be happy to messenger over the file anytime you want to see it."

Voorhees looked around the table. He obviously knew he was outnumbered, and Fowler had offered him a face-saving way out. He nodded. "Okay. I'll take a look at it. If what you say about the Soviets' boosting North Korea's military capabilities is true . . ." Voorhees paused. "Well, I'd have to say that would show that an American troop withdrawal could cause some problems."

Fowler fought hard not to smile. They had him. Voorhees might not be completely convinced, but he wasn't going to oppose the group's analysis.

He glanced down at his watch again. God, it was getting late. It was time to declare victory and get back to his word processor.

He shuffled his notes back into order. "Does anyone have anything else they want to go over for now?" There was silence from around the table.

"Right. Okay, I'll finish putting together a draft position paper on the bill. I should have something to send around for comment by tomorrow night."

Carlson spoke for the others. "When do you need it back?" He looked unhappy. He was probably worried about missing the next Redskins game. Fowler knew he had season tickets.

"Frankly, as soon as possible. Sorry, Ted, but Putnam's really breathing down my neck on this one. And with the bill going into markup, he might not be so far off base. Maybe you can take it to the game with you." Carlson laughed.

Fowler stuffed his papers back into his briefcase. "Seriously, I've got a feeling the clock's running on this one, guys. And we'd better get our playbook written and approved before we get stepped on by Congress."

The other members of the Working Group nodded, gathered up their own notes, and filed out of the room. Fowler headed back to his office.

The meeting had gone pretty well. Unless he'd completely misread the signals, the others agreed that the Barnes bill should be vigorously opposed. There'd be the usual back-and-forth tussle over the exact wording, but in the end he should be able to get them to approve a clear, concise paper recommending that course to the President.

Fowler knew that might prove vital. From what he could gather from the nightly news and in shoptalk around the office, the Barnes Korean sanctions bill was gathering support left and right—though mostly from the left. Unions, church and human rights groups, so-called public interest organizations, and activists of every stripe were out beating the drums, sending in postcards, and holding press conferences. One of the farmers' groups had even come out in support of the Barnes bill. They'd been pissed off by South Korea's refusal to open its markets to

American agricultural products. It was beginning to look as if it were open season on South Korea.

It also looked as if he and his trusty computer were among the few standing in the steamroller's path. He stopped in the hallway, stifled a yawn, and laughed to himself. Talk about delusions of grandeur. He must be catching the "Washington disease"—the curious belief that everything everywhere depended on one's own actions.

He'd have thought he was immune to it, but perhaps it stole quietly into the brain—drawn in from the long, echoing marble corridors, from the flags, the statues of great men long dead, and from the tingling, ever present sensation of power that you felt from the very first moment you wore a security badge.

He walked on, idly fingering the badge hanging from a chain around his neck. It didn't matter. He had a policy paper to write, regardless of whether the importance he attached to it was real or imagined.

Fowler didn't get home until well past midnight.

He came in the door as quietly as he could. The town house they rented in suburban northern Virginia seemed well enough built, but it was small and sounds carried far at night.

He left the hall light off and felt his way along past his daughter's bedroom. He stopped for a moment at her door, listening for a change in her breathing. Part of him almost hoped she'd wake up. Kary was five, growing up fast, and he'd scarcely seen her for the past several months. But he kept moving. She was in school now. She needed all the sleep she could get.

Mandy had left the window blinds in the master bedroom open—letting in a soft white glow from the moon that gave him just enough light to avoid stumbling into the furniture. He undressed hurriedly, draping his suit pants, shirt, and tie over a chair. Fowler shivered. The August heat wave had finally broken only a couple of weeks ago, but the nights were already turning colder.

He laid his glasses, watch, and security badge on the nightstand by the bed and slid under the covers. A warm hand came up to gently stroke his face. He opened his eyes to see his wife propped up on one elbow. She smiled and bent down over him. "Hi, there. Glad you're home."

God, she was beautiful. The moonlight gleamed in his wife's corn-silk-fine, blond hair and illuminated her pert, freckled nose, delicate, oval face, and baby-blue eyes. His heart turned over with a thump, and he felt a sense of childlike wonder that it still did that whenever he saw her. Even after seven years of marriage.

He and Mandy had met as graduate students on a summer studies tour of Japan, and he'd fallen head over heels in love with her in hours—bowled over by the combination of beauty, intelligence, and a husky, Southern voice. He still didn't know exactly what she'd seen in him.

He just thanked God he hadn't completely lost whatever it was, despite the constant strain imposed by the hundred-hour workweeks his job often demanded. And it wasn't just a strain on him, he thought guiltily. He never seemed to be around when Kary was sick or Mandy needed his help. They'd exchanged some cold words over times like that. But so far they'd both been able to find their way back into love out of the cold. So far. Still, there were a lot of days when he regretted the pride and ambition that had made him forsake a quiet, university teaching career for the "glamor" of an NSC staff post.

Fowler reached both arms around her, holding her close, marveling at her warmth. "Sorry I'm so late." He kissed her neck. "I should have called."

She sighed, wriggling closer still so that she lay pressed against him. "It would have been nice. But after I saw the news reports, I knew you'd be late." She laughed quietly. "Don't worry, Dr. Fowler, I didn't file a missing person's report."

He tensed. He hadn't even turned on the office television that evening. "What happened? Was it something about Korea?"

He could almost feel Mandy's surprise. "I thought you knew. They had another riot somewhere over there with more shooting. Someplace called Kwangju, I think. It was on the eleven-o'clock news."

Damn. Goddamnit. The South Koreans were their own worst enemies.

He reached over for his glasses and badge as the phone started to ring.

SEPTEMBER 21—HEADQUARTERS, REPUBLIC OF KOREA ARMED FORCES

Jack McLaren sipped his tea appreciatively and set his cup down. He met the eyes of the four-star general sitting across from him. "*Aju masisumnida*. It's very delicious."

General Park, Chairman of the South Korean Joint Chiefs of Staff, smiled politely. "Your Korean is improving greatly, General McLaren. Someday I am sure I will mistake you for one of my countrymen." Park was a small, dapper man. The uniform fitted his wiry frame precisely. He was obviously in excellent condition.

"Thank you. But you're already much more fluent in my language than I will ever be in yours."

General Park bowed slightly to acknowledge the compliment. "Would you care for some more of this tea? Or perhaps there is something else I can offer you that would be more to your taste?"

Yeah, McLaren thought, how about putting an end to all this pussyfooting around and getting down to business. He controlled the urge to let his impatience show plainly. In Rome, you spoke Italian. In Bonn, you drank beer. And in Seoul, you suffered through half an hour of meaningless pleasantries before it was considered polite to talk seriously.

He had to admit, though, that he'd seen meetings in Washington that might have gone more smoothly had those involved spent a little time getting to know each other better.

But he already knew General Park all too well. Park's combat record as a battalion commander during the Vietnam War had been very good. He'd been deeply involved in politics since then, though, and it showed.

McLaren understood the disdain military men like General Park felt for the fractious politicians and the unending political disputes South Korea seemed to breed, but he didn't see how they thought they could do much better. Hell, you couldn't run a growing, prosperous country along strict military lines forever, and if you developed the kinds of political skills needed to run a democracy, you wound up just being another politician like all the rest. And Park was almost all politician these days.

McLaren drained his teacup and shook his head as Park's aide leaned forward to pour more tea. The Korean general delicately set his own cup back on the tray and motioned his aide out of the room.

Park sat back in his chair. "There, my friend, we are alone now." He smiled. "So we are free to discuss things... candidly, as you Americans would say."

McLaren nodded. "Good. First things first. I'd like to commend your troops for the way they handled that NK commando raid near Ulchin this morning. That was damned fine work."

A group of North Korean commandos had been landed by submarine, with a mission somewhere inland. While not routine, the North launched such a raid approximately once a month. Their usual missions included sabotage and assassination. Whatever mayhem had been planned this time, the heavy defenses that ringed the coast had stopped it cold, right on the beach.

"They were simply doing their duty. But of course I shall be happy to pass your commendation on to their division commander. He will be delighted, I am sure, to receive praise from the commander of all our Combined Forces."

McLaren heard the carefully controlled bitterness in Park's voice but let it pass. He'd known this was a difficult command situation before he'd accepted the assignment to head allied forces in South Korea. The South Koreans, understandably, were increasingly unhappy with a chain of command that put an American general with forty thousand troops in charge of the entire six-hundred-thousand-man South Korean military.

He looked straight into Park's eyes before continuing. "But I can't go along with this last request of yours. There simply are no valid military reasons to pull the 3rd Infantry Division back from the DMZ to the interior."

Park's face was impassive. "I must protest your hasty decision. Surely your staff has shown you the figures on the recent upsurge of attempted communist landings."

"Yes, my South Korean staff officers have shown me their

studies. But I also know that the forces already in place along the coast haven't had much trouble coping with these latest landings. They don't need reinforcements."

McLaren leaned forward. "Look, General. I'm well aware that you want those men posted back in the cities to help you control these student demonstrations. And I'm sure you're equally well aware that my country simply can't countenance the use of regular military forces to put down civil unrest."

"General McLaren." Park's anger was starting to show. "These riots are being sparked by terrorist agitators. My government is not facing simple crowds of unruly students. These radicals are being led by a hard-core communist cadre."

"Bullshit." Damn. McLaren was glad there were no State Department flunkies around to hear his undiplomatic language. But that was what they got for sending a combat soldier on a diplomatic fishing expedition. "Cut the crap, General. I don't doubt for a minute that the bastards up in Pyongyang are salivating over all the trouble down here. But don't try to feed me that stuff about these students being controlled by the commies. It ain't going to wash—here or in Washington."

Surprisingly, General Park smiled. "Very well. If you can speak so bluntly, then so can I. But I shall deny ever having said this, you understand?"

McLaren nodded. Well, well, so Park hadn't really expected him to buy the communist agitator line. Interesting.

"The truth is that my government must restore order in our cities . . . and we must do so quickly." Park lowered his voice. "As you know, we have a . . . how do you say it? A tradition of military intervention to bring order out of chaos."

McLaren nodded again. South Korea's military had jumped into the political fray in 1961 and 1979. "Go on."

"There are officers, junior-grade officers to be sure, but officers nonetheless, who are becoming unhappy with the way the government is handling this latest crisis. They believe we have been indecisive, even weak, in responding to these student provocations."

"So. Have your Defense Security Command deal with these officers. Hell, that's what you've got it for, isn't it?" McLaren couldn't see the problem. The Defense Security Command was a vast, shadowy organization maintained solely to protect the South Korean government from coup attempts by its own military. Security agents were attached to every significant armed forces command, with instructions to keep a close eye on all goings on. And all South Korean officers were subject to rapid and unexplained transfers whenever it seemed that they might be becoming too popular with their troops. It was a system that reduced military effectiveness, but it did provide the government with a powerful check on any overly ambitious officers.

But Park shook his head. "The grumbling is too widespread. If we took hasty action against just a few of these men, the others might be driven into an unfortunate decision."

Uh huh, McLaren thought, an "unfortunate decision" that would end the careers of a certain number of government officials—like General Park, for example.

Park looked closely at him. "So you see, General McLaren, it is essential that we bring this rioting to an end. The Combat Police are having trouble doing that. You must allow us to use our soldiers to restore order. It is necessary."

Cute. Very cute. McLaren knew full well that the government, if it simply wanted soldiers for riot duty, could use its "black beret" Special Forces troops—men who weren't under the Combined Forces Command. But using regular units, units nominally under his orders, would send a signal throughout Korea and around the world that the United States gave its full backing to whatever measures the South Korean government used to quell student dissent. Well, he wasn't going to play that game.

"No dice, General. If your government wants to end these demonstrations, I suggest you rely on the police to do it. And if I were you, I'd tread more carefully in the way you go about it. If you've been following events back in the States at all, you know the Congress is giving the administration hell right now about our involvement over here."

Park sat rigid in his chair for a moment. Then he stood abruptly. McLaren followed suit. "Then, General McLaren, I believe we have nothing further to discuss today. I shall inform my colleagues of your decision."

McLaren picked up his uniform cap and briefcase. "Okay, you do that."

"They will not be pleased. Perhaps our President will want to discuss the matter with your President."

So they were going to try going over his head on this one? That wasn't much of a surprise. But McLaren doubted they'd get any further with Washington than they had with him. "Fine. I'm sure they'll find a great deal to discuss. In the meantime, your colleagues don't have to be happy with my decision. They just have to live with it."

He returned Park's salute and headed out to his staff car. He had an inspection to conduct. And with the mood he was in, he sure as hell hoped the commander of the 4th Battalion, 7th Cavalry had everything ready.

C H A P T E R
8

Intentions

SEPTEMBER 23—PARTY HEADQUARTERS, PYONGYANG, NORTH KOREA

The lights were out all over Pyongyang, leaving the city wrapped in a darkness broken only by the stars reflecting off the Taedong River. All its massive government buildings, monolithic statues, and towering apartment houses merged into simple patches of greater or lesser blackness—without feature, without clear line, without scale.

Kim Jong-Il smiled bitterly as he stood looking out over the city from his office. He knew that these periodic practice air raid alerts and blackouts had little military use. He'd seen the lowlight videotapes made by the American bombers striking Libya in 1986. Denying them the use of city lights as aiming points wouldn't have much effect.

Still, the alerts served as an important instrument of

political control. They demonstrated unity and discipline. They reminded the people of the sacrifices of the past and of the dangers as yet all around. After all, what significance could petty internal grievances have when compared to the threat of an aggressive, imperialist war machine?

Kim turned away from the windows, closed the heavy blackout drapes, and switched on his desk lamp. The small circle of light cast distorted shadows against the wood-paneled walls of his office—shadows he ignored. He'd wasted enough time in useless contemplation. Now was a time for action.

The agent Scorpion's work had borne fruit beyond all his initial expectations. The bloody scenes in Seoul's streets had shattered the South's governing coalition, and they were driving the American Congress out of lockstep with its client state.

He had the wedge he'd sought. Now he had to make use of it.

Kim snapped open the sealed Defense Ministry folder sent over by special courier earlier that evening. It contained a thick sheaf of densely typed papers and annotated maps. The title page bore a simple, boldfaced legend:

Draft Operations Plan:
RED PHOENIX
Most Secret

SEPTEMBER 24—II CORPS HQ, KAESONG, NORTH KOREA

The rumble and clatter of tank treads made it impossible to speak. Lieutenant General Cho Hyun-Jae glanced nervously at the guest beside him on the reviewing stand. Then he swung his eyes back front and allowed himself to relax minutely.

His guest didn't seem angered or bored by the procession of battle-ready armored fighting vehicles Cho had arranged. On the contrary, Kim Jong-Il seemed pleased, almost excited. The hard, set lines around his mouth had softened somewhat, and Cho could see the momentary gleam of white teeth every time a T-62 thundered by the stand.

It was more a battle drill than a parade. A battalion's

worth of buttoned-up tanks pitched and rolled across the torn-up landscape at full throttle, spread out in platoon groups of four. The forty T-62s were followed by wave after wave of tracked BMPs and wheeled BTR personnel carriers, some towing mortars and light antitank guns. ZSU-23-4 Shilkas rolled along with this second echelon, their quad 23mm antiaircraft guns elevated and ready to fire into the black, threatening clouds that covered the sky.

Kim watched it all avidly, and Cho thanked the nonexistent gods that he'd arranged this realistic display of a motorized rifle regiment's combat power instead of the traditional, lumbering military parade. Its effect on the Dear Leader was well worth the precious fuel it consumed.

As the last vehicles roared off the review ground and over a hill, Kim leaned closer and pitched his voice just high enough to carry over their fading engines. "Excellent, General. A most impressive display. Your men typify the five combat readiness guidelines enunciated by my father: tenacious revolutionary spirit; miraculous and elaborate tactics; strong physique; point-blank shooting; and ironbound regulations."

Cho bowed his head, acknowledging the compliment. "Thank you, Dear Leader. I shall relay your approval to my troops."

Kim nodded and half-turned to stare out again across the tread-torn ground. The silence seemed to stretch forever. Then, abruptly, without looking directly at Cho, he said, "Let's take a walk together, General. We have much to discuss, you and I."

For an awful moment the tall, broad-shouldered North Korean corps commander felt his stomach twist in on itself, but he forced himself to appear calm and unruffled. Logically he should have nothing to fear from this man. His military record was distinguished, he kept his personal life carefully uncluttered of any suspicious bourgeois vices, and he'd made his personal loyalties clear years ago by siding with the pro-Soviet faction of the General Staff and the Politburo—a faction the younger Kim headed. Still, Cho knew fear in the presence of this man who had the power to wipe away careers, lives, with the stroke of a pen or a raised voice. Kim was not always logical.

He followed Kim out onto the open ground. The two men

walked for several minutes without speaking, paced by a small cluster of uniformed aides and a phalanx of Kim's heavily armed plainclothes bodyguards, all of whom stayed well out of earshot.

At last Kim stopped, his eyes fixed on the muddy remains of a small, grassy hillock that had been crushed flat by Cho's tanks. "Such power," he half-whispered to himself.

Then he swung round to face Cho squarely. "Such power, General. Tell me, as commander of our Second Corps, you most directly confront our enemies, true?"

"Indeed, Dear Leader."

Kim stepped delicately over a patch of soft ground. "So you understand the danger they pose to our Revolution?"

"Of course." What was all this about? It reminded Cho of the political instruction classes of his school days.

"Your wife is well? She finds your new apartment in Changwang Street to her liking?"

Cho looked at the shorter man in surprise. Why the sudden change of subject? "Yes, Dear Leader. But then she's always been fond of Pyongyang. She's a city girl at heart."

Kim smiled, showing his teeth. "Good. Good."

He clasped his hands behind his back. "Tell me what you think of Red Phoenix, Comrade General."

Cho shrugged. "I helped draft the plan during my last tour on the General Staff, Dear Leader. It was a good plan then and it's a good plan now. In fact, I believe that it offers our best hope for a successful liberation of the South." He frowned as one of Kim's boots splashed mud across his uniform trousers.

"I see." Kim's voice was flat, uninterested. "This plan calls for a surprise attack across the so-called DMZ—an attack launched right out of our barracks. Why?"

"Surprise is the handmaiden of victory," the general quoted. "The South has larger reserves than we do. A sudden, unexpected attack would deny them the time needed to mobilize those reserves. It would also prevent the Americans from shipping in their own reinforcements."

Kim nodded his understanding. They walked quietly across the torn-up field for several minutes more before he asked in a carefully casual tone, "How soon could you be ready to launch Red Phoenix? Two weeks? A month?"

A strange question. So strange that Cho answered honestly, without thinking of possible consequences. He shook his head. "Impossible. We couldn't possibly be ready for several months at least."

Kim pounced on that. "Why not? Have you and your fellow generals been shirking? Where is all this readiness for instant action you've always promised."

The look in the smaller man's eyes made Cho picture an ice-cold bayonet poised at his vitals.

It was a time to be cautious. "We are ready for most contingencies, Dear Leader. You have my word on that. But Red Phoenix has not been our official strategy. Launching it successfully would require moving most of our own second echelon troops closer to the front—all without the fascists noticing. That takes time. There are only so many railroads and only so many hours in the day that imperialist spy satellites aren't overhead watching."

The general gestured at the muddy, ripped-up ground around them. "And that is the other reason, Dear Leader. An armored assault into the South now would quickly bog down in the rice paddies. We wouldn't have the mobility required to carry it out successfully. Red Phoenix calls for a winter war—a war when the fields are frozen and can support our tanks." He stopped talking, conscious that his palms were wet.

Kim dug a boot heel into the soft ground, mounding dirt and torn grass behind it. Then he nodded sharply. "Very well, General. I accept your explanation."

Cho bowed.

Kim looked carefully at him for several heartbeats and seemed to come to some sort of decision. "What I am about to tell you, General, is a matter of the highest State security. You are not to reveal anything to anyone without my express permission. Understood?"

Wordlessly Cho nodded.

"Should you disobey that instruction, you will suffer. And your suffering will extend to all those who bear your name. Is that clear?"

Cho shivered. Now he understood Kim's questions about his wife. "Yes, Dear Leader."

"Excellent." The shorter man turned away from him

while still speaking. "General Cho, I am authorizing you to begin the initial preparations for Red Phoenix."

For a moment the general stared at Kim, transfixed by a flood of contradictory emotions—shocked by Kim's bald, calm, assured words, elated at the thought of the People's Army being unleashed on its enemies after nearly forty years of seemingly endless waiting, and dismayed by the prospect of possible defeat. He carefully studied the man waiting for his answer, swallowed hard, and found his voice. "I shall obey your orders willingly, Dear Leader. But there are . . . practical difficulties. I am—"

Kim cut him off with an impatient gesture. "Yes, yes, Cho. I see them far more clearly than you think I do. As a corps commander, you can't order the second echelon troops forward to a full war footing without the General Staff's approval. Or make any of the other needed preparations for that matter."

Kim reached into his tunic and pulled out a folded sheet of paper. He handed it to Cho. "Within forty-eight hours the General Staff will unanimously approve the order contained on that piece of paper. It declares that the recent unrest in the South constitutes a possible security threat to the People's Republic, and it authorizes any or all troop transfers necessary to meet that threat. I have a similar order for your counterpart at Fifth Corps."

Kim smiled ironically. "You will, of course, ensure that these 'defensive' troop movements mirror the dispositions needed to launch Red Phoenix."

Cho couldn't think of anything to say. Launch Red Phoenix? Prepare for war against the South and against the United States without the formal approval of the Great Leader, the Administration Council, the Central Committee? This was unthinkable. Unbelievable. Unbidden, another word crept into his mind—*daring*.

Kim Jong-Il seemed to read his thoughts. "You find my orders surprising? Dangerous, perhaps?"

"No, Dear Leader. It just seems so . . ."

"Adventuristic?" Kim finished for him. "Perhaps. But why is that bad, my dear Cho? Old men fear adventures. We are not old men, are we?"

Cho shook his head.

Kim smiled. "Of course not." He leaned forward to peer directly up into the general's eyes. "Believe me, Cho. There is an opportunity rising in the South—an opportunity for the reunification of our sacred homeland." Kim clenched a fist. "It must not be wasted. It will not be wasted." Cho could hear the iron determination in the man's voice.

Kim's voice became soft and earnest. "General, forces are at work—military, political, economic factors—that make it imperative that we strike as soon as possible. The imperialists are withdrawing, and until the puppets in the south realign themselves, they will be vulnerable."

He paused. "Also, comrade, I must tell you, in strict secrecy, that even our socialist allies are not to be entirely trusted. Southern gold is making inroads in both Russia and China, and as they slide closer to the South, they lose the revolutionary spirit. We must move now, while they still have the will to support our cause."

Kim stopped talking and let his words sink in. Then he leaned forward again and said, "Ride with me, Cho, and in six months' time you will be a colonel general commanding the First Shock Army. Your future will be assured. You will be a hero of the fatherland." The man's dark eyes flashed. "Reject me and you will fall unnoticed in the mud."

Cho stared into Kim's eyes. Into the eyes of the son of the Great Leader. Into the eyes of the heir to the man who had replaced God in North Korea. He had no choice. Wanted no choice. Lieutenant General Cho Hyun-Jae came to attention and saluted.

A thin-lipped smile spread slowly across Kim Jong-Il's face. He had his general. Red Phoenix was underway.

CHAPTER

9

The Dead Zone

SEPTEMBER 24—CAMP HOWZE, NEAR TONGDUCH'ON, SOUTH KOREA

Captain Matuchek was obviously not in a good mood.

"Goddamnit, Little. Next time I ask you a question during a map exercise I don't want a friggin' military history lecture."

Kevin nodded. And winced. Oh, Jesus, did his head hurt.

Matuchek carried on. "I wanted to know where you would have placed your machine gun teams to support an assault up Hill five seventy-two. I don't give a flying frazzoo about limey Lord Wellington and his patented, Waterloo-style, rear-slope defense. Do you read me, mister?"

Kevin nodded again, cautiously, half-afraid that the top half of his brain would fall right out on his company commander's desk. "Yes, sir. Loud and clear, sir."

"Okay, consider yourself chewed out. I'll take your word that it won't happen again." Matuchek rolled his chair back a few inches and opened a desk drawer. He pulled out a file folder and slid it across to Kevin. "Anyway, you won't be participating in the next exercise. You and your platoon are rotating to Malibu West for a week, starting at oh four hundred hours tomorrow."

Kevin picked up the folder. Malibu? What the hell?

Matuchek chuckled. "Don't look so happy, Lieutenant. You aren't going to see any bikini-clad surfer chicks up at Malibu West. That's the name we use for Hill six forty." He grinned a little wider. "You'll be in scenic bunker accommodations along the DMZ, just a couple of klicks north of the lovely little village of Korangp'o."

"Just us, sir? I mean, what about the rest of the company?" Kevin tried hard to keep his head perfectly still as he talked.

"Oh, we'll be right behind you. In position along the MLR, the Main Line of Resistance. You're pulling outpost duty, Lieutenant. You know, first to fight and first to fall." Matuchek laced the fingers of his hands together on top of his desk and looked slightly smug. "I'll expect to see your platoon on trucks heading out the camp gate at oh two hundred tomorrow. Sergeant Pierce will know what kind of equipment and supplies to take."

At 0200? Two o'clock in the morning? Wonderful. A night road march and his first one at that. But two weeks with the 2nd Infantry Division had taught Kevin not to complain—at least not out loud. Matuchek was a good company commander, but he had a hair-trigger temper and it seemed that right now was not a good time to reveal any more gaps in his knowledge or experience.

Kevin hadn't been able to get the hang of handling the captain yet. Everything that he did seemed to set Matuchek off. The man definitely wasn't the nurturing type. One of the other platoon leaders had told him not to worry too much about it. There was a rumor going around that the captain and his wife back in the States were having "marital difficulties" and that was the real source of Matuchek's discontent.

It was easy enough to believe that the rumor was the straight scoop. Korea was classed as a hardship post—no wives or families allowed. And any two people could grow far apart over twelve months. But understanding the reason for it didn't make Kevin's position as the focal point for Matuchek's temper any easier.

"Okay, Little. That's all for now. Study that folder. You'll find a platoon deployment drawn up by the officer you replaced. Don't bother to change it. He knew what he was doing. Dismissed." Matuchek jerked a thumb toward his office door.

Kevin took the hint and left in search of his platoon sergeant.

Walking across the compound to find Sergeant Pierce was a chore. The ground wouldn't stay still, it just kept rolling up and down, and the bright morning sun sent his shadow lurching ahead of him.

He frowned at no one in particular. Somehow he was

going to have to find a way to get off Matuchek's shit list. The trouble was he wasn't quite sure just how to go about doing that.

Take the map exercise the grouchy bastard was pissed off about for example. Kevin and the other A Company platoon leaders had been simulating an attack to recapture an American defensive position along the DMZ during a hypothetical war. Moving little cardboard counters back and forth on a map to show deployments and assault formations. Kevin had been demonstrating how he would position his platoon's infantry squads and weapons teams to support the attack when Matuchek had suddenly blown up and ripped him up one side and down the other. All because he'd made an offhand comment about how machine gun support wasn't going to do much good because most of the "Aggressor" defense force would logically be dug in behind the hill—protected from direct line-of-sight support fire. It had made sense then. And it made sense now. But maybe he shouldn't have tried to show off by pointing out that deploying on a reverse slope was a tactic going all the way back to Wellington's beating the French at Waterloo. It had seemed like the right thing to say at the time.

Kevin shook his head slowly and then wished he hadn't. The ground didn't stop moving when his eyes did. He'd just have to keep his mouth shut about military history around the CO. Matuchek obviously wasn't much of a scholar.

He'd also have to take it easy next time the other company officers invited him into town with them. Sirroci, Owens, and O'Farrell had called it his "initiation" to South Korea, and they must have hit every bar in Tongduch'on before lurching back to camp. He thought he could remember eating dinner in some tiny cafe, but he couldn't remember exactly what he'd eaten. Judging from the raw, burning feeling in his stomach and throat, it must have been liberally laced with garlic and some really hot red peppers. Of course, from what he'd seen of Korean cuisine so far, that could describe just about anything.

With an effort he tried to stop concentrating on his hangover and to start thinking about just where his platoon sergeant might be closeted at this time in the morning.

Kevin found Sergeant Pierce in the platoon armory supervising a weapons-cleaning detail. Ten men in work fatigues were busy scrubbing away at every moving part of their rifles.

It was one of those boring, routine, and absolutely necessary jobs that occupy most of a modern soldier's time. To keep an M16 up and firing took a liberal amount of 10-weight sewing machine oil and a daily cleaning.

Kevin's ROTC instructors had gone to great lengths to make sure that he knew that a jammed M16 could be just as fatal for its owner as a tank that wouldn't run. That was something Sergeant Pierce obviously agreed with whole-heartedly, and he spent a lot of time making sure that 2nd Platoon's weapons were clean and ready for action.

Kevin poked his head into the small, cramped room and motioned the sergeant outside to give him a quick rundown on their new orders.

"Malibu West, sir?" Pierce was considerate; he kept his voice below its normal booming level.

"That's right, Sergeant. And the captain wants us up and out of here by oh two hundred tomorrow." Kevin knew the sergeant and he were going to be damned busy for the next few hours. The logistics involved in moving forty-five men, their personal gear, two M60 light machine guns, three Dragon antitank guided missile launchers, and a week's worth of supplies up to the DMZ were incredibly complicated. Among other things he had to arrange transportation for his platoon, get the latest artillery support plan, set up his communications— everything, in fact, down to making sure the platoon's mail would get delivered. Just thinking about it threatened to turn his headache into a real bastard of a migraine.

Pierce eyed him closely. "Look, Lieutenant, I'll start pulling things together for the move. That's all SOP anyway."

Yeah, thank God for SOP—standard operating procedures. Anything the Army had to do more than three times was written down as SOP. He could find the information he needed in the Army's bible for troop movements, Army Manual FM 55-30, catchily titled "Army Motor Transport Operations." There were always shortcuts that experienced officers could use that weren't covered in the manuals. But Kevin knew he had a long way to go before he could consider himself experienced.

"You don't need to worry about a thing, sir. The boys have been up to Malibu West so often they could probably load everything up in their sleep," Pierce said.

"Right, Sergeant." Kevin cleared his throat. "You go ahead and get started then. I'll tell Lieutenant Rhee about our new orders and meet you back at the barracks to go over the movement ops order."

Pierce saluted and left whistling. Kevin watched him leave, envying the man's seeming ability to take anything that happened in stride.

He turned on his heel and headed for the two-story, whitewashed BOQ to find his South Korean counterpart, Lieutenant Rhee.

Under the Combined Forces structure set up back in 1978, virtually every American line and staff officer had a South Korean counterpart assigned to handle liaison with the ROK Army. It was a step that had been taken partly for political reasons—to smooth over growing South Korean resentment that an American general always commanded all allied forces. But it was also a very practical concept. In a situation where there were more than fifteen South Korean soldiers for every American, the counterpart system helped make sure that language and cultural barriers didn't impede military efficiency as much as they might have.

When Kevin had arrived at Camp Howze, Rhee had been off attending some kind of staff course, so he'd only met the Korean lieutenant a couple of times. But they'd gotten along fairly well, and Rhee spoke perfect English. So perfect in fact that Kevin felt embarrassed that he'd only been able to pick up a few sentences of phrasebook Korean.

Second Lieutenant Rhee Han-Gil, wearing a crisp, newly pressed uniform, opened the door to his room at Kevin's first knock and waved him in. Except for a cigarette smoldering in an ashtray on the desk, the room looked ready for an inspection by the entire General Staff. Every book was perfectly aligned, Rhee's clothes hung in regulation order, and the sheets on his cot were pulled so tight that it looked like you could bounce even a paper won—the Korean currency—off it. The South Korean lieutenant seemed just as ready for an inspection. He was shorter than Kevin and stocky, but he had a lean, sharp-featured face.

"What can I do for you, Lieutenant Little?" Like most Koreans, Rhee was a stickler for titles. The easygoing, informal way most Americans spoke to each other was completely alien to people raised in a culture steeped in the need to show respect for authority. Rhee would have been shocked if Kevin started calling him by his first name.

"We've got movement orders—short-notice ones." Kevin tried not to let his dislike for Captain Matuchek show. "We're being sent up to some place called Malibu West for a week."

"Ah, yes, Malibu West. I have been there before. I'm afraid that it is not nearly so glamorous as the real Malibu in California must be." Rhee smiled slightly.

Kevin let that pass. He'd never been to Malibu anyway. "Yeah. Well, we're moving out early tomorrow morning, so I thought I'd better let you know. You'll need to be packed and ready to go by oh two hundred."

The Korean pointed to a duffel bag standing in the corner. "Thank you, but there is no need. I am quite ready. But I can make use of the time to coordinate with the units holding the other outposts on our flanks."

"How the hell . . . did Matuchek already tell you we were moving up to the Z?" Kevin asked, irritated that the captain might be trying to make him look like an ill-informed idiot.

Rhee looked apologetic. "Oh, no. The captain didn't tell me anything. It's just that the communists caught my country sleeping once before. We shall never be caught that way again. We're trained to be ready for any eventuality."

"Well, you're way ahead of me on this one," Kevin admitted. He paused, realizing it was probably time to swallow a little more pride. "Look, if you've been up to this place before, maybe you can give me some advice on what to take up there. I mean, besides the usual, my combat gear, rifle, stuff like that."

Rhee nodded. "Of course, I'd be honored to assist you in any way I can." He thought for a moment. "First, I should take a set of extra blankets if I were you. The nights are growing colder and we won't have any heat up at the outpost."

Kevin was surprised. "What? Well, hell, why don't we take a couple of camp stoves with us then?" Christ, you'd have thought some bright Army officer before him would have figured that one out.

Rhee didn't look impressed. "Unfortunately," he said,

"camp stoves produce smoke. And the communists have the unpleasant habit of using smoke as an aiming point for the occasional mortar shell."

Mortars? Oh, brother, this was getting worse and worse. A posting to West Germany would have been so much better. The Russians and their East German puppets might be a dour lot, but at least they didn't lob mortar shells over the inter-German border on a whim.

Kevin shook his head. "Okay, no camp stoves. Blankets instead. Anything else unusual I should bring?"

Rhee flexed his fingers. "Well, you might bring along a deck of cards." He twisted his Korean Military Academy class ring back and forth. "A good game of your American five-card stud always helps to pass the time."

So, Mr. Perfect enjoyed a game of poker, did he? Kevin concealed his surprise. He'd been in the country long enough to learn that the South Koreans were a proud people. It wouldn't do to offend or shame Rhee by making a big deal out of the fact that he liked to play cards. After all, it wasn't as if he had a surplus of friends over here. He grinned. "Okay, you're on. I'll see you on the parade ground at oh one thirty tomorrow."

Rhee smiled back. "As you Americans say, it's a date."

"And Lieutenant," he said as Kevin moved to the door, "I thought your point about the machine guns in today's exercise was very interesting."

"Yeah, well, thanks. But I'm afraid the captain didn't exactly think so."

Rhee didn't exactly smile either, but Kevin could swear he saw an eyebrow twitch upward. "The captain is, of course, a good soldier. Is there anything so perfect, however, that it cannot be improved?"

Kevin sketched a rough salute and stepped out of Rhee's quarters in a happier mood. Things might finally be looking up, and even his hangover seemed to be fading.

So his Korean counterpart liked to play cards. Well, if he was going to be stuck in some godforsaken hole for a week, he might as well make the best of it. Colonels, captains, and majors always seemed to be able to read the least bit of indecision on his face in military matters, but card games were something else altogether. He could hold his own there. Rhee couldn't possibly know that playing poker had supplied him with spending money all the way through college.

He headed back to the platoon barracks. Sergeant Pierce might be perfectly able to handle all the arrangements for the move on his own, but he'd better get some idea of just what was involved. It would beat sitting on his behind in his quarters, moping around. He stopped in his tracks for a second. My God, maybe he was actually getting used to this place.

Kevin remembered that optimistic thought sourly as he watched his platoon assemble on the floodlit parade ground early the next morning. The sun wouldn't be up for several more hours yet, and a cold north wind made the darkness outside Camp Howze seem even blacker. He pulled his fatigue jacket tighter around him, trying to stay warm, and did his best to look alert as Sergeant Pierce called the roll.

The platoon had already loaded their gear on the row of canvas-sided Army trucks parked behind him. Now the men were lined up, shivering at ease, as Pierce took a last check—making sure that nobody got left behind, snug in a warm bunk.

"Walton?" Pierce wasn't shouting, but his voice carried across the parade ground.

"Here."

"Wright?" Silence.

Pierce waited a couple of seconds and tried again, "Wright? Look you dumb bastard, I saw you loading a truck not more than two minutes ago. So answer up."

"Yeah, Ah'm here, Sarge. Guess Ah must've fallen asleep. It's just so cozy here in Ko-rea." The other men chuckled softly. PFC Wright's deep Arkansas twang and deadpan delivery made him the platoon comic.

Kevin waited for the platoon sergeant to come down loud and hard on Wright, but he didn't. Instead, Pierce just chuckled himself and said, "Okay, Funnyman. You think it's so warm? Then I guess I won't hear any complaints from you when you pull sentry duty tomorrow night."

That brought a laugh from the rest of the platoon. "Way to go, Johnny," called someone from the ranks to Wright.

"Thanks for volunteering. We'll be thinking of you while we're freezing in our sleeping bags."

"Aww, Sarge," Wright tried again. "You know Ah got me a delicate type of chest condition. Walking a beat could send mah poor little soul right up to heaven."

But Pierce was waiting for that one. "Well, PFC, be sure to give my regards to St. Peter then. I'll let him know you're on the way." Even Wright broke up laughing. Kevin felt himself smiling in the darkness and tried to stop. He had to maintain his dignity, didn't he? But he could hear Rhee, standing beside him, laughing as hard as all the rest.

"Okay, troops. Settle down," Pierce said. "The sooner we get this roll call finished, the sooner we can get in out of this damned wind." That shut them up.

"Yates?"

"Here."

"Zelinsky?"

"Here, Sergeant."

Pierce shoved his clipboard back under his arm. "Tenshun!" The platoon snapped to attention.

Pierce turned to Kevin. "Platoon present and accounted for, sir!" He saluted.

Kevin stepped out of the shadows and returned the salute. He took a line out of the movies. "Very good, Sergeant. Load 'em up."

The sergeant wheeled back to face the platoon. "You heard the lieutenant. Let's go. Everybody on the trucks!" The men broke ranks and started clambering into the canvas-sided trucks, one eleven-man squad per vehicle.

Kevin pulled himself into the passenger seat of the lead truck. Rhee clambered into the one just behind him, and Pierce took the last truck in the convoy.

The five trucks wheeled off the parade ground and roared out through the main gate. Once on the highway running past the camp, they turned north and lumbered toward the DMZ.

Camp Howze was only about fifteen kilometers behind the DMZ but the trip to the assembly point took nearly two hours. Every kilometer or so they were stopped at fully manned checkpoints, complete with barricades, barbed wire, and machine guns. And at every checkpoint their papers were scrutinized by submachine gun–toting South Korean security troops. Kevin didn't know what made him more nervous, the intense security or the possibility that it was necessary.

At last they turned off the main highway onto a tree-lined dirt road winding up a narrow valley. The corporal driving the lead truck slowed down to a crawl, and the ear-splitting engine noise fell away to a low, dull roar. A helmeted soldier appeared in the headlight's beams, waving a flashlight fitted with a red lens. The driver said, "There's our ground guide."

Reaching forward, he doused the truck's headlights, turning on the dim red blackout lights.

Startled, Kevin turned to ask him just what he thought he was doing.

The man drove and kept his eyes on his guide. "Regulations, sir. We're within five klicks of the Z here and we're not supposed to make it any easier for the North Koreans to know what we're up to."

Kevin had to admit that made some sense. He sat back and tried to act nonchalant as they drove slowly up the valley.

The assembly point was a small clearing just behind the trenches and bunkers of the main line of resistance, the MLR. They were ten minutes behind schedule. Kevin clambered out of the truck cab and walked toward the lone figure who had guided them. Urged on by Sergeant Pierce's low, hoarse voice, his men clambered out of the trucks and formed up in a column of twos. It was still pitch-dark outside. The moon had set and low clouds covered most of the night sky.

The red beam came up and centered on his face.

"Second Platoon from Alpha?"

Kevin nodded, then realized the man probably couldn't see him all that clearly. "Yeah. You the guide to Malibu West?"

"Sergeant Hourigan, sir. Third Platoon, Bravo Company. Lieutenant Miller's waiting back up at the outpost. If you're ready, sir, we should hit the trail. Sunup's in a little over an hour and a half, and we've got some hard walking to do by then."

"Okay." Kevin half-turned toward the column behind him. "Sergeant Pierce?"

"Here, sir. Platoon's assembled and ready to move."

Kevin turned back to their guide. "Okay, Hourigan. Let's do it."

Hourigan led them out through an opening in the rolls of barbed wire strung along the MLR. The ground was rough and uneven, but even in the dark Kevin could see that every tree or tall patch of brush had been cut down or uprooted to provide clear fields of fire for the troops stationed behind them.

Hourigan stopped suddenly, then moved over to the left a few yards. Kevin followed him. The sergeant reached over and tapped him on the shoulder. "See them white stakes up ahead, Lieutenant?"

Kevin nodded.

"Well, there's a pair every few yards. Stay between 'em unless you want to get blown to bits. We're going through the main minefield now."

The column pushed on, moving slower now that they were in the minefield. Kevin kept going, trying to keep pace with Hourigan. He brushed away sweat that was beginning to trickle into his eyes. Jesus, he hadn't carried a fifty-pound pack since basic. He could feel his heart pounding. In the still night air every scuffed rock, patch of dried grass, or broken twig made a noise he could swear would carry for miles.

At last they came out of the minefield and started up a winding trail that got steeper and steeper. They began passing through piles of boulders lying half-buried on the slope. Kevin could feel the straps of his pack starting to cut into his shoulders as they climbed. God, this was a damned high hill. It hadn't looked this bad on the map.

A voice broke through the darkness. "Halt." It was accompanied by the sound of a machine gun's being cocked. Shit.

The sentry called, "Advance and be recognized." The party walked forward in the pitch-blackness. After a dozen steps they heard, "That's far enough. Marbles-Galore."

The sergeant stopped. "It's Hourigan, you dumb son of a bitch."

"I don't give a shit. Give the countersign or you're a deader."

"Zebra-Cardinal."

"Okay, Come ahead." They could hear the safety being snapped back on. Kevin ran a hand across his face and wiped it across the front of his jacket. Damn, what a bunch of paranoid assholes.

The platoon stumbled over the crest of Hill 640 and into the middle of Malibu West. Another column was there, waiting to go down.

A figure wearing black plastic bars stepped out from the head of the other column. "Little? I'm Miller. Glad to see you're here. Look, let's go into the command post and I'll get you settled in before I head down after my troops. Hourigan and your platoon sergeant can get your men squared away."

Kevin still couldn't quite make out the man's face in the darkness, but he could tell that it was getting lighter.

He followed Miller down a couple of steps into a low, lamp-lit bunker. The command post, or CP, was scarcely five feet high, made of green sandbags with a beamed ceiling. Inside, it was barely big enough for the two cots, a table, telephone, and backup radio. And it stank. A mixture of unwashed bodies, damp mustiness, and old food hung in the air. Kevin tried not to breathe in too deeply.

Miller laughed. "I know. It's pretty bad, isn't it? Our laundry and bathing facilities aren't exactly first class up here. Don't worry, you'll get used to it." The other lieutenant had dark shadows under his eyes.

He motioned Kevin over to a low table crowded with a map and a communications setup. "Okay, here are your fire concentrations." Kevin could see a sheaf of plastic overlays with colored-pencil markings showing preregistered artillery firing points and code numbers.

Miller continued on down the table. "Your radio, field phones, sound-powered phones to your squad leaders and the other outposts nearby, one to your company CP back on the MLR, and the artillery direct line." Kevin nodded his understanding.

"Any questions?"

Kevin shook his head, then thought better of it. "Just one. Has it been hectic up here lately?"

"Nah. Pretty damned quiet—for once. Only one alert, the usual 'hold your ass and pray until the all-clear comes.'" Miller stood up, stooped low to avoid the roof. "Okay. That's it then. Good luck and I'll see you back at the camp." He held out his hand.

Kevin shook it, suddenly realizing that Miller couldn't wait to get out of Malibu West. Well, he couldn't blame him for that.

Miller nodded and ducked back out the door up into the cleaner air outside.

Kevin sat down heavily onto one of the bunks. Great, he had a whole week in this combination rattrap and outhouse to look forward to. He dropped his pack off onto the ground by his feet. At least that felt better. Then he remembered that he'd better report the platoon in to Captain Matuchek back in position along the main line. He stepped over to pick up the phone to the company CP.

Now, just where the hell was that list of code names he was supposed to use? Kevin fished around in the pockets of his fatigue jacket before coming up with a small pad of radio codes.

He lifted the field phone's receiver. "Alfa Echo Five Six. Alfa Echo Five Six. This is Alfa Echo Five Two."

"Go ahead, Echo Five Two. This is Echo Five Six." The line was clear of static. Good, he could call for help without much trouble if he needed it. That was reassuring.

"Echo Five Six, Echo Five Two is in position. Say again, Echo Five Two is in position."

"Roger, Two. You're in position. Out."

Kevin put the phone back down on the table and rubbed his eyes. He hadn't gotten any sleep the night before, and he knew he'd have to stay awake at least until past dawn to make a daylight inspection of the position.

He looked at his watch: 0535. The sun should be up in twenty minutes or so. He could see the sky outside growing grayer.

Pierce stuck his head in the door a few minutes later. "I think it's light enough to take a quick walk around now, Lieutenant."

Kevin sat up sharply. It was growing orange outside now. The sun must be coming up over the horizon. Oh, crap. He'd fallen asleep, just nodded right off on his first tour of duty up at the DMZ. He blinked and staggered to his feet, barely stopping himself from trying to stand full upright under the CP's low roof.

He followed Pierce out into a connecting trench dug from

the CP out to the edge of the hill. It tied into the main trench running completely around the outpost. Rhee joined them there for the inspection of their home for the next week.

Malibu West was laid out in a rough oval with a six-foot-deep trench connecting twelve reinforced log bunkers large enough to shelter four men during an enemy air or artillery attack. Each bunker was separated by about fifteen yards of trench. Firing steps along the trench made it possible for troops to use their weapons against a ground assault. Two belts of barbed wire and a minefield completed the defenses.

As an outpost, Malibu West and its defenders were expected to fight pretty much on their own, though with liberal artillery support. Malibu and the other strongpoints like it scattered along the DMZ were intended to make an enemy assault force deploy for an attack before it reached the main allied line. It was hoped they would delay an assault long enough to allow the UN command to bring American and South Korean air and artillery power into play and to move reserves to the right places. In essence, the men holding the outposts were expected to buy time with their lives.

"I've put our two MG's in the far left and far right bunkers on the forward slope. That should give us good coverage to the front. And we've inherited another MG with the position. Lieutenant Miller had it set up to cover the rear slope, and I figured that was a pretty good place for it so I left it there." Pierce paused.

"Sounds good to me." Kevin yawned. Damn, he'd have to start waking up. "Any comments, Lieutenant Rhee?"

The South Korean looked wide-awake. Naturally. "No. It sounds like a reasonable deployment to me. But what about our Dragon teams?" That was a good question. The Dragon teams with their wire-guided missiles were the 2nd Platoon's best defense against enemy tanks and APCs.

"I've got 'em spread out along the forward slope. If the balloon goes up and NK tanks start getting around behind us, we may have to move 'em. But they've got good fields of fire where they are right now."

Kevin nodded. "All right, Sergeant. Good work." He worked his tongue around inside his mouth, trying to clear out the gritty taste he'd acquired during his short, unintentional nap. He looked at Rhee. "I understand there's a South Korean platoon holding the next outpost over from us. Why don't you go over to the CP and make contact with them. Let them know we're here. Okay?"

Rhee smiled and sketched a salute. "No problem, Lieutenant."

"Great. Oh, and then get some sleep. I thought we'd pull three watches until we get settled in. I'll take the first, Sergeant Pierce here can take the second, and you'll take the third. Sound all right to you?"

Rhee smiled even more broadly. "Certainly, Lieutenant. I'm always glad to hear that I'll get some uninterrupted sleep." He saluted again and moved back down the trench toward the CP.

Kevin yawned again and stretched. He'd have to get Zelinsky to make some coffee. In the meantime he could get a look at the terrain around Malibu. He'd studied the map, but you couldn't always trust maps. There was that time he'd gotten lost on a night training march near Fort Lewis . . . it had just been damn lucky that he'd found a gas station where he could ask for directions.

Kevin shook his head to clear the memory. He'd learned his lesson that time. Never trust maps. He clambered up onto the firing step and lifted his binoculars. Let's see. Hill 640, Malibu West, fell sharply away down a rocky slope into a narrow, brush-filled valley. There were gullies running through the valley and up toward a ridgeline to the north. He could just make out what might be some camouflaged bunkers on that ridge.

A hand grabbed his combat webbing and yanked him down off the firing step.

"What the fuck?" Kevin wheeled in fury as Pierce let go of his webbing.

"Sorry, sir." Pierce didn't sound very sorry. "But part of what they pay me for is to make sure that my lieutenants don't get shot on their first day up at the Z."

"And what does that have to do with grabbing me from behind just now?" Kevin was breathing hard. He'd been startled. Christ, he hadn't even heard Pierce come up behind him. The man must move like a ghost.

"Snipers, Lieutenant. The North Koreans take a special pride in potting people staring at 'em with shiny binoculars. You want to look around up at the Z, you use the 'scopes." Pierce jerked a thumb toward a periscope that could be raised above the trench parapet.

"Oh, bullshit. I know that the North Koreans are lunatics, but they can't just go around shooting people. There is an armistice on, you know."

"You know it and I know it, Lieutenant. But I ain't too sure the gooks know it or give a damn." Pierce had his voice pitched low. "Look, sir. This isn't peacetime up here. This is damn close to the real thing. Back when I was just a green PFC, before Vietnam, I was stationed at a place pretty much like this." He paused.

"So things haven't changed much in more than twenty years. What's the point?" Kevin was impatient. It was starting to warm up, the sun was in his eyes, and he wanted some coffee.

"Well, sir, this rear-area general came up for an inspection one day. Now, the lieutenant gave him a pretty good tour of the bunkers, trenches, and all, but this general wanted to see the commies for himself. And he wouldn't hear of using anything like that 'scope over there. So he just jumped up on the firing step and wouldn't listen to the lieutenant asking him to get down. He didn't listen until some commie sniper put a round through his head." Pierce laid a finger on the bridge of his nose, right between his eyes. "Right there, Lieutenant. Knocked that dumbshit general off the firing step and blew what little brains he had out through the back of his head."

"Christ!" Kevin was shocked. "How come I never read anything about that?"

"Hell, I suppose they hushed it up. Damned embarrassing way to lose a general, I guess."

"Well, what happened to your lieutenant?"

"They weren't too happy with him. Wasn't his fault, so they couldn't send him to Leavenworth, but they did shove his ass out of the Army in a godawful hurry."

Kevin thought about that for a moment and then smiled ruefully. "Okay, Sergeant. You've made your point. You won't lose this dumbshit lieutenant the same way."

Pierce grinned back at him, "That's the spirit, Lieutenant. It's just a question of experience. And there's one thing you can say for the Z—you get experienced real quick."

OCTOBER 1—MALIBU WEST, ALONG THE DMZ

After six days Kevin had had enough of Malibu West. Six days of solid boredom. Of not being able to move freely during daylight. Of lousy food and not enough sleep. Six days that were too hot and six nights that were too cold.

The only high points were the daily poker games with Rhee, Pierce, and a couple of the other noncoms. Playing cards with his NCOs might not be regulation, but it helped pass the time. Table stakes were low because it wouldn't do to have officers winning too much money from their subordinates. Still, he'd won more than he'd lost. And it had been nice to see a look of genuine respect on Sergeant Pierce's face for once.

But that had been it. Other than a series of meaningless, routine daily reports and a single, quick inspection by Captain Matuchek, who'd seemed pleasantly surprised to find the outpost still intact, their tour at Malibu West had been about as exciting as guarding a convent somewhere in the Midwest.

That made the call even more shocking when it came.

"Sir!" The hand that was shaking him shook even harder. "Sir!"

Kevin groaned and tried to roll over. It was still dark out and he'd been up past midnight filling out useless paperwork.

"Sir!" It was Jones, his radioman. "Captain's on the phone, sir. Says it's urgent."

Shit. Now what the hell did he want. Probably wanted to bitch about some goddamned form he'd filled in wrong. Kevin threw the blankets off his cot and stumbled over to the phone.

"Alfa Echo Five Six, this is Alfa Echo Five Two. Go ahead."

"Five Two, this is Five Six. Wait one." Great, they woke him up and now they were going to make him wait. But the line came alive again in seconds, and something in Matuchek's voice brought Kevin up straight. "Five Two, this is Five Six.

Go to full alert. Say again, go to full alert. We have a general stand-to all along the Z.''

Oh, Christ. Kevin could feel his heart starting to pound and he was having trouble catching his breath. ''Six, this is Two. Is this a drill? Over.''

Matuchek's wrath came over the phone loud and clear. ''I don't fucking know. And right now I don't fucking care! Just get your men out ón the firing line and clear the goddamned phone. Six out.''

Kevin handed the phone back to Jones and looked around for his M16, flak jacket, and helmet. They were in the corner of the CP, right where he'd left them. Rhee was already up and buckling on his gear.

Kevin turned back to Jones. ''Okay, get Pierce in here. On the double.'' He took a deep breath, but he couldn't seem to get enough air into his lungs. Shit, shit, calm down. He grabbed his flak jacket and started to put it on, then realized he had it backward. He flipped the bulky jacket around and slipped into it. Rhee handed him his helmet.

''What's up, Lieutenant?'' Pierce was in the door to the CP, rifle in hand and looking as awake as if he'd already been up for hours.

''We've got an alert. All along the DMZ. I don't know if it's for real or not, but you'd better get the men up and in position anyway.'' Kevin grabbed his rifle and map case.

Pierce backed out of the CP and vanished down the shadow-filled connecting trench, moving toward the nearest bunker. Rhee headed out the other door. Kevin followed him as far as the main trench, accompanied by Jones, lugging the platoon's commo gear.

The moon was up and nearly full, casting an eerie mix of orangish light and pitch-black shadows across the valley below. Gusts of a cold north wind stirred the brush back and forth and whined through the coils of barbed wire covering the approaches to Malibu West.

Kevin fumbled with the focus on the periscope. Damn it. For all he could make out, the valley down there could be filled with a thousand enemy soldiers. Or it could be empty.

The eleven troopers of 2nd Squad jogged past him, equipment rattling as they fanned out down the length of the trench and clambered up onto firing steps.

"Sir!" Jones's hoarse whisper pulled Kevin's eyes away from the periscope and back down into the trench. "Sergeant Pierce says everybody's up and in position. Nothing else to report."

"Tell Pierce to get back here pronto. And check with Company to see if they've got anything more."

Pierce was there almost before he finished speaking. "We're set, Lieutenant. One of the Dragon launchers is acting up a bit, but Ramos is working on it. Should have it up in a couple of minutes."

"Well, he goddamned well better. Christ, what if we get hit by tanks in the next couple of minutes!" Kevin realized he was starting to sound like he'd lost it and tried to calm down. He got down off the parapet and squatted in the trench next to Pierce. "Look, are we picking anything up on our motion sensors or starlight scopes?"

"Negative. There doesn't seem to be anything moving or warm out there."

"Then this could all be just a false alarm."

Pierce shrugged. "Maybe. Maybe not. Could be a long night, though, whichever way it goes."

A shout from down the line brought them both to their feet. "Flares! Flares to the east!"

Kevin whipped his periscope around to stare down to the right. There, about five miles away, he could see two magnesium flares swaying away south on their parachutes. He found himself praying under his breath. God, oh God, please don't let this be real. Don't let there be a war. Please, God.

"Could be an attack down that way." Pierce still sounded calm. "Might just be an infiltration attempt though." He cupped a hand to an ear. "I don't hear any shooting."

Rhee's voice drifted down the line, high and excited. "Those flares are coming from a point just over Azure Dragon. That's the ROK post on our right."

Kevin yelled back, "Well, get on the horn and ask them what the hell's going on."

"Lieutenant?" Pierce coughed lightly to catch his attention. "Next time you and Lieutenant Rhee want to have a conversation, you might not want to yell it all over creation. If there are gooks down there, I figure they probably know we're awake and ready for 'em now.''

Kevin felt his ears burning. Pierce was right and there wasn't any way around it. He'd made a stupid mistake. The kind that Major Donaldson had warned could get his men killed. He looked down at Corporal Jones. "Uh, pass the word to Lieutenant Rhee that he's to report here after he's talked to that Korean outpost."

They waited for several more minutes, but no more flares popped up to light the night sky, and everything stayed quiet. Rhee came jogging down the trench and jumped up beside Kevin and Pierce.

"I talked to the CO over at Azure Dragon. It seems that one of their new conscripts got overexcited and fired off a pair of flares. He'll be disciplined, of course."

Kevin knew that meant the poor little sod was probably getting the living crap beat out of him. And just at this moment, he didn't care a bit.

Then Jones was grabbing for his elbow again. "Sir! It's the captain!"

Kevin picked up the phone with a feeling of dread. Was this it? Was the balloon going up? "Alfa Echo Five Six, this is Five Two."

"Alfa Echo Five Two, this is Alfa Echo Five Six. Stand down. I repeat, stand down. Resume normal schedule. That was a drill, Lieutenant, a real McLaren Special."

"Acknowledged, Five Six." He tried to sound cool and collected, but he knew that Matuchek had to be able to hear the immense relief in his voice. He could see Pierce and Rhee visibly relaxing at what they could hear of the conversation.

"Well, Lieutenant. Are your britches full of brown organic matter?" Matuchek didn't sound quite as pissed off as he usually did, despite the words.

"Not quite, Five Six. Close, but not quite." Pray God that Matuchek didn't ever find out just how close to the truth that was.

"Well, Lieutenant. If that McLaren Special didn't fill 'em up, I guess we might make a soldier of you yet. See you back at camp tomorrow morning. Echo Five Six out."

Kevin hung up, feeling drained and shaky. But relieved, too. He'd screwed up, but it hadn't been for real. And he still had time to learn.

CHAPTER
10
Revelations

OCTOBER 1—INSIDE THE GREAT LEADER BUNKER, NORTH KOREA

"Comrade General. COMRADE GENERAL!"

Lieutenant General Cho Hyun-Jae opened his eyes. The lights were on, revealing Colonel Chung, his aide, bending over the bed. He came fully awake.

"What is it, Chung?" He automatically started getting dressed. Whatever it was, if it was important enough to wake him, it was important enough to get dressed for.

"Sir, the enemy has just gone on alert. We've seen movement into emplacements . . ."

Cho headed out the door, buttoning his tunic as he ran, with the colonel jogging along behind. The bunker had been constructed so that his quarters were only moments away from the II Corps operations center.

The door was open. Cho slowed down, took a deep breath, and entered an organized pandemonium. Officers and enlisted men were streaming into the room, taking positions at map boards, teletypes, and desks. A huge map occupied one side of the room, detailing the sector of the front around Kaesong, his responsibility. General Chyong Dal-Joong, his second-in-command, stood nearby discussing some point on it with the staff. He saw Cho come into the room and saluted. The rest scattered to their stations.

"Report, General. Another drill?" Cho finished buttoning his tunic collar while studying the array of painted wooden blocks used to show enemy units on the big map.

"Probably, sir. We've seen no movement behind the front line, but all of the imperialist troops have manned their combat positions. It would not be an auspicious time to start the liberation." The left side of Chyong's mouth creased upward in a lopsided smile.

Cho idly wondered how long it would be before his second-in-command's sense of humor landed him in a State Political Security Department detention camp.

He yawned. "I think they know when I am up late and do this just to ruin my sleep. Major Ko!" He beckoned the slim, narrow-faced intelligence officer over to him.

"Major, your observations, please."

"Yes, sir. I believe that this is an exercise. The enemy rotates the troops manning the perimeter on a regular weekly cycle. About once every two weeks he holds an alert. The alert is always in the early morning, and late in the week. Thursday is the most frequently selected day. Only troops in place are ordered to stand to. No additional units are staged forward. That is what has happened this time."

"As far as we know," Cho corrected.

Ko looked a little crestfallen. "Yes, sir. As far as we know."

Cho quoted, " 'Revolution in military thought is built on a base of knowledge, not assumptions.' "

"Yes, sir." Ko bowed sharply, accepting the correction.

Chyong looked at his superior. "Maybe our enemies should read the Great Leader's thoughts. These imperialists are too predictable."

"Or they are trying to put us to sleep. What's our readiness?"

"Excellent. All of our positions were manned within five minutes."

"Hold our troops there until dawn. Have them conduct subunit training in place on what their roles would be in case the imperialists attacked. Also, move the field commanders' meeting up from oh seven hundred to oh five hundred. Since we're all up anyway, let's get an early start."

While Chyong hurried away with his order, Cho pondered the map. The first support units slated for Red Phoenix had just arrived in their new camps near the DMZ. Could the imperialists have gotten wind of the move? He dismissed the thought as irrational. They'd taken great care in scheduling the troop trains to avoid times when American spy satellites were over Korea. The Americans couldn't know anything.

But the worry returned to nag him as he prepared for the morning's special meeting with his field commanders and other newly arrived senior officers. He fought it off, determined to avoid any thought that might shake his confidence and spoil the presentation he had planned. Kim Jong-Il still insisted that Red Phoenix be kept a closely guarded secret, but he had finally accepted Cho's argument that he be allowed to begin molding the proper "aggressive" spirit in his officers and men. This meeting would be a first step in that direction.

STAFF AUDITORIUM—II CORPS HQ, KAESONG, NORTH KOREA

The small, spartan auditorium lay three stories underground, part of the massive complex that housed II Corps headquarters. Six division commanders, their deputies, the general commanding his corps artillery, and the 62nd Special Forces brigade commander sat stiffly in high-backed wooden chairs facing a podium flanked by four-foot portraits of Kim Il-Sung and Kim Jong-Il.

"Attention!" rang in the room as Cho entered. Round-faced and lean, he strode to the podium and nodded to the group.

"I have just returned from a meeting of the General Staff, where we were addressed personally by the Dear Leader. What I have to tell you is welcome news."

Cho chose his words carefully, knowing that they would be taped, transcribed, and shipped to Pyongyang within hours. There they would be scrutinized by Kim for any hint of disloyalty or disbelief.

"You are all aware of the disturbances in the South that have prompted certain 'defensive' measures on our part." He nodded to the three second-echelon division commanders. "Now further developments require preparation for further action on our part."

Cho paused to let the small murmur of comment his words aroused fade away.

"According to our intelligence network, the capitalist forces that occupy the southern half of Korea are preparing to withdraw. They have recognized the corrupt regime in the South for what it is, and like a thief who no longer trusts his partner, they are leaving. As their own economy collapses, drained by their adventurism, the fascist Americans are unwilling to pay the price of their occupation.

"This is not generally known in our nation and must remain so. If the people find out, they may become impatient to liberate their brothers." Cho paused again, studying the faces of his officers. Already alert, his words had caused them to sit up even straighter in anticipation of the orders that might follow.

"The illegal regime in the South has been engaged in a massive military buildup, supported by the Americans. They buy the South's goods, give it military aid, and help the regime when it suppresses legitimate protests against its excesses.

"That buildup has now stopped, and over the next six months the American forces are expected to withdraw completely. It may be that, without its puppetmasters, the regime will collapse of its own weight.

"During the period of withdrawal, moreover, the political situation will be unstable. At any time the oppressed peoples of the South may spontaneously rise up and try to overthrow their leaders. We must be ready to go to their aid. If they are too weak to rise up, we will assist them."

Cho stopped for emphasis. He could see the gleam in his officers' eyes. They could sense that they were on the edge of carrying forward to completion the great work begun nearly forty years before during the Great Fatherland Liberation War. He spoke the next words slowly. "The need for such an undertaking may come upon us as suddenly as the north wind. Therefore, the General Staff has reiterated that it is the sworn duty of each and every soldier to be prepared for swift and decisive action.

"Accordingly, this Army corps will engage in a strenuous series of offensive battle drills over the coming months. Your men and equipment are to be held at a high state of readiness—available to carry out any orders the Great Leader sees fit to issue."

Cho stepped back from the podium to survey his audience. "Questions?"

There were none, and Cho carefully studied the reactions he saw emblazoned on his commanders' faces—eagerness, determination, excitement, and curiosity. Very well. He had momentarily lifted the curtain on Red Phoenix, and his generals liked what they saw.

They would be ready when the time came.

C H A P T E R
11
Signals

OCTOBER 3—COMBINED FORCES HQ, SEOUL, SOUTH KOREA

"Crap!" McLaren crumpled the piece of paper and threw it across the room toward a wastebasket. It missed. He shook his head, he must be getting old.

His aide nodded toward the paper. "Bad news, General?"

"Yeah, Doug." He felt himself wanting to pace and willed himself to keep still. "That goddamned sanctions legislation is still moving through Congress."

McLaren had been following the Barnes bill in the Pentagon's daily news summary ever since it had been introduced. He didn't pretend to understand all the ins and outs of the legislative process, but any good soldier could recognize a steady advance when he saw one.

What the hell was the matter with Congress anyway? Couldn't they see that there was a big, dangerous world out beyond the bounds of their congressional districts? He didn't like what was happening in South Korea any more than the next American, but you couldn't go around threatening to throw away a vital strategic position without having something to replace it. And that was just what Congress was threatening to do.

He'd seen the studies. The sanctions contained in Barnes's harebrained legislation could wreck the South Korean economy if they went into effect—and economic growth was pretty much the sole underpinning for South Korea's political stability right now. Without it, there'd be nothing left to hold the country together. What happened next could make the Seoul massacre look like a tea party. Kim Il-Sung would be licking his chops, ready to exploit any weakness across the DMZ.

Didn't these guys ever look at a map? The Korean peninsula was a dagger pointed right at the heart of Japan. At least that was how the Japanese saw it, and the Japanese were a pragmatic people. Let the Soviets or Chinese get a bigger foothold here and just watch how fast Japan's industrial giants would start selling even more high technology to them—and any export control treaties be damned. The thought was chilling. Take the enormous Soviet edge in sheer numbers of planes, tanks, guns, ships, and submarines. Mix it with a liberal dose of Japanese-supplied high-tech weaponry and sensors, and what did you have? A goddamned nightmare, that's what.

McLaren grimaced. There had better be some people left in Washington with some brains and guts.

"General, do you still want those reports on this week's alert?"

McLaren started. He must be getting feebleminded, standing around worrying about the Washington hive. He had work to do right here. "Hell, yes, Doug. Lay 'em on me."

He walked back around his desk and sat down to start poring through the tangle of reports that, together, would give him a picture of just what had happened up at the Z the last time he'd called a snap alert. What was it they called them—McLaren Specials? He smiled to himself. He knew his officers hated those alerts, but it was good practice for them. You never knew just what those crazy bastards up in Pyongyang had up their sleeves. You had to be ready for the unexpected when you were stationed in South Korea.

His phone buzzed. It was the Signals Room. "Sir, we've got a priority, scrambled call for you. It's Admiral Simpson." McLaren's eyebrows went up. It must be past midnight, Washington time. The Chairman of the Joint Chiefs was working late.

"Put him on." He heard a series of clicks and then a faint wash of static. "McLaren here."

"Hello, Jack, how's tricks?"

"Phil! You old son of a bitch. What's up?" There was a barely perceptible lag as the microwave signal raced twenty-four thousand miles up to a communications satellite in geosynchronous orbit and then back down to the chairman in Washington.

"It's this Barnes sanctions bill. The White House still says it isn't going anywhere this year, but my gut tells me that it just might. Both the House and Senate are getting a case of the electoral willies, and you know how screwed up things can get when they start looking for a foreign policy 'accomplishment' to show the voters."

"Hell, Phil. When did you get to be such a big political panjandrum?"

Simpson chuckled. "Goes with the turf. I've sat in front of so many congressional committees since last year that I'm even starting to talk like one of them."

"God save us."

"Yeah. Well, my wife says she likes it. Says it makes me sound more civilized."

McLaren's grip on the phone tightened for a moment. His wife, Elly, would probably have agreed with Caroline Simpson.

But she wouldn't ever have the chance. Not anymore. He cleared his throat. There wasn't time for sorrow. Not now. "Go on, Phil."

"Anyway, I need ammo to give the President a reason to kick this Barnes bill in the head while it's still young. And what I need from you, Jack, is your best analysis of the situation up North. I need your best guess as to what's going on up there across the wire."

"Hell, a guess is all you'll be able to get." McLaren reached across his desk for a pencil. "Don't you Pentagon boys already get copies of all my intel reports?"

"I want a new assessment drawn up. I know it might not be much different from the last one, but I want something hot off the presses to take in to the President."

"Okay. You've got it. I'll get my J-2 to send an update over the wire ASAP." McLaren made a note. Colonel Logan, his intelligence officer, was going to be busy today.

"Thanks, Jack. I appreciate it. Look, I've gotta run. It's nearly one in the A.M. back here, and Caroline's going to have my butt for breakfast if I stay much longer."

McLaren smiled to himself. He couldn't imagine anyone, even the admiral's formidable wife, putting the fear of God into Phil Simpson. He doubted if the thickset little man with the jutting jaw and impish grin had ever truly been afraid of anything or anyone. McLaren and the admiral had been friends since Nam. His battalion had been stationed down near the Mekong Delta, right beside Simpson's detachment of river gunboats and patrol craft. They'd fought together against the Viet Cong and North Vietnamese regulars, and then they'd moved on to some truly mind-bending carouses in the back-alley bars of both Saigon and Hong Kong. Somewhere along the way they'd formed a friendship that had lasted through years of peacetime, promotions, and duty assignments around the globe. Each man appreciated the other's guts and willingness to buck the conventional wisdom to get results.

"No problem, Phil. I'll talk to you later. And that intel report will be sitting on your desk when you get there in the morning."

There was a pause on the other end of the line, and then Simpson asked cautiously, "Look, are you planning on visiting Washington anytime soon?"

"No, why?" His daughter was supposed to come out to Seoul for Christmas this year. And his son would be at sea over the holidays.

"Well, it's just that this might be a good time to keep out of the States. If you're in town, some smart-ass congressional aide would probably call you to testify in some public hearing on the ROK. And Jack, don't take this wrong, but you come across kinda raw on camera. Know what I mean?''

McLaren laughed, ''Yeah, I know what you mean. I flunked Public Diplomacy one oh one back at the Point years ago, and I haven't ever bothered to take a refresher course.''

''No kidding. I wouldn't ever have guessed,'' Simpson said dryly. ''Later, Jack.''

''Give my best to Caroline.'' McLaren hung up and pressed the intercom button. ''Doug, get Charlie Logan over here, pronto. I've got work for him.''

Logan, his J-2, was a good officer, but he was a little too inclined to slack off if he thought no one was paying attention. McLaren had noticed a tendency to recycle old, approved intelligence reports if the situation hadn't changed much. Logan's laziness wouldn't put his career at risk, but it would probably keep him from getting his star. Well, Charlie wouldn't have a lot of time to goof off today. If the Chairman of the Joint Chiefs wanted a new North Korea intel assessment by breakfast Washington time, McLaren would make damned sure he got one.

OCTOBER 3—THE PENTAGON, WASHINGTON, D.C.

Combined Forces Korea Intelligence Report: Update
Top Secret
Warning: Includes Sensitive Intelligence

SUMMARY: Recent political and diplomatic maneuvering by North Korea could significantly increase the military threat Pyongyang's communist regime poses to regional and U.S. security...

Admiral Philip Simpson nodded to himself. McLaren's J-2 knew how to write a good report. He'd have Carlson pass it on to the NSC staffer, Fowler, for inclusion into the Interagency Working Group's final report to the President. The admiral skimmed through the document, looking for anything new that should be highlighted. He found it on page four.

North Korean Air Order of Battle (continued):

Accumulated evidence shows that an additional North Korean MiG-23 fighter squadron is now fully operational. Analysis of latest satellite photos (see Tab V-1) indicates they are based at the Wonsan airfield. However, recent data indicate that the MiG-23s may not be the only advanced Soviet aircraft now being delivered to the North Korean Air Force Command. Reconnaissance photos in Tab V-9 to 11 show the Soviet freighter *Valentin Zolotarev* at anchor in the top security zone of Wonsan harbor. Three crates (marked A, B, and C on the photos) appear to be the type commonly used to ship aircraft fuselages and other parts. While the precise type of aircraft being shipped cannot be identified, the crates are large enough to contain any of the current-generation Soviet fighter or ground-attack aircraft.

In addition, South Korean National Security Planning Agency (NSP) listening posts on random scan have picked up airborne Russian language transmissions that can be interpreted as showing that a new cadre of Soviet instructor pilots are now operating inside North Korea. Since North Korea's MiG-23 squadrons are now operational, our conclusion is that the new Soviet instructors are training North Korean pilots to fly a new type of aircraft. (See attached transcript).

Simpson flipped to the back of the report, looking for the radio intercept transcript.

Attachment C—NSP Monitoring Station 3, INT/A/R/4537—1235 Hours, 25 September:

Unidentified Airborne Transmitter (Pilot): "Tell that blundering idiot to keep his wings level! And to adjust his throttle. He's wallowing all over the sky like a drunken cow."

Unidentified Ground Control (Control): "(static) . . . Alpha Two reports . . . (unintelligible) . . . starboard engine . . . (static)"

Pilot: "Nonsense. He doesn't know what he's talking about. Tell him to pull his nose up before he . . . (static)"

Control: "(unintelligible) . . . fuel feed . . . (static)"

Pilot: "Better. Nose level. Tell him to bank left twenty-five degrees and go to full power . . . (static) . . . What's his airspeed now . . . (unintelligible)"

Control: "Switching now . . ."

—Transmission Frequency Changed, End of Intercept—

NOTE: US E-3 Sentry Delta five niner five on patrol over the Sea of Japan confirms aircraft at 20–30,000 feet at transmission origin coordinates.

Simpson marked the section for Captain Carlson's attention and sat back in his chair. North Korea and the Soviet Union were getting entirely too chummy for his taste. Not that he could do much about it.

His intercom buzzed. "Admiral, your car is here to take you up to the Hill."

Simpson tossed the report into his out box and stood up, reaching for his briefcase. It was time to go to Capitol Hill and jabber at the Senate Armed Services committee about manpower retention rates. He looked at his calendar. This was his fourth congressional appearance of the week. He often thought it was a goddamned wonder that he ever got any work done.

OCTOBER 4—CNN HEADLINE NEWS

The CNN reporter, a pretty brunette, stood in the marble-lined corridor outside a hearing room in the Rayburn House Office Building.

"This is Connie Marlowe for CNN Headline News. *In a surprise development here today, House Armed Services Committee Chairman Stephen Nicholson announced that his committee would not seek jurisdiction over the South Korea sanctions bill. The move, which caught most Capitol Hill observers off guard, clears the way for the bill to go to the House Rules Committee. From there it would move to the full House of Representatives.*

"The bill's chief sponsor, Congressman Ben Barnes of Michigan, was understandably pleased when I spoke with him earlier."

The film cut to taped footage of a smiling Ben Barnes in the same corridor.

"Naturally I'm delighted that my distinguished colleague

Congressman Nicholson has seen the importance of swift and decisive action by the House in this matter. America's roads and stores cannot continue to be flooded with shoddy South Korean imports while students are murdered in Seoul's streets. We must send a clear message to the South Korean government. No more violence. No more repression. No more free ride."

The picture cut back to Connie Marlowe.

"In other news here on the Hill today, a similar bill moved a step closer to consideration by the full Senate by winning approval from the Senate Foreign Relations Committee. Conservatives have threatened a filibuster if the bill reaches the floor. But Senate Majority Leader Dickinson of Arkansas remains confident that he has enough support to invoke cloture, a move that would shut off any prolonged debate and bring the issue to an up-or-down vote within a set time frame."

The screen split, showing both the CNN anchorman stationed in Atlanta and the reporter in Washington.

"Connie, doesn't it take a two-thirds vote of the Senate to end a filibuster? Does the Korea sanctions bill have that much support in the Senate?"

"You're right, John. Normally, the majority leader's confidence would indicate overwhelming support for the bill. But this is a special case. With the election coming up, a lot of challengers have been pummeling Senate incumbents with charges that they never do any work. So even senators who don't plan to vote for the legislation are eager to avoid a long, wearing filibuster. And right now, it's just not clear who has the votes to win on this issue in the Senate. I'm Connie Marlowe for CNN Headline News."

OCTOBER 6—THE HOUSE RULES COMMITTEE, WASHINGTON, D.C.

"Mr. Chairman, this proposed rule is outrageous and you know it!" Henry Fielding, the ranking minority member of the House Rules Committee sounded angry but not surprised. The white-haired representative from Missouri glared out across the handful of congressional staffers rapidly scribbling notes on legal pads.

The Rules Committee always met in a small, cramped

room to hold the number of spectators down to an absolute minimum. In a way that was a true measure of its power. This committee could make or break legislation in a single hour. It set the terms, the rule, under which a given bill would be considered by the full House of Representatives. Legislation that the Speaker liked would get a rule that sharply limited debate and made it impossible to offer so-called killer amendments. Legislation that the Speaker didn't like wouldn't ever get a rule, period.

To make sure of that, the majority party in the House always maintained a two-to-one plus one edge on the Rules Committee—no matter what the real ratio of Democrats to Republicans might be.

And the Speaker liked the Korea sanctions bill.

Fielding knew the fix was in, but he had sworn to put up at least a token fight. "Mr. Chairman, the rule you and your friends have concocted would prevent members of the House from offering even the most reasonable amendments to this legislation. That is not the way we should be conducting business on this kind of issue. And there is no conceivable excuse for the absurd time limitations you've placed on the debate."

The chairman, Representative Kerwin Bouchard of Louisiana, interrupted him. "Mr. Fielding, the issues contained in this bill have been fully considered in committee." Unconsciously he ran a wizened hand through the remaining strands of his hair. His Southern drawl thickened. "There is no reason for further delay and no necessity for extended debate."

Fielding struck back. "With all due respect, Mr. Chairman, that is nonsense. We're not elected to be rubber stamps for the committees. This is supposed to be a deliberative body, and your rule would prevent a thorough and reasoned consideration of this legislation. The issues in this Korea sanctions bill are too complex and too important to be handled in this callously partisan fashion."

The chairman listened with interest. Fielding at his best was very good. And the chairman had no doubt he would hear the same phrases and arguments again on the floor when the full House debated this rule. But his instructions from the Speaker were clear, and he hadn't gotten this far in the House by crossing the Speaker. He sat back to enjoy the show with complete confidence in the outcome.

It took nearly an hour of pro forma argument, but in the end the committee approved the rule by a party-line vote of nine to four. No one on the inside was at all surprised.

OCTOBER 7—THE WHITE HOUSE, WASHINGTON, D.C.

Putnam tossed the bulky report back across his desk. "Damn it, Blake. This isn't what I asked you for."

Blake Fowler looked down at the document and then back to the red face of the national security adviser. He sat down in one of Putnam's chairs without an invitation.

"You asked for the Working Group's recommendations to the President. And that"—he pointed to the paper—"is what you've got sitting on your desk." The report was nearly two weeks overdue, but even that had required a minor miracle and countless hours of overtime.

The actual writing involved in the analysis of the Barnes Korean sanctions bill hadn't taken more than a couple of days of hard, steady work. But getting the precise wording approved by five cabinet departments and intelligence agencies had been nightmarishly complex. Each wanted to leave its stamp on the report, so each made its own set of editorial changes. Changes that required approval by all the rest, and that often prompted a whole new series of rewrites. Blake had circulated so many different drafts that he now knew every classified-documents courier on the interagency–White House run.

The minor miracle had come in salvaging anything that was clearly written. The members of the Interagency Working Group were solid professionals, but they weren't writers, and they'd all learned to use bureaucratese. In bureaucratese, people weren't affected, "population subgroups were impacted." The risks of full-scale warfare weren't increased, "the probability of significant geopolitical and military interaction" underwent an "upward modification." Blake had dug in his heels to fight off meaningless gibberish like that wherever he could, and he'd won more fights than he'd lost.

But he knew that none of that mattered to Putnam. Putnam

was upset because the State Department had refused to sign off on the report. State's representative, Tolliver, hadn't bothered to attend more than one out of every two or three Working Group meetings, and he'd been a pain in the ass every time anyway.

After a while it had become clear that the secretary of state, a former congressman, was more interested in domestic political polls showing rising public support for some action against South Korea than he was in the foreign policy implications of the legislation. And he wouldn't approve a document that recommended strong administration opposition and a presidential veto if the Barnes bill got that far.

Blake had tried everything he could think of to get the State Department on board—short of soft-soaping the Working Group's recommendations. He'd even made several attempts to get in to see the secretary personally, without result. The man's flunkies had used every excuse in the book. The secretary was always away on "national business," or had an "urgent policy board meeting," and once they'd even tried the old standby that he was "receiving an important foreign delegation." Blake hadn't even been able to secure an appointment with the assistant secretary for East Asian and Pacific Affairs.

The message was clear. The State Department, or at least its political leadership, wasn't interested in getting into a shitting match with the Congress over South Korea. He'd been given a reason for that over a hasty lunch in the White House commissary with a friend from the Arms Control and Disarmament Agency.

"Look, Blake," "Tubby" Barlow had said, "there's no way you're gonna get the boys at Foggy Bottom to risk pissing off the Speaker and the majority leader right now. They're within inches of a new missile agreement with the Soviets. And they aren't taking any chances that some irate congressman might blow the thing because his favorite bill got dumped on by the administration." The way the upper echelons of the State Department saw it, South Korea just wasn't in the same league with a possible superpower arms control treaty.

And so the Working Group had decided to go ahead without State's sanction for their final product. It was either that or come up with nothing at all. From the way Putnam was carrying on, it was clear that he might have preferred that.

"Goddamn it. This thing is practically useless to me the way it is." One of Putnam's reddish-gray curls had broken lose from its hair-sprayed moorings and was flopping around over an eyebrow. The national security adviser impatiently brushed it back into place.

Blake shook his head. "I don't see how you can say that. Okay, State doesn't agree with our recommendations. BFD. Five other agencies do. That's about as solid a bloc as you're ever going to find in any administration."

Putnam glowered at him. "That's not going to cut it with the media, Dr. Fowler. You and I both know that somebody at State will leak the secretary's displeasure with this report to the *Post* or the *Times* and then the shit's really going to hit the fan. The President doesn't like to see headlines that say things like 'Top-Level Rifts Mar Administration Policy.' "

Blake had to admit that Putnam had a point. But it was moot.

The State Department wasn't going to reverse course and approve the report. And the South Korean situation was too critical for the White House to simply sit idly by as the Barnes legislation moved through Congress. Jesus, he hoped there were at least a few red faces over in Legislative Affairs. They'd been telling anyone who would listen that the Barnes bill was just a typical piece of election-year foofaraw. Something introduced to soothe angry voters and then slated for quiet extinction after the ballots were cast. Well, every passing day put that prediction more and more in the column headed by the *Chicago Tribune*'s 1948 election day headline, "Dewey Wins!"

Blake looked back across the desk at Putnam. "So you're not going to present our recommendations to the President?"

"I didn't say that." Putnam reached over and tore off a piece of tape. "The President's asked for a briefing on this Korea thing something in the next few days. My calendar's pretty full, but I'm going to try to squeeze it in somewhere— after I've had time to go through this stuff in a little more detail." Putnam started rolling the piece of tape in between two fingers, wadding it up into a tiny, sticky ball.

Blake wanted to ask why Putnam didn't just ask him to

deliver the briefing. But he already knew the answer. Putnam didn't know much more about Asian and Pacific affairs than the average daily newspaper reader did, but he did understand the mechanics of power. And in Washington, D.C., access is power.

Putnam guarded the right to personally brief the President with jealous vigor. In nineteen months on the job, he'd never yet allowed a member of his staff to lead the President through the tangle of position papers, charts, maps, and satellite photos that made up a typical NSC presentation. His rules were clear and absolutely inflexible. The staff experts prepared the briefing and he delivered it. If Putnam still felt uncomfortable with the material, he'd bring a staffer along. But always with the understanding that they would respond only to direct questions from the President or from Putnam himself.

Blake thought it was a shitty way to conduct business. But he understood Putnam's intentions. It made the red-haired bastard look very much like the all-knowing whiz kid he claimed to be—at least to the President. And that was what mattered.

He looked up as Putnam flicked the little ball of tape off into his wastebasket.

"In any event, Blake, I've got a few edits to make in your report." Putnam smiled. "You've done a pretty good job in putting this thing together, I guess. But it needs a little work to make it more readable. Can't risk putting the Boss to sleep during the presentation, now can we?"

Oh, crap. Putnam's idea of clear prose made federal bureaucratese look like something written by Ernest Hemingway. The man never saw a short, simple, clear word that he didn't think could be replaced by an impossibly long, convoluted clause.

Blake knew there wasn't much point in worrying about it. He and Putnam had tangled over the written word nearly as often as they'd clashed over policy. Beside, Putnam probably wouldn't let him see the hash he'd made of the Working Group's paper until just before they briefed the President.

He was almost right.

OCTOBER 9—THE HOUSE FLOOR, WASHINGTON, D.C.

Jeremy Mitchell watched the flickering totals on the vote board with one eye and kept the other on his boss, Ben Barnes, working his colleagues down on the floor in front of the Speaker's chair. He smiled as the totals changed once again, reflecting another congressman who'd buckled to persuasion from Barnes or pressure from the Speaker.

Getting the Speaker on board had been the best thing he'd ever done. The man was an oily little snake-charming s.o.b., but he knew the rules and procedures of the House backward and forward. And he'd bend any of them to get his way. Mitchell looked up at the section of the vote board that showed the time remaining. It read "0:00." Just as it had for the last twenty minutes or so. He smiled again. Votes in the House of Representatives were usually supposed to last fifteen minutes or less. If a congressman hadn't made it to the floor by then or hadn't made up his mind, that was just too bad. In practice, though, the Speaker controlled time in the House, and fifteen minutes was whatever he said it was—no matter what the clocks might say.

The sharp crash of the chairman's gavel brought his eyes back to the floor. The vote was over. The congressman acting as chairman of the Committee of the Whole took a small piece of paper from one of the clerks. "On this vote, the ayes were two thirty-eight. The nays, one eighty-one. The bill is passed."

Mitchell headed for the door grinning from ear to ear. They'd done it! And now it was up to the Senate. The majority leader's chief aide had already assured him they'd bring the Korea sanctions bill up as soon as it passed the House. Jeremy Mitchell could smell victory. Victory for the bill and victory for Ben Barnes when he ran for the Senate two years down the road.

He was only half right.

CHAPTER
12
Low Profiles

OCTOBER 11—INSA-DONG, SEOUL, SOUTH KOREA

Captain Tony Christopher did not regret coming into Seoul that day. He had planned on a little shopping. But he hadn't planned on spending almost all of his time in the same store.

Back at the base that morning there had been the standard warning about "the possibility of civil disturbances." Fine, he was no fool. But Seoul was huge—more than ten million people lived within its limits. The South Koreans could have a riot at one end of town and still leave enough peaceful city for one Air Force pilot to do some gift-shopping. Anyway, the chance was too good to miss. He only got one day off during the week.

Besides, the warnings had been for the Myong-dong district, around the Catholic cathedral, where there had been protests all week. That was bad luck, of course, because the best department stores were all clustered in the Myong-dong area. And he was getting tired of the cheap, touristy stuff they tried to push on you in the Itaewon bargain shops, near the main U.S. Army base just south of Seoul.

Fortunately the squadron's intelligence officer had put him on to a good thing. He'd suggested taking a look along Insa-Dong, Mary's Alley. Michaels might not know much about his main job—keeping track of enemy aircraft deployments, tactics, and antiaircraft sites—but he did have a nose for bargains on things like handcrafted fans, fine jewelry, and ceramics. Exactly the kind of stuff most women liked. Exactly the kind of stuff that might help Tony smooth things out with his current girlfriend, Maria.

She was a real looker, short, but with jet-black hair falling straight down to below her waist. They'd gone out three times, most recently last night. She was fun, with a good sense of humor, and an appreciation of Tony's flying stories. She also, however, had a tremendous temper—a temper that had been triggered when, lost in thought, Tony had called her Carol.

So at Michael's recommendation, Tony had come up on the first train from Kunsan to Seoul and then hopped the Seoul subway to the Chongno 3-ga station near Pagoda Park. That had been the easy part. Since then, he'd spent a long, hot morning browsing his way up Insa-Dong, combing through the antique shops, art galleries, furniture stores, and jewelry stores that lined the narrow, winding street.

The trouble was, he doubted that he could tell a piece of good Korean craftsmanship from the worst piece of junk ever made. And even a "bargain" from one of the Insa-Dong shops was going to take a pretty hefty bite out of his paycheck from Uncle Sam.

Damn. Tony hated dithering around like this. He'd hoped to make a quick sortie into Seoul for Maria's gift and still have enough time left for a swing through the casino at the Sheraton Walker Hill. He felt lucky and you always had to hit the blackjack tables feeling lucky. But it looked as if he was going to need all that luck just to make the evening train back to Kunsan.

Tony zipped up his jacket. He wanted to get out of the chill wind for a while, but he knew the minute he stepped into a shop he'd be mobbed by a bunch of Korean salesclerks. They were all so godawful helpful and polite that you almost felt compelled to buy something from them. And Tony knew that was the fastest way to wind up stuck with something you didn't want, couldn't afford, and couldn't get rid of.

As he stepped off the curb to cross a side street, a sign in a storefront window caught his eye—LEE'S KOREAN-ENGLISH BOOK-STORE. That was the ticket. Just the place for a breather. He wheeled and started for it.

The bookstore was a godsend all right. It was warm, quiet, and blinds across the store's two front windows cut out most of the sun's glare. Tony closed the door firmly behind him, shutting out the roar as a convoy of trucks loaded with riot police rumbled down the street.

A short, middle-aged Korean standing behind a counter with a cash register smiled and bowed slightly to him. Tony nodded back politely and moved deeper into the shop, glancing idly at the bookracks around him. There weren't any other customers. And there didn't seem to be a whole lot of books by American authors either. Most were by people he assumed were modern Korean writers.

Books with titles like *The Heartless* or *The Grass Roof* didn't have much appeal for Tony—his tastes ran more to murder mysteries and thrillers. He moved to the next rack and started thumbing through a translated Korean government publication called "An International Terrorist Clique—North Korea." It seemed like pretty heavy-handed stuff, but then he didn't have to live full-time in a country that had enemy commandos landing on its beaches.

A sudden increase in the noise coming from outside on the street broke Tony's concentration. He looked up from the propaganda pamphlet to see the little Korean shopkeeper peering intently out through the blinds.

Then he heard the chanting and the muffled, coughing explosions of tear gas canisters. Tony went up to the front and looked out down the Insa-Dong to see a crowd that filled the street from one end to the other.

He had to look hard to see individual people. The first impression he got was one of waving arms and legs, white masks, and streaming vapor. They were just coming into view, but he felt he was close—way too close. Personal safety aside, the ops officer would ream him good if he got tangled up in this mess.

He nodded to the shopkeeper and headed for the door, only to feel the man's hand on his arm. "Please, you should wait here. I think it's not good to go out. You help me put up shutters and we wait here. You not like my books?"

Tony smiled and tried to decide, torn between the desire to get the hell out of there ahead of the crowd and the idea of lying low and riding it out. He looked down the street again. He should have time.

"Okay, brother. But let's snap it up. Just where the hell are these shutters?"

The Korean pointed to a pile of heavy sheet metal panels stacked by the counter. Working quickly, they managed to hoist the shutters onto hooks set over the windows. The shopkeeper left one pair unfastened so he could see out.

Tony tapped him on the shoulder. "Is this going to be enough? I mean, shouldn't you just lock up so we can both get out of here?" He could see other figures locking their doors and scurrying away ahead of the oncoming mob.

"No. I see this before. There are other crowds, more people other places. We run down street, might find another group. This over in two-three hours."

Tony had to admit that the Korean made sense. Maybe sticking it out here was the best idea. He stood next to the man and watched through the shutters as the mob approached. As a pilot, Tony felt totally outside his element. He could feel his pulse speeding up. This was the kind of situation the groundpounders, the infantry, were trained for—not him.

The rioters were individuals now, and he could see green-uniformed Combat Police behind and mixed in with them. They were pushing the demonstrators up the street, clubbing anyone who stopped to fight. They were thorough. Anyone who tried to hide in angles or doorways was cornered and beaten senseless.

It was clear, too, that some of the "rioters" were actually people who had just been caught in the protest, swept up as the police moved in.

Jesus, it was getting really vicious out there. He could see rioters trying to throw tear gas canisters back at the police, and there were other things flying through the air—rocks, bricks, and bottles filled with flaming gasoline.

Several masked demonstrators converged on a policeman who'd gotten too far out in front of his fellows. They ripped his gas mask off, and one of them landed a punch on the man's throat. Tony saw his mouth open in agony for a second before he went down under a flurry of kicking legs.

A patch of color caught his eye, and he saw a Caucasian woman running down the street just in front of the oncoming melee. She was wearing high heels that looked uncomfortable and were slowing her down. Tony had a quick impression of copper-colored hair and a green summer dress.

But the woman was coughing, and unless she ditched the shoes, she wasn't going to get clear.

He didn't stop to think. He just reached out and unlocked the front door. "Hold the fort, Mac. I'll be right back."

The shopkeeper put a hand out, startled, but Tony brushed past him and ducked out onto the street.

The noise and smell hit him first—and he stayed back against the building to make sure nothing else hit him. Christ, the smell. He could feel his eyes tearing up and his throat drying out. He had been caught by tear gas before, back in West Germany during an antinuclear protest outside the base where he'd been stationed. This wasn't as bad, but that was a relative term.

The first groups of rioters were past him, and he could see rocks and bottles flying through the air in both directions. Nothing was aimed directly at him, and as far as he could tell, he hadn't been noticed. He sprinted the hundred yards to the woman flat out. She had stopped, winded, on the sidewalk.

Tony skidded to a stop on the sidewalk in front of her—his eyes half on her and half on the brawl swirling up the street toward them. "Ma'am, come with me! I've got a place back there where we can hole up." He jerked a thumb back toward the bookstore.

She looked at him without much expression at all. "Hole up?" She was breathing heavily and rubbing her feet.

"I mean where we can get out of this mess." Christ, this wasn't any time for an English lesson. He looked nervously over her shoulder as the mob closed on them. "Ma'am, I'd get rid of those heels if I were you. They're nice, but they aren't Nikes!"

She looked at him and then at the chaos behind her. Muttering "There goes one pair of stockings," she kicked out of her heels, scooped them off the pavement, and ran down the street, shoes in one hand and a package in another.

Tony ran to catch up, shouting, "The bookstore on the left!"

This lady was fast. Even with the noise behind pushing him along, he caught up to her only when she slowed to find the shop front.

Tony banged on the door and it opened just long enough for them to duck inside. The Korean slammed it shut as if it were spring-loaded. He looked up at Tony. "This is good. You find your lady friend. Both now safe."

The woman flushed red.

Tony glanced over at her, embarrassed, and then back to the shopkeeper. "I don't know her. I just didn't think we should leave her out on the street."

"I'm glad you didn't. Thank you both." She started to put on her shoes, and Tony reached out a gentlemanly hand to steady her. She stood gracefully on one leg and slipped on one shoe, then switched legs and repeated the process. Tony pulled his hand back before she noticed it.

Hell, she wasn't just pretty—she was damned pretty. She had a nice figure, but what really caught his eye was a mop of curly copper-colored hair. She wore it shoulder-length, and combined with the pale, freckled complexion only redheads can have, she was a knockout. She was tall, only half a head shorter than Tony, and that much taller than the shopkeeper.

And that was an American accent if he'd ever heard one. He straightened his shoulders. "Ma'am, I'm just glad I could help." He reached out again, turning the charm meter up to level three. "My name's Tony Christopher."

She took his hand. "Pleased to meet you, Mr. Christopher. I hadn't counted on running into something like this." She suddenly smiled. "I'm sorry, I should introduce myself. I'm Anne Larson."

Tony was worried. Level three wasn't a killer, but "Mr. Christopher"? Sheesh. He tried level five. "Call me Tony, please."

Before she could reply, something or someone slammed off the bookstore's shutters, making them all jump. Anne whitened. "They're going crazy out there. What's going on around here all of a sudden?"

Tony shrugged helplessly. "I don't know. This is out of my field. Ask me about MiGs or flying, but not this stuff."

They could hear windows breaking across the street. He turned to the Korean shopkeeper. "Say, have you ever seen anything this violent before?"

"No, not before. But all riots bad. Criminals and communists and ungrateful children. They make too much trouble, and everyone suffers. My shop will smell of the gas for weeks."

Anne said, "But the police, they're clubbing people."

The Korean's face tightened. "They bring this on themselves. Protesting the government! They should see how I lived thirty, forty years ago. They go to school and instead of classes they march in the street and throw rocks! They should obey parents and use chance to go to school. I wish I could go to university. They could have better life, build country.'' He shook his head slowly and gestured outside. ''Instead, they tear things up.''

Tony peered through a crack between the window shutters. Groups of students and police were struggling—sometimes attacking, sometimes fleeing. He felt as if he were watching it on television, but the sounds were too real, and you couldn't catch the gut-wrenching stench of the tear gas on television.

He could see several hundred people, mostly white-masked students with some other civilians mixed in, trying to make a stand in the street outside. But a solid line of green-uniformed Combat Policemen were working their way slowly up the street breaking heads.

Squads in phalanx formation charged knots of protestors as they tried to form, firing rubber bullets and closing with clubs. Behind the advancing police line, troopers handcuffed individual rioters, none too gently, and dragged them over to waiting security vans. At the same time, trucks with water cannon and grenade launchers fired at larger groups, driving the mass of people farther up the street. It was a well-organized operation, pulverizing a mass of organized demonstrators into dazed individuals, safely under control.

He and Anne both watched as the police line moved toward the bookstore. As the fighting got closer, details popped out. Two policemen handcuffed a glassy-eyed student, threw him to the ground, and kicked him savagely. Just a few feet away, another demonstrator picked up a tear gas grenade from the pavement and lobbed it back toward the police. He went down with blood streaming from his forehead, knocked senseless by a rubber bullet fired at near point-blank range.

Another had a spray can. As a riot trooper ran at him, the kid pressed the spray button, then held a lighter in front of it. Tony saw a flash and saw the student try to aim his improvised flamethrow at the oncoming policeman. But the helmeted trooper knocked the spray can away with a long billy club, then whipped the weapon down onto the student's unprotected head—smashing the boy to the pavement with a series of short, vicious blows. The man ran on, leaving the kid huddled in agony on the ground.

Tony looked back at the Korean shopkeeper. He was sitting at his desk in the back, quietly working. He wasn't accomplishing much though, since he glanced up every five or ten seconds. When he saw Tony looking, he quickly fixed his gaze on the papers in front of him and did not look up again.

Anne didn't say anything. She just shivered occasionally.

Tony couldn't think of anything to say that wouldn't sound ridiculously out of place. So they stood together, behind the shutters, watching silently as the South Korean riot police broke the demonstration into fragments.

It was over in minutes. Moving with steady precision, the line of police and armored cars advanced past up the block. Like water spraying from a hose, the crowd scattered onto other cross-streets, and as the fighting moved on, the noise outside fell away—leaving an almost eerie quiet in its place.

They waited a few moments more, unwilling to believe that the brutal street battle they'd witnessed had ended so quickly. But it had, and finally Tony looked over at Anne with a questioning look. Anne nodded, seeming almost afraid somehow to break the silence.

Tony looked out through the shutters again, craning to catch a glimpse of the streets down which the riot had flowed. It seemed all clear.

"Hold up for a second," he said, and walked back to thank the bookstore owner for sheltering them. He also wanted to pay the man for the pamphlet he'd been holding crumpled in his hand for almost an hour. The man smiled, came with him to the door, and unlocked it.

He ushered Tony and Anne out onto the street—bowing politely as they both wished him good luck. "Please, do not pay attention to this, this incident." He gestured at the debris-strewn pavement. "Do not judge Korea by these hooligans. They are fools. They do not know what they do."

As they stepped out onto the empty street, Tony half-expected to feel as if he were walking across a deserted battlefield. But the wind had blown the tear gas away and it felt strangely like an early morning, like those quiet, still hours just before people wake up and the stores open for business.

And Tony knew that the stores along the Insa-Dong would soon reopen. There had been a riot, but the police had restored order. At least that's what they would say on the evening news.

Yeah, right. As far as Tony was concerned that was like calling a plane crash "an undesirable ground/air interface."

He looked at his watch. Plenty of time to spare before his train left for Kunsan. Well, to hell with the shopping trip.

He wasn't going to hang around waiting to get teargassed again. He glanced at Anne. She seemed uncertain, hesitant somehow.

"Look, can I get you a cab or help you find someplace? I'm not real familiar with Seoul, but I've got a pretty good map."

Anne looked even less certain than she had before, if that was possible. "Oh, no. No, I don't think so." She paused. "I took the subway to get out here."

Tony smiled. "No problem. I'm heading back that way myself. I'd be glad to see you to the station." He was pretty sure he could find it again.

Anne kept her eyes fixed about the level of his shoes. Tony felt frustrated. Hell, he didn't bite—at least not that often. And he couldn't stand around here in the street forever, waiting for this woman to make up her mind about whether or not she wanted to keep shopping in a riot district.

Finally she glanced up at him, but only for a split second. "Well . . ." Then in a rush, "Thank you, Mr. Christopher, I'd appreciate it." She looked down the street. "I'd feel better with some company . . . to the station, I mean."

He grinned. "Please. Call me Tony. The only time I'm called Mr. Christopher is when I've screwed up. It has negative connotations for me."

That got her. Anne laughed lightly. "Okay, Tony, lead on." He decided he liked the way she said his name. She gave it a musical quality somehow, or maybe it was just the faint hint of a Southern drawl.

Anne considered the man beside her as they walked. She didn't particularly mind his putting the moves on her. He was a pilot, after all. She did mind his assuming that she'd automatically be charmed by his looks and his line.

Still, he had gotten her out of a bad spot, and he was being polite, almost courtly. As they talked, his manner changed her initial feelings. His freshness and honesty made it hard for her to hold anything against him.

They headed south down the Insa-Dong, walking past the still-shuttered shop windows at a rapid clip. Tony didn't want to spend any more time in the area than he absolutely had to.

Anne didn't have any trouble keeping up with him, and Tony found himself admiring her graceful stride out of the corner of his eye.

The streets were still quiet, but after a few blocks they began seeing a few other cautious pedestrians going about their business. Finally they came to a block where the shops were unshuttered, and Tony felt as if a great weight had been lifted from his shoulders. Without realizing it he slowed down.

He nodded at the store windows filled with beautifully painted screens and elegant furniture. "Hardly seems like we're in the same country, does it?"

Anne followed his glance. "No. I don't know how they can do it. How can they just pretend nothing's happened?"

Tony shrugged. He liked the Koreans he'd met so far during his tour. They were tough, hardworking, and friendly. But there was no getting around the fact that they belonged to a completely different culture. Things that struck Americans as wildly out of kilter often seemed normal to Koreans and vice versa. Take the time that Korean pilot had tried to persuade him to order marinated dog for example. Tony's stomach, already unsettled by the tear gas, rebelled at the thought. Whoops.

Don't lose it, son, he warned himself. He had a hunch he wouldn't impress Anne very much by being sick all over the pavement in front of her.

And he suddenly realized, he did want to impress her. Well, why should that surprise him? After all, here he was ten thousand miles away from home, strolling along beside a pretty American woman. Hell, his wingman, Hooter, would probably have already gotten her address, phone number, and room key by now.

But then Hooter was a daredevil son of a bitch all the time—whether he was in the air or on the ground. Tony liked to think he was a bit more tactically minded.

They stopped at a cross-street, waiting for a break in the heavy traffic. That was reassuring. Where there were cars, there weren't likely to be any demonstrations. Korean drivers didn't like seeing their windshields smashed, and they seemed to have a sixth sense for staying out of trouble spots.

He heard a relieved sigh from Anne and smiled. "Yeah. I think we're out of the danger zone now." He paused, trying for just the right emphasis on the key words. "You know, I sure never expected a visit to Seoul to be more nerve-racking than a low-altitude dogfight."

It was the second time that he had hinted about flying. She decided to rise to the bait. "Dogfight? Are you a pilot?"

They started across the street. Tony kept his voice casual. "Oh, yeah. I fly F-16s for the Air Force." He waited, expectantly.

"Oh. That's nice." Anne looked both ways down the road, keeping an eye out for oncoming traffic.

That's nice? That's nice? Tony could hardly believe it. She sounded as if he'd just told her he was a plumber or something. But he had to laugh, mostly at himself. What did he expect her to do—faint dead away at being so near a real, live fighter pilot? Get a grip on yourself, guy.

He looked over sharply at Anne, but she had her eyes resolutely fixed on the pavement again. Damnit. Was she smiling? He couldn't tell, and he couldn't think of any clever way to find out. Damn, damn, and double damn.

He could see the subway station entrance just a block ahead when suddenly Anne's head snapped up, her eyes wider than he'd ever seen them. She grabbed his elbow. "Did you hear that? That popping noise, just now."

Popping noise? What the hell was she talking about? Then he heard it. A long, rolling series of muffled explosions—like cooking popcorn or a string of Chinese firecrackers. It was off to the west, toward the city center, but it was getting louder. The riot was moving back this way, nastier than ever.

He took Anne's hand without even thinking about it. "C'mon." They ran toward the subway station, jostled their way in with a crowd of Korean commuters, and took the down escalator two steps at a time. The station was noisy, crowded with Korean businessmen and shoppers heading home after a long day, but they could hear wailing police sirens rushing past on the street above them.

Tony kept hold of Anne's hand until they pushed their way onto a packed subway car, along with most of the others who'd been lining the tracks. As the train pulled out, heading into the darkened subway tunnel, Anne pulled her hand away—gently but firmly.

The other passengers were restless and just as edgy as Tony and Anne. They'd heard the sirens, and many had heard the shooting off in the distance above the station. As they chattered back and forth in worried tones, Tony wished he'd learned more than phrase-book Korean.

Shit, he knew why they were worried. The train they were on was moving west—right toward the direction of the riot. Tony could have kicked himself. This was the right subway line to Seoul Station, but he could have gone around the other way. Now, he'd put both himself and Anne at risk just because he'd rushed onto the first damned train that came along.

He swore under his breath.

Anne heard him and leaned over. "Don't worry about it. I didn't think either." She was pale but seemed under control.

Tony felt a little better. He just hoped the train's engineer knew what was going on above ground.

The man must have, because he went rocketing through the next station, Chongak, without slowing. Tony could see the huge crowd waiting by the tracks frantically trying to wave the train down. But they were through and into the next dark tunnel in a matter of seconds. Once there, the subway train started slowing to a more normal speed. They must be past whatever was going on.

Tony pulled out his city guide. Chongak Station led out onto Sejong Street, wherever the hell that was. And there would only be one more stop before they got to the railroad station.

He looked over at Anne. "I'm supposed to get off at Seoul Station, but let me get you to your hotel, first."

She got a strange look on her face. "My hotel?" She

shook her head. "I'm not a tourist, I work in the logistics section at Yongsan."

Yongsan. That was the main U.S. Forces military base in Seoul. Just who was Anne, some other officer's wife? He risked a quick look at her hands. No, no rings. So what was she doing at Yongsan?

She must have read his mind. "I work there. For the Army." It shouldn't have, but that took Tony by surprise and it must have showed on his face. Anne frowned. "You've heard that some women are smart enough to make their own way in the world, I suppose." She looked a little taken aback by what she'd said.

Oops. Where the hell was an ejection seat when you really needed one. How was he going to dig himself out of this hole?

The train stopped at the City Hall station, but no one got off and more people forced their way on board.

"Look, I'm sorry." He stopped. Saying he was apologizing for not thinking she was smart enough to work for a living was a lot like being asked if you had stopped beating your wife. It was a no-win proposition.

He started over. "I'd like to get to know you better." The train was starting to brake. His stop must be just ahead. Damn, there wasn't time to do this with any finesse.

"Could I see you sometime, you know, maybe for dinner? I'm not such a bad guy when I'm not stuck in the middle of a riot, honest." He tried to smile. Christ, he felt like a high school freshman again. He hadn't had trouble talking to women for years, so why now?

Anne's reply was immediate. And uncompromising. "Thanks, but I don't think so." She was blushing again. She looked away from his eyes. "I do want to thank you for helping me this afternoon . . ." The train's brakes squealed as it shuddered to a stop inside Seoul Station, drowning out her words.

Tony had to go. The car doors opened and he was being half-carried out by the surge of Korean commuters heading for home. He tried Plan B. "Well, how about meeting some afternoon for lunch? Or maybe you could show me the sights."

He got pushed out of the car before she could reply. The doors slammed shut. Tony tried looking in the windows as the subway train started to pull away, but he couldn't tell whether she was shaking her head no or yes.

He stood watching the train lights disappear out of sight into the darkness. Shit, he hadn't even gotten her phone number.

He caught his train back to Kunsan without any further trouble. And that was almost too bad. He would have welcomed the excuse to really blow up. Instead he had to sit quietly in another compartment crowded with Korean commuters and shoppers.

And the trip back to base gave him more than enough time to replay every line of that last disastrous conversation with Anne Larson.

Tony got back to the BOQ just before seven and washed up. He had to change all his clothing because of the tear gas smell. It wasn't strong, but it was noticeable.

He walked across the hall and knocked on Hooter's door. He heard a muffled, "Come on in, for Christ's sake. Quit trying to knock my door down."

His wingman looked up from the latest men's magazine he'd managed to snag in the PX. Hooter's face creased into a smile. "Hey, Saint! Back from Seoul so soon? Man, you gotta read this article." Hooter tapped the magazine in front of him.

Tony looked down. The article was a natural blonde.

"So how was the big day in the big city? Tell Uncle Hooter all. And spare no details."

Tony weighed the truth with more comfortable fiction and decided on a compromise. "It was okay. I got caught in a riot and struck out with a pretty girl. No big deal."

The fiction part was the "no big deal." It was a big deal, to him. It was more than just the challenge of getting a pretty woman to go out with him. Anne had looks, grace, and a lot of class. He definitely wanted to see her again, and he'd blown it.

C H A P T · E R
13
Double Cross

The dry mumble of the clerk's calling the roll ended, but it took the sharp bang of the Senate president's gavel to bring Blake Fowler's eyes back to the TV picture being broadcast on the C-SPAN cable channel.

He squinted up at the screen: 54–45. The conference version of the Korean sanctions bill had been passed by nine lousy votes. Well, that wasn't much of a surprise. The margin had been the same two days earlier when the Senate passed the bill for the first time. Damn it. He knew for a fact that they could have switched at least six of those votes if the President had declared his opposition to the bill. Instead there'd been nothing but silence from the East Wing of the White House.

Blake knew the kind of pressure that was being exerted to win the President's consent to the Korean sanctions. Phone calls to the White House switchboard. Telegrams. Weekly visits by the Speaker of the House and the Senate majority leader. Barnes and his allies were pulling out all the stops. Naturally. The congressman from Michigan was openly angling to become the next senator from Michigan, and it was no secret that he planned to ride the protectionist, anti-Korea bandwagon all the way into the Senate chamber.

What Blake couldn't understand was the glacial pace that Putnam had set in orchestrating the administration's internal opposition to the sanctions bill. He'd had the Working Group's report in his hands for over a week now. Why hadn't he briefed the President? With the congressional elections coming up in less than three weeks, there wasn't much time left to pull the head of state's mind back from domestic politics to foreign affairs.

He picked up the phone and dialed Putnam's office.

Putnam's secretary was apologetic but unhelpful. "I'm sorry, Dr. Fowler, but he's tied up in a meeting right now. He'll have to get back to you. Can I take another message?"

Blake knew there were already at least ten pink message slips with his name and number littering her desk. "No, that's all right, Liz. I'm just trying to find out when he's planning to meet with the President on this Korea thing."

Putnam's secretary lowered her voice. "Korea? I thought you'd heard. He's briefing the President and the cabinet tomorrow morning. Didn't he call you?"

Blake kept his voice level. "No. I guess it slipped his mind."

"Hold on for just a moment. I'll see if I can pull him away from his congressional guests long enough to ask him about it for you."

He heard the line go silent as she put him on hold. That son of a bitch. What kind of games was he playing now?

Putnam's secretary was back in less than a minute. She sounded embarrassed. "I'm sorry. He said the President has asked that this meeting be kept strictly limited. He's going to do the briefing himself."

Blake hung up slowly. He'd been shut out by Putnam before. But never on something so crucial. Just what the hell was going on over in the East Wing?

OCTOBER 16—THE WHITE HOUSE, WASHINGTON, D.C.

The President looked around the half-empty Cabinet Room while Putnam droned on. It might have been nice for once to have a full complement of his senior advisors present for an important meeting. But the world didn't want to cooperate. Crises, both domestic and foreign, always seemed to drain people out of Washington at the damnedest times.

So, now that he needed to make a decision on this Korean sanctions bill, half his key people were scattered across the globe. The secretary of commerce was in Japan for high-level trade negotiations. And both the secretary of defense and the CIA director were off flitting around Europe briefing the NATO governments on the latest round of conventional arms talks. Even the vice president was out of town on a swing through Sub-Saharan Africa.

That left a small cadre of foreign and military policy experts to canvass—basically just the secretary of state and Putnam. He'd thought about putting this meeting off, but Putnam had assured him that the views of both Defense and the CIA were included in his Working Group's report. The man had also managed to deftly remind him that polls showed a growing public impatience with what they saw as his administration's reluctance to take swift, decisive action on important issues.

The President sighed. He'd campaigned on the promise of "hands-on" leadership and management. Didn't people realize it took time to assimilate all the detailed knowledge that required? He was beginning to envy his predecessor's seeming ability to make snap judgments that turned out to be more right than wrong.

"Mr. President? You had a question, sir?" Putnam had stopped in midbriefing, pointer resting on large-scale map of the North Pacific.

"No, George. No questions just yet. Go ahead and finish your presentation."

Putnam laid the pointer back on the table and stared down at his notes for a couple of moments before continuing. "Let me quickly summarize the Working Group's findings and recommendations, gentlemen. First, the trade sanctions included in the bill would have a powerful impact on South Korea's economy. Given that, it seems clear to me that no rational government would risk their full implementation."

"And," Putnam continued, "they would have little substantive impact on our own economy in the unlikely event that we have to put them in place. Korean products are a convenience—not a necessity."

His eyes strayed over to the Defense secretary's empty chair. "Finally, although the Department of Defense and the intelligence agencies are not especially happy about the bill's troop withdrawal provisions, it's clear that South Korea's armed forces no longer need rely on our protection to deter aggression from the North.

"Plus, there's a side strategic benefit to pulling our troops out of South Korea and basing them in Texas. By reassigning them to the Central Command, we can strengthen our rapid deployment forces and enhance our ability to respond to military crises anywhere in the world."

Putnam turned his gaze on the President, a tall, slender man with thinning hair, an open, friendly countenance, and steel-blue eyes.

"All in all, sir, I think a consensus view would be that the bill is worth signing. A few agencies have expressed some minor concerns"—he flicked the bulky document in front of him—"but I don't believe that any of them are important enough to warrant a presidential veto—and all of the accompanying political heat." He walked back to the table and sat down.

The President sat quietly for several seconds and then looked over at his secretary of state. "Well, what's your view, Paul? Should I sign this thing or not?"

Like the President, the secretary was a big man. Unlike him, however, the secretary fought a constant, losing battle against gaining weight and still had a full head of curly, graying hair. He steepled his massive hands and glanced quickly over at Putnam before answering. "Well, Mr. President, I haven't heard anything from my own experts that would contradict this version of the Working Group's report."

He paused. "I'd sign it, Mr. President. Our back-channel communications with the South Korean government haven't achieved much of anything, and frankly, I don't think this is the right time to anger the congressional leadership by vetoing a bill they've backed so solidly."

"Damn it, Paul. I didn't get myself elected to run scared from the boys back up on the Hill."

"I'm not suggesting that, Mr. President. I'm simply saying that the situation in South Korea is intolerable and growing worse. I don't believe this administration should have to wear that kind of albatross around its neck with an election coming up. Let's pull the security blanket away from Seoul and see how they react."

The secretary held up a single finger. "I'd be willing to bet that they'll come running to us with the kinds of political reforms the bill demands. And in less than a month."

The President looked back at the map of the North Pacific. "I wasn't aware that you supported this legislation so strongly, Paul."

"I don't, Mr. President. I don't like Congress trying to push its nose into our foreign policy any more than I suspect you do. But I also know that there's a time and a place to fight that kind of interference."

The secretary pushed his half-frame reading glasses back up his nose. "This isn't either the time or the place."

He started counting off items on his fingers. "South Korea's in a shambles. The government is increasingly brutal and desperate. The students seem determined to stay out in the streets. There's no denying that the Koreans haven't been trading fairly with us. And two-thirds of the American people want us out of South Korea. Maybe it is time that we tried sterner measures. Certainly we haven't gotten very far using ordinary diplomacy."

"Hell, I can't disagree with you there, Paul. But I don't like this idea of pulling our troops out of South Korea. It could send the wrong message to our other allies. Not to mention Moscow."

"Mr. President," Putnam broke in, "it's unlikely to ever come to that. It takes time to arrange a large-scale military movement. The South Korean government will almost certainly take the actions we're seeking long before our first soldier steps onto a plane heading back to the States."

The President raised an eyebrow and looked around the table at the rest of his cabinet. "Well, gentlemen. Anyone else have anything to add?"

A chorus of shaking heads greeted his question. That was about what he had expected. The secretaries of departments like Energy, Housing and Urban Development, Labor, or Education weren't eager to step into the middle of the foreign affairs turf jealously guarded by State, Defense, and the CIA.

The President sat back slightly from the table and let his eyes slide back to the map. Decision time. He wasn't particularly happy with the answers he'd gotten, but at least his key people were fairly well united for once. He could feel Putnam and the secretary of state staring at him. The President ran over the variables one more time. The bill's economic impact on the U.S.: negligible. Military impact: minor and controllable, at least according to Putnam's Working Group and the State Department. Political impact: positive. The polls showed that. And hell, maybe it would convince the South Koreans to get their act together. Okay, so be it.

He turned away from the map and brought his gaze back to the waiting cabinet. "Very well, gentlemen. I'll sign this damned thing."

Putnam smiled. "Yes, sir. We can arrange a Rose Garden signing with the congressional leadership for either today or tomorrow, Mr. President."

The President frowned. "You'll do nothing of the kind, George. I may be willing to accept this bill, but I'll be goddamned if I'm going to give people like Barnes or the Speaker free publicity for having shoved it down our throats. Clear?"

Putnam turned red and nodded.

"Good. I'll sign it tonight. In the Oval Office. You can have Jack put out a press release tomorrow morning."

The President flipped to the next page on his agenda. "Okay, let's move on to this housing bill coming up in the Senate."

He fought down the urge to reconsider his decision. It was done and that was that. Wasn't it?

OCTOBER 17—OLD EXECUTIVE OFFICE BUILDING, WASHINGTON, D.C.

"He's gone where?" Blake couldn't keep the disbelief out of his voice.

"Up to the Greenbrier for the weekend, Dr. Fowler." Putnam's secretary sounded surprised, too. The Greenbrier was a plush West Virginia resort favored by many in Congress for retreats, conferences, and just plain getaways.

"Well, when do you expect him back, Liz?" Blake swiveled in his chair to keep the afternoon sun out of his eyes.

"Not for a week or so. He's going straight from the Greenbrier on to a speaking tour out across the country. Election rallies. That sort of thing."

"Shit." Blake couldn't believe it. The President signs that goddamned Barnes sanctions bill and Putnam heads out on some kind of victory parade. Something was not at all right in the State of Denmark.

"Look, Liz. Did he have you make a lot of changes to that report I gave him?"

Putnam's secretary was silent for several seconds and then said, "Yes. He rewrote whole sections."

That bastard. What had he done? "Can I get a copy of the latest draft?"

Silence again. "Uh, Dr. Fowler, he . . . well, he said I wasn't allowed to distribute it to anyone but the President and the other people at the cabinet meeting yesterday."

Bingo. "I suppose that counts me out." Blake grimaced. He had to find a way to see what Putnam had done to the Working Group's recommendations.

Putnam's secretary said, "I'm sorry, Dr. Fowler. I'm afraid it does." She stopped and then said, "But I do have an extra copy here on my desk. I haven't had time to log it in yet. And I'm going to have to step out for a few minutes."

Blake hung up smiling. Thank God for Liz Klein. She'd been around the White House through three different administrations and she knew exactly how to play the game. He got up and stuck his head out his office door. "Katie, could you come in here a second. There's something I want you to pick up for me over at the White House."

He sent his secretary off on her semi-cloak-and-dagger mission and then sat down to consider his next move. Whatever he did, he was going to need allies. Powerful ones. People that the President couldn't ignore. And if Putnam had monkeyed around with the Working Group's report the way Blake thought he had, the next several days were going to be critical. He also knew that chances of his staying employed in the administration were just about nil.

He sat waiting for Katie to get back, looking at the picture of his wife and five-year-old daughter.

OCTOBER 19—THE NBC NIGHTLY NEWS

The camera view showed what were now almost routine scenes from the South Korean capital. Masked, chanting students throwing rocks and firebombs at police troops who retaliated with tear gas, water cannon, and billy clubs. Long-distance shots from a chartered helicopter showed the fine, white tear-gas mist billowing above Seoul's city center.

The anchorman's calm, dispassionate tones were in sharp contrast with the televised pictures of complete chaos and random violence.

"Thousands of South Korean students poured out into the streets of Seoul today—the seventh consecutive day of anti-government protests that have virtually paralyzed this city of ten million.

"The demonstrators once again clashed with government security forces in several hours of street fighting that left another sixty people injured, many in critical condition. And there are no signs that the riots will end anytime soon."

The camera cut back to the anchor desk.

"In other Korean news today, a government spokesman lashed out at the new U.S. trade sanctions scheduled to go into effect within the month. According to the spokesman, South Korea, quote, utterly rejects this unprincipled attempt by the United States to interfere in the internal affairs of another freely elected government, end quote. The spokesman went on to say that South Korea's coalition government saw no reason to give in to the impossible demands made by the rioting students.

"However, informed sources report that the South Korean government will soon announce a series of cosmetic political reforms—in the hope that they will placate the rioting students and soothe the angry American Congress.

"Meanwhile, the European Economic Community announced that it would follow the example set by the U.S. in imposing sanctions on South Korean manufactured products. This European action is considered extremely significant by foreign policy and economic analysts because the EEC is the third-largest purchaser of South Korea's exports, after the U.S. and Japan."

The camera cut again, this time to pictures of a flag-waving political rally in Illinois.

"And in Chicago, today, presidential national security adviser George Putnam told a cheering crowd of union members that the U.S. sanctions showed America's commitment to fair trade and to the cause of democratic reform in South Korea."

OCTOBER 20—SEOUL, SOUTH KOREA

General Chang Jae-Kyu, commanding officer of the 4th Infantry Division, stepped carefully through the door of the Han Chung Kak *kisaeng* house. He smiled politely at the young woman who took his officer's cap and overcoat. Charming. And so beautiful. He really must find out her name and ask for her the next time he came here. But not tonight. Tonight he had other business, business that made even the sophisticated pleasures of Seoul's most attractive *kisaeng* pale in importance.

Chang followed the woman down a quiet corridor lined with precious paintings and silk screens. He shook his head, amused that he now found such luxury and beauty so commonplace that he could disregard it.

Chang was a farmer's son, a man of the earth. His family had labored for countless generations, growing the crops that fed Korea's elite city dwellers. The Army had changed all that. It had nurtured and protected him. It had given him a future, just as it had safeguarded the future for all of South Korea. He frowned. And now these effete city snobs, the corrupt politicians and radical students alike, threatened to destroy all that—to emasculate the bulwark of the state and the new order.

Chang straightened his shoulders. They would not succeed. Not without a fight.

The *kisaeng* stopped outside a closed door and bowed. He bowed back and followed her with his eyes as she glided back the way they had come. Truly a study in elegant grace. Well, perhaps there were advantages to cities after all.

He turned, knocked once, and entered the small, smoke-fogged room beyond the door. He knew the officers assembled around the table intimately, well enough to trust them with his life. They were classmates, graduates of the Korean Military Academy.

Chang nodded to them. "Gentlemen. It is good to see you all here."

They grinned back at his formal tone. He studied them for a moment before continuing. General Bae, commanding officer of the 9th Infantry Division, part of the Capital Corps that guarded Seoul. He was tall for a Korean, with a round, moon face. Colonel Kim of the 6th Interceptor Squadron was shorter and had quick, hurried movements. Colonel Min, G-2 for the III Corps, looked uncomfortable. He was as fat as a Korean Army officer ever gets, which is not much.

Most importantly, General Hahn, head of the Seoul District of the Defense Security Command was present. His angular face smiled in anticipation.

It was because of him that Chang and his small cadre could meet here in complete safety. The politicians expected the Defense Security Command to play watchdog over the armed forces. Chang smiled to himself as he looked at Hahn. But what happened when the watchdog turned on its supposed master?

"Are we secure here?" he asked.

"Yes, my men swept it for listening devices just this afternoon. It was clean."

"Good. Then we can get down to business." Chang looked over his assembled friends. "I apologize for rushing this, but time is not our ally. None of us can afford to be missed or brought under suspicion during this time of preparation."

"So you're convinced then that we must move against the government?" Lieutenant Colonel Min didn't sound completely surprised.

"I can see no other alternative." Chang kept his voice low, but the others could hear the steely determination that had won him the nickname the Iron Man during his days at the academy.

He continued, "As officers, we are sworn to defend this nation against its enemies, foreign and domestic. And can any doubt that our country is under attack?"

The others, their minds full of images from the past two months of rioting and disorder, shook their heads.

"No, I thought not. But what have these politicians, these vote-buyers, done about it? Nothing." Chang let the word hang in midair for a moment and then repeated it. "Nothing.

"Oh, they talk a grand game. But instead of swift, decisive action to crush this communist insurrection, the bureaucrats have spent their time running from one place to another, pissing on the fires only when the flames reach their feet." The officers chuckled at his crude imagery.

"And now, what are they planning?" Chang asked scornfully. "I'll tell you. They are preparing a surrender. A surrender to these young thugs and their calls for socialism. And a surrender to America and all its intolerable demands."

The officers murmured to one another, and Chang could see the anger growing.

"So then, I ask you, what else can we do as men who've sworn to guard the nation with our very lives?"

General Bae answered for the others after glancing around the room. "You are right. We must reform the government. And soon."

They all knew what he meant by "reform." He meant a military coup. It was not unthinkable. Twice before in the forty-year-long history of the Republic of Korea, groups of young officers had acted to save the country from corrupt, feuding politicians. They would simply be following in that tradition.

Chang held up a hand. "You're right. There is little time. But we must not act with undue haste. We six alone are not enough to topple the regime."

He smiled and bowed to Hahn. "There are others in the armed forces who share our determination to save this country. With our friend Hahn's help, I shall bring them into the fold in the coming weeks." He paused for a moment. "And when we are ready, we shall move with lightning speed to oust the moneygrubbers of Seoul and restore order."

That won approving nods and smiles from the group. Only Min still looked troubled. "But what of the Americans? Won't they intervene?"

Chang didn't bother to hide his contempt. "The Americans? They've washed their hands of us. Now we owe them nothing. They can do nothing. And once we've ended these disturbances, their corporations will be back begging us to trade with them once again."

He looked squarely at Min. "So. Are you with us, or not?"

In the silence that followed his question, they could all hear faint sirens from outside as the police rushed to quell yet another riot.

Min listened for a moment and then stared straight back into Chang's eyes. "Yes. Yes, I'm with you."

Chang slowly smiled. Now they could begin.

C H A P T E R
14
Riposte

OCTOBER 23—THE WHITE HOUSE, WASHINGTON, D.C.

Blake Fowler sat quietly in the antechamber outside the Oval Office, resisting an urge to pace. He glanced across the room at Admiral Philip Simpson, Chairman of the JCS, who sat conferring with an aide. He double-checked his briefing folder to make sure he had all the documents he would need for this morning's show. Or maybe "showdown" would be a more accurate term for what he had planned.

"Dr. Fowler?" The dark-haired secretary had raised her head from her work.

"Yes."

"The President will see you in just a couple of moments. He's on the phone right now, but it shouldn't take long."

Blake nodded his thanks and sat back. This waiting was the hardest part. At least he hoped so. He was acutely aware that the next fifteen minutes or so would be the most crucial of his entire career. In fact, they could easily be the last fifteen minutes of his government career.

He'd spent the better part of a week preparing for this meeting. First, he'd had to persuade Mike Sinclair, Putnam's deputy, to give him a chance to deliver the President's daily national security briefing. Putnam was still away on his pre-election campaign swing, but he was due back in a couple of days, and Blake knew this would be his last opportunity to get in to see the President. Sinclair disliked Putnam as much as everybody else on the NSC staff, and he'd finally agreed— thinking that Blake, as one of the staff's rising young stars, just wanted a chance to impress the President while the adviser was away. Blake hadn't disillusioned him. But he knew that Sinclair was going to be damned mad when he found out the truth.

Next, he'd sought out the kind of ally he'd need to persuade the President that this was more than just a quibble over words and staff procedures. Admiral Simpson had been the logical choice. He'd supported the Working Group's original recommendations wholeheartedly. He was the nation's senior military officer. And the admiral had a well-deserved reputation as a man who put the truth above political expediency.

But Blake had only met the admiral twice before, once at a Georgetown dinner party and once at a conference on grand strategy for the Pacific region, so he'd been surprised when Simpson agreed to see him the same day he'd asked for an appointment. He'd been even more surprised when the bull-necked little man had readily agreed to come to the Oval Office with him.

Simpson had grinned across his desk. "What's the matter, Dr. Fowler? Haven't you ever come across someone willing to gamble a thirty-year career in the military before?"

"Frankly, Admiral, no, I haven't. At least not in this town."

"Well, I'll tell you, my friend, I'm willing to do this for two very good reasons. First, the President's made a goddamn big strategic error in signing that sanctions bill. Someone's got to try to do something about that, and that someone is probably me. The taxpayers should be able to count on something for the seventy-five thousand dollars a year I get paid. And second, George Putnam is a slimy son of a bitch and it'll be a pleasure to put a stake through his heart."

Blake smiled as he remembered Simpson's words. He just hoped that the admiral's optimism was justified.

The secretary's phone buzzed softly, bringing him out of his reverie. She picked it up, listened for a moment, and hung up. Blake sat up and laid a hand on his folder.

"Dr. Fowler? Admiral Simpson? The President is ready

for you now." She got up from behind her desk to hold the door open for them. Blake could see the same blue carpet with its interwoven presidential seal, high-backed colonial chairs, marble-sided fireplace, flags, and paintings he'd seen a hundred times before in TV newscasts. But it felt different in person. The room seemed to breathe power.

As they walked into the Oval Office, the President got up from behind his desk and came to meet them.

"Phil, it's good to see you again." He shook hands with the admiral and turned to Blake. "And you must be Blake Fowler. Mike Sinclair's been telling me good things about you."

Blake heard himself mumbling something about hoping he deserved Sinclair's praise. Then the President waved them both into chairs and settled back down behind his desk. He put his fingertips together below his chin.

"Now, gentlemen, I'm going to assume that this is more than just a routine briefing. I've only been here a couple of years, but I haven't yet had the Chairman of the Joint Chiefs come in to fill me in on the latest news from Lower Freedonia."

Blake glanced over at Admiral Simpson. The admiral nodded slightly. They'd agreed earlier that Blake should take the first stab at explaining the situation.

"Mr. President, you're absolutely right. We're here about the Interagency Working Group report you were shown before you signed the Korean sanctions bill."

The President frowned. Korea was obviously still a sore spot. Blake had seen some of the private messages that had passed between the White House and the South Korean government and couldn't really blame him.

Blake took a deep breath and pushed on. "The truth is, sir, that the document you saw had been altered."

"Hold it right there." The President held up a hand and glared at him. He looked at his watch. "I've got better things to do than listen to some goddamned staff squabbling. That's what I pay my senior people for. If you've got some beef with the way your copy got rewritten, take it up with Putnam or the chief of staff. Now let's get on with the rest of your briefing. I've got an important meeting in half an hour."

Blake could feel himself flushing. They couldn't leave

without at least getting a hearing on Putnam's treachery, could they? He fought an urge to rearrange his notes. Anyway he looked at it, his days with the administration were numbered. Better to be damned for something he'd done then for something he hadn't. But would the admiral stick with him?

The admiral did. "With respect, Mr. President, Dr. Fowler and I aren't here to complain about the way a few words were changed here or there."

Simpson leaned forward in his chair. "We're here because your national security adviser took it on himself to drastically alter the conclusions reached by the Working Group. I'll be blunt. The recommendations you were shown bore about as much resemblance to what I and the other Joint Chiefs approved as horseshit does to roast beef. And that's got direct consequences for this nation's security."

The President looked up from his desk and Blake could see the curiosity in his eyes. Curiosity and something more. "Go on."

Blake asked him, "Did the report you saw recommend signing the Barnes bill?"

The President nodded.

"Then I think you ought to take a look at what the Departments of Defense and Commerce, the CIA, and the NSA all originally recommended." Blake reached into his folder and pulled out several pages highlighted in yellow.

"These are from the draft we submitted to Putnam."

The President reached over and took the papers out of Blake's hand. He spread them out in front of him and started reading. They could see his frown growing deeper as he read. It took him just a couple of minutes to finish.

He handed them back to Blake without a word and swiveled his chair around to look out the rain-streaked window toward the White House Rose Garden. Blake and the admiral exchanged glances. Now what?

The President swung his chair back around to face them. "Okay, gentlemen. That bastard lied to me. And I signed something I shouldn't have. I certainly wouldn't have done it if I'd seen your analysis first. So what can we do about it?"

Blake looked back at him. "The best thing, sir, would be

to push Congress to repeal the sanctions. And as soon as possible.''

The President shook his head. "Impossible. The House and Senate have gone out of regular session for the election, and the new Congress won't assemble until early January.''

Simpson nodded his understanding. "But you could call a special session—after the election.''

"Not on your life, Admiral.'' The President studied the wall behind the two men for a moment before continuing. "How do you suppose I'd look going back begging Congress to lift sanctions I could have vetoed in the first place?''

Neither Blake nor the admiral answered him, but he must have read their thoughts in their eyes.

"Yeah. I'd look like a clown. Like a regular Jerry Lewis stand-in.''

The President snorted, "Okay, maybe that's too damned close to the truth for comfort. But I'm not going to do something that would just about kill my chances to accomplish anything else in this term. Clear?''

They nodded.

"So. Short of making myself look like a walking jackass, what are my options?''

Blake and the admiral had come prepared to answer this question. The trouble was that they didn't have a hell of a lot to offer.

Blake got up out of his chair without thinking. His days as a student teacher had taught him to feel more comfortable talking on his feet. "Well, sir, Barnes and his legislative strategists have crafted a very tightly written bill. It doesn't leave much at all to your discretion.''

"I've seen the legal analysis, Dr. Fowler. Now tell me something I don't know.''

"Yes, sir,'' Blake said patiently. The President might have heard some of what he was going to say before, but it was vital that he realize just how limited his options were.

"Essentially, the sanctions on South Korea's exports are practically set on automatic pilot. They're almost certain to go into place because there just aren't any loopholes in the legislation for us to wriggle through.''

The President interrupted him with a question. "Isn't there

a possibility, however slim, that Seoul will make the political and economic reforms we're looking for before the sanctions go into effect?''

''Anything's possible, Mr. President. But our analysis rates that as the least likely outcome.'' Blake started to pace.

''Basically, the South Korean government rests on a very narrow knife's edge between two small, but powerful, factions. On one side they've got a hard-line element in their military. The current Seoul government had its origins in a military coup, so they know what can happen if the armed forces aren't happy with what's going on.'' He turned and walked back past the President's desk.

''Now on the other side of the equation, you've got a small hard-core group of radical students. Most of them aren't communists, but they are socialists and they want things that the military and South Korea's industrial conglomerates would find intolerable—virtual unilateral disarmament and reunification with North Korea.''

The President nodded his understanding. ''So they've got no maneuvering room. The token reforms that the hard-liners in the military would accept won't be enough to placate Congress or their students. And the reforms demanded by Congress won't be acceptable to the military.''

''Yes, sir, exactly. What's worse, they probably wouldn't even keep the students out of the streets anyway.''

''Shit.''

''In a nutshell, Mr. President.'' Blake started another circuit past the President's desk. ''The odds, then, are that South Korea's booming economy is going to come to a crashing halt over the next couple of months as their exports dry up. That's going to polarize the apolitical middle portion of the South Korean population. Some are going to side with the military hard-liners, and some are going to break over to the left-wing students.''

He shrugged. ''Where South Korea's internal balance of power will wind up is anybody's guess.''

''And we can't do a damn thing to stop any of this?'' The President's question was almost plaintive.

''Not this year. Not without a special session of Congress.'' Blake came to a halt. ''The best we can hope for is that

South Korea will muddle through until sometime next year. Then you might be able to make a good case for lifting the sanctions on humanitarian grounds. By then, people here will have seen a lot of TV pictures of unemployment lines in Seoul, and they'll have started missing Hyundai cars and Samsung televisions."

The President nodded slowly. "Yes. We'd still face an uphill legislative fight in Congress, but at least I'd hold the moral high ground."

Blake glanced at Admiral Simpson.

The admiral took his cue. "There's one thing wrong with that scenario, Mr. President."

The President looked at Simpson. "What's that, Phil?"

"It assumes that there will still be a South Korea left to concern ourselves with next spring."

Simpson paused and the President arched an eyebrow. "Go ahead, Admiral. You've got my attention."

"Yes, sir. You see, while all of this is going on in the South, we've got to worry about what's going on up in North Korea. Kim Il-Sung and his generals are going to be rubbing their hands over the prospect of a badly weakened South Korea. And they've been piling up the hardware to do something about it." The admiral handed McLaren's latest intelligence assessment to the President and waited while he skimmed through it.

"Jesus, these people aren't fooling around, are they."

"No, sir, they're not. Without our forces along the DMZ as a trip-wire deterrent, they just might be tempted to use some of those brand-new tanks, planes, and artillery pieces."

The President kept paging through the assessment of North Korea's order of battle. "I don't see what we can do about it. The Barnes bill is damned specific there, too. No political reforms, no American troops. We're going to have to pull them out."

Blake tensed. This was the crucial moment. He spoke softly, "Not necessarily, Mr. President. At least not until you've had a chance to reverse the sanctions in the next Congress."

The President's head snapped up. He stared straight into Blake's eyes. "Just what are you proposing, Dr. Fowler?"

Blake chose his words with great care. "Simply this, sir. Unlike the trade provisions in the bill, there is a small opening in the legislative language requiring us to pull our forces out of South Korea. An opening that you might be able to exploit to keep our protective umbrella up long enough to try convincing Congress to find alternatives."

He stopped for a moment. The President's eyes didn't move away from his face. "The bill doesn't set a specific timetable for our withdrawal, Mr. President. Instead, the language calls for a pull-out to be carried out, quote, as expeditiously as possible, unquote."

This was it. The President leaned forward in his chair. "So how does that language give me the leeway I need, Dr. Fowler?"

"I suggest that you interpret that demand as loosely as possible, sir. After all, withdrawing more than forty thousand combat troops, support personnel, and all their equipment is going to be a logistical nightmare. It's bound to take time— several months at the very least."

Blake paused again and then pressed ahead. "And a discreet suggestion from you to the commander responsible for carrying out the move, General McLaren, could ensure that those months were stretched to at least a year. A lot can happen in a year, Mr. President. At the very least we'll have bought time for the South Koreans to adjust to a very different strategic equation."

Blake finished speaking and sat back down in his chair, surprised to find that his hands were trembling slightly. He looked up to see the President studying him closely.

"You are aware, Dr. Fowler, that you've just proposed that I twist the wording of a law beyond all recognition. That I tell a senior military officer to ignore its clear meaning?" the President said in a low, even tone.

"Yes, sir. I know that."

The President turned to Admiral Simpson. "Phil, what do you think of this young man's plan? You know that there are people in Congress who'd love the chance to crucify me if this thing leaks out."

Blake could see the admiral weighing his answer. "Mr. President, both of us have sworn to uphold the Constitution.

And both of us have sworn to defend the United States against all enemies, both foreign and domestic. What Dr. Fowler proposes seems to me to fall into a gray area between those two responsibilities.''

The admiral continued, ''I can't make this decision for you, sir. But I believe that it's a risk worth taking.''

The President sat quietly for several minutes after the admiral had finished speaking. Then, suddenly, he looked over at Blake.

''Did you vote for me in the last election, Dr. Fowler?'' he asked.

Startled, Blake never even considered lying. ''No, sir, I didn't.''

The President smiled thinly. ''Hell. If you can be that honest, I guess I can trust you on this.''

He slapped a hand down on his desk. ''Very well, gentlemen. I'll take your advice. Somebody gave me bad advice, worse than bad, and I made a mistake. We'll delay our pull-out from South Korea as long as we possibly can, and use that time to try and correct the error.''

He stared hard at them. ''But I don't want a single goddamned thing about this on paper. You understand? No memos. Nothing on disk. Got it?''

They nodded.

''Great.''

Simpson looked curiously at the President. ''What about Putnam? If you take any action against the lying bastard, his congressional patrons may guess that we're up to something they'd want to know about.''

The President smiled grimly. ''Don't worry about Mr. Putnam, gentlemen. We'll keep him on in his old job—at least as far as he and the outside world are concerned. But I'll be goddamned if I ever believe a word that man says from now on. He'll attend every national security meeting, but when he speaks, I'm not listening. If I want to know something about this Korean situation, I'll arrange a little private get-together for just the three of us. Clear?''

They nodded again.

The President turned to Blake. ''You know, Dr. Fowler, while this whole troop withdrawal thing is playing out, you're going to have to keep treating Putnam as though he were still your trusted, all-powerful, all-knowing boss. Is that going to be a problem for you?''

Blake shook his head.

"Okay, then. That's settled." The President picked up the phone. "June, I want you to put together some travel arrangements for a member of my staff: Blake Fowler. Yes, I want him in Seoul by tomorrow, if possible."

He hung up and smiled again at Blake. "No need to look so surprised, Dr. Fowler. I'm making you my go-between with General McLaren on this thing. You're going to be in it up to your neck."

Blake couldn't think of anything to say except, "Yes, sir. I sure as hell will be."

OCTOBER 25—EIGHTH ARMY FIELD HQ, SOUTH KOREA

The clattering, ear-splitting roar of the Cobra gunship's rotor hammered through McLaren's helmet as he looked out through the front windshield.

The Cobra skimmed low over rice paddies as it raced toward a jagged ridge flanking the multilane Main Supply Route. Then it climbed, following rising ground in a smooth curve to the left just fifty meters above a hillside orchard. Fallen leaves caught in the helicopter's downdraft swirled high into the air in its wake.

McLaren kept his eyes focused on the small valley they were rushing toward at a hundred and twenty knots. Without looking, he held up his right hand, palm forward. The chopper pilot obeyed his signal and eased back on his collective, slowing the gunship as they flew by the valley's tree-lined entrance.

McLaren studied the ground carefully, first with unaided eyes and then with a pair of binoculars as they orbited past the valley again. Nothing. Not a single radio aerial in plain view. Good, there weren't any telltale signs that might reveal his camouflaged headquarters to an airborne enemy.

He pulled his head back into the cockpit and cut in his

throat mike. "Okay, Jim. You can take us down now. I think I'm getting airsick."

The pilot grinned at him and sketched a mock salute before pushing the stick over to send the helicopter into a long slide up the valley toward a small clearing. They settled in to land in a hail of rotor-blown dust, small pebbles, and dead grass.

McLaren slid down out of the gunship, bent low holding his helmet, and scuttled out from under the slowing rotor blades. He straightened up and strode past a headquarters detail waiting with the netting to conceal his personal chopper from prying eyes.

He returned their salutes and kept going down the path toward the tangle of tents and M577 command vehicles that marked his army's "bare-bones" field headquarters. Bare bones, my ass, he thought, looking at the crowded vehicle park. Still, it was smaller than his predecessors' traveling circuses. Doctrine said an army-level field HQ needed dozens of trucks, command trailers, and personnel carriers to operate properly. But McLaren knew that doctrine didn't mean diddley-squat if it made you a big, juicy, and obvious target for an enemy airstrike or artillery barrage. He preferred to travel light.

His staff looked up when he walked into the main command tent but then bent back down to their work. He'd made it plenty clear early on in his tour that he didn't have time for a lot of meaningless saluting and ass-kissing— especially not in the field.

His aide came up to take his helicopter crewman's head-gear. McLaren shrugged it off and took his old-fashioned steel pot in return. He didn't like the new, plastic-armored "Fritz" helmets prescribed by Army regulations. He'd seen the studies showing they were more effective at keeping out fragments, but there was something unsettling about them nonetheless. He'd told Doug once that a man needed to have steel on his head to feel secure under an airburst. "Damnit," he'd barked, "plastic's only good for two things—model airplanes and some bimbo's shopping trip." He remembered that his aide had smiled gamely and packed McLaren's new-style helmet away for good. Humoring him, no doubt. But what the hell, he was a general and rank should have some friggin' privileges after all.

McLaren settled the steel pot on his head and looked back at his aide. "That fella from Washington get here yet?"

"Yes sir, about half an hour ago. I've got him waiting in your trailer. Do you want me to send for him?"

"Nah. Muhammad will go to the mountain this time. Keep an eye on things here for me, will you?"

McLaren climbed the steps to his command trailer and looked in through the door. The President's highly unofficial "emissary" stood. McLaren liked the look of him. Tall, rangy, and with an open, honest face. Smart enough not to wear a suit out here, too.

He nodded his head toward the hillside rising above the camp. "Let's take a walk."

McLaren and Fowler hiked up through the tall grass far enough to be out of earshot of anyone else in the HQ. McLaren pulled his helmet off and turned to face Blake. "Okay, Dr. Fowler, what gives?"

Blake filled him in, speaking quickly at first but then slowing to emphasize each word as he got closer to the President's "suggestion" that McLaren delay his planning for the congressionally mandated withdrawal from South Korea.

When he'd finished, McLaren stood silently for several minutes, looking out across the hill to the north—toward the DMZ. Then he shook his head in disbelief. "Jesus Christ, Dr. Fowler. I've never heard anything like that in my whole friggin' Army career."

Then he grinned. "But I'm damned glad I finally got the chance to."

Fowler grinned back at him. The general had reacted just the way Admiral Simpson thought he would.

"Just one question. Are we going to let the South Korean government in on this little secret?"

"No. The President doesn't want any leaks on this. And he doesn't want to blow any chance that the government here just might make the reforms Congress is insisting on."

"Okay." McLaren settled his helmet back on his head. "You go back to Washington and tell the President that he can count on the most screwed-up evacuation planning process he's ever seen."

They shook hands and headed back down the hill toward the headquarters of the Eighth Army.

C H A P T E R
15
If at First...

NOVEMBER 2—LOGISTICS CENTER, YONGSAN ARMY BASE, SEOUL

Tony felt like an idiot. It was foolish to feel this way, of course. He had traveled all the way to Seoul to get a second chance at being rejected by Anne Larson. Why should he feel foolish?

He knew she worked at the logistics agency as a computer programmer. The logical thing to do was go up to the headquarters building and ask where the computing facility was. Strangely enough, it worked. The corporal had looked at his out-of-place Air Force uniform a little strangely, then given him directions to building A34.

He walked out of the headquarters with a mix of excitement and anxiety he hadn't felt since his last blind date in high school. Of course he had acted like an idiot in high school.

The base's buildings were old-style brick, obviously designed by a Westerner. They looked a little odd after all the Korean architecture he'd seen, but normal enough in this little island of America. The place was really jumping, with people and vehicles almost filling the sidewalks and the streets.

The Logistics Computing Facility, building A34, looked more modern than most. It was almost windowless, with a fortresslike air. He had to walk halfway around it to find an entrance. After a close inspection of his armed forces ID card, the front desk issued him a pass and gave him directions to

"Miss Larson's office." They didn't ask his business, which was just as well.

After leaving the reception area he went through a door marked AIR-CONDITIONING BOUNDARY—KEEP CLOSED. The temperature dropped by ten degrees and there was a whirr in the air. The corridors were full of people in Army uniforms and civilian clothes. He started looking for Anne immediately, rehearsing what he was going to say. "Okay, Tony, whatever you did on the subway, don't do it now."

The second floor was quieter, with carpeting instead of tile on the floor. He turned the corner into corridor C, wiping his palms.

The first thing he saw was a receptionist's desk, with a nameplate, but it wasn't Anne's—GLORIA BURNS. Miss Burns looked up from a computer printout. "May I help you?"

"Uh, I'm looking for Anne Larson," Tony answered. "She's supposed to be in room two ten."

The receptionist glanced at the phone board. "Miss Larson is on the phone right now. If you'd like to wait, I'll tell her you're here. What did you need to see her about?"

Suddenly Tony felt his face getting warmer. "Ah, it's personal. Just tell her Captain Christopher is here please, ma'am."

He saw Gloria's eyes give him a once-over, and then she said, "Fine. Just take a seat."

There was a couch in the reception area and Tony sat down. He watched Gloria's departing form, which was not uninteresting, go toward a door. The plate next to it said A. LARSON—SUPERVISOR.

The Air Force didn't pay fighter pilots to be slow-witted. Anne was the boss? He quickly reevaluated his opinion of her, based on what little knowledge he had. He was a little ashamed that he had to raise it. "That will teach you, Saint," he said to himself. "Never take a woman for granted."

Gloria was still standing in the door, talking in a low voice, about him no doubt. He couldn't hear Anne's reply, but her secretary (Tony forced himself to think of Gloria that way) came back and sat down. "It'll just be a moment." Then she went back to her printout.

Tony glanced at his watch: eleven forty-five. At least his

timing was good. He hoped to ask her out for lunch. He didn't know how he was going to get her to say yes, but what the hell.

He spent most of his time watching the phone board, and after about three or four minutes the light went out. Miss Burns looked up and said, "You can go in now."

Okay, boy, this is it. Sydney or the bush. He wiped his palms again, uncomfortably aware that the receptionist was watching him from the corner of her eye. He walked up to the open door and stopped short, knocking twice on the doorframe. "Come in." It was Anne's voice.

She was sitting at an L-shaped wood desk covered with papers and printouts. She recognized him immediately. "I knew it." She didn't look pleased.

Tony smiled, looking a little like a child caught doing something he shouldn't. "I came to Seoul to see if you really . . ."

The phone rang and Anne picked it up. "Larson. Yes, I know, I've my two best people trying to figure out what happened." She looked up at Tony, who was doing his best to look pleasant. "Listen, I should have something this afternoon. Is that soon enough for you? I'm a little busy now. . . . I know. I'll call you back later."

She hung up and looked at Tony. "I'm sorry, excuse me. This is not a good time, especially for 'personal visits.' "

"I'm sorry if I said something wrong. I just wanted to see if you would like to go—"

A knock on the door stopped him. A man in shirtsleeves was holding a piece of paper. He said, "Oh, hi," to Tony and looked at Anne. "Have you seen this memo?"

"Let me see it." She stood up and walked over, took the sheet, and glanced at it. "Yes, Harry, I got one yesterday in my mail. It's general routing."

"Well, I just wanted to make sure. See you," Harry said as he left.

She sat down heavily behind the desk, looking somewhat disgusted. "What were you saying?"

"Just that I wanted to talk with you some more, and I was hoping . . ."

"Oh, God!" Anne said softly, looking out the door. She smiled and waved at someone in the hall. Tony turned and looked. A middle-aged woman was pushing a coffee cart down the corridor, waving back.

"Anne, I know you said you didn't like to go out, but I thought maybe you'd like to have lunch. I'd really—"

"Sounds good. Let's go." She stood up and grabbed a largish purse off a corner of her desk. Tony stepped out of the way as she strode through the door, then followed.

"Gloria, I'm going out for some lunch, I should be back in an hour." Her voice sounded normal, but Tony was puzzled. She didn't sound like someone looking forward to a pleasant outing.

"Okay, Miss Larson. Have a good time." Gloria had a funny smile. What was going on here?

They strode down the corridor and stairs with Anne setting a fast pace. It reminded Tony of how she had moved during the riot. She was a little ahead of him, and he felt like an idiot, almost trotting trying to keep up with her.

They went past the front desk and Tony dashed ahead to open the front door for her. This took a major effort, and as his hand pushed it open, he said, "I win."

She looked puzzled for a moment, but he went for it. "Oh, it's okay, I like to jog before lunch."

They stepped outside and she seemed to relax. "I'm sorry, I guess I was moving a little fast. I just wanted to get away from all those eyes."

Tony looked at her with a puzzled look. She took his arm. "Please, let's just walk." They went down the steps. "I know a nice lunch place about a ten-minute walk from here."

"Anne, what do you mean about 'eyes'? Was it something I said?"

"Yes, Tony, but it's not your fault. Gloria is head grape on the grapevine. She told me you said your business was 'personal.' Two seconds after you went in my office half the floor knew I had a gentleman caller. That 'important memo' Harry had to show me was about the coffee fund."

"Oh. Is that why you acted so odd later?"

She nodded. "And the lady with the cart."

"What about the lady with the cart?" he asked. "Was she using the cart as a cover or something?"

"Oh, that's her cart, but she works the main floor, not the second."

"I'm sorry, I've embarrassed you. I just wanted to see if you—"

"You keep saying that, but I said on the subway I wasn't interested in going out. The only reason I'm here now is that you are the lesser of two evils." She added, smiling, "Besides, you are kind of cute."

Tony blinked in surprise, but continued, "Whatever the reason, I do not consider a riot the best place to meet people, but I liked your style. Why should it be such a big deal that I ask you to lunch?"

"Look, I just don't go out a lot, and those bazoos will spend their lunch hour discussing us." She stomped her foot as she walked.

Tony had a flash. "Why is it such a bad time at work?"

"The place is going crazy. My office maintains the software that tracks all logistical movements in and out of Korea. They're doing things that the system was never designed for. Moving stuff in while they move the same stuff out . . ."

With only occasional nods and a yes now and then, Tony followed Anne to a small diner. It was a little crowded, but they found a table. Most of the clientele was Korean, which Tony took to be a good sign.

". . . they're using the most inefficient schedules. I know they are brighter than that. Wait a minute. I've been talking for five minutes."

"Yes, do you feel better? You're a lady who cares about her work."

"You let me blather on for five minutes? I feel like an idiot."

"Would you like to order? They've got *kalbichim*. It's pretty good."

"Why did you let me talk so much?"

"Look, Anne, you're having a hard day—"

"Hard month, more like it."

"Fine. A hard month. I wanted to find out what was bothering you. And everybody likes to talk about their job. You already know what mine is. Now let's order."

"All right." She relaxed a little more, studying the menu.

It was standard Korean fare, heavy on beef and fish, but spicy. She looked resigned. "I'll just have *pulgogi*."

Tony frowned. "You don't sound enthusiastic about the menu. *Pulgogi*'s just marinated beefsteak. You picked this place. Don't you like Korean food?"

"I haven't had much besides *pulgogi* and a few other things. I guess I'm not very adventurous. I really came here because nobody from my office ever comes here."

"Next time I'll wear a bag over my head."

She giggled. "Stop that. I shouldn't be so upset, but—"

"It's been a bad day. Yes, I remember." Tony was pleased that Anne had actually laughed. "Can I make a few suggestions? I've tried most of the things on the menu at least once. I promise, nothing too exotic."

"All right." This time she sounded a little more pleased, even curious. "What are you having?"

"*Pibim-bap*. It's got eggs, rice, meat, beans, lots of stuff. It's good, but it's a little spicy."

"I'll try it, too." She studied the menu with more interest. Most of it was printed with Hangul characters, but alongside each dish was an English transliteration of the name. "What's *myolchi*?"

"Anchovies in a sweetish sauce."

"Yuck."

"No, it's the old salt-and-sweet contrast. It's not bad."

"I'll pass. What goes well with *pibim-bap*?"

"*Yonppuri*. It's lotus root in a sweet sauce. It helps kill the fire."

"Fine, let's order."

While they waited, Tony found out that Anne had been in Korea for three months, working as the systems programming supervisor. "I was promoted in the States and brought over to fill in this job. It's the first time I've been in charge of other people." She frowned.

"You don't like it?" Tony prompted.

"I don't know what to do. I'm much more comfortable working with the computer. I guess I don't work well with groups—certainly not leading a group."

"This is a bad time for learning management skills," he agreed.

The food came, and they ate and talked and laughed a little. They were both equally handy with chopsticks. Tony fought his desire to talk about flying, and instead they talked about Korea, and what they'd seen, or not seen in Anne's case.

"I've been completely wrapped up in my work," Anne said. "Remember the riot? That was my second trip downtown. My first was to the Kyongbok Palace. Nothing since early October."

"Anne, when the U.S. pulls out, you'll go, too, and this is a beautiful country. I've been playing tourist ever since I got here, and I haven't seen half of what I want to. The food, the art, the—"

"That surprises me. I thought fighter pilots just liked to fly and party."

Tony looked a little peeved. "I like both, but I don't fly every day, and I don't party every night. Uncle Sam paid my way over here, and there's not a lot to do besides fly. I want to understand the country and the culture, at least a little."

"You're right," she said. "I'm sorry. I guess I just don't feel comfortable exploring the country."

"I think you just need some practice. I've got a day off next weekend. I'm going to visit an old ruined fort south of here. Would you like to come along? It's thousands of years old."

"I'm so busy right now. I usually work on the weekends."

"Well, what's the deadline on this crunch project? We can just go after it's over."

"Oh, there's no deadline, I just normally work."

"Oh, well, please, take one day off and come out with me to visit the fortress. It's not far, and there's a good restaurant someone in the squadron told me about."

"I really should see some of the country before I have to leave. I may even enjoy myself."

Tony assured her. "You will."

C H A P T E R
16
Tremors

NOVEMBER 10—NEAR THE DMZ, SOUTH KOREA

High on a hill above the full-scale mock-up of a Korean town, General Chang watched the afternoon's scheduled urban-assault exercise move toward its planned climax.

The sharp rattle of automatic weapons fire mixed with the hollow crump of exploding grenades reached General Chang's ears as he lay watching the assault blast its way into the village. He kept his binoculars focused on the lead platoon as it advanced up a narrow street.

Yes, that was the way to do it. One squad back shooting the hell out of likely enemy firing positions while another group dashed forward to close with the next house. The troops flattened against its walls while two men lobbed grenades in through doors and windows. Chang smiled as he saw the soldiers go in firing before the smoke from the grenades had even stopped billowing out of the building. Damn right. Charge in before the bastards inside had time to clear their heads.

Without lowering the binoculars he said, "Make a note. Commend the first platoon. Give them a two-day pass."

His aide, crouching beside him with a pad and pencil, scribbled frantically, adding a new line to his tenth page of notes from this exercise alone. The general must be in a generous mood, he decided. For the conscript soldiers of South Korea's army, a two-day pass was an almost unheard-of luxury. There'd be a lot of celebrating in the barracks tonight, and General Chang, the soldier's soldier, would see his popularity soar even higher.

Chang swung his binoculars over to follow the other part of the assault force. They were also making good progress, grenading their way deeper into the village. He watched and listened as the firing rose to an echoing crescendo and died away into a spatter of individual rifle shots. Then the firing stopped.

"Tango One Five, this is Tango One One," the radio crackled.

Chang took the microphone held out by his radioman. "Go ahead, Tango One One. This is Tango One Five."

"The objective is secure. Repeat, the objective is secure."

Chang thumbed the mike switch. "Acknowledged. Assemble your troops in the town square. I'm coming down. Out."

The colonel tossed the mike back to his radioman, stood up brushing the dirt off his uniform, and headed toward his jeep. He was pleased. The exercise had gone like clockwork, with the village cleared of its hypothetical North Korean or subversive defenders in less than forty-five minutes.

Chang clambered aboard his jeep and settled back as it tore off down the winding, dirt road toward the small group of houses that marked Exercise Area Five. He threw his head back and let the cold air rush over him. Winter was coming on fast and they would have snow soon. He smiled. Many in the cities hated the winter, the icy north winds, the shorter days. But for farmers, the winter was a welcome time—a chance to rest from endless days spent laboring in fields and rice paddies. Chang had always liked the winter.

His jeep, radio aerial whipping in the breeze, slewed around a street corner and braked in front of the infantry company assembled in the village square.

"Attention!" D company of his 1st Battalion straightened in a single fluid motion.

Chang stood in his seat and returned their salute before jumping down out of the jeep. He strode over to the captain commanding D Company. "Fine work, Captain. Your boys looked very good."

"Thank you, sir. We've been working them hard these past few weeks."

Chang knew that was true. Every unit in his division had been given an accelerated training schedule. That wasn't surprising, given the chaos sweeping through the country. And if anyone had noticed that most of the extra combat training centered on urban fighting, well, they'd kept their thoughts to themselves.

He looked the company over carefully. Every man's gear looked in good order and ready for use. These men looked tough and they'd acted tough. He made a snap decision. D Company would lead the column into Seoul.

He studied the captain, too. The man had a good record. His men obviously liked and trusted him. And he was known around the 1st Battalion officers' mess as a rabid political hard-liner. He was just the kind of officer Chang was looking for.

"Very well, Captain. You can dismiss your company now." Then Chang held up a hand. "But before you do, you should let them know that they've just won themselves a two-day pass."

He could see the front ranks smiling proudly, and he knew he'd just won another group of men who would fight for him when the time came.

"Company! Form in a column of twos and head for the barracks!"

The captain's command roar cut through Chang's thoughts. He turned back to the man. "Oh, and Captain?"

"Sir?"

"Join me in my quarters this evening for a drink. We've much to discuss, you and I. Be there at nineteen hundred hours sharp."

The man beamed. "Yes, sir! I'm honored, General."

Chang returned his salute and wheeled toward his jeep. He had other units to visit before this day was through.

NOVEMBER 14—YONGSAN ARMY BASE, SEOUL, SOUTH KOREA

McLaren stood at his window watching the tear gas rise above the city to the north. If Seoul's politicians had thought the cold weather would end the rioting, they'd been damned overoptimistic, he thought sourly. Instead of tapering off, the disturbances were spreading over all of South Korea. From the reports he'd seen, most of the major industrial cities—Pusan, Taegu, and Taejon— were at a standstill.

Of course a lot of that could be blamed on the American and European trade sanctions. Overseas buyers had started breaking their contracts even before the sanctions went into effect, not wanting to get stuck with lot of overtaxed, unprofitable merchandise when they did. As far as McLaren could tell, the only people who were going to benefit from this whole mess were the international trade lawyers who were being called in left and right.

Certainly the sanctions weren't helping South Korea's workers. Large-scale unemployment had been a thing of the past for Korea, but now more than ten percent of the work force had been thrown out on the streets. And the numbers were rising fast. Government projections showed a twenty percent unemployment rate by early December.

The results were predictable, but McLaren didn't find any pleasure in having predicted them. The workers who'd been tossed out on their ears, courtesy of the U.S. Congress, were siding with the radical students. And their protests were taking on an increasingly anti-American tone. In the past two weeks McLaren had seen sixteen of his men hospitalized with injuries after they'd been caught up in riots, and he'd been forced to curtail most leaves. As a result, morale in his command was starting to sag. Korea was already a strange place for most of the American soldiers stationed there, and being kept cooped up in their compounds wasn't helping things any.

McLaren swore to himself. About the only thing that was going according to plan was his effort to bollix up the troop withdrawal planning process. He'd started by letting the routine paperwork pile up on his desk before sending it back down with requests for minor and meaningless changes. And his staff, surprised as all hell at first, had caught on fast. He hadn't had to say a word, but they were now actively doing their best to screw things up along with him. It was too goddamned ironic, he thought. Here he'd worked hard for months to organize a smoothly operating staff, and now they were showing just how good they were by turning a difficult administrative task into an impossible one. Admiral Simpson had joined in as well. Whatever paperwork did get through the maze here in Korea usually came back from Washington stamped UNSAT.

Jesus, George Patton was probably rolling over in his

grave. McLaren smiled slightly at that thought. Hell, if Patton had faced the same kind of situation, he'd probably be down sitting in the clerk's filing room with a flamethrower right now—burning paperwork as fast as he could.

He turned away from the window and moved back to his desk. Normally kept bare, it was now covered with a mass of spilled papers and manila folders. He controlled the urge to sweep it all off onto the floor. Instead he picked up the latest set of draft equipment transfer orders for the 2nd Division's tank battalion. He started reading, making marginal notes to himself from time to time. This was good stuff. The battalion's S-4 had found a way to cut two weeks off the time it would normally take to ship his unit's tanks back to the States. McLaren scribbled a reminder to himself to commend the officer's ingenuity and then scrawled "Disapproved—try again" across the draft. He tossed it back on the stack.

There was one thing about this paper chase that he'd already decided. Officers who'd submitted grade-A plans wouldn't suffer for it. He'd continue to give them high marks for efficiency even while ripping their work to shreds. Of course, that would create a clear paper trail pointing directly at him if Congress started getting suspicious about the slow troop withdrawal and sent its GAO snoopers sniffing around. But McLaren would be damned if he'd screw up the careers of a dozen promising young officers just to protect himself.

If there was going to be any heat from this thing, he'd take it himself. After all, it wasn't as if he hadn't been under fire before for not playing the game the way the Army or congressional bureaucrats wanted it played. McLaren smiled to himself, remembering.

First there'd been that Tactics Review Board they'd stuck him with while he'd been recovering from wounds suffered in the Tet offensive back in '68. He'd issued a minority report criticizing the tendency to rely on firepower to make up for inadequate patrolling and small-unit action. He'd also fired a verbal blast at Washington's interference in field operations. That had earned him—what?—four years in a backwater training unit? Then there'd been his critical review of the Carter administration's first try at building Rapid Deployment Force—a hodgepodge of units that hadn't been very rapid, very deployable, or much of a force. He'd spent the next year in the Pentagon's Manpower and Recruiting doghouse before a new administration had given him another field command.

McLaren grinned. He'd been a good little boy for too long this time. It was time to raise a little hell. His career was at its peak anyway. No one was going to make him SACEUR— Supreme Allied Commander, Europe. He didn't have the diplomatic skills you needed for that job. And no Washington brass hat in his right mind was going to put him on the Joint Chiefs. Nope. Korea was it and it was enough. While wearing his many hats as Eighth Army CO, Commander U.S. Forces, Korea, Combined Forces chief, and others, McLaren commanded nearly 700,000 troops—a force just about the size of the entire regular U.S. Army. Now Congress wanted to end all that, to pull out of the Korean peninsula? Well, they'd just have to wait longer than they'd thought.

McLaren got back to work throwing sand into the gears.

NOVEMBER 17—SOUTHEAST OF SEOUL

Tony Christopher knocked on Anne's apartment door precisely on time. That had been easy to arrange, since he'd already been waiting anxiously in the car for fifteen minutes.

Anne Larson opened the door and stepped out, wearing a stylish fur-trimmed coat with a high collar that elegantly framed her curly mane of copper-colored hair and her fair complexion.

"Hi there." He smiled. "Ready to go?"

She made a quick half-twirl as though modeling her winter coat and smiled back at him. "Definitely. Is this place a long drive?"

"Nah, just twenty or so klicks. I mean, kilometers." Tony stepped aside to let her go first and then followed her downstairs to the front door. As Anne reached for the knob, he reached around her and opened the door, pushing it open a little awkwardly in the close quarters.

She looked slightly surprised but said "Thank you" anyway.

The steps outside were slick following a late-night rainstorm, and Tony offered her his arm. Anne didn't seem to see his gesture and reached instead for the railing. Should have known better, he thought. You'll have to watch showing your semichauvinist streak, old son.

He pointed out his car, parked half a block down. A battered old four-door Hyundai, it had been passed from pilot to pilot as they rotated through his squadron. And despite Tony's best attempts the day before, it was less than sleek.

They walked up to the passenger side and Tony reached for the door handle. This time, Anne protested, "Hey, c'mon, I'm a big girl now. I'm strong enough to open car doors." She smiled as she said it, but she still grabbed the handle before he could.

Mentally kicking himself, Tony looked crestfallen. "Sorry, Anne. I didn't mean to imply that you couldn't..."

Now she looked a little sheepish herself and tried to pass her reaction off with a joke. "It's okay, Tony, I'm just not used to such correct behavior from a fighter pilot." She bent down and climbed in the Hyundai.

Tony shut the door after and moved, frowning, around to the driver's side. Then he shrugged. Can't let it shake you, he decided. Redheads are touchy, right?

Anne leaned across and opened his door from the inside.

The business of pulling out into traffic gave him a few moments to consider his next move. Anne's gentle rebuff had made him realize he was acting like a kid on his first date. Not good.

Trouble was, he wanted to make a good impression. He couldn't use his normal style on Anne. Momentary memories of his "normal" style and Maria filled his thoughts, but he quickly suppressed them.

Okay, Tony, just relax, he thought. He looked over at Anne, who was sitting quietly. When she saw his glance, she smiled quickly but said nothing. He decided to try again.

"I hope you like this place, Anne. The view is nice, and the history's sure interesting."

"I'm sure I will," she said with warmth in her voice. It sounded a little forced, but the feeling was there.

He chattered on, relieved to find a topic he could discuss without anchoring his foot solidly in his mouth. "I read up on Namhan Mountain last night. It hasn't really been used for over two hundred years, but the Koreans first built on the site two thousand years ago."

She whistled softly under her breath. "Two thousand years! I'll bet our ancestors were still wearing skins and running from Roman soldiers back then. How much of this place is still standing?"

Things went easier from that point, and they passed the rest of the forty-five-minute drive exchanging tidbits of history on Korea in general, and their destination in particular. Tony was delighted to find something that both he and Anne could talk about—an interest they shared. Could share, he corrected himself.

In any event, the drive from Seoul seemed much too short. It was a clear winter day, and the road led southeast, climbing slowly. It took half the trip just to get clear of Seoul. The sprawling city had grown to within a few miles of their destination.

As they left the city behind, they started to see Namhan Mountain rising on the left. There were regular shapes visible on the top, which from this distance meant an impressive size.

Luckily the road didn't end at the base of the mountain but instead wound up and around toward the summit. As they climbed, Anne could look back and see the Seoul skyline spreading out behind them. She described it to Tony, who dutifully kept his eyes on the road through the long drive to the top.

They pulled into a parking lot and got out of the car. Although it was a cool day, they were lucky. There wasn't much wind. What there was, was just nippy enough to make them hurry toward the monolithic walls rising ahead.

The sign said "Namhan Castle," or "Namhansan-song" in Korean. It wasn't a castle in the European sense, with turreted battlements and a drawbridge. Instead, high stone walls stretched to the left or right. In some places they were twenty feet or more high.

"Fortress" was a much more suitable word, with all its connotations of immense size and strength. Namhansan-song reminded Tony of the Great Wall of China, wrapped around a single hilltop.

A cozily warm visitors' center supplied them with pamphlets; and they took turns reading aloud the most interesting portions and picking out where to go first.

Tony was a little appalled at the size of the place. The guidebook said there were over eight kilometers of wall, and

Anne sounded as if she wanted to see all of it. Her enthusiasm pulled him along, though. And as they started out on the path, he reached out and she took his hand. It happened without either of them thinking much about it. They walked that way toward the gate.

The old gates were open, and as they neared them, Anne pulled him off to study the wall. It was made of dressed stone, well weathered, but it was impossible for their inexpert eyes to tell whether it was two hundred or two thousand years old.

There were, however, some modern-looking pockmarks on the surface. Anne looked at him questioningly, and Tony tried to puzzle out their meaning. It came to him suddenly.

"They've got to be from the Korean War, Anne. This place was probably used by both sides during the battles for Seoul."

"Such a shame." She sighed. "Imagine this place, thousands of years old, defaced with bullets."

"I don't think the fortress minds, Anne." He smiled. "Remember, it was never built as a monument. It was built for war." He patted the stones. "Thirty years is just an eyeblink for this place."

He took her hand again and they walked inside.

The first thing they did was climb up to a point on the wall that overlooked Seoul. The guidebook had stressed Namhansansong's view, and it hadn't been exaggerating. From their vantage point, Tony and Anne could see the entire Han River valley.

Looking to the northwest, Seoul's skyscrapers, bridges, and sprawling suburbs spread out before them. The Han River entered their view from the right, the northeast, and then snaked its way through the city and off over the western horizon. There was a slight haze over the city itself, charcoal smoke from the hundreds of thousands of households. Some of the taller buildings seemed to thrust right through it.

They stood together, drinking in the view. Neither wanted to leave, so they stood and quietly pointed out various landmarks to each other. As the cold mountain air started to work its way into them, helped by a slight breeze, Tony stood close to Anne and then put his arm around her. She smiled and leaned into him a little.

They started following the walls, walking quickly to warm

up. Marveling at the exhibits, they read the plaques describing various aspects of the wall's history and construction. Tony's disastrous attempts to read the Korean side of the plaques became a running joke as they proceeded.

Suddenly they were back at their starting point, and Tony realized he was very tired. Arm in arm they trudged back to his car.

As he started it up and pulled out of the parking lot, Tony looked over at Anne. "I'm glad we could see the fortress together. It was a great morning."

"Thank you for asking me, Tony." She smiled coquettishly. "Now, where should we go next?"

They spent the drive back deciding.

NOVEMBER 20—SEOUL, SOUTH KOREA

General Chang stubbed his cigarette out in an ashtray and looked slowly around the crowded room, seeking out the eyes of every officer present. None avoided his gaze. He nodded to himself. They were committed and he could trust them.

The conspirators were meeting in the back room of the Han Chung Kak *kisaeng* house again. It was a good cover. No one would question an officer who chose to avail himself of the company of Seoul's most charming women. And if internal security had noticed Chang's frequent visits here, it might even lead them to write him off as nothing more than a middle-aged womanizer. If so, he thought, that would be an impression they would soon regret.

But General Hahn had assured him that the government knew nothing of his plans. Oh, the bureaucrats were nervous enough, jumping at shadows on every side. But they didn't have the detailed information needed to break up his coup attempt. And with General Hahn busy laundering Defense Security Command reports before they reached the higher echelons, they never would.

Chang brought his thoughts back to the matter at hand. The final brief for Operation Purify—the code name he'd selected for the coup. Almost everything was in place. The ten other officers in the room represented the merest tip of the cadre he'd organized. They would be responsible for briefing other groups of supporters at each of their duty stations. Chang was proud of his efforts. In a little over a month he'd managed to recruit middle-grade officers in nearly every major command of the South Korean Armed Forces. That had required a lot of hard work and a lot of risk, and now the payoff was at hand. Within the next few weeks the Republic of Korea would wake to find itself with a new group of political and military leaders—leaders who would rescue the nation from its turmoil.

"The time for action is nearly at hand, gentlemen." That startled them. He could see the surprise on their faces.

Colonel Min spoke first. "General? Are you sure we are ready? After all, we've been meeting for just a month. Can we afford to risk failure with a hasty throw of the dice?"

Others around the room nodded. Chang had caught them off guard. They'd anticipated a more leisurely planning process.

Chang snorted, "Gentlemen, the risks are greater the longer we wait."

He waved a hand at General Hahn. "Friend Hahn here has kept the government's lapdogs off our trail so far, but every passing day brings another chance for them to pick up the scent." Hahn nodded at that.

Chang continued, "Besides, gentlemen, our nation is fast approaching the edge. If we wait much longer, we may not have a country left to save."

That was something of an exaggeration, but only just. Every officer in the room had been appalled by the speed with which South Korea's economy and its political stability were unraveling. Most of the nation's industrial conglomerates, the *chaebol*, had already been brought to their knees by a combination of strikes and foreign trade sanctions. Skilled and unskilled workers of every description had been turned out of their idle factories, ready for exploitation by radical students. Rioting had flared across the peninsula, and the Combat Police seemed unable to contain the growing civil disorder. Hundreds had been killed, thousands injured, and thousands more were in "protective detention." There were even rumors that many of the conscripts who made up the Combat Police force were deserting, taking their skills and weapons over to the rioters.

And now the South Korean coalition government seemed on the brink of collapse. Opposition leaders were demanding more power from the ruling party—power they hadn't won at the polls and power the ruling party wasn't willing to surrender. The National Assembly had been deadlocked in petty political maneuvering for weeks while the crisis outside built steadily.

Chang reminded them of all of that and asked, "Is there any man here who can doubt the need for swift action?"

He turned to Min. "Isn't it better to throw the dice quickly than to be caught with them in hand?"

Min, still uncertain, looked at the others around the room and then down at his locked hands for a moment before replying. "You're right, Chang. We have no choice."

The others muttered their agreement.

Chang spoke slowly. "Thank you, gentlemen. I know that this is a tremendous gamble for us all, but you all know my reputation as a gambler." There were smiles at that. Chang had been known throughout the Academy as a risk-taker, but he'd also been known as a winner.

Chang pulled a map out of his briefcase and unfolded it across the table. The other officers leaned forward to get a better look.

"The key, my friends, is speed. The quicker we act, the less time available for the politicians to react. True?"

They nodded.

"So we must move with lightning speed to decapitate the current regime. That's the only way to do it. Seize the reins of government here in Seoul and the country will follow." Chang stabbed a finger at the capital as he outlined his plan.

A column made up of picked units from his own 4th Infantry Division would move from the DMZ to Seoul down the Main Supply Route. General Hahn would provide the necessary papers to take them through the rear-area checkpoints. Once in the capital, special assault troops would seize the President and his cabinet, the National Assembly building, and the Armed Forces HQ complex. Hahn and his fellow conspirators in the DSC would be responsible for making sure that the government's "black berets," the Special Forces, didn't intervene before these objectives were seized.

Once ensconced in the Blue House, Chang would make a nationwide broadcast announcing the change of government and promising a swift restoration of order and prosperity. That would be the signal for the other plotters to arrest their senior officers and assume full command of their respective units. With luck and careful timing, the governing elite would never know what had hit them.

Chang finished his briefing and sat down. The others stood clustered over the map, tracing out the intricate movements needed to bring the coup off. After a moment they, too, sat down.

Hahn spoke for them all. "It can be done."

Chang smiled. They were ready.

NOVEMBER 24—YONGSAN ARMY BASE, SEOUL, SOUTH KOREA

McLaren looked up from his pile of paperwork. "Come in!"

His aide stepped into the room and saluted.

"Take a pew, Doug. And spare me the formalities."

Captain Hansen smiled and sat down. "What can I do for you, General?"

McLaren glanced out the window before asking, "How are things out there, Doug?"

"Lousy." His aide frowned. "There are barricades up near the National University and the Combat Police aren't even trying to go near them. Instead, they're just trying to keep the city center operating under some semblance of normalcy."

"Shit."

"Amen to that, General. If things get much worse, we may have to consider moving the HQ out to the field—at least until things cool off here."

McLaren grimaced. "I'm not even going to consider that suggestion. The South Koreans would take that as the final sign that we're on the way out. We're gonna stay right here in Seoul until the very last stages of this dumbshit troop withdrawal are completed."

His aide kept a straight face with difficulty. Everyone in close proximity to the general knew that McLaren was playing fast and loose with the congressional mandate to pull out of South Korea. But nobody would admit to knowing that.

"Okay, Doug. I called you in here because I've got a little something I want you to do for me. And it's gotta be done ASAP and on the sly."

Hansen wondered what the general's "little something" would entail this time. The last one had taken several straight twenty-four-hour shifts, a lot of computer time, and gallons of coffee to come up with. But that was the price you paid for working close to someone with stars on his shoulders. There was an old Army joke that if God told you to do one thing and your commanding general told you to do another, you'd better hope God was forgiving because the general certainly wouldn't be.

"I want you to visit every one of our major commands up near the DMZ. Talk to the COs for me and tell them I want to know first thing, and I mean first thing, whenever a South Korean unit makes a troop move that I haven't personally authorized."

"Yes, sir." Hansen was puzzled and didn't bother to try to hide it.

"And I don't want any of our Korean liaison officers hearing about this, okay? This is between you, me, and the people I'm sending you to talk to. Clear?"

"Clear, sir." But Hansen's voice made it obvious that it wasn't at all clear.

McLaren decided to brief him more fully. The U.S. Army had never been big on unquestioning obedience. "Relax, Doug. There's a method to my madness."

McLaren got up from behind his desk and crossed the room to the window. "What I'm worried about is this. With all the shit flying in Seoul and the other cities, I'm convinced that it's only a matter of time before the government tries to bring regular troops in to crush the rioters."

He swung round to face Hansen. "Now, we can't afford to let that happen. For a variety of reasons I don't want to wake up one morning and read about another Seoul massacre, especially not one committed by troops nominally under my command. So I want to know what the government's up to before anything like that happens."

Hansen nodded his understanding.

"Okay, then. Now I don't want our South Korean officers to know I've tightened our reporting procedures because my relations with the government and the General Staff are damned tenuous at best. If they hear we're 'spying' on them, it'd piss them off even more. And that's something I really don't need at this stage.''

McLaren finished. ''All right, Captain, you have your orders. Any questions?''

''No, sir.''

''Okay, dismissed. And good luck.''

Hansen saluted, wheeled, and left to hit the road. He had a lot of ground to cover in the next several days.

McLaren watched the door close behind his aide and turned back to stare out the window again. He had a feeling that there was something ugly out there just waiting to pounce. Something worse than the endless rioting he'd already seen. But what the hell was it?

C H A P T E R
17

Operation Purify

DECEMBER 8—HIGHWAY 37, SOUTH KOREA

As his armored personnel carrier clattered around a gentle curve, General Chang stood high in an open hatch to look back along the road. The hundreds of PCs, trucks, and tanks carrying three battalions of his division stretched behind him in a rumbling, four-kilometer-long column, their dimmed headlights casting dancing shadows across ice-covered rice paddies beside the highway.

He glanced at his watch and then over to the right at the dark, narrow band that marked the Imjin River. They were on schedule, just minutes away from the small town of Sonu. From there a short drive would take the column to the Main Supply Route, Highway 1. Once on the MSR, they would be just forty kilometers from the outskirts of Seoul—a distance he planned to cover in less than three hours.

Chang dropped back down into the PC's red-lit interior. He wormed his way past the radioman and flak-vested body-guards to a small, hinged table covered with maps showing their route to the capital. His aide had just penciled in a small dot to show the regiment's position. They were almost up to the next security checkpoint.

Without looking up from the map Chang reached out and took the papers his aide offered. He thumbed through them, smiling slightly. So far at least, Hahn's forged movement orders had held up beautifully. Then his smile disappeared. The papers were damp. Chang glanced at his aide and frowned as he saw that the man was sweating like a pig, with dark stains discoloring his tunic collar and underarms. It was warm inside the crowded PC, but not that warm. Was the man afraid? Chang's nostrils wrinkled in disgust and he turned away toward the front of the troop compartment. He had no time for cowards now.

The general climbed back up through the hatch to let the cold night air flow over him. Within four hours his troops would be fanning out across Seoul. And an hour after that, he, Chang Jae-Kyu, the son of a rice farmer, would be the new president of the Republic of Korea.

Chang smiled at the thought. Yes, he would be the president. And he would do precisely what had to be done to restore order to his nation's troubled cities. Many of the rebellious students and workers would die, but their deaths would bring countless others to their senses. Then, with calm restored, he and his fellow officers would reform society—bolstering the sense of discipline, self-restraint, and respect for authority that had characterized Korea for countless generations.

He had no doubt that the foreign traders would return once all that had been accomplished. But they would trade on his terms, without arrogant demands that Korea surrender its sovereign right to govern itself as it pleased. Chang shook his head, cutting off that train of thought. It was pleasant to contemplate, but first he and his three thousand troops had more immediate work to do—work that would certainly require speed and determination, and work that might well require gunfire, grenades, bayonets, and blood.

Chang straightened as the PC came over a small rise a few hundred yards from Sonu. He could see barricades, and sandbagged machine gun nests blocking the road ahead. They'd reached the next security checkpoint.

He leaned down in through the hatch and signaled the driver to stop. His radioman was already ordering the rest of the regimental column to halt. Chang swung himself down off the PC and dropped lightly onto the road. He pulled his phony travel orders out of his pocket and strode resolutely forward to speak with the Special Forces lieutenant commanding the roadblock.

DECEMBER 8—YONGSAN ARMY BASE, SEOUL, SOUTH KOREA

The phone rang, jerking McLaren awake and upright in bed with a muttered curse. He'd been up late checking over plans for the next scheduled military exercise. He fumbled on the nightstand for the phone.

"McLaren."

"Sorry to wake you, General." It was Doug Hansen. "But I'm afraid we have a situation developing."

McLaren looked at the luminous dial of his watch. It was past two A.M. "Go on."

He could hear Hansen suppressing a yawn. "I just got a call from one of our battalion COs up near the Z. One of his observation posts has reported seeing South Korean troops leaving their base and heading south. The Twelfth Mechanized Infantry Regiment. They're part of the 4th Infantry Division, commanded by a General Chang. And that's not an authorized movement, General."

McLaren threw the covers aside and swung out of bed, reaching for his pants. "How long ago did they leave, Doug?"

"About two hours ago. It took some time for the report to get passed through channels." Hansen's voice was apologetic.

"Shit." McLaren cradled the phone with his shoulder

while bending over to tie his shoes. "Hell, they could be halfway to Seoul by now."

"Yes, sir."

McLaren started buttoning up his shirt. "Okay, Doug. I'll be down in the Operations Room in two minutes, and I want all the details you can dig up on that regiment and this Chang character. If I'm going to get on the horn and ream that bastard General Park out properly, I want to know what I'm talking about." He hung up.

Goddamnit. He'd warned the South Korean government not to try using their military to fight the rioters. But it looked like they'd gone ahead and decided to try it anyway. He'd just have to hope that an early-morning phone call to the chairman of the South Korean Joint Chiefs of Staff would be enough to persuade them to pull the troops back to base before any shooting started.

McLaren snapped his bedside lamp on and leaned over to stare into the mirror. He ran a hand over his face, feeling the rough stubble. Well, there wasn't time to shave. He threw on his uniform jacket and headed for the door.

The Eighth Army Operations Room was already crowded with half-asleep staff officers getting in each other's way. McLaren paused in the door, looking for Hansen. Christ, what a zoo.

There. He saw his aide on the phone at a desk across the room. He plunged into the room, working his way past his officers and nodding as they greeted him.

Hansen saw him and put the phone down. "Good morning, General." He handed McLaren a file folder. "That's what we've got on this General Chang, and the switchboard is waiting to put your call through on General Park's private line. He's not at his headquarters."

Not at his headquarters? That was strange. If the South Korean government was conducting a major military move, you'd expect its JCS chairman to be at his post—even if it was in the middle of the night. McLaren filed that away mentally as something to wonder about later. There were more immediate concerns.

He leafed through Chang's personnel record. "Give me a quick rundown on this guy. What's he like?"

"He's a good soldier, sir. Very tough, even for a Korean. Saw combat as a captain during the Vietnam War."

McLaren nodded. He'd seen the Koreans fighting in Vietnam at first hand. They had been good. Very good.

"What about his politics, Doug?"

"Real hard-line, General. Just the kind of guy they'd pick to shoot up some demonstrators."

Friggin' great. "Okay, patch me in to Park's line. I'll come on after you've got him on the phone. I'll be damned if I'm going to sit around waiting for him to roll out of bed."

McLaren headed for his office. He didn't want the whole world to hear the kind of language he was going to use while speaking to a four-star South Korean general.

It took three minutes to get Park on the phone.

"Good morning, General McLaren. I assume there's an important reason for this call." Park sounded both tired and irate.

"There certainly is, General." McLaren clenched his teeth, trying to control his own anger. "I'm calling to see just what the hell you and your government are trying to pull."

Park was puzzled. "What? What are you talking about, General McLaren?"

"I'm talking about the mechanized infantry regiment you've got on the road to Seoul right now, General Park. The regiment that's moving without my authorization. That's what I'm talking about."

There was silence on the other end of the phone for several seconds. Then Park spoke again. "General McLaren, please believe me. I do not know anything about this movement."

Damn. It sounded as if he were telling the truth, and it explained what he was doing at his home instead of his headquarters. "Could these troops have been given their orders by somebody else in your government?"

Park was firm. "No one else has the authority to move troops away from the DMZ. And I would have cleared such a move with you first, General."

"Then just what the hell are General Chang and his men up to, General Park?"

"Chang?" Park said slowly. "General Chang? I know this man. They call him the Iron Man. He is one of those officers we have been concerned about. If he is moving toward Seoul, it is without the government's knowledge or consent.''

Suddenly it was clear to McLaren. ''Oh, Christ. He's launching a coup.''

''Yes. I think you are right.'' McLaren could hear shuffling noises as Park got dressed. ''If you will excuse me, General McLaren, I must look to the safety of my country. I must alert the President and my Special Forces commanders. I'll call you back when that is done.''

Park hung up, leaving McLaren holding a dead phone. He put it down and headed out the door back to the Ops Room at a run. ''Doug! Tell the J-3 I want all American commands on full alert, pronto!''

Hansen looked up from a road map of the area around Seoul. ''What about the ROK troops, General? Do we alert them, too?''

''No, just our own men. At least for right now.'' There wasn't any way of telling how many other units were involved in this coup attempt. And McLaren didn't want to let Chang and his fellow conspirators know the cat was out of the bag.

He looked at the wall clock. Park had maybe an hour and a half to organize a reception for Chang's regiment before it reached Seoul. He hoped that would be long enough.

DECEMBER 8—SPECIAL FORCES BARRACKS, SEOUL, SOUTH KOREA

As the black staff car slowed for a stoplight, General Hahn pulled his pistol out of his shoulder holster, checked the magazine, and slid it back into place. He glanced at his deputy, Major Yi. ''You have the papers?''

Yi tapped the briefcase lying between them on the seat. ''They're all here, sir. The arrest orders, authorizations, everything.''

Hahn nodded. He twisted in his seat to look out the back window as the car accelerated away from the light. The truck loaded with his DSC troopers was still right behind them, rolling along Seoul's empty streets. They were just minutes away from the main Special Forces barracks for the Capital Corps.

Once there, he and his men would arrest all the Special Forces senior officers for allegedly plotting against the government. And with the barrack switchboards manned by "loyal" DSC soldiers, the government's frantic calls for help wouldn't be heard until it was too late.

Hahn smiled. Chang's plan had a brilliant simplicity to it. While Hahn's DSC troopers eliminated progovernment officers for supposedly plotting a coup, the real rebels would be pouring into Seoul unmolested. Under the cover of a phony coup attempt, Chang would launch a real one.

But as they rounded the last corner, Hahn's smile faded. The Special Forces Barracks was ablaze with lights. Trucks loaded with armed Black Berets were pulling out through the main gate and turning north toward the city outskirts. They were too late. Someone or something had alerted the government.

Hahn briefly considered aborting his mission, but he knew he was already in too deep to extricate himself. Better to carry on in the hope that he and his men could still grab enough of the Special Forces officers to cripple their command and control before Chang's troops reached the city.

Two sentries in full combat dress waved the staff car to a halt at the gate. One covered the driver with his M16 while the other, a sergeant, walked back to Hahn's rolled-down window and saluted.

"Papers, sir." The sentry had to shout to raise his voice above the roar as another heavily laden truck careened out through the gate.

Hahn fished in his tunic and came up with his identity card. The sergeant took it and studied it under a flashlight. He handed the ID back and then leaned half in through the window to sweep his light around the car's interior. Yi flinched as the beam caught him right in the eyes. Hahn sat impassively, his eyes closed against the glare.

The sergeant stepped back and saluted. "Very good, sir. You may proceed."

Hahn tried to look disinterested. "What the hell's going on, Sergeant? Some kind of exercise?"

"Don't know, sir. Orders. Maybe there's another riot building." The man nervously fingered his slung assault rifle and looked back at the truck now stopped right behind Hahn's staff car.

Hahn followed his gaze. "You can clear them, Sergeant. They're with me."

The Special Forces trooper licked his lips. "I'm afraid I can't do that, sir. Only our own people are allowed into the compound tonight. Your men will have to wait here until someone changes my orders."

"Sergeant, I'm a general in the Defense Security Command and I'm changing your orders. Right now."

"With respect, sir, that's not good enough. Not tonight. You'll have to speak with someone up at the HQ." The sergeant jerked a thumb at a building across the barracks courtyard.

Hahn stared at him for a moment. Was it worth trying to bull ahead through the gate? He glanced quickly at the other sentry. The man hadn't moved an inch during the whole exchange, and he still had his rifle pointed straight at Hahn's driver. No go. And every minute he wasted out here was another minute that let more of these Special Forces fish slip through his nets.

He nodded. "All right, Sergeant. I'll get you your precious authorization."

Hahn turned back to Major Yi. "Stay here with the men until I send for you."

Yi bobbed his head in understanding and got out of the car. The sentries stepped back, clearing the way, and as they did, Hahn leaned forward and tapped the driver's seat. "Let's go."

The car slid ahead into a large, floodlit courtyard jammed with parked trucks and running soldiers. Hahn could see men hoisting heavy equipment onto the trucks, including Dragon missile launchers. That clinched it. The Black Berets knew about Chang's assault column. Nobody carted along antitank missiles to crush a student riot.

His driver parked in front of the headquarters building and got out to hold the door open for him. Hahn climbed out, settled his uniform cap squarely on his head, and marched up the steps into the Special Forces HQ.

He walked straight into an organized pandemonium of

ringing telephones and rushing clerks. Many were out of uniform, and their rumpled clothing made it clear that they'd been rousted out of their bunks not long before. Hahn felt a little more sure of himself. Whatever had alerted the government had done so only at the last minute. That meant they probably didn't have a source inside the conspiracy itself. There might still be a way to pull this thing off.

Hahn grabbed the nearest clerk. "You! Where's the duty officer?"

The man pointed to a door at the end of a long corridor. Hahn released him and moved down the hallway. He pushed open the door and stepped inside.

There was only one man inside the small office, a lieutenant. The lieutenant's eyes widened when he saw Hahn's insignia, and he put down the phone he'd been holding. He had dark circles under his eyes and he'd missed a button while putting on his shirt.

"Where's your CO, soldier?" Hahn said harshly, tossing his briefcase onto the man's desk.

"He's up with the column, sir. I can raise him on the radio if you'd like." The lieutenant reached for the phone he'd just set down.

Hahn shook his head. "No good. I need to talk to the senior officer here in this compound, right now."

The lieutenant looked even more worried. "Well, that's me, General. Everyone else is on the road."

Curse it. Hahn could feel his part of the plan slipping away from him. How much did the government know?

"Okay then, Lieutenant. Maybe you can tell me what all this fuss is about."

The man looked surprised. "I'd have thought you'd know more about that than I would, sir. All I know is that General Park called my colonel about half an hour ago and told him to get every company and heavy weapons team we had on the road north."

Hahn grabbed his briefcase back off the desk. There wasn't any further point in hanging about here. Arresting one junior officer wasn't going to put a crimp in the government's reaction. He was just exposing himself to unnecessary risk. He had to get back to DSC headquarters and warn Chang about the

Black Berets waiting for him. Maybe they could switch the assault column to an alternate route.

"Very well, I'll talk to your commander later. Carry on, Lieutenant." Hahn returned the man's salute and left the office, shutting the door behind him.

The lieutenant stared at the closed door for a moment. What had that been about? What was a senior DSC officer doing showing up at the compound with a truck full of armed men?

Well, there was only one way to find out for sure. He picked up the phone again. "Corporal, get me General Park's adjutant."

DECEMBER 8—MINISTRY OF NATIONAL DEFENSE, SEOUL, SOUTH KOREA

Across the city, the Ministry of National Defense was hastily being prepared for a state of siege. The dress-uniformed guards who normally patrolled outside the squat, reinforced concrete headquarters were gone—replaced by troops in full battle dress. They were busy throwing up sandbagged machine gun nests in the streets around the building and on the roof. Armored personnel carriers now blocked the ministry's main entrance.

Brigadier General Kim Tong-Ki turned away from the windows and put the phone down. He looked across the office at his boss, General Park. "Sir, I've just had a very strange conversation with the duty officer at the Special Forces barracks."

Park looked up from the map he was studying. The first elements of the Special Forces group stationed in Seoul had just reported reaching their blocking positions. Park was trying to decide how far he could trust the other units in the capital garrison. The obvious answer was not very far at all. There was no telling how far Chang's conspiracy reached.

"Yes, go on." Kim could hear the strain in his commander's voice.

"It seems that a General Hahn, a DSC man, showed up there a few minutes ago with a whole truckload of troops. He was looking for the unit's senior officers, and he left when he heard they were already gone. Does that mean anything to you, General?"

"Not a thing. But we can soon straighten it out." Park waved an aide over. "Go find General Lew in the Operations Room and tell him I need to see him."

Kim nodded his understanding. Lew ran the Defense Security Command. If anyone knew what this General Hahn was up to, it would be him.

Lew, a compact, muscular man, was as puzzled by Kim's news as General Park had been. He shook his head. "No, I didn't send him up there. In fact, I've been trying to reach him for the last hour myself. He's one of my best commanders, and I wanted to put him on alert."

Park stood motionless for a moment, stroking his chin. He looked at Kim. "What's the last reported position of this rebel column?"

"Ten kilometers north of the outlying districts. They passed through one of our checkpoints about ten minutes ago."

Park and his senior officers had made the decision not to alert their routine security posts along the MSR. None of them were strong enough to put up much of a fight against Chang's three thousand crack troops. At most they might have been able to delay his advance by a few minutes, and that wasn't worth losing the chance to pull a bigger surprise on the renegade colonel when he got closer to Seoul.

Park considered the timing carefully. If they hadn't been alerted, Hahn and his men would have been inside the Special Forces compound roughly half an hour before Chang's column reached the capital. No one would have been expecting them, and no one would have stopped them from doing whatever they had planned. It might be coincidence. But could he take that chance?

No. Better to wrong what might be an innocent man than to risk the loss of a government. He turned to Kim. "Pass the word to the security forces. Arrest General Hahn."

DECEMBER 8—THE MAIN SUPPLY ROUTE, SEOUL, SOUTH KOREA

They were right on time, moving at a steady twenty kilometers per hour down the multilane highway. The frost-covered fields and rugged hills of the countryside were beginning to give way to tall, block-long apartment buildings, sprawling factories, and huge, flat-roofed warehouses. It was still dark and Chang could see stars sparkling in the icy black night sky. But the crescent moon was sinking lower on the horizon, and the sun would rise in less than three hours. If he had been a poet, he would have been moved by what he saw.

Instead, he thumbed a switch on the microphone. "All units. All units. This is Tango One Five. Five kilometers to Point Alpha."

He switched off and handed the mike back down to his radioman in the troop compartment. Point Alpha was the code name he'd chosen for the intersection at which his column of PCs, trucks, and tanks would split, with each unit moving separately to its assigned objective. He would personally lead the battalion heading for the Blue House to arrest the President.

He felt a hand on his leg and looked down. His aide stood below, hunched over and swaying as the PC rumbled down the highway.

"We're almost up to the final checkpoint, sir. Any change in instructions?"

Chang shook his head. "No. I'll handle this one personally. But tell Captain Sung that I want his best platoon ready to move in if there's any trouble. I don't want our fat friends in the ministry alerted to the danger just yet."

The man nodded and dropped down into the crowded troop compartment. Chang settled back to enjoy the ride. Everything was going according to plan.

The last checkpoint on the MSR loomed out of the darkness, a row of reflector-topped barricades stretched across the road. He could see a few black-bereted figures moving behind the barricades, their assault rifles slung across their shoulders. The lights were on in the guardhouse built beside the highway. Chang's PC slowed to a halt a few yards in front of the roadblock, and he clambered down off the vehicle. He stretched, checked to make sure he had his papers, and started walking toward the guardhouse.

Suddenly he found himself speared by a dazzlingly bright light that threw his shadow back along the road for yards. His eyes closed involuntarily in the glare, and he raised a hand to try to block it out. Some bastard had turned a searchlight on him.

"General Chang." The megaphone robbed the speaker's voice of any individuality. "This is Colonel Lee of the First Special Forces Group. You are under arrest for plotting against the security of the state."

Damn. They had been betrayed. It was the only explanation. Who was it? Was it that DSC bastard Hahn? Chang stood still for a moment, stunned.

"You will come forward with your hands raised above your head. And you will order your troops to dismount from their vehicles without their weapons. Any man carrying a weapon will be shot without further warning."

Chang heard boots slamming down on the pavement ahead and equipment rattling, and through half-open eyes he saw the barricades lined with fully equipped Black Berets. Most of their weapons were pointing at him.

His lips tightened. Quite an honor. The government considered him so dangerous that it made him the personal target of more than a hundred riflemen and machinegunners. A thought crept into his head through the shock. Perhaps they were right to fear him. After all, these men were also soldiers. They could not be happy with the chaos they saw around them. Why should they be his enemies and his undoing?

He straightened up and slowly brought his hands down toward his sides. He turned his head away from the searchlight's glare, seeking out the line of troops ahead of him.

"Soldiers of Korea!" Chang's voice carried easily through the night air. "Fellow soldiers."

He paused, searching for the right words. "Do not let yourselves be turned into unthinking pawns for these corrupt politicians! Don't help these ink-stained bureaucrats use you as a shield while they destroy our country!"

He took a step closer to the barricades. No one fired. He wished he could see their faces, could see the effect his words were having.

"Join us!" Chang waved an arm back toward the silent column of vehicles massed behind him. He saw movement out of the corner of an eye. There were government troops in position along the sides of the highway as well. It had been a thoroughly planned ambush.

"Join us to oust these fat ones who sit idle while you are beaten by communist mobs. Join us to restore order in the streets and prosperity to our nation." He was within a few yards of the barricades now. It was working. He could see rifles beginning to waver, and he could hear muttering from the men ahead of him.

Chang took another step forward and started to smile. He was going to do it. He was going to bring these men over to his side. All it would take were a few more carefully chosen words. He opened his mouth to speak.

Two hundred yards away, Colonel Lee brought his night-vision glasses down slowly. He'd set up his CP on a flat-roofed warehouse to get a better view of the action. That had been a mistake. Now he was too far away to counteract the man's oratory. The Special Forces officer shook his head. Chang was good. He'd hit just the right note, and Lee could see his men wavering, starting to turn toward rebellion.

Now there was only one way left to stop that. He looked at the sergeant lying prone on the roof next to him. "Do it."

The sergeant nodded and lifted the sniper rifle to his shoulder. He squinted through the scope for a moment and squeezed the trigger.

The bullet caught Chang in the throat, tore through, and exploded out the back of his neck.

There was no pain, but Chang found himself falling backward onto the pavement. He couldn't feel his arms or legs, and when he opened his mouth to cry out, he couldn't get any air into his lungs.

Oh. Chang knew he'd been shot, knew he was dying. Time seemed to slow; he could see the stars overhead spiraling down to earth. Sons of bitches. They'd never given him a chance. It was over.

Chang was dead before the gunner aboard his APC came out of shock long enough to trigger his .50-caliber machine gun. But he avenged his general twenty times over as the burst caught men at the barricade and threw them back in a spray of blood and shattered bone.

A Special Forces heavy weapons team on the left flank

saw the carnage and slammed a Dragon missile into the APC's side. It exploded, ripping through the PC's thin aluminum armor and hurling it over onto the pavement upside down and on fire.

Then the other Black Berets opened up, flaying the trapped column with antitank missiles, grenades, and machine guns. It was a slaughter. Chang's men were in a tightly packed march formation with their vehicles spaced just far enough apart for safety during the drive south. It was a formation that guaranteed disaster under fire.

Drivers who tried to wheel out of the column to escape the crossfires laid down by the Black Berets either collided with the vehicles in front or back or were shot dead. Canvas-sided trucks were shredded by machine-gun fire that butchered the soldiers trapped inside. Men who'd dropped onto the pavement were cut down before they could lift their rifles. High-pitched screams from the wounded echoed above the gunfire. A tank, trying to escape, ground its way over a loaded truck, crushing it into a crumpled mass of blood-soaked steel. Seconds later, a Dragon missile caught the tank and blew its turret off, sending flames roaring into the night sky. Trucks and APCs exploded, throwing flaming gasoline high into the air. Smoke from burning vehicles billowed above the highway, blotting out the setting moon.

By the time Colonel Lee got his men back under control, Chang's column was a tangled mass of wrecked and burning vehicles and dead and dying men.

Chang's coup attempt was over. But the retribution had just begun.

CHAPTER
18
Reactions

"Attention!" The sergeant major's roar echoed over the snow-covered parade ground. One thousand men snapped to attention, their shoulders thrown back and posture ramrod straight. For a moment the sergeant major studied them, his narrowed eyes looking for any weakness or imperfection.

Satisfied, he wheeled and threw a rigid salute to the group of officers facing the assembled troops. "Battalion present and ready for inspection, sir!"

General Bae returned his salute casually. "Very good, Sergeant Major. We'll begin now."

The man dropped his salute and fell in behind Bae as he walked along the ranks, checking uniforms and weapons at random. Occasionally he stopped to have a name taken either for commendation or for punishment. But only occasionally.

Bae smiled thinly to himself. The battalion was in good fighting trim. Ready for anything. The phrase echoed in his mind: *ready for anything*. This was the unit he had planned to take to Seoul to reinforce Chang's coup attempt if necessary.

The general continued his inspection but his mind was far away, concentrating on a more urgent problem. What had gone wrong with Chang's plan?

Chang was dead. That was certain. Bae had heard the news from a friend in the Defense Ministry. But there'd been a complete security clampdown on exactly what had happened along the MSR north of Seoul. All Bae knew for sure was that a five-kilometer stretch of the highway was still closed—forcing supply convoys coming north to detour around it. And the 4th Infantry Division's camp was quarantined, surrounded by a thick cordon of heavily armed Black Berets.

The general had avoided making any contact with the other plotters since the abortive coup, feeling certain that the DSC's spies would be watching combat officers even more closely now. In a few days, perhaps, it might be safe to arrange a meeting to try to pick up the pieces. Bae shook his head slowly. Chang had been their inspiration. He wasn't sure how many of the others would have the stomach to try again now that the Iron Man was gone.

Behind him, the sergeant major frowned as Bae walked right by a private with traces of weapons lubrication oil staining his tunic. He stopped, gave the man a ferocious glare, and then hurried on after his general. Something was bothering the Old Man all right.

Bae finished his walk-around and started moving toward the small cluster of officers nervously waiting for his verdict on their troops. Then he stopped.

Two black staff cars had just driven through the main gate. They were followed by three canvas-sided trucks. The car lurched off the camp's main road and turned toward the parade ground. The rest followed it, their tires crunching over the compacted surface of snow and ice.

Bae started moving again but one hand dropped, almost unconsciously, to rest on the pistol holster at his right side. The sergeant major followed suit.

He rejoined his officers as the staff car pulled up and slid to a stop in a spray of snow and gravel. The trucks stopped right behind it, and Black Berets carrying submachine guns jumped down off them, fanning out to cover the little group of officers.

Once they were in position, the staff car's doors popped open. Bae's eyes narrowed. There could only be one reason for all of this, but surely they were making an unnecessarily large production out of what should be a simple procedure. Why hadn't they simply waited until his inspection was over?

A small, nervous man wearing a thick officer's overcoat and carrying a swagger stick levered himself out of the rear door of the staff car. He shivered in the cold air and pulled the overcoat tighter around him. Then he flipped open a file and studied it for a moment. Bae's officers clustered around the general, waiting for him to take the lead.

Finally the man walked over to them, followed closely by two submachine gun–toting guards with DSC collar tabs. He stopped, facing Bae. "General Bae?"

Bae stood silent for a moment and then nodded.

One side of the thin man's mouth curled upward and he reached into his pocket for a single, folded piece of paper. He handed it to Bae. "I'm General Kim of the DSC. Those orders come from General Park himself, and they authorize me to take command of your division."

Bae studied them and then looked up sharply. "For what reason has General Park done this?"

Kim smiled. "For a very good reason, General Bae." The smile disappeared. "You're under arrest for treason."

Even though he'd been half-expecting arrest since the failure of Chang's coup, the words still shook Bae and he stepped back a pace.

One of the DSC troopers with him stepped forward and yanked Bae's pistol out of its holster. The other kept Bae's officers covered with his SMG.

Bae stood rigidly still as the guard frisked him for other weapons. Kim smiled pleasantly again. "What? No protestations of innocence and wronged honor? You disappoint me, General."

Bae said nothing. How had they known? Chang had told them he'd never kept written notes, so someone must have talked. But who? Chang was dead. Who had betrayed him?

Kim nodded to the DSC guard who now had his SMG trained directly on Bae. "Take this traitor to the car."

Bae swallowed, trying to clear his throat. "May I have a moment to inform my family of what has happened? I give you my word as an officer that I shall not attempt to escape."

The DSC general laughed, a harsh, braying sound. "Don't worry yourself. They'll be informed of your fate. And your word means nothing to me." He nodded to his guards. "Take this dog away. The sight of him sickens me."

Bae was stripped of his coat and hustled away into a waiting car. As it drove off, Kim turned back to face the shocked officers. "Very well, gentlemen. Now that this unpleasantness is behind us, we can get on with my other business here today."

He looked at the battalion commander. "We will start with your battalion. Have your companies return their weapons to the armory. The entire division is confined to quarters until I've had time to sort out this mess to my satisfaction. Clear?"

The battalion commander nodded quickly. Kim was satisfied to see the man's hands trembling. Good, it was time to throw fear into these soldiers. Fear would keep them in line until he'd had the chance to purge this unit of every traitor and malcontent.

He stood back to watch as the process was begun.

DECEMBER 11—MINISTRY OF NATIONAL DEFENSE, SEOUL, SOUTH KOREA

McLaren waited while the uniformed aide cleared away the tea and then looked hard at General Park. "You do realize how goddamned stupid your government's behavior is right now, don't you?"

Park spread his hands. "I'm not quite sure what you're referring to, General."

"Come off it, Park. I'm talking about the mass arrests made by your security forces. I'm talking about the way your DSC goons are ripping the guts out of your command structure."

"There have been arrests, yes." Park laced his fingers together and sat back in his chair. "But surely that is an internal matter, General McLaren. It does not concern you or come under your authority."

"Bullshit!" McLaren's fist crashed down on the low table between them. "You've thrown half the best officers in your Army, Navy, and Air Force into detention camps, and the rest are too busy looking over their shoulders to run their units properly."

"I'm well aware that the necessary steps my government has taken to quell General Chang's rebellion may have affected some elements in our officer corps." Park's eyes shifted away from McLaren's face and then came back. "But they are necessary, General. The rot was widespread and we must burn it out."

"Damnit, man, you're burning the heart out of your army." McLaren lowered his voice. "Have you been up to the DMZ lately? Have you seen what's happening up there?"

Park shook his head and said stiffly, "Matters of state have kept me here in the city."

"Well, let me tell you, General Park, your 'necessary measures' are a fucking disaster for military preparedness. I've never seen morale so low. Christ, how do you expect the troops to react to seeing their officers hauled off under guard?"

"Loyal officers have been left in command. That should be enough."

McLaren shook his head. "No, it's not. You really think your troops are going to follow a bunch of HQ Milquetoast ass kissers into battle?"

"If it is necessary, yes."

McLaren took a deep breath. Time to calm down before he throttled the obstinate s.o.b. "General, it's my duty as Combined Forces Commander to ensure the readiness of all the units under my authority. I can't do that while you're stripping them of the most experienced and dedicated officers. So I'm asking you, in my official capacity, to suspend these arrests and to release all the officers who haven't been directly tied to General Chang's coup attempt."

Park's lips thinned. "You pick a strange time to . . . how do you say? . . . throw your weight around, General. You and your men will be gone from my country in a few months, and your authority will end with your departure. Why should we pay any heed to the advice of those who are deserting us?"

McLaren had no answer for that. It would have to come from Washington.

DECEMBER 12—CAMP HOWZE, NEAR TONG DUCH'ON, SOUTH KOREA

Kevin Little knocked once on Rhee's door and waited.

No one answered, but he could smell cigarette smoke. The South Korean lieutenant hadn't been at Captain Matuchek's morning commander's meeting. He hadn't been at dinner the night before. And he hadn't signed out through the gate guardhouse. That left only one place he could be.

Kevin knocked again. This time the door opened.

"Lieutenant Little?" Rhee sounded surprised. His English, usually perfect, was a little slurred. "Whad can I do for you?"

Kevin pushed the door open wider. "For starters, Lieutenant Rhee, you could let me in out of the hallway here."

The South Korean nodded slowly and stepped back out of the way. Kevin closed the door behind him and studied both Rhee and his quarters carefully. Though normal looking by most standards, they were a shambles when judged by the impossibly high standards that he knew Rhee set for himself.

Rhee stood swaying slightly in the middle of the small room. His eyes were red-rimmed and bleary, and the top button of his uniform shirt was undone. The sheets on Rhee's cot were slightly rumpled, as though he'd been lying on top of them and had gotten up without bothering to straighten them out. A lit cigarette smoldered in the ashtray on the desk, perched atop the twisted, crumpled remains of more than a dozen others. An open bottle and a half-full glass of clear liquid sat next to the ashtray.

The room smelled like a hellish combination of rum and furniture-polish remover. Kevin recognized the smell from trips to Korean restaurants and bars that had always been followed by monstrous hangovers. It was Soju, a cheap, grain liquor. He looked from the glass to Rhee. "A bit early in the day, isn't it?"

Rhee lowered his own gaze. "Perhaps." He let the word hang there.

"You missed the captain's meeting this morning."

Rhee's head snapped back up. "Did he ask where I—"

Kevin interrupted him. "I told him you were out running down a missing equipment requisition for me."

The other man's eyes fell again and he sank back onto his coat. "You should not have lied for me, Lieutenant. I have failed in my duty. To drink when I should be at my post is . . . unforgivable." The South Korean's voice faded completely.

Kevin stared at Rhee's slumped shoulders and felt his irritation vanish. He pulled the chair away from the desk and sat facing his liaison officer. "Look, Rhee, you've got to snap out of this funk. Just what the hell is wrong?"

"General Chang's coup attempt . . ."

Kevin felt cold. They'd all heard the scuttlebutt about the

slaughter outside Seoul and the DSC's ongoing wave of mass arrests. "Jesus Christ, Rhee, you weren't involved in that, were you?"

"No." Rhee shook his head slowly. "I was too junior to be involved. I had no hand in it."

"Well, then, you haven't got anything to worry about." Kevin forced a cheerful note into his voice. "This'll all blow over in a few more days and things'll get back to normal." He winced. That sounded fatuous even to him.

Rhee locked his fingers together and stared at his clasped hands. "I do not think so, Lieutenant. My country being destroyed from within before my eyes, and I can do nothing. My friends and relatives are being thrown out of work in the midst of the winter. And I can do nothing for them. Now the Army, our last bulwark against the enemy, is being broken on the wheel." He raised his bloodshot eyes to Kevin's face in a mute appeal. "And what can I do to prevent this? Nothing." His eyes strayed toward the Soju bottle.

Kevin stared at him for a second, framing his reply carefully. He had to find a way to rouse Rhee from his depression. If Matuchek found the South Korean in this state, there'd be hell to pay—both by Rhee and by Kevin. Another thought crossed his mind and chilled him further. If any of the DSC men in the area heard about this reaction to Chang's coup, Rhee would probably find himself on a short ride to a long prison term, guilty or not guilty. Kevin shook his head. He really didn't have any choice. He had to get Rhee back to some semblance of normal, and fast.

He spoke slowly, emphasizing each word as he thought of it. "Look at me, Lieutenant." Rhee's eyes swung back toward him. "Neither one of us is in a position to do much about the big things that are going wrong over here. I'm not the president, so I can't undo that stupid trade bill. And you're not a general, so you can't call off this DSC witch-hunt. Right?"

Kevin saw the South Korean starting to pay attention to him. Encouraged, he continued, "But that's not what they're paying us for. They're paying us to soldier. And you're a damned good soldier, Lieutenant Rhee. You're a hell of a lot better at this game than I am." He narrowed his own eyes and stared hard at the Korean. "Or at least you are when you're not drunk."

Rhee hung his head in shame again.

Kevin softened his voice. "C'mon, Rhee. Everybody screws up once or twice. But you can't let it grind you down."

The South Korean slowly lifted his head. He stared back at Kevin for a moment in silence and then answered, "You are right, Lieutenant Little, I should concentrate my energies on the things that I can affect. On the platoon and on my own preparedness." He shook his head in disgust. "I've been indulging in nothing more than weak self-pity. That was foolish and wrong."

Rhee stood abruptly.

Kevin followed suit.

"If you'll allow it, I'll get cleaned up and join you for the rest of the day's schedule." Rhee suddenly bowed slightly to him. "I must apologize for my behavior today, Lieutenant. And I must thank you for your kindness."

Embarrassed now, Kevin awkwardly sketched a return bob of the head. "Ah hell, Rhee. No need for that."

He turned toward the door and then turned back with a sudden grin. "After all, I didn't want to get left facing Sergeant Pierce and Captain Matuchek on my own."

Slowly Rhee returned his smile. "I see. Well, that is understandable. They are indeed a formidable pair. But perhaps they will meet their match in us." He reached out and recapped the bottle of Soju.

The South Korean lieutenant was a soldier once again.

DECEMBER 13—THE WHITE HOUSE, WASHINGTON, D.C.

Blake Fowler slid General McLaren's telex across the desk to the President and sat back in his chair. He waited while the President skimmed through it.

"You're sure this general knows what he's talking about?"

Admiral Simpson answered, "I've known Jack for a long time, Mr. President. He's not a genius at spotting political trends, but he's a damned fine soldier. And if he says that South Korea's turning its army into mush, well, I believe him."

The President turned to Fowler. "What do you think, Blake?"

"I've got to concur with the general's assessment. The reports we've picked up show a complete government overreaction to this coup attempt. They've already arrested everyone fingered by some internal security chief who was in on it, and now it seems that they're hauling off any officer who's shown any signs of competence— just on general principles.

"The results out in the field aren't good. Morale in most units has hit rock bottom. There are even unconfirmed reports that some battalions have refused to obey orders from their new officers. The government's Special Forces are supposed to have come down very hard on them."

The President shook his head. "Why are they doing this? Hasn't the South Korean government got enough trouble in its streets without looking for even more by wrecking its armed forces?"

"That's just it, Mr. President. That's exactly why they've reacted so badly. The government has always counted on the military as its bulwark against the mobs. Now that's gone. I'd say that South Korea's leaders are feeling increasingly isolated and increasingly paranoid—with some justification, of course, because there are people out to get them."

Simpson nodded. "That's why I agree with General McLaren that we've got to find a way to calm the government over there down. Maybe it's time we sent someone over there to assure them that we're not pulling out anytime soon."

"Damn." The President picked up a letter from his desk and flipped it so that Blake and the admiral could see the congressional seal embossed at the top. "I got this from our fine friend, the Speaker, this morning." His tone made it clear that he considered the Speaker of the House anything but a friend.

"He writes that the congressional leadership is, quote, gravely concerned by the continuing turmoil in South Korea, unquote. He goes on to say that they're most concerned that American troops still in the country might get caught up in this 'cycle of violence.' And they're asking for an immediate troop pull-out, with every last American soldier to be out of South Korea by the end of January."

"That's impossible." Blake looked at the admiral for confirmation of what he'd said.

"Blake's right, Mr. President. Even if we hadn't been holding things up, there'd be no way to meet that kind of timetable. It'll take months alone just to ship our heavy equipment back across the Pacific.''

The President nodded. "They know that. The letter goes on to propose leaving the equipment there in storage until it can be moved. But they want our people out as fast as possible." He tossed the letter back onto his desk. "Naturally this 'private' letter has already been released to the press."

Goddamn all congressmen. Blake knew that the Speaker's letter had probably been dreamed up by some congressional staffer as the ideal way to exploit South Korea's troubles to get some TV time for the Speaker and his favorites. Congressmen were always looking for a way to stay in the public eye when the House and Senate weren't in session. All right, that was understandable. But their publicity stunt had just drastically narrowed the President's options.

Blake looked across the desk. "So I suppose we can't take the chance that our reassurances to the South Korean government might leak?"

The President nodded again. "Dead on, Dr. Fowler. If the leadership hears that I'm delaying the pull-out after they've publicly asked me to expedite it, they'll have no choice but to seek legislation setting an explicit timetable. And that's something we can't risk, true?"

"Yeah." There wasn't anything else Blake could say.

"Okay, then. We'll just have to hope that the government over there comes to its senses soon. Maybe the North Koreans will do us a favor and try some kind of commando raid—something that'd bring the military back into favor."

Admiral Simpson shrugged. "Anything's possible with those sons of bitches, Mr. President. I know Jack's got his boys on rotating alert just in case something like that happens."

"Good." The President rolled his chair back a few inches and opened a drawer. He pulled out a folder and laid it open on his desk. With a quick flourish he signed the bottom of one of the papers in the folder. "There. That's the one other thing I can do, gentlemen."

He smiled at their puzzled looks. "I've just taken one of your earlier suggestions, Phil." He handed the paper to the admiral. "That's an order putting MAC on standby alert. Ostensibly I'm doing this to boost our ability to evacuate speedily should the situation in South Korea deteriorate further. Ostensibly.'' He emphasized the last word.

Both Blake and the admiral knew what he meant. Putting the lumbering C-5 and C-141 troop transports of the Air Force's Military Airlift Command on alert would also increase their ability to reinforce South Korea during a crisis. It wasn't much, but it was probably the best they could hope for given the current political situation.

Blake just hoped they weren't sending the wrong signals overseas.

DECEMBER 14—PYONGYANG, NORTH KOREA

Lieutenant General Cho Hyun-Jae was puzzled.

At the last meeting between Kim Jong-Il and the forward army corps commanders in late November, intelligence reports had made it clear that the Americans weren't planning to pull their forces out of the South until at least the next spring. Given that, Kim had agreed that Red Phoenix should be postponed until the next year. As a result, orders had been issued to slow down the troop redeployments, munitions stockpiling, and training exercises associated with the plan. They would continue, but at a slower, more relaxed pace less likely to unnecessarily alert the South's puppet government.

Now, just two weeks later, came Kim Jong-Il's urgent middle-of-the-night summons to Pyongyang, compelling Cho to take a hair-raising, mountain-hopping flight north strapped into the back seat of a MiG-19UTI trainer.

He had been met at the Pyongyang East military airfield by a plainclothes security detail and driven through the capital's empty streets in a motorcycle-escorted black sedan. The quiet around him had made no impression on Cho. There were few vehicles, even in the daytime, for Pyongyang's broad four-lane boulevards.

But the car hadn't deposited him at Kim Jong-Il's offices at Party Headquarters as usual. Instead it had turned into the underground garage beneath the Presidential Palace—a building reserved largely for ceremonial purposes. Cho's disquiet had been increased by the sight of other parked staff cars in the garage, cars carrying the flags of almost every major military command in the Korean People's Army. He'd wondered what the devil was going on. Some briefing connected with the attempted coup in the South?

Now, looking around the huge, marble-walled room at the other grim-faced men seated nearby, Cho began to doubt that initial assessment. The room was filled with top-ranking officers from every service, and entire General Staff, the National Defense Commission, and even the drab-suited members of the Party's Central Committee and its Military Commission. It seemed unlikely that the nation's entire top-level political-military apparatus would have been assembled at such short notice for a simple briefing.

He caught the eye of his counterpart at the V Army Corps and raised an eyebrow in a silent question. The man shrugged back, his face carefully expressionless beneath the savage scar left by an American bomb four decades before.

Martial music suddenly sounded over hidden loudspeakers, pulling Cho's attention back to the small, raised dais flanked by giant-sized portraits of Kim Il-Sung and his son. The assembled officers and party leaders snapped to attention as the room's main doors opened and Kim Jong-Il strode in to stand near the platform. He inclined his head slightly to acknowledge the salute and stood stiffly waiting, his eyes fixed somewhere in the middle distance.

The blaring military march continued, and the Great Leader himself, Kim Il-Sung, came through the doors, moving slowly, haltingly. Cho stifled a gasp. The elder Kim had aged dramatically since his last appearance at the Party Congress. The news photos taken in recent months must have been retouched to conceal the new, deeply etched lines on the Leader's face, his thinning white hair, and dark, shadowed eyes. Kim moved cautiously down the center aisle, stopping briefly to clasp hands with some of the men in the room. Always the old men, Cho noted.

When he reached the platform, Kim Jong-Il stepped forward to help his father up the low stairs to the microphone, the perfect picture of a devoted son. The elder Kim motioned his generals and party colleagues to their seats before speaking.

"Comrades!" The Great Leader's voice was low, rasping as he read a prepared text without looking at his audience.

"Comrades! The forces of history have created an opportunity for greatness. An opportunity for liberation. An opportunity we cannot afford to lose."

Liberation? Cho glanced sharply at Kim Jong-Il. The man's cold eyes were shielded by his thick glasses, but the general could sense the younger Kim's smug sense of triumph.

"The corrupt puppet regime of the South is starting to crumble and its bandit military is crumbling with it. The people of the South are ready to rise against their oppressors. Accordingly, after careful consultation with the Military Commission of the Central Committee, I have decided to commit the armed might of the Democratic People's Republic to a renewed revolutionary struggle to liberate the southern half of our beloved fatherland."

Officers and party officials around the room stirred in their seats, thrown into consternation by the Great Leader's words.

"To assure the unity of purpose and direction required by this historic decision, I am appointing the beloved Dear Leader, Kim Jong-Il, as acting chairman of the Military Commission. His authority is my authority. His voice is my voice. . . ." The elder Kim's own voice trailed off into silence as he came to the end of his script. He stepped back from the microphones and glanced uncertainly at his son, who bowed and moved forward to take center stage.

"Comrades!" Kim Jong-Il's voice was vibrant, assured, full of confidence. "I assure you that our Great Leader's trust in me is not misplaced. Final victory is within our grasp. We have but to seize it."

The younger Kim stopped, letting the silence build tension. Then he broke it. "Military operations against the South will commence at oh two hundred hours on the twenty-fifth of December. The plan will be Red Phoenix."

The excitement Cho had felt as Kim Jong-Il spoke suddenly flowed down his throat into an icy-cold spot in the pit of his stomach. A hasty attack? Eleven days to complete the planning and preparation for an operation recently postponed for at least a year? He stared at the younger Kim in shock. It could not be done.

Kim's eyes met his briefly and roved on across the confounded leadership. "Comrades! Now is the time to strike hard and strike fast. Delay could be fatal. The puppet armies of the South are in disarray—torn by faction and mutiny. Their

American masters are abandoning them. Already America's air transports have been mobilized to speed their evacuation."

Kim paused again, his eyes bright behind his lenses. "Comrades! The South is ours for the taking!"

Or so it appeared, he cautioned himself.

At first, the opportunity provided by this renegade fascist general and his attempted coup had seemed almost too good to be true. He'd been prepared to ignore the opening, preferring to wait until the American evacuation was complete. But then, as intelligence report after intelligence report showed confusion and dismay spreading throughout the South's military, Kim Jong-Il had changed his mind. Such a chance might never come again in his lifetime. The enemy army would recover its morale in a few short months, and even without its American backers, it would remain a dangerous foe. Better to strike now, while the opening existed, than to wait for another chance that might never come.

Kim was all too aware that time was not on his side. His father was aging rapidly, and with each stage of the old man's decline, Kim Jong-Il stood more exposed to his political enemies. Every instinct in him screamed for immediate action. The military situation was as good as it would ever get. The South's puppet government was reeling, hammered hard by its supposed friends. And most importantly, his own survival might rest on a successful war that would bolster his authority as North Korea's absolute ruler. It was enough. He had always been something of a gambler.

He stepped forward to the very edge of the dais. "Comrades! We stand on the brink of reunification with our brothers in the South. One sturdy push will smash the armies of our enemies into fragments—impotent fragments incapable of stopping the forces of history. Our forces!"

Cho saw Kim's eyes swing back to settle on him. He felt the force of the man's personality, the power of his oratory, flowing across the room into his own body—reinfusing confidence where there had been doubt. Kim was right. The opening was there, waiting to be used. And they could be ready. Oh, it would be difficult. There could be no doubt of that. Schedules would have to be compressed, risks taken, perfection subordinated. But it could be done. Red Phoenix could be readied and launched by the twenty-fifth. Slowly Cho smiled—a smile he saw repeated on other faces across the room. It would be a fitting Christmas gift for the imperialists.

CHAPTER
19
The Dragon Stirs

DECEMBER 17—KIMPO INTERNATIONAL AIRPORT, SOUTH KOREA

"Mr. Sik?"

The North Korean commando major turned to face the security man. "Yes?"

"Your papers are in order." The South Korean held them out and gestured toward the baggage claim area. "Your luggage has also been cleared."

"Thank you." The major bowed, holding back a smile. Scorpion had been right. These fascists were so busy looking for traitors in their own military that their normal security measures had been relaxed. Now, with this last contingent flown in from Japan, his assault team was complete. And not one man had been picked up or even questioned by the authorities.

He moved past the checkpoint toward Baggage Claim through a crowd of Japanese businessmen. Not even a bloody coup attempt and continued riots could keep these capitalists away from their money-grubbing ways, he thought. Well, all that would soon change. Soon discipline, order, and unity would be restored to this weak-willed land. And they would be enforced by the North Korean Army.

The commando major picked up his bags and walked outside to call a cab. His men were assembling at a safehouse right in the heart of Seoul. And once there, they would wait for the orders that would unleash them. The major smiled openly now. He was ready.

DECEMBER 18—KYONGBOK PALACE, SEOUL

There was almost no wind, which was a relief for Tony. He had been standing outside the Kyonghoe-Ru for almost twenty minutes. It was cold, a few degrees below freezing, and a light snow had begun to fall. Of course, he had arrived early. As it was, the snow softened the cold and made it just crisp, instead of raw.

The Kyonghoe-Ru was a centuries-old meeting hall on the grounds of the Kyongbok Palace. Sitting in the middle of a now-frozen artificial lake, it was reached by one of three graceful stone bridges on the eastern shore.

Tony walked a beat up and down the eastern side of the building, both for warmth and to keep a lookout to the north and south. The lake lay to the west, so she would not come from that direction.

The building was two stories high, but the bottom floor was open, supporting the upper with forty-eight stone pillars. The building was covered with beautiful ornate carvings, and perched on the edges of the roof were *chapsang,* "ridge beasts," guardians too intent on their task to brush off the dusting of snow.

The snow continued to fall gently, muffling traffic noises. It also hid objects in the distances, softening outlines and washing out colors. The few people visiting the palace today were indistinct forms, moving quickly from one building to another.

He saw her coming down the mall from the east. Her red hair was a spot of color in the snow. She wore a long green coat and brown leather boots, both trimmed with fur. Moving quickly, she seemed sure of her destination.

Tony stood by the shelter of the hall until she was closer, then walked toward the center span of the bridge and waved.

Anne waved back, smiling, and ran to the east end of the center bridge. Suddenly she stopped, looked left and right, considering. She walked over to the end of the left-hand bridge, and Tony followed, waiting by the western end. She waited until he had stopped, waiting for her, then ran to the far span on the right.

Tony looked at her, shook his head, and trudged somewhat theatrically to a point opposite her. He stood there, arms crossed, waiting for her next move, and she walked over as if nothing had happened.

When she reached his side, he took her hand and they walked silently under the sheltering overhang of the roof. Her shoulders were sprinkled with snowflakes, and ones that had landed on her hair had melted to small, clear drops of water. They hugged, and she allowed him to kiss her once.

She looked at his leather flight jacket and gloves. "Aren't you cold?" Frowning, she reached out and held a hand over his bright-red ear. "It's like ice."

As she looked him over, she spotted a package he was trying to conceal. It was gift-wrapped, and as soon as he realized his efforts were in vain, he handed it to her.

"I'm sorry, I didn't get yours yet. I won't have it until our date on Christmas Eve." She looked at it and then at Tony. "Can I open it now?"

"Yes. Go ahead. It's very appropriate."

He leaned against a pillar and watched as she tore open the package and opened the box. Inside was a scarf covered with green and silver dragons.

"Tony, it's beautiful!" She ran up and hugged him, then shook her hair to get most of the water droplets off. She tied the scarf over her head and announced, "Now I'm ready for the weather! Thank you, Tony."

"Well, it wasn't much." He'd only spent his last day off canvassing Kunsan from one end to the other, but he wasn't going to tell her that.

"I hope you like mine as much as I like this." She was running her hands over the soft fabric. "I haven't known you long enough to know what you like."

"Don't worry, Anne, there will be other Christmas presents."

"Yes, there will."

He took her hand and they started on their way.

DECEMBER 24—THE LIBERATION TUNNEL, NEAR THE DMZ, NORTH KOREA

The blacked-out train groaned to a slow, shuddering stop inside the tunnel entrance. Dim lights came on as a massive blast door slid across the tracks—sealing it away from the outside air.

The train had come down from the north, moving slowly under a rising moon. Never hurrying. Never racing around curves, through villages, or across mountain bridges. Doing nothing that would call attention to itself or to its cargo. At last it had come gliding down from the hills into this huge, steel- and concrete-faced cavern.

The blast door locked in place across the tunnel mouth and bright arc lights flared to illuminate the cavern. Shrill whistles blew, and uniformed men moved under shouted orders to unload the train's hidden cargo. Some worked in teams to yank aside heavy tarpaulins concealing squat T-55 and T-62 tanks loaded on flatcars. Others slammed boxcar doors open to get at the artillery shells, mortar bombs, and small arms ammunition stacked inside.

No delay could be tolerated. There were deadlines to be met, schedules to be kept. This last train had to be back on its normal route long before the next imperialist spy satellite swung high overhead to spy on the fatherland.

Other soldiers carrying AKM assault rifles, RPK light machine guns, and full combat packs poured out of the passenger cars just behind the engine. They wore the shoulder flashes of the 4th Guards Division. Some carried bulky, Soviet-made SA-7 SAM launchers slung across their backs. Every man's pockets and pack bulged with extra ammo clips, rations, and grenades. As they jumped down out of the cars, officers formed them into ranks and led them away down a long, darkened corridor stretching south.

Heading into the darkness beyond the train, the marching men tramped past row after row of camouflaged tanks, M-1974 self-propelled guns, and tracked BMP and wheeled BTR-60 troop carriers parked in the main corridor and in large galleries off to both sides. Small groups of leather-helmeted tank crewmen and steel-helmeted infantrymen were clustered around officers giving final briefings and exhortations. A heavy, almost intoxicating, mix of diesel fumes and engine exhaust hung in the air, stirred only faintly by ventilating fans spaced at fifty-meter intervals along the high, arching roof.

The main corridor stretched for more than three kilometers, cut straight through the east-west ridge marking North Korea's side of the Demilitarized Zone. It came to an abrupt end at another massive blast door, and the column turned left into a side passage leading to another, much narrower tunnel continuing south—under the DMZ.

This tunnel sloped downward and it grew darker with each step forward. Their officers now led with flashlights to show the way. The air grew thicker, and the noise behind them fell away—sinking to a dull, murmuring mix of voices, clanking tank treads, and idling engines. The men in front could see lights bobbing up and down ahead down the corridor. Officers went down the column whispering harsh warnings about the need for silence.

Finally the column halted at the foot of a long, gently sloping ramp leading up—up toward the surface. Up toward the enemy. Sweating combat engineers were manhandling jury-rigged blast doors into place, and far ahead, at the very end of the tunnel, the assault troops could see other engineers moving with careful precision to place explosive charges against the roof.

It was nearly time.

Time for war.

C H A P T E R
20
Decapitation

PFC Williams was bored. Bored and cold and dead-tired. He yawned, his breath visible in the chilly night air, and tried to shift the M16 slung over his shoulder into a more comfortable position. The rifle wasn't that heavy, but after several hours of walking a sentry beat it was starting to dig into his back whenever he turned to make another circuit of his post.

The private stopped at the edge of the brick wall and stared out toward the Itaewon district just beyond the compound. He could almost hear snatches of off-key Christmas carols mixed with off-color rock-and-roll favorites drifting out of the bars. Of all the rotten luck. Pulling guard duty on Christmas Eve. And right when HQ had finally lifted its restrictions on GIs going off-post.

He shifted his rifle again. Boy, this was really stupid. Walking a beat like this didn't make sense. Not anymore. Not with all this high-tech stuff the Army could lay its hands on. Why didn't they just rig a few low-light TV cameras to cover the perimeter and let somebody sit somewhere nice and warm to watch them?

He came to the end of another circuit and started back the other way, cursing softly under his breath and leaving a fine mist floating in the air behind him. He wanted to go someplace and get warm, but with his luck that'd be the one time the sarge checked up on him. And then he'd wind up pulling guard duty on New Year's Eve, too. Instead, Williams decided that he definitely, definitely wasn't going to reenlist. He'd put in the rest of his time in this man's Army and then he'd head back home—back to Seattle. He started imagining what he'd do first in civilian life. First, sleep for a week. No interruptions. No reveille. Nothing. Then he'd find a girl and . . .

Williams never heard the soft, warning scrape on the wall behind him. The last things he felt were strong arms pulling him backward, and then something terribly cold and sharp sawing at his throat.

The North Korean commando major lowered the American's body to the ground, knelt beside it, and wiped the man's blood off on his dead back. He snapped his fingers twice, signaling the rest of his men forward over the wall. They made it without raising any alarm and dropped softly one by one beside him, fanning out in a half-circle while unslinging their submachine guns.

The major smiled to himself. This was going to be even easier than it had been in rehearsal. The mission planners had been right. The Americans were fast asleep, caught napping because they'd chosen to celebrate this bourgeois holiday.

His sergeant crouched next to him and held out a clenched fist. The team was in. They'd cut right through perimeter security without any problem. Now they had to find their targets and strike fast and strike hard.

The North Korean scanned the mostly darkened compound around him, trying to compare it with the maps and photos he'd studied back at Special Forces HQ in Kaesong. Ah, there it was. He pointed the house out to his sergeant, who nodded. The major smiled again in anticipation. In the next five minutes they were going to win a war that hadn't even started yet. And they were going to do it with a few carefully placed knife thrusts and gunshots. The liquidation of the American butcher McLaren and his senior command staff would plunge the imperialist forces into confusion— confusion that would aid the first waves of the Great Fatherland Liberation Force now sweeping forward to the attack.

He rose to his feet and gestured his men forward toward the darkened house on a low hill. They stood, reslung their weapons, and followed him at a trot. Each man carried a razor-edged commando knife ready for instant use. This was to be a silent killing—silent at any rate until the first Americans managed to raise an alarm.

DECEMBER 25—COMBINED FORCES COMMANDER'S QUARTERS

McLaren paused by the window in his darkened study. He drew on his cigar, brightening the slow-burning tip momentarily, and looked out across the base without seeing much of anything. For once he was content just to stand still, to relax, to savor the slightly acrid taste of the cigar. Better make this one last, Jack boy, he told himself. This is it for another year.

The doctors had warned him to cut down. Cancer. Emphysema. None of those words had held much fear for McLaren—not after the corpse-strewn battlefields he'd seen in Vietnam. And cancer, well, cancer had taken his wife from him, and she'd never smoked a day in her life. But he'd followed their advice; pressure from his daughter had seen to that. Over the years he'd worked himself down to this one cigar, a cigar he reserved as a sort of Christmas present to all his old vices.

He sucked in reflectively, held the smoke for a moment, and blew it out, forming a perfect circle. It floated up past the window and McLaren's eyes followed it. He used to keep his children quiet for an hour or more just watching him do that. The thought saddened him. It had been a long time since they'd had the whole family together. Not since Elly's funeral in fact. He pushed the memory away.

He had hoped to see his daughter for the holidays this year, but the events of the last few weeks had persuaded him to have her cancel the trip out from Washington.

McLaren drew on the cigar again and blew another smoke ring. But this time his eyes followed it only halfway up the window. He froze. There were men moving out there—black-clad men slipping from building to building, working their way in from the perimeter. They were coming toward him.

His mind came awake. He'd seen men moving like that before. Sliding from shadow to shadow with speed and in silence. Cong assault teams crossing the fields outside his battalion's firebase to wreak havoc on the sleeping Americans. Rangers and LRRPs crawling through the jungle to repay the favor. SAS men putting on a counterterrorism demonstration. Only this wasn't Vietnam and it wasn't a demonstration. He came out of his trance. Don't just sit there, dumbshit, move! He grabbed for the desk phone and stubbed his cigar out.

"Sir?" The operator's voice was drowsy.

"Security." McLaren lifted the phone off the desk and crouched down. No point in making himself a bigger target than necessary. He wished that he'd thought to keep a personal weapon in this room instead of upstairs in his bedroom.

He heard the phone ringing in the base security office. Once. Twice. Three times. Answer the phone, goddamnit.

"Security. Captain Miller." The man sounded out of breath and more than a little irate.

"McLaren here." He could almost hear the man coming to attention. "I want a full alert. Now. Total illumination of the compound. This is not a drill, Captain. We've got intruders on base and you can assume I'm a priority target."

He could hear Miller starting to gobble something at him, but he cut him off. "I don't have time to chat, Captain. I've got a situation here. Carry out your goddamned orders!"

He could see a small group of men gathering across the way. They were now less than fifty yards from his quarters. They'd surround the house of course, and trying to make a break for it would be suicidal. McLaren had no doubt that these guys would be the first team. He could surprise one or two of them, maybe, but his only hope would be a quick response by the security team he'd formed two years ago to deal with just this kind of attack.

McLaren's mind was racing. There'd be no way his men could possibly respond to the alert in anything less than a minute or two. Plenty of time for the NKs or whoever it was outside to make an initial attack. He had to find a place to hide. Someplace that would give him an edge in this first combat. Jesus, ain't this the way of the world. Make it to army commander and find yourself scrabbling around in the dark worrying about men with knives.

McLaren left the phone lying off the hook on the floor and scuttled out of the room toward the stairs leading up to his bedroom. He took them two at a time, trying hard to make as little noise as possible. At the top of the landing he dropped to his stomach again and reached up to turn the doorknob, pulled the bedroom door open just wide enough to slide through, and then pulled it closed again. Staying well out of the line of sight from the window, he crawled over to the plain old army footlocker he kept beneath his bed.

Time. Damn it, he needed more time. Those bastards outside were almost certainly on the way. Where the hell were Miller and his security team?

McLaren fumbled for a second with the catch but then got it open. He felt around inside the locker, ignoring the pistol and the M16. This was going to be close-in fighting. Down-and-dirty stuff. His hands found a familiar shape—a Mossberg 500 shotgun—and slid it carefully out of the retaining straps. It was already loaded. Strictly against regulations of course, and against every principle of weapons safety. But McLaren had always thought that if he needed this thing, he'd need it damned quick, with no time to waste. He grimaced. Well, by God, he'd been right about that.

Maybe a minute had gone by now. No time to waste. McLaren got carefully to his feet and slid around the room, staying out of the half-light pouring in through the window. He found the right ceiling panel, climbed onto a chair, levered it aside, and pulled himself up and through into a small windowless attic. He rolled away from the opening and lay still for a moment, trying not to pant for air. Jesus Christ, he thought, I'm getting too old for this shit.

The sirens going off outside made him jump. McLaren rose to a half-crouch and cradled the shotgun. Captain Miller had finally managed to get the alarm out. Well, good. The combination of bright arc lights flaring all over the base and ear-splitting sirens screaming would almost certainly throw the NKs into some confusion. Trouble was, they'd also redouble their efforts to get him before someone else got them. And they wouldn't waste time in being fancy about it.

He was right. McLaren heard the glass in his bedroom window shatter and saw a small round object sail in to land squarely on his bed. He threw himself flat away from the opening as the grenade went off with a thunderous *WHUMP.*

The shock wave bounced him an inch or so off the attic floor and then back down. Smoke and dust swirled in the air.

He pulled himself across to look down into his bedroom just as a North Korean commando rolled in from the doorway and opened up with his submachine gun, shredding the tattered, burning fragments of bedding with a hail of soft-nosed bullets. When the man stopped firing and started forward to check his target, McLaren braced the shotgun, aimed, and pulled the trigger. The blast threw the North Korean back in a welter of blood and killed him instantly.

McLaren rolled hastily away from the hole as bullets fired blindly from below tore through in a cloud of splinters. Shit, there were others down there. He lay flat against one side of the attic and kept his shotgun trained on the opening. He'd send the first NK through to hell. They'd have a hard time getting at him. Unless . . .

McLaren didn't waste time completing the thought. The grenade bounced in and rolled toward him just as he twisted round to get his feet in front of him. He kicked out desperately and connected, sending the grenade skittering away back down through the open ceiling panel. He heard screams as it went off and hunched himself back even farther into the narrow gap between the roof and the attic floor.

He could hear firing off in the distance.

DECEMBER 25—YONGSAN ARMY BASE, SEOUL

The North Korean major crouched behind a parked Hyundai and feverishly snapped a new magazine into his submachine gun. Bullets spanged off the metal chassis and whined away into the air. He finished reloading, looked over at the man next to him, and jerked his head toward the direction of the fire. They both jumped to their feet and sent precise three-round bursts crashing in through the windows of the barracks just ten yards away. Broken glass cascaded out onto the snow-covered lawn.

Moans coming from a tangle of half-dressed bodies sprawled in an open doorway attracted the major's attention, and he fired another burst into them. The moans stopped.

He heard a muffled explosion from behind him and smiled

exultantly. That would be his assault team finishing off the American general. Someone had raised the alarm, but it hadn't mattered at all. If anything, it was making their job even easier. All over the compound, half-drunk and half-asleep Americans had rushed out to see what was happening, and they'd walked right into the deadly crossfires laid down by his men.

The major pulled another magazine out of his belt and wished they'd been able to carry more. He wanted to kill more Americans. This was like slaughtering sheep.

Suddenly the man crouching next to him grunted and fell over onto him as bullets scythed along the side of the car. Shit. The major rolled out from under the body and lay sighting back the way the bullets had come. He could see helmeted troops advancing up the street, ducking from car to parked car as they moved toward him. Americans who'd broken past his flank guards.

The major edged away from them around the rear bumper of the car he'd been using for cover. He popped up and fired a quick burst before dropping back down. The Americans flopped to the ground, pinned down by his fire. He grinned. Now for a quick dash away from the car and into the darkness. This was the kind of cat-and-mouse fighting he'd trained for. The imperialists wouldn't even know what had hit them. He got to his feet to run.

Corporal Hughes saw the movement up ahead and lifted the cardboard-tubed LAW he carried to his shoulder. He squeezed the trigger and closed his eyes against the backblast.

Some instinct made the North Korean commando leader turn his head to look just as the 66-millimeter light antitank rocket slammed into the passenger side of the Hyundai and exploded. Flame sheeted over him, but fast-moving steel and fiberglass fragments killed him before he had the chance to scream.

The Americans clambered to their feet and continued to advance, ignoring the smoking corpse that had been tossed out into the middle of the road.

DECEMBER 25—COMBINED FORCES COMMANDER'S QUARTERS

He had dust in his eyes and throat now.

McLaren didn't know how much time had passed since the

last grenade had gone off. But it didn't matter. All that did matter was that they hadn't tried anything for a while and it was making him nervous.

The alert sirens had stopped, and he could hear more firing off in the distance. Then a series of muffled, coughing explosions. Some of it seemed to be moving closer. He stayed silent and kept his eyes on the opening.

More gunfire from below. Heavier sounding than the SMG fire that had ripped up the attic floor and shredded his bed.

He heard feet clattering up the stairs.

"General?" An American-sounding voice. But was it a trick to get him to reveal his position? He brought the shotgun up again.

"General, this is Sergeant Corey. The house is secure, sir. Mackerel Six."

McLaren started to relax. Corey was one of his security team people and he'd used the right codeword. "Coming down, Sergeant. Shark Seven."

He crawled over and swung himself out and down through the open ceiling panel. Corey and two of his troopers were there in full gear, weapons out, and their faces were drawn and tight. One of them was shaking almost uncontrollably. McLaren ignored that. He looked around the room. The acrid smell of burning cloth and charred flesh was stronger, and he could see blood spattered across the walls. Two dead Koreans in black camouflage gear lay crumpled on the floor—one near the door where McLaren's shotgun blast had thrown him and the other half-entangled in the burning bed, killed by his own grenade.

He swung back to face the sergeant. "What's the situation?"

Corey's eyes came back into focus. "We think we've got most of them, sir. There's three more dead downstairs where we got 'em as we came in. Others outside." He stopped, seemed at a loss for words.

"Go on, Sergeant." McLaren kept his voice as gentle as he could. Corey had never been in combat before.

"I've lost a lot of my boys, General. Captain Miller's dead. Took a round in the head as we set off. I lost more out there. Kip. Mike Andrews. A lot." McLaren could see the tears in his eyes.

He reached out and put a hand on Corey's shoulder. "You

did real well, Sergeant. I want you to know that." He looked around the shattered room. "Now let's get the fuck out of here over to the Ops Room. This ain't the end of it. Not by a long shot."

The arc-lit compound outside looked as though it had gone through a full-scale pitched battle. McLaren could see bodies dotting the snow-covered walkways and parade grounds. Some were surrounded by clusters of medics and stretcher bearers, but others, too many others, were simply being covered with white sheets. He shook his head wearily. They'd been caught flat-footed and a lot of his men had already paid for it. Smoke from a burning building somewhere off out of sight drifted south, pushed by the north wind.

The Operations Room was in complete chaos when McLaren came in through the door. Half-dressed staff officers crowded the room, each trying to do two or three things at once. Some were slapping situation maps up on the walls and ripping them down almost as fast. Others were standing around in small groups, demanding in loud, high-pitched voices to know just what the hell was going on. He scowled. These idiots were going to have to learn how to act calmly during a crisis. He looked around for his aide and found him standing in one corner working to sort things out.

Hansen put down the phone he'd been holding. "Glad to see you're all right, General."

"Yeah. Me, too." He could feel himself starting to shake. Always happened after a fight. "Did they hit anything else?"

Hansen nodded. "Just got the word. They got into the Signals Room before the alarm went out. Killed everyone in there with knives or their bare hands. And then they blew the shit out of our commo gear. Major Gunderson said to tell you that they're routing our traffic through the Navy until we can get spares set up out of storage."

"That it?"

"No way, General." Hansen pointed to another map just going up. It was a map of Seoul dotted with hastily drawn red circles. "Each one of those dots represents a reported terrorist or commando attack. All carried out in the last half hour."

"Jesus." McLaren whistled softly. He stepped forward to get a better look. "Give me the details."

Hansen flipped through his scribbled notes. "Okay. First, an attack on our embassy." He looked somber. "They broke past the marine guards and killed the ambassador, his family, and a lot of the senior staff. There's still fighting going on, but it's just a mop-up operation now."

McLaren could feel himself growing cold as Hansen's recitation continued. A raid on the South Korean Ministry of Defense. The main Seoul telephone exchange blown up. Senior government officials murdered in their own homes, including a South Korean corps commander and several Air Force generals. Only one conclusion fit the pattern he could see developing.

He broke away from Hansen and plunged into the middle of the Ops Room, looking for Gunderson, his duty signals officer. "Sam! Drop whatever the hell you're doing and send an alert signal to all commands!"

The tall, thin Tennessean looked up from an equipment inventory list. "Sir?"

"You heard me, Major. Get off your ass and—" McLaren was interrupted by a huge, rattling explosion that shook the room. Some of his officers dived under their desks, but others followed him in a rush to the window. There, off to the west, an orange fireball several hundred feet high roared into the night sky.

Then, suddenly, the lights all across the compound winked out, leaving everything in darkness. And McLaren could see the lights going out all across Seoul. A power loss or a government-ordered blackout? They could now hear the air raid sirens wailing.

McLaren nodded and turned to an open-mouthed Major Gunderson. "Clear enough for you? Get the word out to all commands and then to Washington. Tell them we're at war. If they don't already know it by now. And then get to the goddamned shelters."

McLaren pulled Hansen out of the tangle of officers heading for cover. "Doug, get the word out for me. I want the field headquarters activated and my chopper ready to go. I'll be damned if we're all going to get stuck here while there's a war on."

Hansen nodded and turned away, but McLaren stopped him again. "Oh, Doug? One more thing."

"Yes, General?"

"Merry Christmas." They ducked as a string of explosions rattled across the compound.

CHAPTER
21
Wave One

DECEMBER 25—OVER THE YELLOW SEA

Chun Pak-Lee was tired. It had been a long flight, and he was overdue at the navigation ship. He had increased speed, but with this plane that didn't mean much.

The plane in question was an An-2. NATO had assigned it the name "Colt," but it should have been "Barrel." It was a biplane, an honest-to-God biplane, and if Lee didn't think that was unusual in an age of jet fighters, it was only because of his exhaustive training. He knew what the craft could do, and it was perfect for this mission.

The Colt has excellent low-altitude and low-speed characteristics, can carry a large load, and is cheap and simple to operate. It was designed in Russia, but the Democratic People's Republic of Korea had received many of them. One of its strengths, though, was not speed. Its frame and fuselage were steel, but its wings were covered with fabric.

He *had* to make up the loss. Timing was everything. His comrades were depending on him to place them at the right time and the right spot with an accuracy measured in seconds.

The water flowed by him, less than a hundred feet away. He had to stay low to avoid visual and radar detection. It was a clear night but there was little moon, and he saw the water more as a dark mass than moonlit waves. The air was bumpy, especially this close to the surface, and the strain of holding such a low altitude for over two hours was tremendous.

There it was! A light on the horizon. He made a minor course correction, then pressed a button that made a directional light flash forward under the fuselage. It was answered. Good. It was his boat.

The light on the horizon was a North Korean fishing boat, loaded with navigational gear. It was much too sophisticated for normal use, but it would provide the landmark he needed. For precise timing he needed precise positions, and the biplane's navigational gear wasn't up to it.

He marked his time overhead and made a rapid mental calculation. As Lee adjusted his speed, he waggled his wings to his comrades below, and turned to his final heading.

All right. Nine minutes to the objective. He called back to the rest of the troops, then started his final procedures. He put the few maps and documents he had in a weighted pouch and tossed them out the window. He checked his own assault rifle and grenades, then tightened his harness.

The coast was exactly as he expected it to be. He'd seen enough pictures and maps to know every point and light on it. He lowered his altitude even more, until he was skimming the wavetops. He called back, "Five minutes!"

As he crossed the coast, Lee started his approach list. Climb to thirty meters. Cut engine, open fuselage fuel dump valves. That would lessen the risk of fire. The sudden silence was almost restful after the hours of noise. It would be a short rest.

Tony heard someone screaming. He rolled over and considered the issue. The party was getting loud, but nobody should scream like that. But he wasn't at the party. He was asleep. Someone was screaming in his room. He opened his eyes. Nobody was in his room, so the screaming was outside. It wasn't screaming. It was the alert siren. If this was someone's idea of a joke . . .

The phone rang once and he grabbed it. "Captain Christopher here."

"Sir, this is Luther at ops. We have a general recall. This is not a drill."

"It fucking well better not be, on Christmas Eve." Then Tony realized what that meant.

He jumped into a set of coveralls and pulled on his boots in seconds. The sirens had not stopped, and they lent even more urgency to his movements. As Tony ran to the door, there was a mild vibration, followed by the sound of an explosion. And another. Then a chain of rumbling.

Hooter lived two doors down. He and Tony shot out of their rooms almost simultaneously, along with most of the other residents. Most were pilots or wing staff, pulling on whatever clothing was at hand. Nobody stopped to see if their doors were locked behind them. Tony had not stopped moving and was in the corridor heading toward the stairs. Only an idiot would take the elevator, and besides, the stairs were faster.

Running down the stairs was not the best therapy for his head. Most of the fuzziness was masked by the adrenaline, but he'd partied hard and gone to sleep at one. He didn't feel his best.

"Saint!" came echoing down the stairwell, and he recognized Hooter's voice.

Tony called up, "Meet you outside."

Pilots spilled out of the exits and jumped into cars and jeeps. An explosion rocked the BOQ as he ran out the front door. Sure as shit ain't no drill, Tony thought. It came from over by the ROK Air Force compound, maybe the tower. It was followed by a rapid sequence as a stick of bombs landed. Suddenly the stick was multiplied by fifty—more bomb explosions, and the base's SAM defenses started launching, leaving bright lines across the horizon. Tony looked up and saw arrowhead forms, lit at the rear by the flames from their afterburners. They were followed by tracers from Vulcan cannon near the base. They added a sound like ripping metal to the jet engines' roar.

Men were pouring out the door. Tony spotted one other man from his flight and called to him. "Boomer! Come in my car." Hooter came running up, and as the three got in, other pilots piled in until there was one lying across the three in back.

Dangerously overloaded, Tony beeped the horn twice and slammed the car into reverse. He screamed out of the lot and suddenly realized there were absolutely no lights on anywhere in the base. Headlights filled the road, but there was no other illumination. The idea of being the only visible lights on a base under attack appalled him, but he saw no alternative.

He drove down the main road, heading for the squadron building. The Korean Air Force compound was on his right, with the ocean beyond. Streaks and tracers from both sides of the road pointed to the positions, or imagined positions, of enemy aircraft. Jets were coming in low, some on burner, but even the ones without burner had hot, bright exhausts. They were firing cannon, dropping flares to confuse infrared SAMs, and launching missiles.

They bumped over an inactive runway and passed the wing's dispersal area. The arches blocked a lot of the view, but there were fires, and two columns of smoke, lit by sparks and red glows. Lights and vehicles moved about, seemingly at random.

They turned right into the squadron building's parking lot. As Tony braked and pulled up, Creature came running up waving a flashlight. "Everybody to the squadron theater! Shadow's running a mass brief in two minutes."

They went into the ops building and saw a beehive of activity. Every one of the squadron's personnel was bent on some urgent task. Some were in civilian clothes. Tony's eyes were drawn to Airman Vance by a white bandage on his lower arm. He wondered if anybody else had been hit.

The theater was a smallish auditorium with an elevated stage. Lieutenant Colonel Robbins, "Shadow," was the squadron's commanding officer. He was stocky with sandy hair. Standing quietly, he held a clipboard and looked at his watch periodically. On the minute he waved his arm once and the conversation in the room stopped instantly.

"Everybody listen carefully. I've only got time to say this once. North Korea is making a general attack, all over the DMZ. The base has been hit once, by how many aircraft I don't know, and one commando attack. We think all the commandos are dead, but we lost two arches and three aircraft are out. The Thirty-fifth is going to total base defense until we know the situation. Flight leaders will take charge and stack at five-thousand-foot increments, starting at ten thousand feet. We're surging everyone.

"All birds have cannon and at least two nine limas. Some

may have more. Watch takeoff. We've got wreckage one-third
of the way down, a Colt biplane that the commandos landed in.
We're all lightly loaded so it shouldn't be a problem. Use
combat takeoffs. Don't go below five thousand without clearance, the SAM crews are authorized to—''

BRAAANG filled the room as the klaxon went off. The
pilots scrambled out the door with Robbins shouting behind
them, ''Watch out for friendlies! The ROKs are up, too!''

Tony and John headed for the alert shack. Pilots were
running in, then back out with their flight gear. It had taken a
few cannon hits, judging by the cratered wall and shattered
window. ''Boomer,'' Lieutenant Carlson, was still with them,
but there was no sign of his element leader, Captain Owens. He
decided to fly as a three-ship rather than waste time finding
him. They fumbled with their lockers and pulled on their
g-suits and vests. Except for their helmets, they let the rest of
the stuff lay.

The three pilots ran out the door toward the shelters,
intending to take the first armed and fueled aircraft they came
to. Luckily things were more organized than that.

Kenneth Beam, the ops officer, ran up. ''Saint, you've got
five seven nine, Hooter take four nine two, Boomer has four
nine four. They're in F, I, and J. They've got full fuel and gun
ammo, and two nine-limas each. Where's Viceroy?''

Tony shrugged. ''I don't know. Is he in the building?''

''I haven't seen him. I'll send him up to you when he
arrives. You guys are Showtime flight. Pancake will give you
vectors on button two. Go!''

Most of the shooting had stopped by this time. The initial
raid had tried to suppress the base defenses and the command
and control net—radars, radios, and the control tower. Some
attention had been paid to the flight line. The North Koreans
had used MiG-23s for the first wave—fast, but carrying a
relatively light load. They all knew the main raid was only a
few minutes away.

As Tony and Hooter ran past shelter D, they saw it
collapsed on top of its F-16. There was a form lying on the
concrete, covered by a jacket. Hooter looked over at Tony,
looking grim. ''We're gonna kick butts, Saint.''

Tony tried to cool him off. ''Just stay loose, John. It's

gonna be a long war." They were all making their first combat flight. He had hoped for a calmer start.

Tony stopped and looked over at Bob Carlson. "Boomer" was a relatively low-time pilot, and Tony was worried about how to fit him into a practiced fighting pair. Finally he decided on simplicity. "Boomer, stay on my left and back a bit more than normal. If things get too hot, fall into trail. Keep a lookout to port. Hooter will cover your six. Let's do it."

They split and went to their shelters. The crew chief for 579 looked incongruous in civilian clothes and flight safety gear. Tony sprinted up. "Anything I should know about?" he asked.

Sergeant Kawamoto was confident. "No sir, it's a good bird. I've preflighted it."

"Great." Tony started up the ladder and bounced into the cockpit. He hit the starter and got the INS spinning up.

As soon as he connected his helmet radio leads, the speakers were filled with chatter. Everybody wanted to say something immediately. And this was only the ground frequency!

He finished a highly abbreviated checklist and waited for a break in the chatter. "Flight one, go, out." Releasing the brakes, he moved the throttle forward.

Hooter's nose was already halfway out of the arch, and Tony rolled out onto the taxiway with his wingman in trail. Tony craned back over his shoulder looking for Boomer, and finally he saw him shoot out of his shelter and quickly taxi up. He fell in line behind them. They could hear jet engines everywhere, and there were almost continuous roars from the direction of the runway.

Tony switched to the tower frequency. It wasn't nearly as crowded. Must be a good man on the net. He waited a moment, then called in. "Tower, this is Showtime with three Falcons."

"Roger, Showtime, the runway has been cleared for all outbound Falcons. You are number one for takeoff."

As they reached the end of the taxiway and turned the corner, they saw a glowing pile a few hundred feet in front of them. It looked like the skeleton of a biplane, crumpled and sagging from the heat. They continued rolling up the runway, and as they got closer, they could see bodies, some half-charred, off to the side of the runway. Tony said, "Wait a minute," and braked.

It looked a little tight. Just as he was going to inch closer, an airman with a flashlight ran up from the side and waved him forward. He pointed the light over to the side, and Tony could see where they had added some metal matting to one side of the pavement.

They taxied over the matting gingerly and lined up for takeoff. Tony called the other two ships. "Combat departure. Go."

They were lightly loaded, thank God. Even with afterburner they were barely past takeoff speed when they hit the end of the runway. The combat turn was a little shallower than usual, but they made it.

As they climbed, he looked at the sky. He hadn't stopped for a weather report. There were scattered clouds at high altitude, maybe thirty thousand feet. No problem for his flight, but he hoped there weren't any surprises in the forecast.

He led first flight, so they would orbit at ten thousand feet. Second flight would be at fifteen thousand, and so on. Tony felt almost honored. Any bandits would probably come in at low altitude, so he was closest to them and might be the only one able to hit the gomers before they made their attack. Of course they were also the closest to all those SAMs and Vulcans. Something to remember if they got in a scrap. That thought made him pause. "Showtime flight, verify IFF is on, out." He looked over and saw both planes waggle their wings in answer.

IFF stood for "Identification, Friend or Foe." The electronic box sent out a coded pulse that told friendly radar screens that they were friendly aircraft. If they were shot down by their own side, it wouldn't be his fault.

They reached ten thousand and leveled off, throttling back until the engines were almost idling. Since they didn't have to go anywhere, the idea was to minimize fuel used and maximize time aloft. He started a long, slow turn, looking alternately at the horizon and his radar screen. His abbreviated formation maintained position behind him.

As they started their third circle, Tony and the rest of his flight heard their call sign. "Showtime, this is Pancake. Steer two nine five." Tony immediately turned to the new course, increasing his throttle to cruise speed. Pancake hadn't said why they should head west, but there was only one reason to do so: bandits.

"Pancake" was the ground-based fighter control station. The staff analyzed the radar picture and tried to predict where the inbound aircraft were going to attack. It was not a simple task. Not only did mountain valleys block many radar beams, but the enemy used jamming and feints to confuse the issue.

Pancake probably had enough info to want the Showtimers moving west, but nothing hard, Tony thought to himself. He tried to imagine John's mood right now. He had always been tight with the enlisted crews. Hooter was solid, though.

Boomer was aggressive enough, but he didn't have a lot of experience in night air combat. With only the radar and occasional silhouettes of an opponent, dogfighting became much more difficult. It was best to make a fast, slashing attack, then get out of Dodge before someone got in a lucky shot.

"Penguin, Cadillac, Universe, Showtime, Castle, this is Pancake. Multiple bogies at five thousand to ten thousand feet, raid count thirty, speed four hundred at fifty miles. Steer two eight seven, buster."

Jesus, Tony thought, they're really calling in the clans! Thirty aircraft, probably one-quarter are escorts. We've got about fifteen.

Buster meant full throttle, but not afterburner. He increased speed, the pressure at his back almost reassuring. Suddenly his radar scope was filled with contacts. The computer sorted them out and locked onto the nearest plane. Forty miles out, closure rate of 900 knots. "Pancake, Showtime has lock."

"Roger, Saint. Cleared to engage. Get some."

A diamond symbol on his HUD told him where to look for the target. It was about two thousand feet lower than he was, which put it below the horizon and hard to spot. They were approaching from the target's front, a little to the right. There were three other aircraft close by, probably a flight of four like his own should be. "Hooter, take the right man, Boomer, the left. Clear to fire nine limas at max."

Automatically Showtime flight spread out into line abreast. They would fire Sidewinder missiles at maximum range, almost ten miles. "It isn't the best angle," he thought. "Better would be dead aft, but it's in the envelope. Twenty miles out."

He spared a glance at his wingmen, then at the horizon. They were just visible in the dark, still in position. No other aircraft could be seen. Dawn was still five hours away.

Tony got a growl at fifteen miles. The seeker "saw" the target, even though the missile's motor couldn't carry it that far. He held it for a few seconds as they closed the gap. With the seeker's signal still filling his earphones, he heard a *BEEP-BEEP-BEEP.*

"Shit!" He pressed the shoot button on his stick, with the HUD readout at 12.2 miles. At the same time he called, "Showtimers break left!" and pushed the stick over hard. He tensed his muscles and took short breaths as the g's increased.

There was a switch-plate on the left wall of the cockpit, next to the throttle, that released chaff, bits of metalized plastic that could confuse a radar-guided missile. Tony banged it with his fist twice. Suddenly there was a *WOOSH* and Tony looked back to see a line of flame about a hundred feet behind him. The *BEEP*ing stopped.

He heard a *SLAM* and his heart turned to lead. Automatically he looked to the left, the engaged side. There was a bright ball of flame, right where Boomer ought to be.

"Saint, Boomer's gone!"

Radar-guided missiles meant interceptors. Where were they? He looked at his scope. "Hooter, Bandits at two three zero are probably the fighters."

"Rog. You have the lead."

They closed at burner. It was too dark for a visual ID, but Tony had a good lock. There were three aircraft, all small. Range was seventeen miles with a closure rate of over a thousand knots.

They both automatically armed Sidewinders and fired a few seconds later. Tony went vertical, with Hooter following. His plan was to roll into the opponents after he saw the results of the missile attack. He looked back down for the aircraft maneuvering or missile explosions, but he saw nothing. He scanned the sky frantically and saw a flash of wings at his level!

It was too dark to see the type, but he saw two fins against a lighter sky. It was maneuvering with him, which meant a capable aircraft and a capable pilot. He maneuvered, trying to maintain energy and get in firing position. Meanwhile, they climbed.

The thing had two engines, and they were both on burner. Tony throttled back and saw him pull ahead. "He must have lost me," Tony thought.

Hitting the cannon select, he started lining up for a shot. The pilot would realize his error any second.

"Saint, there's one behind."

"Rog." The plane's tail filled his HUD and he fired. There was no flash, but the aircraft suddenly spun wildly to the right. He started to follow it down—

"One's behind, at your seven, break left!" Tony pushed left on the stick and leveled out, turning hard. Hooter was behind and to his right.

"Can you get a shot?"

"I'm going to guns. Turn harder, he's lining up!"

Tony was already pulling seven plus g's. The harder an aircraft turned, the more speed it bled off. He was going to start slowing down, which could make him an easy mark. He put the aircraft in a shallow dive to gain some speed back, cranking the stick even harder. His head was pushed back by forces nine times normal. "Get him, Hooter!"

"Rog."

Even in the steep diving turn, Tony jinked and slid, trying to spoil the pilot's aim. He looked over his shoulder and saw the bastard nimbly following his maneuvers. "Anytime, Hooter."

"Rog."

Tony continued to jink, watching his altitude decrease. The fight had started at about eight thousand. He was now at sixty-five hundred and had the choice of either diving into the SAM envelope at five thousand or pulling up and losing—

"Shooting." *BLAM!* Tony looked back and saw a beautiful explosion. A black shape fell out of it, tumbling. He leveled out and called to John. "Hooter. Take the lead. Head back toward base, and climb to ten thousand." Executing a gentle turn, he fell in on his wingman's right. While Hooter did not "lead" their flight, he was capable of taking the lead position, and right now he had the only missile left. This seemed like a good time for him to be in front.

Tony started scanning the sky, looking for any more bandits. They were alone. He thumbed his frequency switch. "Pancake, Showtime, splash two high-performance MiGs. Vector, over."

"Roger, Showtime steer zero five five, bandits exiting the strike area. Buster, over."

"Showtime, roger, out." Hooter's tailpipe glowed brighter as they increased their throttle again. Tony glanced at his fuel gauge with a little concern. Pancake was pushing them all over the sky, and they did not have an infinite amount of gas.

Tony had been too busy to listen to the radio chatter. All of the squadron's fighters were on the same frequency, and now he tried to piece together the battle around them.

"Owl, break right!"

"Watch for the Fishbed, he's at your nine." He recognized Sanchez's voice, so he didn't check his own left.

"Clear to fire."

"Splash two!"

"Saint, I'm locked. Negative IFF zero six two at ten miles."

Tony looked at his screen. The contact was northeast, and easy to sort out of the confetti on the screen. The contact was probably climbing up after making its attack. Yep, the altitude was increasing. They were at his five o'clock, almost dead aft.

Hooter's voice came over the circuit. "Tone."

There was a flash at the Falcon's left wingtip as the motor fired. Tony forced himself to cover Hooter's blind side, watching for threats to the pair while John earned his pay.

They were close enough to the target to see bits of the airframe fly off as the warhead detonated. It was a Fitter, an older attack jet. As it rolled left slowly, there was a flash as the ejection seat fired the pilot out of the crippled aircraft and into the dubious safety of captivity in South Korea.

Tony headed them toward base. They called in and were told to orbit. "Runway is fouled, ETR ten minutes."

"Rog." He was glad they had headed back. He looked at his fuel gauge. "Hooter, what's your fuel?"

"Eight fifty."

That was much better than his. "Tower, Showtime lead is critical fuel, five fifty pounds, over.

"Roger, Showtime flight is number two for landing. ETR five minutes."

He wondered who was number one, and what fumes he was burning. All they could do was wait. Pacing was hard in a fighter cockpit, but Tony did his best. He reviewed the scramble, Boomer's loss, his own narrow escape, Hooter's marksmanship. The war was not off to a good start.

"Showtime cleared to land, steer one five two. Brake hard on landing, over."

"Rog." Tony and Hooter turned toward the base, being very careful to follow the tower's instructions. They were flying through a narrow "safety lane" where antiaircraft crews were barred from firing. In theory, at least. Outside the lane it was open season.

Tony looked at his gauge. Two hundred pounds.

The runway lights appeared and they lined up for a straight-in approach. As they closed, Tony saw something blocking some of the lights. A dark blot resolved itself into a Falcon-shaped wreck, half-on and half-off the runway.

They immediately flared, hard and early. Tony thought it was one of the best landings he had ever made, actually starting on the underrun area. He chopped throttle, then leaned on the brakes. Hooter was on his right, and he looked over to see him running almost on the grass. Tony steered over, glad for the clearance.

The wreck resolved itself. It looked like the port gear had failed, the aircraft spinning as the wing hit the ground. The canopy was off, indicating that the pilot had ejected rather than stay with a potential fireball.

Suddenly Tony's attitude shifted. Yesterday this was an accident investigation and a maintenance hassle. Now it was a valuable combat aircraft out of action for several days.

They taxied in quickly. There were piles of debris swept off to the side of the taxiway. Tony had never seen so much activity. Work lights were on in every arch. Another change was that everyone was wearing a sidearm.

Kawamoto was waiting. He pointed to Tony's empty wing rails and clasped his hands over his head. Tony cut the engine and rolled to a stop. Suddenly he was weak, too tired to even take off his helmet.

The sergeant ran up with the ladder, then climbed up and knocked on the canopy. Tony looked over and pushed the release, feeling as if he were moving a safe.

"HOT SHIT, sir! Here, drink this." He handed Tony a Styrofoam cup.

Tony gratefully took it and drank. Expecting coffee, he was slightly startled. Chicken soup.

John came running into the shelter waving a tape cassette. "Saint, that was wild! Three morts each! We paid those bastards back, the first installment anyway."

Tony looked over at him. "What do you mean? You got two, I got one."

"Negats, my leader. All our initial shots hit. I saw three flashes as we turned off. Your second shot on the fighters hit, too. I climbed after you did and saw it go in."

Well. Gee. Tony considered. They lost Boomer, but had killed seven between them, assuming Hooter was right. Hooter had excellent eyesight. Chicken soup or victories, Tony's strength started returning.

"Hooter, you've just demonstrated the true value of a wingman." He climbed out of the cockpit and lowered himself down the ladder. Hooter was studying the seat of his flight suit.

"What are you looking at?"

"Just looking to see how full it is."

"Funny, very funny. Well, you're entitled, it wouldn't be there if you hadn't smoked that sucker." They started walking toward the ops building.

"Saint, those were MiG-29 Fulcrums."

"It's possible. Russian, two tails, twin engines."

"Screw that. I saw him, silhouetted. Nothing else but."

"Fuck."

"My sentiments exactly. How many do you think they have?"

"Three less, thanks to us."

The ops building was busy, but well organized. Beamer took their tapes and told them to follow him. They went to a briefing room. It was dark and half-filled with pilots watching the videotape of a mission. Tony recognized Ninja, a lieutenant in the second flight. He was describing a double kill on two unsuspecting MiG-23s.

Beamer pointed them toward a table on the side. It was covered with sandwiches, soup, doughnuts, and coffee. They had time enough to load up and get a couple of bites before their turn came.

Tony talked his way through the tape, with Hooter filling in. They fast-forwarded through everything but the combats.

"Okay, here's where I dropped back." He slowed, then paused the tape. Filling the large-projection screen was a black, angular shape. Twin tails and two engines were easily visible.

Pistol was the squadron intelligence officer. "Look at the gap between the engines. That, gentlemen, is the ass end of a MiG-29 Fulcrum."

Beamer looked at him. "George, your briefs haven't included anything on this aircraft."

"Sir, current intelligence says the North Koreans haven't reached operational status with their Fulcrums."

"Current intelligence is hosed." He sighed. "All right. Dupe this tape and send it up the line. Prepare a brief on the Fulcrum and recommended counters and have it ready to pass out in an hour." He looked at Tony.

"Saint, dawn's in about three hours. We're going to provide air support to the western sector of the line, north of Seoul. Takeoff is at oh six thirty. You're leading four ships. The mission planning cell will give you the rest of the details."

That was the first mission.

22

Red Phoenix

DECEMBER 25—NEAR THE DMZ, NORTH KOREA

The North Korean gun crews crouched motionless beside long-barreled artillery pieces and squat, openmouthed mortar tubes. Others stood beside truck-mounted, multiple-barrel rocket launchers. Outside their hardened shelters, they could hear jets roaring overhead on the way south, but the gunners were content to wait. Their moment was coming.

Deep inside a command bunker, the general of artillery studied his watch and then nodded to an aide holding a telephone. "Move into firing positions."

The aide hooked the phone into the general command circuit and passed the order to the hundreds of battery commanders all along the DMZ who had been waiting on the same circuit.

The order stirred the waiting gun crews into frantic activity. Some men ran to open heavy blast doors that protected their shelters, while others levered the guns forward into their firing positions. The Ural-375 trucks carrying Soviet-designed rocket launchers rolled out into the open and parked with their launch tubes swung off to the side to protect the vehicle itself from blast damage. Mortar crews jumped down into firing pits that held their weapons and stood ready by them.

None of the gunners could see the enemy. The same snow-covered ridges and hillsides that protected them from enemy observation limited their own view of the areas their shells would strike. Once the battle was joined, they would rely on the data gathered by forward observers in the front line and passed back through the artillery chain of command.

Secure in his bunker, forty kilometers behind the DMZ, the general of artillery smiled, imagining the havoc his guns would wreak on the Americans and their Southern puppets. He had organized what would be the heaviest barrage seen since the end of World War II by concentrating more than 6,000 artillery pieces, 1,800 multiple rocket launchers, and 11,000 mortars against the imperialists. With an average of 500 gun tubes per kilometer of breakthrough front, he would overwhelm the enemy fortifications with a shock wave of explosive fire. All told, the first salvo alone would send nearly 2,000 tons of high-explosive smashing into their bunkers, command posts, artillery parks, and supply depots. And his men would be firing four to six salvos a minute. The imperialists would be annihilated.

Annihilated. He savored the thought as the second hand on his watch marked the hour. It was time. The general turned to his aide and barked, "All guns. Open fire!"

With a thunderous, rolling crash, thousands of artillery pieces fired at the same moment. And even as the first wave of shells arced up and over into the predawn night sky, the gunners were already racing forward to reload. Their next rounds would be in the air before the first salvo exploded on the imperialist positions.

OUTPOST MALIBU WEST, ALONG THE DMZ

Second Lieutenant Kevin Little dreamed of rain. Not a soft, whispering spring rain. A hard, cold winter downpour, with thunder and searing lightning to back it up.

The thunder threw him out of his cot and onto the CP's dirt floor.

He came awake to find himself scrabbling on his knees and coughing in dust-choked air. The whole dugout seemed to be rocking back and forth, swaying first one way and then the other. A tiny Christmas tree his men had decorated toppled over in a heap of tinfoil and broken ornaments. He grabbed for the table with his maps and phones as a small, battery-operated lamp fell over and smashed. Jesus, what was this? An earthquake?

But the real answer came as his mind sorted out the separate parts of the unearthly din outside the small bunker. Dull, muffled rumbling from the north, high-pitched, whirring screams passing overhead, and a continuous, ear-splitting succession of explosions from the south. It was artillery fire.

Kevin grabbed for his helmet and flak jacket. Got to get out. Get out before this place came down around his ears. He looked around and saw Rhee fumbling into his own gear. The Korean lieutenant had a wild-eyed, disbelieving look on his face—an expression that was probably mirrored on his own. Oh, God, this had to be a nightmare. Please, make it a nightmare.

The door crashed open and Sergeant Pierce burst into the CP followed by Corporal Jones, the platoon's signalman. Both Pierce and the corporal were in full combat gear, and both were wearing white camouflage snowsuits over their uniforms. Kevin could see the sky paling to a predawn gray through the open door.

Pierce pushed Jones over toward the commo gear and turned to Kevin, "Let's go, Lieutenant! We've got big-time trouble in River City here. Got arty coming down all over the place behind us."

Kevin stood uncertainly, having reconsidered his earlier decision. Now it seemed incredibly stupid to run out into the middle of an artillery barrage. Better to stay here; the bunkers were designed to protect people from this kind of stuff.

Pierce saw his momentary indecision. "It ain't landing on us, goddamnit. It's those poor rear-area slobs who're getting dumped on. But we got North Koreans pouring around us like fucking ants. If we don't do something about it, we're gonna be eating NK kimchee for the rest of this frigging war. Now let's go!"

The sergeant didn't wait for a reply. He just turned and headed back up the communications trench toward the forward slope.

Rhee snagged his white camouflage jacket with one hand and lurched out through the door carrying his rifle in the other, heading for his position with 2nd Squad along the rear slope of the hill. Kevin bent and pulled his own jacket out from underneath his cot. Then he followed Rhee out into an icy maelstrom of windblown dust, snow, and smoke.

It was bitterly cold, and Kevin could feel the chill air bite down deep into his lungs as he jogged up the communications trench. The bombardment was even louder outside. A constant pounding that rumbled through every part of his body, not just his eardrums. He could feel his teeth rattling from the concussions. But he knew that was only half-right.

He was scared. Scared worse than he'd ever been before in his life. Something in his brain kept telling him to turn around, to run for cover while there was still time. But another part of him resisted, remembering the look in Pierce's eyes. He kept stumbling forward.

The main trench was crowded with the other men from his platoon. Pierce moved among them, cajoling them into their gear and pushing them into their assigned positions. But he held them back below the trench's firing steps.

He saw Kevin and nodded. "Take a look through the scope. You'll see we've got company." He had to yell to make himself heard through the howling din of the barrage.

Kevin turned the trench periscope into position. My God. The whole northern horizon was a flickering sea of light, an artificial sunrise made by the massed artillery firing from behind ridges and hills.

He swiveled the scope down to look at the ground around the outpost. It took him a moment to comprehend what he saw. Then he understood. He was looking at his worst nightmare come to life.

The rough, broken ground below Malibu's small hill was crawling with North Korean infantry, tanks, and APCs. A part of him automatically started trying to count them. Fifty, no, sixty tanks at least. He couldn't make out the exact types through all the dust and smoke, but they all had guns. One lay immobile, spewing a cloud of oily, black smoke. Must've hit a mine, thought Kevin. He stared transfixed at the spectacle laid out to either side of the small hill topped by Malibu West. Row after row of infantry, looking like black ants in the distance, marching south in open order, followed by waves of wheeled and tracked personnel carriers. At the very edge of his vision the enemy's ordered lines were breaking up under what looked like an American artillery fire mission—bright, orange-red flashes opening like short-lived flowers as time-fused shells burst in the air. It gradually dawned on Kevin that he was seeing the forward elements of what could only be an entire North Korean motorized rifle division.

Pierce followed the direction of his scope and tapped him on the shoulder. "We've got some troubles a little closer to home, Lieutenant. Down by the wire."

Kevin adjusted the scope and almost dropped it. North Koreans in snowsuits were worming their way through the barbed wire at the base of the hill. They were less than a hundred and fifty meters away. There were other troops crouched behind them. A company of infantry at least—around a hundred riflemen and machinegunners.

Good Christ. Where was the American artillery? Why weren't they chopping these bastards down with high explosive and white phosphorus? Then he remembered that calling in the artillery for this sector was his job. The platoon's attached forward observer had been rotated home weeks ago, and he hadn't been replaced because of the Army's scheduled withdrawal from Korea.

Kevin pulled his eyes away from the periscope, looking for his signalman. The ops plan for meeting a North Korean surprise attack gave him at least one artillery battery in direct support, with up to a full battalion on call. Plus whatever close air support could be arranged. That was a lot of firepower, the kind of firepower he was going to need to keep the NKs as far away from him as possible.

"Jones!" The signalman's head snapped up from his phones. He had a pale, set look on his freckled face. "Get me the arty. We've got a fire mission."

Jones nodded and lifted one of the phones. "Charlie Victor Two Seven, Charlie Victor Two Seven, This is Alpha Echo Five Two."

Kevin waited, watching Pierce as the big, gray-haired sergeant moved down the trench encouraging the men. "Got arty coming anytime, boys. Stay cool. Wait for the word. Hold your fire."

"Sir!" It was Jones. "I can't get through. All the lines are dead. That stuff"—he gestured over his shoulder to the explosions still racking the main American line—"must've cut the wires."

Shit. "Switch to the goddamned radio then." Kevin could

feel the panic bubbling up inside him. Oh, God. He wanted to be sick.

Jones bent over his radio, but Kevin could hear the confused squeals and hissing static pouring out of it. They were being jammed. Jones worked frantically, changing frequencies to find one still in the clear.

"Lieutenant. Those people down there are getting awfully close. Where's the arty we're supposed to have?"

"We're blocked. The phones are out and the radio's jammed." Kevin kept his words clipped, trying to conceal the fear he felt.

Pierce just nodded. "Right, we'll do this the old-fashioned way then. On our own." He turned and headed back down the firing line. "Okay, boys. This is it. When I give the word it's rock-and-roll time. Pick your targets. Get their heavy weapons men first unless you want an RPG up the ass." One or two men laughed nervously. The others nodded grimly.

Kevin turned back to the scope. The closest North Koreans were only forty meters away and coming on fast, though bent low under the weight of full packs. It struck Kevin that they weren't planning on going back to their own lines for food or ammo resupply. They must be pretty sure they'd push on right through his platoon on their way south. And for some reason that made him mad enough to momentarily push down the panic welling up inside.

He looked down the trench line toward Pierce. The sergeant gave him a thumbs-up, and Kevin pumped a clenched first back and yelled, "Let's do it."

Pierce's bullroar cut through the unearthly din from the North Korean artillery barrage landing behind them. "Up and at 'em! Fire! Fire!"

All along the forward perimeter, troopers from the platoon's 1st and 3rd Squads jumped up onto firing steps and cut loose with their M16s. Many fired their rifles on full automatic, wasting rounds as the recoil kicked the barrels higher and higher above their targets. Two of the platoon's M60 machine guns joined in, hosing down the front slope of the hill in steady, regulation bursts. The concentrated fire cut the first rank of the North Korean assault company to pieces. Men trying to charge up the steep hillside were bowled over or thrown back to fall in crumpled heaps as bullets found them. Others dropped to the ground, looking for any kind of cover they could find. Only a few tried to shoot back with their AK47s and AKMs, but they were soon killed, wounded, or pinned down by the sheer volume of fire pouring out of the American-held trench.

Satisfied that his men had held off the first rush, Pierce shifted the platoon's fire back down the slope into the North Koreans still struggling through the barbed wire and minefields. Caught bunched up like that, they were slaughtered. Through his scope Kevin could see them falling. Those left alive started to edge backward, away from the hill. A North Korean officer came running forward to rally them, but he went down with a bullet in the face.

Whistles shrilled from down by the wire, and the surviving North Koreans began moving back, leaving a trail of bloody, writhing bodies on the ground behind them. Pierce let the platoon shoot until they were outside effective range—about two hundred and fifty meters—and then roared, "Cease fire! Cease fire! Save your ammo. You'll need it later."

Kevin was elated. His earlier fears had faded as quickly as they'd broken the North Korean attack. He looked up and down his line. Not a man had been hit. They'd smashed an enemy infantry company without suffering a single casualty.

He grinned at Pierce as the sergeant came up to him. "Well done, Sergeant."

Pierce nodded, his own face carefully expressionless.

Kevin could hear moans from the North Korean wounded left behind on the hillside. Time to be humanitarian about this. "Tell the medic I'd like him to see what he can do for those poor bastards out there."

Pierce was astonished. "You gone nuts, Lieutenant? This ain't the end of it." He gestured in the direction the attack had come from. "That was just a probe. Now that they know for sure we're here, they're going to make us wish we weren't."

He leaned forward to bring his face closer to Kevin's. "And next time they're gonna give us a dose of that arty."

BELOW MALIBU WEST

Senior Lieutenant Park Sung-Hi of the North Korean People's Army couldn't see the body of his company commander from where he lay. In fact, he couldn't see much of anything at all.

Park and the remains of his platoon had been driven back from the American outpost to a place where a small fold in the ground offered cover from the imperialists' murderous fire. One of his men hadn't made it all the way to safety, and his body lay sprawled half in and half out of the shallow ditch. Park gripped his AKM assault rifle tighter and tried to burrow deeper into the frozen snow.

Technically his captain's death had given him command of the company, but there wasn't much left to command. Just the four, no, five men huddled on either side of him. There were undoubtedly others left alive and unwounded, but they'd either sought cover elsewhere or kept running. For their sake Park hoped that the men who'd run stopped before they got back to the company's Start Line. The commissars of the Main Political Administration had made it clear that would-be deserters would be dealt with harshly.

The North Korean lieutenant lay in the snow and considered his options—none of which seemed particularly palatable. He could try again to take the hill with what he had left. And that was suicidal madness, of course. The Americans were too well dug-in. Or he could wriggle back to the company's communications gear, report the failure of this attack, and ask for support from a higher headquarters. That was the militarily sensible thing to do, but it might be viewed as cowardice by an unsympathetic political officer.

He bit his lip while trying to decide what to do and spat the blood out onto the snow. Oddly enough, the pain helped clear his mind. Better to be shot for trying to do the right thing than to be killed while doing something utterly foolish and wasteful. He would call for help.

3RD MOTORIZED RIFLE DIVISION HQ, NEAR THE DMZ

The North Korean division commander smiled all the way through his staff's situation report. The attack was going well, much better than he'd dared hope possible. His first echelon tank and infantry battalions had already broken into the first enemy defensive line in three separate places. Casualties in some units had been heavier than expected, but others had suffered only minimal losses. And according to the reports, whole enemy units had collapsed under the weight of the unexpected attack. The Special Forces and the artillery had done their work well.

He leaned over the map table to get a better look. The grease-penciled wedges showing his spearheads were being erased and redrawn as new information came in. They were now well on their way to their first day objectives. Excellent. But then his smile faded. One of the American hilltop outposts had not yet been seized.

He tapped the map. "What is the problem here, Comrade Colonel?"

His deputy moved closer, his eyes magnified behind thick glasses. "We've just had a report from a platoon leader outside that position, sir. It was supposed to be taken by a company strength surprise attack before our barrage began, but there was some sort of delay as they moved through our forward lines. Consequently, the attack failed. The platoon leader is now requesting artillery support and reinforcements."

"Casualties?"

"Extremely heavy, sir."

"Hmmm." The general rubbed his chin absentmindedly. He hated the idea of diverting resources from the main attack to reinforce failure. Doctrine spoke against that. But on the other hand, the American outpost sat squarely on his flank. From there its defenders could call down artillery onto his resupply units and lines of communication—and that might cause delays he couldn't risk. He made up his mind.

"Very well." He studied the map. "Order the Twentieth Rifles forward to attack this hill. The Americans there have defeated a company. Now let's see how they fare against a full battalion. And tell the artillery that I want a hurricane preparatory barrage on the imperialist position. I want their fortifications pulverized. Understand?''

His deputy nodded sharply and hurried away to issue orders for the second attack on Malibu West.

OUTPOST MALIBU WEST, NEAR THE DMZ

Kevin Little was beginning to wish that he hadn't been so quick to pull his men back inside their bunkers. He could still hear the artillery landing to the south, but everything around Malibu West was quiet. What if the NKs were sneaking back up the hill while they just sat here? Kevin knew that Pierce had put an OP—an observation post—out on the forward slope to give the platoon advance warning. But what if the two men in it had been surprised? Or what if they were looking in the wrong direction? It had been over an hour since the last attack. What the hell was going on?

He could hear Jones muttering into the radio. "You got anything, Corporal?"

The radioman twisted round with his earphones still on. "Not a damned thing, sir. Every time I find a clear frequency and start talking, the frigging gooks come in and mess it up."

Kevin swore under his breath. What a clusterfuck. Here he was sitting blind in this little hole on a hill, and he couldn't get through to anyone to get some help or to find out what was going on. None of his ROTC lecturers had ever warned him that it would be so hard to communicate on the battlefield.

He jumped up. Enough of this waiting shit. "Tell Pierce I'm going to check the OP personally." He'd just make sure his observers were on the job and come right back.

"But sir!" Jones started to yell something as Kevin pulled the bunker door open. Then he heard it.

An enormous howling arcing down out of the sky. Falling right on him. Kevin froze, one hand on the door, the other holding his M16.

Jones knocked him flat onto the CP floor just as the 152-millimeter shell exploded outside.

The shock wave tore the air out of Kevin's lungs and

throat and buried him in a tidal wave of dirt and smoke. He blacked out.

He came to seconds later, aware first of the dirt caking his face and then of a heavy weight holding him down. The ground bucked up and down as other shells landed around the hill, but he couldn't hear the explosions. He'd been deafened by the first burst.

He shifted uncomfortably beneath the corporal's weight. Why didn't Jones get off him? Then he felt something warm and sticky pouring onto his neck. And there was a hot, coppery smell mixed in with the sharp, acetone odor left by the shell burst.

Kevin wriggled frantically out from under his signalman and rolled him over. Jones was dead.

A fragment thrown by the North Korean shell had spiraled out at several hundred meters a second, catching the corporal just below the eye and tearing through into his brain. Kevin stared for a moment at the ragged mess left of the man who'd saved his life, then he spun away on his knees, retching. In all his worst dreams he'd never imagined it would be this bad. Jones was dead because he'd done something stupid.

After a moment Kevin crawled over and pushed the door shut with shaking hands. He leaded against it for a second, feeling the bone-rattling vibrations thrown by the artillery pounding his hill. Then he scuttled over to the radio, carefully keeping his eyes off Jones's body. The bunker rocked under a near miss, spilling dirt through cracks in the reinforced log roof. He had to get help. The platoon needed support.

His hearing was coming back. Kevin could make out muffled explosions now as North Korean salvos landed on Malibu West. He fumbled with the radio, setting it back to the main tactical frequency.

"Charlie Victor Two Seven, Charlie Victor Two Seven, This is Alfa Echo Five Two. Repeat, this is Alfa Echo Five Two. Over." Kevin was ashamed of the high-pitched quaver he could hear in his voice.

Nothing. He switched to an alternate frequency and tried again, praying for an answer.

"Alfa Echo Five Two, this is Charlie Victor Two Seven. Over." The American artillery officer's voice crackled through the headphones.

Thank God. "Victor Two Seven. I have an immediate fire mission. Pattern Hotel. Repeat, Pattern Hotel." Pattern Hotel would create a horseshoe-shaped curtain of American high-explosives around the base. That should keep the NKs from crawling up under the cover of their own barrage.

Victor Two Seven's answer was quick and horrifying. "Negative, Echo Five Two. Half my guns are gone. The rest of us are pulling out. We've got NKs coming down around our . . ." The artilleryman's voice faded in a spray of hissing static as North Korean jammers swept across the frequency.

Kevin stared at the radio for a moment. Then he heard a whistle from one of the sound-powered phones that linked his outlying positions to the outpost. He grabbed it.

"Little."

"This is Donnelly, Lieutenant!" It was one of the men he'd assigned to the OP. "We're in deep, sir. Me and Smith can see two NK companies assembling down in front of us. And we seen another one moving around the flank a minute ago. What should we do, Lieutenant?"

Kevin could hear the fear in Donnelly's voice and it matched his own. Three North Korean companies. God, that was at least three hundred men coming against his forty or so troops. This was not the way it was supposed to work. Where was the artillery and air support those rear-area bastards had all promised Malibu West would get?

"Lieutenant?"

He started. He hadn't answered Donnelly's plaintive question yet.

"Lieutenant? It looks like the arty's starting to lift. What should we do?"

Kevin could hear the noise from outside diminishing. Not much time left now. "Okay. Get back inside the perimeter. Get back to the trench!"

He switched connections, trying to get Pierce's bunker. Had to let the sergeant know what was going on. Had to find out what he should do. Nothing. Christ, didn't anything work around here?

Kevin put the phone down slowly. He was going to die. And it just wasn't fair. Not at all.

Everything went quiet. The shelling had stopped. Then he

heard the whistles blowing from all around his hill. This was it. Kevin grabbed his M16 and headed out through the bunker door.

Malibu West looked like a moonscape now, full of smoking craters, partially collapsed trenches, and smashed bunkers. Kevin could hear moans from all around him: "Medic! Medic!"

Rifles fired from the forward slope of the hill, rising quickly from a few isolated shots to a continuous, crackling roar. The North Korean attack was coming in. He ran down what was left of the communications trench and stumbled into the firing line.

His troops were up on the edge of the trench firing as fast as they could down the hill. But this time, they were being answered by the harsh rattle of North Korean automatic rifles and heavy weapons. And Kevin could see Americans lying dead or wounded along the trench floor.

"Lieutenant!" Pierce grabbed his shoulder. "You all right?"

Kevin suddenly realized he was covered in Jones's blood. He must look like a walking corpse. He leaned forward to yell in the sergeant's ear. "I'm not hit. Jones . . ."

Pierce nodded in understanding. "Yeah. Well, we got a whole shitload of troubles, Lieutenant." He half-ducked involuntarily as a grenade went off just outside the trench, spraying them with dirt and ice-cold snow.

"We're holding 'em for now. But Kostowitz and Ramos are down. Along with a bunch of others. The Dragon teams took a direct hit on their bunker. And we're shooting up our rifle ammo too damned fast."

A GI next to him suddenly screamed and fell back away from the firing step. Most of the man's right arm had been shot away. Kevin stared at the corpse in shock.

"Lieutenant! Snap out of it! There's others still alive who need you." Pierce pulled him away from the body. "Look, we gotta have some support."

Kevin shook his head. There wasn't going to be any support. He pushed Pierce away and jumped upon the dead man's firing step to get a better look at what they were facing.

The first wave of the North Korean assault had gotten to within twenty meters of the trench line before being stopped. But instead of retreating back down where they'd come from, the survivors had taken shelter in new shell craters on the slope, and they were laying down covering fire for a second wave now forming up inside the outpost's barbed wire.

An NK light machine gun burst tore into the ground in front of him, and Kevin ducked back below the lip of the trench. A 1st Squad trooper groaned and toppled back to the bottom, cursing and clutching at his stomach. Kevin couldn't remember the man's name. He looked away as the firing rose to a new crescendo.

BELOW MALIBU WEST

The North Korean major winced as the medic pulled the bandage tighter around his lacerated upper arm. It was ironic that his first wound of the campaign had come from his own country's artillery. But it had been worth it, the major thought. He'd pushed his men right up to the edge of their own barrage—accepting casualties from friendly fire to close with the Americans before they'd had a chance to shake off the effects of the bombardment.

The medic finished tying off the wound, and the major pushed him away, half-rising to a crouch to look over the edge of the gully his command group occupied. He could see the rocky hillside carpeted with bodies, but enough men had survived the first rush to pin the Americans down inside their trenches. Good.

He glanced around for the commander of his second company, "Captain Han!"

The man scuttled over to him, eyes wide under the lip of his Russian-style steel helmet.

"You will take your company forward on my signal. We'll wait for Koh's attack to go in first. That should draw off enough of the fascists for you to close with their trenches. Clear?"

Han nodded. "Yes, Comrade Major." He scurried back along the gully to pass the word to his platoon leaders.

The major watched him go and then slid back down to check his watch. Captain Koh's 3rd Company should be in position behind the American-held hill any minute now. Soon they would find out how the imperialists held up under a two-pronged attack.

OUTPOST MALIBU WEST

Kevin was starting to regain his confidence when the sound of firing mixed with grenade explosions surged from behind them. That goddamned third North Korean company! Now they were under attack from all sides at once. He couldn't hear a lot of American return fire from Lieutenant Rhee's position either.

Movement from down by the wire caught his eye. A second wave of snowsuited North Koreans were worming their way through, getting ready to lunge up the hill. Kevin looked frantically up and down the trench. He barely had enough men here to hold the NKs as it was. He didn't have anything to spare for the rear slope. Could the South Korean lieutenant hold his ground without reinforcements?

He grabbed Pierce. "Check with Rhee. See what's going on back there."

The sergeant nodded and ducked back up the communications trench toward Rhee's position. Kevin turned back to the forward slope.

He walked up and down the trench, trying to encourage his troops. "Keep it up, guys. Keep it up. You're murdering the sons of bitches." Yeah, sure. He felt like a liar for even saying it.

The fire from his line fell away as men were hit or ran out of ammunition. And now the North Koreans were taking advantage of it, advancing by short rushes from cover to cover—working their way up the hill.

A grenade landed on one of his machine gun positions and silenced it. Kevin raced over to try to get the gun back into operation, but there wasn't anything he could do. The machine gun's barrel had bent under the full force of the grenade burst. The gunner and his loader were both dying.

He lost track of time. The battle seemed to have been going on forever, although he knew that couldn't be true. He tried to swallow and couldn't. Where was Pierce? He needed the sergeant's advice and steadiness. He didn't think they were going to be able to hold here much longer.

Kevin looked around frantically. His line was down to about half strength, and the North Koreans weren't going back. What should he do?

Bugles blared from the other side of Malibu West. Kevin spun around and saw Sergeant Pierce skidding down the slush-filled communications trench, arms pumping and head down. He put an arm out and the sergeant stumbled to a stop. Pierce nodded his thanks and gasped out his message, "NKs inside the perimeter. We gotta throw 'em—"

Pierce's head suddenly exploded, sending a spray of brains and blood over Kevin's uniform. The sergeant crumpled into his arms. Oh, Christ. Pierce had been shot from behind. Through sudden tears Kevin saw North Koreans flitting up the communications trench toward him. He couldn't move or speak. The men nearest to Kevin stared in shock at the body. Some dropped their M16s into the frozen mud.

Time started running again. Still holding the sergeant's body, Kevin looked up and saw a grenade flying into the main trench. He threw himself to the ground as it went off. The explosion rolled Pierce's corpse over on top of him and tossed another man dead across his legs.

North Koreans jumped up onto both sides of the trench, firing down inside it at full automatic. Kevin could hear his men screaming and trying to surrender. He lay still in the mud, trying to control his breathing.

The firing stopped. Everything was quiet for a moment, and then Kevin heard a chorus of groans from what had been his line: "Medic! Medic! I'm hit."

Laughter drifted downwind, harsh guttural laughter. Someone shouted an order in Korean and rifles cracked. Moans turned into screams and then into silence.

Kevin tried to stop the tears he felt dripping into the blood-soaked ground under his face. Corpses don't cry. He heard more loud voices as men jumped down into the trench, their combat boots squelching into the mud. He held his breath.

The North Koreans were making sure of their handiwork. Kevin didn't look up, but he could hear men moving down the line toward him. Every now and then they stopped and fired a burst into an American who'd been wounded or lying doggo. There were fresh screams.

The boots were coming toward him. Oh, God. Please make them think I'm dead, please, Kevin prayed without moving his lips. The boots stopped. Don't move. Whatever they do, don't move, Kevin told himself. He heard a dull, meaty thunk from his left and then something cold and sharp sliced across his ribs. A bayonet. He bit down the pain and stayed still, waiting for the bullet that would end everything.

But the bayonet pulled back and the boots moved away down the trench. They thought he was dead.

There were isolated pistol and rifle shots from around the perimeter as they finished off others who'd survived the attack, but the North Koreans didn't come back. Kevin lay amid the bodies of his men, alone with the knowledge of his failure.

Malibu West had fallen.

CHAPTER
23
First Kill

DECEMBER 25—ABOARD THE
USS *JOHN YOUNG*

Commander Michael Deveroux, USN, studied the plot carefully. His ship, a Spruance-class destroyer, had slipped its moorings and left the South Korean navy port of Chinhae an hour earlier. Now they were ten miles outside the harbor, moving south at fifteen knots through a narrow passage between the islands of Kadck-do and Koje-do.

The start of the war had caught almost everyone in Chinhae by surprise. Everyone that was but the North Korean commandos who'd infiltrated the port. The crew of the *John Young*, anchored there on a port call, had come awake to the harsh rattle of automatic weapons fire and then the unending, thundering roar as a fuel storage depot went up in a towering ball of orange-white flame. One South Korean frigate fueling from the depot had been caught by the blast and she'd turned turtle, the water hiding the mangled metal of her upper works.

Deveroux shook the image out of his mind. He had his own ship to look out for now.

Seventh Fleet's orders had been clear and concise. "Proceed at best speed to Yokosuka, Japan." Once there, Deveroux had no doubt that they'd be ordered to serve as a convoy escort or formed into a battle group sortieing against the North Koreans. Well, good. They hadn't asked for this war, but the shooting had started and the *John Young* would get a chance to show her stuff.

Right now, though, she had to make it to Japan. It was only a ten-hour run across the Korea Straits, but Deveroux knew that might be a very long and lonely ten hours. North Korea had a sizable diesel-electric sub fleet and dozens of fast attack missile craft—any of which might be out there lurking in wait for his ship.

He'd asked for air support, but all of the Seventh Fleet's P-3 Orion ASW aircraft were fully engaged. And South Korea's S-2F Tracker squadron had been hammered hard by a North Korean air raid earlier that morning. Essentially his ship was on her own.

Outside, the sky was paling to a predawn gray, but it was always dark inside the dimly red-lit Combat Information Center. Deveroux swept his eyes over the ship's status boards. Hull-mounted passive sonar operating. Active sonar on standby. Surface and air search radars operating, sweeping the sky and the sea for enemy contacts. He looked across at the antisubmarine warfare officer. "How are the water conditions?"

"Still lousy, sir. You know what this area's like. Strong currents, shallow water, mixed-up salinity. And there are dozens of wrecks on the bottom. Jap freighters we sank during World War II. Passive detection's lousy, but we can't turn on active sonar without getting blanked by our own reverberation. It's gonna be tough to hear anything out there, Captain."

Deveroux nodded. "Yeah. Well, at least the North Koreans will have the same problem. Hell, those old Romeo-class boats of theirs will probably have to rely on periscope sightings instead of that crappy sonar they've got." He studied the plot again. "How's the LAMPS helicopter doing?"

"He's been aloft for forty-five minutes. We'll be launching his relief in another fifteen, sir."

"Well, ensure we have continuous coverage till we get into deeper water. With the LAMPS's radar we should be able to pick up a periscope in time."

"Yes, sir." But the ASW officer didn't sound especially convinced.

"Captain." It was his executive officer and navigator, calling down from the bridge. "We're almost up to that chunk of rock they call an island."

The passage they were steaming through held only one obstruction. A small, barren point of land rising above the water midway between the two larger islands that bounded the passage out into the Korea Strait proper.

Deveroux made a decision. "Very well, let's put it to port." They would pass the small island to the right, well away from the main track to Pusan. He suspected that South Korea's main port was probably not a very healthy place to get closer to at the moment.

"Aye, aye, sir." The *John Young* heeled slightly as she came around on her new heading.

ABOARD THE DPRK *GREAT LEADER*

"I have a passive sonar contact, Comrade Captain." The sonar operator's voice was jubilant. "Bearing three five zero degrees."

Senior Captain Chun Chae-Yun smiled slowly. The enemy vessel had done precisely what he'd thought it would—turn to avoid Pusan. And now it was coming into his sights.

He looked around the crowded control room, marveling all over again in its clean, modern equipment. Acquiring this latest-model Kilo-class submarine from the Russians had been another brilliant stroke by the Great Leader for whom it was named. Its sensors were much better than those on the Romeo-class subs, and its anechoic coating made it almost impossible to detect in these shallow waters.

He had taken advantage of that to lie hidden near a small island in the middle of this passage out of Chinhae, the main South Korean naval base. Long hours of waiting had followed, waiting for the first enemy vessel to fall into his trap. Now the waiting was almost over.

"What's our battery state?"

"Ninety percent, Comrade Captain." Excellent. They had more than enough battery power to maneuver against this contact.

"Very well. Left standard rudder. Come to course two seven zero degrees." The *Great Leader* swung right, closing on the sonar contact and moving slowly at five knots to reduce the chance of the enemy's sonar detecting them.

Five minutes passed endlessly. Chun could feel his heartbeat accelerating as the sonar operator continued to report contact. The technician worked with the signal, analyzing it and comparing it with known signatures.

"Contact positively identified as a Spruance-class destroyer. Screws turning for fifteen knots."

His first officer asked, "Should we come up to periscope depth for a visual sighting?"

Chun waved the suggestion away. "No. They haven't heard us yet. Let's not give them a chance to see us either."

Another minute passed. Chun watched his control room crew feeding bearings and other data onto the fire control computer. It would determine the position, course, and speed of the target and compute the firing angles for the sub's torpedoes.

Any moment now, Chun thought. It is a short-range solution. The torpedoes will travel quickly, and there will be little warning time. Out of the corner of his eye he saw a green light appear on the computer console.

"We have a firing solution, Comrade Captain! Contact now bearing three four one degrees. Course one eight zero degrees, still fifteen knots. Estimated range at twenty-three hundred meters, torpedo run time ninety seconds."

Chun wheeled to his weapons officer. "Fire!"

The *Great Leader* shuddered as two ET-80 wire-guided torpedoes were shot out of their tubes and accelerated toward the American ship at fifty knots.

USS *JOHN YOUNG*

"Shit! Sir, we've got hydrophone effects bearing one three five—evaluated as torpedoes inbound!"

The sonarman's shout almost stopped Deveroux's heart. Oh, my God. He grabbed for the bridge intercom. "Mr. Hall, torpedoes bearing one three five!'' He didn't have to tell the conning officer what to do.

He looked at the ASW officer. "Stream and activate the Nixie!" The torpedo decoy might fool one or more of the incoming torps. The water was really too shallow to stream it normally, but right now he didn't care if it bumped on the bottom.

As he sprinted out the door of CIC toward the bridge, he felt the ship heeling to the right, away from the oncoming torpedoes. A vibration in the deckplates told him they were building up speed as well.

Deveroux arrived on the bridge in time to hear a *thump* sound as one of their own port torpedo tubes launched a Mark 46 down the enemy torpedoes' bearing. The Mark 46 didn't do well in shallow water, and without a fire control solution, it was just a shot in the general direction of the enemy. But the other captain didn't know how well-aimed it was. Maybe it would throw the enemy sub off. Maybe.

He picked up a phone. "Get a Flash message off to Seventh Fleet and Chinhae!" He could feel the ship accelerating, slashing through the water faster and faster. C'mon, baby. Show your stuff. Dodge those bastards.

The intercom from the sonar shack came to life. "Captain, I show two torps, bearing one two five and decreasing range. Both are pinging on us. One is drawing left. The other's bearing is steady. The LAMPS is dropping a sonobuoy pattern."

Deveroux didn't reply. There wasn't anything more he could do.

DPRK *GREAT LEADER*

"Comrade Captain! The Americans have fired on us. Torpedo running, bearing three three one degrees."

Chun nodded philosophically. That was to be expected. "Have ours acquired the destroyer?"

"Yes, sir."

"Very well. Cut the wires." The weapons officer moved to obey, cutting the thin wires that had allowed him to control the movements of the torpedoes lunging for the American ship. Now they were on their own, homing on their target with the data gained by their own active sonars.

"Right full rudder. Increase speed to fifteen knots. Release a decoy." Chun began issuing the series of commands that would take his submarine out of danger. They should be able to avoid this American torpedo. If not? Chun mentally shrugged as he watched the display showing his own weapons closing on the enemy. If not, at least they wouldn't be going to the bottom alone.

USS *JOHN YOUNG*

It was a race. A race between life and death. A race the American destroyer was losing. The ship was trying to get out of the seeker cone of the enemy torpedoes, turning and accelerating to degrade the enemy sub's fire control solution. But the laws of geometry and physics were inexorable, the range too short, and the surprise had been too complete.

It took two minutes and nearly two nautical miles, but the North Korean torpedoes ran their target down. One missed—running behind the destroyer and attacking its Nixie noisemaker trailing a hundred yards astern. The other had locked on to the *John Young*'s hull and it hit.

The torpedo smashed into the ship forward of the stern, and the explosive power of its 270-kilogram warhead lifted the *John Young* up out of the water in a cloud of smoke and spray. A column of water fifty feet high announced the sub's presence to Chinhae and Pusan harbors.

The warhead tore a twenty-foot hole in the ship's port side, spraying fragments that penetrated the steel decks and letting water into the after berthing compartment. Just aft of the torpedo's point of impact, the *John Young*'s Sea Sparrow missile launcher was shaken loose from its mount and thrown high into the air, catapulting into the water to starboard.

In tenths of a single second, the blast rippled through the ship from one end to the other, tearing equipment from its mountings and throwing men into steel bulkheads or machinery.

Unfortunately for the American destroyer, its second LAMPS helicopter was fully fueled and loaded with a torpedo, preparing to relieve its comrade aloft. The force of the explosion bounced the aircraft around in its hangar like a bean in a bottle, mangling the fragile machine and spraying jet fuel all over the area. Sparks touched it off, engulfing the after part of the *John Young*'s superstructure in flames.

Most of the men in the ship's berthing compartment were killed instantly—by the blast, by fragments it threw, or by the concussion. Other survived long enough to drown as the sea poured in through the enormous hole torn by the explosion.

The shattered destroyer crashed back down into the water and started to settle by the stern. Damage control efforts would fail but would keep the warship afloat long enough to allow for an orderly rescue by other vessels in the area.

DPRK *GREAT LEADER*

Senior Captain Chun stepped back from the periscope in satisfaction. It slid down into the deck.

The images of the sinking American destroyer had told their own story. It lay motionless in the water, its stern already almost completely submerged, and he could see yellow life-jacketed figures floating in the water alongside. The destroyer no longer posed any threat to his vessel or his country.

In contrast, the *Great Leader* had evaded the American torpedo with relative ease. Chun doubted that it had ever acquired his submarine.

After the American Mark 46 had stopped running, he'd ordered his planesmen to bring the submarine up to periscope depth. This was his first kill and he'd wanted to get a good look.

Now, though, it was time to leave. The Americans had undoubtedly radioed news of the attack, and Chun was sure that retaliation would soon be on its way. He wanted to be long gone when it arrived.

"Right standard rudder. Come to one five zero degrees. Set a course for Pusan." He had other targets to hunt down.

CHAPTER
24
Activation

The first flash bulletin transmitted instantaneously to more than a thousand newspapers, radio stations, and television networks around the world could sketch only the barest outlines of the disaster:

"WAR BULLETIN! INVASION—SOUTH KOREA! The peaceful silence of Christmas morning in Seoul has been brutally shattered by a massive North Korean invasion launched without warning or apparent provocation. Following deadly predawn air raids and commando attacks on most of South Korea's major cities, tens of thousands of invading North Korean troops have surged across the demilitarized zone separating the two countries. Radio Korea reports heavy fighting all along the 600-mile-long border, and government officials here in Tokyo confirm that Japanese listening outposts are picking up transmissions indicating that titanic air, sea, and land battles are now raging across the length and breadth of the Korean peninsula.

"Seoul has declared martial law, and all communications into or out of the country are now under tight military control. No word has been received from any of the independent journalists in the South Korean capital. A U.S. military spokesman has refused detailed comment but has confirmed that American air and ground forces are fully engaged in the fighting. All U.S. bases in Japan are now reported on full alert.

"So far, there has been no official Washington reaction to the morning's developments.

"Meanwhile, in a propaganda broadcast heard here, North Korea's Radio Pyongyang has claimed that its 'heroic People's Army' has repulsed a South Korean invasion and is now engaged in pursuing its beaten remnants back across the DMZ.

"More information to follow as it becomes available.

"REPEATING. WAR BULLETIN! INVASION—SOUTH KOREA! The peaceful silence of . . ."

DECEMBER 24—THE WHITE HOUSE SITUATION ROOM

Fowler squeezed his way past the secretary of defense and made it to a chair near Admiral Simpson, ignoring a glare from Putnam. He'd never seen the Situation Room so crowded. The Joint Chiefs, most of the cabinet, the intelligence directors, their principal advisers, and senior members of the President's personal staff were all crammed into this one subterranean, cigarette-smoke-fogged room.

A projection map system on one wall showed a large-scale display of the Korean peninsula. Red arrows and circles showed reported North Korean air, land, and sea attacks. Blake knew the overall pattern by heart since he'd spent the past two hours sifting fragmentary incoming reports to piece it together.

"Ladies and gentlemen, the President of the United States."

The chief of staff's words brought everyone in the room to their feet, and the buzz generated by more than a dozen heated, low-voiced conversations died away as the President strode in and took his place at the head of the conference table.

"Okay, okay. Let's get right to it. We've got a lot of ground to cover and not much time to do it in." The President motioned his National Security Council members to their seats, ran a hand through thinning hair, and then tugged at his shirt collar to loosen it.

His attire added a further touch of unreality to the crisis. Washington time was fourteen hours behind Korean time, and news of the North Korean attack had arrived during the first dance at the White House Christmas Eve Ball. The President had come straight from the ballroom floor to this emergency session of the NSC as soon as the reports had been confirmed through secure communications channels. He was still wearing white tie and tails.

Most of the cabinet secretaries and senior White House staff were similarly dressed, and the Joint Chiefs were all in full uniform. Blake regarded his own wrinkled shirt and hastily knotted tie ruefully. He'd been at home surrounded by torn wrapping paper and his daughter's new toys when the calls started coming in. There hadn't been time to throw on anything better before a Federal Protective Service squad car pulled up outside his town house to take him on a siren-screaming ride across the Memorial Bridge and through Washington's slush-choked streets.

He pulled his attention back to the present as the President continued speaking.

"Admiral, we've all seen the initial messages from General McLaren, but not much more than that. So why don't we start this show with a rundown on what you know about the current military situation."

Simpson nodded and rose briskly to his feet. "Certainly, Mr. President."

He walked over to the projection map and picked up a light pen pointer. "Exact details are still hard to come by, but it is clear that we've been hit with a general North Korean offensive across the DMZ at these points." The light pen highlighted areas along the western half of the DMZ.

"These ground attacks were preceded both by a well-orchestrated series of commando attacks and by air raids on our airbases, command and communications centers, and supply depots." Simpson nodded to the display operator, and dozens of points across the length and breadth of South Korea glowed bright red.

The admiral nodded grimly at the murmurs that swept through the Situation Room. "Yeah. We'd always worried about North Korea's commandos, but we'd always counted on the ROK's tight internal security to help control the threat. Obviously, what we didn't figure on was that the ROK's security force might be too busy cracking down on its own military to keep an eye out to the North."

Simpson turned back to the display. "Okay. The current

situation is this. General McLaren has activated his field headquarters, but communications are still somewhat screwed up. What we do know is that North Korean armored spearheads have penetrated our MLR at these points." Blobs of light sprang into existence on the map. "Casualties are reported to be heavy, and some of our forward positions have either been surrounded or overrun." He shrugged his shoulders. "No one knows for sure."

"We've also got some initial reports that suggest that some South Korean units folded up under the first attacks and are pretty well out of it. But that's also unconfirmed."

Simpson looked at the President directly. "That's all I've got right now, Mr. President. I'm sorry there isn't more, but we're still trying to get a better fix on things."

The President nodded and turned to the secretary of state. "Any more news from your side of things, Paul?"

The secretary looked ashen. The ambassador to South Korea had been one of his closest friends. "I'm afraid not, Mr. President. The survivors at our embassy are trying to sort things out, but things are still very confused. The ROK government also had a number of its own people killed in the first wave of these terrorist attacks."

The secretary made a visible effort to pull himself together. "I would recommend a direct call to the South Korean president as soon as possible. Something to let him know we're backing them in this crisis."

The President nodded. "Agreed. And I'll want to talk to the Japanese prime minister right after that. But not until I can give them a fairly detailed overview of the actions that we're taking." He looked at his communications people. "Set up a secure channel for use after this meeting."

He swiveled his chair back around to face the rest of the NSC and signaled the display operator. The map expanded suddenly to show the Soviet Union. "All right. It's pretty clear that things are bad enough in Korea. Now, what I want to focus on is this. Just what the hell are the Russians up to? Are they a party to this North Korean invasion? Is this just a prelude to something bigger?"

There was a momentary silence around the table as everyone waited for someone else to take the first crack at the President's questions.

Finally Blake cleared his throat. Time to stick his neck out.

"Yes, Dr. Fowler?"

Blake looked up from his notes. "Well, Mr. President, I'd have to say that the best guess is that the Soviets were just as surprised by this attack as we were." He heard a contemptuous snort from Putnam but ignored it. The national security adviser had been cut out of Pacific policy planning for months, knew it, and wasn't happy about it.

"Is that just a plain guess, or do you have something to back it up?"

"Mr. President, I can't tell you that we have anything solid yet, but I think it's the most reasonable interpretation of the facts—at least based on the signals data the NSA has been picking up."

Blake pushed his glasses back up his nose. "About an hour after the North Korean air and commando attacks began, the NSA intercepted an emergency signal from the Soviets' Far East Military District HQ in Khabarovsk to Moscow. They've been in almost constant communication since then. But the pattern is consistent. Short transmissions from Moscow followed at intervals by longer transmissions from Khabarovsk. Based on that, I'd say that Moscow is asking pretty much the same sort of questions you're asking, and that the Far East district is doing its best to find out the answers."

The President considered that for a moment, looking at the map. "Okay. Sounds reasonable. Do you have anything else along those lines?"

Blake nodded. "Yes, sir. Our satellites and recon aircraft have picked up signs that some of their Far Eastern Voyska PVO air defense squadrons have been put on a higher state of alert—but not their Long Range Aviation bomber units. Again, that's consistent with a defensive and not an offensive reaction— at least for the moment."

"So there aren't any immediate signs that the Soviets are planning to jump into this thing."

"That's about the size of it, Mr. President." Blake flipped his notepad to a new page. "In addition, we've picked up similar signals from the Chinese. Their Shenyang Military Region fronting North Korea has gone on a defensive alert, but nothing beyond that.''

The President sat back slightly. "Well, good. We may only be facing a local crisis, then.''

Blake nodded. "So far, Mr. President. But if the Soviets or the Chinese scent real success developing in the North Korean offensive . . .'' He shrugged. "At that point all bets are off.''

"Fine, so be it. Now then, that leaves the question of what we can do to make sure these North Korean bastards don't succeed. Admiral?''

Simpson looked up. "I've had my planning staff and the other Chiefs put together a list of options. In the short run, I think it's essential that we commit our F-15 squadrons based in Japan and Okinawa to the air battle. The ROK's Air Force took heavy losses in the first raids, and our F-16 wing at Kunsan is almost certainly being worn down by sheer numbers. And I'd like to get a task force from the Seventh Fleet steaming to the area right away. North Korean subs and missile boats have already started trying to interdict the sea routes into the ROK.''

"Approved. Send the F-15s and the Seventh Fleet in ASAP.'' The President waited while Simpson handed a note to an aide before continuing. "Okay, Phil. What are my other military options?''

"Well, I think we should start sending ground unit reinforcements to McLaren. He's only got the Second Division over there right now, and infantry tends to get chewed up pretty fast in this kind of fighting.''

Blake agreed with the admiral. The South Koreans could mobilize a lot more men than the U.S. could possibly ship in, but every extra man would count. Besides, it would send exactly the right signal to Pyongyang, Moscow, and Beijing by demonstrating American resolve.

Simpson continued, "With your permission, Mr. President, I'll alert the commanders of the Sixth Light in Alaska, Seventh Light at Fort Ord, and the Ninth Motorized at Fort Lewis for movement to the ROK. The ready brigade from the Twenty-fifth in Hawaii is already loading.''

He nodded toward the Marine four-star general to his left.

"The commandant says the Third Marine Division on Okinawa is already packing, and the prepositioned cargo ships at Tinian will sail within six hours. They have the equipment for a heavy brigade already loaded. He has also alerted the First Marine Division at Camp Pendleton, and some of the Force Troops Pacific at Twenty-nine Palms."

The President toyed with a pen and asked, "Do we have enough sea- and airlift to move all those troops?"

Simpson shook his head. "Not even half of them. But I'm sure we can get help from the Korean merchant fleet and from their national airline. I'd also like permission to begin mobilizing the West Coast elements of the National Reserve Defense Fleet and a limited portion of the Civil Reserve Air Fleet. I expect the airlines will cry bloody murder for a few days, but we're gonna need the transport."

Again the President sat thinking for a moment and then said, "All right. Let's do it. Cut the orders and I'll sign them."

"Excuse me, Mr. President." Putnam leaned forward in his chair, his face flushed and his voice barely under control, obviously smarting at having been ignored in the discussion so far. "Shouldn't you consult with our allies and with the congressional leadership before taking these steps? I mean, we don't want to go this thing alone."

Blake frowned. The President saw it and motioned to him to respond. "It would be wise to consult with our allies as soon as possible, Mr. President. But there's no need to give them a veto over our discussion here. The actions you're taking now are all covered under the UN Security Council resolutions passed back in June and July of 1950 calling on member states to meet North Korea's aggression with force. They've never been rescinded. So, technically, our allies have the same obligations with regard to South Korea that we do."

Blake pointed to the map. "But no one else has the ability to transport the needed troops and equipment into the Pacific region. In practical terms, then, we're going to have to go it alone anyway."

Putnam's face purpled. "That may be true. But what about the Congress? Under the War Powers Act—"

"Come off it, George!" The President cut Putnam off in midsentence. "No administration has ever recognized the War

Powers Act as constitutional, and I'm not about to start now. Christ! You think I want the North Koreans believing I'll have to go hat in hand to the Congress to keep our troops there longer than a lousy ninety days?''

He slapped a hand down on the table. "Not a chance, Mr. Putnam! This is a question of national security, and I'm acting on my authority as commander in chief. I'll meet with the congressional leadership later." The President stared icily at his national security adviser. "Does that give you some kind of problem?''

Putnam subsided into an embarrassed silence while the other NSC members looked carefully away. Blake glanced down at the conference table to hide his own grin. The President had obviously grown tired of pretending to respect Putnam's opinions.

"All right, does anyone have anything else we should discuss right now? I'm going to have to make a statement to the public before long and I'd like to work on it." The President looked around the table.

Simpson nodded. "Yes, Mr. President. One final matter. I'd like to raise the DEFCON status of all our forces in the Pacific. There's no reason we should assume that North Korea's attacks will be confined to our facilities and troops in the ROK.''

The President shook his head slowly. "I'm sure you're right to worry, Phil. But I don't want a general Pacific Command alert just yet. That might provoke an unnecessary Soviet reaction. Stick with an alert for our forces in and near Korea and Japan for right now. I want to try to keep this thing bottled up there as long as possible, okay?''

He stood and everyone stood with him. "All right. Let's break this up for now, but I want this room continually manned by a crisis team. And I want you all ready to meet again as needed, clear?''

Heads nodded around the room. "Good. Okay, these North Korean sons of bitches have caught us with our pants down. Now let's pull them up and kick their teeth in." Both his voice and face conveyed grim intent, and muttered agreement from other NSC members echoed across the Situation Room.

Blake hoped that would be enough.

DECEMBER 25—THE OVAL OFFICE, WASHINGTON, D.C.

The makeup artists had done a wonderful job, thought Blake Fowler, as he studied the President from off to the side—from off behind the tangle of cables and cameras now cluttering the Oval Office.

The Chief Executive's bleak, haggard look and worried expression were gone, replaced by what appeared to be calm, rested confidence as he addressed the nation:

"My fellow Americans, by now many of you have heard the first reports of fighting from the Korean peninsula. I must tell you that those reports are accurate and that we are once again engaged in a desperate struggle to preserve the cause of freedom in our world.

"Beginning before dawn today—on this day sacred around the world as the birth day of the Prince of Peace—communist forces from North Korea brutally and without warning attacked a wide range of civilian and military targets inside the Republic of Korea. Their assaults have also been directed at American diplomats and American soldiers serving the cause of liberty and peace under the auspices of the United Nations. Many of our fellow countrymen have already lost their lives while heroically resisting this vicious and utterly unprovoked aggression."

The President stared directly into the cameras and his voice hardened as he spoke. "Their sacrifices will not be in vain. North Korea will pay a heavy price for this dastardly aggression. They have fired the first shots in this conflict, but I assure you that we shall fire the last.

"And with God's help and our own commitment and courage, the cause of freedom will triumph in the Republic of Korea. Together with the other members of the United Nations and with the courageous Korean people, the United States of America will resist this communist onslaught with every proportionate means at its disposal.

"We shall not rest until we have once again secured the blessings of peace and liberty for the people of the Republic of Korea.

"Accordingly, I have declared a state of national emergency for the duration of this conflict. Effective immediately, all ships and aircraft registered under..."

Blake turned to go. The crucial words had been spoken. America was going to war.

DECEMBER 25—THE KREMLIN, MOSCOW, R.S.F.S.R.

The General Secretary of the Communist Party inclined his head gravely toward the general standing by the large wall map of the Northern Pacific. "Thank you, comrade. That was a most concise and enlightening briefing."

The General Secretary swept his eyes around the elegant, wood-paneled room with its polished brass lamps, thick carpets, and priceless paintings. Not exactly the sterile, modernist room one would have thought would house the top leadership of the world's most powerful Marxist state. The irony never failed to amuse him slightly.

His eyes focused on a thickset, bull-necked man at the other end of the table. The director of the KGB looked more like a butcher or farmhand than a master spy, he thought. And judging by its most recent efforts, that description of the KGB's master might well be accurate. He put his thoughts into words. "Well, Viktor Mikhailovich, I'm glad that we had the benefit of your marvelous intelligence assessments to prepare us for news of this war."

The KGB director flushed at his heavy sarcasm. "The North Korean regime's actions have always been difficult to predict, Comrade General Secretary. Every report I've submitted on the situation has included a note to that effect."

"Oh, very true, Viktor. Naturally it was only our own foolishness"—the General Secretary gestured around at the assembled Politburo—"that made us read phrases like 'the likelihood of open warfare is negligible' and assume that they were correct. Shall I read from your most recent submission, Viktor?"

The director stayed silent.

"Very well." The General Secretary adjusted his reading glasses. "Ah, here it is. Quote, instead of offensive action, the

Democratic People's Republic of Korea will almost certainly pursue an escalating campaign of terror and subversion designed to add to the increasing chaos in the South, end quote.''

He looked up at the director. ''So, a completely accurate document, eh, Viktor? Assuming that is, of course, that one counts an invasion by over six hundred thousand troops as 'an escalating campaign of terror.' '' He smiled with his lips pressed tightly together. Now he could see the veins standing out on the man's neck.

Abruptly he dropped the matter. Pushing the director of the KGB into a premature heart attack would be satisfying but hardly productive. ''Very well, comrades. You can see that we have a problem. Our North Korean friends have taken it upon themselves to open a war with the United States. The question we must face, therefore, is what our response to all of this will be.'' He gestured at the map, opening the floor to discussion.

The defense minister was the first to speak. ''With respect, Comrade General Secretary, I think that we should view this as a golden opportunity. As our briefing showed, the North Korean offensive has been astonishingly successful so far. With judicious assistance on our part, they could win this war—crushing the American puppet regime and humiliating the United States.''

The defense minister shoved his chair back and moved to the map. ''The strategic benefits of such a victory are obvious and might even exceed those we reaped after Vietnam.'' His hand moved across the map, touching briefly on Japan, the Philippines, Taiwan, and on down to rest on Singapore. ''By again shattering the American image as a reliable ally, a North Korean victory would force Japan and all of the emerging economic powers in Asia into a more neutral posture. A posture that would make it easier for us to expand our presence in the region and obtain important advanced technologies.'' The defense minister's dark brown eyes gleamed beneath heavy eyebrows at the thought.

He continued, ''By driving the Americans out of Korea, comrades, we could also roll them back halfway across the Pacific. Out of their offensive bases in Japan and the Philippines. The benefits to our defense of the motherland and to our ability to project power in the Pacific unhindered would be incalculable.''

The foreign minister, a lean, impeccably dressed man, objected, ''Come now, comrade. You're not proposing direct intervention against the Americans? That would be madness....''

''No, no.'' The defense minister's voice was impatient, irritated. ''General war with the United States is out of the question. I know better than you that the strategic correlation of forces does not yet decisively favor us. When our antiballistic missile system is fully in place, perhaps then—but not yet.''

The General Secretary thought it time to take a hand in the discussion. ''What are you proposing then, Andrei?'' He kept his tone friendly, even solicitous.

''That we maintain the supply of advanced armaments that we are presently providing, provide spare parts, and replace combat losses.''

''Why should we provide any help to them?'' one member objected. ''They didn't provide us with any warning of their actions.''

The defense minister stared at the man. ''We must continue to help them for the same reasons we sent assistance in the first place. If we do not bribe Kim's regime with weapons and assistance, he will look to the Chinese for support. North Korea will move into the Chinese sphere of influence, and comrades, the last thing we need is a Chinese ally on our border.''

He let that sink in, then continued, ''Comrades, I do not believe the North Koreans can win a modern technological war without our support. They know that, and once they are totally dependent on our stream of weapons, we can dictate any terms we choose. We will control them.

''While we must increase our own support to Kim, we can help them reduce the flow of supplies to the puppet South Korean regime.''

The foreign minister raised a finely sculpted eyebrow. ''And just how do you propose to do that?''

''By putting pressure on the Japanese. The Americans need their airspace, airfields, and ports to ship supplies and reinforcements to South Korea. A strongly worded diplomatic note to Tokyo protesting their intervention in this Korean 'internal struggle' might force the Japanese to assert total neutrality. And that would choke off the American resupply effort.''

The General Secretary asked, "You think a diplomatic note would have that much effect on the Japanese?"

"Yes." The defense minister's lips creased into an unpleasant smile. "If it were accompanied by intensive air, sea, and naval infantry maneuvers off their coast."

He shrugged. "Who knows? Perhaps we could even offer to return the Kuril Islands to them?" That raised smiles around the room. They had been seized by the Soviets at the end of World War II and held by them ever since. They would never willingly give it up.

"Go on, Andrei. We're listening." The General Secretary leaned forward in his chair.

"Well, we could also provide the North with useful military intelligence on U.S. movements in the Pacific. RORSAT data. That sort of thing." The defense minister's eyes fixed on a small aircraft symbol attached to the map near Pyongyang. "And finally, Comrade General Secretary, we could 'allow' our MiG-29 instructors already in North Korea to serve as 'volunteers' and participate in the air battle. That kind of tangible support would count for a lot with our little yellow comrades. It would certainly give our crews some valuable combat experience."

The foreign minister frowned. "Comrades, with all due respect to the defense minister, I said this was madness before and I say it is madness now! We are on the verge of a new long-range arms agreement with the Americans—an arms agreement on terms favorable to us. This is not the time to reignite the Cold War!"

One hand smoothed his tie, half-unconsciously. "And even more importantly, the Western banks are only now again starting to lend us the money we need. It took us nine years to repair the damage we suffered for intervening in Afghanistan. We should not repeat that folly now."

Heads nodded gravely around the table, the KGB director's among them.

The General Secretary turned to his defense minister. "Well, Andrei? What do you have to say to that?"

"That my friend, the foreign minister, is wrong. That he is shivering at shadows." The defense minister brought a heavy fist crashing down on the table, making some of the older Politburo members jump. The gibe about Afghanistan must have cut deep, thought the General Secretary.

"The Americans are weak-minded, forgetful fools. They won't dare link your precious arms talks with South Korea. And even if they did, they'd soon be back at the bargaining table. Their own internal politics will see to that."

That much was true, the General Secretary admitted to himself. The American capacity for self-delusion never failed to amaze him. He pondered the matter while the debate raged on around him, back and forth across the conference table.

Not all of the defense minister's arguments were wholly convincing, but the General Secretary had been intrigued by the possibility he held out of greater trade and technology transfers with the new Asiatic economic powers. Trade and new technology that would speed the work of revitalizing the Soviet economy.

He tapped a fleshy finger reflectively against his chin. The Asian countries, while economic giants, were military pygmies. Once stripped of American protection, they'd be easy enough to keep in line with a judicious mix of outright pressure, internal subversion, and fancy diplomatic footwork.

The thought pleased him and he studied the other men around him through slitted eyes.

In this matter the Politburo's own factional politics were fully as important as the facts of the matter. And judged in that light, realism dictated a decision in favor of the defense minister. Despite all the General Secretary's efforts, his position remained tenuous—dependent on a shifting coalition of votes. The armed forces were a crucial part of that coalition. They'd supported his reforms so far, believing they would lead to greater military strength in the future. If he thwarted their will now, how long would their support last?

Not long, he judged. The General Secretary nodded to himself. Together he and the defense minister had enough votes to force a consensus from the Politburo—despite the foreign minister's objections.

The Soviet Union would support its "fraternal socialist neighbors" in North Korea.

But something nagged at his thoughts. Another factor that would have to be evaluated. Ah, yes. China.

He reminded himself to ask the KGB and GRU to step up their intelligence-gathering operations in Manchuria. It might even be worth another diplomatic push to ease tensions with the revisionist bastards in Beijing. It didn't seem likely that the Chinese would be able to do much to influence events in Korea, but there wasn't any point in risking an unpleasant surprise.

The General Secretary turned his attention back to the ongoing debate. Although he now knew which policy he would follow, it was still important to observe the formalities.

DECEMBER 26—BEIJING, THE PEOPLE'S REPUBLIC OF CHINA

The Premier of the People's Republic of China walked deep in thought across the windswept pavements of the Forbidden City. A security detachment trailed along behind him, shivering in the winter cold.

The Premier had no doubt that most of his bodyguards hated these slow, seemingly aimless, noontime strolls through the squares and palaces of the old Imperial compound. But he found them useful. They gave him time by himself to think.

Of course, they also served another purpose. They demonstrated his relative youth and good physical condition. Many of the others in the ruling Politburo were well past their prime. Some, including his two chief colleagues, the president and the Party's general secretary, were either past or closing on eighty.

By itself, his youthfulness gave him no great advantage. Despite over forty years of Marxist rule, the people of China retained a traditional veneration for the elderly and automatically ascribed the virtue of wisdom to them. In fact, that attitude toward age had even insinuated itself into the Party. And the Premier had to admit to himself that he shared some of that peasant reverence for the old—despite the years he'd spent in the Soviet Union training as an engineer and administrator.

Still, this daily demonstration of good health acted as a reminder to his colleagues and younger members of the administration that he would be around for years to come—long after the first generation of the Revolution was dead and buried. And that was useful. It gave him an edge in the fierce internal struggles that often racked the Party out of public and foreign view.

Though that edge had most certainly not shown itself during the morning's debate on Korean policy, the Premier reminded himself as he turned a corner and began climbing the steps toward one of the Forbidden City's magnificent inner courtyards. Behind him, one of his bodyguards slipped and skidded on a patch of ice hidden among the cobblestones of the walkway. He ignored the man's stifled curses and muttered apology.

No, he thought, this morning's Defense Council meeting to adopt China's position on this mad North Korean adventure had been even more of a hidden wrestling match than such meetings usually were—with all the participants circling watchfully, waiting for that one opening that could lead to victory.

No one had found it. And the result had been an unsatisfactory compromise. A compromise he himself disliked despite having been its chief proponent.

It was, however, the only realistic policy China could follow at this stage in the renewed Korean War. The Politburo was just too evenly split among the conservatives, moderates, and Party liberals to adopt a less equivocal position.

The Premier nodded to himself as he emerged from a vast gateway topped by a stone-carved Imperial dragon. The policy he'd urged and won was the best of the immediate alternatives available to China. And it was the best precisely because it could be altered to match ebbs and flows in the complicated military and political game being played out in Korea.

China had been losing the competition with the Soviets for influence in North Korea for years. She simply did not have enough of the high-tech weaponry Kim Il-Sung and his son lusted after. And the Premier knew that the failed assassination attempt launched by his predecessor against the elder Kim had been the last straw. It had given the younger Kim the power he needed to throw North Korea firmly into the Soviet camp.

Given that, some of the more liberal and moderate members of the Politburo had argued for open opposition to North Korea's aggression. They were openly contemptuous of Kim's antiquated Stalinism and "cult of personality." But the Premier had squelched that talk swiftly. The Party hard-liners still had more than enough power to successfully resist action they would see as a betrayal of their fellow communists in Pyongyang. Especially when the North Korean offensive seemed to be going so well. And China could not risk yet another internal power struggle in the midst of a serious international crisis.

At the same time, his nation could not afford to openly support North Korea's actions. First, it wouldn't gain them anything in Pyongyang—the Soviets were too firmly entrenched. More important, open support for the North while it was killing American soldiers in combat would almost certainly cost China its hard-won commercial links to the U.S.—trade agreements vital to the PRC's continued economic growth. That was too bitter a pill for even the hard-liners to swallow.

Even the alternative of declared, open neutrality was unacceptable. In fact, perhaps the most unacceptable option of all. A declaration of disinterest in a war being waged in its own stated sphere of influence would make a mockery of China's claims to status as a world power.

And that was why the Politburo had finally adopted his suggestion that it adopt no clear-cut position. Instead, it would ship Kim Il-Sung the weapons and supplies he'd requested while officially terming the war "an internal affair to be resolved by the Korean people." And the Premier planned a quiet chat with the American ambassador to help the U.S. understand his position. Such behind-the-scenes diplomacy might help avert an American overreaction to China's logistical support for Kim's invasion. Or, at any rate, so he hoped.

The compromise, while unsatisfying, was at least susceptible to change should the battlefield situation itself change. And the Premier's technically trained engineer's mind regarded that flexibility as a virtue in and of itself.

He glanced at his watch. It was time to turn and head back to his office for his scheduled meeting with the Rural Electrification Committee. With an effort he shoved the considerations of war and international politics out of his consciousness— making way for thoughts about small hydroelectric dams and coal-fired power plants.

China had made its decision. Now it would await events in South Korea's snow-covered hills and frozen rice paddies.

DECEMBER 26—3RD MARINE DIVISION HQ, OKINAWA

Major General Andrew Pittman, USMC, handed the FLASH message from Washington to his division ops officer, the J-3. A frown creased his weather-beaten face and crinkled the bushy, black eyebrows that were his trademark and most prominent feature. His Texas twang was even more pronounced than usual after a full night without sleep. "Well, what do you think, Brad? How much longer before we're packed up and ready to ship out for Pohang?"

Tall, stick-thin Colonel Owen Bradley Strang scanned the priority message from the Joint Chiefs of Staff and handed it back to his boss. He ran a hand over his shaved scalp, absentmindedly ruffling long-gone hair. "Breaking every rule and shortcutting every procedure the way we've been doing it since the commandant called?"

Pittman nodded.

The colonel shrugged. "We'll have the two infantry regiments, the First Amphib battalion, the Headquarters battalion, and the Third Recon aboard ship with all their gear within the next twenty-four hours. The artillery, Divisional Support Group, and the Seventh Commo battalion will take longer. *Peleliu* has been rerouted from Subic Bay, and once she's in, we'll have more space for the heavy equipment."

"Best guess, Brad."

Strang looked out down the truck-choked road leading to the harbor. Storm clouds had rolled in on Okinawa toward midnight, bringing with them gusting winds and periodic rain squalls. Even with the sun up, the Navy's harbor master had been forced by poor visibility to keep the furnace-white arc lights along the quays burning. And in their glare, Strang could see more than a score of gray-painted Navy amphibious ships pitching and tossing in heavy, gray-green seas.

As the trucks carrying troops or equipment crawled through the traffic up to the harbor's main gate, Marine and Navy

officers in rain slickers and camouflage ponchos assigned their
cargoes to specific ships. The division would sail from Okinawa
combat-loaded, with vital stores and gear dispersed so that
losing any given ship to enemy air or sub attack wouldn't
cripple the Marines before they could reach the battlefield.

Strang turned back to his commander. "With the weather
playing up like this, it's going to take us at least seventy-two
hours to get everything saddled up." Even that was a miracle
made possible only by constant practice and detailed prewar
planning. Strang thanked God for the annual Team Spirit
exercises they'd held in South Korea.

Both men fell silent as a rain-laden burst of wind rattled
against the window.

Then Strang cleared his throat. "Of course, we could
always break the division up. Sail now with most of the troops
and let the heavies follow on afterward."

But Pittman shook his head. "That's a no go, Brad. I
talked to the admiral earlier this morning. The Navy's classified the whole Korea Straits a high-threat area, and he doesn't
have enough escorts available to adequately guard two convoys." He drummed his fingers on the desk, beating out a
martial-sounding tattoo. Then the general looked up. "Okay.
Seventy-two hours it is."

He scribbled a hasty reply to the Joint Chiefs' message
and handed it to Strang for coding and transmission.

The colonel had his hand on the doorknob when he heard
Pittman's voice from behind him. "One thing, Brad."

Strang turned. "Yes, General?"

"No screw-ups. Anything not aboard in seventy-two hours
is gonna get left on the beach. And I don't want to leave
anything on the beach, clear?"

The colonel nodded. "Aye, aye, sir. I hear you loud and
clear." The Marines were going to war, and Pittman wanted
every rifle, every grenade, every piece of equipment in there
with them.

TRAVIS AIR FORCE BASE, FAIRFIELD, CALIFORNIA

Northern California's low, rolling hills were also being soaked by cold winter rains—rains thrown by a Pacific storm moving inland to dump snow on the High Sierras.

The rain puddled on Travis Air Force Base's extralong, reinforced runways, taking on an oily sheen in the flood-lit night.

One puddle on the main runway vaporized, cast into a million infinitesimal droplets by the backblast from the four mammoth jet engines of a Military Air Command C-5 transport plane. The C-5 rolled on in a thundering roar as its engines reached full thrust and it picked up flying speed, lumbered heavily into the air, and arced gently over onto a westward course.

The plane's engine noises faded, their place taken by the howling, high-pitched screams of other C-5s and C-141s, as they taxied onto the slick tarmac for takeoff or waited motionless while troops and gear of the Army's 7th Light Infantry Division were loaded on board. A ceaseless flow of buses and trucks from Fort Ord—the 7th's stateside base—rolled off Highway 80, through the main gates, and onto the field to add to the long lines of combat-ready soldiers waiting their turn to clamber aboard a troop carrier.

The airlift to South Korea had gotten underway as soon as a significant number of the division's scattered troops and the MAC plane crews could be recalled from their Christmas leaves. Many men were still enroute, caught by the crisis at home in cities and towns all across the U.S. As they trickled in, haggard and wan, already sapped by jet lag and family worries, the nonstop cycle of loadings, takeoffs, and landings continued. It would go on without respite for another ninety-six hours.

CHAPTER 25

The Big Picture

DECEMBER 25—EIGHTH ARMY FIELD HEADQUARTERS FORWARD, NORTH OF SEOUL

McLaren walked into the tent almost unannounced. A few people near the door noticed his entry and started to straighten to attention, but he waved them down. Everyone was too tired and too busy to waste time with Regular Army bullshit.

McLaren was tired, too, but not as exhausted as he had been earlier. Once they'd got the Army's field HQ up and running, he'd bugged out for a four-hour nap in his command trailer. He'd long ago learned the old soldier's lesson that you should grab sleep whenever and wherever possible. It had been drummed into his head as a company and battalion commander in Nam.

He scanned the worn faces of his staff. It was obvious that he'd have to start enforcing the same kind of sleep discipline on them. He didn't want men too tired to think straight trying to run his army's logistics or write operations orders.

McLaren saw Hansen in the far corner and caught his eye. His aide nodded and moved to the front of the large, wood-floored tent that served as the HQ's Operations Center. Hansen stepped up onto a low platform backed by wall-sized maps.

"Gentlemen, the general would like to get this afternoon's brief underway." Officers around the tent looked up at Hansen's words and moved to find chairs.

McLaren sat in the front row.

Normally briefings were set-piece affairs, the presenters in their best uniforms, following a ritual older than they were. Everyone afraid of making a mistake in front of the big boss, but wanting to do their best, too. The room was always as still as a church, except for the briefer's voice and the whirr of a projector showing carefully prepared slides.

That kind of protocol had gone right out the window when real bombs started dropping. Now there were people running in and out with printouts and other scraps of paper. Everybody was in cold weather gear and BDUs, mottled baggy uniforms that were worn in combat. Everyone wore a sidearm. And now a chance to sit down meant a chance to eat.

A paper plate materialized in front of McLaren. Corned beef sandwich, chips, and pickles. His stomach growled, reminding him that he hadn't put anything in it since early last evening. He picked up the sandwich and bit into it, chewing wolfishly. Some of his own fatigue fell away at the first taste.

Still chewing, he glanced up at the short, portly officer waiting to kick the briefing off—Colonel Logan, his J-2.

McLaren didn't like the expression on Logan's face. He was worried, a little wide-eyed. Well, let's see what we've got to be worried about.

"Good afternoon, sir. I'm going to start with a short rundown on what we now know of the North Korean drives and their order of battle." Logan looked down at his notes, took a deep breath, and said, "Finally, I'll try to indicate likely courses of enemy action over the next several days."

In other words, McLaren thought, he's gonna try to predict what the bastards will do next. Good luck, Charlie.

Logan walked over to a map that had been taped up on the tent wall. It showed all of the DMZ and the upper third of South Korea. McLaren leaned forward, eager to get the big picture. He had been out of circulation for four hours.

"North Korean forces are making attacks all along the DMZ. They've had their greatest success in the west and have gained the most ground there." Logan tapped the map with a pointer, indicating an area running from roughly Tongjang in the west to Ch'orwon in the east. "This is flattest terrain and the easiest to attack over, especially with the rice paddies frozen. Their assaults along the eastern portion of the DMZ haven't been backed by the same level of firepower or Special Forces support. We're evaluating those as holding attacks— intended largely to pin down our troops in the east."

McLaren nodded to himself. No surprises there. South Korea's geography closed off a lot of North Korea's offensive options. The mountains and razor-backed ridges running down the eastern half of the Korean peninsula formed a natural barrier to ward off any would-be attacker.

Logan continued his dry-mouthed recitation of the available facts. "In the west, we face two main attacks. One launched down Highway One by the North Korean Second Corps, and the other moving down Highway Three along the Uijongbu Corridor. That one's being spearheaded by the enemy's Fifth Corps. Both corps have been heavily reinforced. We've identified elements of at least two armored, four mechanized, and eight infantry divisions in these attacks."

There were gasps around the room. Neither enemy force had been listed on the Eighth Army's prior OB charts as containing more than half that strength. Somehow the North Koreans had been able to double the number of their troops along selected portions of the DMZ without alerting either American or South Korean intelligence.

"The enemy's Fifth Corps drive has already captured Yonch'on. In the west, they've pushed up to the outskirts of Munsan." Logan looked soberly at the assembled officers. "In other words, the North Koreans are already across the Imjin River."

McLaren scowled. That was bad. The Imjin had always been viewed as a principal backstop for the allied forces deployed along the DMZ. Prewar staff studies had estimated it would take the North Koreans a minimum of two days to push that far south. They'd done it in less than sixteen hours.

And Munsan was a quarter of the way to Seoul. Seoul was the center of it all. It had a population of eleven million in a country of forty million people. Damn the geography that placed the political, cultural, and economic center of the country within forty kilometers of a hostile border.

Logan finished describing the known positions and strengths of the attacking forces. They were pushing hard, using Soviet steamroller tactics—attacking everywhere until they found a weakness, then concentrating everything at that point. McLaren listened to his J-2 with half his mind. The other half was busy considering options. The North Koreans were showing they could play the Soviet ball game well, demonstrating a dangerous grasp of speed and offensive firepower. But there were weaknesses, too. Weaknesses he and his troops would have to be ready to exploit. Soviet tactics weren't too flexible. If they could find ways to seize the initiative, to disrupt the smooth unfolding of the North Korean plan, they should be able to throw the enemy commanders off balance.

McLaren filed the thought away for future consideration and turned his full attention back to the briefing. The J-2 had moved on to a discussion of the new North Korean equipment they'd identified so far. One of Logan's assistants came up front with a slide screen and another turned on a slide projector. The first image was a fuzzy black-and-white shot, so blurred it was only a collection of angular shapes. It was an airplane.

"This was taken from the videotape of a fighter that fought last night. This is a MiG-29 Fulcrum, a Soviet design that has been recently added to the enemy inventory. It's a very advanced aircraft, a match for our F-16s. But that's not all. The Soviets have provided the North Koreans with other weapons."

He put up another slide. In color, it showed several tanks against a typical Korean winter landscape. "These are T-72 tanks, one generation advanced over the T-62s that we thought were their newest models. It has a bigger gun, better armor, and is much faster than the T-62. This is a complete surprise to us."

A buzz of conversation swept through the crowded Operations tent, and Logan waited for it to die away before continuing, reacting to the irritated disbelief he'd heard from his fellow staff officers: "Yeah, I know." He looked at the general.

"Sir, I am very embarrassed that we didn't know about this new equipment in the enemy's inventory. We had some information from ROK Army Intelligence that the stuff was present, but it was disregarded because we couldn't confirm it by our own sources. We're reevaluating our data, but we don't know what other surprises we may have overlooked.

"On the bright side, they can't have too much of this new equipment. Therefore, we can expect that it will be reserved for important attacks, and its appearance may signal enemy intentions." McLaren saw several of his officers making a note of Logan's observation.

The lights came back up.

"Okay, Charlie, whip out your crystal ball." McLaren tried to make his voice lighter than he felt. He'd always disliked senior officers who let their pessimism infect those around them. He was determined not to make that same mistake.

"General, there can't be much doubt that the North Koreans intend to carry this thing through all the way. They've committed an enormous percentage of their available military resources to this operation—their whole Special Forces outfit, and a sizable chunk of the regular Army, Navy, and Air Forces. And satellite data shows heavy rail traffic heading south from the second echelon encampments around Pyongyang, Wonsan, and Hamhung. Clearly, they're trying for a knockout punch before our reinforcements from the States arrive and before our reserves here complete their mobilization."

Logan laid his map pointer dead center on the large, orange blotch that marked South Korea's capital city. "Now. Seoul is the first big prize, and the NKs have two choices—either head directly for the city or use their two assault columns to envelop and surround it." McLaren agreed with his assessment. It wasn't brilliant military insight, but he was probably correct. The North Koreans weren't going to be subtle. They didn't need to be. They had numbers and momentum on their side.

Brigadier General Shin, deputy J-3 for the Combined Forces Command, took Logan's place on the platform. His chief, Brigadier General Barret Smith, was still enroute back to the ROK from a Christmas leave in Japan. Shin's precise, cultured, perfect English painted a bleak picture of the situation the American and South Korean troops faced.

Casualties in first-line units had been heavy—more than thirty percent in some battalions. And North Korean commandos had inflicted significant losses on a number of extremely important rear-area units. The troops facing the enemy thrusts down Highway 1 and Highway 3 urgently needed reinforcements, replacements, and resupply.

For example, the South Korean brigade holding Munsan, a strategic road junction, was under attack by at least two enemy divisions with heavy air and artillery support. After nearly a day of continuous fighting, its three infantry battalions were down to half strength. The brigade's commander and most of his senior staff officers were dead. Antitank and small arms ammunition were running low. Without immediate assistance, the senior battalion commander reported that Munsan would fall within four to six hours.

"Unfortunately, gentlemen"—Shin's face was impassive—"we don't have any help to send. Not that can get there in time to matter. All our available forces are fully committed."

Similar situations were being duplicated all up and down the line. No out-and-out North Korean breakthroughs had been reported so far, but it could only be a matter of time before their tanks started tearing holes in an ever thinner allied defense.

Additional American ground troops were on the way, but they couldn't possibly begin arriving in significant numbers for several days. The same thing went for South Korea's hastily mobilizing reserves.

McLaren shifted in his chair, pushing his empty paper plate off to one side. "What about the air situation? We need replacement aircraft and pilots almost as much as we need troops."

"F-15s from Kadena, Japan, will be arriving shortly, General. We've been notified by Washington that other U.S.-based squadrons will be airborne later today. They should be available for combat missions within twenty-four hours. Your Navy also reports that two carriers, the *Constellation* and *Nimitz*, are on the way. *Nimitz* is the closest, but her attack squadrons and fighters won't be in range until the day after tomorrow."

McLaren sat back, pondering. Not a pretty picture, but not Fort Apache, either. "Okay, we've got a lot of help coming, but we're on our own for at least the next few days. We've got to slow down the North Korean push with what's on hand."

He got up and strode to the front of the tent, getting a closer look at the map. "General Shin, I want you to assume that Munsan will fall to the enemy. Start preparing the next main line of resistance here." His finger stabbed the small town of Pyokche, just fifteen kilometers north of Seoul. "Reinforce it with whatever odds and ends you can scrape together."

McLaren turned to face his officers. "That road junction is the key, gentlemen. If the enemy's assault column presses its drive past Pyokche down the MSR, we're looking at a direct push to grab Seoul. If it swings southeast, toward Wondang or thereabouts, we're in for an envelopment and we'll plan accordingly."

He folded his hands behind his back. "All right then. We've already ordered the evacuation of American noncombatants and unattached civilians. It's time for the next logical step. Put out the word to all U.S. installations in Seoul to prepare for evacuation. Headquarters and command functions will go to Taegu, all the support stuff to Japan."

He looked over at the Air Force liaison officer. "Jim, your boys have done well so far, but I'm gonna need everything they've got."

The colonel nodded. "Yes, sir. We have thirty aircraft shuttling between Kimpo and Japan now. There'll be twice that many in eight hours, and we'll double that again in sixteen. We're even calling up Reserve C-130 units."

"Good, but see if you can even push that. Given the current pace of the NK advance, I can't guarantee the safety of the airfield for more than two or three days, and there's a lot of people to move."

He heard helicopters clattering overhead, growing louder, and saw Hansen signaling him from the back of the tent. His "guest" was arriving. Time to wrap the brief up with a quick pep talk. "Okay, gentlemen. That's it for now. But I want you to keep this in mind. They got the drop on us, but we can hold these bastards. Every hour we can delay the enemy buys time for our reinforcements to arrive. And when we get enough troops on hand we're gonna kick these s.o.b.'s back across the Z with their tails between their legs."

McLaren looked around the tent. Everyone was writing, looking at the map, or looking at him. They looked slightly less unsettled, and that was about all he could expect right now. "Anybody got anything else?"

Nobody spoke.

"All right then. Let's get down to it."

The assembled officers scattered back to their duties. McLaren pushed through the crowd toward Hansen.

"General Park and his entourage are here, sir."

"Great. Okay, Doug, separate out all the ass-kissers and bring 'em here for a minibrief on the overall situation. Make 'em feel like they're doing something."

Hansen grinned and asked. "What about the general?"

"Get him up to my command trailer. Park and I have a few things to go over in private. Mano-a-mano."

Hansen grinned wider, sketched a quick salute, and left. McLaren followed him out the tent and then headed for his trailer. This was going to be touchy.

The Chairman of the South Korean Joint Chiefs showed up on his doorstep a few minutes later. Park wore impeccably tailored combat fatigues, a cold weather parka, a holstered .45, and a helmet he took off as soon as he stepped inside the narrow-bodied trailer.

McLaren met him with a firm handshake and led the Korean over to a canvas-seat director's chair. He settled into a similar chair and willed himself to be patient through the next several minutes of meaningless pleasantries as Park conveyed his government's gratitude for the aid being sent by the United States and repeated the ROK's firm commitment to the unified command structure.

That was what McLaren had been waiting to hear, and he used it to raise a crucial issue: the release of the South Korean officers being held in detention camps for their part in General Chang's abortive coup. He wanted them back in the field, commanding their units.

Park was outraged. "What you ask is impossible! These men are traitors, conspirators."

McLaren kept his tone level, but he spaced his words out enough to let Park hear the determination behind them. "I'm not—asking—anything, General. The situation we face is critical. Meeting it is going to take a one-hundred-percent effort from every man in this country—Korean and American alike. And without the officers you've got rotting in those camps, a lot of my ROK units aren't operating up to par. I don't want any more fiascos like the one up at Kangso this morning."

The word on that had come through just before the staff briefing. A South Korean infantry battalion commanded by a major whose only obvious military credential was unquestioning loyalty to the Seoul government had been ambushed enroute to the front. The major had panicked and fled—leaving his troops to try to fight their way out of the trap without any command coordination or support. Three hundred of them had been killed by a force of North Korean commandos probably mustering less than half of that number. A total of twenty-three NK bodies had been recovered from the ambush site.

"We can't afford that kind of exchange ratio, General Park. Hell, we just plain can't afford to let a bunch of political amateurs try to play combat soldier while there's real shooting going on.

"Now I'm not talking about the officers that were actually conspiring with Chang. They can hang, they should hang." McLaren leaned forward. "But we both know that DSC cast its net pretty wide after the coup attempt. You know many of the men being held. A careful reevaluation of the information that led to their arrest should show that most of them are loyal to the government."

Park frowned. He'd been around long enough to know that what McLaren said made sense. He had fought in Vietnam and knew how valuable experienced leaders were. He sat quietly for a moment, obviously considering his response. McLaren waited, knowing he held the upper hand on this one.

A minute passed in uneasy silence until Park said, "Very well, General McLaren. I'll speak to the President and present your case to him. I think I can get them released."

The Korean looked up from his folded hands. "But I must warn you, General, that my government will hold you responsible for their actions should they betray us again."

McLaren nodded calmly. "I wouldn't expect anything else." He stood abruptly. "Now that's settled, let me show you what we're up against."

He led the way back to the Operations Center.

THE ARMY LOGISTICS CENTER, YONGSAN ARMY BASE, SEOUL

Anne Larson looked at chaos. The systems programming division could be a little crazy, especially if the computer went down, but this went beyond all reason.

First there were the phones. North Korean commando targets in the Seoul area had included communications centers and automated switchboards, and now the phone service was all snarled up. Her people were spending five minutes just trying to get through to someone on the other side of town. And a lot of the phone numbers for supply and combat units were unusable, because the troops were in the field and there was no way to reach them.

On top of that, and despite the lousy communications, it seemed like every logistics officer in the ROK was determined to get a complete list of everything in his inventory. She scowled. If they'd been doing their jobs, they wouldn't have to ask her. One low-level idiot had even called demanding a data dump of everything stockpiled in Korea! She'd hung up on him, hard.

Anne punched a button on her terminal, sending a main-gun-barrel spares list for the 1st of 72nd Armored into the already overloaded print queue. She rolled her desk chair back and stretched, wincing slightly at the pain in her lower back.

It had been a long night and an even longer day. Tony hadn't been able to get leave from Kunsan so she'd had to make an appearance at the office Christmas party by herself. An hour surrounded by buzzed, hard-up, and horny junior staff officers had seemed like an eternity. She'd stuck it out long enough to avoid being talked about and then left—half-angry with Tony for not being able to be there and half-angry with herself for feeling lonely. Three months before she would have taken the whole thing in stride.

It had taken her a long time to go to sleep. She was deeply disappointed in not spending the evening with Tony. She missed him and missed sharing the holiday with him. She hadn't even been able to give him his present. As she tossed and turned her last thoughts were of him.

The alert sirens had woken her an hour later.

At first she'd thought the high-pitched wail rising and falling above Seoul was something to do with Christmas, some Korean custom she had never heard of. But the sirens kept on and on—ending in a tremendous, rattling explosion that had knocked books off her shelves and lit up her bedroom window for an instant with an eerie, orangish light. Then she'd heard jets loud and close overhead. Tony had told her that aircraft were never allowed to fly over Seoul.

She'd still been sitting upright in bed half-asleep when the jet engine noises roaring all over the city were suddenly mingled with sharper cracking sounds. Shrapnel from antiaircraft shells bursting overhead had started pattering down on the street outside, sounding a lot like a hard, metallic rainstorm. And while her conscious mind sorted out all the obvious clues, Anne's subconscious had already had her moving. Out of bed and into her clothes. She'd been fully dressed by the time she allowed herself to think the answer. They were at war.

Just thinking the word "war" made Anne's stomach turn over. She shook off a mental picture of herself ripped apart by bombs. She thought about Tony trapped in a flaming cockpit, trying to get out... stop it. That wasn't getting her anywhere. Anne rolled back to her keyboard, fingers punching up a new menu without conscious thought. Her mind drifted back again to the events of last night.

At least she hadn't gone running out into the street in panic like a lot of her neighbors. Instead she'd sat by the telephone, trying to get through to the base general information number. Nothing. Every time she tried calling, the line was either dead or busy.

After nearly an hour of frantic dialing, Anne had given up and retreated to the apartment's tiny kitchenette to consider her next move. The U.S. Armed Forces–Korea radio station was silent, off the air, and she couldn't make out any details in the Korean language broadcasts spewing out of the government-owned stations. Without any solid information, one side of her mind had wanted very much to stay hidden in the apartment. But another side had argued that she would be needed at the Logistics Center and should report in for work.

She'd been right in the middle of this internal debate when the phone started ringing. Anne had grabbed for the receiver, started to speak, and then stopped in midword as she realized it was a computer-generated call relaying a taped message.

"This is the Eighth Army Information Center with an urgent message for all civilian contract personnel employed at the Yongsan base. At oh two hundred hours this A.M., North Korean forces commenced open hostilities with U.S. and South

Korean troops stationed along the Demilitarized Zone.'' Well, it's official, she thought. The recording continued, ''Accordingly, the base commander has declared a general alert and ordered all base employees to report to their respective work stations.

"However, civilian employees are cautioned to avoid using personal or public transportation. Special buses are being dispatched to pick you up at your place of residence. Wait for the bus dispatched to your location. All employees with dependents should bring those dependents with them. Make sure that you have the following items: your military ID card, passport, special medical information and prescriptions, and a minimum kit with spare clothing and portable personal valuables. Each person boarding a bus will be limited to one, repeat, one suitcase.'' Anne had sat still while the taped message recycled and repeated.

For a moment after hanging up, she hadn't known whether to be relieved now that she knew for sure what was going on or even more frightened. She'd finally shelved the question and started packing, figuring there'd be time enough later to sort out her feelings.

Beep. Anne pulled out of her reverie and glanced at the screen. Damn, she'd misentered a whole field of data. Start thinking, woman. She shook her head and started over again.

Now the bus ride, she thought, that had been frightening. She'd been picked up just before dawn by a green-painted Army bus escorted by a street sweeper to push shrapnel fragments aside and a jeep filled with M16-toting MPs. The trek to Yongsan had been an hour-long, circuitous crawl through Seoul's streets. They'd stopped every so often to load on more of her coworkers and their families.

The capital's boulevards had been strangely empty of the normal, morning rush-hour traffic. And Anne had seen fully equipped South Korean soldiers posted at every major intersection. Storefronts all along their route were still covered by roll-down metal shutters.

Their arrival at Yongsan's main gate had only reinforced her uneasiness. MPs in bulky flak jackets had boarded the bus and scrutinized every passenger's identification. Others stood on guard on the pavement outside, weapons at the ready. And she'd glimpsed still more troops hurriedly building sandbagged machine gun nests at intervals along the perimeter fence.

Anne shook her head slowly, remembering the blackened, torn, and gutted buildings, the debris-strewn streets, and the shattered windows she'd seen on the way from the gate into the Logistics Center. The place looked as if it had been hit dead center by a tornado.

It hadn't taken long, though, for word of the North Korean commando strike to sweep through the crowds of newly arriving civilian workers. Rumor had magnified both the numbers and the casualties they'd caused.

As if the thought had been a premonition, she heard someone yell, "Commandos! There's gook commandos outside!"

Oh, God. Anne hit the save button on her computer, jumped out of her chair, and ran to the window, along with the rest of the staff. Ed Cumber, one of her programmers, stood shaking, pointing outside at a truck parked in front of their building. Korean troops in full combat gear were jumping out the back and taking up positions along the street.

Anne started to back away from the window, then stopped and looked closer. There were American soldiers intermingled with the Koreans, talking calmly, sharing cigarettes with them.

She shook her head and looked disgustedly over at Cumber.

The tall, bleary-eyed programmer shrank a little under her gaze and tried to defend himself. "Well, I thought . . . I mean, they were jumping out of the truck, and they . . ."

"I don't want to hear about it, Ed. Just because everybody else is panicking doesn't mean we should," she said sternly, aware that she'd jumped the gun just like all the rest.

Phones were ringing in the office while everybody stood and looked at the motionless Korean soldiers.

"Back to work!" They scattered.

Anne moved back to the computer terminal she'd taken over earlier that morning, but she altered course when she saw her secretary waving her over. Gloria was on the phone, listening intently and scribbling notes. "Right, right, uh huh, got it. Okay, I'll pass the word."

She hung up as Anne came over.

"It's official, Anne. We're supposed to prep for possible

evacuation. They're going to start sending all civilian contract workers to Japan sometime in the next forty-eight hours.''

Anne stood still for several seconds. Japan. She was going to get out of this mess. Then her mind whispered, But what about Tony?

C H A P T E R
26
Evasion

DECEMBER 25—OUTPOST MALIBU WEST

Kevin Little had never been so cold.

At first the freezing Korean winter air had been a minor annoyance as he lay motionless, playing dead. But now it had become a sharp, stabbing pain—spreading slowly from the bayonet slash through his parka across his whole body. Each short, controlled breath he took moved the icy air farther up his back, sucking away warmth and leaching away his life.

Kevin had always heard that freezing to death was painless. Now that it was happening to him, he knew that wasn't true.

He had to get up and move. Movement meant warmth and warmth meant life. But movement could also mean death if the North Koreans had left sentries behind to guard the hill.

Kevin lay still, listening for the slighest sounds around him. He'd heard the North Koreans evacuate their wounded and march south, away from Malibu's smashed bunkers and trenches. But he hadn't been able to make up his mind about the answer to the crucial question. Had they all gone?

Kevin wasn't sure how long he'd been lying there beneath his platoon sergeant's corpse. Time had stopped meaning very much. How long had it been since his platoon had been wiped out? An hour? Two? Three? He couldn't read his watch without moving his arm.

A new wave of cold agony swept through him. Kevin clenched his teeth against the pain. He had to get up. Now. Before the cold sapped his strength so much that it began to feel warm. Before he started falling asleep in its chill embrace.

Awkwardly he crawled out from under Pierce's body, forcing himself first to his hands and knees and then into a crouch, his back against the sandbag-reinforced trench wall. Teeth chattering, he looked at the wreckage of his platoon.

Bodies were heaped down the length of the trench, lying crumpled and twisted wherever the killing bullets had thrown them. White, bloodless, unseeing faces stared at the sky.

Kevin closed his eyes and brushed roughly at the tears frozen to his face, as if he could brush away the images surrounding him. He'd failed his men. He'd led them to disaster. And now he was conscious of a terrible, almost overwhelming sense of shame that he'd survived. It had all happened so quickly. Only a few seconds had elapsed between the moment Pierce was killed and the final collapse of Malibu West's defense. But during those few chaotic seconds he'd been overpowered by a wave of horrible, mind-numbing fear, caught completely unable to think of what to do next. Playing dead during the massacre had been an instinctive reaction, a last grasp for personal survival.

Kevin clenched his fists and moaned softly. Now he could think again and wished that he couldn't. His mind kept replaying those last horrible seconds, over and over. Pierce falling in slow motion, bleeding, dead. The grenades going off nearby. Men screaming and dying. Men he'd been responsible for.

He shook his head in despair. He'd panicked and lived while they'd died. Now the most he could do was save himself. And maybe not even that. He bit his lip and levered himself slowly to his feet.

Sounds were starting to make themselves clearer to him, and he realized that he could still hear the thumping roar of North Korean artillery from across the DMZ. It wasn't a continuous, ear-splitting barrage anymore. Instead, the guns fell silent for moments at a time as new targets were sought, identified, and marked for destruction. Then the guns fired again, sending streams of high-explosive shells screaming across the sky toward the south.

Suddenly Kevin froze. He'd heard footsteps from the communications trench off to his left. The North Koreans had left sentries behind. His left hand fumbled for the 9mm Army-issue pistol holstered at his waist. It wasn't there. He looked around frantically and saw the Beretta lying in the muck by Pierce's body. Oh, shit.

He heard the footsteps again, closer this time. Kevin tensed. There wasn't time to run. He'd have to try taking the North Korean with his bare hands. He felt a wild urge to laugh and suppressed it. He'd barely passed his ROTC Unarmed Combat classes. What chance did he have now?

He pressed back harder against the sandbags, willing himself invisible and knowing it wouldn't work.

Footsteps again, crunching in the frozen mud at the bottom of the trench. Out of his half-closed eyes, Kevin saw a man step out of the communications trench and start to turn toward him. Now!

He lunged forward with a strangled yell, knowing he wouldn't make it. The man was already turning, moving fast, bringing a rifle up toward him. Then Kevin saw his face and faltered.

It was Rhee, a battered and bloody Rhee, but Rhee nonetheless. His South Korean liaison officer.

He saw the recognition in the South Korean's eyes at the same moment. The rifle slid out of Rhee's hands.

"You're alive?" Rhee's voice was hoarse, and Kevin saw the long, jagged cut running down the right side of his head. Dried blood streaked the South Korean lieutenant's torn snowsuit.

Kevin nodded, not trusting himself to speak for a moment.

Both men stared at each other, panting, waiting for the fear-invoked adrenaline rush to subside.

"What happened?" Kevin jerked his head back the way Rhee had come.

Rhee shook his head and winced. "I'm sorry. I don't know." He paused, obviously trying to remember something, and then continued in a hoarse whisper, "I was in my . . . my bunker. There was a flash. An explosion."

The South Korean looked around slowly at the bodies

heaped around them. "When I came to . . . everything was like this . . . everyone dead."

He stared back at Kevin. "How did you survive?"

Kevin laughed, a bitter, coughing laugh that turned into a choked-back sob. "Me? I chickened out. I played dead while they killed my men."

Rhee shook his head. "You must not blame yourself, Lieutenant. We were overwhelmed by vastly superior numbers in a lightning attack. No one else could have done any better against such odds."

"I should have done something." Kevin heard his voice break. "God, there must have been something I could have done."

"There was nothing to be done," Rhee said flatly. "The communists outnumbered us by more than ten to one. They had absolute artillery superiority. We were short of ammunition and completely surrounded. The result was preordained. Victory was beyond our grasp."

Kevin turned away, feeling irrationally stubborn and oddly irritated by Rhee's attempts to find excuses for him. "Nice try, Lieutenant Rhee, but I screwed up. End of story, okay? Forty men are dead because of me. Because I panicked."

The South Korean moved in front of him again. "You cannot dwell on it, Lieutenant. Your reaction was normal. Anybody else would have done the same." He tapped his chest. "I would have done the same."

He leaned closer. "Come, Lieutenant Little. There is much that we must do if we are to get out of this. We may have been defeated, but we are both still able to fight on. And we shall avenge our men a hundred times over."

Kevin closed his eyes again and sank back against the sandbags. Avenge their men? They'd be lucky to survive the next couple of hours. Right now, he just wanted to sleep. Funny, the air felt warmer somehow.

Hands grabbed him and shook him. Kevin opened his eyes to find Rhee's face inches away. "Come on, Lieutenant! There is no time for self-pity. You're alive. Now stay that way!"

The South Korean's voice hardened. "It's going to take both of us to get out of this. If you want to fall apart, do it later, after we're back in our own lines."

Kevin felt anger surge through him, driving back both the cold and sorrow. "Goddamn you, Rhee. Let go of me!" He pushed the South Korean's hands away and straightened up.

Still angry, he turned away and grabbed an M16 off the trench floor. He didn't see the wan, sorrowing smile cross Rhee's face and vanish.

He turned back to the South Korean. "Okay, Mr. Rhee. Just what the fuck do you suggest we do to get out of this mess?"

Rhee kept his face expressionless. "First, I think we must get off this hill. The communists have gone for now, but they'll be back. You can be sure of that."

Kevin nodded, grudgingly accepting the sense of Rhee's argument. "Okay. But we can't move very far in daylight. We'd be spotted in minutes."

"True. But we can try to get into cover in a gully or a patch of brush. Somewhere out of sight and out of the way. After that?" The Korean shrugged and moved away from Kevin up onto a firing step to study the ground around Malibu West's small, rocky hill.

Kevin followed him.

North Korean tanks and troop carriers were still pouring south over the open fields around them—the passage marked by the sound of rumbling engines and squealing, clanking treads. Canvas-sided trucks followed, bouncing and lurching across the torn, roadless ground.

Suddenly sunlight flashed off a canopy as a jet roared low over them and then dropped even lower, screaming west toward the closest North Korean column. The plane pulled up sharply and banked as its bombs found their targets. A pair of trucks disappeared in searing, orange-red explosions.

The jet dived again for the safety of the hills and vanished, pursued by streams of tracers and by airbursts from larger-caliber antiaircraft guns. Oily smoke from the flaming trucks billowed into the sky above the North Korean column, but other trucks and tanks were already detouring around them— still driving south.

Kevin and Rhee slid back down to the bottom of the trench. Kevin raised an eyebrow at the South Korean, his question silent but clear. Well? Which way should they go?

Rhee jerked a thumb to the southeast, and Kevin nodded

his agreement. There'd been fewer North Korean troops visible in that direction.

The two men grabbed their weapons and hauled themselves over the lip of the trench, staying low. Then they crawled down the hill to the southeast, looking for somewhere to lie hidden until the sun went down.

Malibu West lay abandoned behind them.

DECEMBER 26—SOUTHEAST OF MALIBU WEST, SOUTH OF THE DMZ

Kevin clutched his M16 tighter and crouched lower in the snow-choked ditch, scanning the darkness. Where was Rhee?

The South Korean had gone on ahead nearly ten minutes ago to scout out the little village and side road their maps showed right ahead beyond the small rise to his front. What was keeping him?

Kevin knew that he and Rhee had been lucky so far. They'd lain undetected in a clump of dead brush through the rest of Christmas Day while a North Korean assault column rumbled south just a few hundred meters away. Once night had fallen, they'd wriggled out of the brush and jogged southeast, guiding themselves by Rhee's compass and by the bright flashes of the North Korean guns still firing from beyond the DMZ.

Late at night, clouds had rolled in from the north, covering the sky and raising the temperature enough for a light snow to begin falling, settling in over the whole battlefront. They'd welcomed both the relative warmth and the cover from prying eyes it provided.

Now, though, the snow was a hindrance. Fast-falling flakes made it almost impossible to see anything more than a few meters away. Kevin peered out into the swirling darkness, alert for the slightest sound or sign of movement.

Snow crunched somewhere off to the right. Kevin twisted toward the sound, his fingers seeking the M16's safety.

"Little?" Rhee's voice sounded even more hoarse and strained than it had before.

"Here."

Rhee dropped down into the ditch beside him.

"Well?"

318 • / LARRY BOND

318 • / LARRY BOND

318 • / LARRY BOND

318 • / LARRY BOND

318 • / LARRY BOND

318 • / LARRY BOND

318 • / LARRY BOND

318 • / LARRY BOND

318 • / LARRY BOND

318 • / LARRY BOND

318 • / LARRY BOND

318 • / LARRY BOND

318 • / LARRY BOND

318 • / LARRY BOND

318 • / LARRY BOND

318 • / LARRY BOND

318 • / LARRY BOND

318 • / LARRY BOND

318 • / LARRY BOND

318 • / LARRY BOND

318 • / LARRY BOND

318 • / LARRY BOND

318 • / LARRY BOND

318 • / LARRY BOND

"We can cross through the village safely enough. There's no one there to . . ." Rhee faltered for a second and then went on, "Come, you'll have to see it for yourself, and we have no time to waste."

The Korean lieutenant clambered out of the ditch and moved off into the night. Kevin followed.

He understood what Rhee meant when they reached the outskirts of the lifeless village. A North Korean tank column must have rolled right through the middle of the place, machine guns blazing. The killing had been indiscriminate, wanton.

Old men, women, and children lay scattered in and around their wrecked homes, cut down without reason or pity. The new-fallen snow mercifully covered most of the torn bodies and hid much of the horror.

But not all of it. Kevin's face tightened when he saw the huddled figures of a mother and her three children lying still against the bullet-riddled wall of the village shrine. Bastards. They'd pay for this. And for his men.

He shook Rhee's shoulder, pulling the Korean lieutenant away from the nightmare around them. They had meant to look for food, but all he could think of was leaving this place. Rhee wiped the tears from his face and led the way out of the village into the rice paddies and orchards beyond.

They had to find a place to hide before the sun came up. Artillery continued to thunder off to the north.

NEAR TUIL, SOUTH KOREA

The North Korean company commander watched impatiently as his crews stripped the camouflage away from their T-55 tanks. It was all taking too long for his taste. The sun would be up in a matter of minutes, and he'd wanted to be on the way well before first light.

The North Korean captain frowned. If he'd had his way they would never have stopped for the night. His T-55s had infrared searchlights mounted beside their 100-millimeter guns. They could have pressed the attack onward through the darkness and snow. And he was quite sure that kind of unrelenting pressure would have cracked the imperialist defenses ahead of them wide open.

The captain's lip curled. But no, his battalion commander had explained, the infantry units accompanying the attack were exhausted. They had to rest. They would all drive on together first thing in the morning.

Well, screw the infantry. Those damned footslogging weaklings had given the fascists a four-hour respite. Four hours to strengthen their defenses, resupply, and rest. Now he and his men would have to pay a heavier price in blood and burned-out tanks to make the same gains they could have made with relative ease in the night.

To top everything off, his battalion commander had forbidden anyone to bivouac in the small village they'd shot up. The fool had been afraid the imperialist artillery batteries might have the area zeroed-in. So instead of warming themselves inside captured houses, he and his men had shivered sleepless inside their tanks.

He slapped the side of the turret in frustration. "Come on, you puling swine. Move!"

His men raced even faster to fold and stow their white camouflage nets. Their company commander's morning temper tantrums were infamous. All his urgings, however, couldn't do much to speed the moment when they could start turning over their T-55s' powerful, water-cooled diesel engines.

And when the sun rose blood-red, only five of the company's eight remaining tanks had their diesels revving at full throttle.

The captain muttered angrily to himself as he waited for the other tank commanders to get their armored behemoths underway. His breath steamed in the frozen air. The temperature was dropping again.

Something flickered at the corner of his eye and he turned, squinting painfully into the rising sun. Nothing. Nothing. There.

He stood rooted in place for a moment, mesmerized by the oncoming shapes. Then he grabbed for the twin handles of the turret-mounted DShK-38 heavy machine gun and bellowed, "Air raid warning—EAST!"

BLUE DRAGON FLIGHT, 25TH SQUADRON, ROK AIR FORCE

Major Chon of the South Korean Air Force smiled beneath his oxygen mask as his American-built A-10 Thunderbolt II lifted its ugly nose above the ridgeline and dropped back down in a gentle dive toward the ice-covered rice paddies below.

He glanced quickly right and left. The three other planes of his flight were pacing him, flying in a line-abreast formation to maximize their chances of sighting a worthwhile ground target.

Chon smiled again. This was more like it. Much better than yesterday.

The first day of the war had been a disaster for the ROK's lone A-10 ground attack squadron. Right at the start, North Korean commandos had crash-landed right on Yanggu's runways and fanned out across the field, shooting up and grenading barracks, maintenance shops, a Vulcan antiaircraft battery, and the nearest I-Hawk SAM battery. They'd inflicted heavy casualties and damage before Air Force security troops had killed them.

The air raid that followed had been even worse. The 25th's A-10s were still taxiing out when a squadron of MiG-23s roared in out of the mountains—laying a string of concrete-piercing bombs across the now-defenseless base and its aircraft shelters. The bombs had turned three of the squadron's twelve planes into flaming wrecks and had grounded the rest until the base's shattered runways could be repaired.

That was bad enough. But then the Air Force staff gurus in Seoul had given first priority to the ROK's fighter and air defense squadrons. As a result, specialized runway repair crews hadn't arrived at Yanggu until late in the day—near dark. And by then the crews had been so exhausted that it had taken nearly six hours to fill in the holes and restore the runways to operational status.

That was all in the past now, though, and Chon expected today's tank-killing missions to erase the stain on his squadron's honor. They'd been ordered up into the predawn gray to hunt down enemy armored units that had been spotted late yesterday moving in to overrun some of the few troops still holding firm against the North Korean onslaught.

Chon scanned the low, undulating ground rushing toward him. Small, scattered clumps of trees, a snow-covered road and rice paddies, houses on the horizon—a tiny village. Ah. There they were. He spotted clouds of steam and exhaust smoke rising near the village where a cluster of T-55 tanks and other armored vehicles were gunning their engines to dispel the growing cold.

He broke radio silence. "Blue Dragon flight, this is Lead. Target at two o'clock. Attack in sequence."

Chon banked right and dropped lower, lining up for a quick strafing run. The other three A-10s followed suit. He thumbed a switch on the stick, setting the plane's internal decoy dispenser system to AUTOMATIC. Now the A-10 would pop an IR decoy flare every couple of seconds through his attack run. With luck, any heat-seeking SAMs fired at him would be attracted to the flow of fast-burning magnesium flares instead.

The South Korean major settled his thumb back on the trigger for the plane's GAU-8 30mm rotary cannon and watched the cluster of enemy tanks and APCs grow larger in his HUD's target reticule. His thumb tensed, waiting.

NEAR TUIL, SOUTH KOREA

Lying half-hidden in a nearby drainage ditch, Kevin Little and Rhee watched in amazed relief as the first dark-green, flat-winged A-10 screamed down out of the sky toward the North Korean tanks, trailing an incandescent stream of slowly falling flares.

They'd taken shelter in the ditch early in the morning, too punch-drunk to spot the camouflaged T-55 company just a hundred meters ahead. When the tank engines had coughed to life, each had known they'd had it. Their improvised hiding place was right on the enemy's line of march, and the North Koreans couldn't possibly miss them once the tanks started rolling.

The A-10 fired and its nose disappeared in a blaze of light as it threw a hail of heavy, depleted-uranium slugs toward its targets.

The slugs vaporized snow and threw up fountains of new-made mud in a straight line pointing right at the parked T-55s. Then the bullet stream slammed into the thin top armor of the first tank, slashed through steel, and fireballed it—throwing burning diesel fuel and armor fragments high into the air. A second tank exploded, and a third sat lifeless and immobile, shredded from end to end.

The A-10 roared overhead, picking up speed as its twin turbofans went to maximum thrust. Its companions came in close behind, completing the slaughter. More North Korean tanks and APCs were ripped apart.

Kevin's eyes followed the lead plane pulling up out of its strafing run. As it raced low over a white-cloaked orchard, a streak of orange flame leapt out from among the dead trees—darting after the Thunderbolt. Christ, North Korean infantry must be bivouacked in the grove, he thought, and one of them had fired a hand-held SAM to try to avenge his tank-driving comrades.

Aware of the oncoming missile, the A-10 suddenly jinked hard left, climbed sharply to clear a low ridge, and spewed a new cluster of flares. The SAM veered off, closing on one of the decoys.

The cleanup Thunderbolts saw the missile launch and banked right to strafe the orchard it had come from. Short cannon bursts from each hammered the orchard into a splintered tangle of fallen trees and dead men.

Kevin heard new explosions cracking nearby and tore his horrified gaze away from the carnage in the woods. He glanced back toward the lead A-10 just as it suddenly disappeared in a wall of smoke and flame.

45TH MEDIUM ANTIAIRCRAFT BATTERY, NEAR TUIL, SOUTH KOREA

Altered by the tank company commander's last bellowed warning, the 45th's gunners frantically swung their six S-60 towed antiaircraft guns through an arc, trying to lead Chon's snub-nosed A-10. The jet was moving too low and fast for precise aiming. They could only try to throw a proximity-fused barrage ahead of the speeding plane and hope that it ran straight through the deadly cloud of explosions and spiraling fragments.

Each gun only had time to lob three shells toward the selected aim point before Chon's wingman spotted their muzzle flashes and strafed the battery into oblivion.

Most of the North Korean gunners didn't live to see it, but they got lucky.

One of the eighteen 57-millimeter shells burst just above and behind Chon's A-10. The explosion tore the plane's starboard engine off and sent fragments slicing through A-10's armor, deep into its fuselage—tearing through control cabling, hydraulics, and fuel tanks. The fragments didn't cause any fires or internal explosions that would have destroyed the jet outright, but they did damage or destroy too many vital systems for it to remain flyable for long.

BLUE DRAGON FLIGHT LEADER

Chon swore under his breath as he wrestled to regain control. The unexpected flak burst had ripped the stick out of his hands and tossed the A-10 into a dive. Now, without its starboard engine, the plane bobbled through the air like an epileptic duck.

The electronics for his HUD were out, gutted by a shell splinter, but he could see the ground rushing upward and his backup altimeter spinning down as the plane lost altitude.

Grunting with the effort, Chon pulled the ungainly A-10's nose back level less than a hundred meters above the snow-covered ground and risked a quick glance at the instrument panel. Red MALFUNCTION warning lights blinked on almost every crucial indicator. No good. He could feel the aircraft growing less responsive with each successive maneuver. It was time to get out.

He pulled the wavering A-10 up into a shallow climb, feeling the stick shudder in his hands as the vibrations grew worse.

"Black Dog Nine, this is Blue Dragon Leader. Over." He paused, waiting for a response, and watched the altimeter climb slowly past seven hundred meters while his airspeed bled off—dropping from over 300 knots to just under 200 in seconds.

"Blue Dragon Leader, this is Black Dog Nine. Over." The airborne controller's voice sounded calm, impartial, almost soothing.

"Black Dog Nine, Blue Dragon Leader declaring emergency. Triple A hit east of Tuil. Ejecting. Out.'' Chon put his hand on the ejection handle.

"Roger your last, Blue Dragon Leader. SAR on the way. Good luck.'' The voice sounded a little less detached, a little more human now.

As the shuddering A-10 leveled out, Chon paused for just a split second to thank whatever gods were looking out for him. With a SAR—search and rescue—chopper on the way to him now, all he had to do was survive the ejection and any North Korean reception committee that might be waiting for him on the ground.

He tapped the 9mm pistol in his shoulder holster once and punched out.

NEAR TUIL, SOUTH KOREA

Kevin saw the A-10 pilot's chute blossom over the village moments before oily, black smoke from the burning tank company blotted out visibility. He shook his head, knowing that the pilot didn't have a chance. The North Koreans would probably be on top of him before he could even shrug out of his parachute harness.

Rhee saw the drifting parachute, too, and scrambled up out of the ditch. Kevin followed him, ready to move away under cover of the smoke.

But Rhee had other ideas. Instead of heading south, toward safety, he lurched off north through the virgin snow with his M16 at the ready.

Kevin stumbled after the South Korean lieutenant. "Where the hell are you going?"

Rhee glanced sidelong at him and snapped the safety on his M16 off. "To help the man who helped us."

Oh, Jesus, Kevin thought, we're gonna put our necks on the chopping block for a flyboy we've never met. But he jogged forward with Rhee, unslinging his own rifle as he ran. He was too tired and too cold to argue—too tired to even feel much fear at the thought of death. A stray thought flashed through his brain as they crested a low rise and came out of the smoke. Did most soldiers do the things they did in war because they were too damned fatigued to know any better?

There wasn't time to think the question through. The parachute was lower, sinking rapidly toward the cluster of houses that marked the small village they'd come through the night before. The wind shifted slightly and the chute skimmed low over the tangle of tiled roofs and stone walls to collapse in a billowing mass of windblown silk a couple of hundred meters ahead.

Kevin saw the pilot roll over, stand up, and start frantically tugging at the chute's harness to free himself. He ran faster and stumbled as Rhee put out a hand to stop him. The South Korean pointed to the right, toward other shapes emerging from the smoke—four North Korean infantrymen who'd survived the slaughter in the orchard.

Damn. Now what? Rhee leaned close to him and said, "Keep moving. We can flank them. They'll think we're part of that." He pointed back over the rise toward the burning tank company.

Kevin nodded and they ran forward again through the ankle-deep snow, angling slightly to close with the enemy soldiers moving in on the A-10 pilot still struggling with his balky chute.

Kevin watched the North Koreans carefully as he and Rhee closed with them, waiting for the sudden shout that would show they'd been spotted and identified.

It didn't come, but Kevin could feel the sweat beading on his forehead. Anytime now. They came down off the hill onto low, flat ground carpeted by frozen rice paddies and waist-high, snow-covered dikes. The North Koreans were still running on open ground as Kevin and Rhee slithered down the first embankment and half-ran, half-slid across the ice to the next.

The four North Korean infantrymen were within thirty meters when Rhee suddenly flopped down on a paddy dike and brought his M16 up to his shoulder. Kevin did the same, and the movement caught the attention of one of the enemy soldiers. The man goggled at Kevin, yelled something to his comrades, and started to lift his AK47.

Rhee fired a three-round burst into the North Korean. One bullet caught the man in the stomach, and he screamed and toppled to the ground, wriggling in short-lived agony. Rhee's shots echoed back from the village and surrounding low hills.

The other three were turning in shock when Kevin fired—a long, scything, uncontrolled burst that emptied his magazine and kicked up the snow all around them in a white mist. Two were thrown back dead, but the third dropped to his stomach, seeking cover. While Kevin frantically tried to snap a new magazine into his M16, he saw the muzzle of the North Korean's automatic rifle swing toward him and flash.

A bullet moving at supersonic speed cracked through the air near his head. Shit! Kevin jammed the magazine in place and started to bring his M16 around. He knew he wasn't going to make it. The North Korean's next burst couldn't possibly miss.

He gasped as Rhee fired, hammering the ground around the North Korean. Bright-red blood spilled out into the snow. Both Kevin and the South Korean lay motionless on the dike, looking for signs of movement. There weren't any. The whole fight had taken less than ten seconds.

Footsteps crunched in the snow behind them and they whirled round. It was the A-10 pilot, gun in hand and a broad smile plastered across his flat-featured face. Kevin could see an angry-looking bruise puffing up on the man's left cheek.

"I owe you my thanks, gentlemen! I won't ask what you're doing here. Wise men don't question heaven's gifts."

Rhee stood up, slung his rifle across his shoulder, and saluted. "It was our pleasure, Major."

Kevin was speechless. They'd just killed four men, four human beings with fathers and mothers and others who loved them, and now these two were acting as if they'd just met in some fancy restaurant in Seoul. He could feel himself starting to shake, and he fought down a sudden urge to vomit. Suddenly he could almost hear Pierce's voice, loud and booming in his ears. Don't be an asshole, Lieutenant, it said. They would have done the same to you. Remember your platoon. Which would you rather be? Innocent and dead? Or alive and able to feel guilty?

Kevin straightened. His hands were still shaking, but he no longer felt gut-wrenchingly sick. If that North Korean's bullet had been one inch closer . . .

Rotors beat off to the south, the sound rising above the crackling flames still consuming the smashed North Korean tank company. The pilot heard it, knelt, and shrugged a small radio off his shoulder. He extended its collapsible aerial and thumbed a switch.

"Blue Dragon Leader. This is Echo Two-Niner. We have your signal. Identify yourself. Over."

"Chon Sang-Du. Major. Four five four niner two three."

A pause. Then the radio squawked again. "Confirmed, Blue Dragon Leader. Stand by for pickup."

Chon glanced up at Kevin and Rhee and then bent to the radio. "Roger, Echo Two-Niner. Two friendlies also at this location."

"Copy that, Blue Dragon Leader." The rotors clattered closer.

Chon looked up again at Kevin and Rhee. "Can I offer you two gentlemen a ride?"

Rhee grinned at the Air Force major and gave him a thumbs-up.

All three turned as the search and rescue UH-1H Huey helicopter lifted above the hill, hovered overhead for a moment, and then settled in to land amid a rotor-blown snowstorm.

As they hurried toward the waiting chopper, Kevin felt the tension drain away. They were getting out in one piece. Back to their own lines. He was safe.

He was wrong.

CHAPTER

27

Hard Target

DECEMBER 27—OVER THE FEBA

Tony Christopher looked down at the white, dirty-gray, and brown landscape twenty thousand long, cold feet below his

Falcon. They were crossing the "forward edge of the battle area"—the FEBA—in a relatively quiet sector and it showed. No explosions. No missile trails. Just a few burnt-out tanks and trucks littering the ground. The grunts were well hidden on both sides, either for warmth or for safety.

He glanced up into a layer of hard-edged white cloud just over his fighter's canopy. The Falcon's air superiority gray camouflage paint blended nicely with the deceptively solid-looking ceiling overhead. The air was smooth, and the F-16 slid through it like a tiger stalking silently through tall grass.

Tony's eyes flicked over his HUD indicators briefly and then resumed their routine scan of the airspace around and below his plane, looking for the telltale shimmer of movement that might reveal a hostile. They were flying this mission on the Mark I Eyeball detector—for the moment, at least. He and the other Falcon pilots in this formation all had their radars off to avoid alerting the NKs to their approach. Tony hoped that the F-15 Eagles flying top cover and Stingray, the E-3 AWACS plane orbiting well to the south, were keeping a sharp lookout on the high side of the clouds.

Tony flew onward, trusting to his instincts and experience to warn him if something went wrong. One part of his conscious mind disengaged itself from the purely mechanical task of flying the airplane and started reviewing the mission coming up. Any way you cut it, this one was going to be a bitch.

"MISSION SUMMARY: Provide flak suppression and close air cover for South Korean F-4s assigned to destroy divisional artillery 2 kilometers west KUWHA." It had looked easy enough on paper earlier this morning. Easy that is until you stopped to think about what those words really meant.

Tony knew all too well. It meant coordinating the movements of nearly fifty aircraft from different units. Reconnaissance planes to take prestrike photos. Tony's F-16s for defense suppression. South Korean F-4D fighter bombers to make the actual attack on the primary targets themselves. American F-15 Eagles for high cover. An irreplaceable E-3 AWACS for control and long-range radar warning. And finally, more recon aircraft to photograph the results of the strike. Their photos would show if they had to go back in and do it again.

It all formed an intricate dance, and Tony knew his place

in it. He'd practiced often enough in peacetime, and it had worked well enough in the war, so far.

This target, though, was an especially difficult one. "Divisional artillery" for the North Koreans meant 152mm howitzers buried in concrete emplacements, called HARTs, for hardened artillery sites. The guns were always guarded by multiple batteries of automatic weapons and sometimes even SAMs. And as soon as enemy radar picked them up, there'd be fighters added to the other defenses. All in all, not a fun time.

He didn't envy the South Korean F-4 Phantom crews their task either. The recon photos the squadron's intelligence officer, George Michaels, call sign "Pistol," had laid out at the predawn mission briefing had shown what they were up against.

There were three batteries of 152mm guns, each with four pieces. Each gun sat secure in its own concrete emplacement, protected by a roof nearly two meters thick and by armored blast doors to the front. The gun areas were further protected by thick earthen dikes. Each HART also had tunnels connecting it to its neighbors and to well-stocked, underground magazines. Cratering those minifortresses was going to take split-second precision—precision the South Korean pilots might find hard to produce with tracers reaching out for them and SAMs flying all around.

Tony shook his head slowly. That made the squadron's defense suppression role vital to the overall success of the mission. He glanced back at the other planes pacing his Falcon. Each had six Rockeye cluster bombs hanging under its wings. Rockeyes were designed to scatter explosive bomblets that could damage antiaircraft guns and SAM vehicles, kill their crews, and knock out fire control radars. While the eight F-16s assigned to the mission couldn't hope to destroy all the sites defending the HARTS, they could suppress and disrupt enough of them to give the F-4s the "quiet" time they needed.

And in all likelihood the F-16s would be called on to do even more than that. Besides their air-to-ground ordnance, all of his planes carried a centerline drop tank and two Sidewinders on their wingtips. They'd loiter over the battle area after their attack runs and intercept any NK fighters that tried to break up the Phantoms' HART tap dance. Stingray, the AWACS plane aloft, could warn them of approaching enemy aircraft and give them a steer.

There was someone else in on this little party, too. A converted cargo plane, call sign Rivet. Tony didn't know much about its capabilities, but the grapevine said it was covered with antennas and most of its crew spoke Korean. He and his pilots had been instructed to treat any Rivet calls as gospel.

Tony glanced down at his INS display. It was vital that they arrive at the right location and right altitude within thirty seconds of the planned time. Timing was everything in this kind of mission. It wouldn't do at all to screw up during his first flight with a new rank.

A new rank. Tony still couldn't believe it. The squadron CO, Lieutenant Colonel "Shadow" Robbins, had called him over into the planning area that morning, before the brief. He'd assumed that Shadow wanted to see him about something connected to the morning's mission. He'd been wrong.

Robbins had stood as Tony walked over to his desk, looking him over. "How are you feeling, Saint?"

Tony remembered stifling a yawn. Six hours sleep wasn't enough to regenerate the nervous energy expended in flying and fighting at high speed, not with lives depending on each and every decision. But he'd answered the CO's question the only way he could. After all, everybody was short on crew rest. "Fine, sir. What can I do for you?"

Shadow's next words had brought him fully awake. "Quite a bit. First thing is, stand at attention!"

He'd braced, wondering just what the hell was up and noticing that all activity had stopped in the Mission Planning Cell. He'd also glanced out the corner of his eye and seen people filling the doorway.

The answer to his unspoken question had come seconds later when Robbins picked up a telex and started reading. "In accordance with the secretary of the Air Force instruction dated twenty-seven April 1986, combat personnel serving in billets may be promoted to ranks required for proper execution of those duties. Therefore, by order of General G. F. Taylor, Commander Eighth Air Force, you are promoted to the rank of major, with all the privileges and responsibilities of the rank. And I'm making you ops officer effective immediately."

Major Christopher. Tony mouthed the words beneath his oxygen mask, after first making sure that his radio wasn't transmitting. They had a nice ring to them, but he hadn't really wanted the promotion—at least not the way he'd gotten it. Stepping into Kenneth Beam's dead shoes seemed like kind of an unlucky thing to do. And the burst of applause from the other members of the squadron clustered at the briefing room door had made him even more uneasy. Still, he knew that the squadron needed an excuse to celebrate, to feel happy. It was one way to help forget all the empty chairs in the pilots' mess.

And Hooter—well, Hooter was just Hooter, Tony thought, grinning to himself. Trust his wingman to bring him down to earth. The tousle-haired little runt had been waiting for him in the ready room, kneeling, and as Tony had come close, he'd bent at the waist and touched his head to the floor with his palms on either side.

Tony hadn't had any choice but to laugh. "Hooter, you've been over here too long."

"Just showing proper respect for the exalted status of my flight leader." He'd stood up, dusting off his knees and reaching out to shake Tony's hand. "Congratulations, Saint."

"Yeah. Well, I'll believe it when I see the first paycheck."

"What? You mean they pay us for this?"

"Very funny. Suit up."

He glanced sideways. Hooter's Falcon hung there, perfectly positioned. Then he looked down at the INS again. Six minutes out. Time to start concentrating.

Tony reached down into the cockpit and turned his secondary radio to the mission frequency. The primary would stay on the package frequency throughout the mission, but he wanted to be sure that he could hear Bookmark, the F-4 Phantom strike leader flying with the main group of aircraft.

Five minutes out. Tony waggled his wings and reduced power. Pointing his Falcon's nose down, he found the crossroads that marked the start of his run in to the target area. He glanced sideways and behind him. Good. The four F-16s of Garnet flight led by Captain Gunther, call sign "Dish," were breaking off, swinging wide to come in on the target from a different compass point. His own Diamond flight would come straight in from the south.

Tony followed them with his eyes for a second while the altimeter unwound and then looked back behind him. Right on schedule, the second pair in his flight had split off and were settling in two miles astern. Viceroy and his new wingman, Saber, would cover the two lead Falcons while they made their run, and then Tony and Hooter would return the favor. Each aircraft would make only one pass, unloading six cluster bombs on the target and then get out. Making a second pass on a now-alerted enemy was a good way to get splashed.

They were at their attack height. Cruising at one hundred feet down an undulating, rock-walled valley. Tony checked the time. They were early, by one minute. Tony flashed his formation lights and turned left, starting a lazy, time-consuming circle. He looked behind to make sure that everyone had gotten the word. Dropping even lower, he watched the navigation system's prompts and the planned approach route. As the INS time reached zero, Tony hit the throttle for full military power. The others followed him.

Even fully loaded the Falcons accelerated from three hundred to six hundred knots in seconds. As they reached full speed, the valley ended, opening up into a rolling, tree-covered plain.

The HARTs were dead ahead with flak guns on top of the bunkers and nearby hillsides. And as soon as the screening valley walls fell away, Tony's radar warning receiver lit up. The sky was filled with tracers and puffs of black smoke. The flak had been firing at the reconnaissance aircraft. Tony could see two plane-shaped black specks pulling away quickly, then he turned and gave his full attention to the formation's target.

The recon photos of the area had shown its being guarded by twin 23mm cannon, single-barreled 37mms, and one battery of 57mm cannon. This last group was Diamond flight's target. He turned onto final bearing, with the battery firing a few miles ahead.

Tony felt an urge to drop down, but he fought it. The Rockeyes had a minimum safe release height. If he flew any lower, he might collect a few fragments himself. He glanced right and saw that Hooter had moved from behind and beside him to a position just abreast and about a hundred feet away.

The F-16 bucked and he was suddenly glad he wasn't

flying any lower. The air was rough this close to the ground. Keeping one eye on the altimeter, he checked the release settings on his Rockeye weapons. The computer would drop them in sequence, timed so that they formed a line over the target and the bomblets sprayed uniformly over the entire area.

The North Korean 57mm guns were laid out in a circle, with a still-turning dish radar in the middle. Tony lined up on the near side of the circle, just to the left of center. He focused his attention on the closest flak gun, lining it up in the center reticle of his HUD. The bomb "pipper" was a small circle now at the bottom of his windscreen, creeping slowly upward. Tony moved his thumb to the weapons release. This wasn't going to be a lob-toss attack. Just a straight, old-fashioned, and effective bomb drop.

Two miles out, then one mile. At six hundred knots the ground was a blur. Everything was lining up, except that the turbulence kept wanting to throw him off. A black puff appeared off to port. The battery had noticed the incoming attack, but it was too late. As the bomb "pipper" crossed the gun barrel, he pressed the bomb release on his stick. There were six small shudders as the weapons left the racks. He spared a glance to his right and saw the fifth and sixth Rockeyes tumbling down from Hooter's plane.

As the two planes sped off, the casings opened and small one-pound bomblets sprayed out. Each weapon could cover an area a hundred and fifty feet wide and three hundred feet long. With the preset release pattern, and the route flown by the two planes, the areas overlapped. Each casing had two hundred and fifty bomblets in it.

Looking over his shoulder, Tony saw the ground being kicked up by thousands of small explosions. Like lethal fire-crackers, the bombs would explode on impact, damaging or destroying equipment and killing anyone they hit. In addition, the bomblets sent out fragments that could slice through armor plate, much less guns or nearby personnel. Smoke covered his target. Yeah, that was one flak battery that wouldn't give the Phantoms any grief.

Tony pulled away from the target. He had an urge to climb, to claw up into the air and away from the dangerous ground just beneath him. He fought it because the first aircraft to show itself at altitude would attract the attention of every gun in the area. The idea was to hit them from different directions, and to split the defenses by staying so low they couldn't all see you.

He banked right and throttled back a little, with Hooter dropping back and falling into trail. That way Tony could maneuver suddenly without having to check on his wingman's location. He looked for Viceroy and Saber and saw them starting their run.

They were going for a group of ZU-23s, large-bore, twin-barreled machine guns. ZU-23s didn't have radar, and there were so many of them that they were normally not worth the ordnance expended to kill them. These, though, were right on the exit route for the main strike group.

The two jets flashed over the ground, and Tony saw cluster bombs fall from their wings just before the area erupted in dust and smoke. As the F-16s turned away, a smoke trail came from off to Tony's right and streaked toward Saber's aircraft.

"Saber, SAM, break right!" Tony called, and increased his own right bank. He fought against the sudden extra weight on his chest, looking for the source of missiles. There it was. A wheeled vehicle with a boxy shape on top—that had to be the launcher. He hit a button on his stick and saw CANNON appear on the Falcon's HUD.

"Hooter, I'm going for the launcher."

"Rog."

Christ, a mobile SAM launcher. It hadn't been there in the prestrike photos. There might be others. Hooter would follow him in and make sure that there weren't any other surprises waiting for them.

Tony locked his radar on the vehicle and a small square immediately appeared on his HUD, centered on the launcher. A circle also appeared, showing where the computer thought his bullets would hit. He came left a little and pulled up slightly.

As he closed, the aspect of the launcher on top of the vehicle changed, and he realized it was pointing at him.

The aiming circle moved over the box and he fired, just as a puff of smoke appeared in the launcher box, followed by a streak of flame, heading straight toward him. The F-16 shuddered as its cannon fired, and Tony saw the launcher obscured by dust and smoke. He rolled violently, popping a string of flares, extremely conscious of the ground just below him.

He looked back and Hooter was gone.

There he was. Off to the right and back, Hooter had seen another launcher. He was firing, a plume of white smoke streaming back from the nose of the plane. Hooter's bullets didn't kick up smoke and dust. Instead, the vehicle fireballed. Tony pulled in behind his wingman and told him to take the lead.

"All units, this is Bookmark. Rebound, out."

That was it. The main group was going in to make its run on the HARTs. Tony called, "Diamonds, join on me."

They would take station on the edge of the area and fend off any fighters until the strike group got away. He switched his radio to the Phantoms' frequency, so that he could monitor the progress of the raid. The instant the Phantoms cleared, his Falcons would be out.

"All units, this is Stingray. Multiple bogies bearing three zero zero Bull's-Eye twenty miles, level fifty, out."

Goddamnit. The AWACS had spotted incoming NK aircraft. It looked like Diamond flight wouldn't get time to form up. "Bull's-Eye" was a map reference that allowed them to radio locations in the clear without revealing their own position. "Multiple" meant more than four, and "level fifty" meant five thousand feet. Twenty miles meant they had to move fast.

Tony gave a new order. "Diamonds, engage by pairs, out." He snapped on his radar and selected a missile. The first job was to "sort" the enemy fighters—find them, figure out how many there were, and what they were up to.

As Tony and Hooter swung their F-16s around to the right bearing, their radar scopes lit up with contacts. Tony did a fast count and then made a radio call. "Bookmark, Diamond Lead. Twelve inbound, I'll keep them off you."

"This is Bookmark. Roger out." The South Korean sounded unperturbed. Tough guy.

Tony's HUD had selected a target rapidly coming into range. He slid out from directly behind Hooter but stayed back so he could cover his "leader's" rear.

As they closed, he listened to the incoming Phantom

strike. The South Korean pilots all spoke English and used it on frequency. There were sixteen F-4s, attacking the gun sites in pairs.

"Bookmark, this is Dragon Lead. Targets at ten o'clock."

"Roger. Watch the Triple-A to the right."

Tony checked his panel. Their radar warning receivers hadn't lit up so they were probably up against IR homing missiles. That was fine with him. An infrared missile locked onto its target's heat and closed in and exploded. But the Russian-built missiles the NKs used had to lock onto the hot tailpipe of a jet before they could home in. The AIM-9L Sidewinders his Falcon carried were more sensitive and could attack from any angle, including the front. Advantage to Tony, he thought.

The SHOOT prompt came on and he fired, seeing a missile flare off Hooter's rail as well. The enemy fighters were close enough to see now, round bodies and thin wings—MiG-212 Fishbeds. His target had seen the inbound missile and started a hard turn to the left, trying desperately to evade it. At first the Sidewinder looked as if it wasn't going to follow, but then it veered sharply, passed over the enemy plane, and exploded. The MiG-21 broke in half and the pieces spun away.

Hooter's shot had hit as well. His target appeared intact, but Tony saw it fall away with an empty cockpit. The pilot had ejected.

Tony concentrated on following Hooter. The Falcons and MiGs were really mixing it up now, forming a "furball" of maneuvering aircraft five miles across and ten thousand feet high. The air was filled with white missile smoke trails, gray-black explosions, and a few parachutes.

The Phantom strike was still in progress. But he couldn't tell how well it was going. He heard things like "Three and four going in" and "Break left!" but that didn't tell him if the bombs were hitting the target. One thing, though. There were other mobile SAM launchers in the area. The pair he and Hooter had hit had jumped the gun. Most had waited for the Phantoms to show up before firing.

Tony felt frustrated. He was supposed to be package commander, managing the overall situation, not just playing aerial cowboy with a bunch of MiGs. He decided to let Hooter look for targets. He called on the package frequency, "Any Garnets unengaged?"

The answer came back quickly. "Garnet One and Two are clear." He recognized Dish's voice.

"Roger, Dish, backstop the Phantoms. Engage any leakers."

Two clicks of the microphone switch answered him. Tony felt a little better. Eight Falcons could keep a squadron of MiGs busy, but some would slip through. Dish and Ivan would stay between the furball and the strike group.

Tony followed Hooter as he extended, pulling away from the mass of whirling aircraft. "Saint, I'm going hard right and try to lock up with a nine lima."

Tony clicked his mike switch twice and slid from behind and right into trail. If Hooter was going to do hard maneuvering, Tony wanted to be out of the way. They came around and went into a gentle climb. Hooter's voice came over the circuit. "I've got one up high. Fox Two."

The missile left Hooter's wingtip as he spoke, guiding on a glint several thousand feet up, about a mile away. Tony saw the Sidewinder's smoke trail as it merged with the glint and exploded. The contact disappeared from his scope.

"All units, Rivet. Floggers enroute your area. Out."

Wonderful, Tony thought. He looked over at the dogfighting aircraft, now breaking up. He'd been following the radio chatter subconsciously, and they must have killed six or seven bandits, with at least one F-16 hit and unaccounted for. That was bad enough, but they'd also used up most of their missiles, and the MiG-23 Flogger carried long-range, radar-guided missiles. This was not the time to tangle with them. "Stingray, this is Diamond Lead. We are fully engaged, request Topaz engage new inbounds, over." Topaz was the high-altitude F-15 Eagle flight.

Stingray's voice was unsympathetic. "Topaz is busy, too. You're on your own, Diamond." Terrific.

He followed Hooter through a barrel roll. He was doing his best to stay behind his wingman, watch his back, and monitor the package frequency. The sky was still full of airplanes, and half of Hooter's violent maneuvering could be considered collision avoidance.

Tony heard a particularly urgent call. "Viceroy, break

left!'' He snapped his head around and saw a missile in flight, a red streak that suddenly joined with an F-16. The Falcon fireballed, and bits of airplane flew out of the red-and-black cloud. There wasn't any chute. Oh, God. A picture of Viceroy's wife flashed into Tony's brain as he pulled hard left away from the smoke cloud. Concentrate. Concentrate.

"Diamond Lead, is your IFF on? Over." It sounded like Stingray's voice. Tony knew his IFF was turned off. The "Identification Friend or Foe" was a device that sent out coded radar pulses that showed up on a radar controller's screen. It was standard procedure to turn it on near a friendly base, but an IFF was always turned off in Indian country, to avoid sending out radar pulses that would reveal location and identity to an enemy.

The controller repeated his message. "Diamond Lead, this is Stingray. Ensure your package has IFF on. Authentication echo sierra. Over."

"Diamond Lead, roger out." Tony shook his head and flipped a switch on his panel. "All Diamonds and Garnets, this is Diamond Lead. Turn on your IFF. Out."

He clicked the microphone switch again. "Diamonds, join on me, we're heading north." They successfully disengaged from the dogfight, and Hooter waggled his wings and slid off to the right. Tony pulled up to take the lead position. He checked his left and saw Saber sliding into the number three slot. Tony and Saber each had one missile left. Their only hope was to stay low and hide until they could mix it up with the incoming Floggers.

The MiG-23 was a totally different beast from its older brother, the MiG-21. It wasn't very maneuverable, but it had a decent radar, and its radar-guided missiles gave it a distinct edge at long range. It was fast, too, especially on the deck.

Tony decided to check on the other half of his group. "Garnet Lead, what's your status?"

"Engaged with a few bandits, one wounded bird. Fuel state near bingo. Over."

Yeah. Tony knew his own group was near the edge, too. Think positive. "Roger, Garnet. Position your group to the north. Catch what we miss. Out."

Tony set his radar for maximum range scan, and sure

enough, there they were. He counted ten bandits, thirty miles out and high up, maybe ten thousand feet. His radar warning receiver was lit up, too, with a solid wedge white from the radar strobes of the oncoming fighters.

One more thing to do before the clash. "Stingray, this is Diamond Lead. Request tanker support, over." And probably towing services, too, Tony added mentally.

"Stingray, roger out."

The range was down to twenty miles, and Tony lost more altitude. They were getting close enough for the Floggers' radar to pick them up, but he hoped that by staying low, in the ground clutter, they . . .

A white trail appeared out ahead of his planes, suddenly snapping down out of the cloud cover overhead. It was a long way off, near where the enemy fighters should be. There was a second, and then smoke trails started to appear too quickly to be counted. What the hell? He looked at his scope. There were only four MiG-23s left now. Those had to be missile trails, but from what? Nothing else showed on his radar scope. The trails seemed to come from the east.

The Floggers were turning left, heading toward the unknown source of the missiles. Tony knew they hadn't seen his flight, and he called, "Diamonds, full throttle!"

He went to full military power himself. Screw the fuel. He selected a target and called on the mission frequency. "Stingray, incoming bandit count is now four. Diamonds engaging."

"Roger, Diamonds, Navy Thunder flight, F-16s engaging. Check missile fire, over."

A strange voice acknowledged the call. The Navy? Our Navy? Jesus, those must be Tomcats from a carrier off the coast. With their Phoenix missiles, they could hit a fighter a hundred miles away. No wonder he hadn't seen the launching aircraft.

Their fortuitous appearance was allowing Tony to execute a beautiful bushwhack. He was sure every one of those NK pilots was heads-down in the cockpit, trying to find the shooters on his radar screen.

"Saber, take the left-hand bird, I've got the outside right." Tony didn't wait for acknowledgment but fired. The Sidewinder headed straight for a MiG-23's hot tailpipe and blew the back end of the aircraft off. The rest spun down out of control. He didn't see a chute. Chalk one up for Viceroy.

Saber's missile had also guided, and there were only two contacts left. They were splitting up, diving for the deck, afterburners lit up. They were heading north. Tony watched them go, bright flame flaring aft. The Diamonds' fuel state wasn't up to a high-speed chase.

Besides, the Phantoms had done their work. The last F-4s were just making their attacks. He ordered the Diamonds to disengage, and with the Garnets, they trailed the Phantoms out of the area. They didn't have enough fuel to cover the poststrike reconnaissance aircraft. The spyboys would just have to take their chances.

The egress route was west of the target, but close enough for Tony to see a cloud of gray dust and black smoke hanging over the area. There was another blotch, off to his right, on a hillside. As he got closer, he could see the remains of a Phantom that had slammed into the ground. He couldn't see if the canopy was in place.

As his flight passed the wreck, Bookmark called. "Diamond Lead, we have two wounded birds. Request close escort, over." It looked as if they weren't finished.

The F-16s tanked on the south side of the DMZ, and Tony counted noses. Owl was missing, his wingman losing sight of him during the big dogfight with the Fishbeds. Dish's own wingman, Ivan, had taken a piece of flak in his left wing. He was still airworthy but had to reduce speed or the vibration would shake him apart. Viceroy was gone, too.

Two for fifteen or so. He guessed that was an acceptable loss ratio. It didn't feel like it though. In silence the F-16s joined on the limping Phantoms and turned for home.

KUNSAN AIRBASE, SOUTH KOREA

The ops office was quiet now. The day's last missions had been flown. Fourteen hours of grueling planning, preparation, and flying—all mixed in with desperate minutes of high-g combat. By rights, Tony should be asleep, worn down by responsibility and exertion. But he couldn't sleep.

He was too worried about Anne. He'd been able to push

her face out of his thoughts in the air, but his fears for her had come back as soon as he was on the ground. She was still in Seoul, and the North Koreans were pushing hard to take the city. Combined Forces HQ said they were still about two days away, but NK heavy guns had been shelling Seoul from Day One. The worst of it was, he couldn't do anything to help her.

The phone rang again. Come on, Anne or somebody, answer. This was the first clear line he'd been able to get in three days of trying.

Ring. Answer it. Please, God.

"Logistics Center." It sounded like her. It had to be her.

"Anne?" He heard the quaver in his voice and tried to still it.

"Tony! Oh, Tony." He heard her take a deep breath. "Are you all right?"

His heart jumped slightly. She was worried about him. About him. "Yeah. Oh, yeah. Look, Anne, I'm fine. No problem." He hurried on. "But what about you? I mean, they're hitting the city pretty hard."

She sounded calmer. "They aren't shelling near us, Tony. They've been hitting the defenses and military bases. We're pretty safe."

"Only 'pretty safe'? Jesus, Anne, the gomers are moving on Seoul."

There was a pause. Then she said, "I know. But don't worry, Tony. They're going to fly us out, move the entire operation to Japan. They've already started moving records and such. We'll go anytime now. One bag apiece, just the essentials. You know the drill."

His pulse started slowing. Evacuation. Thank God somebody in the high command had some brains. "Are you taking the scarf I gave you?"

He could almost see her smile. "Yes. Look, Tony, I'm going to be fine. I'm more worried about you. Really, how are you doing?"

"I'm flying, Anne, that's all I can tell you. I'm doing okay."

He heard voices in the background. Then she said, "Tony, I've got to go now. Work to do. I'll let you know where I am when I get to Japan."

"Okay..." He searched for the right words but didn't trust himself to say them.

"I'll miss you, Tony. I'll call as soon as I can."

There was a click, then silence, and he put the phone down reluctantly.

C H A P T E R
28
Evacuation

DECEMBER 28—SEOUL
LOGISTICS BASE

The orders came late in the day. Anne hadn't gotten much sleep lately, and there was a dullness behind her eyes. She had to read them twice before she understood them.

Waving one hand over her head, she called, "Everyone! Listen, we just got the order. We move out at eighteen hundred." She saw their panicked expressions and looked at her watch. It was 4:10 P.M.—1610 hours military time.

Everything had come to a dead halt, and she saw no reason to start it up again. "All right, if you can't finish it in five minutes, pack it away. Trucks will pull up at six o'clock to take us to Kimpo. We're going to Misawa, Japan, and set up there.

"Gloria, keep taking messages. We can't tell anyone we're evacuating, so it'll just be awhile before we get them their data."

The office had changed in the last four days. Everyone had moved their belongings, one bag each, into the office. The enemy had closed steadily on the city, until fighting could be heard almost constantly to the north.

Last night she had told Tony that they had not been

shelled, that the North Koreans had more important targets. The base had been shelled twice since then. Stray rounds had come within a few hundred feet of the computer center. There had been no damage, and nobody hurt, but she had felt the barest introduction to combat. From an infantryman's point of view, this was not even close. But she wasn't a soldier, and neither were her staff. She wondered what Tony must feel, being shot at daily since the war started.

There were blackout curtains on the windows, and the basement had become an air raid shelter and dormitory. They had worked hard to keep track of the logistics situation, which had included reversing the flow of matériel out of Korea, managing the stream of supplies coming into the war zone, and searching supply bases worldwide for critically needed items.

They had been on twelve-hour notice for days, trying to be ready to shift the entire operation to Misawa's computers as quickly and smoothly as possible.

She had planned the transfer carefully. All the data was being copied onto tapes, and two copies of each tape were being made. That would take most of the hour and fifty minutes they had. Twelve hours' notice. That was a laugh.

She paused. In a way it was good. It would minimize the time that they were unable to operate. The Army had already started setting up a site at the airbase there, and thank heaven they used the same type of computer. An hour to the airport, another hour to load, then it was about a two-hour flight to Misawa. Another hour to get to the base's computers, and an hour to load the software and data. With luck, they would be back in business by breakfast. It would be a long night, though.

The trucks came early, with a mixed U.S. and Korean escort. In addition to the vehicles for the logistics center's personnel, there were two more full of soldiers, and an armored car at the front. The lieutenant in charge loaded them as if the plane were waiting at Kimpo airport with its engines turning over.

They loaded in the cold dark, with no lights and apparently no organization. Anne and the other supervisors tried to keep their people together, but she wouldn't be sure if they'd succeeded until they got to Kimpo airport. Finally a soldier half-threw her onto a truck. She felt like a side of meat going into a freezer.

It was dark in the back, and what little light there was disappeared when they lowered the canvas flap on the back. That caught her in midstride, and she would have fallen but for friendly hands catching her. Anne groped and half-stumbled her way to a seat, landing just as the truck started moving.

She followed the turns the truck made in her mind and tracked them until they turned right outside the main gate. All she could think of was how cold the seat was. It didn't get any warmer.

There were frequent stops, and once, sirens. Finally her curiosity got the better of her and her seatmates. They loosened the rope tying the canvas top to the side of the truck body and raised it enough to peek through.

The crack was small, and they were moving so slowly that there was no rush of cold air. After being in the dark truck for so long, the blacked-out city looked almost light.

Anne saw buildings damaged by bombs or artillery. Once an entire row of shops was leveled, but even the lightest damage would have been the lead story on the evening news back home.

There had been little effort at cleanup. From the looks of the rubble, it had just been pushed out of the street. Some of it was still smoldering.

A dusk-to-dawn curfew was in effect. This had been ignored inside the busy Yongsan Army Base, but outside, it was strictly enforced.

Every major intersection had a checkpoint, and armed patrols walked the streets between them. Additionally, she sometimes saw weapons poking out of building windows. She knew that most of the post-1950s construction in Seoul had included features that would allow them to be used as bunkers. The city was being turned into one giant fortress.

In the almost total blackout, the city looked dead. Ten million people lived here, but the only signs of life were armed soldiers and occasional convoys like theirs.

They stopped at an intersection where some sort of road-block had been set up. She couldn't see the head of the column, but there was a sandbagged gun emplacement on the two corners she could see, and a barrier across each entrance to the intersection.

There were two Koreans dressed in civilian clothes standing at one of the corners. Both were men. They had their hands in the air, and they were being searched none too gently by a soldier while another covered them with an M16 rifle. The truck started up, and her last view was of the two men being knocked to the ground.

As they went down one street, movement caught her eye, and she saw soldiers at work outside a building. As Anne studied their movements, she realized they were wiring the foundation with explosives.

It took almost an hour to reach the airport, by which time Anne didn't know if the truck was actually warming up or she was just going numb.

There was more security at the airport, including tanks and antiaircraft guns. They pulled up to the main terminal, gratefully unloading into its heated interior. Unsure of what to expect, Anne was startled to see a Korean Air Lines ticket agent waving her over.

The agent asked for identification from each member of the party, examining it closely before returning it. One person did not have an ID card, and Anne had to sign a temporary ID form, taking responsibility for her.

After the last staff member had been verified, Anne said, "How long will it be until our flight takes off?"

The agent replied, "We can't tell, ma'am. Not until tomorrow morning, at least."

There was a general commotion and several voices repeated Anne's question. "But what about our orders? We're on twelve-hour notice for immediate departure. . . ."

"Miss Larson, that means the Air Force wants you here twelve hours before scheduled flight time, just in case they get more sorties than they plan on. I've been here for four days, and I guarantee that barring miracles, you will not be on a plane before dawn tomorrow."

She should have known. She knew how logistics worked. Try to have the cargo to be shipped present well before the scheduled flight time. So what if the cargo spent all night at an airport? All they could do was wait. She hadn't even brought a book for the flight, just a manual to review upload procedures.

They filed past the security station. The metal detectors were of course being used, but instead of civilian guards, no-nonsense Korean soldiers with submachine guns watched everyone.

Once she was past the metal detector, Anne looked down the long corridor to the departure area. It was full of people, with rope barriers set up to control their movements. The logistics staff morosely took up their positions at the end of the line. It was going to be a long night.

It was impossible to sleep. About every half hour everybody had to move forward five feet, or some new group of evacuees appeared, asking questions and bemoaning their fate. Even if they could have settled down inside, the roar of jets outside was incredible. The concourse was glassed-in, so they could see the operations on the field.

Cargo planes landed constantly. Every three minutes a four-engined transport, either a C-130 or C-141, would roar in. After a while she noticed that there were occasionally longer gaps, after which a monstrous C-5 would lumber in. As one would clear the runway, another landed. On the parallel runway next to it, cargo aircraft took off.

Every half hour or so, a cargo aircraft would taxi up to their gate. She watched through the glass as troops or light equipment unloaded, while fuel trucks drove up and attached hoses to the aircraft. Evacuees would stream aboard, chivied by Air Force personnel. The ramp would go up, the hoses detach, and the plane would taxi away, headed for takeoff. Total elapsed time was fifteen to twenty minutes, depending on how fast the evacuees moved aboard.

As a logistics expert, Anne could appreciate the organization and timing involved. There were delays, of course. Twice mechanics had to be called to work on some part of an aircraft, but they had come on a run and had worked frantically to correct the fault. They'd succeeded though, and airplanes continued to land and take off.

She had almost dropped asleep once, when suddenly sirens went off all over the base. The few lights that were on went out, and she heard the roar of jet fighters. Nothing else happened, and after about ten minutes the lights came back on.

She dozed as best she could, and watched the people she worked with, and who worked for her. It was interesting to see who complained, who accepted their fate, who helped out. She knew she wasn't in the last category. Few were, especially as the night wore on.

Dawn finally came, and they had shuffled and moved into what would have been a waiting area for departure under more normal circumstances. They started to get themselves organized, and the group in front of them went through a door. They were next.

Another cargo plane came and went, and an Air Force tech sergeant came out and said, "Army Logistics staff. Follow me for boarding."

Smiling and relieved, they went through, expecting to march into the cargo door of an aircraft. Instead, they went into a large room with metal walls and grease stains on the floor. From the signs on the wall, Anne guessed that it had been used for storing maintenance equipment. It was noisy, but when Anne saw the source, she was glad. Someone had moved two gas heaters into the otherwise unheated building.

All the maintenance gear had been removed, and the floor had been marked off into several large areas. The sergeant started calling off names, in alphabetical order. As each person answered, he checked their ID again, then handed them a battered index card. He pointed over to an empty marked-off space and told them, "Get in it and stay in it."

Anne's turn came, and she looked at her card. Hand-lettered, it said "C-141, 50." She would be the fiftieth person on that aircraft, and they now knew it would be a C-141 Starlifter. She saw one group ahead of them and knew it wouldn't be long now.

Their square started to fill up, first with her group, then a group of civilians who turned out to be Air Force maintenance contractors. The area looked full, but the Sergeant checked his clipboard and called out, "Seventeen!"

A side door opened and another group of civilians came in. These were obviously dependents, mothers with children in their arms or clinging to them as they walked.

The last people were worming themselves into the area when the sirens went off again. Anne was near a window and saw people running for cover. Suddenly four fighters appeared in her field of view and split off.

They had to be MiGs, she thought, because they were firing. She saw one drop bombs and bank away. She suddenly felt herself being pulled to the ground as the explosives hit. The shock wave shattered the glass and spread fragments over everyone in the building.

There was a second explosion, much closer. The walls started to shake, and the Air Force people started shouting "Out! Everyone out!" There was a double door on each side of the building, leading out to the field, and people poured through it.

She moved with the crush of people and was outside in seconds. As she emerged from the building, Anne felt a wave of heat to one side and looked over to see a cargo plane on fire. One wing tip touched the ground, and the front of the plane looked chewed up.

The cargo door was open and soldiers in camouflaged uniforms were running out of the plane. Some helped injured comrades, and there were several inert forms lying on the ground near the back.

Anne looked around the field. Antiaircraft guns were firing, making a sound like ripping metal. She followed one line of tracers and saw a delta-winged fighter jinking. Another stream of tracers joined the first, but the fighter barrel-rolled away.

She followed its flight path and saw its target. A four-engined shape was turning, diving, trying to get out of the MiG's path, but the fighter followed easily. A smoke trail appeared in front of the attacker, and then a second one followed.

The cargo plane turned, trying to perform a break maneuver that would take a fraction of a second for a fighter. It was far too slow, and both missiles hit on the starboard wing. It broke away, spinning crazily, and the rest of the aircraft fell, trailing smoke.

She didn't see if the MiG escaped. Looking at the airfield, she saw fires, columns of smoke, and craters in the runway, and at least two cargo aircraft had been destroyed, with full loads of human cargo.

An Air Force lieutenant came up to her. "Miss Larson? You and your group should come back inside the main terminal. We're closing the airfield."

They would have to find some other way of getting out of Seoul.

DECEMBER 29, KUNSAN AIRBASE

Tony dragged into the ops building, feeling as if he were nine hundred years old. The last mission had been a good one, a close air support flight that had turned into an air-to-air hassle with another two kills for him and no friendly losses. If he weren't so tired, he might actually smile.

He noticed a commotion around the situation board. The progress of the NK offensive was posted on a large map, updated by the intelligence officer. Pistol was taping up a message, which was being read with intense interest by other pilots and ground crew.

"Pistol, what's all the excitement?" Tony wasn't too tired to be curious. Besides, if it involved the war, it was his business to stay informed.

"Big raid at Kimpo, Saint. The gomers massed enough aircraft to get past the CAP and attack the field."

Tony's chest felt cold. Anne was supposed to be getting evacuated through Kimpo. "How much damage did they do?"

"Pretty bad. They bombed the runway and the main terminal, which was packed with evacuees. Worse still, they got four transports on the ground and shot down one that had just taken off. Total killed is going to be over five hundred. They've closed the airfield until further notice. I think they'll start diverting stuff down here..."

Tony turned and walked away. There were enough people listening to Pistol so that nobody noticed his abrupt departure.

His office was mercifully close. He ignored several message slips and dialed two numbers. One was Anne's apartment, the other the logistics office where she worked. There was no answer at either.

C H A P T E R
29
Juggernaut

DECEMBER 29—NEAR MUNSAN, SOUTH KOREA

Lieutenant General Cho stood by the roadside watching his troops march south down the thoroughfare the imperialists called Highway 1 or the Main Supply Route. He stood in the shadow thrown by a wrecked South Korean M-48 main battle tank.

The tank and its crew had been killed on the first day of the war as they tried and failed to stem the North Korean offensive. Its twisted gun barrel still pointed north along the highway. The three T-62s it had destroyed before dying were already gone, pulled off the battlefield back to rear-area repair shops. They would fight again. The M-48 would not.

The wind veered slightly suddenly, and Cho's nostrils twitched as they caught the faintest smell of death rising from inside the tank. He was immediately thankful for the freezing temperatures that had delayed the onset of corruption and decay. Seeking fresher air, he stepped away from the M-48 and stood motionless again, silhouetted by the setting sun.

Cho clasped his hands behind his back and smiled. Tanks, trucks towing artillery pieces, APCs, and other vehicles jammed every lane on the highway, rolling steadily on their way to the front nearly twenty kilometers ahead. Columns of marching infantry paralleled the highway on both sides, pushing through the snow to leave the road to their mounted comrades.

Red Phoenix was working. The frozen ground and iced-over rice paddies were giving his men a mobility undreamed of in the warmer summer or spring months. And Korea's harsh winter weather was playing its part by degrading the enemy's air attacks on his columns—making it difficult for South Korea's surviving F-16s and F-5s to find their targets.

Cho knew that the same weather hampered the North's air forces even more, but he had never counted on their support to win this war. A draw in the air battle would satisfy him and leave the ultimate outcome in the hands of his tank and infantry commanders.

He lifted his binoculars and scanned the low hills rising at irregular intervals on either side of the road. Every elevation in sight was occupied by camouflaged ZSU-23-4s, 57mm flak batteries, and their associated radars—his backup defenses should enemy aircraft leak through the MiG-29, MiG-23, and MiG-21 interceptors loitering overhead. Heavier antiaircraft guns and SAM sites farther back provided added protection.

Cho knew that some of his units had been hit hard from the air, but his air defense commanders had assured him that the imperialists were paying a high price in planes for every attack. He knew their claims were almost certainly exaggerated, but even so the toll of downed aircraft had to be wearing away the American and South Korean squadrons—loss after loss that would eventually render them ineffective.

Satisfied for the moment with the apparent readiness of his air defenses, he turned on his heel and faced south, studying the heavy black smoke cloud roiling high into the sky on the horizon. A huge cloud formed by burning villages and hundreds of wrecked vehicles. And he could hear a dull, muffled, thumping noise as his artillery continued to pound the retreating enemy, sending still more smoke and dust into the air.

Cho slowly lowered the binoculars to his chest and looked again at the landscape around him. The smoke pall staining the sky had reminded him that war, however successful or necessary, carried a bitter price. He could see that easily enough in the shattered buildings along the roadside and in the twisted corpses and abandoned, burned-out tanks and vehicles, strewn across the countryside. He could read it in the weary, vacant-eyed troops huddled around small fires off the highway—the remnants of his two first-echelon infantry divisions.

According to his reports, both divisions had lost nearly

seventy percent of their effective strength in four days of continuous fighting. But they'd inflicted equally heavy losses on the enemy units opposing them.

Cho made a mental note to see that they were refitted and brought back up to strength with reinforcements as soon as possible. He would need every man he could lay his hands on.

"Comrade General! A message from General Chyong at the forward HQ!"

He turned and took the message flimsy from his thin-faced aide-de-camp. He frowned. The young man would simply have to learn to work calmly and more quietly. War was too important for high-pitched voices.

But the frown vanished as he read Chyong's message. Advance elements of the II Corps were nearing Pyokche—barely fifteen kilometers from the outskirts of Seoul. Soon his troops could begin veering southwest, aiming to cross the Han River at Kimpo. Excellent. In just five days they had breached the puppet government's fortifications and driven more than twenty-five kilometers against heavy opposition.

His counterpart at V Corps was having a slightly harder time of it as his divisions pushed down the Uijongbu Corridor. But even so, his columns were reported to have captured Chon'gong—a village twenty kilometers south of the DMZ and right at the mouth of a long valley leading right to the heart of Seoul. Soon the V Corps would also begin to swing away from the puppet regime's capital, moving at an angle to cross the Han to the east.

The offensive was going well. With luck and skill the People's Army would soon be able to encircle the imperialist forces massing to defend Seoul from the attack they'd dreaded for decades. An attack that would not happen. Cho had no intention of throwing his troops into the kind of meat-grinder house-to-house fighting that would be necessary to take Seoul by direct assault. Instead, the war plan he'd helped develop envisioned using the city as bait to draw the enemy's armed forces into a trap. They would be pocketed when his II Corps and V Corps arced around Seoul to the east and west and joined hands at Suwon, twenty-seven kilometers south of the enemy capital.

With the bulk of its forces cut off from supply and

surrounded by the People's Army, the Southern regime would have little real choice but surrender.

Cho came out of his reverie and snapped his fingers, summoning his aides and driver. He'd spent enough time playing the wide-eyed tourist. There was work to be done back at the main headquarters—reports to be written for Pyongyang and plans that had to be laid for the next day's attacks.

Things were going to get more complicated as the follow-on troops of the III Corps moved into the attack in this sector. Once it was committed to battle, Cho would move up to command both the II and III Corps as Colonel General of the newly formed First Shock Army. The First Shock Army, Cho repeated silently to himself. Truly, Kim Il-Sung's spectacled son had fulfilled his promises.

Now Cho would fulfill his. The South would fall.

SOUTH OF SHINDO, NEAR THE SOO ROYAL TOMB, SOUTH KOREA

The Main Supply Route was jammed bumper-to-bumper with canvas-sided, two-and-a-half-ton trucks, jeeps, fuel tankers, ammo carriers, and military vehicles of every description—all moving south at a snail's pace intermingled with carloads of frantic civilian refugees.

McLaren looked at the chaos on the road and knew he was looking at a beaten army.

His South Korean and American front-line units weren't beaten yet. They were still fighting, surrendering ground reluctantly, meter by meter, and making the North Koreans pay in blood for every advance. But they were being worn down, submerged by the North's superior numbers and massed artillery, and McLaren didn't have much help he could send them.

The first reinforcements from the States—battalions of the 6th and 7th Light Divisions—were starting to arrive by air, but it would take them at least a day to organize and get up to the front. And McLaren wasn't even sure how much they could do once they got there. Both the 6th and the 7th were basically light infantry forces; units designed for rapid transport overseas, with few of the heavy antitank weapons or artillery pieces needed to meet the kind of armor-heavy assault the North Koreans were making.

South Korea's several-million-man reserve force was also mobilizing, but the nationwide mobilization had been slowed by the confusion caused by the North's surprise attack and by the political disturbances that had preceded it. Many of the already assembled reserve units were tied down chasing North Korean commandos who'd infiltrated by sea and by air to attack U.S. and ROK rear-area installations.

And now this. McLaren clenched the stub of his unlit cigar between his teeth. Things were bad enough up at the front without this rear-echelon bug-out. He wasn't sure who or what had started it, but it seemed like just about every supply unit, maintenance detail, field hospital, and Army paperchaser within earshot of the war had decided to retreat at the same time. They'd loaded up on anything with wheels and an engine and spilled out onto the MSR in a honking, panicked mass. The South Korean units that were supposed to control the roads had been totally swamped.

And they were blocking the goddamned road! Every friggin' inch of it. Troops and supplies trying to get forward to where they were most needed were having to detour off onto little, winding country lanes or go cross-country through the built-up snow and ice. This traffic jam was costing valuable time—and that cost lives.

"Doug!"

"Yes, General?" Hansen materialized beside him, notepad in hand.

"Get on the horn to Frank Collier and tell him I want this mess straightened out, pronto!" Hansen took rapid notes as McLaren outlined exactly what he expected the Eighth Army's J-4 to do. "I want at least a company of MPs here to start these people in some kind of order. They won't be able to stop them short of the bridges over the Han, but they can at least clear some lanes going north. Clear?"

Hansen nodded.

"Okay. I want more MPs on the other side of those bridges as a reception committee. They're to stop these bastards and get 'em back in—" Someone just up the road leaned on his horn and kept leaning, cutting McLaren off.

His temper snapped.

With Hansen tagging alongside, McLaren stormed up the road toward the offending vehicle—a jeep occupied by a heavy-jowled, sweating American lieutenant colonel and a slim, shaking, freckle-faced PFC driver. The bird colonel stood high on the jeep's front seat, frantically and futilely trying to wave the stalled traffic ahead out of the way.

The driver saw McLaren coming and guiltily took his hand off the jeep's horn.

"Damnit, Greene! Keep honking!" Spittle flew out of the lieutenant colonel's mouth as he turned to yell at his driver.

"He'll do nothing of the kind, Colonel."

The man looked up angrily. "And just who the hell do you think . . ."

He noticed McLaren's four stars for the first time and paled even further.

McLaren saw the crossed cannons on the man's uniform collar and pounced. "What's your unit, Colonel? And why aren't you with it?"

The lieutenant colonel's mouth opened and closed without making any sound.

"Son?"

The PFC stammered out his answer, "We're with the Two thirty-sixth Artillery, General, sir."

McLaren wheeled on the lieutenant colonel, who'd collapsed back onto the seat. "Your guns are back that way, Colonel, firing support for my forward battalions." McLaren pointed north. "Now suppose you explain just why the fuck you aren't up there with 'em."

The man's lips quivered as he tried to form a coherent reply, "Had to . . . had to report to HQ. Wanted to arrange more, uh, more ammo . . ."

"Bullshit! You were running, mister!" McLaren glared him into silence and turned toward his aide. "Captain Hansen!"

"Yes sir."

"Place this man under arrest for desertion in the face of the enemy. He's relieved of his command, effective immediately."

Hansen stepped forward and led the shaking, teary-eyed officer out of the jeep toward McLaren's waiting command vehicle. McLaren leaned closer to the jeep's driver. He spoke more softly. "Now, son. What I want you to do is to wheel this jeep out of this mess and make your way back to your unit. Is your battalion's XO still there?"

The PFC nodded. "Yes, sir. Major Benson's in charge, sir."

"Good. Okay, now you tell Major Benson what's happened. And you tell him from me that he's got the battalion now. Got it?"

The PFC nodded again, even more vigorously this time.

"Great. Okay, son, get on your way. And good luck." McLaren stepped away as the driver snapped him a quick salute and started pulling the jeep off the highway onto the shoulder.

He watched the young private disappear north up the side of the road past the stalled traffic toward the battleline. Then he turned and headed back toward his waiting aides. He had a lot more to do to try to unscramble the situation he and his troops faced.

SOUTH OF PYOKCHE, SOUTH KOREA

Captain Lee watched Pyokche burn.

An ROK mechanized infantry battalion had held the town for nearly two hours against overwhelming numbers of North Korean tanks and infantry. Dug in among Pyokche's tile-roofed houses and small shops, they'd tossed back wave after wave of attackers—buying time for Lee's combat engineers to dig defenses south of the town.

Now, though, the resistance inside Pyokche was collapsing. The surviving North Korean attackers had pulled back from the open fields surrounding the town and called on their artillery to finish the job. The heavy guns had responded, and after a brief, blessed lull, shell after shell had screamed down into the town—smashing houses, collapsing trenches, churning even the rubble into a sea of unrecognizable debris.

Lee had listened to the frantic screams of the defenders over the radio, and he'd known that they couldn't hold much longer. No one could be expected to last long in the inferno the communist barrage had created. So he'd left the radio to spur his engineers on.

Some were using the bulldozer blades on their mammoth

CEVs—combat engineering vehicles—to scrape out firing positions for the mixed bag of South Korean and American tanks left to block the North Korean advance. Others were scattered across the open ground behind the town, laying a thin screen of antitank and antipersonnel mines.

Satisfied that they were working as fast as was humanly possible—and perhaps a bit faster—Lee had come back to the M-113 armored personnel carrier that served as his command vehicle. Infantry squads were desperately digging in on either side of his APC. Dig fast, he thought, you haven't much time left.

A voice on the main tactical net confirmed his unspoken thought. It was the battalion commander inside the town calling his brigade commander farther back along the highway. In the background Lee could hear shells crashing on Pyokche, an uncanny echo of the same explosions he could hear with his own ears. "Alpha Foxtrot Four Four, this is Alpha Charlie Two Three. Enemy columns forming up for attack. My strength at thirty percent. Repeat, three zero percent. Request permission to withdraw. Over."

Lee waited while the brigade commander acknowledged the message and gave his permission. It wasn't long in coming. No battalion that had lost more than half its strength in such a short time could possibly fend off another determined attack.

He switched to the frequency assigned to his own engineering company. "Bravo Four One to all Bravo Four units. Withdraw to main position. Repeat. Withdraw to main position. Acknowledge." He wasn't going to leave his men out in the open.

The South Korean combat engineer listened to his platoon leaders confirm his order and then switched back to the main net.

"Alpha Foxtrot Four Four, this is Charlie Two Three. Request smoke to cover our withdrawal. Over." Lee nodded to himself. A sage request. Even a thin artillery-laid smoke screen would make it safer for Pyokche's surviving defenders to evacuate their positions.

"Charlie Two Three, this is Alpha Foxtrot Four Four. Negative your smoke request. Say again, smoke is unavailable. Over." Listening, Lee swore to himself. Nothing was working right. Ammunition expenditures for all weapons had been far above prewar estimates, and he knew that supplies weren't getting forward the way they were supposed to. Now the remnants of the mechanized infantry battalion in Pyokche faced a kilometer-long retreat across open ground without cover.

Minutes later, Lee stood high in the M-113's commander's cupola watching his engineers filter back through the thinly held foxholes and firing positions that marked the new front line. He shook his head wearily. There weren't enough infantry, tanks, or heavy weapons here to hold a determined North Korean attack for more than half an hour. It hardly seemed worth the sacrifices Pyokche's defenders had made and were still making.

Lee lifted his binoculars and focused on the town, watching through the smoke and dust as rubble fountained skyward under the enemy's barrage. Suddenly the barrage stopped. An eerie silence descended across the landscape as the smoke and dust drifted away from the ruined town.

The radio crackled. "Charlie Two Three to all Charlie units. Execute withdrawal now!"

Lee's grip on his binoculars tightened as he saw scattered figures emerging from the rubble, running for the safe lanes through the minefield his engineers had laid. Others clung to a handful of battle-scarred M-113s racing at high speed to cross the open ground.

One of the APCs suddenly lurched to a halt and burst into flames. Lee spun round and saw the snout of a T-62 poking through the smoking rubble of a wrecked house on the outskirts of Pyokche. The North Koreans had arrived.

An American M-60 tank in defilade to his left also saw the enemy tank. Its 105mm main gun whined, swung right, and recoiled as it sent a SABOT armor-piercing round smashing into the North Korean tank. The T-62 exploded.

The revenge was short-lived. Muzzle flashes winked among the ruins of Pyokche as North Korean machinegunners opened fire. Dozens of the men sprinting toward safety were spun around and dropped into the snow. Some escaped the slaughter. Enraged by the sight, men all along the line opened up, flaying the ruins, trying to cover the survivors.

At last the firing died away. The broken fragments of the

mechanized infantry battalion crossed into friendly lines and shelter while the North Koreans stopped shooting to avoid giving away their positions.

Lee waited, studying the corpse-strewn ground in front of Pyokche. Wounded men writhed in agony or crawled bleeding toward safety. Their moans could be clearly heard in the eerie silence.

Any minute now, Lee thought. Soon the North Koreans will lunge out of the town and we'll have a brief chance to repay them for this butchery. He knew it would be in vain, though. Reinforcements from other parts of the front were arriving too slowly. The first determined communist attack would find it easy to punch a hole through the defenses he and his men had built.

Worse yet, his engineers would have to ride the attack out. The brigade commander had made it clear that they couldn't even pull out of the line to start working on new field fortifications to the south. There were so few infantry left in fighting shape that he needed the engineers to man key battle positions. Lee and his men would have to fight and die as common footsloggers—no matter what specialized skills they possessed.

Time passed. Ten minutes. Half an hour. An hour. Lee grew impatient. What were the communists waiting for? Why hadn't they attacked? They must know how weak we are, he thought, why haven't they come to finish us? Every minute they delay gives us more time to recover. He cocked his head, listening.

Firing had erupted somewhere off to the northeast some time ago, but he hadn't paid much attention to it. Now, though, he could hear that it had intensified—escalating from a few isolated rifle shots to a deafening mix of heavy artillery, tank cannon, and continuous automatic rifle fire. It sounded like a major assault was going on, but in the wrong direction. Away from Seoul.

He grabbed his binoculars and swept them across the fields, the rice paddies, and the still-smoldering ruins of Pyokche. Sunlight flashed momentarily on shovels rising and falling. He focused the binoculars, seeing dirt and snow being thrown out of waist-deep holes by North Korean infantrymen. There couldn't be any doubt of it. The communists were digging in. They weren't going to attack.

Relief washed over the South Korean combat engineer. He and his men weren't going to die—at least not yet. The relief was followed, however, by a feeling of unease. What was the enemy up to? He chewed on the thought for a long while without coming up with a satisfactory answer.

EIGHTH ARMY FIELD HQ, NEAR KURI, SOUTH KOREA

Night had fallen.

Artillery rumbled off in the distance, muffled by the high hills between the HQ and the battle zone.

McLaren looked up from the map at his senior staff officers, clustered around him in a semicircle and blinking in the dim light. They all looked haggard, worn down by five days and nights without enough sleep and filled with constant tension. It hadn't helped that they'd already been forced by the North Korean advance to shift the HQ lock, stock, and barrel from its initial wartime location.

He shifted his gaze to the Army's operations officer, the J-3, a tall, stick-thin major general who'd kept a flat, nasal New England accent through a thirty-year career in different postings around the world. "Well? What do you think, Barney?"

Major General Barret Smith unfolded his arms and took the unlit pipe out of his mouth. "I think your assessment earlier was right on the money, Jack."

The J-3 stepped to the map, tracing the enemy's movements with a finger. "Okay, the NKs have been driving hard for five days straight down Routes One and Three—right toward Seoul. Suddenly the pressure's eased up, and now we're getting reports of fierce attacks from here"—his finger tapped the map near Pyokche—"almost due southeast, toward the Han River—and away from Seoul."

He continued, "Plus, we're seeing something similar up along the Uijongbu Corridor. Only there, the NK attacks are driving southwest." The J-3 stopped and shook his head. "I'd say it's pretty clear that they're trying to pocket us inside Seoul."

Other heads nodded around the staff circle.

"Right, gentlemen." McLaren stepped forward again. "Now I do not believe in playing the game by the enemy's rules or doing what he wants us to do. So what we are going to do is this . . ."

The staff listened as he outlined his plan. Except for a thin screen, all the South Korean and American combat troops north of the Han River were to withdraw. The South Korean Capital Corps and an assortment of reserve and home defense units would stay behind to garrison Seoul, but McLaren wanted everyone else out of the intended North Korean pocket. He would let the North Koreans close their trap on thin air.

He jabbed the table with a rigid forefinger to emphasize the point. "Everyone goes, gentlemen. Tanks, artillery, infantry, supply units, field hospitals. Everyone. Is that understood?"

Heads nodded. All but one.

"Yes, General Park? You have an objection?"

The South Korean chairman of the Joint Chiefs looked much older than his years. "Yes, General McLaren, I do. What you propose is unacceptable to the government of the Republic of Korea. Seoul is the nerve center of our nation. It contains a quarter of our population. We cannot risk its capture by the communists."

McLaren lit a cigar to buy time while studying the faces of the other South Korean officers in the room. One or two looked as though they agreed with Park. The others were less sure.

He drew on the cigar and then took it out of his mouth. "General, with all due respect, my decision is final. We will not dance to North Korea's tune. They want us to risk and lose everything we've got to hold on to a single city. We aren't going to do that."

"But my country—"

McLaren cut him off. "General, your country exists so long as an army remains intact to defend its freedom. Lose that army and you will lose this war."

Park looked unconvinced.

The J-3 joined in the debate. "Frankly, General Park, I doubt very much that the North Koreans will dare attack Seoul so long as our main army remains in the field. If they do, the forces we're leaving behind should be able to hold them off for quite a while. You've prepared the city for a siege by stockpiling food, water, and ammunition. I suggest we make use of those preparations.''

The Korean waited for him to finish and then said stiffly, ''That is not a decision we should make here. I must consult my president before agreeing to your plan.''

McLaren puffed on his cigar and eyed Park for a moment without speaking. Then he said, ''Very well, General. That's certainly your privilege. In the meantime, however, my orders stand. And they will stand until I get word to the contrary from my president. Is that clear?''

Park nodded abruptly.

''Good. Captain Hansen will make arrangements to get you into Seoul to confer with the President.'' McLaren turned to face the rest of his officers. ''All right, gentlemen. We've got a lot to do. I want to see the plans for the withdrawal from Seoul immediately. Let's move!''

The officers scattered. McLaren put a hand out to stop his J-3. ''Hold on a sec, Barney.''

''Yeah, Jack?''

''We both know it's gonna take a helluva long time to move our troops through Seoul. The roads are still clogged with rear-echelon crapouts and refugees. We've got to hold the NKs on the Han until they can get clear. Right?''

Smith nodded.

''Okay, so what I want is this. Get together with the J-1 and comb through every noncombat unit you can lay your hands on. I want every spare man who can carry a rifle on the line ASAP. Form 'em into provisional units and send 'em up to the river. Scrape up some officers to command them.''

Smith looked at him closely. ''Jack, you know those boys are going to get chewed up pretty bad, don't you? I mean, you're sending supply clerks up against T-62s. That's kind of an uneven proposition.''

''Yeah''—McLaren stubbed his cigar out on the table—''I know.''

He looked at the red arrows pushing down from the north toward Seoul. ''But they're all I've got left right now.'' He turned to face his J-3. ''Time, Barney! We've gotta buy time.''

NAHA HARBOR, OKINAWA

The frigates sortied first, upping anchor on a cold, clear morning, just before dawn. Their job was to "sanitize" the Naha harbor channel, sweeping the water and the seabed for hostile submarines. North Korea's Romeo-class diesel boats had never operated this far from their own coastal waters, but that wasn't any reason to take chances. Every American naval officer had the lessons of Pearl Harbor drummed into his skull from the first day of his service to the last.

Admiral Thomas Aldrige Brown, USN, watched the four Perry-class and two aging Knox-class frigates under his command slip out of port. His breath hung in an icy haze around him. Christ, it was cold out here. It would grow colder as his task force moved north, and colder still once the ships reached the open ocean. There wasn't much wind blowing across the motionless aircraft carrier's bridge wing at the moment, but Brown knew how raw it would be once they were underway, moving into the teeth of a twenty-plus-knot wind.

He shivered and pulled the parka his wife had packed tighter around him. She'd had a devil of a time finding one that fit his tall, gaunt frame. His eyes followed the tiny frigates as they steamed out toward the gray ocean beyond the harbor. Good God, he thought, this was a far cry from the hot, hazy confines of the Persian Gulf, his last duty assignment. Cold air, cold water, cold steel.

Brown turned on his heel and left the bridge, headed for the warm, darkened confines of the USS *Constellation*'s Flag Plot. The Flag Plot contained the computers, display screens, and staff he would need to fight a modern battle at sea. A battle Brown hoped he wouldn't have to fight. But if he did have to fight one, he was certainly glad he'd have the *Constellation* along to fight it with. He smiled to himself, knowing that was an admission he'd never willingly make in public.

Brown had cut his teeth commanding the frigates and destroyers that he still thought of as the real Navy. As a junior officer and then a ship's captain, the massive aircraft carriers he'd escorted around the world were just targets, troublesome beasts to be protected from all manner of threats—planes, missiles, submarines, and other warships. Now he had his flag, and his thinking had expanded with it. Now it was comforting to know that he could call on a powerful air group to reach out and strike down enemies while they were still hundreds of miles away. The admiral reached the Flag Plot and stepped over the hatch coaming past a pair of armed Marine sentries standing at rigid attention. The Plot's dark, stuffy warmth was welcome.

Brown unzipped his parka and moved to study an electronic map covering part of one wall. The map displayed the jagged outlines of Naha harbor and the positions and status of all his ships. Once they were at sea, it would also show the positions of every aircraft aloft and of any neutral or hostile contacts the task force's radars or sonars detected.

Right now the map showed the harbor filled with ships. Most were naval vessels, including the better part of the Pacific Fleet's amphibious ships. Most had traveled at flank speed to reach Okinawa on time, then loaded troops and equipment of the 3rd Marine Division all day and all night. It had been a straight and exhausting grind, but now, at last, they were ready to pull out.

Brown knew that the task force he commanded was going to be the largest assembly of ships seen in these waters since the Korean War. The First Korean War, he corrected himself. The troops his warships escorted represented a mobile, powerful punch that could be landed anywhere there was a coastline. Not that they planned an immediate amphibious assault. They had no planned target. Instead his orders directed him to get the Marines and their transports safely to Pohang, a port on South Korea's east coast. The classified war reports he'd seen made it crystal clear that the Combined Forces Command desperately needed every division of fresh troops it could lay its hands on.

Still, it wouldn't hurt to give the enemy a few more worries. The amphibious command ship *Blue Ridge* would join the rest of the group south of Japan to boost the appearance of an impending landing operation, and if *Wisconsin* could make the rendezvous in time, the battleship would be along to provide welcome gunfire support. It wouldn't be the first time these coasts had seen her.

A phone buzzed. "Sir, it's the screen commander."

Brown took the phone from his flag lieutenant. "Yes, Mitch?"

"Admiral, the screen has taken stations around the harbor. The inner zone is clear."

Brown sneaked a look at the map display. Every ship had steam up and was ready to proceed. "All right, let's get underway."

He hung up and turned back to the map to watch their departure at second hand. As the heavies came out of the harbor mouth, the ships of the outer screen would expand to maintain an unbroken ring of sensors around their charges.

Constellation came out first, followed by gray-painted Navy amphibious ships and chartered cargo vessels. Land-based Marine fighters and Navy patrol aircraft covered their exit. As soon as the carrier, known as *Connie* throughout the fleet, reached open water and could get up to speed, her own planes and helicopters would take over the job—a job they would keep until the convoy reached its destination.

Every neutral ship in the immediate area had already been overflown, visually identified, and then positively tracked. One was not neutral, at least as Admiral Brown defined the term. The Soviet intelligence trawler *Kavkaz* was steaming in slow circles, twenty miles off Okinawa. Its captain undoubtedly intended to follow the American ships, once they'd sortied.

In addition to its role as a tracker and full-time shadow, *Kavkaz* was loaded with electronic equipment designed to detect and analyze any radio, radar, or sonar emission made by the task force. That was standard, and expected.

Normally a group like that led by the *Constellation* would leave at night, under full EMCON, emission control. Nothing— not a single radar, radio, or active sonar—would radiate unless absolutely necessary. The task force commander would strive to deny his opponent as much information as he possibly could. Then, as soon as he was clear of the harbor, the admiral commanding would use every trick in or out of the book to shake any unwelcome tagalong like the *Kavkaz*. The standard idea, Brown thought, was to leave the other side as uncertain as possible about your composition, your location, and your intentions.

Not this time, though. Before leaving the harbor Brown had ordered every radar and sonar possible to be on and emitting. There were several reasons for this. First, as far as most of the world was concerned, this was peacetime, not wartime. He couldn't sink or shoot down anything without a positive ID, not only as potentially hostile but positively threatening. For that he needed information only active sensors could provide.

Second, the National Command Authority, which was Pentagonese for the President, wanted everyone to know where this force was and where it was going—within limits. It was a highly visible signal of America's resolve and determination to stand by its South Korean ally. And the limits had already been set. With the President's permission, Brown had declared a one-hundred-nautical-mile exclusion zone around his task force. The Chinese and the Soviets, and in fact all shipping and aircraft, had been warned to keep clear. Anything that came too close would be shied away, and if it insisted on approaching, it would be sunk or blown out of the sky. There were some Soviet missiles with ranges of three hundred miles, but the North Koreans weren't supposed to have any of those. One hundred miles should provide an adequate safety margin.

But the *Kavkaz* was going to be a problem.

Brown watched as the map display shifted, showing the oddball assortment of warships, amphibious ships, and merchant vessels forming up off the Okinawa coast. It was taking longer than he would have liked, and the Soviet spy ship showed no signs of withdrawing to the edge of the declared exclusion zone. Surprise, surprise.

He wanted the Soviets to know he was enroute to Korea, but he'd be damned if he wanted them sniffing up his backside all the way there. The admiral swung away from the display and signaled his flag lieutenant. "Get me the captain of the *Thach*."

ABOARD USS *THACH*

The captain of the USS *Thach*, a Perry-class frigate, grinned into the phone. "Aye, aye, Admiral. We'll herd the bastard away."

He put the phone down and looked across the three miles separating his ship from the ungainly Soviet intelligence trawler. "Mr. Meadows, lay us a quarter-mile to port of that seagoing abomination."

His executive officer smiled dutifully and issued the necessary helm orders. He sometimes thought his captain had read *Moby Dick* once too often. The frigate heeled slightly as it came around on a new course, closing with the antenna-festooned *Kavkaz* at fifteen knots. At a range of just under five hundred yards, she turned again and ran parallel with the Soviet vessel. *Thach*'s captain leaned casually on the cold, metal railing and nodded to a rating standing nearby with a signal lamp. "Okay, Mahoney, do your thing." The carrot-haired rating grinned back at him and started flashing out the message his captain had just drafted: "This is U.S. Navy warship *Thach*. You are inside a declared maritime exclusion zone. Alter course immediately to leave the zone."

Kavkaz's captain kept them waiting for a couple of minutes before replying. Mahoney read the signal aloud as it was blinkered over. "This is a Soviet ship in international waters. You are interfering with our right of innocent passage."

"Innocent, my ass!" muttered the American captain. He scribbled a testy response and waited while Mahoney sent it over. He hoped the kid wasn't going to try to "burn up" his opposite number by sending so fast the Russian couldn't follow along. It was a favorite game among signalmen, but this message was something he wanted the Soviets to ponder.

"*Thach* to Soviet ship. I repeat, this is a maritime exclusion zone. Failure to comply with my order will be treated as a violation of said zone. You will leave immediately."

"We have no information on such a zone." The American captain nodded and smiled grimly. This kind of bullshit could drag on for hours, and Admiral Brown had made it all too clear that he wanted results, not negotiations. The Soviets had been duly notified. Now he would make the notification a warning. He pushed a button on the squawk box. "Guns. Prepare to fire a shot across that son-of-a-bitch's bows." The *Thach*'s gunnery officer had been waiting for just such an order, and everybody on the bridge heard the alarm bell and the mechanical whine as the frigate's single-gun 76mm turret slewed toward the *Kavkaz*. This time the message got through.

ABOARD THE USS *CONSTELLATION*

Brown watched the dot representing the Soviet intelligence trawler pull away from his formation. Its captain had made it clear that he was doing so only under protest and because of a "Yankee threat to initiate unprovoked hostilities." The admiral knew that the Soviets would soon broadcast TV pictures of an American warship "bullying" an unarmed vessel, but it didn't really bother him very much. Maybe that was precisely the right kind of signal to send to potential adversaries around the globe.

Kavkaz really was dragging its heels, though—moving away so slowly that it would take most of the day for the trawler to clear the exclusion zone.

Brown didn't push it. As soon as he was satisfied that the Soviet ship really was leaving, he recalled the *Thach*. Just to keep the *Kavkaz* honest, every so often a pair of armed attack jets would overfly the ship—low. Until they were exactly one hundred nautical miles away, he wanted that seagoing collection of Soviet intelligence agents to know they lived at his sufferance.

Brown studied the display as his task force turned onto its primary course. The distance from Okinawa to Korea's east coast was roughly six hundred nautical miles, and at an average speed of twelve knots, the trip would take just over two days. He expected the real North Korean threat to begin once they left the East China Sea and entered the Yellow Sea near the Korean coast. The admiral rubbed his eyes and wondered just how much sleep he would get until then.

A radar operator suddenly sat up straight in his chair. "Airborne contact, range one eighty miles, no friendly IFF."

Not much, Brown judged, moving toward the command phone.

CHAPTER
30
The Bridge

DECEMBER 30—NEAR HANGJUSAN CASTLE, SOUTH KOREA

The battered Army three-quarter-ton truck ground its way across the Haengju Bridge along a single lane reserved for northbound traffic. Tanks, trucks, jeeps, and artillery pieces moving south packed the other three lanes, crunching over sand laid on the highway to improve traction. Temperatures all over Korea were falling, and chunks of ice now bobbed and spun in the Han River, rolling westward toward the Yellow Sea. It was quickly growing into the worst winter in recent memory.

Once across the bridge, the truck turned out of traffic onto a small access road winding southeast with the river on one side and towering, snow-dusted evergreens on the other. Dozens of other vehicles moving along the same road had already melted the snow on its surface into a slippery, slushy gunk, and it took the driver several minutes of frantic gear-shifting to force the truck up the road to its destination.

"This is the end of the line, sir. HQ of the First of Thirty-ninth."

Second Lieutenant Kevin Little stared at the ramshackle collection of tents nestled among the tall green trees. For a moment the scene summoned up half-forgotten memories of family ski trips in the Washington Cascades. He held on to the memories like a lifeline as he climbed out of the heated cab and stood shivering in the raw air. Rhee slid out beside him. Then he pulled his gloves off, zipped his white camouflage jacket all the way up, and struggled to pull the gloves back on over fingers that were already growing numb. It didn't do much good. The weather was getting worse and the wind cut deep through every layer of clothing he had on.

Kevin had seen the frostbite cases piling up at the field hospital they'd been sent to after the search-and-rescue chopper picked them up behind enemy lines. The medics had said that most weren't serious, but he'd seen some men who were going to lose fingers and toes—no matter what the doctors did for them.

He and Rhee had been lucky. Each had escaped with a minor case of exposure, a few cuts, and some bruises. Nothing that two days of enforced bed rest and hot food hadn't been able to put right. But now they were going back into the thick of it. He shivered again, though not from the cold this time. The thought of seeing more slaughter sent a chill up his spine. He'd seen enough in his first battle to last a lifetime.

"We'd better report in." Rhee's breath steamed.

"Yeah." Depression settled in over Kevin, a mantle of gray despair and self-doubt so tangible that he felt his shoulders slump beneath its weight. He'd failed up on Malibu West. What use could they possibly have for him now?

He heard the Korean lieutenant ask a passing GI the way to the battalion CO's quarters. Kevin felt lower than he'd ever felt before in his life, and he was content to let Rhee lead him deeper into the cluster of camouflage-netted tents.

Major Donaldson was waiting for them in a small, tarp-floored tent crowded with maps, radio gear, and a charcoal-burning camp stove. The short, square-jawed major had been running the battalion since the first day of the war. The old CO, Colonel Harriman, was on his way home minus a leg, thanks to a North Korean 152mm shell.

Donaldson greeted them with a quick, tired smile that didn't quite reach his eyes and waved them over to chairs clustered around the stove. He didn't waste time on small talk but started right in asking questions about what had happened at Malibu West. Kevin had already written up an after-action report back at the field hospital, but the major wanted to hear it firsthand.

When Kevin told him about the jamming that had made it impossible to call in artillery support, Donaldson grimaced. "Goddamn if I don't know just what you mean, Lieutenant. The NKs were able to do the same thing all up and down the

Z." The major rocked back slightly on his camp stool. "Well, I can tell you that we've been paying some pretty serious attention to those jamming units since then."

He smiled thinly. "A little radio triangulation and a few quick salvos of eight-inch arty fire usually works wonders for the commo situation." He waved Kevin on with his report.

Kevin told him everything—all the way up to their pickup by the SAR helicopter. He could hear the strain in his own voice but felt oddly removed from it all. Almost as though it had happened to someone else in some other place at some other time.

When he finished, Donaldson sat silently for several seconds, his eyes fixed on Kevin's face as though searching intently for something hidden there. Then he leaned forward and laid a gentle hand on Kevin's knee. "Now look, Kev. What happened to your platoon happened in other places, too. And I want you to know that I believe you did everything you could under the circumstances. You personally led your troops up until the last possible moment in the middle of the worst kind of nightmare any commander could face. No one could ask for more than that. If you hadn't played dead when you did, the results would still have been the same—except that I'd be short another platoon leader. As it is, you're here and alive and I can use you."

"But—"

Donaldson interrupted him. "No buts about it, Kev. It wasn't your fault. You understand me?"

Kevin nodded as if he did.

"Good. Okay, then. Let's get down to brass tacks." The major pulled his hand back and stood up. He stepped across the tent to a map covered with cryptic grease-pencil markings. The two lieutenants followed him.

In short, clipped sentences Donaldson brought them up to date on the overall situation facing the Combined Forces. Put simply, it was grim. North Korea's armored spearheads were driving hard, gaining ground and inflicting serious casualties on the units trying vainly to stop them. More troops were desperately needed.

South Korea's vast reserves were mobilizing, but the process of getting them to the fighting front had been badly disrupted by NK commando attacks and by the need to secure logistics centers, headquarters sites, and communications facilities against new raids. American reinforcements were on the way, but they would be slow in arriving. Even with every available cargo and troop carrier plane pressed into service, it could take up to ten days to ship a full division by air. The units coming by sea would take even longer to get there. It took time to bring mothballed cargo ships back into service, time to load them, and even steaming at full speed the ships would take at least ten days to cross the Pacific. All of which meant that the Combined Forces' retreat wasn't likely to stop anytime soon, Donaldson told them.

When he came to the high command's decision to pull back south of Seoul, Rhee's face tightened and the South Korean stood rigid as a statue. Kevin suddenly remembered that Rhee's family lived in one of the capital's northern suburbs.

Donaldson traced the route of the North Korean column pushing west of the city. It was headed straight for them. Notations on the map showed its steady progress. "Now that is what we're up against. We've got to slow this column down. The roads through Seoul are completely choked with refugees and other units, and there's still a lot of our guys on this side of the Han. And that bridge"—Donaldson jerked a thumb over his shoulder back toward the span they'd crossed earlier—"that bridge is the only one left standing west of the city. It's the only way a lot of our people are going to make it out."

The major tapped the map again. "Okay, that's one reason we have to buy time. The other's just as important." He ran a finger along the riverline. "This is our next main line of resistance. But it's just a hollow shell right now. The engineers are working fast and we're getting more troops there as quickly as possible, but it ain't gonna be quick enough unless we can put a crimp in dear old Uncle Kim's advance up here." He pointed to the red arrowhead in Wondang—just six kilometers up the main highway.

Both Kevin and Rhee nodded their understanding. Things were pretty bad all over.

"Now that's where you come in. I need two officers to command a provisional company I've formed from the battalion's service units."

Kevin's heart sank as Donaldson ran through the forces he

was expected to lead into battle. Seventy-four supply clerks, maintenance techs, and MPs serving as riflemen, organized in two below-strength platoons, and a scratch weapons platoon made up of six M60 machine gun teams and four Dragon antitank missile teams. Even with the platoon of South Korean M-48 tanks Donaldson promised to attach, the provisional company sounded like a half-baked abortion that wouldn't last ten minutes up against the North Koreans. A picture flashed in front of his eyes, the dead heaped at the bottom of Malibu's main trench. It was going to happen again.

He glanced quickly at Rhee. The South Korean had an eyebrow arched slightly but showed no other sign of perturbation. How could he stay so cool?

"We'll give you as much support as we can, Kev. You won't be out on your own, that I promise you."

Kevin shifted his gaze back to find Donaldson looking closely at him. He nodded and tried to smile. He'd heard that promise before and knew just how far it went. Not far at all.

Donaldson looked at him, his face serious. "I wouldn't ask you to go back on the line so soon, Kev, but I haven't got anyone else. Matuchek's got his hands full over at what's left of Alpha, and I'm already short a company commander. I'm short lieutenants, too. O'Farrell's dead, three others are wounded, and another's MIA."

The major stepped back from the map. "I'm afraid you're it, mister. Lieutenant Rhee will continue as your liaison officer and second in command. Sergeants Bryce, Geary, and Caldwell will be your platoon leaders. Any other questions?"

Kevin couldn't think of anything more to say and Rhee stayed silent.

"Great. All right, the trucks will be here inside an hour to move you up to the front, so you've got that long to get some chow, meet your troops, and get acquainted." Donaldson held out a hand. "Good luck to both of you, and I'll see you on the other side of the Han."

First Rhee and then Kevin shook his hand, saluted, and left the tent.

THE KIMPO AIRPORT CUTOFF, SOUTH OF WONDANG, SOUTH KOREA

Kevin lay on his stomach in the snow, flattened behind a log just inside a copse of evergreens covering a low hill above the highway. Montoya, his new radioman, huddled beside him, teeth chattering in the cold. Troops of his 1st Platoon were spread out on either side in a line through the trees, crouching low in firing positions hastily scraped out of the frozen ground. They'd only had time to lay a few logs over their holes for overhead protection against artillery fire. To his left a two-man Dragon team sheltered behind a clump of brush, just at the limit of his vision. To the right the squat shape of an M-48 tank lay partially concealed by white camouflage netting. Rhee squatted behind the tank, ready to relay his orders to the South Korean crew inside.

Kevin lifted his binoculars and scanned the ground to his front. The hill fell away gently, sloping down to the multilane road leading to the Haengju Bridge. Beyond the highway the landscape opened up into a checkerboard pattern of diked rice paddies broken only by a raised railroad embankment running parallel with the highway. Helmeted heads bobbed above the nearest rice paddy dike where his 2nd Platoon was supposed to be lying hidden and then disappeared as quickly as they'd surfaced.

Without taking his eyes away from the binoculars, Kevin snapped his fingers and held out a hand for the radiophone. Montoya pushed it over to him.

"Echo Five Two, this is Echo Five Six. Keep your people down. We're gonna have company in a bit, and I don't want to give 'em anything for free. Over."

Sergeant Geary, the 2nd Platoon's CO, answered himself. "Roger that, Six. Out."

Kevin handed the phone back to Montoya. Shit, these people were green. They were going to get sliced apart by the North Koreans. He didn't even know their names. He held the thought for a second and then wondered what they thought of him. Nothing good, that was for sure.

The story of the massacre on Malibu West had run through the battalion like wildfire, and he'd seen the looks thrown his way by the men of his own company on the ride north. He knew what they saw. A washed-out wreck. Before leaving Battalion HQ, he'd seen himself in a mirror and been shocked. His eyes were red-rimmed and bloodshot, his face was deathly pale, and he'd developed a nervous tic on his left cheek. The nerve pulsed irregularly, tightening the skin for an instant and then releasing it. How could anyone draw confidence from someone who looked like that?

He shook his head. No way. No one could or would. Move on, Kevin, the thought came. Move on. There's nothing you can do about it. They'll either follow you or they won't. But you've got to act as though they will.

He lifted the binoculars again, surveying the rest of the battle positions he'd picked for his troops. The 1st Platoon held this low, forested hill; 2nd Platoon's squads were deployed along the other side of the road. He'd divided the machine guns and Dragon missile teams of his understrength Weapons Platoon among the two rifle platoons. The three attached M-48s were spread out in a rough arc along the fringe of the woods—a deployment that gave them good fields of fire out into the rice paddies beyond. The trucks that had carried his troops up from the battalion HQ waited behind the hill, hidden on a narrow side road. Kevin had pressed their drivers into service as extra riflemen. He wasn't sure how useful they'd be in a fight, but at least it would keep them from abandoning the company when the first shells started dropping.

Other hastily formed companies were dug in to the east and west of his force—in position to cover his flanks if the North Korean advance guard spilled off the highway.

He shifted his gaze north up the highway, seeing the smoke drifting lazily away from Wondang. A mixed bag of American and South Korean armored cavalry units were up there, dueling with advancing North Korean tanks and infantry. They'd bought enough time for his men to arrive and filter into hastily prepared positions, but the price had been high. Now they were getting ready to break off the battle, dash back south, pass through his positions, and cross the bridge.

Kevin frowned and felt the nerve in his cheek jump. Once that happened the North Koreans would be on the move—coming on fast to cut off any stragglers left on this side of the Han.

Montoya nudged him. "It's the major, Lieutenant."

Kevin took the handset. "India One Two, this is Echo Five Six, over."

Major Donaldson's voice crackled through the receiver. "Covering force is pulling out now. Stand by for handoff. Over."

"Roger, Two. Out." Kevin felt his hands trembling. The enemy was on the way. He lifted the handset again. "This is Echo Five Six. Handoff imminent. Keep an eye peeled for friendlies and hostiles and hold your fire until I give the word. Acknowledge."

Kevin listened as his platoon leaders signaled their understanding and rose to his knees to get a better view down the road. Smoke shells were bursting now at the edge of his vision, providing cover for the grab-bag armored cavalry squadron trying to break contact with the enemy.

He focused the binoculars as the first vehicles emerged from the gray smoke pall hanging over the highway, racing toward his positions. One by one they sped past. A battle-scarred M-60 tank, several M-113 APCs packed with troops, another damaged M-60, and then a pair of ITVs—M-113s modified to carry TOW antitank guided missile launchers. A last M-60 rolled back down the road, its turret facing backward, ready to fire at the first North Korean vehicles to appear out of the smoke.

The radio crackled again. "Kilo Two One, this is Kilo Two Eight, November Kilos in sight. Three Tango Seven Twos. Repeat, Three Tango Seven Twos. Engaging now—"

The transmission ended abruptly and Kevin watched in horror as the M-60 lurched to a halt and burst into flame. The top hatch blew skyward as ammo inside the tank cooked off.

"Oh, shit, man." Montoya sounded sick. "Oh, Jesus."

Kevin clicked the transmit button on the handset. "Echo Five Six to Five Two. Hold your fire. Repeat, hold your fire. Do not engage the November Kilos. Out." He wanted to keep the 2nd Platoon hidden as an ace in the hole.

He let go of the handset and rose to a low crouch. "Sergeant Bryce!"

A helmet down the line turned. "Lieutenant?"

"Pass the word to the Dragon teams. Tell 'em to open fire as soon as the first NKs come in range. Hit their tanks first. Got it?"

Bryce nodded and scuttled off to relay his orders. Kevin

glanced at Rhee. The South Korean grinned and gave him a thumbs-up signal. He'd already briefed the tank commanders on what they were expected to do. Kevin nodded and dropped back behind his log.

Shapes were appearing at the edge of the smoke, resolving into low-hulled tanks with long-barreled 125mm guns pointed south down the road: T-72s. Five of them. This was modern, first-line equipment. The M-48 tanks opposing them were over twenty years old and had 105mm guns. Two veered to pass to the left of the burning M-60, and the other three rolled off the road to the right, treads squealing as they reformed into line.

Other vehicles appeared out of the drifting smoke. Troop carriers. Tracked BMPs and wheeled BTR-60s. Kevin grimaced. There wasn't much doubt of the importance the North Korean high command attached to this attack. That was the first string out there.

The T-72s swept closer, and the range dropped rapidly, 1,200 meters, 1,100, 1,000. Christ! They were in range, why hadn't his Dragon teams fired? Kevin started to get to his feet.

WHOOOOSH. Flame leapt out from the Dragon position to his right as a missile left the launcher and streaked toward an oncoming T-72. The tank started turning, trying to evade it, but the Dragon gunner saw the attempt and corrected his missile's flight. It slammed into the T-72's hull and exploded. For a second the tank kept rolling with smoke streaming out the back. Then it ground to a halt and sat immobile, wreathed in flame.

CRACK! The M-48 to his right fired its cannon. Kevin swiveled, looking for the target. There. Another T-72 sat motionless, caught with its vulnerable belly exposed while climbing a rice-paddy dike.

Another Dragon team fired off to the flank, but its target tank suddenly disappeared in a cloud of whitish-gray smoke. Must've popped its smoke dispenser, Kevin thought. The missile plunged into the smoke cloud and missed. Damn.

CRACK! An M-48 farther down the line fired at a T-72 that had closed to within five hundred meters. *WHANG!* The 105mm round glanced off the North Korean tank's bow armor and bounded high in the air. The T-72 came on and fired back.

The M-48 exploded, spewing orange flame and metal

fragments through the trees. There were screams from some of the infantry foxholes near the wrecked tank. "I'm hit! Oh, GOD! I'm hit!"

Kevin dropped flat to the ground, pressing his hands to his ears, trying to shut out the sounds. It was happening again, just like Malibu West.

"Lieutenant! Lieutenant!" It was Montoya, nudging him, holding out the radio handset. "It's Echo Five Two."

Kevin looked up. The RTO was crouched with his back to the log, staring at him like a little lost puppy dog. Somehow the sight gave him a sense of purpose. Montoya needed him. Maybe they all needed him.

He grabbed the handset. "Two, this is Six. Over."

Geary's voice quavered audibly; he'd been shaken by what he was seeing. "Six, PCs to your front are unloading troops."

Kevin grabbed his binoculars and focused them on the open ground below the hill. No good. The smoke from the two burning T-72s blocked his view. The other three had disappeared. Had they pulled back?

He swept the binoculars from right to left, searching for signs of movement. There. He could see shapes moving in the smoke—men carrying AKM rifles, RPK light machine guns, and RPG-7 launchers. Engine noises were audible above the crackling flames. Troop carriers backing up the North Korean infantry he could now see clearly. They were only four hundred meters away and trotting in fast.

"Sierra Echo Two One, this is Juliet Echo Five Six. I have a Delta Tango for Yankee Delta two three zero six seven five. Over." Kevin called in a DT—a defensive target artillery fire mission. He wanted to see how the North Koreans liked a dose of their own medicine.

"Roger, Echo Five Six. Stand by." The NK infantry kept moving forward, hunched over under the weight of their gear. BMPs and BTRs were visible now, nosing out from the smoke.

The BMPs and BTRs were armored vehicles, designed to carry infantry. Kevin had forgotten what the letters stood for, an abbreviation of their Russian designations. The Soviets rarely gave their equipment sexy names like "Patton" or "Bradley."

The BTR was an eight-wheeled armored box with a

machine gun on top. It was big and could carry fourteen men. The BMP was a nastier beast but could only carry nine troops. To make up for the difference, it carried a small turret with a 73mm gun, an antitank missile launcher, and a machine gun. It had better armor and was tracked, so it could go places the BTR couldn't. Both could swim across rivers.

The radio spoke: "Shot, out."

Kevin heard a high-pitched howling arcing overhead and saw dirt spray skyward behind the advancing North Koreans. "Echo Two One, this is Six. Drop fifty and fire for effect!"

He dropped back behind cover as the first time-fused shells whirred over and exploded in midair, showering deadly fragments across the wave of North Korean infantry charging toward the hill. A dozen or more dropped into the snow without a sound, mowed down like standing wheat at harvest time. Others were thrown back screaming, torn apart by splinters.

Kevin felt the ground rock. A shell burst two hundred meters away, hurling dirt away in a black cloud. Then another exploded, closer in. Holy shit! Those weren't American shells. The North Koreans were responding in kind, walking their own artillery in on his positions.

"Cover! Cover! Incoming!" He threw himself back into a shallow foxhole and dragged Montoya in after him. Evergreen needles slashed at his face. They hadn't had time to strip the branches off the logs providing overhead cover for their holes.

WHAMMM! WHAMMM! WHAMMM! WHAMMM! Shells burst all along the fringe of woods sheltering the 1st Platoon. Treetops exploded as North Korean guns found the range, spraying clouds of whining wood and metal splinters across the hill. A foxhole with two GIs crouching low inside it suddenly disappeared in a flash of bright white light, leaving nothing but a smoking crater.

The noise was deafening, maddening. Kevin and Montoya coughed as dirt thrown by a near-miss cascaded into their foxhole.

"Echo Five Six, this is Two. Over." He could barely hear it.

He wriggled round to get at the radio strapped to Montoya's back and had to shout to make himself heard. "Two, this is Six! Go ahead."

"NK infantry stopped. But the BMPs are still closing with you."

It was time to show his ace. "Two, this is Six. Open fire! Say again, open fire!"

"You got it!" Geary sounded excited now. He and his men had flank shots on most of the approaching North Korean vehicles. BMPs started going up in flames as Dragon teams hidden among the rice paddies found the range.

WHAMMM! WHAMMM! WHAMMM! Enemy shells continued landing all over the hill, shaking the ground, toppling trees, blasting foxholes—killing and wounding men crouching helpless under the barrage. The 2nd Platoon's missile teams and machine-gunners were wreaking havoc on the North Korean vehicles, but they kept coming, surging forward toward the pinned-down 1st Platoon. Kevin knew he had to get his men out from under this artillery fire or they'd be overrun. But how?

TARGET ACQUISITION BATTERY, 3-35 ARTILLERY, SOUTH OF THE HAN RIVER

"Target, sir!" The corporal's yell brought the captain's head back inside the darkened radar van.

"Where?"

The corporal leaned closer to his green-glowing monitor, pounding keys as the van's onboard computer evaluated radar traces made by the North Korean shells pounding Echo Company's hill. In a microsecond it backtracked along their projected trajectory, compensated for known temperature and wind velocity, and flashed the estimated position of the North Korean battery on-screen. It was in range.

The captain grabbed his command phone. "Fire mission! Counterbattery!" He squatted to look at the corporal's computer monitor. "Target at Yankee Delta six five eight two three zero!"

He carried the handset over to the van's open door, looking down into the shallow valley where the four surviving guns of Battery B were deployed.

"Target laid in." The battery commander's voice was flat, all emotion ground out by more than ninety-six hours of near-continuous combat and heavy losses.

"Fire at will!"

Battery B's 155mm self-propelled howitzers crashed back, flinging four HE shells toward the North Korean artillery battery sixteen kilometers away. Four more followed fifteen seconds later.

BATTERY 3, 2ND BATTALION, 44TH ARTILLERY REGIMENT, NEAR PYOKCHE, SOUTH KOREA

The North Korean artillery captain froze in shock as the first American shells exploded on and around his battery's gunline.

His second-in-command had quicker reflexes. He dove to the bottom of a slit trench dug next to the CP and stayed there for a full minute as the ground trembled from hit after hit. When the barrage lifted, he raised his head cautiously above ground level to survey the damage.

He glanced back at the CP and quickly averted his gaze from the bloody scraps of flesh that had once been his captain. Things weren't any better anywhere else. One D-30 howitzer had taken a direct hit and sat mangled on its central firing jack, with its seven-man crew lying dead beside it. Four of the battery's five remaining guns were also out of action, and more than half his gunners were dead or severely wounded. Moans rose from the wreckage.

The North Korean lieutenant stared at the carnage for a moment and then went to help the wounded. The attacking force his howitzers had been supporting would have to fend for itself. Battery 3 was out of action.

1ST PLATOON'S POSITION, SOUTH OF WONDANG

At first the silence was overpowering. But then, as Kevin's hearing returned, other sounds of the battle came flooding back—the rattle of machine gun fire from 2nd Platoon's rice-paddy dikes, sharp explosions as American proximity-fused shells continued to burst in midair over open fields now carpeted with North Korean dead, and the grinding squeal of

North Korean BMPs lumbering up the slope toward the woods he and his men held.

Kevin wriggled out from under the logs of his foxhole and sat up. Montoya followed him.

Trees had been blown down all around their position, sheared off by the North Korean barrage. The next foxhole over wasn't there anymore; an evergreen had landed right on top of it. Kevin swallowed hard and looked away from the thin red smear oozing out from under the fallen tree.

Burning vehicles dotted the ground below his hill. A handful of BMPs, a scattering of wheeled BTR-60s, and five T-72 tanks sat motionless, spewing smoke. But three BMPs were still advancing, spraying the woods with machine gun fire and rounds from their 73mm cannons. Kevin couldn't see any return fire from his own positions.

He craned his head, looking for the M-48 tanks attached to his command. One sat afire in the woods nearby. A thick, black column of smoke marked the funeral pyre of a second farther down the line. But where was the third? They needed armor support to stop the BMPs from overrunning the hill.

A soldier bellycrawled over from behind a splintered tree stump. It was Rhee.

Kevin reached out and pulled him into cover. "Where's the fucking tank?"

Rhee's face was grim. "Gone." He pointed over his shoulder. "It fled and abandoned us."

"Shit!" The BMPs were closer now, shooting up the forward edges of the wood. Kevin could see his men now. They were starting to give ground, slipping back through the trees. Echo Company's defense was collapsing all around him. He felt the nerve under his left cheek twitch again. Another failure.

Three men ran past, one without a rifle.

Bastards. Kevin stood up and yelled, "Get back on the line! Goddamnit, we can hold 'em! Get back in your holes!"

They swept by without answering. Others were following them.

Kevin jumped up out of the foxhole. He felt Rhee's hand on his leg, pulling him down, but he shook it off. He moved to intercept the troops heading away from the oncoming BMPs.

One carrying a LAW slung over his back came right at him. Kevin stepped into his path and held out a hand to stop him. "Hold it right there, soldier. We need that weapon."

The man shoved him aside without even looking and snarled, "Fuck off!"

Kevin felt something explode in his brain for just an instant. Something infinitely cold and infinitely hot. An anger greater than he had ever known before surged through him. He gave in to it and threw himself at the soldier's back—knocking the GI flat into the snow.

Kevin got to his knees first and wrenched the cardboard-tubed antitank rocket off over the man's neck, tearing away skin and the soldier's helmet. The lead BMP was pushing its way into the mangled woods just twenty meters to the right, roaring up and over fallen trees.

Ignoring the white-faced GI on the ground, Kevin scrambled to his feet and ran toward the North Korean infantry combat vehicle, swinging the LAW up and onto his shoulder as he ran. He could hear himself shouting something at the top of his lungs, but he couldn't make out the words.

Snow spurted all around him, and wood splinters sprayed off a tree to the side. A second BMP had spotted him and was firing its coaxial machine gun. Kevin ignored it, really conscious only of his target and the white-hot rage he felt.

He got to within ten meters of the lead BMP and slid to a stop, feet plowing through the snow and churned-up mud. He braced and aimed, focusing along the length of the LAW toward the BMP's massive, armored flank.

"Bastards!" Kevin screamed, and pulled the trigger. The 66mm antitank rocket roared out of its launch tube and slammed into the BMP. It ripped through sixteen millimeters of steel armor and exploded inside. The BMP shuddered to a halt with smoke pouring out of its firing slits.

Kevin stood staring at it for a second and then felt himself knocked to the ground. Machine gun bullets cracked overhead, ripping branches off the evergreens around him and tearing away deeper into the woods. Kevin rolled over and came face-to-face with a grinning Lieutenant Rhee. He opened his mouth but couldn't think of anything to say.

Rhee shook his head and waved a hand at the woods

around them. American soldiers were settling back into fox-holes, their weapons out and ready. Kevin saw one man raise another LAW, point it downslope toward the second BMP, and fire. It hit, but the BMP kept coming. A second soldier off to the flank saw it and fired a third antitank rocket. This one burst near the driver's slit and sent fragments ricocheting around the interior of the North Korean vehicle. It rolled on for a few meters more and then juddered slowly to a stop.

The last BMP abruptly popped its smoke dispensers and reversed rapidly away from the hill, jinking from side to side to throw off the aim of any American missile teams zeroing in on it.

Kevin sat up slowly and then levered himself to his feet, looking at the wrecked vehicles and corpses scattered across the hillside and through the woods. He could hear faint cheering coming from the rice paddies occupied by his 2nd Platoon, but the men of his 1st Platoon sat silent, relieved just to be alive. He reached down and helped Rhee to his feet, gradually realizing that a smile was spreading across his face—an expression he hadn't worn for what seemed like an eternity.

He looked down at his hands and saw that they were steady. No more trembling. They had won—at least this round. They'd stopped the North Koreans cold.

Kevin turned on his heel and started back through the tangle of shredded trees, looking for Montoya. His orders still stood. They'd bought some time. Now it was time to fall back to the next battle position and do it again.

NORTH OF THE HAENGJU BRIDGE, NEAR HANGJUSAN CASTLE

"Drop one hundred, right fifty."

The spotting round sent chunks of asphalt flying as it gouged a crater in the highway. Kevin clicked the transmit button. "Got it! On target! Let 'em have it!"

More artillery rounds screamed in, blasting the road and the open ground around it. North Korean infantrymen scattered in all directions, seeking cover where there was none. Earth and fragments of torn bodies fountained high into the air.

Kevin stopped watching the barrage and wriggled back

into his foxhole to consider his next move. Echo Company and the units covering its flanks had fought steadily all day, gradually giving ground in the face of repeated North Korean attacks. Each time the pattern had been the same. Bloody the NK columns from concealed positions. Force them to waste time deploying for a more deliberate attack and then beat a quick retreat down the road to the next set of defensive positions.

It had worked. They'd bought time for the other units fleeing across the Haengju Bridge. But the price had been high. Sergeant Caldwell, his Weapons Platoon leader, was dead. Bryce, the 1st Platoon leader, had been medevacked two hours ago, bleeding from a dozen shrapnel wounds. All told, nearly thirty of his men were out of action—dead or seriously wounded.

Kevin rubbed a weary hand across his face, feeling the bristles of his beard mixed in with caked-on mud. How much longer could he ask his troops to go on taking losses like that? They were being ground up by this constant fighting. How much longer would they have to hold? This hill was the last barrier between the North Koreans and the Han.

He squinted west into the setting sun. Not more than an hour of daylight left. He turned to look down the slope behind him. There were still trucks crowding the bridge, but the traffic seemed somewhat lighter.

"Sir. It's Major Donaldson." Montoya nudged him gently.

Kevin took the handset and clicked the transmit button. "India One Two, this is Echo Five Six, over."

Donaldson sounded tired, too. "Stand by for withdrawal. Say again, stand by for withdrawal."

Kevin shook his head, not quite understanding. He felt as if his head had been wrapped in cotton. What was that? Withdraw? How? When? He clicked the transmit button again. "One Two, this is Five Six. Request instructions."

"Okay, Kev." Donaldson spaced his words out carefully. "Foxtrot and Bravo are pulling out now. They're clear of NK contact. What's your situation? Over."

Kevin sat up higher in the foxhole. The fire mission he'd called down had ended. There were bodies thrown all around the road, some motionless, others writhing in agony. The scattered survivors of the NK infantry company he'd spotted were in full retreat—scampering back up the road as fast as their legs would carry them.

He lifted his binoculars, looking farther up the highway toward the low, rolling hills he and his men had left behind an hour before. He could see shapes moving among the trees. Tanks and other armored vehicles forming up for another attack.

He lowered the binoculars, thinking hard. "Two, this is Six. Estimate three zero minutes before next NK push, over."

"Understood, Kev. Start your people across in five minutes, but leave a force to cover the bridge approaches until everybody's clear. Got it?"

Kevin acknowledged and signed off. He handed the radio back to Montoya and looked around for Rhee. The shorter man's steadiness and absolute reliability made him the perfect choice for the task Kevin had in mind. The South Korean lieutenant had shown himself to be a damned fine combat leader—one who could be counted on to inspire his men and use them well in the heat of battle. Just as important, he'd proved that he had brains as well as guts. During the day's fighting, the dapper South Korean had earned his assigned slot as Kevin's right-hand man a hundred times over.

Rhee was crouched beside one of the three remaining Dragon launchers. He saw Kevin's wave and scuttled over.

Kevin filled him in on the situation and gave him his orders, trying to use the formal tone he knew the South Korean liked. "Lieutenant Rhee, I want you to lead the boys across. Leave me one Dragon team, one MG team, and a rifle squad. We'll follow after you're on the span. Clear?"

The South Korean nodded.

"Okay, then. Get moving." Rhee rose to a crouch, but Kevin stopped him with a hand. "But keep everybody out of sight as long as you can. I don't want the NKs to know we're going until we're long gone."

Rhee nodded again and moved off to get the company organized and loaded onto its trucks.

The exhausted men of Echo Company needed no urging to leave their foxholes behind and crowd onto the waiting vehicles. One by one the trucks pulled out onto the road and roared off down toward the bridge and safety.

Kevin spread his remaining eleven men out in a thin skirmish line along the crest of the hill. Montoya crouched beside him in the foxhole that served as his CP, turning every five seconds or so to see how far the company had gotten. Kevin kept his eyes on the woods to the north.

He didn't have any illusions left. Another North Korean tank attack would sweep through this last squad as if it weren't even there. The most they could do would be to give a little warning to the men waiting to blow the bridge.

Minutes passed. The signs of movement in the woods were increasing. The NKs could come anytime now. He glanced at his watch. Come on, Rhee!

"Echo Five Six, this is Five Four." It was Rhee.

Kevin grabbed the handset. "Go ahead, Four."

"We're on the bridge."

Kevin felt relief wash over him. He stood up and cupped his hands. "Second Squad! Let's get the fuck out of here. Let's go, people!"

He watched the woods while his troops grabbed their weapons and jogged downhill toward the last truck. The driver already had its engine running. Men swarmed over the tailgate, turning once they were on board to help others up.

Oh, God. Tanks were emerging from the tree line, forming up for the attack. Ten, eleven, twelve . . . Kevin counted them rapidly. There were at least two North Korean tank companies moving toward him.

"Lieutenant!" It was Montoya yelling at him from the truck. "C'mon, sir. We gotta get out of here!"

No shit. Kevin spun away from the oncoming North Korean tanks and sprinted hard for the waiting truck. *KARRUMP. KARRUMP.* Dirt kicked high behind him. NK mortars were zeroing in on the hill. He ran faster, arms pumping out from his sides.

KARRUMP. Rock fragments and splinters whined overhead, thrown by an explosion to his right. Kevin skidded to a stop, panting, at the back of the truck. Hands reached down to pull him aboard as the driver put it in gear and raced away toward the bridge. Behind them the hill they'd been defending disappeared in a sea of blindingly bright flashes as the NK heavy artillery opened up.

WHAMMM! The truck careened around a shell crater and roared onto the empty bridge. Kevin sat up amid his men as they swayed from side to side under the low canvas roof. Gray-white smoke billowed high in the air above the hill. The North Koreans were laying a smoke screen to cover their attack. He smiled crookedly. They were wasting a lot of ammunition on people who weren't there anymore.

The truck crossed over to the south side of the Han and slowed, turning off onto an access road running along the riverbank. The driver slammed on his brakes, fighting a skid, as he turned a corner and came face-to-face with a row of concertina wire laid across the road.

"Everybody out! Out! Take cover over there!" Grim-faced combat engineers waved Kevin and his men out of the truck. They jumped down over the tailgate, some falling to their knees in the mud, and staggered over behind a snowbank.

"Blow it!" Kevin looked up at the voice and saw an engineer wearing colonel's insignia staring intently at the bridge. He followed the man's gaze.

WHUMMP. WHUMMP. WHUMMP. WHUMMP. Kevin covered his ears as the series of explosions grew louder and closer together, rippling across the bridge from north to south. Whole sections of the roadway buckled and then flew upward, spinning end over end before splashing into the river below. Others simply sagged and then fell over, crashing into the water in a spray of white foam and ice.

When the smoke cleared, the Haengju Bridge lay in ruins, torn and ripped into a mangled mass of twisted steel and shattered concrete, poking above the water here and there. Tanks appeared momentarily on the hill to the north of the river and then backed hastily out of sight. The North Koreans would have to find another way across.

ABC WORLD NEWS TONIGHT

The camera view showed a computer-generated map of South Korea, with red arrows showing the known positions of the attacking North Korean columns.

"Defense Department sources admit that, although the enemy's advance has been slowed, it is still continuing. Ac-

cording to these sources, American and South Korean troops are currently engaged in what is called a 'determined fighting withdrawal.' Other people tell us that's what used to be called a retreat.

"For other news of the day's events, we go to ABC's Karen Fuchida near the small town of Benicia, California."

The camera cut away to an aerial view of row after row of gray-painted merchant ships riding motionless at anchor against a backdrop of flat marshland and low, rolling hills. As the helicopter moved closer and swooped lower, work crews could be seen swarming over several of the vessels.

"Civilian contract workers continued their 'round-the-clock' efforts today, as they pushed relentlessly to ready these ships of the nation's 'mothball fleet' for sea. Once they're ready to go, these ships will join others already carrying much-needed cargo to the troops fighting in South Korea."

The camera view shifted again, this time to the main street of a small town nestled among snow-covered cornfields in Iowa. Men in green uniform fatigues moved purposefully around a square, brick building.

"Meanwhile, National Guard and Reserve units around the country received orders putting them on standby alert for possible movement overseas. There wasn't a lot of flag-waving enthusiasm, just a lot of quiet determination. ABC's John Peterson asked one Guardsman about his feelings."

The camera cut to a close-up of one middle-aged man in full gear.

"Sure I'm hoping this thing gets settled without us. I've got a wife and couple of kids to think of. But I guess this is what they pay us for and all. So, if the country figures they need us, why, I guess we'll go. Nope, not much doubt about that."

The man seemed to stand taller as he spoke.

CHAPTER
31
Task Force

Captain Nikolai Mikhailovitch Markov looked at the sonar display and smiled. His position was perfect: his Tango-class submarine was loitering at three knots directly in the path of the American task force. He had a full battery charge, and fleet headquarters had given him detailed information about the composition and arrangement of the enemy ships. All was well with Markov's world.

He was a small, thin man, well suited to the cramped quarters of a submarine. His broad, Slavic face was pale from weeks submerged. In his early forties, he had served in the Navy since he entered the Nakhimov Secondary School in Leningrad as a teenager. Sea tours had alternated with years ashore at other academic institutions. He'd served aboard the *Dribinov* for many years, beginning as navigation officer, then *starpom,* or executive officer, and finally as captain. He knew his ship, and what it could do for him.

His orders from the fleet command were clear. *Konstantin Dribinov* was expected to approach the American task force undetected, penetrate its ASW screen, and make a simulated torpedo attack on a high-value target—preferably an aircraft carrier or an amphibious command ship. The key word was "simulated." At the point where Markov would normally launch torpedoes, he would instead launch a flare that could be seen on the surface.

It was a dangerous game. The Americans would be doing their best to detect any submarine, warn it off, and if it closed to attack range, sink it.

In a sense, his land-bound superiors were risking his submarine, and several other boats, to show the United States that its ships were not invulnerable. Markov didn't mind. That was the kind of game the Americans often played with Soviet ships. Maybe it was time to start turning the tables. And the shallow East China Sea was a good place to do just that. The U.S. Navy's weapons and sensors were all oriented toward "blue-water" operations, where the water was always over two hundred meters deep and often over two thousand meters. In fact, the American Mark 46 torpedo, their standard antisubmarine weapon, couldn't even function effectively in shallow water. All too often its active sonar would home in on the nearby seabed instead of a target submarine. In addition, Markov knew that U.S. ships used powerful low-frequency sonars, with ranges measured in hundreds of kilometers through open water. But in shallow coastal seas, those same sonars were practically blind. Their sound beams tended to bounce right back off the nearby seabottom, blanking out the American sonar operators' screens.

In contrast, his submarine was at its best under those same conditions. The *Konstantin Dribinov* was a diesel-electric design, first built in the 1970s. When operating on battery power, it was one of the quietest submarines afloat—a silence enhanced by a rubber anechoic coating designed to absorb sound waves. Just as important, its sensors were fairly modern by Soviet standards, certainly much better than those carried by the Romeo-class boats used by his North Korean comrades. And unlike the larger nuclear subs, the *Dribinov* could maneuver easily in shallow water. Its hull was only 92 meters long, and at periscope depth it needed a mere twenty meters of water to stay submerged.

At the moment Markov's planesmen were holding the *Dribinov* just below periscope depth. He planned to wait, watch for a good opening in the American screen, and then make his approach. He was confident. After all, he'd practiced the same kind of maneuver against Soviet surface forces dozens of times.

ABOARD USS *CONSTELLATION*, IN THE EAST CHINA SEA

As he'd feared, Brown hadn't gotten much more than an occasional and unsatisfactory catnap. Lack of sleep wasn't improving his judgment any, and it certainly wasn't helping his temper, but the habit of command was too deeply ingrained. He couldn't make himself risk missing something that might affect the safety of the ships under his authority. Their first radar contact had proved to be a Chinese Yun-8 Cub. The Cub was a four-engine patrol plane, actually nothing more than a converted transport mounting an old surface search radar. It had proved more circumspect than the *Kavkaz* and appeared perfectly willing to respect the hundred-mile exclusion zone.

Its Soviet counterpart hadn't been so polite. The Soviet plane, a Bear D flying out of Vietnam's Cam Ranh Bay, had appeared at extreme radar range, headed straight for the center of the task force. Brown had been ready for that, and the Bear had been intercepted by two F-18 Hornets a hundred and fifty miles out. One took station behind the Soviet patrol plane, while the other F-18 flew close alongside. The three planes flew in formation until they were just a hundred and ten miles out. Brown had been preparing a harsher response when the Bear suddenly altered course, circling slowly just outside the exclusion zone.

Both the Bear and the Chinese Cub had since acquired permanent companions. At least one Hornet loitered near each of the lumbering aircraft, just in case. If any more trailers appeared, Brown thought he might be tempted to sell tickets. The admiral ran his reddened eyes over the Flag Plot's status boards for the thousandth time. It seemed quiet enough now. Maybe he had time for another nap.

WHISKEY THREE, OVER THE EAST CHINA SEA

The S-3 Viking patrol plane known as Whiskey Three orbited at low altitude ahead of the task force. It didn't look dangerous. The S-3 was a boxy, twin-engine plane that wouldn't last a second in a dogfight with an enemy fighter. It was slow, low-powered, and relatively unmaneuverable. But it was death on submarines. Every Viking carried sonobuoys, torpedoes, and a half-dozen different sensors, all designed to find and fix hostile subs before they could do any damage. The petty officer manning Whiskey Three's surface search radar suddenly started and leaned closer to his screen. He'd seen a small blip appear momentarily out in front of the formation. There it was again. A radio aerial, maybe. Or possibly a periscope or radar detection mast. Whatever it was, it wasn't friendly.

He keyed his mike. "Contact report! Possible sub bearing zero one five degrees. Twenty miles."

Forward in the cockpit, the S-3's pilot whistled sharply and banked right, heading for the contact's reported position at two hundred and fifty knots. The game had started.

ABOARD USS *CONSTELLATION*

Brown stared at the ASW display screen. Whiskey Three's contact report had caught him just heading for his cot. The submarine the S-3's radar had spotted was roughly sixty miles ahead of his lead ships, directly on their intended track. So far, they hadn't been able to determine its nationality or type, but it sure wasn't a U.S. or any known friendly submarine.

Whiskey Three was on station now over the sub's last known position, running cloverleaf search patterns at low altitude.

Brown looked at his ASW controller. "Get Whiskey Three some backup. As soon as they've localized the sub, they're to use depth charges to force it to the surface. Tell 'em to start with a salvo a thousand yards away and halve the distance with each attack. Whoever's down there should get the message pretty damn quick." The gray-haired commander nodded his understanding and moved to obey his admiral's order, but then turned back to ask, "What if the sub doesn't break off, Admiral?"

"If he gets within twenty miles, we'll sink the bastard."

ABOARD *KONSTANTIN DRIBINOV*

Markov cursed himself for his impatience. He'd raised his radar detection mast to check the direction of the approaching American task force. Well, they were up there, all right, emitting signals as if they were putting on some kind of electromagnetic fireworks display. But something else had been up there, too. Something he should have been more wary of. The *Dribinov*'s radar detector had immediately lit up with a strong signal from an antisubmarine patrol plane—a signal so strong that the American aircraft must have detected the mast in the seconds it was above water.

Now he was being forced to expend precious battery charge moving away from his planned position. He had to hope that the *Konstantin Dribinov* could get clear of the upcoming American search before it really got underway.

But Markov's hopes were quickly dashed. "Comrade Captain, sonar reports active sonar contacts ahead and to both sides. Distance is between two and three thousand meters." His first officer's voice was apologetic.

Markov stared at the chart as his officers laid in the contact bearings reported by his sonar operator. The pattern that emerged was all too clear. He could see that the American patrol plane must have laid a circle of active sonar buoys all around the spot at which he'd raised his radar detector.

Markov picked his next course of action straight out of the Red Navy's manual of submarine tactics. He'd have to look for a gap between the American sonobuoys, all while staying as close to the bottom as he could and relying on the *Dribinov*'s anechoic coating to absorb some of the sonar pings' energy. With a little bit of luck he and his crew could still wriggle free of this net.

His voice was crisp and assured as he issued a quick series of orders. "Helmsman, left standard rudder. The rest of you, plot the rest of those sonobuoy positions. Let's see if they're behind us as well. Find me the largest interval between the buoys and quickly!" He turned to the lieutenant manning the depth gauge. "Vladimir, what's the water depth here?"

"Eighty-two meters, Comrade Captain."

"Very well. Make your depth eighty meters." The Dribinov circled, carefully, like a big cat gauging the strength of its cage. Markov knew he had to move fast. In another minute or two, the American ASW aircraft would undoubtedly start to drop buoys in the center of the circle. Right on top of them.

He studied the plot more closely. They'd taken cross bearings on the buoys to precisely determine their position. Ah, yes. He pointed at a spot along the ring outlined by the American buoys. "There. Right full rudder. Steady on course one nine three.

But just as they settled on their new course, his sonar operator called excitedly, "Comrade Captain! New active sonar signals to port, very close! They've almost certainly detected us."

Damn the Yankees. Their reflexes were faster than he'd assumed they would be. "Right full rudder. Increase speed to ten knots." They'd have to evade the hard way.

Suddenly there was a new sound rumbling through the sub's metal hull from directly ahead. Throughout the control room, pale, set faces turned to stare at the hull. They knew what that sound was—a depth charge explosion. They'd heard enough of them in training. This was a low rumble, a sound only with no shock.

Markov was puzzled. If they had a good idea of his location, why drop a weapon so far away? Suddenly he smiled. It was a warning. Well, he would use that warning time to break free of their sensors and resume his approach. The Dribinov and its captain weren't out of tricks yet.

ASW PLOT, USS CONSTELLATION

Brown watched over the air controller's shoulder as the situation developed. Two S-3 Vikings were working the contact now, and another two were on deck, ready to take over when the first pair ran out of sonobuoys or depth charges. He had ten S-3's in his deckload, and he'd use as many as he needed to blanket this character. The controller pointed at his screen. "Sir, he's turning south and speeding up. Buoys thirty-four and thirty-five are fading."

"I don't think the first depth charge convinced him we're serious, Tim. Lay another pattern of active buoys."

"Whiskey Four's already enroute, Admiral. We're laying an east-west line ten miles wide, then we'll turn them on all at once, just like last time."

Brown nodded his agreement, feeling the excitement of the chase again. ASW work had always been his favorite.

ABOARD *KONSTANTIN DRIBINOV*

Markov was taking a chance. Running at fifteen knots used a lot of battery power, but by turning east and moving fast, he might be able to avoid the next pattern of buoys. He knew the Americans had more coming. They were the best way to find a submarine in these shallow waters, and they'd worked the last time. His plan was to be where the buoys weren't.

He knew what he was up against. ASW aircraft dropped sonobuoys into the water by parachute. And they were so small—only about twelve centimeters in diameter and less than a meter long—that they made no discernible noise when they splashed down. Once a buoy was in the water, it extended a radio antenna from the top and unreeled a hydrophone from the bottom. Normally the hydrophone could be commanded to go either shallow or deep, but in this place there was only shallow water. That greatly simplified the task of the Americans hunting him.

Markov also knew that a newly placed buoy wouldn't start pinging until the controlling aircraft told it to. This time the American plane must be waiting until it had laid the whole pattern, whatever its shape.

He desperately wished he knew the location of the aircraft and its pattern. He could use his periscope to spot the plane, but that meant slowing the *Dribinov* down and exposing its periscope mast to radar and visual detection. That was suicide under these conditions.

He stopped. No, not suicide. They were not going to kill him, only warn him away. Well, he had a little warning for them.

"Comrade Captain! New active signals. Behind and to starboard."

Markov glanced at the sonar display and made an instant decision. "Deploy a decoy! Left full rudder! Steady on course zero four five." He turned to the sonar operator hunched over his display. The man had one hand clapped to his earphones while the other danced across his controls. "How strong is the signal? Are we being detected?"

The sonarman shrugged. "Unknown, sir. We were nearly beam-on to one of them. We should be out of range quickly, though."

ASW PLOT, USS *CONSTELLATION*

"We've got him, sir, on the edge. The joker zigged on us."

Brown pulled at his jaw. "Can we drop on him?" The air controller didn't hesitate. "Yes, sir. Five hundred yards?"

"Yeah. How precise is your fix?" Brown wanted to scare the bastard out there, not kill him. Not yet.

"Good, sir. It's a strong return. Present course is zero eight zero, speed is . . . one knot. . . . " The controller's voice faltered.

Crap. Brown had seen this stunt before. "That's not the sub. That's a decoy!" This sub driver was smart. He'd popped a noisemaking decoy out of one of his signal ejectors and probably turned the other way, hoping the Americans would follow the wrong one. Well, they had. The controller started giving directions to his planes. "Whiskey Four, this is Alpha Whiskey. Pattern Charlie Three, centered on datum." He looked at Brown. "Sir, if we keep using circular patterns, the S-3s are gonna run out of buoys in a hurry."

Brown pondered that, but only for a few seconds. "Keep it up. We've got ten aircraft, and we're going to use them. I'll start arranging resupply flights of sonobuoys from Japan and the Philippines. If I have to, I'll strip the Pacific, but I'm not letting any sub close to this force."

"Aye, aye, sir." The controller nodded and turned back to his task. The admiral's answer was the only one that made sense, but there were going to be a lot of busy supply officers from here to Pearl Harbor.

ABOARD WHISKEY FOUR

The S-3 Viking wheeled into position to lay its sonobuoy pattern. From the outside it looked pretty slow. All the action went on inside the subhunter's cabin.

Whiskey Four's tactical coordinator, or TACCO, sat on a computer display that showed all known information about the contact and the units "prosecuting" it. He heard the order from the *Connie* for a new sonobuoy pattern and keyed it onto the screen. The tactical computer looked at the plane's position, the contact's last known course and speed, and the ordered buoy pattern. Its microprocessors began calculating the positions of the buoys in the water, including such factors as the sonar conditions and the plane's distance from the sub's assumed position.

Up forward, Whiskey Four's pilot sat with his hands in his lap as the computer took over the controls and started banking the S-3 toward the plotted position of the first buoy it planned to drop. He controlled the surge of irritation he always felt when the TACCO's toy turned him into a passenger. It was difficult, but good ASW work required absolute precision, and five years of experience had taught him that only a computer-controlled buoy drop could guarantee that kind of accuracy.

In the plane's belly a burly crewman loaded buoys into a bank of launch tubes. As each slid into place, the S-3's tactical computer gave it a quick burst of instructions—how deep to lower its microphone, which radio channel to use when sending data back, and a slew of other commands needed to make it work.

When Whiskey Four reached the computer-selected start position, it released its first buoy. The canister slid down the launch tube and out into the aircraft's slipstream. A small parachute snapped open and the sonobuoy slid downwind into the water. Others followed at regular intervals. The TACCO watched as small symbols appeared on his screen, marching slowly in a circle around a moving symbol that showed where the enemy sub might be.

He waited until the Viking had dropped the last buoy in this pattern and then leveled out of its long bank. With a smile on his face he pressed a key and imagined the sound waves that were now radiating outward through the cold water below. Knock, knock, tough guy.

ASW PLOT, USS *CONSTELLATION*

"Four's got a solid return, Admiral. Course one seven zero, speed four knots."

Brown smiled. "He's still trying to work south. Persistent bugger, I'll give him that." His smile disappeared. "Okay, Tim. Drop another charge, this time five hundred yards in front of him." The admiral leaned closer to study the ASW plot. The sub driver out there had guts, maybe too many to keep pussyfooting around like this. "How close is he now?"

"Forty-two miles from *Constellation*. Thirty-five miles from the forward edge of our screen." The ASW controller sounded just a tad impatient. Brown knew he should back away and let his subordinates do their jobs. They couldn't find it easy trying to work with him staring over their shoulders. He allowed himself a minor twinge of conscience over that and then refocused his mind on the hunt.

He tapped the aircraft status board, pondering his next move. Then he nodded to the ASW controller. "All right. Let's give the Vikings some help."

ABOARD *KONSTANTIN DRIBINOV*

The rumbling had been louder this time, and Markov well understood the message it carried. He'd used up ten percent of his battery charge trying to break free of the last field, and he'd almost succeeded. Almost.

But now the rumbling explosion of the American depth charge rang in his ears like laughter. All right. He would use their own laughter against them. "Full speed. Steer for the place where the depth charge exploded."

His control room crew leapt to obey.

Markov was gambling again. He knew the depth charge explosion would rumble through the sea for several minutes, and the water it had roiled would return confused echoes to the American active sonars. The *Dribinov*'s high-speed propeller noise should be cloaked by those echoes—allowing him to merge his sub with them, wait for the echoes to fade, and then motor away quietly. The Soviet crew listened carefully, and Markov slowed the sub's electric motors as the rumbling subsided. Two minutes later the *Dribinov* reached the "knuckle" in the water formed when the depth charge exploded. A little turbulence remained, gently rocking the sub's mass left and right. "All stop," Markov called out softly. Knuckles did not move.

He looked at the gauges showing the submarine's battery charge level. That minute and a half at full power had considerably reduced his battery charge. The same power that would last for days while creeping at three knots could be used up by an hour's dash at twenty knots.

His first officer followed his gaze and arched an eyebrow in an unspoken question. Now what? Markov spread his hands, careful not to bump anything that might make noise. They drifted for five minutes in complete silence, hoping the search would move away from them. At last Markov ordered, "Speed thrcc knots, course one eight zero." Dead south, toward the Americans again.

"Comrade Captain, I have new active sonar transmissions, to the west." The sonar operator smiled. "They are weak, at least five or six kilometers distant."

"Excellent." Markov turned back to his first officer. "You see, Dimitri, the Americans are not unbeatable. Now we'll simply move south until we can hear their task force, find a hole in their sonar screen, and then—"

PIINGG! Almost too high to be heard, the pulse was so strong that Markov didn't need the sonar operator to tell him that they had been detected.

"What direction?" he called.

"Bearing two one seven." Shit.

PIINGG!

"Full speed, hard left rudder." Markov was running out of tricks. Now all he could do was try to get away from this latest active sonar, and do it as quickly as possible.

PIINGG! This was getting annoying. How many sonobuoys did the Americans have anyway? "Classify that damned noise," Markov demanded. The operator studied his scope, analyzing the frequency and type of the sonar signal bouncing off the *Dribinov*'s hull. "It's not a buoy, Comrade Captain. It's a dipping sonar, of the kind mounted on American helicopters."

ASW PLOT USS *CONSTELLATION*

"Hotel Two is still holding, Admiral. Three is almost in position." The controller controlled his excitement, trying to concentrate on the complicated hunt.

"Great. If Three gets a solid contact, have Two leapfrog and drop a depth charge at two fifty." The symbols on the screen showed one helicopter moving into position, slowing until it was in a hover. It was lowering a cable mounting a powerful, high-frequency sonar into the water, right in front of the submarine's predicted position. Unlike the low-frequency sets the ships carried, the helicopter's sonar wasn't degraded by shallow water.

As soon as the SH-3H Sea King known as Hotel Three turned on its sonar, it detected the sub, moving at high speed away from Two's position. Bracketed between the two pingers, it altered course to the right, racing ahead at twenty knots.

Brown was impressed. This guy was still trying to move south. "Okay, have Two drop and move Whiskey Four and Six in to backstop the helos to the south." The symbol for Hotel Two changed shape as it reeled in its cable, then took off at eighty knots under the direction of Three's sonar operator. Twenty knots was fast for a diesel submarine, but no sub could outrun a helicopter, and getting away from two was at least twice as hard.

Brown and the ASW controller listened in on the radio circuit. "Hotel Three, steer zero seven three magnetic. On top in thirty seconds." The helicopter's rotors and engine could be heard in the background.

"Roger."

"Hotel Three, correct to zero six nine. You are on top now, now, NOW."

"Weapon away!"

ABOARD *KONSTANTIN DRIBINOV*

This explosion was closer, and so loud that for a moment Markov thought they had dropped right on top of his submarine. When he recovered his composure, he ordered all compartments to check for damage, more for drill than because he expected any.

While he waited for reports from his officers, Markov stared at the plot. What had once seemed possible was now clearly beyond the capabilities of his submarine. Now that the Americans had his position fixed so precisely, they'd never let him break clear—not with both fixed-wing aircraft and now helicopters hovering right over him. And even if he could, it wouldn't do much good. The *Dribinov*'s battery charge was down below sixty-five percent. Another hour or so of hard maneuvering would leave his submarine powerless unless he came to periscope depth, switched to diesel engines, and started snorkeling. And the moment he did that, anybody with a decent sonar within range would know exactly where he was. Snorkeling was noisy.

"All compartments report no damage, Comrade Captain."

Markov thanked his first officer absentmindedly and came to a decision. Political second-guessers in Moscow might interpret it as simple cowardice, but it was only military common sense. The American "warnings" were getting stronger, and he couldn't know if the next one would be aimed to kill or just "very close." Technically the Americans would be within their rights if they sank him without further notice. The *Dribinov* was inside a declared exclusion zone, and as "an unidentified submarine" it could be sent to the bottom at will.

His orders were to deliver a message, but the orders hadn't included losing the messenger in the process. It was time the *Dribinov* became an "identified submarine."

PIINNG.

Markov took a deep breath, held it for a second, and then shrugged. "Surface. Take us up, Dimitri, and rig for diesel power. We've lost this game."

ASW PLOT, USS *CONSTELLATION*

The admiral sighed with relief as he listened in to the excited chatter of the ASW copter crews. Their intruder was a Russian, all right—Tango-class. Brown hadn't expected to find any North Koreans out this far, but it was nice to know he wouldn't have to kill anybody this time.

After the last attack Hotel Two had reported the sub's surfacing. Now as Brown watched, the display changed, showing the Soviet submarine moving east at fifteen knots, away from the task force's track.

He allowed himself a small pat on the back. His people had done well. The Soviet sub had been forced to surface more than thirty miles ahead of the task force. Nobody hurt. And at its present speed, his formation would put the Tango well behind it in about four or five hours. Until then an armed ASW aircraft would escort the Russian boat, ensuring that it stayed on the surface and headed in the right direction.

He shook his head wearily. The Soviets seemed determined to press their luck against his ships. First on the surface, with the *Kavkaz*, and now with that plucky diesel-electric boat. What would they try next? He doubted they'd give up so easily.

He was right, and the Soviet countermove materialized even as he walked away from the ASW plot board.

"Sir, we have nine aircraft at thirty-seven thousand feet, three hundred thirty miles. Speed is four hundred and sixty knots. They're headed directly for us. Negative IFF."

Well, Brown could probably have guessed the last. Best not to take chances. "Sound general quarters. Launch another four Hornets to back up the CAP, and then get some tankers up. Our birds are gonna need some juice pretty soon." If they were hostile, he'd have a hot reception waiting for them. If they were just testing his reflexes, he'd show them that they were still lightning quick. His eyes swept over the air display. The *Constellation*'s air warfare coordinator had already vectored the two Combat Air Patrol fighters on the threat axis to intercept.

"Admiral, we've detected Down Beat radar emissions. The bogies are probably Backfire bombers." The carrier's electronic warfare officer looked a little pale, but his training was still holding.

Brown was concerned but not alarmed. The Soviets often used American battle groups as live targets for training exercises. He'd seen it in both the Mediterranean and the Pacific. They did it to make a point, or to harass a formation. Both of these in our case, he thought. Well, let 'em come in and play. If the Soviets wanted to make a serious attack, they'd have sent at least three times the number of supersonic bombers now closing on his formation. No, this was just another game.

He listened to the GQ klaxon echoing through the carrier and watched as MANNED AND READY appeared by every weapons mount and sensor system in the task force. The Soviets wanted to practice? Fine. Brown and his ships would get some more practice in, too. He moved to the antiair plot and started snapping out orders.

CHAPTER

32

Roads South

DECEMBER 30—KIMPO AIRPORT, SEOUL

"Miss Larson?"

Anne looked up, startled by the Army officer's question. She was still sitting on the floor in the main terminal, in the same spot where she'd tried to sleep all night. After the airfield had been shut down, she hadn't been able to find anyone with new orders for her group, and there'd been no way to get anywhere. She'd tried butting her head against obstinate officialdom for many hours before giving up and storming back to her people where they sprawled on the floor. It had been a long night for all of them. Sleep hadn't been easy to come by with the muffled thumping of heavy artillery growing ever louder to the north. But now maybe somebody had remembered where they were.

The Army officer standing above her wore black "railroad tracks," or captain's bars, on the collar of his camouflaged uniform. The name sewn over his tunic pocket read HUTCHINS. He was a little shorter than Tony but looked personable enough.

"Miss Larson?" he asked again.

"That's right," she said, and stood up, feeling every aching muscle. "Are you from the base? My people and I need transport back to..."

Hutchins held up a hand to stop her. "I'm sorry, ma'am, but we're not going to be able to get you back to the base. The Army's orders were to evacuate you, and that's exactly what I'm supposed to do. I've got a cobbled-together platoon and enough trucks to carry you all waiting outside. The new evacuation airfield is Kunsan, and my orders are to get your group there.''

Anne shook her head. That couldn't be right. Kunsan was over two hundred kilometers south of Seoul. There had to be closer airfields. She dug into her memory. "Can't you get us out at Ch'unch'on or Suwon? It'll take hours to get to Kunsan.''

"My orders say Kunsan, Miss Larson," Hutchins's tone was apologetic, but firm. "Both those other fields are getting too close to the front lines. Besides, Kunsan's supposed to be pretty heavily defended. It's the safest place in South Korea right now.''

Anne stopped herself from arguing. What the captain was saying made sense. She didn't know what had made the upper-ups choose Kunsan as the primary air logistics point, but at least they had sense enough to defend it. Not like here. There were pillars of smoke still visible around Kimpo's runways if you wanted to look for them. She didn't.

She glanced down at her watch and then at the hollow-eyed people sprawled across their luggage all around her. "Okay. When do we leave?''

Hutchins smiled ruefully. "Right now, I'm afraid. The NKs are still moving south, and the Army wants your group and a lot of other people out of Seoul immediately.''

Everyone around had heard their conversation, and with a soft groan her people got up and arranged themselves. Carrying the precious computer tapes, now more out of date than Anne liked to think about, they followed Hutchins through the crowded terminal.

The airport's normal office arrangements and passenger procedures had been completely superseded by preset wartime plans, and now last night's air raid had confused things even more. They walked by offices set up on makeshift desks in the concourse and past crates packed with military gear and documents stacked all along the walls. Civilian evacuees like themselves clustered in every spot of open floor space.

Hutchins led the party down a motionless escalator, through an unlit corridor, and suddenly into the open through an unused loading dock. They gasped as they came out into a howling wind that cut right to the bone, and they hastily buttoned up against the unexpected cold. A half dozen trucks sat idling by the roadside, a much more beat-up group than the ones they'd ridden in out to Kimpo.

The soldiers who were supposed to serve as their escort matched the appearance of the trucks. In fact, if anything, they looked even more ragged. Anne could see two wearing blood-stained bandages, and the tall, black sergeant bellowing orders was in civilian clothes. The only sign of his rank was an armband with three stripes taped to it. The weapons the soldiers carried were even more varied, a mix of M16s, old M14 rifles, and even a few riot guns.

The dismay she felt must have been mirrored on her face, because Hutchins answered her unspoken question. "No, ma'am, they aren't regular infantry. If they were, they'd be up on the line."

He kept his voice low. "About half of them are from an artillery battery that was wiped out the first day. The rest are from supply or administrative units, and two of them that I know of were in the stockade for a little excessive celebrating on Christmas Eve." He smiled crookedly.

She didn't smile back. "And just what did you do before the war started, Captain Hutchins?"

Hutchins looked her in the eye and said, "I was adminis-trative assistant to the Second Infantry Division's civil affairs officer." He saw her lips tighten and shook his head. "Look, Miss Larson, I know what you're thinking, but don't try to read a book by its cover. I've been through the Infantry School, and I speak passable Korean. That's one reason I got this job. Trust me."

He turned away to face the others in her group. He raised his voice to make sure they could all hear him. "Look, we don't plan on doing any fighting. All we've got to do is load you people onto the trucks and see you safely to Kunsan. My men and I will do our best to make the trip as fast and safe as we can."

Hutchins smiled thinly as they started grumbling. "Count your blessings, people. My men and I haven't slept in twenty-four hours."

Turning his head back over his shoulder, he called, "Sergeant Evans! Load 'em up!"

The grumbling didn't stop, but the civilians moved to obey. They'd had enough of being this close to the war. Evans chivied them into six different groups and assigned each to a different truck. Their complaints got even sharper when they climbed into the backs of the frigid, canvas-sided vehicles. The cold morning sun hadn't done anything to warm the trucks up. And just like those on the trip out to the airport, they'd have to be warmed by human body heat. Veterans now, Anne's logistics staffers made sure the flaps on the backs of their trucks were securely tied down.

This time Anne didn't have to ride in the back. Hutchins asked her to sit with him in the cab of the lead five-ton truck. She squeezed in beside the captain and his driver, a cheerful-looking PFC named Bell, gratefully. It might be cramped and uncomfortable, but at least the truck cab had a heater.

Hutchins was the last one in, and as soon as the door slammed behind him, they roared off, bumping over a half-plowed access road littered with debris.

As they drove away from the airport, Hutchins explained their route on a marked-up map. They wouldn't be allowed to use Highway 1, the main north-south artery between Seoul and Taejon. Instead the convoy would have to parallel it on smaller roads, first to a town called Anyang, then to the walled city of Suwon, and south from there.

"With luck, we'll be past Anyang by early afternoon, and Suwon by nightfall."

Anne looked at her watch, then at the map Hutchins had unfolded across his lap. Anyang was only about twenty kilometers away, and it was just after nine in the morning. "Why so long to get to Anyang?"

Hutchins corrected her. "Oh, we'll get to Anyang in about an hour, but it's one of the major traffic control points. After that, it'll probably take us a couple of hours to reach the checkpoints and then get passed through. After that, our main problem should be traffic." He shrugged. "I really don't know much about what the roads are like outside the city."

Anne had the feeling he knew more than he was telling her, but she decided not to press it. Hutchins was in charge, and she'd just have to trust his judgment, at least for the time being. She slumped back against the seat to stare out at the passing scenery through the truck's half-fogged windows. Bell had his defroster going full blast, but it wasn't doing much good.

They made fairly good time for the first few kilometers.

All nonessential civilian vehicles were banned from the streets, and military convoys like theirs had absolute right of way.

Things started changing once they left the city limits. They drove south on a two-lane road, through a countryside dotted with tiny farms, rice paddies, orchards, and small villages. War hadn't touched this area much yet, Anne thought, as they drove through the main street of one village. Women and children were still walking out of shops with bags and bundles. But then she realized just how wrong her first impressions had been. Every house in the village had its windows boarded up, and there were armed police on every street corner. What was more, she couldn't see a single young or middle-aged man wearing civilian clothes. They'd all been called up for active duty.

Bell started cursing monotonously under his breath as he drove. The traffic was getting thicker, with civilian carts and cars jammed with women, children, and old men slowly giving way only when he leaned on the truck's horn. Everything was heading south. Occasionally Hutchins would yell something in Korean out the window, but it didn't help much. Nobody wanted to risk getting stuck in the snow heaped along the roadside.

Their inching progress finally stopped altogether, and Hutchins snapped at Bell to stop hitting his horn. They sat with the engine idling for several more minutes without seeing any signs of movement in the packed mass of vehicles blocking the road ahead. At last the captain scrambled down out of the cab and motioned Anne to come with him.

Reluctant to leave the warmth of the cab, but curious about the delay, she zipped up her jacket and followed him around the back of the truck. Most of Hutchins's men were in the back, including his sergeant. "Evans, we're blocked in solid. Send two men forward to see what the holdup is."

The noncom nodded and picked out two men, who, unsmiling and silent, picked up their weapons and jumped out. Anne followed them with her eyes as they threaded their way forward through the traffic jam. They were out of sight within a couple of hundred meters.

She shook her head. If she had to be out here in the cold, she wanted to at least be able to see what was going on. Anne moved back through the freezing slush to the front of the truck. She climbed up onto the front bumper and from there up onto the hood.

Hutchins saw what she had in mind and followed her. He helped her up onto the roof of the truck cab and stood below on the hood himself. The extra couple of meters of height made all the difference in their line of sight.

Ahead, the road wound off to the left, following a shallow valley. For at least a kilometer it was packed with motionless carts, vehicles, and people. Beyond that a bend blocked their view, but she could see a makeshift-looking sign with something scrawled on it in large Hangul characters.

Hutchins was looking at it through binoculars and translated. "Military Control Point. No civilian traffic beyond this sign without a pass." He lowered the glasses and looked at the mass in front of them. "They're not letting civilians pass, but the civilians aren't leaving."

He shook his head slowly. "Jesus, what a way to run a railroad. We've got to get moving. Right now the North Koreans are moving south faster than we are."

He saw the look on her face and hastened to add, "Don't worry, Miss Larson, we'll be moving again soon enough. And remember, the fighting is still all north of the Han."

Anne nodded, knowing that the captain's words were intended to reassure her. They didn't. Suddenly she shivered. The wind was growing stronger and colder, cutting right through the jacket a salesman had once assured her would stand up to a Chicago winter. She thought wryly that she should have remembered to ask the man how Chicago compared to South Korea.

Hutchins steadied her as she climbed down to the road. Remembering how cold the rest of her people must be, Anne started to work her way from truck to truck, telling everyone about the delay while keeping the back flap as tight as possible. For the most part everyone was comfortable.

After a seemingly endless twenty minutes, the two privates came back, accompanied by a Korean corporal. He saw Hutchins, braced and saluted, and then launched into a rapid-fire report in Korean. The captain replied in the same language, and the corporal turned and trotted back through the crowd.

Hutchins caught Anne's eye. "There are two more convoys in front of us. They're using military police to clear a path through the traffic, and they expect to be up to us in about an hour."

They waited, taking turns climbing up on the cab to check the MPs' progress. After forty-five minutes with no sign of activity, Anne gave up and crawled back into the cab to try to get some sleep. Bell, an old campaigner, was already snoring.

She tossed and turned, fighting her frustration with the knowledge that she'd done everything she possibly could. It didn't help much. She knew that every hour away from her computer would mean more work sorting out the chaotic supply situation once they did finally reach Japan.

She fell asleep making a list of things to do once she got there. The only thing was that Tony's face kept coming between her and her list.

ABOARD THE DPRK *LIBERATOR*, IN THE YELLOW SEA

"Sonar reports high-speed screws bearing two six five degrees, Comrade Captain."

Captain Min Sang-Du's head snapped up from the chart laid out before him. "All stop! And pass the word to all compartments for complete silence."

He straightened and stood listening as the faint whine of the *Liberator*'s electric motors died away. The sound of the air recirculation system faded away next. The crew of his Romeo-class submarine would have to subsist on increasingly foul air until this latest danger had been avoided. With the heads malfunctioning the way they were, Min wasn't sure anybody would notice.

At last, satisfied that his orders for silence were being obeyed, Min stepped out of the cramped plot office and moved forward to the Sonar Room. For some unknown reason, the Soviet naval architects who'd designed the Romeo class had seen fit to cloister the submarines' sonar operators in a tiny, inaccessible compartment without an intercom. As a result, sonar information had to be relayed by voice to the control room. And Min didn't want to risk bellowing questions back and forth while someone on the surface was hunting his boat.

"Contact now bearing two seven two degrees." The lieutenant manning the Feniks-model passive sonar had his eyes closed while he fiddled with the gain and frequency controls.

"Evaluation?" Min didn't bother asking about range. Passive sonar couldn't provide that kind of information without a lot of bearing cross-checks. And besides, the Feniks sonar his submarine mounted couldn't hear anything much more than five kilometers away in these confined waters. Whatever was up there was already much too close for comfort.

"Contact evaluated as a destroyer, type still unknown. Screws turning for an estimated ten knots. No active sonar operating."

Min rubbed his chin reflectively. The enemy destroyer wasn't actively hunting them, then, at least not yet. Perhaps he'd ordered absolute silence just in time.

He closed his eyes, trying to recall all the information shown on the chart back in the plot office. They were still sixty kilometers from their objective, and he had only a little more than twelve hours to reach it. There wasn't much margin for error built into the mission timetable, and he couldn't waste a lot of time lying doggo like this. Even arriving as little as half an hour late would force him to abort the mission. And that was something the admirals in Pyongyang would probably not forgive.

"Contact now bearing three zero five degrees and fading. It seems to have missed us, Comrade Captain!" The sonar operator's voice was jubilant.

Min opened his eyes and smiled. Another barrier passed. He clapped a fatherly hand on the sonar operator's shoulder. "Good work, Comrade. Keep it up and we'll all avoid becoming Heroes of the Revolution for a long time to come!"

The captain made his way back to the main control room and motioned to his first lieutenant. "Sung, go tell our passengers to start preparing their gear. I now estimate that we'll arrive at the objective on schedule."

Min watched the man scurry aft and hoped his confidence was well placed. They still had a long way to go.

ANYANG MILITARY CONTROL POINT, SOUTH KOREA

Anne woke up suddenly, not sure at first what had startled her. Then she heard it again. A deep, menacing rumbling off some distance, but moving closer fast. She sat up and gasped as she saw the cause. Artillery shells were bursting in the fields ahead off to one side of the road, flinging dirt, smoke, and flame into the air.

She could see Korean civilians abandoning their stalled cars and trucks and streaming off to either side, taking shelter inside farm buildings and ditches along the road. Hutchins jumped down off the cab and pounded on the door. "Out! Get out! Take cover!"

He sprinted back down the length of the convoy, with PFC Bell right beside him. Anne scrambled out after them, feeling her heart pounding fast.

"Shit!"

"Get outta my goddamned way!"

The soldiers poured out of the truck, swearing at each other in their haste. One groaned and collapsed, clutching a sprained ankle. Sergeant Evans and another man grabbed the moaning private and dragged him away as the explosions moved closer.

Anne followed them as they half-ran, half-skipped over to a low earth bank that marked the edge of a frozen rice paddy.

She'd barely clambered over onto the other side when there was a roaring, whooshing sound. She didn't need to be a veteran to know what was coming, and she fell flat to the ground.

WHAAAMMM! The shell exploded just as her body hit the cold earth, and she felt the ground buck beneath her. Heat and air rushed over her head, deflected by the earth piled to one side. The combination of the shock wave in both the air and the ground pushed and pulled at her body, and for a split second, it bounced her into the air. The force of the explosion surprised her. It reminded her of being caught by a strong wave at the beach and driven facedown into the sand.

She opened her eyes and mouth and immediately discovered another similarity: she was coated with dirt and dust. Most of the troops were already kneeling, looking at the other side of the bank. She got to her knees and followed their gaze. The shell had come down just fifty meters off the road and torn a still-smoking crater two meters across out of a rice paddy. The snow had been blasted off an area more than twice as large.

Sergeant Evans saw the look on her face and grinned. "The good news about being so far behind the lines is that they don't shell you very often. The bad news is that when they do, only the big stuff can reach far enough."

WHOOOOSSH.

"Down!"

WHAAAMMM! WHAMMM! WHAAMMM! More explosions rocked the ground all around the road. Anne lay flat, praying. She'd never been particularly religious, but it seemed like a logical thing to do at the moment.

The noise faded, leaving behind an eerie mixture of crackling flames, moans, and the whistling wind.

Evans raised his head and cocked an ear, waiting. When nothing more hit the ground for a couple of minutes, he stood up and shouted, "Okay, people. All clear. On your feet. Check yourselves and your buddies. Let's go!"

Anne rose to her feet and stared at the scenes around her. The six trucks in their convoy looked unscathed, but the artillery had found the range farther back along the road. She saw a blazing pile of scrap metal canted over in a field and took several seconds to realize that the wreckage was a Hyundai that had been blown off the road by a North Korean shell. Several bodies lay motionless around one crater, the white snow rapidly turning bloodred. She could hear children sobbing from somewhere ahead.

Anne swallowed hard and started toward the cries, but Hutchins stopped her with an outstretched hand. "There's nothing you could do up there, Miss Larson. Look after your own people."

She started to protest and then stopped. Hutchins was right.

The captain kept talking. "Go on, count noses. Make sure you see every person in your group. If people ran off by themselves and got hurt, nobody may have seen it." He turned away to do the same thing for his own men.

As her staff filtered back from their hiding places, Anne walked from truck to truck, checking off each person's name on the transportation order as she saw them.

They'd been lucky. Only one of her people had been hurt. Ed Cumber had taken a shell fragment in his chest. He lay along the side of the road, clutching his chest and swearing. Gloria crouched beside him, looking worried. Anne knelt beside her and with shaking fingers peeled away Cumber's jacket to look at the damage. Fortunately the splinter had been slowed down so much by his winter coat and other clothing that it was only a superficial wound. Gloria didn't seem very relieved, and it suddenly struck Anne that there were other reasons for her concern.

She pushed the thought out of her mind. Interoffice romances didn't seem very important with people lying dead and dying all around them. Together they helped load the wounded man into one of the trucks where Hutchins's medic could inspect the injury more thoroughly. He slapped a bandage on over the wound and shook his head. "Hell, I've gotten worse cuts shaving."

Anne moved away from the truck slowly. Up till now she'd never really thought about how her responsibilities had changed with the transition from peace to war. Normally she supervised her staff's office work and left it at that. But now, suddenly, she found herself responsible for their safety, for making sure they were fed and had places to sleep. She shook her head. This wasn't the kind of job that she'd trained for. Anne decided she'd start watching Hutchins and Evans more closely. She had a lot to learn.

Except for the PFC with the sprained ankle, Hutchins's men hadn't suffered any injuries, but one of the convoy's six trucks had been laced with fragments. Two tires were flat, and it wouldn't start. She asked the captain if it would be a problem.

He shook his head. "I don't think so. We can get it fixed. The concussion probably knocked loose some of the..."

A Korean officer, a lieutenant, appeared out of the crowd and saluted Hutchins. The American straightened up and returned his parade-ground salute. "Yes, Lieutenant?"

The Korean's English was word-perfect. "Sir, can your

people board immediately? My men will have cleared a path for your vehicles in a few minutes." Even as he spoke, a group of soldiers in battle dress appeared out of the crowd. They started shoving people off the road in both directions. Under their direction cars were driven off the road and carts were dragged off into the open fields. They were efficient, and any Korean civilians who argued suddenly found themselves looking into the muzzle of a bayonet-tipped rifle. Watching, Anne felt guilty that so many people were being threatened to clear the way for her group.

Hutchins started giving orders. "Miss Larson, get your people loaded. Sergeant, we'll have to tow that damned truck. Get the one ahead rigged up." Everyone scurried to obey, eager to get moving and out of the cold. And away from the carnage behind them.

Anne watched from the cab as they moved slowly through the mass of silent, weeping people. Bell cursed quietly as he wove his way around occasional obstacles and a shell crater that forced him off into the snow. His cheerful disposition had vanished somewhere back up the road.

At last the roadblock appeared, a massive-looking fortification of cement blocks and sandbags. Two tripod-mounted machine guns faced north in front of a dugout large enough to hold a dozen or more men. The headquarters building sat off to one side, with a South Korean flag flying defiantly overhead.

As they stopped at the roadblock, another South Korean officer approached, and when he saw Hutchins, they exchanged simultaneous salutes, followed by a handshake. "I am Captain Sik. May I see your travel orders, please?"

The Korean examined all the papers with the care of someone buying a used car. Every person in the convoy had to produce identification, and Sik went so far as to check the copies to ensure that they were all identical. It took almost twenty minutes to plow through the paperwork.

"Captain," Hutchins asked, "how's the road up ahead?"

The South Korean looked up from the last few sets of ID he'd been inspecting. "Relatively clear, but I would advise you to stay close together and to avoid stopping. Many people are trying to get rides south in military vehicles. They have tried to block some trucks with trees or other obstacles." He shrugged.

"Unfortunately, I don't have enough troops to man the road-blocks and patrol the roads."

He handed the sheaf of papers back and added one more piece of his own to the stack. "Your papers are in order, and I have heard about the order evacuating U.S. civilians from Seoul, so I have not been very strict with you. But please validate your pass at each checkpoint. A new order has come through ordering the arrest of anyone moving south without authorization."

As they climbed in and drove off, Anne muttered to Hutchins, "So he wasn't strict with us. Hah!"

"Nope. He wasn't," Hutchins replied with a deadpan expression, arms folded across his chest. "He didn't have his men search the trucks. He didn't search us. And he didn't check our vehicle markings against the unit issuing our orders. He might have phoned back to verify them, too."

He jerked his head back in the direction they had come from. "Did you see the third-degree every Korean civilian was getting? Even a signed pass and valid ID card might not get you past those guys. You might be carrying contraband, or have some other suspicious reason for wanting to go south."

She looked at him unbelievingly, so he continued, "Look, this country is losing the war right now. I've heard stories of Korean and American units folding and running, or being overwhelmed by sheer numbers. So you can bet the government isn't going to allow everybody to suddenly decide to visit their uncle Kyung in Pusan. The roads have to be kept clear for military traffic." Hutchins realized he'd been preaching and stopped in embarrassment.

They drove on in silence, past a ragged line of civilians walking south in the cold—mothers carrying their babies, older children carrying household goods and family treasures heaped on their backs, and old men and women staggering along beside them. Anne kept her eyes on the road ahead. She knew they couldn't possibly carry any of the refugees lining either side of the road, but that didn't soothe her conscience very much.

Now that they were past the control point, the traffic wasn't too bad, and they made good time to the junction with Highway 47. As they turned south off the highway onto a narrow gravel road, Anne looked at the map with concern. The sun was already starting to sink lower in the west, gleaming over a landscape that again looked peaceful.

"Shouldn't we have stayed on the road to Suwon?"

Hutchins tapped the map. "Suwon's a major airbase, and I don't want to be anywhere nearby if the NKs decide to raid it. A convoy like this would be a fat target for some MiG. We have absolutely no protection against an air attack."

She sighed. Hutchins was right again. And infuriatingly so. Anne settled back into a fog of her own thoughts as they drove through a host of tiny, look-alike villages—through Yamok, Chaan, and Paran. The farther from the war they got, the more peaceful the landscape looked. She looked for details that would tell her why it looked less troubled, but she finally decided it was her own lessened tension.

She finally relaxed enough to think consciously about Tony. It occurred to her that he must be wondering why she hadn't already called from Japan. Well, with any luck she'd get a chance to see him in person before they were flown out of Kunsan. Anne frowned. She'd have to find a way to get word to him somehow. Maybe she could call when they stopped for gas. . . .

WEST OF TAECH'ANG, SOUTH KOREA

The boat slid up onto the beach quietly, gently scraping far enough inland so that a chance wave couldn't carry it back out into the Yellow Sea. Eight men in wet suits rolled off onto the wet, white sand. They crouched in a rough semicircle, hastily stripping plastic coverings off their weapons while scanning the area for signs of movement.

Nothing. Only the soft crash of waves breaking offshore. The moon hadn't risen yet and low clouds covered most of the stars. The North Korean commando team leader waved his men into action. One scuttled inland a few yards and dropped back to a crouch with his automatic rifle at the ready. The others pulled waterproofed packs out of the boat and then peeled off their wet suits.

They wore South Korean army uniforms. The team leader, now wearing captain's bars, studied the luminescent numbers on his wristwatch. Two minutes. It was time to go. He signaled the sentry back into the boat.

As the man struggled into his scuba gear and settled in at the helm, the others pushed the lightweight boat off the beach and around so that its bow pointed seaward. From the stern a specially quieted engine sputtered, then caught, and the boat slid out to sea through the surf. It submerged just offshore, leaving only a faint, rippling wake behind.

The captain smiled to himself. So far, everything had gone according to plan. The *Liberator* had dropped them off at exactly the right position to make their run in to the beach, and Pyongyang's information on the beach patrol schedules had been perfect. He dropped to one knee, unfolded a small map, and studied it with a small, shielded penlight.

Yes, they'd landed in the right spot. The fascists mined all but a few beach approaches that were carefully guarded at night, but there were always paths left through the minefields for use by sentries and patrols. One lay just a few dozen meters inland to the south.

He snapped off the penlight, folded his map, and rose to his feet. His men stood with him, slung their M16s, and picked up their waterproofed packs. There wasn't any further point in acting furtively. They were now just another South Korean army unit patrolling the beach.

With the captain leading, they moved off into the darkness in single file. He kept his eyes on the ground in front as they walked. Sand. Sand mingled with clumps of grass. A small rise off to the right lined with barbed wire. There. Two short, red-flagged stakes marked the beginning of the path through the minefield—their path into the so-called Republic of Korea.

The eight men headed east, off the beach and onto the flat inland plain. They walked more quickly now, making sure only that they stayed between the pairs of stakes planted every few yards. The captain paused to check his watch again. Five minutes since they'd landed. They were still on schedule.

"Halt!" A high-pitched, nervous voice came out of the darkness ahead of them. The captain and his men froze. There wasn't supposed to be a guard post on this path. Other raids and infiltrations were supposed to have distracted the imperialists' attention away from this landing site.

"Advance and be recognized." This time the voice was accompanied by the sharp click of an M16's safety being snapped off.

The captain kept his hands well away from the pistol holstered on his waist and stepped forward slowly. "Beach patrol. Captain Yi."

A flashlight came on and centered on his face—blindingly bright. He blinked. "Get that light out of my face, you fools. And stop acting so surprised to see us."

The flashlight went out. That was better. The captain could just make out a sandbagged foxhole a couple of meters ahead. He edged closer. There were two South Korean army privates in the foxhole, but only one had his rifle up and trained in the right direction. The other was nervously shifting a flashlight back and forth from one hand to the other. The captain smiled. They must be reservists hastily recalled to arms without adequate training.

"Sorry, sir. But we weren't expecting a patrol for another hour." Was the rifle barrel aimed at them starting to drop?

The captain took another step forward. "They've changed things around. Weren't you notified?"

One hand reached slowly into his tunic and pulled out a short, broad-bladed commando knife.

The young South Korean soldier with the flashlight didn't see it. The flashlight beam had ruined his night vision. "No, sir. I'm sorry about the light. I'm afraid you startled us." The captain saw him turn and bend down to pick up an object. A field telephone? He tensed.

"I'll just report you in to HQ, sir. That way the other outposts won't be so jumpy." The private lifted the receiver.

As he did, the captain lunged forward and down into the foxhole, shoving his knife into the man's throat up to the hilt. Blood spurted out over his hand and uniform sleeve and the private gagged, frantically pawing at him before falling back limply against the sandbagged walls. The captain jerked his knife back out and wheeled to face the other sentry. But the man was already dying, his larynx crushed by a steel-tipped kick. The commando who'd delivered the kick grinned, his teeth gleaming in the darkness. The captain grinned back.

He unfolded his map again, looking for their objective. He

traced a line toward it, looking for potential obstacles. One road, a low rise, the village of Taech'ang proper. Nothing more than that. The Chosan River bridge lay just an eight-kilometer jaunt away. He smiled. He and his men would be in position in a matter of hours.

The captain put his map away and took his rifle back from another commando. He looked down at the dead South Korean sentries. The unexpected encounter had been an inconvenience, but it wasn't necessarily a fatal one. They'd police the area to remove all signs of a struggle and carry the bodies away with them. With any luck the South Koreans would assume their men had simply deserted.

They wouldn't think that for long, but the captain and his men didn't need long. Besides, he doubted that the fascists would be able to find them anyway. After all, they'd be hiding in plain sight. He held the thought and started issuing the necessary orders. His commando force had a bridge to visit before the night was through.

CHAPTER
33
Search

DECEMBER 31—SOUTH OF PARAN

The sound of the truck was comforting. They were moving south, and Anne could feel the distance between the war and her increasing, stretching thinner and lighter. She could also feel the pull of Kunsan. For everyone else it was just an intermediate stop on their way to Japan, but they didn't have friends there.

Anne tried to eat her spaghetti and meatballs as they

drove. Hutchins had handed her an "MRE" and told her it was dinner.

MRE stood for "meals, ready to eat" and was the U.S. Army's replacement for the legendary "C" ration. It was a green plastic bag the size of a large book. Her first problem was tearing open the thick plastic. In the end she had to borrow Private Bell's razor-sharp bayonet.

Inside were other pouches. One held the dinner, labeled "Spaghetti and Meatballs." Another held dried fruit. There were other packages with cheese and crackers, utensils, and so on.

Hutchins had commented on her luck. The dinners were designed to be mixed with hot water, which was of course unavailable in a moving truck. The spaghetti dinner did not need water. There were other problems, though.

Whoever had designed the spoons had neglected the fact that she was digging into the large dinner pouch. Almost immediately her hand had become covered with sauce. It didn't taste bad, but it was messy. She ate it slowly, to help pass the time.

She had looked at the map when they passed through Paran. From there to Kunsan was about 160 kilometers, a hundred miles. They were crawling, but even at ten miles an hour they would pull into Kunsan well before dawn.

She looked at the map, willing a straight and smooth path, and a warm one while they were at it. In the cold moonlight she could see the snow-covered rice paddies stretching off on either side of the road. It was a peaceful, quiet scene, but she could see no comfort in it.

NEAR THE COAST HIGHWAY, SOUTH OF TAECH'ANG

The ground near the coast was flat, which Yi hated. Not a valley or a ridge to hide behind; the best they could get was a small gully that ran in the direction they were going. Much of the march had to be made in short rushes, with one team covering the other. It was slow and tiring work.

Each man was dressed in a South Korean Army winter uniform, but instead of the standard white camouflage smock, they wore black. They would put on the white ones later, when they were in position. Concealment was more important now.

They also carried M16 rifles with plenty of ammunition, and standard South Korean field packs. In addition, each man, Yi included, carried another thirty kilos of "special equipment."

This was evidently a popular area, Yi thought. He had seen many signs for bathing beaches, hotels, cafes. Even covered with snow it was picturesque.

His musings were interrupted by the sergeant's signal. All clear. Yi and his three men ran forward at a crouch, the light snow muffling their footsteps.

He fell flat next to Yong, the sergeant. Yong pointed silently out ahead, toward a gravel track stretching across their path. Frozen rice paddies lined the road on either side. They waited, watching the road for about ten minutes, seeing no movement. Yi held up one open hand, then clenched his fist and pumped it up and down. Four commandos ran across the road while Yi and his team covered them.

No sign of movement. He gave the signal and sprinted across the road, sure that Yong and his group were watching and covering him.

The coast road was his landmark. Once across it, they would turn south and head for the Chosan river. They would then follow the river inland to their target.

NORTH OF ONYANG, ON HIGHWAY 39

Anne was awakened by Bell, who was cursing again as they drove downhill. "Captain, the transmission's getting worse. It's even money whether I can get it out of first gear at the bottom of this hill."

Hutchins had been asleep, too. He straightened up in his seat, stretching as much as the cramped cab allowed. He looked at the map while Anne held a hooded flashlight. They had made good progress, covering sixty-five kilometers from Anyang in about three hours.

The captain looked at his watch and made a decision. "We'll pull into Onyang and stop for repairs. We have to gas up anyway, and we can fix the cooling system on that other five-ton truck, too."

Bell smiled. Onyang was only a small town, but it would have decent food, maybe a few beers, a nap . . .

"Quit dreaming, Private. We're going to fix these vehicles and get back on the road ASAP." Hutchins's tone was stern. Bell was one of the two men that had come from the stockade. He was a good soldier but would goof off any chance he could get. That's why the captain had taken him as his own driver, so he wouldn't get many chances.

Anne asked, "Captain, where will we get the vehicles fixed in Onyang?"

"We'll have to find a civilian garage and hope he has the right parts. These trucks use a lot of parts from civilian vehicles, so—"

"I know about the parts, Captain. What I need to know is if they will have a phone I can use."

Hutchins shrugged. "I guess so."

Anne smiled.

AT THE CHOSAN RIVER BRIDGE

Captain Yi looked over the situation. They had followed the river east to Highway 21. The two-lane asphalt road was the major north-south artery on the west coast, and his job was to make traveling on that road a dangerous business.

A concrete bridge crossed the river, which was about twenty meters wide at that point and about three meters deep. The water was moving fast enough to keep it from freezing.

There was a low rise that overlooked the highway and the bridge. Yi's squad waited about one hundred yards back, at the base of the rise, shivering. The bridge was guarded, of course, but this wasn't a major bridge or a major river.

The area was lighted, so his binoculars were more useful than his night-vision scope. There was a small building near the bridge, big enough for a few men. A small sentry box at one end had two men near it.

From their uniforms they looked like Provincial Police, responsible for security in the Korean interior. The Army only guarded the coast. These police, though, were much more than "traffic cops." For one thing, they carried M16 automatic rifles.

There was another man pacing back and forth between the building and the bridge. He was wearing a camouflage uniform, probably Territorial Army. It made sense, Yi thought. Back up the police with reserve units.

The soldier, probably a noncom, ducked under the gate and started across the bridge. Yi moved his glasses ahead of him and saw what he expected: two sentries at the other end as well.

The commando crept backward down the slope, quietly, carefully, until he was about twenty-five yards back from the crest. He then spun around and sprinted down to where his men were hidden.

"It's as we expected. Two at each end, one more in charge. The guard shack probably has two men in it, but no more than four. They are Provincial Police, so we have to change uniforms. Let's go."

The plan had been practiced a dozen times. Without instructions the party moved down to the water's edge, well away from the bridge. They took out Provincial Police uniforms and changed clothes. One private removed a small bundle from his knapsack. Another removed a rope from his pack and tied one end securely around a tree.

There was a hissing sound, which seemed as loud as a steam leak in the quiet night. As the inflatable raft took shape, two men assembled paddles and tied the other end of the rope to the boat. They placed it in the water and climbed in.

Wordlessly they pushed off with their paddles and let the current carry them downstream. The other commandos slowed their progress by slowly letting out the rope, while the two men steered their way across.

In five minutes the boat was grounded on the opposite bank. Yi and the remaining men did not wait to watch them pull the craft into the bushes. They knew their job.

The captain brought his men back to the rise and pointed out their targets, then the approach route. The brush had been cleared around the road, but it almost reached to the guard shack. And nobody was watching the rear of the building.

There was nothing complicated about the approach to the building, but it was tiring. The dark made them slow down to a crawl, to reduce the chance of stumbling, and the biting cold made it hard to hold still. Yi was in front, not because of any desire to lead by example, but because there he could set the pace and react quickly to any changes.

It was hard work, even with the training. Pick each spot carefully, nothing that can make noise or cause you to stumble. Remember that five other men behind have to step where you step, careful that . . .

If he hadn't been moving so slowly he would never have been able to stop. Moving in a low crouch, he had already raised his left foot to bring it forward when he saw a line across the snow. He froze. Any regularity had to be man-made, and anything made by man around here was a threat, until proved otherwise.

He leaned forward carefully, with his followers holding their uncomfortable positions behind him. As he changed his position, starlight caught the line and it glinted. It was a wire.

Following it back to its ends, he found one anchored to a rock, and the other to a trip flare. Not a mine, but almost as deadly to their mission. If he had touched the wire, it would have sent a magnesium flare fifty meters into the air. Without surprise they would fail without having started.

It was a simple device, and he quickly disarmed it. Pointing it out to the man behind him, he moved forward again.

Reaching the back wall of the building was a relief, a chance to stand up straight and pull off the black camouflage smocks. They put on white smocks, the same as those worn by the South Koreans.

From this point on everything depended on speed and luck. Yi watched the noncom walk back from the far side of the bridge. He had to wait until the bulk of the building was between the man and him.

His men had moved into position, flattened near the corners of the building. He took one last look and followed the movement of the South Korean noncom. The man passed out of sight and Yi raised a small flashlight. Shining it across the river, he flashed a coded signal, hoping his men were in position to see it. He started counting.

One. He put away the flashlight and pulled his pistol. Two. Yi checked the silencer as he moved to the corner of the building near the sentry box.

Three. Yi and two of his men fired at the two sentries, each man shooting two or three times, until they started to fall. He heard small *whup* sounds behind him, the rest of his team firing at the noncom. He looked across the bridge but could not see the two sentries there. Had they been killed, or just taken cover?

No shots, from this side or the other. Assume success. They stepped quickly out from behind the building, still hugging the walls. Yi relaxed a little when he saw three forms crumpled on the ground. He snapped his fingers and pointed to the guard shack.

The sergeant and another commando flattened themselves on either side of the door. Yong gave a signal, and they opened the door quietly and slid through. Yi did not follow, instead concentrating on the far end of the bridge.

There. A light shone briefly at the far end. Two short, one long. They'd done it!

Yong came running up just in time to see Yi smiling. He stopped and reported. "Three men. No problems."

Yi didn't waste any more time celebrating. "Get the bodies out of sight. Look for any papers or documents. Clean up any bloodstains. I'm going to see what's in the guard shack."

He looked around at the mayhem his men had caused, then allowed himself one more smile. "And Sergeant, get those sentry boxes manned. We've got a bridge to guard."

For their side.

IN ONYANG

Hutchins cursed out loud. Bell cursed at the truck, Anne cursed to herself. Onyang was a town of about two thousand people. It had one garage, operated by a Mr. Moon, who absolutely refused to get up on a cold night and open his establishment. In the end Hutchins had to threaten him with arrest at bayonet point before Moon would cooperate.

Reluctantly the proprietor unlocked the door, but he absolutely refused to help in any way with the vehicles. Evans took over then. "All right, this is now a U.S. Army motor pool."

While the sergeant organized the repairs, Anne's staff took

shelter in a small hotel, filling the small building. Anne found the night clerk, who spoke excellent English, far more helpful than Mr. Moon. He directed her to a phone, and she tried calling Tony. It was exciting, then frustrating, as she called his BOQ, then squadron offices, trying to reach him.

There was no answer at his BOQ. He was "not available, ma'am," when she called the squadron. She knew that meant he was flying. All Anne could do was leave a detailed message saying where she was and that she should arrive in Kunsan a few hours after dawn, and that she was scheduled to be flown out to Japan that evening. The airman said Major Christopher would get the message as soon as he returned. She hung up.

The two broken-down vehicles barely fitted inside the garage. Anne stayed there, pacing and fuming inside as the time passed. She knew she should be fatalistic, but they'd lost half an hour just getting into the garage. They had been working for an hour since then.

The truck with the cooling problem had been easy to fix, but the other! Bell hadn't imagined his problems with the transmission. Metal from worn gears had worn and chewed the works until the question was why it had worked at all. Bell, still cursing under the truck, wanted a new transmission.

They didn't have one. Mr. Moon gleefully informed them of that, and that he had no parts for that kind of truck, and they could leave now, thank you.

Two hours later the convoy rumbled back onto the highway. Some of Anne's frustration ebbed as the convoy left Onyang and started moving through the countryside.

Sitting in the dark cab, with Hutchins asleep on one side and the dark rice paddies on the other side, there was time to think. The airman had called him "Major" Christopher. She was pleased and proud for Tony, and for herself as well. She seemed to have picked someone with real ability and . . .

Wait a minute. What were her feelings for Tony? Why was she so frustrated about getting to Kunsan on time, if not to see him? What was she going to say to Tony in Kunsan when she did see him? What would he say to her?

Too many questions. She sat in the cab, musing and rehearsing and analyzing and discarding until she drifted off to sleep.

* * *

A sharp jolt woke her, bumping her head against the window hard enough to see stars. Rubbing the sore spot, she opened her eyes as Hutchins started chewing out his driver's lack of skill.

She looked at her watch. Almost two hours had passed. "Where are we?"

Hutchins paused long enough in his tirade for Bell to answer. "We should reach Kwangch'on any minute, ma'am."

She found it on the map and showed it to Hutchins. It was far enough down the coast to lift her spirits. She might get to see Tony yet, not that she knew what to say to him.

Hutchins took the map, trying to determine their exact position, and Anne started to look for landmarks. It was something to do.

One of the first things she saw was a highway marker, illuminated by the truck's headlights, with "29" on it. "Captain, where does that put us?"

Hutchins glanced at the sign, then studied the map. His studious expression was suddenly replaced by anger. "It puts us on the wrong highway! We're supposed to be on Highway Twenty-one, not Twenty-nine!

Bell tried to look at the map as well, but Hutchins pulled it away. "Just drive, Private."

He studied the situation for a few minutes. "Which way did you turn in Hongsong when the road forked?"

Looking like a student unprepared for a pop quiz, Bell answered, "Right?"

It took another ten minutes to stop the convoy, turn the trucks around on the narrow two-lane road, and head back in the other direction. Hutchins drove while Anne navigated, and Bell curled up next to the door in not-so-distant exile.

Hutchins was irritated but hopeful. "We should still get you into Kunsan before noon."

Anne was not comforted. Half her day with Tony would be gone.

KUNSAN AIRBASE, 35TH TACTICAL FIGHTER SQUADRON

Tony Christopher held the message Airman Rice had handed him and studied it for the third time. The airman carefully edged away toward a side door. "Luther, how did she sound? Was she sure she'd be here?"

"Sir, I wrote it all down just like she said it. 'I am enroute by convoy to Kunsan from Onyang for air evacuation to Japan tonight. Expect to arrive by dawn. Will call when I get there. Hope to see you. Anne.'" It had been easy to memorize the message. Rice had repeated it to the major four times.

She was alive. She was all right. She hadn't been shot down or bombed at Kimpo. Intellectually he had known that she was probably okay, but there had been a chance, a probability he didn't like thinking about. And she would be coming to Kunsan, then leaving that night.

"Before dawn." Well, he needed to sleep, but he needed to get some work down as well. His duties as ops officer had cut into his flying. He was only flying one or two missions a day now, and he did paperwork in the morning. He would be free to see Anne, but only if he got his desk clear first. There were some things he wanted to tell her.

He got busy. Flying was more important than paperwork, but it still had to be done. The adrenaline started to wear off from his mission, and his excitement about the message, and he started yawning. He kept at it, though, knowing that he would not sleep.

"Major. Major!" Somebody was shaking his shoulder. He looked up and saw Airman Rice standing over him. He looked apologetic.

"Sorry, sir, but they'll stop serving breakfast soon, and I wondered if you wanted to get anything to eat."

Groggily, Tony said, "Thanks, but I'm not hungry." He started to put his head back down, then suddenly sat bolt upright. Breakfast ended at eight o'clock.

Rice was already heading for the door when Tony called to him. "Have there been any other messages?"

"No sir, not a thing."

Tony sat at his desk and calculated. It had been an hour

since dawn, and he had his first mission brief at fourteen thirty. And all he could do was wait.

"Hey, Saint, why so worried? We got a big mission on?" Hooter's entry into a room was never quiet.

"Anne's coming to Kunsan."

"She's safe? That's great news! When will she get here?"

"She was supposed to be here an hour ago. She's being evacuated out to Japan through the airbase here, and her convoy was supposed to arrive before dawn."

"When does she leave?"

"Tonight." He showed John the message, his frustration apparent.

"I see your problem. What have we got, six hours before the brief?" Suddenly John brightened. "I've got it! Victory through air power!"

Tony was baffled. "What in hell are you talking about?"

"Relax, Saint, I've got it all figured. I know an Army aviator, 'Chips' Nicholson. He's a helicopter pilot, and he'll do anything for two bottles of Scotch."

Tony was still confused. "So?"

"So, since she can't get here in time, let's go find her. Chips can fly north, find the convoy, and set you down."

Hooter pulled out a map lying on Tony's desk. "Look, there's only one way to get from Onyang down here. And Onyang's only seventy miles away. That's an hour in the chopper, and she's probably well south of there by now. We can take off, fly there, and be back by lunch."

Tony sat, considering. He usually made decisions quickly, but this was not his style. There wasn't anything to worry about. The risk of enemy activity was slight.

He looked up at Hooter as his wingman paced the room. "What will Shadow think?"

Hooter shook his head. "My fearless leader, uncertain? Shadow won't know."

Tony thought about the risks, and the risk of not seeing Anne. "Okay. Let's do it. By the way, why 'Chips'?"

"He got his helo too close to a tree once. Luckily he was close to the ground. You go find the hooch, I'll make a phone call."

*   *   *

Tony felt at home on the flightline, but looking at the helicopter, he felt a little uneasy. Like most aviators, he regarded rotary wing aircraft as a momentary aberration of aerodynamics. Any minute now everyone would realize that they really couldn't fly.

Lieutenant Nicholson was a savvy-looking pilot who greeted Hooter warmly, exchanging punches to the shoulder and friendly insults. Tony was introduced, with Chips saluting smartly. When Chips heard Hooter say "fourteen kills," he was ready to do the favor for free.

"But since you went to all that trouble, I wouldn't want to seem ungrateful. Hop in." He collected the bottles and stowed them in a safe place.

John took the copilot's seat and Tony the crew chief's jump seat in the main cabin. The lieutenant started the turbines and they quickly spun up to full power. The UH-1 "Huey" usually transported twelve troops, in addition to the crew, so with only three men aboard, it leapt into the air.

Tony could see Hooter pointing out the route to the pilot, and he put on the intercom headset. "Hooter, there must be more than one convoy between here and Onyang. How will we spot hers from the air?"

"How many will have trucks full of American civilians?" John answered. "Don't sweat it, Saint."

The weather was clear, and with the doors closed the temperature was comfortable inside the chopper. The engine noise was another story, though, and Tony kept the headset on to block out some of it. They quickly passed over the airbase, the city itself, and then the Kum river just to the north.

The traffic into the city was heavy, but a convoy of military vehicles would be easily spotted among the civilian passenger cars and trucks. They flew north.

HIGHWAY 21, SOUTH OF KWANGCH'ON

Anne hated the sunlight. They were late, and their progress now was so slow they would be lucky to reach Kunsan at all. Bell was driving again, and cursing every time he had to shift gears.

They were driving through a narrow cut, with the road

narrowing from two lanes to one. The road was a downgrade, which kept Bell very busy trying to manage the balky transmission.

As they listened to the driver's profane monotone, loud honking started coming from the back of the column. Hutchins quickly halted the convoy, sure that some disaster had struck.

They piled out of the cab and ran toward the back. The honking continued for a few moments, then stopped as they reached the end.

Surrounded by a small crowd of soldiers and passengers was a jeep, occupied by one passenger. A lieutenant colonel, he was climbing out from behind the wheel and did not look happy. "Who's in charge of this mob?"

Hutchins saluted. "Captain J. F. Hutchins, sir, Provisional Transport Detail."

The colonel's laundered, sharply creased battle dress and cold-weather gear contrasted wtih Hutchins's rumpled uniform. His combat boots were the old-style leather kind and were finely polished. The name AYERS was stenciled over the breast pocket. While Hutchins's captain's bars were embroidered in black thread on his collar tabs, Ayers's rank insignia were polished silver metal, oversize, and shone from not only his collar tabs but from his helmet as well.

"Captain, your lack of intelligence is only matched by your lack of military bearing and your obvious inability to maintain discipline. I am enroute to a vitally important conference, and your slow-moving circus has slowed from a crawl to a stop."

Hutchins started to open his mouth to answer, but the colonel was just drawing a breath. "Since you decided to stop and delay me even further, all I can do is report your performance to your superiors and hope that they aren't as incompetent as you are."

He took Hutchins's name, rank, serial number, and parent unit, then climbed back in his jeep. "Captain, I want you to get these junk heaps moving at top speed. If I miss that meeting, it may adversely affect the course of the war, and it will be your fault. Now move!"

They started the convoy up and pulled out of the cut as fast as the transmission would allow. Occasionally a honk or two from the back would exhort them on. They reached the end about five minutes later, and they heard a roar as the jeep's motor passed the convoy.

Colonel Ayers was sitting straight upright, at attention in the seat. He ignored the column and roared off to the south.

Hutchins had returned wordlessly to the cab, and Anne and Bell had followed suit, unsure of what to say as the officer sat expressionless. Finally, just after the colonel drove out of sight, Hutchins said, "You know, it's hard to think of that man as the end result of millions of years of evolution."

Colonel Ayers roared ahead, mentally ticking off a list of charges to bring against that dim-witted officer. Obvious lack of discipline. Ever since the war started, everyone had been getting sloppy. Uniforms, procedures, and especially courtesy toward senior officers such as himself had been given short shrift.

Well, he wasn't going to let things go to pot. If he had to remind every man he saw about military courtesy, and take down every name between here and Chonju . . .

His musings, combined with a high speed, managed to carry him through Taech'on and the smaller village of Taech'ang. He was rehearsing the presentation to the morale board when he came to a checkpoint at one end of a bridge.

He beeped his horn and waved for them to open the gate, but the barrier stayed down and a Korean soldier came up and saluted.

Ayers didn't bother returning the gesture. "Let me pass, man. I have to attend an important conference in Chonju!"

The soldier was unimpressed. "Certainly, sir, but I must see your orders and identification card, please."

"My ID card?" He fumbled for the papers and identification. "Isn't it obvious that I'm an American senior officer?"

The man reached for his papers. "Sir, you might be a North Korean saboteur. They are extremely clever and often disguise themselves as our soldiers."

He examined the papers. "You are Colonel Ayers? We have a message for you, sir. Could you please follow me? It's in the guard shack."

"Of course, Private. Lead on." He followed the Korean into a small building set off the road.

Inside, an officer was sitting behind a desk. The name on his uniform was YI.

The soldier looked at Yi and spoke in English. "Sir, this is Colonel Ayers. I believe there is a message for him?"

Yi stood and saluted. Ayers, glad to see the formalities being observed, returned the salute, but he was baffled by a sudden sharp pain in his right side. He turned his head and looked down, just in time to see a knife sink into his ribs up to the hilt.

His last thought was an amazed protest: "But they had been so polite!"

Yi looked down at the body and smiled. A lieutenant colonel. "Sergeant, get him out of here."

Sergeant Yong knew what to do. He called to the "off-duty" commandos in the building and started giving orders. The corpse was carried out by a back door and the small bloodstain wiped up. Yi himself started the jeep and drove it off the road to a small stand of trees.

A small vehicle park was growing there, out of sight of the road. He pulled up alongside a row of trucks. Some were empty, but most had carried cargoes of food, spare parts, or ammunition. One bloodstained vehicle had been filled with men, but Yi's commandos had gunned them down as they sat in the back. Fifteen replacements would never arrive at the front.

The North Korean was pleased with his work. It had been a productive night and morning. They would continue to ambush military vehicles for as long as they could.

They had not molested civilian traffic. It was not their job to create terror, and it would also speed their discovery. They had even let a few trucks go through because civilian cars had been lined up behind them waiting.

Eventually a convoy too big or too well armed would survive their attack, but until then this road was no help to the South, or their imperialist backers. He especially hated Americans, because without their help they could have liberated the southern half of the peninsula years ago.

That reminded him to look at the dead American colonel. Grabbing a small bag that had belonged to the officer, he hiked over to a spot under the trees. They had dumped all the bodies there, covering successive layers with snow. As he approached his bloody handiwork, Yi was glad that this was not a summer offensive.

Yong had just finished searching the dead officer. "Nothing, sir. He was a minor staff officer for American Second Infantry Division. All he had were these travel orders, and an agenda for a 'Morale Conference' tomorrow at Chonju."

Yi tossed him the bag. "Search this, too." But he didn't expect to find anything. His disappointment showed in his tone. Their first lieutenant colonel, and he had been a nobody.

OVER HIGHWAY 21

They had been aloft for about twenty minutes, flying north at sixty miles an hour, two hundred feet off the ground. Tony was torn between professional interest and personal frustration. He normally didn't fly this low or this slow, except when he was landing. It was easy to search at this speed.

This hadn't let him find Anne, though. They had seen almost no military vehicles, and the few they had seen were clearly not the group of trucks they were looking for.

Both John and Tony were looking while Chips piloted, following the two-lane road. Up ahead in the distance they could see the highway narrow to one lane as it crossed a bridge. Tony half-expected to see the convoy pulled up, waiting for its turn to cross. It wasn't. He was looking farther up the road when Hooter called him.

"Hey, Saint, there's a bunch of trucks pulled up off the road to the right. Looks like we found them."

Chips heard Hooter's comments and immediately swung over to take a closer look at the vehicles. Tony had swung his binoculars over at once to look for Anne, but he could see no movement near them. He saw two covered cargo trucks, but also an open flat-bed, a tanker truck of some sort, a jeep...

"Hooter, this isn't Anne's convoy. They aren't the right vehicles, and there aren't any people around."

"Picky, picky. I don't know, Saint, this is the closest thing to a convoy we've seen. Do you want to set down and check it out?"

Tony wanted to be sure this wasn't their convoy. "Chips, can you take us down for a closer look?"

The craft slowed and circled, approaching the vehicle park at a slow walk. Tony scanned the collection. Maybe it was Anne's convoy and some other trucks mixed together. Some sort of rest stop?

One vehicle caught his attention. Its top was ragged and looked as if it had been camouflaged.

Hooter was scanning the rest of the area, already convinced that this was a waste of time. He was about to tell Tony that when he spotted a dark patch, growing as the snow covering it was blown off.

"Saint, look over to the right." His tone was confused, and concerned. Tony moved across the cabin and focused on the area. The patch quickly resolved into shapes, but he kept on looking at them, hoping he was wrong.

Yi and his men watched from the road as the helicopter circled, then descended out of sight. It was obviously the enemy. Running ahead, he waved his men into the trees. They heard the craft and saw it again, lower, almost stationary over the abandoned vehicles.

Quickly he dashed from tree to tree, keeping the trunks between himself and the aircraft. His men followed his movements, stalking the helicopter as if it were a living thing. The snow it blew around helped hide them, but that was also his downfall.

They saw the aircraft hover, then pivot to face the spot where they had dumped the bodies. There could be no doubt.

He called out "Fire!" and raised his own rifle, aiming for the cabin.

Chips, Tony and Hooter all stared at the bodies. They were piled on top of one another, rather neatly, Tony thought absentmindedly. The longer they hovered there, the more snow was blown away and the more corpses became visible.

Hooter had been counting out loud, punctuating the litany with exclamations: " . . . thirteen, fourteen, fifteen, Jesus, sixteen . . ."

There was a *zing!* sound, and reflexively Tony turned toward it. It was followed by a few more, and a *zingzingzing-Crack* as the window crazed on the port side door.

Chips didn't wait for an analysis. He pulled hard on the collective and pushed the nose over, not waiting to climb. As soon as the Huey was moving forward, he started to slew the tail left and right, steering as evasive a course as his speed and height allowed.

Tony was not buckled in and found himself hanging on to a bracket. Reaching for one of the seat belts, he was knocked loose from his hold by a sudden shock. The helicopter shuddered, and there was a screeching sound. The floor under him was canted to the left, and he finally had to pull himself hand over hand to his seat.

His headset had ripped off when he fell across the cabin. As he strapped in, he looked forward to see John motioning for him to put it on.

As soon as he complied, he heard Chips's voice. "The left engine is out!"

Hooter broke in, "We're clear. No more firing."

Chips was a busy man. The helicopter was lightly loaded, so the remaining engine could provide enough power to keep them airborne. Barely. The questions was, what else had been shot off?

Tony was in the unusual position of being in a broken aircraft, but he wasn't at the controls. All he could do was trust Chips and hang on. The Army pilot quickly scanned the controls and tried to listen to the remaining engine. "We're airworthy, but I've got to set it down soon. Temperature on number two is a little high."

Tony was more worried about what they had seen. "Those have to be North Koreans back at the bridge. Call on the guard frequency and put out a warning."

They continued north while Hooter used the radio.

TAECH'ANG

It was just a small village on a two-lane road. Since the principal industry was farming, it looked asleep in winter, even during the day. Surrounded by now-frozen rice paddies, they were through it in a few minutes.

Anne welcomed it, seeing it as another milestone. Each landmark passed meant that they were that much closer to

Kunsan. It was ten-thirty. If there were no more interruptions, they would be in Kunsan by lunchtime.

AT THE CHOSAN RIVER BRIDGE

Yi tried to be fatalistic, but he couldn't. Curse whatever luck had let the helicopter see the bodies. They had emptied their rifles at it, but M16 rifles just didn't have the range or hitting power to bring down an aircraft. Still, they had crippled it, which wouldn't prevent it from sending out a warning.

The helicopter would radio a warning, and enemy troops would show up. They would attack his position, and he would kill as many fascists as he could, then he and all his men would be killed. There had never been any question of how the mission would end, just how long it would take. And they weren't the only special forces unit in the North Korean Army.

Their mission had already succeeded. Because they had interdicted this bridge for a while, the guards on all the bridges would have to be increased, and also on tunnels, junctions, any choke point. Any South Korean soldier would be suspected of being a North Korean saboteur, and no truck driver would be certain of reaching his destination.

"Sergeant!" Yong came running up. "Are the charges to the bridge wired?"

"Yes, sir. And the vehicles and bodies are both booby-trapped."

"How about the rest of the explosives?"

"Being wired now, sir. Another five minutes at the most."

Yi looked grim. "We are ready. Tell Corporal Soo to watch the bridge and to blow it if he sees anything approach from the south. Who were you going to put in the outpost?"

"Private Suh, sir. He's very reliable."

"I know. Get him up there. Everybody not on 'sentry duty' should be watching for the enemy. Otherwise, let's continue as before. We'll kill as many of the enemy as we can."

TWO KILOMETERS SOUTH OF TAECH'ANG

Chips stomped around on the frozen ground. "How long before those troops get here?"

Hooter answered. "Half an hour, tops. They have to come from Taech'on. Counting time to saddle up, that's pretty quick."

"Yeah, well, it's damn cold, there's enemy commandos in the area, and I've got a busted helo to explain."

Hooter was unconcerned. "When they hear how you detected that North Korean outpost while flying an emergency medical mission, you'll probably get a medal."

Tony had to ask, "'Medical mission?'"

"Sure, Saint. If you had missed your girl, you would have had a broken heart." He turned to Chips. "They'll believe anything. Don't worry."

All they could do was wait. They passed the time checking the damage to the helicopter, trying to stay warm, and waiting to see who came down the road first.

Tony heard them first. "Listen, engines." They were coming from the north.

Anne was trying to tear the envelope of an MRE open. She had planned on skipping breakfast, but hunger and Hutchins's lecture about "eating when you can" had won her over. Her teeth had proved inadequate to the task, and finally she had borrowed Bell's bayonet again.

The convoy, with her truck still in the lead, came around a bend in the road. There was a clearing on the right with a helicopter in it. Hutchins told Bell to slow down, and she spotted three men by the nose of the craft, waving at them.

The captain ordered Bell to pull over and stop, and they all climbed out. Anne stepped out and saw—TONY?—and two other men coming over.

Hutchins couldn't understand. Miss Larson had seemed like a reserved woman, certainly not the type to display affection for complete strangers.

Hooter and Chips explained the situation to Captain Hutchins and his men while Tony and Anne strolled off to talk. After an initial explanation, Anne's head was whirling. She didn't know what to talk about first. His trip to see her, the attack by the commandos, or her trip from Seoul. So she didn't talk about any of these things. She just listened and looked at Tony.

Their wanderings had taken them back behind the Huey, out of plain sight of the convoy. He was pointing out the damage to the aircraft when he stopped and changed the subject.

"Anne, I was really worried when I heard about the attack on Seoul airport. I . . . it's hard to explain."

She smiled. "Don't try. I think I understand."

"No, Anne, I have to tell you how scared I was when I learned about the attack on Kimpo."

He paused and looked into her eyes. "I thought I'd lost you." She looked down at the ground, avoiding his gaze, but he continued, "I don't want to ever lose you, Anne. I love you."

She looked up at him and smiled. "You sure proved that. A helicopter?"

"Anne, I had to see you." He explained about the timing.

"Tony, I'm glad you came, but I don't know how I feel yet. I haven't got my feelings sorted out."

"Mine are definitely sorted, but I understand. I just had to tell you where I stood."

"Well, I kind of like where you're standing. But a helicopter?" She peered at the machine. "It looks damaged."

"I'm hoping I can hitch a ride with your convoy after the bridge is cleared. I don't have any way to get back to Kunsan."

"I'm glad. We'll have time to talk."

"Hey, guys!" Hooter's call invaded their world. "The Army's here."

They walked back to the road. Pulled up next to Anne's convoy was a new group, four vehicles crammed with Korean soldiers and weapons. Hooter and Chips were talking with a burly-looking captain, who stood lopsidedly. Hutchins and Evans were still deploying their men around the area, in case there were any commandos nearby.

"Tony, this is Captain Cha." Cha saluted briskly. "Chips and I have been filling him in on what we saw."

Cha picked up the conversation. "Yes, sir. It's almost certainly a group of enemy infiltrators. My men and I will clear them out. It cannot be more than a few men, and I have a reinforced platoon.'' He looked at the three pilots. ''Would you like to accompany us?''

The Americans exchanged quick glances and simultaneously said, ''No thanks.'' Tony added, ''I'll leave ground combat to the professionals.''

Cha actually looked disappointed, seemed about to persuade them, but changed his mind and boarded his jeep. ''We will drive up closer to the bridge and then deploy. This shouldn't take too long. We will send a messenger back when the road is clear.'' Saluting, the captain and his troops roared off.

AT THE CHOSAN RIVER BRIDGE

Captain Yi knew that there would be some sort of attempt to clear the bridge, and he was going to make them pay dearly for this piece of territory. They would never get the bridge back, but even the ruins would be expensive.

Private Suh waited in a camouflaged spider hole three hundred meters up the road. He was isolated from the bridge by a small rise, and his hole was dug into the edge of a copse of trees. He had found the time to line his hideout with pine boughs, and outside of the cramped quarters, it was moderately comfortable.

He had been waiting for over an hour, ever since the American helicopter had escaped. He heard the engines, and his rush of excitement and fear at the approach of the enemy was mixed with relief.

A jeep appeared first, then three trucks. The lead jeep held an officer and had a machine gun over the back. As he watched, it pulled off the road, with the officer motioning to the vehicles behind. It slowed and stopped, exactly where his captain had said it would.

The waiting was hardest. If they had dashed off quickly, he might have been helpless, but they were in no hurry to unload. As soon as the last truck had come to a stop, he pushed the plunger.

A claymore mine weighs about ten pounds. It is the size and shape of a telephone book and is not supposed to be buried in the ground. It has two prongs that a soldier pushes into the ground. This allows it to sit on one edge, while a wire runs back to an electric firing switch. One side says "Place Toward Enemy."

It is a directional mine. On detonation, plastic explosive fires hundreds of steel balls several hundred feet in a fan-shaped pattern.

Based on Yi's estimate, the commandos had planted five of them in an arc, facing the road. A mixture of snow, smoke, and fragments filled the air, followed by screams and *splang*ing sounds of metal balls hitting metal.

Suh waited. As the mist thinned, the horror it hid was revealed slowly. Men lay sprawled in the snow, red patches outlining their forms. He could see at least a dozen bodies, and he knew that as yet, he could not have been detected.

The postblast silence was filled with moans and cries, and Suh waited a few minutes for the leaders to appear, to start giving orders and get the men organized. Then he started shooting.

They all heard the explosion, and the firing. Tony and Anne and everyone else listened for the smallest sound, trying to follow distant events. After the first explosion and gunfire, there was nothing.

Hooter bounced up and down a little bit. "Short fight. I guess there weren't too many bad guys." He smiled.

The others ignored him. Tony looked at Hutchins. "That didn't sound like what I would have expected."

The captain agreed. "It didn't sound good."

"Should we check it out?"

Hutchins, more from courtesy than need, considered the question. "No, Major. We don't know the situation and might stumble into something. Even if everything's okay, Cha wouldn't like having his elbow joggled."

He looked at Hooter. "If that was all of the fight, they'll send word back. EVANS!"

The sergeant came running over. "Sir!"

"Double-check the perimeter. Make sure there's no way for a man to be taken alone, and no way for a man to slip in between our men."

To no one in particular he announced, "We will sit tight."

* * *

The soldier appeared twenty minutes later. They all heard the call from one of the lookouts, but there was no real need for a warning. He staggered up the road, doing his best to hurry, but slowed down by wounds and shock and half-frozen to boot.

The sergeant started snapping orders. "Get him in the truck! Hughes, get your aid kit! Murphy and Rodriguez, scout down the road and find out what happened. Shoot at anything that moves."

Hutchins, Evans, and the aid man disappeared into the truck while the others waited outside. Anne kept on looking up the road, feeling the cold grow with her uncertainty.

After five minutes Hutchins and Evans jumped out of the truck. Anne ran up with a questioning look, and Hutchins answered, "He'll probably live."

"What happened?" she demanded.

"They walked into some sort of ambush. Most of them are killed, the rest are wounded. The Korean says they only got one man."

Sergeant Evans came up to the officer with a walkie-talkie. "Sir, Murphy's reached the spot."

Hutchins took the radio. "This is Six, over. . . . How many?. . . Okay. Sit tight and watch the road to the south. We're on our way." He turned to the sergeant and nodded.

Evans started giving orders. "Saddle up! Everybody into the trucks."

Anne got the story from Hutchins as they rode forward. "It was a massacre. Murphy says the area is secure, but they need help. My men and I will have to tackle the commandos.

"Anne, you and your people can't fight, but we will need anyone who knows first aid. You can stay back and help the wounded while we move up."

Anne protested. "Why don't we just wait for more troops?"

"Our radios are too weak to call for help. Since the nearest detachment reacted, it would be even longer before anybody else could respond. Hours probably. That gives those bastards too much time. Besides, I'll be damned if I'll stand by and let someone else do my fighting while I've got effectives."

They saw the carnage spread out along the road, and Anne

felt something twisting her insides. She felt flushed and stared at the soldiers' wounds, imagining them on her body.

Hutchins shook her shoulder. "Don't think about it, Anne. Just keep busy. You can't get sick if you're helping them."

The scene changed to one of organized confusion. The wounded were found and moved into the comparative warmth of the trucks. The dead, frozen into grotesque shapes, were stacked off to one side. Evans had his men throw up a defensive perimeter, while the pilots scavenged weapons and equipment.

It was an impressive pile, including antitank rockets, a heavy machine gun and two lighter ones, and ammunition. Evans's eyes gleamed and he started distributing it to his men. Tony and Hooter refused to take rifles. They each had a pistol and fervently hoped they wouldn't have to use them.

One volunteer from Anne's staff and a lightly wounded soldier were sent back up the road to report to Taech'on.

Evans made his report. "Sir, there were thirty-eight Koreans here. Twenty-one are dead. Ten are seriously wounded, the rest are walking wounded. Cha is dead and his sergeant is incapacitated."

Hutchins was shaken by the losses but looked determined. "Will they fight?"

"No question, sir. I recommend giving them another few minutes to thaw out and eat, but they're mad, sir. They'd go alone if we weren't here."

There was a popping sound from the south that quickly exploded into rifle and machine gun fire. Evans yelled, "Hold your positions!" and sprinted over in that direction.

Hutchins looked at the pilots. "I think we've spent all the time we're going to get. Let's go."

The captain kept it simple. Forming a skirmish line, he had his men advance in a line on both sides of the road. Moving from tree to tree, they knew they were up against the best the enemy had. They had to depend on numbers. Hutchins had briefed them all to watch for more claymore mines, and their progress was slowed as every man searched for trip wires.

It wasn't enough. A man's scream of fear was cut off as he tripped a mine. The sound of an explosion was replaced by rifle fire. Everyone fell flat as bullets whined around them. The commandos' numbers were impossible to determine, but they were making their presence felt.

Tony blew snow out of his face and looked for Hooter. Like any good wingman, he was back a little and to one side.

Crawling backward, Tony moved next to John and punched him in the shoulder. Hooter looked at him questioningly, and Tony pointed over to where the mine had detonated.

Tony turned without waiting for an answer and started crawling. Off to his left, men lay or crouched in the snow, firing at targets he couldn't see. The effort of moving while staying flat to the ground tired him but kept him warm as well.

In front of him the snow was streaked with brown and gray. His eyes followed the lines back to the source, where a small depression was the only sign of the mine's presence. He crawled a little farther, and another sign of its presence revealed itself.

The man lay on his back, half-covered by snow and debris. Tony could see a dark patch on his chest, and his face was bloody, dripping onto the snow.

As the pilots crawled up to him, he moaned. At least they hadn't crawled all this way for nothing. Bullets whizzed over them, and it was obvious that the first thing to do was get him out of here.

Grabbing his arms, they started crawling away from the fighting. Occasionally a rifle bullet would remind them of which direction to go.

They reached a small fold in the ground, and Tony yelled for Hughes. The aid man came running and professionally eased in to attend the wounds.

After a few minutes the soldier moaned and his eyelids flickered. Hughes sounded positive. "He's got two light wounds. The one in the chest needs surgery, but he should make it fine. Thank you, sirs."

They had heard other men fall. Tony started to head back. "Come on, Hooter. No rest for the weary."

Yi looked at his command. With seven men at the start of the fight, the odds were against him. He was down to two now, himself and a private on the detonator for the bridge. There was no point in waiting any longer.

*   *   *

Tony and Hooter were resting between trips, congratulating themselves on not getting hit themselves, when there was an earth-shattering *KABOOM!* They could see a large cloud of smoke and dust to the south.

Hutchins jumped up and shouted, "That's it! They've blown the bridge! They know they've lost."

As Hutchins's men had advanced, each trip to their impromptu aid station had gotten longer. Tony was creeping forward, with Hooter behind him, when he realized that they could see a small building, and that someone in it was shooting.

They flattened, Tony wiping snow off his face again. Looking left and right, he could see the troops pouring fire into the doors and windows. This went on for some time, when suddenly there was a whooshing sound and a smoke trail drew a line from the trees to the building. A second joined it, and the twin explosions tore chunks out of the walls, blew out the windows, and finally collapsed the roof.

There was no more firing.

C H A P T E R

34

Crossings

DECEMBER 31—SOUTH BANK OF THE HAN RIVER, SOUTH KOREA

McLaren focused his binoculars on the far side and listened to the tempo of the shelling. It was shifting, moving back from the rear areas toward the river, and increasing in volume as heavy mortars and other guns joined in. He nodded to himself. His instincts had been right. The North Koreans were trying to bull their way across the Han quickly—without a prolonged preparatory barrage.

He glanced at Hansen, who lay flat on the snowbank beside him. "Doug, make sure all commands are on their toes. It's going to hit the fan any minute now."

Hansen nodded and wriggled away toward the M577 command vehicle sheltered in a clump of trees. He dropped back into the snow a moment later.

"They're as ready as they can be, General." Hansen stopped talking and lowered his face as a shell whirred overhead and exploded two hundred meters behind them. When he looked up again, McLaren saw a deep frown. "Look, General. Staying around is crazy. There isn't anything more you can do here—'cept get killed, that is."

McLaren knew his aide was right. He had an army to run, and he couldn't do it with North Korean shells dropping all around his ears. But something in him resisted the idea of leaving. He'd grown tired of watching pins move back and forth across a bloodless map. It had grown too clinical, made him feel too detached from reality.

He'd come up to see the battle, to get a feel for what his troops were really going through. And McLaren was convinced that he needed that understanding. How else could he realistically appraise his units' ability to carry out his orders? Prewar staff analyses of things like the effects of heavy artillery fire on unit morale and cohesion were one thing. It was quite another to hear the shells coming in, to see the explosions, and to witness the terrible carnage they could cause. Nothing he'd seen during his three tours in South Vietnam had quite prepared him for the terrible reality of this full-scale, flat-out war. That had been a different kind of fighting.

KARRUMPH. KARRUMMPH. KARRUMPH. Shells burst in the ice on the edge of the river, spewing clouds of gray smoke that drifted and merged with the freshening wind. The North Koreans were trying to build a smoke screen to cover their assault force.

They were unlucky in the wind. It was strong enough to thin and rip any screen almost as fast as it was laid. McLaren kept his binoculars on where he knew the far bank to be, waiting for a gap in the acrid-smelling smoke big enough to see through.

There. Squat, boat-hulled vehicles swarmed into view and trundled down the slope to slide into Han. They bellied through the ice-choked river, moving fast on twin engine-driven waterjets. McLaren identified them as BTR-60s—amphibious, wheeled APCs that could carry sixteen troops each. They vanished into gray obscurity as more smoke shells exploded along the near bank.

He hadn't been able to get a good fix on their numbers, but if the NKs were following Soviet doctrine as rigidly as they had up till now, there was at least a battalion's worth of armored vehicles out there swimming the river toward his position. Other North Korean battalions were undoubtedly attacking at other points along the Han—all probing for the weak spot.

McLaren smiled grimly to himself. If they got across, they'd soon realize that his defense line was weak along its entire length. In some places battalions were defending frontages that staff theoreticians would have thought too wide for brigades. And that meant that his troops couldn't afford to lose this fight on the Han. Every enemy assault had to be driven back into the river before the NKs could start laying pontoon bridges to bring their heavy armor across.

He shook his head. If his men could just blunt this North Korean drive, they'd buy him a badly needed day to strengthen his defenses and assemble more of the reinforcements arriving hourly from the States and from South Korea's reserve depots.

The engine noises from the river were audible now, even under the noise of the barrage. McLaren rose to his knees, studying the slit trenches and foxholes occupied by his first line of defense—Dragon teams and the infantry to guard them. The Dragon launchers were equipped with thermal sights that would let their crews see clearly through the now-ragged North Korean smoke screen. They would carry the fight to the NK assault force while his M-48 and M-60 tanks stayed hidden.

Seconds passed. C'mon, c'mon. Let 'em have it. Don't let 'em get in too close. The Dragons couldn't hit anything within three hundred meters. McLaren willed himself to patience. He had to assume that the infantry commanders below him knew what they were doing.

A team fired off to his left, the flame from its missile reaching through the smoke for an unseen target. McLaren followed it with his eyes and saw the gray smoke wall glow orange for a moment. A hit! Then another Dragon team fired. And another after that. Others followed suit, too fast to keep track of.

A rift appeared in the rapidly thinning screen, and through it McLaren could see the shattered remains of the North Korean assault force. Three BTR-60s were dead in the water, spinning rapidly downstream with the current. Several others were on fire, tilted over half-in and half-out of the water along the far bank. Another rolled over and capsized, the flames that cloaked it bubbling into white, hissing steam. Swirling foam marked the watery graves of still other APCs. Survivors splashed vainly in the icy water for moments before being pulled under, overcome by the cold and weighed down by their equipment. Only a handful of BTRs still came on, emerging from the smoke as they neared the riverbank.

The lead North Korean vehicle reared up out of the water and exploded as a round from an M-60 tank found its target. Others were marked down and destroyed in the shallows. It was a slaughter. The BTRs had armor that could stop machine gun fire. They weren't intended to stand up to tank cannon—and they didn't, at least not for long.

McLaren sat watching the last BTR-60s burn on the water's edge while Hansen reported the results of the other attacks. They were all the same. The North Korean hasty assault had failed. Now they would have to spend precious time assembling their heavy artillery and armor before making another attempt.

McLaren had his day.

THE NORTH BANK OF THE HAN RIVER

Colonel General Cho slowly lowered his binoculars. The 27th Mechanized Infantry had been one of his best battalions. He turned and looked steadily at his deputy, who now commanded

Cho's old II Corps. "I fear the smoke screen was an error in judgment."

Lieutenant General Chyong nodded, his face carefully impassive. "I agree. The smoke didn't interfere with the fascists' missile systems at all. Instead, it only ensured that our own tanks and support weapons couldn't provide sufficient covering fire."

The two men turned and walked side by side down the hill toward their waiting command vehicles. They ignored the ambulances racing across the ground ahead of them, each filled with maimed survivors of the failed attack. Deaths and wounds were the currency of war, and neither Cho nor Chyong knew of any way to avoid them.

"You know the imperialists will use this delay to strengthen their defenses."

"Undoubtedly."

"Pyongyang will want our full assessment of this setback. Can I assure the General Staff and the Dear Leader that your next attack will succeed?"

Chyong didn't hesitate. "Yes." He saw Cho's raised eyebrow and continued on, "Given twenty-four hours to deploy and zero in, my heavy artillery should be able to pound the enemy's forward defenses to pieces. In addition, I shall not repeat this morning's mistake. There will be no smoke screen blinding us the next time. My assault waves will go in covered by direct fire from our own tanks and missile teams."

Cho nodded in satisfaction. "Excellent. I shall inform Pyongyang of your confidence."

Chyong held out a hand. "There is one thing more, however, my friend."

"Yes?"

"The Americans will undoubtedly send their aircraft to attack my bridging units in their staging areas. I have concentrated all my available SAMs and mobile flak batteries to protect them, but that may not be enough. It would be helpful if our Air Force could lend a more active hand in this battle."

Cho nodded again, more slowly this time. Chyong's carefully phrased point was well-taken. At this crucial stage of the campaign, friendly air cover was even more important than usual. And so far at least, North Korea's MiGs had been less successful than he would have liked. They were inflicting losses on the Americans and their South Korean puppets, but their own casualties had been horrendous.

Fortunately it appeared that steps were at last being taken to remedy their deficiencies. Or so Pyongyang had promised in its latest string of dispatches to his field HQ. He glanced sidelong at Chyong as they reached the parked command vehicles. "I will see what I can do, comrade. "More than that I cannot promise."

Chyong smiled gravely. "More than that I cannot ask."

He glanced back at the last vestiges of smoke drifting downwind and then saluted. "Very well, then. Give me twenty-four hours to prepare and I shall give you a firm bridgehead across the Han."

Cho noted how the setting sun burnished the stars on his subordinate's shoulders. For his own sake, he hoped that Chyong's confidence was warranted. Every passing day gave the imperialists more time to recognize the trap he was preparing to spring. Cho also knew that every day that passed without significant territorial gains would be viewed as a day of failure by Kim Jong-Il. It was unfortunate that the Dear Leader's definition of military success was so limited. Unfortunate, but too late to change.

Cho returned Chyong's salute and then climbed back into his command vehicle for the ride back to headquarters. He had more work to do before the evening staff meeting.

KOKSAN AIRBASE, NORTH KOREA

Colonel Sergei Ivanovitch Borodin strode confidently onto the stage, noting the mood of the assembled squadron. He was pleased by what he could see in their eyes—eagerness, anticipation, determination. These North Koreans were by no means the best pilots he had ever commanded, but they were unsurpassed in their ability to absorb losses and remain undaunted. And now he had something to give them that was worthy of their courage.

He reached the center of the stage and stood without speaking for a second, aware that all eyes were on him. Finally he lifted a single hand and signaled the five armament technicians waiting just offstage. They came forward, pushing a dolly occupied by a single long, narrow wooden crate.

Borodin waited while murmurs swept through the crowded auditorium. Then he spoke. "Comrades! I present to you the weapon that will help us win this battle for command of the air. Will you do the honors, Comrade Captain Kutusov?"

The senior armament technician nodded and bent to release the base of the crate so that the other four men could lift the casing up and bring the object inside into view.

The air-to-air missile they lifted was two meters long and weighted about sixty kilograms. Its four large rear delta fins gave it maximum maneuverability—maneuverability reinforced by triangular canard controls indexed in line and by the four small rectangular fins spaced around its IR seeker head.

Borodin let his enthusiasm for the weapon show in his voice. "Comrades, this is the AA-11, arguably among the world's most advanced infrared homing missiles! It has a maximum front aspect range of approximately eight kilometers, and a rear aspect range of nearly five kilometers. It does not limit you to a rear attack. With it mounted on your aircraft, you will have a weapon that matches the performance of the American Sidewinder!"

Borodin paused, seeing sharklike grins appear on the face of every combat pilot in the room. So far in the war, they'd been forced to sit helpless while closing with the enemy as all-aspect American IR missiles knocked their comrades out of the sky. Now all that would change. They, too, would carry a weapon with a seeker head sensitive enough to home in on the heat emitted from the front of an enemy plane. And they would no longer be sitting ducks from the front.

Borodin matched their smiles with one of his own. "The first shipment of these missiles has arrived from the Soviet Union, comrades. We will carry them on our next mission against the imperialists!"

He stepped off the stage as his North Korean counterpart moved up to brief the squadrons on the new set of tactics they'd devised to take advantage of their new missiles' capabilities. While the North Korean spoke, Borodin fished a small notepad out of his flight suit and finished writing up a rough account of his last action. The South Korean F-5E he'd downed this morning made his score four so far—two F-5s, an American F-16, and an F-4 Phantom. One more and he would be an ace, one of only a handful since the Great Patriotic War. The thought brought another smile to the Russian pilot's lips.

JANUARY 1—RED DOG LEAD ABOVE THE YELLOW SEA

Commander Kerwin "Corky" Bouchard, USN, scanned the sky around his F-14A Tomcat, counting aircraft as they launched from either the *Nimitz* or *Constellation* and orbited about five miles from the two carriers. He shook his head in wonder at the number of planes filling the airspace around him. Twelve F-14 Tomcats and ten F-18A Hornets as escorts. Twelve F-18s carrying HARM antiradar missiles for use against NK SAM and antiaircraft fire control systems. Eight more Hornets flying as flak suppressors armed with rocket pods and cluster bombs. Then the strike force itself, twenty-two A-7E Corsairs and 18 A-6E Intruders. All accompanied by four EA-6B Prowler electronic warfare aircraft. Four fat-bellied KA-6D tankers circled as the formation assembled, passing fuel to planes that had been launched first. Finally an E-2C Hawkeye was aloft to control the strike.

Ninety aircraft all massing for a single, maximum-effort Alpha strike against the North Korean bridging units moving toward the Han River. There would only be time for this one, mammoth attack. U.S. weather satellites in geosynchronous orbit showed a storm front moving down out of the Siberian wastes—bringing with it high winds, hail, and snow that would put an end to normal flight operations until the skies cleared.

"Red Dog Lead and Duster Lead, this is Roundup. Proceed." The strike commander's voice came through Bouchard's earphones.

He keyed his radio mike twice to acknowledge and waggled the Tomcat's wings to signal the rest of the strike escort. Then he banked right, heading for the Korean coastline one hundred and fifty miles ahead at four hundred and fifty knots. The F-18s slid lower and out in front, while his F-14s stayed high and behind. Two Prowlers followed, ready to jam enemy radars and radar-guided missiles if MiGs appeared to contest the air.

"Corky, I'm still getting that goddamned Mainstay on my scope. Even with the jamming, it's got us for sure." Lieutenant Mike Esteban, his RIO, radar intercept officer, sounded pissed.

His frustration was understandable. The Soviet AWACS plane had been loitering arrogantly just outside the task force's declared exclusion zone for hours, escorted by a pair of Su-27 Flanker fighters out of Vladivostok. Everyone aboard the two American carriers knew that the data the converted Il-76 transport was collecting was being passed straight back to the North Koreans, but there wasn't anything they could do about it—outside of assigning a pair of Tomcats to keep a close watch on the single Prowler now busy trying to jam the Mainstay's powerful radar. That was bad enough. But then to top it all off, the Soviets also had a Tu-16 Badger F aircraft aloft. The Badger F was an electronic intelligence aircraft capable of keeping tabs on every signal the task force emitted.

Bouchard clicked his intercom switch. "Yeah. Well, life's rough, I guess. Keep an eye peeled. The next-door neighbors are gonna come knocking at our door anytime now."

ABOARD THE *MAINSTAY*, OVER THE YELLOW SEA

The four-engined Ilyushin-76TD made another gentle turn, cruising in a racetrack holding pattern at forty thousand feet. As the AWACS plane banked, the large radar dish mounted horizontally atop its fuselage reflected the sunlight, and one of the Su-27 fighter pilots escorting it turned his eyes away, half-blinded.

It was dark inside the Mainstay's main Air Command and Control compartment.

"The American jamming is degrading our systems greatly, Comrade Colonel, but we have firm contact with an estimated ninety-plus aircraft. All heading for the coast. This is clearly what we've been waiting for."

Colonel Lushev frowned at Kornilov's impertinence, but he bit down the harsh reply that first leaped into his mind. The lieutenant was undeniably the best radar operator aboard, and his skills demanded a certain amount of tolerance for his unorthodox behavior. The colonel leaned closer to the repeater scope in front of him, trying to make something out himself of the glowing green splotches and sweeping strobes it showed. He couldn't and shook his head. Kornilov's abilities were remarkable.

Lushev swiveled his chair to face the plane's radioman. "Transmit this information to Pyongyang immediately." He hoped that the little yellow bastards could make good use of it. The Americans needed to be taught a lesson.

He swung back to face the repeater scope, fighting down an all-too-familiar craving for nicotine. The Mainstay's electronics were too delicate to cope with an atmosphere laced with cigarette smoke. He would have to wait until they were back on the ground in Vladivostok.

RED DOG LEAD

Bouchard could feel the tension increasing. They were sixty miles out and closing rapidly on the South Korean coast. The strike target was only fifteen miles inland, so if the North Koreans were going to pull anything it would have to be soon. He glanced to either side. The eleven other Tomcats were perfectly positioned. Sunlight glinted off canopies ahead and below. The F-18s were still keeping pace.

"Red Dog, this is Roundup." Bouchard tensed at the sudden transmission from the Navy strike controller. "Multiple bogies bearing three one zero, seventy miles, level forty. Out." The E-2C's radar had just detected enemy fighters slipping into the open from out of Korea's rugged mountains.

Bouchard made an instant decision and keyed his mike. It was pretty clear that the North Koreans knew exactly where they were. There wasn't any further point in trying to stay hidden. "Red Dog flights, this is Red Dog Lead. Light 'em off and let 'em have it."

His F-14s would turn on their powerful radars and engage the enemy at maximum distance with their AIM-54C Phoenix missiles. The F-18s would stay silent, and Bouchard hoped they might be able to slip in closer without being noticed by the oncoming North Koreans.

Behind him, Esteban flicked the switches needed to activate the Tomcat's AWG-9 radar and bent over his scope, studying the information it showed. "Corky, I read two groups of bogies. Twenty-two in the first, and twenty following ten miles behind."

"Rog. Get me a lock on two of the lead group." Bouchard arched his thumb toward the firing switch on his stick. Each Tomcat in the escort group carried two Phoenix missiles for just such an occasion.

"Coming up."

ABOARD THE BADGER, OVER THE YELLOW SEA

The Badger's twin turbojets had been droning for hours, lulling many among the huge plane's flight crew into a kind of stupor made up as much of boredom as it was of fatigue. There was little enough to look at. Just scattered clouds in a brilliant blue sky. And two American F-14s keeping station on them as they orbited. The Badger's crew had seen their share of the twin-tailed American fighters before. The Tomcats were always nearby whenever a mission took the converted bomber near a U.S. Navy carrier task force.

None of the signals intelligence crewmen seated at the consoles jamming the Badger's fuselage was the least bit bored. This was the opportunity of a professional lifetime. They were kept busy intercepting and recording every burst of electronic noise the Americans sent out. Radar emissions. Radio transmissions. Everything. Watching two American aircraft carriers launch a real combat mission was proving most instructive.

Suddenly the senior technician's fingers stopped drumming the face of his console and he sat bolt upright. "Comrade Major! I'm picking up midcourse guidance signals for American missiles. Phoenix missiles aimed at our fighters!"

The major was an intelligent man and he didn't waste time going through the chain of command. Instead he leaped for the radio himself.

FULCRUM LEAD, OVER NORTH KOREA

Borodin heard the distinctive tone of the American radar in his ear phones as it swept over his MiG-29 and smiled. His plan was working. He'd deployed two squadrons of MiG-21s out in front of his twenty MiG-29s, hoping that the Americans would waste their long-range missiles on the older and less capable planes. It was hard on the MiG-21 pilots, but what the hell. None of them were Russians.

"Fulcrum Lead, this is Badger Four! Missiles inbound from American fighters!"

Borodin keyed his mike to acknowledge and switched frequencies. "Fishbed Lead, this is Fulcrum Lead. Red Sector!" He gave the code phrase that would alert the MiG-21s to their danger. At the same time, he hit the MiG-29's throttle, accelerating to close with the lead group. The other Fulcrums followed him as his airspeed crept closer to six hundred knots.

They would mingle with the survivors of the first group as it came within standard radar missile range of the American escort force.

FISHBED LEAD, OVER THE NORTH KOREAN COAST

The North Korean colonel leading the MiG-21 squadrons squinted into the nearly cloudless blue sky, searching desperately for signs of the incoming Phoenixes. With a top speed of nearly 2,400 miles an hour, the American missiles could be expected to reach him in less than ninety seconds from launch.

There. He saw contrails streaking down out of the sky ahead, just as his radar warning receiver burst into a high-pitched *beep-beep-beep*. At least one of the American active homing missiles had locked onto his plane.

"All aircraft! Take evasive action, now!" The colonel yanked his MiG-21 into a hard, seven-g climb to the left, putting Soviet theory into practice. The theory said a rapid pitch-up maneuver could defeat the Phoenix. The twenty-one other planes under his command followed suit, pulling tightly to the left or right and climbing as they worked to evade the enemy missiles.

Most were successful. The AIM-54C Phoenix was designed primarily to kill lumbering bombers, not agile fighters. Its incredibly powerful motor gave it tremendous speed and range, but the motor burned out within seconds after launch. As a result, the missile often lacked the "oompf" needed to follow a highly maneuverable fighter at long range as it climbed.

Theory only went so far, however, and six pilots weren't fast enough or lucky enough. They died as missiles slammed home.

RED DOG LEAD

"Red Dog Lead, this is Roundup. Splash six bogies."

Bouchard shook his head angrily. He'd hoped for more kills from the Phoenixes. There were still thirty-six enemy fighters out there and now they were much closer. He'd have to bring the F-18s into play sooner than he'd wanted to.

Esteban called from the backseat. "Corky, the rear group is merging with the lead batch. Range now forty-five miles. One thousand knots closure." The rival groups of fighters were racing toward each other at incredible speed, covering nearly seventeen nautical miles with every passing minute.

He keyed the mike again, this time calling the Hornet commander ahead of him. "Black Dog Lead, this is Red Dog Lead. Engage the enemy at maximum range."

He heard twin clicks as the F-18s signaled that they'd heard and understood him. Behind him, Esteban muttered to himself as he selected new targets for the Tomcat's four AIM-7M Sparrow missiles. This wasn't going to be as easy as firing Phoenixes. The Sparrow was a semiactive radar homer. In other words, the missile guided on the radar beam sent out by the plane that launched it. And that meant a plane firing Sparrows had to keep its target "painted" with a radar beam until the missiles hit. All of which required flying straight and comparatively level right into the teeth of the enemy. Esteban had always defined that as a real hard way to earn your flight pay.

FULCRUM LEAD

Borodin pulled his Fulcrum alongside the MiG-21 belonging to the North Korean colonel just long enough to give him a thumbs-up signal. Then he dropped back and to the left as the formation spread out, seeking room for the wild evasive maneuvers they would soon have to make. The last transmission from the Mainstay had shown that they were coming into the launch envelope of the Americans' Sparrow missiles.

He glanced down quickly at his own radar screen. Nothing. Just a myriad assembly of randomly moving splotches and dots. The American jammer aircraft were really very good. Still, they should soon reach the point at which his Fulcrums' radars would be strong enough to "burn through" the jamming and lock on to the enemy fighters up ahead. And when that happened, he would have a little present for them—the two AA-7 Apex radar-guided missiles slung under each MiG-29.

Beep-beep-beep. Shit. The Americans had a lock-on. Borodin looked up from the inside of the cockpit and started scanning the sky in the arcs his radar warning receivers showed the attack would come from.

RED DOG LEAD

"Red Dog Lead, this is Black Dog Lead. We show MiG-29s intermingled with the MiG-21s." The F-18 squadron CO's calm voice crackled in Bouchard's ears. MiG-29s! All right, Corky my boy, he thought, you're gonna be hassling with the primo of the primo today.

Estenban called from the backseat, "Got 'em. We've got lock-ons! Range now thirty miles!"

Yeah. Bouchard thumbed the firing switch twice and felt the F-14 shudder slightly as two Sparrows dropped out from under the wings and ignited. His eyes followed the bright, white smoke and flame trails as they tore toward the still unseen oncoming MiGs. Other missile trails reached out from his Tomcats and from the Hornets. Happy New Year, Uncle Kim.

FULCRUM LEAD

Borodin saw it, slicing down out of the sky right toward him. A tiny speck growing larger and larger through his MiG-29's canopy. He tensed his stomach muscles and held his course, watching the missile come for him. There were other trails in the sky, but he didn't care about those. Under this kind of attack, it was every pilot for himself.

Now! Borodin yanked hard left on his stick and pulled sharply back, throwing his Fulcrum into a tight, climbing high-g turn. He grunted as the g's hit but kept his head cocked to keep an eye on the American missile through the turn. At the same time he kept his thumb busy on the stick's decoy dispenser button, popping out bundle after bundle of chaff—clouds of thin strips of metalized Mylar film that would look like an airplane to the enemy radar.

Yes! Borodin saw the missile trail bend away, following one of his chaff clouds. He craned his neck around and saw the Sparrow explode well behind and below his plane. Then he snapped his head back around, searching rapidly for any more missiles targeted on his Fulcrum. There weren't any.

Voices came over the radio. Desperate voices. "Ten, turn right. Right! You've got one after you!"

"I can't shake it!"

"Turn harder, you fool!"

Borodin looked to his right and saw a MiG-29 diving away, afterburner blazing. A billowing white smoke trail suddenly crossed his vision and merged with the fleeing MiG. The Sparrow exploded in a ball of orange-red flame and the frantic voice in his radio stopped.

He came wings level and looked all around. The sky was crisscrossed with smoke trails and dodging aircraft. He looked down and saw another burning MiG tumbling out of control toward the water. Damnit.

Borodin counted noses quickly as his squadrons reformed, still heading for the American fighters. They'd lost three MiG-29s and another two MiG-21s. Eleven planes lost without knocking a single American bastard out of the sky.

He felt a cold rage gripping him and fought it down. Don't

go berserk, Sergei, he told himself, your turn is coming. As if in proof, a box suddenly appeared on his HUD, up and to the right. His radar had at last locked on to an American aircraft! The range was now eighteen miles—inside his AA-7 envelope. Borodin tapped the trigger twice and smiled as his own missiles flared off toward the enemy. Now they would hit back and hit hard. Other Fulcrums were launching as well.

RED DOG LEAD

"Oh, shit!" Bouchard spun the Tomcat up and away as an Apex streaked past and started turning after him. "Do something, Mike!"

"Doing it!" Esteban was already busy punching out a stream of chaff to confuse the incoming Russian-made missile.

Bouchard tightened his turn and saw his airspeed bleeding away. Crap, they might dodge this missile, but they'd be dangerously slow if another one came after them. He went to afterburner.

Other Tomcats and Hornets were busy dodging, too, spiraling away from the radar missiles launched by the MiG-29s. Esteban had his head craned practically all the way round, watching the Apex turning after them. "It's still coming, Corky!"

Fuck this. Bouchard rolled back out of his right turn to the left and pulled up even more sharply. The missile lost track of the F-14 and veered off into nowhere.

Two Tomcats and an F-18 weren't so fortunate and fell into the ocean wreathed in flames. The score was evening out. Now there were nineteen American fighters left to tangle with the thirty-one NK planes closing on them. The Hornets reduced speed to let the F-14s catch up. They would go in together.

FULCRUM LEAD

Eight miles. Borodin throttled back slightly. They would be in IR missile range shortly, and he didn't want to have too big a heat signature when the missiles started flying. He glanced back behind him and made sure that Moskvin, his wingman, was still in position. Satisfied, he brought his eyes back to the

MiG-29's HUD, searching the box his radar had placed around the closest American plane. Six miles.

Ah. Borodin's mouth tightened as the enemy fighter came into view, rushing toward him at over five hundred knots. Twin tails, swept-back swing wings. An F-14! It would be his fifth confirmed kill. He slid his thumb over to the switch that would fire an AA-11 Archer right into the Tomcat's face.

Three miles. The missile warbled in his earphones. Its seeker head had found the enemy and was tracking. He fired and saw a similar streak of flame pop out from under the F-14's starboard wing.

RED DOG LEAD

"God!" Bouchard couldn't believe it. The MiG-29 had fired an IR missile at him from the front and it was guiding on him. Where'd these bastards get those things? He pulled hard left, grunting as his weight quintupled in seconds, trying to follow the MiG and line up for a shot while Esteban popped flares to decoy away the enemy missile. It swung away and exploded one hundred yards behind the turning Tomcat. Bouchard felt the shock wave ripple through the F-14 and ignored it as he fought to bring the plane around on the MiG's tail.

C'mon round, baby. C'mon round. Almost. Bouchard's thumb reached for the firing button.

"Left!" Esteban's frantic shout brought his head around as orange-white tracers sprayed across the Tomcat's flight path. He jerked the stick hard left, turning toward the new threat. There. A gray-white camouflaged MiG flashed past and rolled away. He'd lost the first MiG somewhere in the sun. Jesus, this was turning into a mess.

THE FURBALL, OVER THE YELLOW SEA

Jets were all over the sky, turning, diving, climbing, weaving, and falling in flames. The air battle between the MiGs and the American fighters had turned into a constantly changing series of deadly, short-range duels. Move and countermove. Shot and return shot. At such close range the North Korean and Soviet edge in numbers more than made up for their slightly inferior aircraft and weapons.

An F-14 blundered into the path of an AA-11 and blew up, throwing pieces of itself in an arc hundreds of yards across. Seconds later an F-18 avenged its counterpart with a quick cannon burst into the belly of a rolling MiG-21. A second MiG soon fell prey to a Tomcat-launched Sidewinder, and another nine lima tore the wings off a scissoring Fulcrum.

The edge shifted back quickly, though, as a Soviet-piloted MiG-29 turned inside an F-18 and got off a high deflection shot that shredded the Hornet's cockpit and sent it spiraling down into the sea.

As the air battle continued, more planes on both sides tumbled away on fire or simply blew up. Losses, fuel consumption, and missile and cannon ammo expenditure were all appalling. But the American F-14s and F-18s were doing their job. They were keeping the MiGs fully engaged, protecting the heavily laden strike aircraft now approaching the Korean coast.

DUSTER LEAD, OVER THE SOUTH KOREAN COASTLINE

Commander John "Smokey" Piper, USN, glanced down out the cockpit of his A-6E Intruder as it crossed the coast, six thousand feet above the spray-marked merger of slate-gray seas and white, snow-covered land. He clicked his mike and said, "Duster is feet dry." His message confirmed to the carriers at sea and the E-2C aloft that the strike planes were over land and just fifteen miles away from their targets.

Piper looked ahead into a maelstrom of white, gray, and black smoke puffs dotting the sky as North Korean antiaircraft guns sought out the incoming strike. He saw hundreds of tiny flashes on the ground and watched an F-18 pull up and away from its bursting cluster bombs. Another far off to the right fired a HARM missile toward some unseen, but still-operating radar site. The missile ignited on the rail, then seemed to disappear as it flew forward and climbed. It would dive on its victim from high altitude. The Iron Hand flak suppressors had their hands full on this one.

Voices over the radio told their own story.

"Strawman, this is Comanche. You've got a SAM launch in your six, break left now! I'll hit the site."

"Breaking! Can you see any others?"

"Nega...SAM! SAM! Five o'clock low. Keep breaking left!"

Piper heard the second pilot's voice quavering under the heavy g's he was pulling. "Can't shake it! Can't—"

There it was. A flash low on the horizon, followed by a searing orange ball of flame as the American plane slammed into the ground at over five hundred knots.

"Pirate, this is Comanche. Strawman's down. No chute."

"Affirmative, Comanche. Watch the Triple-A on that hill to the left. I'm rolling in on it now."

A new INS prompt came up on Piper's HUD, and he turned his attention away from the radio. They were within seconds of starting their attack run. He glanced across the Intruder's crowded cockpit and his eyes met those of his bombardier, Lieutenant Commander Mitch "Priest" Parrish. Parrish lifted his oxygen mask for a moment and grinned at him. Then the bombardier bent forward again to stare at the A-6's radar screen, while one hand stayed busy configuring the attack computer for their run.

Piper checked to make sure his wingman was still in position just aft and to the right. "Orca" Jones would stay there through the whole attack to watch for SAMs or unexpected flak positions.

He pulled the Intruder into a gentle left turn, aware that behind him nineteen other pairs of A-6s and A-7s were arcing around to come in on the target area from all points of the compass. The "wagon wheel" attack had worked well for the Navy over Vietnam. Now they'd see how well it did over Korea.

Piper started searching the rolling hills and open rice paddies ahead for signs of the truck-mounted pontoon bridges and GSP amphibious ferries they'd come to destroy.

II CORPS FORWARD HQ, NEAR THE HAN RIVER, SOUTH KOREA

Lieutenant General Chyong crouched lower in his slit trench as an American attack plane roared low overhead, streaming flares behind it. Another followed seconds later. He cursed when he saw that they were aimed straight for a small stand of trees occupied by some of his precious bridging units.

The lead American plane climbed sharply and then banked away, flinging a pair of bombs off its racks. Both flew straight into the woods and exploded. The second aircraft began its turn away and then shuddered as shells from a nearby ZSU-23-4 battery found the mark at last, though too late to save their engineer comrades in the woods.

The wounded American jet flew on for several seconds with heavy, black smoke pouring out of its belly, then rolled over onto its back and nose-dived into a hill. Its companion accelerated away, chased futilely by several shoulder-launched SAMs.

Chyong rose from his crouch, staring at the bomb-splintered woods. Four more of his invaluable PMP bridge sections had been destroyed. How many more had fallen prey to the gray-painted American jets crisscrossing his operations area?

He started to climb out of the trench to find out, but an aide knocked him down as another American plane suddenly appeared out of a small valley to the left and turned toward them. Chyong and the young captain clung to the bottom of the trench while the jet's cannon roared, smashing a camouflaged radio van parked less than fifty meters away.

Then, as quickly as it had come, the plane disappeared. And as Chyong's hearing came back to normal, he was conscious first of the fading sound of jet engines from the west and then of the crackling flames consuming his bridges. The American air raid was over.

DUSTER LEAD OVER THE YELLOW SEA

Piper keyed his mike. "Duster is feet wet."

Then he scanned the air around his Intruder, counting noses as the strike planes, Iron Hands, and flak suppressors reformed for the flight back to the carriers. Five were gone, counting Orca Jones, and another seven trailed smoke, showing that they'd been hit by North Korean guns or SAMs.

Piper was shocked by their losses. Seven of Corky Bouchard's defending fighters had also been splashed, and several others had been recovered on board either the *Nimitz* or

the *Constellation* in a near-crippled condition. His A-6s and
A-7s had hit their assigned targets, hit them real hard in fact.
But the results were Pyrrhic to say the least. With twelve aircraft
downed and an unknown number of others permanently wrecked,
the two carrier air wings operating off Korea were going to be
mighty fragile instruments of war until they got replacements.

He glanced across the cockpit and saw that Parrish had at
last pulled his face away from the radar screen. The bombardier's eyes were closed, and he had his left hand tightly wrapped
around the small, gold crucifix he always wore round his neck.
Piper quickly returned his eyes to his instruments. He could pray
later. Right now, he had to get this bird back on the deck.

II CORPS FORWARD HQ

Chyong moved out of earshot of the field hospital where
medics were working on the badly wounded.

"Well? What do you have to report, Colonel?"

The engineer's face was grim. Many of those screaming
under the doctors' knives were his own men. "The Americans
have wrecked more than half of my pontoons and nearly half of
my amphibious ferries. With what I've got left, I can't support
both crossing operations you have planned."

"What about the spares back with our second echelon?"

The engineer shook his shaved head. "I'm sorry, Comrade
General. If you could postpone the attack for another day, we
could have them in place, but not otherwise."

Chyong considered that, but only for a moment. Cho's
words had made it clear that further delays wouldn't be tolerated by Pyongyang. So he would have to gamble. He'd wanted to
launch both a primary and an alternate attack across the Han in
order to divide the enemy's attention and defenses. It had been
a good plan, but happenstance, as always in war, dictated a
change in plans. So be it.

He stared at the engineer. "Do you have enough equipment to support a single-crossing operation?"

The man nodded cautiously.

"Very well, then. We'll attack tonight. As scheduled.
Make sure your bridges and your men are ready. I'll want
heavy tanks crossing the river by first light."

"And the storm, Comrade General?"

Chyong studied the sky. Heavy, dark clouds were rolling in from the north and the wind was rising again. Small flecks of snow were starting to fall, with more said to be on the way. He turned back to face the engineer. "The weather will be the same on both sides of the Han, Colonel. We attack as planned."

7TH LIGHT INFANTRY DIVISION HQ, NEAR CH'UNGJU, SOUTH KOREA

Major General Frank Connor turned angrily on his ops officer, "Goddamnit, Art! It doesn't make sense!"

The shorter man spread his hands. "I agree, sir. But General McLaren confirmed our orders personally."

"Shit!" Something was way off base here, Connor thought. He'd seen the daily situation maps. The allied forces needed every man they could spare up along the Han River defense line and pronto. And what were he and more than two-thirds of his troops doing? Sitting on their backsides in the same, camouflaged camps they'd been sent to just after arriving by air from the States. And that, according to his ops officer, was just what McLaren wanted.

Conner paced past the headquarters tent entrance and stopped, watching the last, red rays of sunlight streaming over the mountains surrounding Ch'ungju. He frowned. What was Mad Jack McLaren waiting for?

JANUARY 2—ECHO COMPANY HQ, SOUTH OF THE HAN RIVER

"Sir?"

Kevin Little came instantly awake and reached for the M16 at his side. "What is it?"

Montoya stuck his head through the tent flap. "It's Major Donaldson, L-T. On the radio."

Kevin wormed out of his sleeping bag, teeth already starting to chatter as the cold hit him again. His eyes and mouth felt gritty, as though they were filled with sand. Six hours of uninterrupted sleep had helped, but it couldn't make up for everything that he had lost since the war started.

He rose to a crouch, threw on his parka, and followed Montoya out of the pup tent.

Echo Company lay at rest in a small hollow between two hills several kilometers south of the river line. The hills weren't much to speak of, but they were high enough to block the wind, and Kevin was thankful for small favors. His men had been on the edge when they'd been pulled out of the line. Another few hours of straight duty and they would have been too slaphappy to do much more than wave hello to the North Koreans.

It was snowing again. Kevin felt the soft, wet flakes striking his face, but he couldn't see them. The moon was down and it was pitch-dark under clouds that covered the whole sky.

The only light came from the north, a flickering, eerie half-light reflected in the clouds that Kevin would once have thought was lightning. Now he knew it was only North Korean heavy artillery pounding the poor bastards deployed right up along the Han.

But the battle noises seemed louder than they had when he'd gone to sleep. And now the faraway rattle of small arms fire mingled with the crashing sounds made by impacting artillery.

"Here, L-T." Montoya led him over to a truck with its engine idling. The RTO had obviously decided to set his radio watch up in something that had a heater. Smart thinking.

Kevin clambered into the cab and picked up the handset. "India One Two, this is Echo Five Six. Over."

"Echo Five Six, wait one." An unfamiliar voice.

Then Donaldson came on the circuit. "Kev? Sorry to wake you, but we've got a situation here. A Bravo Oscar situation, understand?"

For a second, Kevin didn't. His brain seemed to be working at about half-speed, or maybe less. Then it clicked. Bravo Oscar. The military phonetics for the letters *b* and *o*. Bug-out. Retreat.

He pressed the transmit button. "Two, this is Six. Message understood. Over." He wanted to ask why, but this didn't seem like a good time to play "20 Questions."

Donaldson answered him anyway. "The NKs are across

the river, Kev. J-2 said they couldn't do it without bringing up replacement bridges, but they did it anyway. Only came across at one point, but they've thrown everything into it and our guys can't stop them. Both the Second of the thirty-sixth and a ROK battalion have wrecked themselves trying. Anyway, the NKs will have their armor across by morning."

Damn. "Understood."

"Okay, then, Kev. Get your people saddled up. Brigade wants us on the road in two zero minutes. We're going back to Point Little Rock to set up a new line. Out."

Kevin signed off and then fumbled inside his tunic for the list of new geographic code names they'd been issued just that morning. He ran his finger down the columns until he found Point Little Rock. Jesus Christ. They were going all the way back to Suwon, an ancient, walled city south of Seoul.

He sat in the truck cab for a moment, feeling cold despite warm air blowing through the dashboard vents. He was caught up in a total disaster. They were losing Seoul. Hell, they were losing the war.

JANUARY 1—THE WHITE HOUSE SITUATION ROOM

General Carpenter's soft Georgia drawl rolled easily across the ear. His words weren't so comforting. "There's no way round it. Out projections show our pilot losses reaching the critical point. These strikes against hardened targets in North Korea are bleeding us dry."

The Air Force Chief of Staff clicked to the next slide. "To keep our squadrons in the ROK up to strength, we're going to have to start cutting into the pool of combat-qualified pilots we've earmarked for Europe should a crisis erupt there." Carpenter paused and looked over at his Navy counterpart. "I understand the Navy's in a similar fix."

Admiral Fox nodded somberly. "A few more raids like this last one and we'll have to start stripping pilots out of our Atlantic Fleet squadrons." Fox, the Chief of Naval Operations, was a medium-sized man who still wore his white hair in a crew cut. He also wore aviator wings on his uniform.

Carpenter studied the assembled NSC crisis team carefully, measuring out each of his next words. "Put simply, ladies and gentlemen, we no longer have the human resources to be everywhere at once."

Murmurs swept through the Situation Room. The implications of Carpenter's report were both clear and troubling. The longer the war in Korea went on, the more pilots would be lost. The more pilots lost, the weaker the U.S. Air Force and the Navy's carrier air wings would be if the conflict escalated. And the longer the war went on, the more likely it would escalate.

The assistant secretary of state for East Asian and Pacific Affairs stopped tamping down his pipe and looked up, impatience clearly written across his face. "Why can't you meet your needs by calling up some of your reserves, General? I'd always heard that most of the airline pilots in this country learned how to fly in the Air Force. Surely you've kept track of those men?"

Carpenter kept his tone level. "Yes, we have. A lot of 'em are in the Air National Guard squadrons that we've already called up. But those who weren't will have to get some pretty intensive refresher training. And that takes time—time we're not likely to get."

Blake Fowler leaned forward in his chair. The President had asked him to chair the crisis team in Putnam's place. Putnam, meanwhile, was up on the Hill soothing Congress, and the President had made it clear that he was expected to stay up there until further notice. The Chief Executive apparently didn't want his so-called national security adviser in a position to cause more damage to the nation's interests. At the same time, he wanted to avoid a messy personnel crisis while trying to cope with a major war. So, officially, Putnam still had his job, even though Blake had to all intents and purposes replaced him.

Blake found it an uncomfortable position to be in. It smacked too much of the kind of petty political infighting and intrigue that he'd always despised. And he wondered, now that backroom maneuvering had worked to his advantage, whether or not his outlook would change. He hoped not. He'd rather reside in academic obscurity somewhere than turn into something resembling George Putnam.

He nodded to the Air Force general. "Have you got anything else to give us right now, General?"

Carpenter shook his head. "No. Not right now. I just want to make sure that the President knows how thin we're getting stretched. This thing is sliding across the edge of being a purely local crisis."

Blake nodded. Carpenter's assessment on narrow grounds matched his own broader-based view of the situation. The Soviets were growing ever bolder in their support of North Korea. Satellite photos clearly showed trains loaded with new artillery, replacement tanks, and aircraft rolling across the border at Hongui. And Warsaw Pact merchant ships laden with military gear crowded North Korea's ports.

China's support for Kim Il-Sung's invasion was somewhat more tepid. But it was there, nonetheless. Chinese munitions trains packed the yards at Sinuiju. Blake had seen the transcript of the meeting between the PRC's premier and the American ambassador to Beijing. The language used had been convoluted, carefully obscure, but the message it conveyed had been clearer. Continued North Korean victories would bring continued Chinese support.

And now the North Koreans were across the Han River barrier and driving south. McLaren's latest telex made it clear that he expected Seoul to be completely surrounded within hours. Where things went from there, Blake couldn't imagine. So far, every success the allied forces had gained had been only temporary—with each small victory followed short hours later by some new setback.

Blake shook his head and turned to the crisis team's next agenda item. The U.S. and South Korea were going to have to start winning some soon, or this war was going to flare out of control.

C H A P T E R
35
Boiling Point

JANUARY 2—THE WHITE HOUSE, WASHINGTON, D.C.

"Idti napravo!"

"Smotri Pozadi!"

Blake Fowler watched the frown on the President's face grow deeper as he listened to the taped voices and bursts of static. The Chief Executive seemed to have aged at least ten years in the nine days since casualty reports began streaming in from Korea. Fatigue and tension had worn new furrows in his face, his hair had thinned noticeably, and the eyes that had looked so open and honest in TV campaign commercials were now red-rimmed and darkly shadowed. Looking at him, Blake decided that the only thing that must be worse than governing the United States during a war was governing it during a war that was being lost.

When the tape came to an end, the President sat quietly for a moment, staring across his desk at a point somewhere off in space. Then he reached out and laid a finger on the printout in front of him. "And this is a verbatim transcript and translation of what I've just heard?"

"Yes, Mr. President. One of our signals intelligence aircraft intercepted those transmissions from the MiG-29 fighters engaging Navy jets over the Yellow Sea two days ago."

"Why'd it take so damned long to get here?"

Blake didn't react to the President's irritation. It was understandable, if unfair. "Rivet intercepts literally thousands of hours worth of enemy communications, sir. It takes time and a lot of expertise to ferret out the wheat from the chaff. They found this transmission at two o'clock this morning, our time."

The President eyed Blake angrily for a second longer, then his gaze softened, and he wearily nodded his understanding. He swung round toward the Oval Office window. Snow cloaked the Rose Garden. The high-backed chair muffled his voice when he spoke again. "The U.N. Security Council is meeting again tonight to discuss the situation in Korea, isn't it?"

"Yes, sir. At seven o'clock. The Soviets have been delaying things with procedural motions, but they've run out of those."

The President swiveled back to face Blake. He put a hand on the cassette tape player in front of him. "Well, what do you think about using this in the debate?"

Blake considered his answer carefully. "The intelligence community will object, sir, but—"

"I'm not asking them. I'm asking you."

"Yes, Mr. President, you are." Blake took his glasses off briefly, polished them with a handkerchief, and put them back on his nose. "I think we should play every last second of this intercept. Normally, it's vital to protect intelligence sources and methods, but the North Koreans know we have things like Rivet. We wouldn't be fooling anybody by denying it. We've used them in the past to prove our case. The political impact of those tapes outweighs normal security precautions."

He paused, feeling slightly uneasy at speaking of politics so glibly. It made him sound like George Putnam. "The truth is, Mr. President, this war's being fought on more than just the physical level. We've got to win both the international PR and global political battles as well."

The President nodded again. "Agreed. Hell, I'd just like to win somewhere sometime."

Blake stayed silent. He understood the President's frustration and concern. He'd also begun to catch a glimmering of the strategy McLaren seemed to be pursuing and approved of it. He just hoped they could keep the lid on things outside Korea long enough for the general to put his plans into effect.

"All right then, we'll send these up to New York by special messenger." The President's eyes narrowed. "And that's not all I'm going to send. I want those Russian bastards to know just how seriously we view this." He picked up the phone. "June, get me the secretary of state, please."

He put a hand across the mouthpiece and looked closely at Blake. "Paul Bannerman helped get us into this mess. Now maybe he can help get us out of it."

Before he could reply, Blake heard a voice from the receiver and kept quiet as the President started speaking. "Yeah, hello, Paul . . . Yes, I've heard them . . . Yes, we're going to use them . . . When? Why, hell, tonight, that's when. Look, Paul, I want you up at the Security Council for the debate . . . Yes, I want you to lead our side of it . . . Instructions? Give them hell . . . Nope, that's it. Those are my instructions. You know what to do. Good luck, Paul. I'll be watching."

The President hung up slowly and looked steadily across the desk at Blake. "Now we'll see just how far my so-called friend in Moscow's 'earnest desire for peace' really goes."

PERMANENT MISSION OF THE PEOPLE'S REPUBLIC OF CHINA TO THE U.N.

For once the scrambled phone connection to Beijing was miraculously free of atmospheric interference.

"Do you have any questions?" The Premier's tone made it clear that he didn't expect any. He sounded tired, worn out by an all-night debate that had lead to this call.

"No, comrade. Your instructions are clear and I shall carry them out without hesitation." The ambassador stood holding the phone while watching the rush-hour traffic stream past below his Manhattan office. He eyed his watch. It was indeed fortunate that this last-minute call from the PRC's Politburo had caught him preparing for the evening's scheduled Security Council meeting. In another few minutes he would have been enroute to the Council chambers and out of reach of secure communications.

"Excellent. Speak with me when you are done. The time will not matter." The phone went dead.

The ambassador hung up slowly and then reached out and activated the intercom on his desk. "Send Comrade Chin in at once. We have some work to do before the debate begins."

THE U.N. SECURITY COUNCIL CHAMBER, NEW YORK

The high-ceilinged chamber was packed, every seat and aisle filled with diplomats from around the world, reporters, and security guards. A hundred whispered conversations rose from the crowd and mingled in a murmuring roar like that of the surf crashing on shore. This would be the first Security Council meeting on the situation in Korea that could be expected to go beyond dry procedural squabbling.

Paul Bannerman, the U.S. secretary of state, settled into the seat normally reserved for the Chief of the U.S. Mission to the United Nations and mopped delicately at his brow with a monogrammed silk handkerchief. The White House had quietly alerted the major TV networks to the fact that major diplomatic fireworks were in store for this session, and they'd all risen to the bait. His speech would be broadcast instantly into a hundred million homes all across America and into hundreds of millions more around the world. And Bannerman knew that sweat was the price he would pay for that kind of audience.

TV cameras needed light and lots of it, and the harsh, white lamps brought in by the networks had already turned the Security Council chamber into a steam bath. Despite that, everyone around the circular row of desks reserved for the Council's five permanent and ten elected members still wore close-fitting, immaculately tailored wool suits. As always, diplomatic formality took precedence over comfort.

Bannerman kept his eyes on the U.N. Secretary General as members of his technical staff wheeled in the audio equipment he'd requested. The Secretary General had been briefed on what he planned and hadn't seen any alternative but to comply. Bannerman knew that the U.N. chief ordinarily disliked theatrics, but he'd had to admit that these weren't exactly ordinary circumstances. He sat up straighter as the Irishman cleared his throat and leaned closer to the microphone. "Mr. Secretary, the Security Council is assembled. Please proceed."

Bannerman nodded and slowly laid his prepared remarks on the desk, moving deliberately to ensure that all eyes were on him before he spoke. He stayed seated while speaking, as the rules prescribed. Keeping delegates in their chairs was supposed to help keep tempers in check and prevent passions from being inflamed. He wasn't sure that it ever made much difference in the end.

He began simply. "Mr. Secretary General, fellow members of the Security Council, and people of the world. This meeting is being held in a time of great crisis. Not just a crisis in my country or for the beleaguered Republic of Korea. No, not just for us. The events of this past week concern all members of the United Nations interested in peace and liberty and justice."

Bannerman paused, surveying the crowd around him. The Soviet ambassador sat quietly, with an expression of carefully uncamouflaged boredom plastered across his face. The secretary hardened his voice and looked straight at the Russian. "We're meeting tonight to respond to the naked aggression launched by North Korea in violation of an armistice secured by this very body.

"But first, I must raise a related issue of the highest possible consequence. I speak now of the actions taken by a member of this Security Council to assist North Korea's aggression—actions that violate the spirit, if not the letter, of the resolutions adopted by the United Nations in June and July of 1950." Bannerman paused again, listening to the murmurs that swept through the Security Council chambers at his words. Then he continued, "To be blunt I'm referring now to the Soviet Union's decision to intervene militarily against the United Nations forces defending the Republic of Korea."

A roar swept through the chamber at his words, a roar of outrage, shock, and shouted disbelief.

"Mr. Secretary General!" The Soviet representative was on his feet now, all pretense of uninterest tossed aside. "This is outrageous. My country will not tolerate such preposterous allegations, wherever they may originate from!"

"Mr. Vlasov"—the Secretary General's voice was firm—"you are out of order. The American representative has the floor at this time. You'll have ample opportunity to respond when it's your turn to speak." He looked at Bannerman. "Please continue, Mr. Secretary."

Bannerman dipped his head in gratitude. The Secretary General didn't always see eye to eye with American foreign policy, but he was always scrupulously fair. Bannerman scanned the chamber and then focused his eyes on the Soviet ambassador.

"Despite the protestations of the Soviet representative, my government is most assuredly not making wild or unfounded allegations. We have proof. Categorical and undeniable proof. Proof that Soviet pilots have engaged in combat with American planes in both international and South Korean airspace. We'll play this evidence for you now." He gestured to a technician standing by the audio equipment.

The man flicked a single switch and the tape began playing, translated simultaneously into the five official languages of the United Nations. First, a flat American voice identified the source of the sounds that would follow. "The radio transmissions on this tape were made by aircraft engaged in combat with U.S. Navy warplanes over the Yellow Sea at thirteen fifteen hours on one January."

Then the voices came on—urgent Russian voices carrying warnings of missiles or American planes and triumphantly reporting kills. All in the Security Council chamber sat quietly, listening intently to the entire recording. Only the Soviet ambassador paid scant attention, scribbling a note that Bannerman saw passed to the Chinese representative. The PRC's ambassador read through it impassively and handed the note back to an aide without comment.

When the Rivet tape ended in a faint wash of static, Bannerman let the silence build. He was surprised to find himself actually enjoying this. It took him back to his days as a junior prosecutor, long before he'd stepped into the murky world of politics. He leaned closer to the microphone. "Fellow members of the Security Council. What you've just heard isn't a fake or fabrication. It is a matter of the utmost concern to us all. By its actions, the government of the Soviet Union has involved itself in direct hostilities against American forces serving under U.N. auspices."

Bannerman pulled a sheaf of paper out from the stack in front of him and adjusted his half-frame reading glasses. "Accordingly, the United States moves that the Security Council adopt the following resolution..." The language of the resolution was as dry and legalistic as all U.N. documents always were, but its meaning was clear. By adopting the resolution, the Security Council would find the Soviet Union in violation of the U.N. Charter and of previous Security Council resolutions. Such a finding would authorize individual members of the U.N. to take any and all actions necessary to force the Soviets to end their support for North Korea's invasion—actions up to and including economic and military sanctions. Bannerman secretly doubted that the resolution could achieve that end, even if it were passed.

U.N. resolutions usually weren't worth the cost of printing them. But it would be an undeniable slap in Moscow's face, a slap that might awaken some of the less militaristic members of the Politburo to the risks they were running with this Korean adventure.

He finished speaking and sat back to wait for the Soviet ambassador's response. It wasn't long in coming.

"The Americans have spoken of proof and played a paltry few minutes of cassette tape as if that were sufficient. But is it? I ask you to ask ourselves this: What have you heard? A few voices speaking Russian. Some static. And a claim that all of this came from planes engaged in combat." The Russian paused, and Bannerman had to admire his poise. Vlasov's earlier show of temper had faded as completely as a summer storm, and now his narrow, handsome face showed only good-natured amusement.

"The Americans have a saying, my friends, 'Is it real or is it Memorex?'" Vlasov continued, having deliberately misquoted the well-known ad line. "Well, I suggest that what we have all heard tonight is Memorex—a tape of deliberate falsehoods created by the electronic specialists of the American CIA and NSA."

Bannerman started to object, but the Russian held him off with a waved hand. "No, no, Mr. Secretary. You've had your turn at this. Allow me mine."

Bannerman shrugged and sat back in his chair. He had a ready response to the Soviet allegations of forgery. Some snippets of the same transmissions had also been picked up by Japanese radio listening posts, and the Japanese government had assured Washington that it was prepared to back American claims that the Soviets were intervening in the war.

"But even if these unfounded allegations were true, it would not matter, and this Security Council would not be justified in adopting the absurd resolutions proposed by the United States.'' Bannerman started, suddenly realizing that Vlasov had stopped speaking off the cuff and was now reading from a prepared statement. He frowned. The implications of the switch were clear and unpleasant. Moscow must have been ready for its involvement in the fighting to become public knowledge. And that suggested that the Politburo's hard-liners were prepared to go a long way to back Pyongyang's war.

''Even if individual Soviet citizens were engaged in actively defending a fellow Socialist state against South Korea's aggression, their efforts as volunteers would have nothing whatever to do with the Soviet Union itself. The precedents are clear, and I need hardly remind the United States of some of the more obvious ones—for example, the service of the American Abraham Lincoln Brigade in the gallant struggle against fascism in Spain.''

Vlasov smiled unpleasantly. ''In any event, the position of the Soviet government is clear. We are not in any way involved in this struggle, but our citizens are perfectly free to do as they wish.'' He looked up from his written statement and spread his hands. ''That is, after all, the essence of a free society, is it not?''

Then, abruptly, he finished. ''The Soviet Union urges the defeat of this ridiculous and insulting resolution forthwith. We stand ready instead to work for a real and lasting end to this imperialist aggression against the Democratic People's Republic of Korea.''

Bannerman was astounded. The Soviets were not only virtually admitting their involvement, they were practically daring the Security Council to try to do something about it. He'd expected them to make a more prolonged argument in an attempt to confuse the issue.

His chief aide leaned forward from the seat behind and touched his arm. ''Looks like they've got the Chinese veto in their pockets.''

The Secretary nodded. No U.N. Security Council resolution could pass without the approval of its five permanent members—the United States, the Soviet Union, France, the United Kingdom, and the People's Republic of China. Both the U.S. and the Soviet Union were parties to this dispute and therefore ineligible to vote, and both France and Britain clearly intended to side with the U.S. That left the PRC as the swing voter on the Council.

No measure it voted against could pass. And clearly the Soviets were confident that, in this case at least, they had China's support. So confident that they didn't feel it worthwhile to prolong debate.

Bannerman wasn't surprised by that. China hadn't openly sided with Kim Il-Sung's war, but it hadn't been very discreet about its munitions shipments to him either. His Pacific Region specialists back at State had estimated the probability of a Chinese veto at around ninety percent. Only that NSC man, Fowler, hadn't been so sure. At Fowler's urging, they'd decided to avoid embarrassing China by dropping all references to the PRC's support for North Korea in the proposed resolution or in his written statement. Well, thought Bannerman, the President's new fair-haired boy was finally going to be proved wrong about something.

He turned his attention back to the debate. It didn't last long. Two of the Soviet Union's surrogates, Cuba and Poland, made fiery but pro forma denunciations of the resolution—denunciations that Bannerman found easy to counter. Other countries around the circle made their customary speeches counseling the superpowers to show patience and restraint. And that was that. Neither side saw any advantage in a prolonged, confusing debate or in the intricate negotiations that often produced compromise resolutions without meaning or force. The United States wanted a straight up-or-down vote on its motion, and the Soviet Union saw little to fear in that.

The Secretary General looked bemused, as well he might, thought Bannerman. Chairing the Security Council emergency session must often seem more like running a marathon than supervising a debating society. But not tonight.

"Does any member wish to speak further on this issue?...No? Well, then, the question now arises on the resolution proposed by the United States." The Secretary General arched a single, white eyebrow, obviously waiting for someone to object to his haste. No one did. The silence lasted until he began the roll call. "Brazil?"

"The Federative Republic of Brazil votes aye."

"Poland?"

"The Polish People's Republic opposes this needless and irresponsible resolution."

Bannerman's aide kept a quick, scratch-pad tally as the vote went on.

"The United Kingdom?"

"Her Majesty's government votes aye."

That put them over the top with nine votes. Now only China's veto would stop the resolution from carrying. He folded his hands and waited for it. At least he'd gained the President a solid propaganda victory. And Bannerman knew that was about all the U.N. was good for these days. The Harvard-educated internationalist in him regretted that. The realist schooled in Washington, D.C.'s corridors of power knew such regrets were meaningless.

"The People's Republic of China?"

Bannerman looked across the circle at the Chinese ambassador, a tall, spare man clothed in a fashionable gray suit and red tie. The man's dark eyes met his as he spoke. "China abstains. We shall neither oppose nor support this resolution."

The American secretary of state felt his jaw dropping open and closed it hurriedly. The room around him was in an uproar as the observer's gallery realized what had just happened. The resolution had passed. He felt one of his aides clap him on the shoulder and saw the others grinning. He could also see the consternation on Vlasov's face as the Russian grabbed one of his assistants and started working his way through the crowd toward the Chinese delegation.

Somehow the Secretary General's soft brogue cut through all the hubbub in the Council Chamber. "The vote being nine to four, the motion is carried and the resolution is adopted. The Council will reconvene tomorrow evening at the same hour to consider its implementation."

The Chinese ambassador stood calmly and began making his way out through the crowded aisles, ignoring the pandemonium all around him—a mass of shouting reporters, TV Minicams, and stunned fellow diplomats. Bannerman watched him go and saw a broad-shouldered Chinese security guard shove Vlasov's messenger bodily out of the way as the Russian tried to get closer.

Bannerman sat motionless in his chair, his mind working

furiously despite all the commotion surrounding the American delegation. He'd felt the pieces in the international diplomacy game shift under his hands just now. Not because of the resolution. That was only a simple scrap of paper—devoid of real power. But China's abstention . . . now that was something real.

THE OLD EXECUTIVE OFFICE BUILDING, WASHINGTON, D.C.

Blake Fowler agreed wholeheartedly with the secretary of state's assessment—something that would have surprised and disconcerted both men had they known of it. China's position on the war seemed to have changed, however imperceptibly, and that had to be followed up.

He leaned across his desk and snapped off the small, portable TV perched precariously on one of his bookshelves. That done, he dropped back into his chair and rolled far enough away from the desk to poke his head out the door. "Katie, would you get Bob Gillespie, Harry Phelps, and that new guy, Kruger, up here right away? Say in"—he looked at his watch—"ten minutes or so?"

His secretary stopped in midyawn, nodded, and reached for her phone.

Fowler rolled back into his office, stopped, and then rolled back out. Katie was just starting to punch the Gillespies' number into her phone. She paused as he stuck his head through the doorway again. "Yes?"

"Ask them to bring everything on the PRC they've got easily to hand—political data, economic status, military readiness, all that kind of stuff."

"Right."

Fowler went to work preparing for the meeting. It was tough to concentrate. His thoughts were jumping from one possibility to another and back again in a rapid, whirling sequence. He'd had an instinct about China and now it might really be panning out. He started paging through a pile of recent State Department, CIA, and academic analyses on China's internal politics, but something nagged at him. Something he'd left undone.

It took him a few minutes to figure out what it was.

He got up out of his chair and leaned around the door. "Oh, Katie? Thanks."

She smiled briefly and turned away to finish logging in another stack of NSA intercepts. Blake went back to work, doggedly trying to cram a mass of data on China into his overtired brain, information that he'd ignored while concentrating on South and North Korea for all these months.

Something important was happening inside the PRC's carefully guarded government buildings, and he'd damned well do his best to find out just what exactly was going on.

JANUARY 3—PARTY HEADQUARTERS, PYONGYANG, NORTH KOREA

Kim Jong-Il could smell the man's fear and relished it. Its sickly sweet odor was a welcome reminder of the power he still wielded. It had helped him control the terrible wave of anger that had overcome him when the news from New York arrived. It had been news of a betrayal of the blackest sort. Kim clamped his lips together tightly at the thought. He must be careful, he knew, careful to control the rage surging just below the surface.

At least until he had a worthy target for his hate. It wouldn't do at all to prove his foolish doctors right by suffering a heart attack—not during this most crucial of times. His political enemies would take full advantage of any weakness he showed.

Kim grimaced. He didn't have time for these wasted thoughts. He stared at the man waiting rigidly at attention. "Well? Speak up. What is it?"

His aide's voice quavered. "Your pardon, Dear Leader, the ambassador has arrived for his meeting."

Kim nodded abruptly. "Show him in. And tell Captain Lew to stand ready. One cannot be too careful when dealing with creatures of this kind." He dismissed the aide with an impatient gesture and concentrated on the matter closest at hand—Colonel General Cho's latest report from the front.

"The ambassador from the People's Republic of China."

Kim heard the Chinese diplomat ushered in, but he kept his eyes focused on the report in front of him. Let the swine wait. Let the man stand, stewing in the shame that rightly belonged to his whole mongrel country.

The news from the front was good. The jaws of his trap had swung shut below Seoul, and Cho's troops were pursuing the beaten imperialist armies as they fled south. Casualties were heavy, of course, but that had been expected. In any event, individual lives were of little importance in the greater scheme of things. No, the news was very good, and Kim almost smiled as he skimmed through the report.

But then he heard a delicate cough from the other side of his desk and his good humor vanished. Everything was going well, save on the international front. One cowardly act by the damned Chinese had unnecessarily embarrassed his Soviet allies and had made it somewhat more difficult for them to give him the aid he required. He kept reading.

At last he snapped the report binder shut with a single decisive motion. The crash it made seemed to hang in the still air of his silent office. Slowly Kim Jong-Il raised his head to stare at the diplomat waiting quietly in front of his desk.

He was disappointed. The Chinese showed no signs of fear or shame. Not even embarrassment or anger at the rude treatment he'd been accorded. Instead, the man stood calmly, his legs splayed apart as if he were some sort of peasant lounging at rest. Again Kim felt the anger rise up inside him. The insolent bastard. How dare this so-called ambassador stand there without showing the slightest sign of contrition for the treacherous actions of his nation.

"Well? What is your business with me? I'm busy, as I'm sure you can see."

The ambassador inclined his head, more a nod than a bow. "I'm grateful for your time, Comrade Kim. My premier and Politburo have instructed me to deliver this." The ambassador stepped forward suddenly, coming right up against the desk with something held out in his hand.

Kim half-reached for the panic buzzer by his knee and then stopped. It was a piece of paper, nothing more. He took it and ran his eyes over the major headings: Munitions, Armored Fighting Vehicles, Artillery. He pursed his lips. Why, this was a Chinese proposal to dramatically increase its logistical support of North Korea's war effort.

"What is the meaning of this?" Kim demanded. "This directly contradicts your government's refusal to support us in the Security Council."

The Chinese ambassador shrugged almost imperceptibly. "I assure you that my country's actions in the United Nations were not directed at your nation, Comrade Kim. We simply had no wish to be linked so closely with a Soviet indiscretion. Our support for your war of liberation is as strong as ever."

"As weak as ever, you mean!" Kim could feel his temper slipping out of control, building toward a towering rage. He let it. "For your information, Mr. Ambassador, this Soviet 'indiscretion' you refer to is its willingness to side openly with us—instead of hiding in the shadows as your country has done!"

The ambassador was unruffled. "There were other considerations in—"

"I'm sure there were," Kim interrupted, all concern for self-control cast aside. "Considerations like the almighty Yankee dollar and your capitalist kowtowing to the Western bankers! You Chinese have finally sunk back to your old role as bootlickers for your imperialist masters."

"Surely that is unfair, comrade. We've sent thousands of tons of valuable supplies across our common border, without the slightest discussion of any need for payment. And now" —the ambassador pointed to the paper lying on Kim's desk— "we are fully prepared to increase even that already generous level of support."

That was too much. Did these swine truly believe he could be bought like some common street whore? Kim grabbed the PRC's weapons offer and crumpled it into a ball. "That is what I think of your pathetic attempt to bribe your way into my friendship!"

The man simply looked at him without any expression at all. "Shall I report to my government that our offer of additional assistance has been refused, comrade?"

The room turned red and Kim threw the wad of paper into the man's face in a fury. "Yes! And report it in person. Your presence in the People's Republic is no longer welcome. You are expelled!"

The ambassador nodded. "Very well, comrade. My gov-

ernment will undoubtedly submit another representative for
your accreditation at the earliest possible moment.''

Kim struggled for control. The damned Chinese hadn't even
flinched when the paper struck him. He took a deep breath, held
it, and let it out slowly. Then he said coldly, ''Your government
may do as it sees fit. And I may even consider its request—though
I fear my calendar is somewhat full for the moment.''

He pressed the buzzer on his desk. ''Send Captain Lew in.''

Lew wore no badges of rank, as befitted his status as an agent
of the State Political Security Department. ''Yes, Dear Leader?''

Kim didn't waste words. ''Escort the ambassador to his
embassy and from there to the airport. Under no circumstances
will you allow him to communicate with anyone save his own
diplomatic staff. Do you understand me?''

Lew nodded sharply. The Chinese ambassador remained
motionless, apparently uninterested in this extreme breach of
protocol and common diplomatic courtesy.

''Good.'' Kim's lips thinned. ''Now, get this man out of
my sight.''

He dismissed the matter from his mind. He didn't need the
Chinese. The Soviets had far better weapons and had been far
more willing to part with them. They had shown themselves
worthy of his trust and his exploitation. He would rely on the
Soviets—for the time being.

BEIJING, THE PEOPLE'S REPUBLIC OF CHINA

The Premier regarded the telexed report from the Pyongyang
embassy with a wistful smile. Kim Jong-Il was so painfully
predictable—not like his father at all. At least not as Kim
Il-Sung had been at the height of his personal power. He shook
his head slowly. The younger Kim was so intemperate, so
arrogant.

A thought struck him. Perhaps the North Koreans really
believed they could win this war without China's assistance? It
was possible. Their naïve self-confidence must certainly have
been buoyed by their apparent victories so far. After all, the
North's armies drove deeper into the South with each passing
day.

On the surface, then . . .

The Premier smiled more broadly. He'd known many apprentice engineers who'd looked only at the outside of a seemingly solid concrete dam without ever imagining the dangerous fissures that might be spreading throughout its interior. And Kim Il-Sung's bloated son was more an apprentice than most.

Well, the apprentice had made his first clear error. The Premier carefully folded the telex and slipped it into his briefcase. Many of his colleagues on the Politburo would be deeply interested in its contents—deeply interested indeed.

He rose to his feet easily, heading for the morning's scheduled Defense Council meeting. The dance was changing, spinning into new form, and the Premier wondered whether all its participants would be quick enough to learn its new steps.

Somehow he doubted it.

C H A P T E R
36
Rear Guard

JANUARY 3—ECHO COMPANY, WEST OF SUWON, SOUTH KOREA

Kevin Little saw a sea of flame ripple across Suwon as more North Korean shells landed—smashing tile-roofed houses and tearing huge gaps in its ancient stone walls. Other explosions rocked the summit of Paltal Mountain, near the old city's center. Temples, pavilions, and fortresses that had taken years of hard labor to build were being destroyed in minutes. He shook his head. The allied troops guarding Suwon weren't anywhere within a kilometer of the North's barrage. They'd abandoned the city's historic center in a vain effort to preserve it from destruction. The North Koreans weren't being so accommodating.

"Hey, Lootenant? Do you suppose we could get on with this? I ain't exactly up here to play tourist, you know. See, I cain't go back to my CO without your John Hancock on this here form to show that I dropped the stuff off at the right unit. Okay?"

Kevin turned away from the growing firestorm and back to the portly, double-chinned sergeant waiting impatiently, clipboard in hand. Something about the man had struck him as odd, and it had taken a while for the pieces to fall into place. Now he knew what it was. The sergeant's combat fatigues looked brand-new and unwrinkled. Odder still, the man was clean. To someone who hadn't been within half a klick of a working shower for days, seeing the supply sergeant's shiny and well-scrubbed face was like running head-on into an alien from outer space.

He shook off the shock and shook his head. "No, it's not okay, Sarge. I'm not signing for anything until I'm satisfied that it meets my military requirements."

The shorter man frowned and Kevin tried making himself clearer. He could tell vaguely that he was starting to lapse into meaningless jargon. He was getting too tired for all of this. "Look, I can't fight my company properly without enough ammo, and the load on your trucks gives me less than half my basic supply."

More shells burst over the city and the supply sergeant flinched at the noise. He looked worried. "Hell, I'm sorry, Lootenant. But I just plain don't have any more ammo to give you right now. Nobody else has any more."

Goddamn the Army. Kevin felt the fury bubbling up inside him. Not enough men. Not enough time. And now not enough frigging ammunition even to fight properly. He fought against showing the anger he felt. The sergeant wasn't the problem, just a symptom.

He felt his jaw tightening and grimly eyed the crates his troops were hastily hauling out of a pair of mud-spattered three-quarter-ton trucks.

The sergeant saw his face and shrugged apologetically.

"Brigade's promised us more before nightfall. But the roads are a mess . . . so I don't know how much stock to put in that."

"Shit."

"Yeah. Amen to that, Lootenant." The sergeant looked back down the slope to where GIs were frantically digging foxholes and trying to clear fields of fire through the undergrowth. Kevin waited silently while the man came to some kind of decision. "Look, I've got a couple of boxes of claymores on the trucks. They ain't spoken for yet. Maybe I could let you have those."

"I'll take 'em." Kevin didn't hesitate. Echo Company was stretched way too thin along this line, and a few strategically placed claymore mines might come in real handy indeed. Used properly, a claymore could do a world of hurt to an enemy infantry unit. It wasn't hard to figure out why. When it was triggered, a claymore's pound of C4 plastic explosive hurled six hundred steel balls out in a sixty-degree arc to its front—literally scything down anything or anyone within its burst radius. Echo could use that kind of firepower.

The supply sergeant tugged at his lower chin thoughtfully. "You've got them." He nodded abruptly. "Okay, then. I'll just go down and tell the boys to hurry it up. Got my rounds to make, and I don't want to stay here in your hair too long, after all."

Kevin knew the man really meant that he didn't want to risk getting caught up in the next North Korean attack, but he couldn't blame him one bit. Nobody in his right mind would willingly hang around to be shot at.

He returned the sergeant's salute and watched him move off down the hill toward the now-nearly-empty trucks. Then he swung away impatiently, looking for his squad and platoon leaders. He had a defensive position to finish laying out and too damned little time to do it in.

2ND BATTALION, 91ST INFANTRY REGIMENT, NEAR UIWANG, NORTH OF SUWON

Captain Chae Ku-Ho of the North Korean People's Army waited patiently while his battalion commander scanned the horizon through a pair of East German–manufactured binoculars. The major was very proud of those binoculars, and Chae understood his pride. They were superb instruments.

"Magnificent! Magnificent! Can you see it, Captain?"

"Yes, Comrade Major." The smoke pouring from a hundred fires obscured Suwon and billowed high into the atmosphere, mixing with heavy, gray storm clouds that still covered the sky. There would be more snow soon, Chae decided.

"And look at that blacker stuff rising beyond the city. That's fuel oil and aviation gas burning. The imperialists must have fired their airbase to prevent us from capturing it. We have them on the run, Captain. They're already beaten in their own minds."

Chae agreed with his commander but didn't see the point in saying anything. The enemy troops might be mentally defeated, but they still had to be physically destroyed for it to mean much. He waited patiently until the major had seen enough.

At last the man lowered the binoculars and turned to face him. "Very well, Chae. Let's not waste any more time. Your orders are simple." The major pointed to the low, tree-covered hills rising to the west of Suwon. "The division's axis of advance runs straight through there. And we've been selected to spearhead the advance." He paused.

"A great honor, Comrade Major."

The man nodded. "Yes. In any event, Chae, I want your company to lead the battalion. Intelligence assures me that we can expect only light opposition from isolated enemy rear guard forces. The rest of the fascists are running back down the highway as fast as they can."

Chae had his own doubts about the major's intelligence reports, but he remained silent. The Main Political Administration's agents had unpleasant ways of dealing with officers suspected of defeatism or insufficient ardor. .

"What about tank support, sir?"

The major waved his question aside. "The tanks are being sent further west, where the ground is more suitable for their use. We won't need them. This will be infantry work only, Chae. We'll rout the enemy out with the point of the bayonet!"

"Yes, Comrade Major." Chae was careful not to let any

expression show on his face. "I'll get back to my troops, then."

"Indeed, Captain." The major's tone grew colder. Perhaps he'd sensed Chae's lack of enthusiasm for his leadership. "I'll expect your column to be underway within twenty minutes."

Chae saluted and headed back to his company's bivouac inside the still-smoldering ruins of Uiwang. He shivered in the wind and grimaced. At least he and his troops would have a brisk six-kilometer march to warm themselves with before going into the attack. The People's Army's trucks were too valuable to risk to enemy fire.

ECHO COMPANY

They were as ready as it was humanly possible to be. Or so he hoped, Kevin Little admitted to himself. Anyway, there wasn't time to do any more work preparing the position. He checked the magazine on his M16. It was full, but he only had six more in the pouch attached to his combat webbing. He patted the ammo pouch to make sure it was still there and for the thousandth time, he silently cursed the fouled-up supply situation. Where the hell were all those planeloads of ammo and other gear that the scuttlebutt said were landing every few minutes from the States?

Seven magazines wouldn't last long in the kind of firefight they'd soon be facing.

A two-man OP sited along the treeline to the north had reported several infantry columns marching south toward them. And Battalion had passed along similar reports from the other companies holding this part of the line. There wasn't much doubt about it. They were going to get hit.

Kevin trudged wearily through the ankle-deep snow, just putting one foot in front of the other—taking stock of his company's situation for one last time. He'd had his troops dig in just behind the crestline of the small, tree-covered hill they'd been ordered to hold. The hill itself would block the line of sight for any North Korean observers and force the NK commander to commit his own forces without much idea about where the company's main strong points were.

Not that there were many of those. Major Donaldson had

scraped together a few more replacements for him, but he still had less than sixty men left to hold a position more suitable for a full-strength rifle company with attachments. As it was, he'd been forced to put everyone up on the line just to avoid leaving gaping holes in his defense. The idea of fighting without having some kind of reserve left Kevin feeling cold. It reminded him too much of the fiasco on Malibu West. That had been one of his mistakes up there, too.

He shook off the thought. This wasn't the time or place. Maybe later. Maybe after the war, always assuming he lived that long.

His 1st and 2nd Platoon leaders—Corporal McIntyre and Sergeant Geary—just nodded when he stopped by their fox-holes to go over the battle plan. They looked haggard, dog-tired and hollow-eyed. But then, hell, so did everyone else in the company. Five days and four nights out in the open under extreme stress and in arctic temperatures had pushed the troops to the edge of their endurance. Many were coming down with bronchitis, severe chest colds, or pneumonia. Kevin knew that, by rights, fully a third of his men should have been in the hospital for treatment. The trouble was, he couldn't spare them—any more than he could spare himself.

He kept going, half-walking, half-sliding downhill through the snow toward the weakest point in his line—a brush-choked ravine that cut between the hill held by his company and the one occupied by Matuchek's Alpha Company. A frozen, narrow stream turned and twisted its way south at the bottom of the ravine, and the tangle of small trees, shrubs, and tall grass its waters had fed made movement difficult and observation next to impossible. It was the perfect place for a North Korean infiltration through his position.

Knowing that and knowing what exactly to do about it were two very different things, but Kevin had done his best. He'd scraped together a blocking force by stripping the 2nd Platoon of a machine gun team and four precious riflemen. These six men now held positions along either edge of the ravine, ready to pour a vicious crossfire into any NK troops moving up through the dense underbrush.

He'd done more. He'd had the blocking force emplace no fewer than six claymore mines along the gully—ready to shred the vegetation and anyone in it with a total of 3,600 plastic-explosive-driven steel balls. It would be enough to give the first North Korean attack down the ravine a very bloody nose indeed. It wouldn't be enough if there were a second or third assault.

Well, he'd have to worry about that later. Kevin moved back up the slope toward the two-man foxhole that served as his CP. Montoya was already there, helmet pulled low over a green scarf wrapped around to cover his ears. The RTO just shook his head when Kevin asked if there were any new orders from Battalion.

"What about Rhee? Any word on him?"

"Not a peep, L-T. Maybe he's wangled himself a cushy staff job."

Kevin grinned at Montoya's stab at humor, but he didn't really find it too funny. Rhee had been summoned earlier in the morning to the temporary Brigade HQ at Yongju-sa—Dragon Jewel Temple—a Buddhist temple complex several miles south of Suwon. The orders hadn't explained why and they hadn't given Kevin any indication of when he could expect Rhee back. Goddamned rear-area dips, Kevin thought savagely. They probably wanted the Korean lieutenant to fill out some pointless requisition. And now he was short his second-in-command just before going into battle.

He felt uneasy at the prospect. This would be the first time he'd gone into action without Rhee at his side, and Kevin knew how much he'd come to rely on the South Korean's calm, good humor and guts. Damnit.

"L-T. Hey, L-T." Montoya laid a gloved hand on his shoulder. "The OP's coming in."

He took the handset. "Echo Five Six to Echo Eyes. Give me a sitrep. Over."

"Echo Five Six, this is Eyes." Kevin could hear the man panting into his mike as he and the other sentry jogged back to the company. "We're coming in. First November Kilos were just about four hundred meters from our position. Strength estimated at one, repeat, one battalion. No tanks or PCs."

"Acknowledged. Five Six out." Kevin handed the mike back to Montoya. "Pass the word to all posts that we've got bad guys on the way with friendlies in front of 'em. Tell everybody to hold their fire until I give the word.''

WHOOOOSH. WHAMMM. WHAMMM. WHAMMM. The howling din of artillery landing somewhere to their front drove Montoya and Kevin to the bottom of their foxhole—an action duplicated by everybody else in Echo Company. It took several seconds to realize that the shells weren't exploding around them, and several more before anybody cared to raise his head above ground level.

Kevin wriggled out of the foxhole and bellycrawled up to the crestline of the hill. Forty-year-old pines, oaks, and willow trees blocked much of his view, but he could see well enough to realize that the North Korean shells were tearing up the whole northern edge of the forest. He almost smiled. Major Donaldson had been right. Trying to defend from there would have been tantamount to committing suicide. It was too bloody obvious a target for enemy artillery.

He slid back down to the CP and started issuing orders to his platoon leaders. Once the NK heavy guns were done shooting up the forest, their infantry would be coming through the fallen and splintered trees—straight toward his positions. The North Koreans would have scouts out in front, and Kevin wanted to make sure they got a warm reception. He had McIntyre and Geary deploy a fire team each along the crest, ready to hose down the first NKs to show themselves on the ground below the hill.

That done, he settled back inside his foxhole to wait. There wasn't anything else he could do.

1ST COMPANY, 2ND BATTALION

Chae scrambled over a massive tree trunk blown down by the artillery barrage and waited for the rest of his headquarters group to catch up. The three infantry platoons of his company were already a hundred meters ahead, pushing deeper into the forest. Everything was quiet, except for the crackle of a dozen small fires set by bursting shells, and Chae didn't like it.

He motioned his second-in-command over for a hasty conference in the shadow of a pine tree whose branches had been stripped off by a near-miss. Senior Lieutenant Koh didn't like the situation any better than he did. He thought they were walking face forward into a trap.

"Agreed. So I want you to take a squad and scout ahead. Don't try to engage the fascists closely. Just find out where they are and we'll let the mortars and artillery deal with them."

Koh nodded sharply and jogged on ahead through the trees to catch up with the lead platoon. Chae followed at a more moderate pace with his staff sergeant and runners tagging along beside him. He didn't see any point in rushing in to get his head blown off—major or no major.

ECHO COMPANY

Kevin went from man to man along the crest with the same warning. "Three-round bursts tops. Make every shot count. No rock-and-roll. What you've got in your ammo pouches is all you'll get. Shoot it all off and you'll have to throw snowballs at the bastards. Understood?" He'd wait for the nod and then move on to say it all over again.

He came to the end of the line, gave his speech to the wide-eyed private there, and started to scuttle away. Suddenly the PFC grabbed the lieutenant's boot and pointed downslope toward a clump of bushes that had started waggling. Kevin dropped flat and twisted around to get his M16 lined up on the spot.

A Russian-style pot helmet emerged from the bushes, followed by the rest of an AK-armed soldier. Kevin squinted right and left and saw more North Koreans strung out in a skirmish line at the base of the hill. He counted at least ten—a squad then, with more somewhere behind.

He tried to stop breathing, willing the North Koreans farther up the slope. Please God, don't let anybody open up until they're a little closer, a little more out in the open, he prayed silently. He heard the PFC beside him swallow convulsively and resisted an impulse to hit him. Sounds carried too far here under the trees. Come on closer, you bastards.

Now. Kevin yelled, "Fire! Fire! Fire!"

The eight other men along the crest started shooting, and he squeezed off a three-round burst at the same moment. His target, the first North Korean he'd spotted, tumbled backward down the hill. The man's helmet fell off and rolled away to rest beneath a bare-branched willow tree.

Others were down as well, thrown off their feet by the first salvo of American rifle fire. A few survivors had burrowed into the snow, firing blindly back up at the top of the hill.

Kevin felt snow spray across his face from a near-miss and took careful aim at one of the prone NKs. He pulled the trigger once and felt the M16 jump in his hands. A hit! Blood spurted from the North Korean's shoulder, and the man rose involuntarily to his knees clutching at the wound. Another bullet from someone else along the crestline threw the wounded man back dead.

He looked to either side, hunting for new targets. Nothing. Just six or seven crumpled bodies bleeding into the snow. The surviving North Koreans had pulled back into cover. He took his finger off the trigger and lay waiting.

An M16 cracked off to his left. Then another. Firing at nothing. Kevin put his energy into a single, harsh, penetrating whisper. "Cease fire! Stop wasting your ammo, goddamnit!"

The shooting stopped, replaced by an eerie silence broken only by low moans from somewhere out in the forest to their front. Kevin waited for his hearing to come back to normal and for his heart to stop pounding so loudly.

He cocked his head, listening. There. Muttered voices. Feet crunching in the snow. Equipment rattling. There were more North Koreans among the trees, moving up to the attack. A lot more. They'd make a rush soon.

Kevin made an instant decision. He didn't have enough men to hold the crest against a concerted attack. "Back! Get back to your holes. Move it."

The two American fire teams slid downhill into their foxholes, joining up with the rest of Echo Company. They'd meet the next North Korean assault when it came over the top of the hill.

1ST COMPANY, 2ND BATTALION

Senior Lieutenant Koh lay ashen-faced while the medic worked on him, trying to stem the loss of blood from his wounds. "As you suspected, they were waiting for us. At least a platoon, perhaps more." He gasped as the medic pulled a bandage tighter.

"Lie still, comrade." Chae put a hand on his second-in-command's shoulder. "You did well. Now we'll smoke the bastards out with a few rounds of artillery fire, eh?"

Koh nodded weakly and closed his eyes. Chae looked sharply at the medic, who simply shrugged. The lieutenant's wounds were beyond his ability to treat, and the nearest aid station was more than an hour's march away. It was all in the hands of chance—Koh would live or die as fate dictated.

Chae stood up and stared around the small hollow that held his command group and the battered remnants of his scouting force. His first two platoons were already deployed in a skirmish line about two hundred meters below the top of the American-held hill. The men of the 3rd Platoon, his reserves, squatted on their haunches just outside the hollow.

He snapped an order to his sergeant and headed back the way they'd come. He needed artillery support to press the attack and only the battalion commander could make the necessary arrangements.

2ND BATTALION HQ

"Absolutely not! There's no time for such foolishness. It would be a waste of valuable ammunition and time. Drive them off that hill with a lightning attack."

Chae was astonished. He'd known his commander was overconfident, but until that very moment he hadn't been sure that the man was a simpleton as well. "Comrade Major, the enemy position is a strong one. An unsupported infantry attack will only fail. We must have artillery support."

The major's eyes narrowed. "Comrade Captain. My orders to you were explicit, were they not? Are you disobeying a direct command?"

Chae knew he was within moments of being placed under arrest—an arrest that could only have one result: his execution. And that left him with a choice of two equally unpleasant alternatives. He shook his head slowly. "No, Comrade Major. Your orders will be carried out."

The major smiled. "Excellent, Captain. Excellent." He

patted Chae's shoulder. "I'm sure there's nothing there but a small delaying force. One sharp attack by your company will overwhelm them and clear the way for our continued advance."

Chae could only nod.

"Very well, Chae." The major glanced at his watch. "I'll expect your assault to get under way in twenty minutes. We've still got a lot of ground to cover today. Division expects us to reach the fascist government's Agricultural Experiment Station by nightfall. And I don't intend to disappoint them. Is that clear?"

"Extremely so, Comrade Major." Chae saluted and wheeled away sharply, seething internally. He and his troops would just have to do their best and hope for the best. He'd send his 1st and 2nd platoons in on a wild rush. Perhaps they'd be able to get in among the Americans holding the hill without suffering crippling casualties. And if that failed, at least he'd still have the 3rd Platoon on hand with which to try something else.

ECHO COMPANY

The bugle's high-pitched, discordant shriek echoed eerily off the surrounding tree trunks and branches.

"Here they come, you bastards! Get set for it!" Kevin flicked the M16's safety off and made sure it was set for semiautomatic fire. He crouched lower in the foxhole.

WHUMMMP! Dirt and snow thrown by an NK grenade sprayed up along the crest of the hill. More grenades burst in quick succession, flashing brightly in the half-light under the overhanging trees. A fragment whined over his head. Above it all, the bugle continued to sound.

There they were. Kevin saw the first figures silhouetted against the skyline, bayonet-tipped assault rifles in their hands. M16s and M60 light machine guns crashed repeatedly along the row of American foxholes, and North Koreans fell or were tossed backward. Others dropped flat and tried to return fire.

Heavier-sounding AK shots mingled with the lighter-pitched cracks made by M16s.

An American private gurgled and suddenly clutched with bloody hands at a throat that wasn't there anymore. Another screamed in anguish and fell back holding a shattered forearm.

But the North Koreans were caught in the open without good cover and they were dying faster.

Kevin shot a man trying to crawl behind a tree and yanked the now-empty magazine out of his rifle, fumbling to insert a new one. Five left. Something round flicked through his line of sight and thumped into a tree just beyond his foxhole. He ignored it and took quick aim at an NK standing full upright, arm extended from the throw.

"Grenade!" Montoya screamed, and dragged Kevin to the bottom of the hole.

WHUUMMMP! The ground shook and both men felt the blast punch the air out of their foxhole. Fragments gouged dirt out of the sides and sprayed overhead. Their ears rang.

"Asshole!" Kevin reared up and pumped three shots at close range into the North Korean preparing a second grenade. The man died with a look of absolute surprise frozen on his face.

Another grenade exploded farther down the line, and Kevin heard men screaming in agony. His men. Kevin cursed and kept firing. Empty. Eject. Reload. Four magazines left now.

The North Korean fire didn't seem so loud now. Visibility was down to just a few meters, but it seemed that there were fewer muzzle flashes up along the crest. Bodies sprawled everywhere along the slope.

He saw a North Korean trying to roll back over the top of the hill and fired again—kicking up a miniature snowstorm all around the man. He couldn't tell if he'd hit him. Another NK tried to run. Four rounds hit the man at the same instant and threw him bodily against a bullet-pocked oak tree.

He ripped another empty magazine out of the rifle and reloaded again. Three left in the pouch.

Kevin scanned a sixty-degree arc around his hole, looking for new targets. He waited for the smoke and dust to thin. There were't any new targets. The bugle had stopped sounding. The North Koreans were gone.

"Cease fire! Hold it! Hold it!" His hearing was coming back, but slowly, too slowly. He could just make out McIntyre and Geary screaming at their men to call them off. They sounded as if they were a thousand miles away.

Kevin shook his head from side to side, trying to clear the
last of the ringing out of his ears. He eased his finger off the
M16's trigger and leaned heavily against the foxhole's dirt
wall, breathing hard. Echo Company and its rookie commander
had won another skirmish. He felt a surge of triumph and
elation and almost laughed out loud for the sheer joy of it.
Then he suppressed the feelings as quickly as they had come.

The trouble was the North Koreans would be back for
more soon enough, and his troops had already shot off half
their ready ammunition. One more attack would burn up the
rest. And then what would he do? Kevin didn't have the answer
to that one, but he knew that he'd have to think of one pretty
damned quickly. There was an enemy commander out there
somewhere in the forest already planning his next move.

1ST COMPANY, 2ND BATTALION

Chae stared at the shattered fragments of his 1st and 2nd
platoons in rage. Nearly seventy men had been thrown away to
no useful end, slaughtered because the battalion commander
was a fool of the first magnitude. The Americans over the hill
were too well dug-in to be dislodged by a frontal attack. He
would have to find another way to get at them.

He frowned. The moans from the wounded were distracting.
He turned to his staff sergeant and snapped an order. "Get the
wounded on their way back to the aid station and rejoin me
here after that's done."

"You"—he pointed to the corporal now leading what was
left of the 1st Platoon—"take your able-bodied men up to the
base of the hill and keep the Yankees occupied. Don't expose
yourselves, but don't let them see how few of you there really
are. Understand?"

The corporal saluted and wheeled to gather his troops and
go forward again. Chae felt his anger grow again. These
soldiers were too good to be led by an incompetent like the
major, a puffed-up idiot with his pretty binoculars. He growled
at an orderly and took his AK assault rifle from the man. The
Makarov pistol holstered at his side marked him as an officer,
but it wasn't the proper weapon for this kind of fight.

He waited until the skirmishers he'd sent ahead to pin

down the enemy started firing. Then he turned to the lieutenant commanding the 3rd Platoon. "Follow me. And keep silent. The first man to make a sound will spend what's left of his miserable life breaking rocks in a work camp."

Without waiting for a reply, Chae moved off through the trees, angling left toward the ravine he'd spotted earlier and marked as a possible way through the American defenses. If he could get in behind the Yankees, he could repay them for the massacre of his men in their own coin. The 3rd Platoon followed him in a column of twos.

ECHO COMPANY

The isolated spatters of rifle fire made it difficult to hear.

"Say again your last, India One Two. Over."

The shooting died away for a moment, allowing Kevin to make out Donaldson's voice through a thin wash of static. "I need a sitrep, Five Six. Over."

"Understood, Two. Attack was by a company-size formation. We're still getting sniper fire, but no heavy weapons stuff. I have two Kilo India Alphas and four Whiskey India Alphas who need evac. Over."

"Okay, Kev. We'll get a jeep on the way. The air boys tell me we can't get a dust-off in through those trees so it'll be a few minutes."

Kevin swore under his breath at that. One of his wounded men could die before a jeep pushed its way over the rutted, narrow tracks they called roads in this part of South Korea. He clicked the transmit button. "Roger, Two. Tell 'em to make it fast. What about my request for ammo resupply?"

"Understand your situation, but I have nothing to give you at this time. We're hunting for some more, Kev, but I can't make any promises." Donaldson sounded harried. He'd probably been getting the same urgent request from each of his other line units.

Kevin clenched the handset tighter. He needed ammo to hold this position. Didn't any of the higher-ups give a damn about that? "Two, I can hold through one more attack like that last one, but that's it."

"Understood. Do what you can. Two out."

Kevin tossed the handset back to Montoya and slung his M16. He'd been jawing with the useless high command long enough. He'd better inspect his line for new weak spots before the North Koreans tried their next move. And the ravine was the most likely place they'd try it. He set off at a fast, angry walk with Montoya in tow.

1ST COMPANY, 2ND BATTALION

Chae crawled carefully through the narrow gap, moving cautiously to avoid rustling the snow-covered bushes on either side. Sweat trickled into his eyes and he stopped to wipe it away, conscious of the small sounds of movement from all sides as his troops continued their painstaking progress down the ravine past the enemy-held hill. Gunfire rattled in the near distance where his other platoons were still skirmishing with the Yankees, and Chae allowed himself a short, breathless prayer that his ploy would work. Then he put his hands back down in the snow and slid forward again. Soon they would be able to strike the Americans from the rear and send them running.

ECHO COMPANY

Kevin heard it first, a soft, whispering hiss as something knocked the snow off an overhanging limb. He glanced quickly around; there wasn't any wind, though from the look of the sky there soon would be. And every animal for miles around must have already been frightened away by the noise of the fighting. That left only one other possibility.

He flattened himself and motioned for Montoya to do the same. One hand tapped the shoulder of the corporal in charge of the ravine detail, the other pulled his M16 closer.

The corporal, a tall black man named Reese, nodded his understanding and waved slowly to attract the attention of the sentries stationed above the other side of the ravine. They waved back and slid down deeper into their camouflaged foxholes.

Kevin waited.

Ten meters below and to the front, something moved. It changed shape and then grew clearer—a single North Korean soldier bellycrawling through the tangle of brush and tall grass with serpentlike care. Reese laid his thumb on the switch that would trigger the claymores, but Kevin quickly shook his head. This was just a scout. There would be others behind him, and he wanted to catch the whole group in the ambush if possible.

The North Korean came closer, and now Kevin could see and hear a dozen other signs of movement in the ravine just below his vantage point—a rustling bush, a metallic clank, a moving shadow among others motionless. He held his breath and let it out slowly, stealthily. Closer. Closer. More North Koreans were visible now, crawling quietly into range.

One of the machine gunners posted behind a fallen tree coughed—a light sound loud in the still air. Kevin saw the North Korean scout's eyes widen and his mouth open to shout a warning.

"Reese!"

Reese jammed a thumb down on the claymore trigger—setting off the whole daisy-chained string of six with a thunderous roar. A moving curtain of steel shrapnel sleeted the length of the ravine at just above ground level, shredding vegetation and human flesh with equal ease in a horrible kaleidoscopic spray of green, white, and reddish pink. The mines killed almost every North Korean within their burst radius and left the survivors stunned.

The other GIs opened up at the same moment, pumping round after round into the ravine. More North Koreans fell, knocked down dead or wounded. Screams reached above the chatter of the M60 and the crack of M16s.

"Pour it on! We've got these bastards!" Kevin jammed a new magazine into his rifle and kept shooting.

He heard Reese panting the same words over and over again as he fired: "Yeah, take it! Yeah, take it!"

The M60 stopped chattering. It had jammed when its loader let the ammo belt twist through his hands.

2ND COMPANY, 2ND BATTALION

Chae heard the American machine gun stop firing and tore the pin out of a grenade. He held it a second longer, rolled right, and hurled it toward the enemy foxhole. Three. It sailed perfectly through the air and fell in between the two Americans trying frantically to unjam their weapon. Two. One saw it, tried to grab it, and missed. One.

The grenade went off and the explosion catapulted both men out of the hole, bleeding from a dozen wounds.

Without the machine gun the American fire seemed much lighter to Chae. The North Korean captain glanced to either side. Bodies lay all around, heaped on top of one another in some places. But there were survivors and they were starting to shoot back at the Americans dug in above the ravine. Chae counted quickly. He had perhaps half a platoon left in shape to fight. If they could push through here, he might still be able to win this battle.

ECHO COMPANY

An AK burst kicked dirt up right in front of Kevin and he rolled away. That was too damned close.

He stopped rolling and squinted down the M16's sight, squeezing off another burst. The rifle fired once, then twice, and then the bolt clicked on an empty chamber. He hit the release and tore the magazine out, automatically reaching for another in his ammo pouch. There wasn't one. Oh, my God, now what?

"L-T! Catch!" Montoya yelled and tossed him another magazine.

"Tell McIntyre we need another fire team down here, now!" Kevin spotted an NK trying to crawl forward and shot the man through the head.

"Medic!" One of Reese's men was down, bleeding from the mouth and chest. Things were getting tight. He had just four riflemen left and the North Korean return fire was getting heavier. Something had to give.

Something did.

Suddenly there were men wearing green camouflage gear and old-style U.S. helmets kneeling at the edge of the ravine, firing down into the North Koreans below. All were Orientals. Kevin took his finger off the trigger and stared at them. South Koreans? Where'd they come from?

Rhee dropped to the ground beside him, a grin spread all

across his lean, sharp-featured face. "Third Platoon, reporting in as ordered, Lieutenant Little."

"Jesus Christ, who the hell are these guys?"

Rhee ducked as an AK burst cracked low overhead, but he kept smiling. "Forty KATUSAs attached to the company, Lieutenant. That's why they wanted me back at Brigade HQ—to pick these men up and lead them to the front."

"Fantastic." KATUSAs were Korean troops attached to the U.S. Army, and they were exactly what Echo Company needed. Kevin started to relax as he watched Rhee's troops push the North Korean attack down the ravine. The gunfire faded as more and more of the NKs took to their heels, dragging their wounded with them.

Kevin sat up. "How much ammo do you people have?"

"Not much." Rhee's smile faltered. "The rear area is a complete madhouse, Lieutenant. Nobody seems to know where anything is."

"Swell. Okay, call your boys off and string a couple of squads along the edge of this ravine. Keep one squad back." Kevin grimaced. "That'll be our company reserve."

Rhee nodded and moved away to carry out his orders.

"Montoya?" Kevin looked for his RTO and saw him trying to clear a jam from his M16. "Montoya! Get Battalion on that radio of yours. I've got some serious talking to do with the major."

2ND BATTALION HQ

Chae limped into the small clearing at the head of a ragged band of fifteen men, almost all wearing bloodstained bandages. He brushed past a sentry and walked up to the major standing at a fold-up map table.

The major looked up from the map he was studying in surprise. His mouth thinned. "Chae, what are you doing here? Why aren't you up attacking with your company?"

"This is my company, or what's left of it." Chae's voice was flat, emotionless. "The attack has failed."

The major stared at the tiny group of soldiers in front of him. Something in their faces seemed to frighten him. "I . . ." He broke off and moistened his lips with his tongue. "I see.

Well, then, we'll...uh, we'll have to try something else, Captain." He forced a sickly smile. "I'm sure your men fought very bravely. They are to be commended."

Chae felt his right hand twitch toward the revolver at his side and forced it down. The swine wasn't worth it. "Yes. They fought well, Major. I'm taking them back for a rest now. I'll need replacements for my losses as soon as possible."

The major waited for him to continue, but Chae had finished. He turned without saluting and moved away, toward his waiting troops.

"Captain..."

Chae turned. "Yes, Major?"

The man still looked pale. "What about the hill? What...?"

Chae was brutal, past caring that he'd crossed the line into insubordination. "I don't know, Major. I'm sure you'll think of something." He swung round and walked away, half-expecting a bullet in the back.

It didn't come.

ECHO COMPANY

"Can you hold, Echo Five Six?" Donaldson's voice filtered through the static.

"Negative, Two. We're down to less than two clips per man and barely a belt per machine gun. That's just not enough." Kevin rocked back on his heels, staring across the hillside to where his men were stripping the North Korean dead—collecting their rifles and ammunition. If another attack came in, his company would have to use the NKs' own weapons against them. It wasn't an acceptable situation.

Nearly ten minutes went by before Donaldson came back on. "Very well, Six. Foxtrot, Alpha, and Bravo are all in the same shape. I've been on the horn to Brigade, and we're pulling back to resupply. With me so far?"

"Affirmative, Two."

"Okay. Charlie Company's going to cover the withdrawal, so be ready to pull out when they get there. We'll re-form at the Yangju-sa temple complex and try to set up a new line anchored there. Got it?"

"Loud and clear, Two." Kevin was glad to be going but

was sobered by the thought that they were yielding another six or seven kilometers to the North Koreans. He shook his head. They could stop those guys if they could just get some reinforcements and enough supplies to do the job. He signed off and rose to his feet to organize Echo Company's retreat.

KUNSAN AIRBASE, SOUTH KOREA

Taxiing C-5s and C-141 Starlifters threw gigantic shadows under the floodlights illuminating Kunsan's hard-surfaced runways. Howling jet engines made conversation and even thinking difficult.

McLaren squinted into the glare and shaped his face into a mask of tremendous anger aimed at the hapless officer in front of him. "I don't want to hear any more goddamned excuses, Frank. I want this frigging mess sorted out. And I mean as in yesterday, mister. Do you read me?"

The man started to say something and stopped as a C-5 roared past on the runway and lumbered awkwardly into the air. When the noise level dropped, he went on, "General, we're doing our best. But we've got one MAC aircraft landing every three minutes or so. And every one of them has thirty to one hundred tons of cargo aboard that we've got to unload and stow before it can turn around and go back for more."

McLaren grimaced. "Look, I've got infantry battalions that are running out of ammo at the worst possible fucking times. I've got tanks that don't have enough gas to move. And I've got artillery batteries that don't have enough rounds to fight off a troop of NK Boy Scouts."

He moved closer to the supply officer and poked him in the chest with an outstretched finger. "So I don't care how many hernias your men get. I want my men properly supplied, or by God, I'll see you in hell, personally."

The man took a step backward. "But General, it isn't as easy as all that. We're getting the planes off-loaded without any problem. That's just a muscle exercise. The trouble is sorting out what we're getting. The people back stateside are loading everything from medical kits to bullets to spare uniforms into each cargo."

"So?"

A Starlifter touched down and braked hard immediately, screeching down the runway to a stop. Trucks were moving toward the cargo plane before it had even stopped rolling.

"We can get the stuff out okay, but there's just time to pile it off to the side before the next plane lands." The officer shrugged. "I don't have the manpower or the computer power available to keep track of everything once it's on the ground. And that's the bottleneck, General."

McLaren smoothed his features out into a cold, impassive stare. "So who's not doing their job?"

"Normally routing comes out of the logistics office in Seoul. They know what's on each plane and who needs it. My guys unload it and put the required crates on the designated trucks and away it goes."

"In other words, you just unload it and load it again," McLaren prompted.

"Yessir." The officer brightened. "I don't have the men or the organization to find out what's on each plane or to match it up with the requisitions. The staff in Seoul has been evacuated. They're here on the base, I think. They're scheduled to fly out to Japan tomorrow morning, and set up in . . ." He realized that McLaren was staring at him intently.

"Yes, sir. I'll countermand those orders."

"Good thinking. I don't want any more foul-ups. If those are the people to fix this mess, get them on the job, now." He nodded toward the flight line where forklifts were busy hauling cargo pallets out of the refueling C-141. "Pass my commendation along to your boys for their work."

"I will, General."

McLaren nodded and started to swing away. Then he stopped. "Oh, Frank?"

"Yes, sir?"

"I don't want to have to come back here again. Is that clear?"

The supply officer straightened. "Absolutely, sir."

McLaren returned his salute and moved off toward his waiting helicopter. He saw the look on Hansen's face. "You think I was too hard on the man, Doug?"

"Well, General . . ." Hansen stopped, but it was clear that he did.

McLaren grinned at him. "Prerogative of rank, Captain. When a general throws a temper tantrum, it's called 'exercising command authority.'" He clambered into the Cobra and buckled himself into the copilot's seat. "Let's get back to HQ. We've wasted enough time here."

The gunship lifted and clattered off into the night sky. Another snowstorm was expected before midnight.

KUNSAN MILITARY TERMINAL

Anne looked at the disorder around her. Not her own group. They had adapted well to this ridiculous situation and almost looked on the MAC terminal as home now. Almost all were asleep, curled up as best as comfort allowed. They had been stuck here for four days, caught up in the logistic logjam they were supposed to be solving.

First there had been problems with the paperwork catching up with their move to Kunsan. Then there were priority squabbles, then wounded being evacuated. Weather complicated everything. If she hadn't been so familiar with the supply system, she would have thought it impossible.

The airfield was a mess. Crates, boxes, equipment were piled everywhere. Every hour of delay added to the chaos they would have to fight when they finally arrived in Japan.

Meanwhile, they sat at the airport. She remembered Kimpo Airport, and waiting for another airplane. Intellectually she knew she was safer here, but her imagination put smoke columns wherever she looked.

She waited for the airplane and hoped Kunsan really was well-defended.

Tony had insisted that it was, four days earlier at lunch. They'd arrived just after noon that day, and after they said good-bye to Captain Hutchins and his men, the entire staff had been invited to the Officers' Club for lunch. Tony and Anne had taken a small table some distance away from the main group. Anne was sure her staff were gossiping about them, but she couldn't hear it, so she didn't care.

"Please, Anne, don't worry about air attacks. The 'Kun'

hasn't been hit since the third day of the war. We've even got a Patriot SAM battery guarding the place.''

"Should you be telling me that?" she asked.

"Doesn't matter," he said, talking around a mouthful of salad. "The NKs already found out about it—the hard way."

"Oh."

They were sitting at a table with tablecloths and silverware, having the salad bar and sandwich special, and Anne marveled at how novel it all seemed. She imagined what it must be like for men really in the field, who had lived in the killing cold and mud for over a week now.

They talked, mostly about what Anne would do in Japan, and Tony's experiences there. Tony was trying to clue her in on the best places to go. "There're a lot of great restaurants in Misawa. Just outside the main gate, if you take a left—"

"Tony, I'm going to be working twenty-hour days when we get there. I'll be lucky if I have time to eat. I may even be too busy to miss you." She smiled when she said it, though.

"I guess you'll be too busy to think about us, then." He smiled back, but his expression was serious.

"Please, Tony, too much has happened. Things need to calm down."

He looked sour. "It could be a long time."

"Don't worry, I'll call, and write every day." It was her turn to look unhappy. "I worry about you."

He waved her off. "Don't worry. I'm not going to get my butt shot off. They say if you survive the first ten missions you're good for the duration. I hit the tenth three days in. Besides, the NKs are running out of airplanes."

He looked at his watch, then sighed. "I've got a briefing in twenty minutes. I've got to go."

"And who knows when we'll be together again," she said.

"Soon, Anne." He stood up to leave and she got up as well. Stepping around the table, she came up and embraced him.

Surprised, he hugged her back but protested, "Isn't this a little public?"

"I don't care."

"Well, I do. Let's go outside."

As they walked to the door, Anne suddenly felt very sad,

more than she wanted to admit, at going to Japan and leaving Tony.

Just outside there was a grassy area with a few bare trees. There were plenty of people about, but they were all strangers, too busy with their own concerns to care about two people kissing good-bye.

She wondered where Captain Hutchins was now and then worried about Tony. He had come by to see her twice for a short while, but they were hurried visits, overlaid with her concern for his safety. Moreover, he couldn't really console her. She was right, combat flying . . .

An Air Force general was coming toward her, with a group of junior officers and enlisted men in tow. He was tired, but determined, and definitely looked in charge. He strode up to her briskly and she fought the urge to salute.

"Miss Larson? I'm Frank Sheffield, base logistics officer." He saw the recognition in her face. "Yes, ma'am, I'm in charge of that disaster outside. Your orders have been changed. We're going to have you set up shop right here in Kunsan."

Raising his voice a little, he said, "Sorry, folks, no trip to Japan this time. Lieutenant!"

A short, chunky officer stepped forward. The general introduced him. "This is Lieutenant Pettigrew. He will act as a liaison between your group and me.

"Miss Larson, the supply situation in Korea is critical. Field units are short of everything while cargo piles up at airfields and ports, and transport assets are being wasted."

He pointed out the window. "That scene is being repeated all over Korea, and I need you and your people to sort it out. We can't afford to delay another minute."

He softened his tone. "You can have anything you want, and the lieutenant is here to see you get it. We're giving you the aircraft maintenance records offices. Nobody's keeping track of the stuff properly, anyway. Lieutenant, take over."

Without waiting for Anne's reply, the general and most of his entourage left, leaving the lieutenant and two enlisted men behind. The young officer stepped forward and offered his hand. "I'm Tom Pettigrew, ma'am. If you and your people will come with me, I've got some buses waiting outside . . ."

He couldn't understand why everyone screamed. Luckily it was a short ride across the base, just long enough to fill in the young officer on the group's adventures to date. And the buses were heated.

Anne tried to get a rein on her emotions. Another change, to set up right here in Kunsan. If it was so important, they could have told them about this days ago. She wasn't sure that there wouldn't be another change, either.

She hoped this one was real, though. Being on the same base with Tony! It was too good to be true. There had to be another change in the works.

Half of her staff was here with her, sitting in the first bus. She decided to get a head start. "Claire, you take the computer center and tell me where we stand. Bill, make up a building plan and assign work spaces for everyone. Set aside some large room as a sleeping area."

They pulled up outside a concrete-block building and hurried inside, eager to get out of the cold and see their new offices. The previous tenants were still packing, signs of a hurried departure everywhere.

Anne started directing the setup. The chance of actually doing her job, helping to straighten out the supply situation, excited her. It was going to be a long, hard night, the third in a row. She had a list of things to do as long as her arm. But she had to make a phone call first.

C H A P T E R
37
Technical
Difficulties

Tony knew it had been going too smoothly. Seeing Anne almost daily, reinforcements arriving, fewer fighters opposing them. Something had to go wrong.

The afternoon mission was no pushover; airfields never were. This was not a standard package. To keep the element of surprise there would be no warning by reconnaissance or jammer aircraft. Hugging the sides of the valley, Tony's Falcons would make one run, dropping their bombs and then escaping before the defenses were fully alerted. It sounded like a good plan, Tony thought. He had thought it up, briefed it, and was now leading it.

Seeing the hillsides whizz by on either side didn't leave much time for second thoughts, but he knew they were taking a risk. The only concession he had made was to have two F-16s stand by along their exit route. Armed for air-to-air combat, they would cover his group's escape and maybe bushwhack any aircraft taking off with revenge on their minds.

The inertial navigation system showed that the last waypoint was coming up. They had been heading generally north, skirting known defenses and using the valleys to stay below enemy radars. Watching the readout, he checked the map strapped to his knee and looked at the hills around him. There was a notch on the right, and he started a gentle turn toward it.

Behind him were ten other Falcons, five pairs spaced at two-mile intervals. His was the easiest position, the lead. Normally he would have taken the rear position, but navigating to the target was also his responsibility, and that could be done only from the front.

The war had been going well in the air. American fighters were doing their jobs, and Soviet-supplied aircraft couldn't replace the pilots the North Koreans had lost. Tony had nineteen kills to his credit now, but hadn't made one in two days. He didn't expect to make one on this mission either. It was air to ground, all the way.

Their target was an airfield close to the border. Intelligence said that a squadron of attack aircraft, among other things, was based there.

With the number of enemy fighters reduced, UN airpower was being used to hit targets well behind the lines, enemy assets that helped keep their offensive rolling. These included road junctions, bridges, ammo dumps, and airfields. Especially airfields.

This one was located on the floor of a valley where three mountain ridges came together and petered out. The aircraft were kept in hardened shelters dug into the side of one of the ridges. It was heavily defended, with gun and missile batteries sited near the runways and on the hills around.

As tough as it was, it was better to attack them here than wait until they were in the air. The enemy would use these planes to reinforce attacks and exploit breakthroughs. In spite of friendly air defenses, the NK planes could do a lot of damage after they took off.

It had been a long flight. There was a lot of turbulence, both from the wind off the mountains and the sun's uneven heating of the ground. They would be attacking late in the day, when there was just enough light for the fighters to see their target, but less for the gun crews trying to pick them out of a darkening sky.

He interrupted his musings to check the time, then the armament display. His HUD was set up for air-to-ground mode, and the two bombs were already armed. The thousand-pound weapons would be dropped in one fast pass, and besides the mandatory cannon and the Sidewinders, these were his only ordnance.

The notch had widened out into its own valley, and Tony felt a roller-coaster sensation as he followed the rise and fall of the terrain. He waggled his wings and started down. From here to the target the map said the ground was flat. They would halve their altitude of two hunded feet, and Tony was going to do his best to stay below that.

They reached the initial point, and Tony blinked his running lights on, then off. Turning slightly, Tony quickly lined up on the approach bearing to his particular target. He spared one glance over his shoulder and was rewarded by a glimpse of Hooter exactly where he should be, then he moved the throttle to full military power.

The jet leaped forward, shooting out onto the valley floor like a projectile from a gun. Behind him, separated by ten-second intervals, pairs of fighters would be pouring out of the gap.

His radar warning receiver lit up instantly. He set the countermeasures dispenser on AUTO. It would kick out chaff and flare cartridges according to a predetermined pattern until he turned it off or until it ran out. The gun and missile crews had their radars up, which was not unexpected. The question was, were the crews alert? Where were the directors pointed?

Tony was busy trying to spot his target, a set of camou-flaged doors carved in the eastern slope of a ridge. The long shadows from the setting sun should make them easier to spot, but it was hard to look for long in a jet moving at over six hundred knots. Especially one only a hundred feet off the ground.

"Hooter, I see it. I'm coming left a squidge." He heard two clicks in answer and hoped that his wingman saw his target as well.

There were dark half-circles in the hill. The blast doors were inset a few feet, and the edges of the tunnel were throwing shadows onto them. Perfect. He swung the cursor up and locked his radar on the nearest opening.

They had been over the airfield for ten seconds, and the receiver had grown brighter. A *beep-beep* filled his phones, joined instantly by Hooter's call "SAM left! They're going for the Two pair."

Hooter had spotted a smoke trail headed for one of the planes in the pair behind his. That was Dish and Ivan.

Tony couldn't do anything to help. He and Hooter were committed. Luminous symbols were crawling across his HUD, showing the target, the course to steer, everything else he needed to put a pair of bombs within five feet of where he wanted them. Ten seconds more and they would be on top.

"Saint, I can see the launcher. It's a Gecko at seven o'clock."

The SA-8 Gecko was a modern battlefield missile on a mobile launcher. It was a dangerous opponent, equipped with an optical backup in case its radar was jammed. Hooter's voice rose in pitch. "Ivan's hit!"

Tony clicked twice in acknowledgment. He was too busy to talk. Five seconds to go. Flak bursts and tracers were starting to appear and were closer than usual. By this time in the war, the gun crews were getting experienced.

And they were well placed. Someone had guessed how an attack would be made. The SAM launcher was well sited to engage aircraft as they entered, and the guns covered the part of the attack run where they would have to fly straight and level.

There. The pipper had crawled down a line until it crossed the target. RELEASE appeared in the lower left corner and Tony pressed a button on the stick. At the same time he pushed the throttle all the way forward. The increased thrust pushed him into the seat just as he felt the two bombs leave the aircraft.

Two BLU-109 bombs arced toward the target. Designed to penetrate reinforced concrete, they had thick, hard cases. If either one hit the twenty-foot-wide door, it would go right through and explode inside.

He pulled up and to the right, hard, and watched the indicator run up from one g to seven times the force of gravity. He was grunting, tensing his muscles to fight the pull when a white smoke trail passed over and in front of his plane.

The bastard almost had him. His first thought was the launcher that Hooter had called earlier, but this came from a different direction. Probably another unit from the same battery. They had launched optically to avoid warning their target. Waiting until the aircraft finished their run, they fired the SAM as he was turning and climbing, either too busy maneuvering to see the launch or too close to the edge of his envelope to do much about it.

It was blind luck it had missed him. Hooter was still pulling out of his run, so he couldn't have seen it either. Tony made a decision and instead of leveling out and then diving back down, he kept climbing. "Hooter, SAM launcher on the right. I'm taking it."

He heard the two clicks as he thumbed his stick and the CANNON prompt appeared on the HUD. Tony craned his neck overhead and followed the thinning smoke trail back. There. The wheeled launcher was parked on a level spot, "above" and to the right.

He pulled hard and rolled right, swinging the sky and ground over to their customary positions. It was a steep shot, but he fired and saw hits. SAM launchers were never armored, and hitting the delicate electronics might keep it out of action for a little while, even if the vehicle wasn't destroyed.

He pulled out, higher than he would have liked, and turned to the exit heading. Looking left and back he could see smoke rising from the shelters. As he craned his neck back farther to see Hooter, black puffs appeared around him. The aircraft shook, as if it had hit a bump, and suddenly rolled hard left. The right side of the cockpit starred in three places, and the air outside took on a whistling sound.

"I'm hit! Tuba, take over." Tuba was the alternate package commander, and he acknowledged Tony's call.

Tony automatically corrected and brought the wings level, but he paused a moment, afraid to look at the instruments. His limbs felt frozen. He knew he had been hit, but how bad?

He gently tried the controls, first the ailerons, then the rudder. Both responded normally. Pushing his nose down, he headed south, which was the exit route anyway. Rule number one for a wounded bird was to get out of Indian Country.

At six hundred knots he was quickly away from the airfield. The air defenses were concentrating on the aircraft now attacking, so Tony's only problem was getting his damaged Falcon home. A quick scan of the instrument panel showed him one obvious concern. Oil pressure was falling.

Throttling back to cruise power, he called his wingman. "Hooter, I'm hit, losing oil pressure. Look over my right side."

"Rog, Saint." Hooter's plane pulled up quickly until he was flying abreast of Tony's fighter, fifty feet apart and two hundred feet off the ground.

"You've got a couple of good-sized holes in the fuselage," Hooter reported. "Come up a bit so I can check your belly."

Tony climbed fifty feet, and Hooter slid underneath and looked him over. "Yep, big black streak coming back from a hole. Something big hit you, maybe a five seven."

"Rog, Hooter, probably the oil pump."

Without oil pressure the engine would not get enough lubrication; the bearings would heat up and soon freeze. It wouldn't happen immediately, but the chance of making a safe landing at base was almost nil.

They could hear the rest of the raid making its attacks and breaking off as well. Tuba, the alternate commander, had led them out along the planned route, while Tony had taken another, so that if enemy fighters showed up, they would be drawn to the larger group and ignore Tony and Hooter.

Normally they would call for combat rescue, but they were still too far north. He would have to fly south another fifteen minutes before he would be in range for a pickup.

All Tony could do was nurse his crippled bird as far south as possible. His fighter was a valuable machine, and if he could make it to an airfield, it could fight again. Also, any landing, on a road or even a cowpath, was better than a wheels-up into a rice paddy or bailing out.

And the longer he stayed in the plane, the closer to friendlies he was. Every minute in the air was worth a day of walking on the ground. In open country, that is. Most of Korea was mountains and valleys, and the time to work through the country below him would be measured in weeks, not days.

Survival classes notwithstanding, Tony was determined to stay with the bird until the last possible second. He started a gentle climb, not wanting to throttle up but still milking every bit of altitude he could without losing speed.

Consulting his map, he saw the closest airfield that could take him was Taejon. Of course he had to bypass Seoul and the front, but one thing at a time.

He climbed above the valley walls and turned to the south. In a few minutes he would be across the old DMZ.

According to the engine temperature, a few minutes might be all he had. He compared it with the earlier temperature and computed the rate of increase in his head. No way he would make it to base. Underneath the aircraft the terrain rose and fell like a stormy sea. Nowhere to even try a wheels-up. "Hooter, I'm losing the engine."

His wingman's voice was both encouraging and desperate. "Hang in there, Saint. Don't leave until the engine falls off."

"I won't, buddy, but I'm setting up for an ejection, while I have the chance." Tony heard two clicks in response.

He looked over at Hooter's aircraft. He was flying abreast and slightly above him, doing his best to look for threats and monitor Tony's status. In the cockpit he saw his wingman give him a thumbs-up gesture.

Okay, so he was leaving work a little early today. First he hit the switch that wiped out his IFF codes. If that black box survived a crash with the codes still loaded, the enemy would learn a lot. The only documents in the cockpit were a small code card and his map. He stuffed those in his pocket. He would shred the card and bury it after he landed.

After he landed. Tony forced himself to think positively. The Aces II was a very smart seat and had gotten a real workout since the war began. If the pilot survived the initial hit and was able to pull the ring, the seat was certain to get him out of the aircraft.

The problem was that in order to clear a fast-moving jet fighter, the seat had to move even faster. If not, the ejecting pilot would be struck by the tail of his own plane and certainly killed.

About half the pilots that had ejected so far had suffered some sort of injury on ejection: compression fractures of vertebrae, dislocated shoulders, even concussions.

At six hundred knots air is almost as solid as the ground. Something as nonaerodynamic as a man in a seat would be whipped by winds that made a hurricane look tame. Add little or no oxygen and freezing temperature of a parachute landing, and a pilot becomes very reluctant to leave his nice, safe damaged fighter.

Tony had a lot of things going for him, though. He was uninjured, could set his airplane up at the optimum altitude and speed, and would have time to brace himself for the ejection shock.

He looked at the gauge and saw the temperature still rising. Not as quickly, but things would start to fail soon. He put his visor down and tightened the knob as hard as he could, then tightened the chin strap on his helmet. Next, the bayonet clips that attached the oxygen mask to his helmet. A lot of pilots had their masks ripped off, and he needed it to protect his face from the slipstream.

The throttle was still set for cruise speed, about five hundred knots. He pulled it back, reducing the thrust almost to idle. This wouldn't cover ground as quickly, but reducing the speed from five hundred to one hundred knots would make the ejection a much less brutal process.

As the airspeed fell, his climb slowed, then he started to lose altitude. To compensate he pulled up more and more until his speed stabilized and the nose was angled thirty degrees in the air.

Tony felt intensely vulnerable. Slow, power fading, over enemy territory—all he could do was hope nobody noticed them. Hooter was taking a risk, too. If they were bounced by more than two aircraft, John would have his work cut out for him, both defending Tony and covering his own behind.

Settling into his seat, he pressed his spine tight against the seat back and made sure his feet were set squarely on the rudder pedals.

Almost throwing his head back, he jammed it against the headrest, then settled it in, making sure that he was facing straight ahead and wasn't offset to either side.

About two steps away from punching out, Tony used his peripheral vision to look at the temperature gauge. Still climbing, but not there yet. Was there a funny sound in the roar of the jet behind him?

Screw the head position. He checked Hooter and saw him still flying above and ahead, probably wishing he had a towing hook. Feeling a little more desperate, he looked over the ground below. Ridges and valleys alternated, with lakes and occasional groups of trees occupying what flat land there was.

In a way he was glad. Air Force instructors said that if you were behind the lines, try and bail out over rough country. It would slow the progress of enemy units trying to reach you, give you lots of places to land, but was not a problem for the rescue chopper.

Well, what if the chopper can't get to you? He'd have to make it out on his own. He looked at the temperature gauge and immediately snapped his head back against the headrest.

"Hooter, it's almost showtime."

"Rog, Saint. Can I do anything for you?"

"Mark my posit and then get the hell out of here. A circling jet will only attract attention. I'll try and work south so the rescue people can get to me."

"Roger, copy."

"And tell Anne."

Tony heard two clicks. There was definitely a new note to the roar of his engine, but he stayed with the aircraft. Every second in the air brought him closer to recovery. The gauge was now past the red line, but the number was meaningless. Essentially, any moment parts of the engine would decide to take a separate vacation.

He felt a shudder and had to correct to bring the wings level. No point in risking a clean ejection. He said, "Punching," and snapped his elbows back against the seat. His hands fell down onto the yellow-and-black-striped loop between his legs. He grabbed it hard, took a breath, and pulled.

Nothing. Shit! The hit must have taken out part of the circuitry. Time for Plan B.

He kept his right hand on the loop, still pulling. Moving his left arm only from the elbow down, he moved his hand over to the side of the cockpit, just under the canopy rail. He knew where the switch was by touch and did not even risk turning his head to find it with his eyes.

His fingers found the cover and flipped it up. There was a simple toggle switch underneath. This was normally used on the ground only, to raise the canopy. He flipped it up.

He heard a motor behind his head start to whine and snapped his left hand back to the loop. He saw the canopy frame start to move, and then daylight appeared under the front. The whistling sound increased to a roar.

The slipstream suddenly caught the raised edge of the clear bubble. The mechanism was designed to hold the hundred-pound canopy up against gravity, not down against thousands of pounds of pressure. The mechanism was pulled apart, the hinges at the back sheared off, and the canopy was torn away from the airplane.

Tony was exposed to the hundred-knot wind for only a few thousandths of a second. Two short lanyards led from the canopy to the ballistic charges under the ejection seat. Unlike the primary circuit, with its torn wiring, these worked. The lanyards went taut.

Tony felt the seat move beneath him. Used to seven or nine gravities during violent maneuvering, the seat threw him out of the fighter with an acceleration of thirty-three g's.

The force of the blast shocked him and distorted his time sense. He felt the single shock of the explosive start to fade, but suddenly it was augmented by the rocket motor on the base of the seat. This only fired for a few tenths of a second, but the straps in front tightened as it pulled him back as well as up, slowing his forward speed. He saw the cockpit sides pull away from him and was suddenly surrounded by open sky.

He looked at his aircraft as it pulled away from him. The cockpit looked odd and empty without the canopy, and the ejection rail stuck out well above the line of the fuselage. It was in a slow left roll, preventing him from seeing the damage to his ship.

He was disappointed and desperately wanted to confirm that the damage to the Falcon was fatal, that there was no way he could have made it back to base. The fighter was desperately needed, almost as much as the pilot that flew it, and its loss would make everyone's job that much harder.

The slipstream was still buffeting him, but it no longer felt like a wild animal tearing at him. Tony felt a motion behind him and realized the seat was falling away, having done its job. There was a rustling sound, and he looked up in time to see his chute deploy in apparent slow motion.

He didn't believe it. The damn thing actually worked! The circular canopy was half green, with orange and white quarters filling out the circle. Tony gazed at it, admiring the way they had spaced the colored sections, the way it looked in the light from the setting sun. . . .

The setting sun. Night. On the ground! Tony snapped out of his daze and looked down. The rocky hillside was rushing up at him. He took a few moments to look around, to try and get the lay of the land.

It was a snow-covered slope, patches and streaks of brown showing through where the ground was especially rough. And there were pine trees dotting the slopes, with a large patch right under him.

He pulled on a pair of red handles, and a vent opened on the back of his chute. He might be able to steer clear. He looked at the setting sun, trying to mark the western direction against a prominent landmark.

The land sloped down to a river. If the ground wasn't so rocky, it would be a pleasant valley to farm. The river ran roughly north-south and would serve as a good guide for his travel.

He heard a roar and saw Hooter's Falcon fly past. The jet was close enough for Tony to see Hooter's thumbs-up gesture, and Tony was sure he could see Tony's wave and clasped hands over his head. Hooter would carry his location and the fact that he ejected safely back to the squadron.

The fighter flew off down the valley, leaving Tony alone. He missed the freedom of flight, the feeling of control over his destiny. He looked down, watching the ground rush up. His control would be much more limited, for the time being.

KUNSAN AIRBASE

He had taken the time to clean up and change after the debrief. Walking into Anne's office wearing a flight suit was a little too melodramatic for his taste. Hooter knew where to find Anne. He and Tony had visited her twice during mornings off from flying.

In spite of the hour the building was lit up and busy, with people coming and going. From the outside it looked like any of the office buildings on base, but someone had nailed a hand-lettered sign that said LOGISTICS over the original AIRCRAFT MAINTENANCE RECORDS. Under the board with the single word painted on it, someone had added another sign: HELP WANTED, APPLY WITHIN.

Anne's receptionist, Gloria, said that she was in a meeting, but after seeing John's expression she went to call her. John had carried bad news before, worse news than this, but it was never easy. He put on an expressionless mask that he saved for occasions like this and waited.

Anne came out of a hallway door, dressed in blue jeans and a sweater. She looked tired, with a fresh layer of concern about whatever had called her from the meeting. She saw Hooter and almost stopped in midstride, but she caught herself.

Walking toward him, she asked, "Where's Tony?" but she knew the answer when he didn't answer immediately. In the last few strides her expression changed, as she tried to maintain control, and realized how hard that could be.

Hooter waited until she came closer, then said, "Let's go to your office."

"But what's happened? What about Tony?"

"Please, Anne, let's talk in your office." All the question in her manner disappeared, and her face became a mask even more expressionless than John's.

They walked around a corner, down a short hall. Stepping into a small office, John let her go in first, then gently closed the door behind him.

She watched him closely, and after waiting half a moment, she said, "Tony's plane was hit." It was a statement, not a question.

"Yes. But I saw him bail out. As far as I know, he's healthy."

She took a deep breath. "Thank God. When I saw you, I was so afraid it was something else." Even now she couldn't say that Tony might have been dead.

Hooter sketched out the mission, how Tony had been hit, and the ejection. Her initial relief was worn away as Hooter described the location: rough country, well behind the lines, and in winter. He was also out of rescue helicopter range.

John tried to talk about smaller things: Tony's work at the squadron, standard rescue procedures, the progress of the air war in general.

She followed his lead and they chatted for about five minutes. Finally, when there didn't seem to be any more point to it, she mentioned her meeting and he excused himself.

Anne didn't return to the meeting. After Hooter left, she sat at her desk and tried to understand what she felt. She knew she was tired. The stress of her job, the importance of her task, had kept her working twenty-hour days. One of the bright spots in these two days had been the visits by Tony. Seeing someone outside of her job, outside of the war, was something she had cherished.

Tony would show up in the morning, sometime after breakfast. They would talk for a while, and then he would have to go back to the squadron. With the two buildings on the same base, he was never gone long. Besides, everyone in the squadron knew where to find him.

They had talked about their interests, past experiences, their beliefs and goals. She had learned more about him in those few short chats than in all the dates they had gone out on.

Now she would have to make it without his help, and she didn't know if she could. There were things she hadn't said, on the road to Kunsan or here in her office. Next time she saw him, they would have something new to talk about.

JANUARY 6—WEST OF P'OCHON, SOUTH KOREA

Tony marched and tried to figure out if he was lucky or unlucky. On the unlucky side, he'd lost his $16-million fighter, had to bail out in the middle of an enemy-occupied area, and now had to walk across frozen hillsides until he could reach his own lines.

On the plus side, he was healthy, except for a sore arm from that damned tree. He was south of the DMZ by at least twenty miles. That meant he was in friendly, if occupied, territory, and presumably the locals wouldn't come after him with a pitchfork.

That about did it for the plus side. He remembered a few more on the minus side, though. It was dark, and he didn't have the faintest idea of where he was.

In the immediate sense he knew his location. He'd been marching along the side of this godforsaken hill for about three hours and was reasonably sure he was heading south.

In larger terms, he didn't know where to head for. He still had his map, but it was impossible to read until he had some light.

He probably should stop anyway, he thought. He had survived the ejection process relatively intact, but he knew it had taken a lot out of him. He felt a little light-headed and had to stop frequently to rest. Only a desire to get clear of his wrecked aircraft had kept him moving.

It took him another half hour of moving south before he found a likely spot to hide. A small stream had undercut its bank, providing a spot just big enough for a man to lie down.

Tony used his survival knife in his off hand to hack off some pine boughs. Even in his fatigued state he was careful to take them from several trees, and to stay on bare ground as much as possible.

He enjoyed hacking at trees. The damn trees had snagged his chute, slamming his right arm against the trunk hard enough to give it a really good bruise. He was sure it wasn't broken, but it was very, very sore.

The pine tree was a lot taller than his chute and had left him dangling twenty feet off the ground. He'd looked a little ridiculous hanging there, with an inflatable raft hanging just off the ground, and his survival kit actually resting on the snow.

Luckily the Air Force included fifty feet of nylon line in the parachute pack for just such eventualities. It had loops and buckles that allowed a pilot to lower himself to the ground. Of course, it was a little harder in the dark with a sore arm, but he'd made it down after about ten minutes.

Another twenty minutes were needed to deflate and hide the raft, shred and bury his code card, and pack up his chute and survival kit. Every move made his arm ache, and grabbing tree limbs involved a lot of moving.

He hacked off enough branches to pad the ground, with enough left over to lean against the bank and hide him. Wrapping himself in his chute

He hacked off enough branches to pad the ground, with enough left over to lean against the bank and hide him. Wrapping himself in his chute with the green part showing, Tony settled in for the night, relatively warm and delightfully horizontal.

He woke up to sunlight filtering through the pine branches over him. Disoriented, he started to get up and looked around, then froze when he remembered where he was. Checking his watch, he realized he had slept nearly nine hours.

Lowering himself carefully onto the branches under him,

he listened for movement, voices, anything. The branches concealing him also served to block his view of the area round him.

Tony waited and listened, deciding after about five minutes that he was alone. While waiting, he became aware of his own body. His arm hurt like fire, most of the joints in his body were complaining, and he was hungry.

Once he was sure it was safe to do so, he solved the last problem first by digging into his survival kit. Munching on a fruit bar, he pulled out his map.

Never having done any orienteering, and using an air navigation chart, and being unsure of his general position, he was pretty pleased with the results. He was almost certain of which valley he had bailed out over, and he could follow his general direction of travel in the night. On the scale of the map, it was hardly a line.

Tony estimated at least fifty miles to the friendly lines. If he could cover twenty, then somehow alert combat rescue, they could home in on his emergency transmitter. He was keeping it safely off until he absolutely turned it on. The NKs could home in on it just as easily as his people.

Okay, at least two days' travel, maybe seven. Better get started. He'd have plenty of time on the way to figure out how to contact his side.

Reluctant to leave the warmth and security of his hiding place, he stepped out and creakily stretched, looking around carefully for any sign of movement. The change from predator to prey was jarring, but he was fatalistic. In fact, he felt almost optimistic.

His plan was to keep moving south until he came to an east-west highway that crossed the ridge to his right. Besides moving south, he had to go east, or he would end up near Seoul, obviously not a good idea these days.

He made good time, the marching helping to fight the cold. After about two hours the road appeared on the horizon, and Tony dropped prone as he watched for movement or vehicles.

After fifteen minutes he hadn't seen a thing. Judging from the size of the towns on each side of the ridge, there probably wasn't a lot of traffic between P'ochon and Sinpai. Still, roads were roads. They would be patrolled.

He approached carefully, slowing to about half his marching speed. In the end he didn't have to risk the road. There was a low spot in the ridge and he decided a climb was better than the road. The trees covered him, and by midafternoon he was over the top and had a good view of the land ahead of him.

In addition to the tree-covered landscape, he saw a small cluster of buildings. Dropping to his knees, he tried to make them out but could only tell that there were several, they were small, and they appeared to be permanent structures. That meant the inhabitants had to be South Korean, and presumably friendly.

It took him the rest of the afternoon, making dashes from cover to cover. That was fine, because he would rather make the final approach in dusk.

He crouched in cover about twenty yards from the edge of the small settlement. There were three small houses, one barn, a long, low building built into the hillside, and some small sheds. There were lights, and smoke coming from the chimneys.

He had seen a few people about, all women or old men. They had been doing chores, a lot of them connected with the long building.

Finally it was fish or cut bait. Either he could sneak into one of the outbuildings and try and hide there for the night, or approach the people here.

He risked discovery hiding in one of the outbuildings, and the locals might have useful information. Such as if there were any NK units around here.

A middle-aged woman came out of the nearest house, heading for the barn. Bundled against the cold, she carried two buckets and strode quickly toward the building.

Tony waited until she had gone inside, then ran to the door. He pushed it open, slowly, to see a dark, wood-beamed interior with stalls for farm animals. Stepping up to a trough, the woman was just about to pour a bucket's contents into it when she turned her head to the sound of the door opening.

"Nu gu sayo . . ." She had started to say something to whoever she thought was coming into the barn. When she saw the tall American, she froze and grabbed the edge of the trough to steady herself. Tony smiled and bowed, and she automatically bowed back, then caught herself.

Her rapid-fire Korean was so much gibberish to Tony, and

he tried to calm her, slowly and softly asking if anyone spoke English. She quieted, and finally on the third repetition she pointed over to a hay bale and made a sitting motion. As soon as Tony sat down, she set down the bucket and ran out of the barn.

All Tony could do was wait. Either she would bring help, or the enemy. On the off chance that it was bad news, he got up and flattened himself against the wall next to the door. He drew his pistol and worked the slide.

A few moments later she reappeared with an older man following her. She looked at the hay bale, puzzled, then sensed a movement to her right and saw him holstering his pistol and stepping forward. The woman frowned but shrugged her shoulders, then stepped out of the way.

Tony bowed to the older man, who smiled and said, "You are among friends. I am Sook Yon-Gil. This is my sister-in-law." She bowed again, then left.

Tony was surprised. Many Koreans in Seoul spoke some English, but this was a long way from the big city. "Your English is excellent."

Mr. Sook smiled and bowed. "I worked with the American Army in the last war. How may I help you?"

Tony explained who he was. What he needed was obvious.

Mr. Sook was direct. "You can stay here tonight, Major. My sister-in-law will bring you dinner, and you can sleep in the barn. We are the only ones who know of your presence here. It is best if most of the family does not see you."

Tony was aware of the risk they were taking. "Are there any North Korean units around here?"

"No, not since their initial passage." The man scowled. "We have nothing here they care about, and they were still barbarians. My brother has a broken arm, thanks to them."

The woman came back in with a covered basket and began to set out food. Mr. Sook continued, "Eat and rest. I must discuss this with my brother and brother-in-law. I will come back later. We don't get much news about the war."

Tony relaxed and tried to eat slowly. The survival kit rations were neither hot nor filling. The meal was, and delicious to boot. Mr. Sook returned as Tony was finishing, accompanied by his two male relatives. The pilot rose as they came in.

The three men stepped in, formed a line, and then bowed deeply. Reflexively, Tony returned the bow and waited.

Mr. Sook was obviously the oldest of the three brothers and the head of the family. His expression was solemn, and contrite. "Major Christopher, I am ashamed. My brothers have reminded me that I failed to thank you for what you are doing. All three of us fought in the last war. Two of my brothers died. Our two sons were called up when the communists invaded us.

"We can help you to reach safety much more quickly than by walking south. We are . . . 'sending a message.' With luck, we should have a reply by evening tomorrow."

They would not explain further but asked him for news about the war. Tony provided them with an overview while Sook translated, then the Koreans started asking more detailed questions.

Some were about cities and towns, and others about military units. He was glad when he could say that he didn't know if a city had been occupied. When he did know, the news was usually bad.

The conversation wandered, and finally Tony was yawning so much that they excused themselves.

His "bed" was an alcove in a stack of hay bales, arranged to conceal him completely once he was inside. He was asleep in seconds.

A bright light in his eyes and harsh voices in Korean yanked him out of a deep sleep. The hay bales above him had been removed, and a black-suited man, armed with a pistol, was holding a flashlight and inspecting him closely.

Tony struggled to sit up, and the man stepped back. There were two more like him, while Mr. Sook and his entire family stood to one side in the barn.

The black-clad men were obviously soldiers, and probably Koreans. They not only wore cold-weather gear, but also knitted hoods that covered all of their faces except their eyes. One, possibly the leader, was conversing in harsh tones with Mr. Sook, while another stood near Tony, and the third covered the door. They were armed with communist-made AK-47 assault rifles.

His heart sank, and he tried to decide what to do next. His

pistol was within reach, but the possibility of killing three
armed men was poor, and how many of the Sook family would
be hurt, but wouldn't they suffer for collaborating with the
enemy, but the thought of just accepting capture . . .

The leader saw Tony moving and came over. He stood at
attention, saluted, and said in accented English, "Good morning, Major. I am Lieutenant Kim of the South Korean Army
Special Forces. We can get you back to your own lines. Are
you able to travel?"

"Yes," Tony said automatically, still recovering. With
that, they gathered his possessions, Tony said thank you and
good-bye to the Sooks, and they set off into the night.

Tony was full of questions. "I don't understand. The lines
are miles away. How did you get here?"

"We didn't come here, sir. We stayed behind when the
communists advanced."

"But the farmer said it would take until late tomorrow for
help to come."

"We have a system set up with all the citizens here. They
knew that if they left a sign in a certain location, they would
get 'help.' They were told it would take twenty-four hours. We
are much closer than that, but there is no need for them to
know everything."

"What happens next?" Tony asked. They told him.

They hiked the rest of the night, about three hours, and
around dawn Tony was blindfolded. Another half-hour march
followed, with Tony's stumbling progress supported by a man
on each side.

Finally they took off the blindfold and Tony found himself
in a solidly constructed underground bunker. It had a bunkroom,
a kitchen/mess hall, storage rooms, and several other sections
he wasn't allowed to see. In fact, he never saw the entrance,
from either side.

They waited there all day, and then at nightfall they took
another hike, this one about two hours long.

Lieutenant Kim had used satellite communications to arrange a rendezvous. With what, he wouldn't say. He just kept
them moving, checking more and more frequently on a large-
scale map of the area. Finally he took out a small device and
started pacing. Tony realized it was a portable inertial naviga-

tion unit. Their rendezvous would be precise, almost to the yard.

Kim finally signaled a halt and deployed his men as pickets around the area. They waited.

Tony didn't see or hear the helicopter until it was almost on top of them. It came up over a small rise, no more than twenty feet off the ground, and moved toward them. Kim pointed something that looked like a flashlight at the helicopter, but no light shone.

It had the desired effect, though. The machine slowed and altered course to head directly toward the Korean.

Tony knew it was a helicopter, but in the faint starlight it looked more like a monster or a dragon. There were bulges all over the nose of the craft, a long probe sticking fifteen feet out in front, and protruberances on the sides as well.

Kim waved him over. "This is your ride home, Major." He shook hands with Tony, then handed him a package. "These are messages and personal letters. Will you deliver them for us?"

"Of course, Lieutenant. Can I do anything else for you or your men?"

"No sir, just kill communists. Good-bye." They saluted.

Even now, with the helicopter landing nearby, it was nearly silent. He got a closer look as it landed and recognized it as a Pave Low special operations helicopter. He could see large drop tanks under the side sponsons, miniguns in the doors, and a Sidewinder!

He had heard about them, even seen one now and then at an airfield. They had infrared TV, terrain-following radar, armor, jamming systems, and enough weaponry to fight their way out of a jam. They were used for special operations, inserting or extracting people behind enemy lines . . .

Sort of like him.

The helicopter's wheels touched the ground, and as if operated by a switch, a door opened and a red-lit interior was visible. The light seemed bright after the pitch darkness. A crewman waved to him, and he ran over. Wind from the rotors buffeted him but he hardly felt it as he ran to the ship.

The crewman tossed out a few crates, then grabbed his arm and pulled him up and inside. The door slammed and he felt the craft rise. Almost immediately it started moving forward and didn't seem to rise anymore.

Tony looked around. The original CH-53 was big enough to carry a small truck, but this one's innards were filled with electronics consoles and ammo boxes.

The crewman handed him a headset and Tony put it on. A few moments later he heard, "Hello, Major. Captain Wells here. Welcome back."

Tony was grabbing for support as he heard those words. The craft had moved suddenly down, sideslipped, then climbed. Answering as best he could, he said, "Glad to be here, Captain. Are we having problems?"

"None, sir. We are away clean and making good time. Would you like to come forward?" The machine went through a roller-coaster bump.

"Yes." Curiosity replaced uncertainty, and he unplugged the headset. Moving forward, he pulled aside the curtain that blocked even the dim red light from reaching the cockpit.

His eyes adjusted further, and by the dim light of the instrumentation he made out the two pilots. At first he couldn't make out their faces, then realized they were wearing masks, or goggles. They had to be infrared goggles, designed to give the wearer vision in low light. Or no light.

He looked forward and was rewarded with the breathtaking view of the hilly landscape only fifty feet below him rushing by at a hundred and fifty miles an hour.

The instrument panel was twice as complex as his fighter's. He recognized a terrain-following radar display, a thermal-imaging TV picture, and computerized map display. It looked more like the bridge of the *Enterprise*.

He firmly believed they needed it. A hill loomed up in front of them, and the craft neatly banked without changing altitude or losing speed. In midmaneuver the pilot reached around to shake Tony's hand. "Glad to see you, Major." He waved at the panel and the view out the windscreen. "Sorry this isn't as exciting as one of your ships, sir."

Tony forced his voice to remain calm. "That's all right. How much more of this before we climb to cruising altitude?"

"We'll stay at this height all the way back. The avionics can handle this easily, and we don't like even our own side to see too much of our operations. Another hour and a half and you'll be back at your squadron.''

The flight back was the hardest part of his trip.

C H A P T E R
38
Dire Straits

JANUARY 7—ABOARD THE USS *O'BRIEN*, IN THE TSUSHIMA STRAIT

Captain Richard Levi, USN, sneaked a glance at the barometer as he came on the bridge. It was still holding steady, a reading confirmed by the nearly cloudless sky and by the gentle, rolling motion of the *O'Brien* as she steamed toward Pusan at twelve knots. His compact frame easily followed the motion of the deck.

His bridge crew stiffened slightly but didn't react in any other way. Levi didn't like a lot of fuss in normal times, and he especially didn't like needless ceremony under war conditions. People busy saluting and clicking their heels were all too likely to miss that first crucial warning of an incoming missile or torpedo.

He nodded to his executive officer and stepped out onto the bridge wing, leaning out over the rail to look back at the three boxy cargo ships trailing placidly in his Spruance-class destroyer's wake. One wore the dull-gray paint scheme that marked it as a Navy Sealift Command ship, but the others stood out in bright colors designed to please the eye and attract paying customers.

Together the three merchantmen carried a vital cargo—a major share of the 25th Infantry Division's heavy equipment. The 25th's personnel had been flown into South Korea over the preceding week, but they would remain as useless as if they were still in Hawaii until equipped with the tanks, artillery, and APCs loaded aboard the *Andrew T. Thomas*, the Liberian-registered *Polar Sea*, and the Danish-flagged *Thorvaldsen*. Seventh Fleet's orders were clear. All three had to get through.

U.N. Forces were fighting hard on the peninsula, but they were still being forced backward, away from now-besieged Seoul. Scuttlebutt said the ground pounders needed all the help they could get to avoid being shoved into the sea. The 25th's heavy weapons were part of that help.

Levi put his back to the chill, five-knot wind sweeping across the destroyer's superstructure and looked east, his eyes hunting for the other part of his command—the tiny, Perry-class frigate *Duncan*. There she was. He could just make out a slightly darker patch of gray rolling up and down above the gray-green sea. He'd put the *Duncan* about four miles out on the convoy's eastern flank. Out where her hull-mounted SQS-56 sonar had a better chance of picking up an NK diesel sub moving in for a sneak shot inside the *O'Brien*'s "baffles," an area aft of the destroyer where the noise of her own engines and screws deafened her sonar.

The wind veered slightly and strengthened, whining through the radar and radio antennas clustered above the destroyer's bridge. Levi ignored the noise and squinted into the morning sun climbing skyward beyond his companion frigate. Sunlight glinted off a Plexiglas canopy. *Duncan* had one of her two SH-60B Seahawk helicopters up, laying a passive sonobuoy line several miles to the north and east of the convoy's track—right along the most likely angle of approach for an enemy sub looking for an easy kill.

But not the only one. Wings winked silver at the edge of his vision and then dipped from view. Seventh Fleet had allocated a P-3C Orion to the escort and he'd stationed it well to the north—twenty miles or so ahead of the small group of UN vessels bound for Pusan. The P-3 had been systematically laying successive lines of passive buoys, trying to clear a path for the *O'Brien* and her invaluable charges.

North and east were covered as well as they could be under the circumstances. And Levi had brought his convoy as close to the western edge of the island of Tsushima as he possibly could without running them aground. The water was so shallow at that point that any damned NK sub trying to stay submerged would have to be half-buried in the mud. He could pretty well rule out that direction, at least until they emerged from alongside the island. He'd have to rearrange his escorts and air assets when that happened. He also planned not to worry overly about his back. Any diesel submarine coming in from the south, chasing after the convoy, would either run its batteries out or make so much noise snorkeling that it would be easy to hear, pinpoint, and destroy.

Levi blinked rapidly, clearing the dazzling afterimages left by looking too near the sun out of his eyes. With a last, quick glance around the horizon, he turned and reentered the comparative warmth of the *O'Brien*'s bridge. They were coming into the danger zone and it was time for him to get back to the ship's Combat Information Center. It was also time to move a little more cautiously. Levi didn't plan to walk into an ambush with his eyes shut or his sonars less than one hundred percent effective.

"Mr. Keegan?"

"Sir?"

"Slow to eight knots, and signal the rest of the convoy to do the same."

"Aye, aye, sir." His executive officer nodded to the rating standing by with a signaling lamp. The *O'Brien* would keep radio silence for as long as possible. There wasn't any point in handing the North Koreans a free fix on the convoy's position. Levi intended to make them work for it.

ABOARD THE DPRK *GREAT LEADER*, WEST OF TSUSHIMA

Senior Captain Chun Chae-Yun studied the plot carefully, conscious of the need to keep a confident, relaxed expression on his face. It had been a long war already for the *Great Leader* and its crew. Many of the junior ratings were starting to show signs of the enormous strain imposed by the need for constant noise discipline and by the high state of readiness required on a war cruise. So, under the circumstances, it was vital that he set a good example by remaining unrattled—no matter what happened.

Chun had to admit that it was hard to control his mixed feelings of dread and excitement as the prospect of new action loomed nearer. After several successive victories during the first days of the war, most of the *Great Leader*'s maneuvers since had been wholly devoted to its own survival—and many of its fellow submarines hadn't been so fortunate. One by one they'd fallen prey to American and South Korean aircraft or to hunter-killer groups of enemy frigates and corvettes. They'd exacted a heavy toll of imperialist merchant shipping and warships, but the exchange ratio remained lopsided and tilted in entirely the wrong direction.

Now, the latest signal from the high command offered a chance to avenge those defeats. Intelligence agents in the Japanese port of Yokosuka had signaled the departure of a small but important convoy. Such a convoy could have only one destination—the imperialist supply base at Pusan. And so Chun's *Great Leader* and two older, Romeo-class boats lurked in its projected path, ready to send the American convoy to the bottom of the Tsushima Strait. A small squadron of three fast attack boats—Osa-class boats armed with Soviet-made SS-N-2C Styx surface-to-surface missiles—waited north of the island, equally ready to pounce on any survivors left afloat after the submarines struck.

Chun had placed his newer, more capable Kilo-class sub in position to cover the western approach to Pusan. The two Romeos waited to the east of Tsushima—forced by their inadequate sonars to rely heavily on periscope sweeps to visually detect an oncoming enemy. Even so, the Americans should find it impossible to slip by them unobserved. Or so he hoped.

He pondered the chart again, rubbing his chin reflexively. Perhaps it would have been better to have concentrated his entire force north of Tsushima, close to Pusan's outer approaches. It would have exposed his units to more risk of detection, but it would also have made it more likely to find and strike the American convoy before it reached the safety of the harbor. Perhaps . . . Chun shook his head almost imperceptibly. Such thoughts were of little use now. His first plan was undoubtedly the best. Second-guessings were a waste of time and energy. He had a battle to prepare for . . .

The navigator's voice broke in on his thoughts. "We've reached the westernmost edge of our patrol circuit, Comrade Captain."

Chun looked up from the chart. "Very well. Come about to zero nine zero degrees. Maintain a speed of five knots." He caught his first officer's eye. "Make another inspection of the boat. Ensure that all compartments are fully prepared for noise discipline and for possible damage control."

They could expect to make contact with the enemy force at any moment now. The *Great Leader* would be ready.

ABOARD THE DPRK *LIBERATOR*, EAST OF TSUSHIMA

Captain Min Sang-Du stared at the chronometer hung on one wall of the *Liberator*'s tiny plot office. Where the hell were the Americans? He'd run the calculations over and over in his mind and on the chart. Given the last known course and speed of the American convoy, he should have sighted them by now. So what were they up to?

Had they gone west of Tsushima? That possibility didn't concern him very much. Such a course would take the imperialists straight into the waiting torpedoes of the *Great Leader*. True, that would rob Min and his crew of their share of the glory, but glory was overvalued when the fate of nations was at stake. No, it was the other possibility that bothered Min. The possibility that the Americans were slipping farther to the east than expected—and might already be crossing behind him on their unimpeded way to Pusan. Any captain who allowed that to happen could expect the worst from the naval security service, and he would receive it.

Min shivered in the cold, clammy air. The air inside the *Liberator*'s cramped hull was growing fouler and damper by the hour. Condensation ran off the walls, even off some of the equipment. He leaned over the chart once more and penciled in a hypothetical new course for the American convoy—one that would carry them well away from his current patrol path—and then stood back to look at his handiwork. Yes, that seemed right. And at twelve knots, the imperialists could be . . . there. He marked the spot and made a decision. The Americans were not here, therefore they must be there.

The North Korean captain made his way back into the crowded Control Room. His first officer waited, eyes questioning.

"Comrade Sung, lay us on course zero three five."

The submarine heeled slightly as it spun slowly through the water, turning to the northeast.

ABOARD *SIERRA FIRE*, OVER THE TSUSHIMA STRAIT

The P-3C Orion shuddered slightly as it hit a small pocket of turbulence. Sierra Five was flying low, cutting through a zone where the hotter air rising off Tsushima ran into colder air held over the ocean. It was hunting submarines, flying low over a twenty-mile-long line of previously dropped sonobuoys, listening in at each in turn for the first sound that might warrant a Mark 46 torpedo.

The Orion shuddered again, this time sloshing hot coffee down the front of the second sonarman's flight suit as he tried to slide back into his chair. He swore viciously and tried mopping at the spilled liquid with the corner of an air navigation chart.

The first sonarman didn't pay any attention. He was too busy punching the intercom button. "Skipper! I've got something on number ten, a very weak signal. Could be a diesel boat creeping."

Sierra Five banked even more sharply as it came around to head back up its sonobuoy line. More coffee spilled onto the second sonar operator.

Up in the cockpit the pilot leveled out of his climbing turn and dropped the Orion's nose to lose altitude. They were closing on the plotted position of Buoy 10 at more than three hundred knots.

"MAD on?"

"MAD is on," Sierra Five's tactical coordinator confirmed. The cheap LOFAR sonobuoys they'd dropped had such a limited range in these noisy waters that any sub they detected with them had to be very close indeed. Close enough so that the Orion's magnetic anomaly detector—its MAD—should have a good shot at picking up the slight distortion of the earth's magnetic field caused by a submarine's metal hull.

"Passing number ten . . . Now!"

The P-3 roared low over the gray-green sea. An onboard display suddenly spiked upward.

"Madman! Madman! Positive contact! Smoke away!" A smoke float tumbled away from the Orion and ignited, settling onto the water to mark its prey.

"Drop a DICASS." The tactical coordinator wanted a firm fix and he wanted it fast. A DICASS buoy could go active and get both a bearing and range on a detected target.

The Orion banked steeply again, trading airspeed and altitude for a tighter turn. The buoy popped out of its belly and swayed down into the water.

"New buoy number fifteen is on. Target! Bearing one three five, range four hundred yards!" The sonarman fought to keep his voice from cracking with excitement.

Sierra Five settled back into level flight, this time aimed right at the submarine picked up by its active sonobuoy.

"Weapon away!"

Nobody aboard the Orion saw the splash as its Mark 46 torpedo hit the water. They were too busy preparing for another attack run.

DPRK *LIBERATOR*

"Torpedo in the water! Bearing three three zero!"

The sonarman's shout froze Min for a crucial half-second. Then he turned and screamed at the helmsman, "Right full rudder! Flank speed!"

The submarine tilted abruptly as it turned and accelerated toward its meager full speed of fourteen knots. Min pulled himself across the control room and into the plot office. He sighed. It was as he'd thought. The water was too shallow to allow any serious maneuvering in the vertical plane. He'd have to try to outturn the American torpedo and hope it lost him. Not that there was much chance of that.

"Torpedo still closing, Comrade Captain!" Min could

hear the fear in his first officer's voice and knew the same hopelessness. Still, they had to try.

"Left full rudder then!"

The *Liberator* heeled in the opposite direction as the helmsman executed his order immediately. One man at least hadn't panicked. That was something. He waited, bracing himself for the impact.

"Torpedo screws fading, Comrade Captain! It has lost us!" Cheers greeted the sonarman's report.

Min smiled tightly. He would let the poor fools celebrate. They would learn the truth soon enough.

SIERRA FIVE

"That first torp missed, Skipper. Still running, but it's moving away from the contact."

The P-3's pilot, a burly Naval Reserve commander with the name LAMBROS stenciled across his flight suit, looked at his copilot and smiled. "Ya know, the biggest ASW mistake the Japanese made during Word War II was giving up too soon. I'm not making the same mistake." His hands pulled the Orion into another turn.

"Madman! Madman!"

"Weapon away."

DPRK *LIBERATOR*

The cheers faded into a collective groan.

"Right full rudder!" Min turned to his first officer. "Raise the radio mast."

"But . . ." Sung looked confused. "Comrade Captain, the enemy will see it . . . especially at this speed!"

"Idiot! Do you think that will matter? Listen!" The *pings* of several active sonars could be heard clearly, even above the noise made by the *Liberator*'s laboring screws. "Signal all units that we are under attack. And do it while there is still time."

Min watched his lieutenant enter the Radio Room and then leaned back against a bulkhead to await his fate. They had been lucky once. They wouldn't be lucky again.

SIERRA FIVE

"A hit!"

Water fountained skyward in a column of white foam, dead fish, and pitch-black oil. The P-3's pilot winced slightly watching it. He had an active imagination and could easily visualize how the Mark 46's high-explosive warhead had killed the enemy submarine—it must have ripped the sub open like a gutted trout. He stared at the oil-coated waves rippling away from the impact zone. There wouldn't be any survivors. Not in the middle of that.

With an effort he pulled his eyes and mind away from the dead submarine. "Signal the *O'Brien*. Tell 'em we got the bad guy."

"Aye, aye, Skipper." The tactical coordinator's voice was jubilant. "That's one down and surely more to go."

ABOARD THE DPRK *REVOLUTION*

Commander Sohn Chae-Hwan studied the message flimsy. "You're sure this is all that was sent?"

The signals rating nodded. "Yes, Comrade Captain. Just the call sign for the *Liberator* and those words, 'under attack.'" He flinched as a dollop of spray sluiced across the Osa-class missile boat's open bridge. He'd grown too used to his warm cubbyhole belowdecks and didn't like standing outside, fully exposed to the cold sea.

Sohn dismissed him with a curt gesture and turned to look at the chart for the *Liberator*'s last known position. He had to assume that the submarine had been sunk by whatever enemy had attacked it. And that left just one Romeo-class antique in the probable path of the American convoy. He sneered. It was unlikely that one ancient diesel submarine would be able to do much on its own.

He glanced up from the chart, studying the stubby silhouettes of the other two missile boats that made up his command. The original plan hadn't called for the Osa squadron to attack until the mop-up phase, but the original plan had just gone by the boards. The *Liberator* sunk without even exacting a price for its loss. Disgraceful.

But perhaps a sudden attack by the twelve SS-N-2C Styx missiles his boats carried could sow enough confusion to give that last Romeo a fighting chance. It was worth trying.

He snapped out an order. "Signal the squadron. New course is two three five degrees. Full speed ahead!"

Sohn felt the *Revolution* leap under his feet as its three-shaft diesel engines roared into life. The three missile boats turned southwest, toward the northernmost tip of Tsushima Island, racing ahead at thirty-six knots.

USS *O'BRIEN*

Levi watched as a rating updated the CIC's plot, showing the P-3 moving further north to lay another sonobuoy line across the northern tip of Tsushima Island. Another seaman entered the convoy's current position.

He turned to his ASW officer. "Well, what do you think, Bill?"

"I think we're right on the edge of game time, Skipper. I sure as hell don't think that NK sub was out there all alone. He'll have company around somewhere."

"Agreed. Okay, then. Let's get the *Duncan*'s helo down for refueling. But tell Vandermeier I want his replacement in the air first. I want continuous coverage to our east. Clear?"

The ASW officer nodded.

Levi glanced at the air status board. They hadn't been updated yet. He frowned. "What's the latest on our own birds?"

"Hotel Three is at plus-five. Ready to launch at your order." The ASW officer followed Lev's frown and frowned himself. Somebody was being slow.

"What about Two?"

"Still down. They're trying to get that cracked rotor casing off for repair, but it looks like an all-day job."

Levi's frown grew deeper. His second SH-2F Sea Sprite had been out of commission off and on ever since leaving Pearl two weeks before. What the hell use was a helicopter that wouldn't ever fly? "Well, try to light a fire under them down there, Bill. You know the old saying, 'For want of a helo . . . ' "

The ASW officer grinned. "Aye, aye, Skipper. Consider the pyre lit." His grin faded. "But I don't think it's going to do much good."

"Yeah, well. At least it'll make me feel better. So get it done." Levi turned his attention back to the plot, trying to guess where the NKs would come from next.

DPRK *GREAT LEADER*

Senior Captain Chun pondered the fragmentary message relayed by East Sea Fleet Command at Wonsan. "And there has been no further contact with the *Liberator*?"

"No, Captain."

Chun dismissed the man with an absentminded wave. Min and his submarine had almost certainly been sunk. If they'd survived, *Liberator* would have made a more detailed contact report by now. Min was—no, had been—a veteran captain, one of the best. Meanwhile the *Great Leader*'s patrol along Tsushima's west coast had been completely undisturbed. Not a single sonar contact. Not a single significant periscope sighting.

The possibility that had been growing in his mind crystallized into a certainty—the Americans were transiting Tsushima's east coast. And he and his submarine were in exactly the wrong place. Chun stepped to the Control Room's plot table.

He laid out a course that would allow them to intercept the Americans to the north of Tsushima and then frowned, calculating times and distances. It would be at least a six-hour run at ten knots—a run that would leave the *Great Leader* dangerously short of battery power.

Diesel-electric submarines were the quietest on earth when operating on batteries, but endurance runs at speed weren't exactly their forte. Kilo-class subs such as his could carry two-hundred hours' worth of charge in their massive battery stacks, but increased speed meant an increased battery drain. At ten knots the *Great Leader*'s electric motors would consume ten hours' worth of charge for every hour of operation. It went up from there. An hour at fifteen knots ate fifty hours' worth of charge, and using the sub's maximum speed, sixteen knots, would drain every battery aboard in just two hours. The *Great Leader*'s batteries could be recharged while snorkeling and running on diesels, but diesels were noisy. And noisy submarines didn't live long.

Still, he didn't have much choice. The high command's orders were explicit. This convoy must be stopped—at all costs. Chun faced his officers. "Left rudder. Bring us to new course zero zero three. And increase speed to ten knots."

For a second the assembled officers stood motionless, surprised by his sudden decision to abandon the *Great Leader*'s slated patrol area. Then they scrambled to obey. They would go north.

ABOARD SIERRA FIVE, NEAR THE NORTH END OF TSUSHIMA

"Buoy number twenty-two down and marked. Drop point for twenty-three is coming up . . . now!"

"Buoy away!" A small parachute blossomed from beneath the P-3's belly and drifted toward the ocean. In the aircraft above, the tactical coordinator watched the computer screen as a small symbol appeared, with "23" next to it. Sierra Five was just passing the small village of Toyo on the rocky northeastern tip of Tsushima Island, laying a new sonobuoy line from the southwest to the northeast. Four more buoys would complete the line, and then the P-3 could circle around to begin its patrol, always listening for the minute sounds—a noisy propeller, a hatch slammed shut too fast, a metal tool dropped on a metal deck—that could signal an enemy's approach.

"Uh . . . Skipper?" It was one of the crewmen acting as lookouts through the side windows.

The pilot clicked his intercom switch. "Go ahead, Charlie. What's up?"

"I think maybe I just saw something up north. Pretty far out there. All I could see was some kind of blinking or flashing." The lookout sounded vaguely apologetic for having disturbed him.

Something to the north? On the surface? Maybe he'd made a mistake in leaving the P-3's radar off. It had seemed unnecessary to have it on and all too likely to alert any enemy sub with

ESM—electronic intercept—capability. Sierra Five's commander clicked his intercom switch again. "Let's get the radar going, Mike."

"Warming up now." Aft in the Orion's electronics compartment, the petty officer assigned to run its APS-115 surface search radar flicked a series of switches and listened to the low hum as his gear came on line, going from standby to active status in seconds. Blips appeared instantly on the screen. "Contact! I've got two, no, three radar contacts bearing zero one six, range approximately twenty-three miles. Definitely small surface contacts, not periscopes."

Up in the cockpit, the pilot glanced at his copilot. "Japanese or Korean fishing boats, maybe?"

His second-in-command looked up from leafing through a thick collection of charts and photocopied briefing papers. "Not in that sector. Not legally, anyway. The Pusan sea lane's been posted off-limits since Day One."

"Skipper!" It was the radar operator. "Contacts now bearing zero two zero. Their track is two three five, speed thirty-six knots!"

Those weren't fishing boats. They were moving too goddamned fast. The P-3 banked hard right to come around on an intercept course. "Sparks, tell the O'Brien the good news. Frank, get your Harpoons ready to go. Looks like we've got targets for 'em."

"Coming up, bossman." The tactical coordinator had his face nuzzled up against a radar repeater scope, studying the contacts he was about to try to kill. Three distinct ships, each separated from the others by about a mile of open water. Three targets . . . and two Harpoons slung under Sierra Five's wings. Well, two out of three wouldn't be bad.

"Range eighteen miles and closing."

The copilot had binoculars up to his eyes, sweeping the sea ahead of them. "Got 'em. Dead ahead. Small patrol boats. Probably Osas by the look of 'em. Definitely not friendlies."

"Okay, that's good enough for me." The P-3's pilot spoke firmly. "Nail the creeps, Frank."

DPRK *REVOLUTION*

"Aircraft! Due south!"

The lookout's shout brought Commander Sohn's head around in time to see the two tiny flashes from under the P-3's wings. "Missile warning! Hard right rudder! Come to new course two seven zero. Alert the *Retaliation* and the *Avenger*!"

Sohn held onto the bridge railing with both hands, braced against the tilting deck as the *Revolution* came around on its new course. Its two sister ships followed suit, turning in line abreast and throwing spray high into the air in twin roostertails.

Revolution's gun turrets whined, spinning round to face south. The North Korean commander grimaced. Even though he'd ordered the radical turn to unmask both his boat's twin-gun 30mm mounts, he knew they'd still have a difficult shot against the enemy missile. The briefings he'd received had said that the Harpoon could skim the waves at more than five hundred knots. Since his guns had a maximum effective range of just over a mile and a half, that meant they would have less than ten seconds to try to knock an incoming Harpoon into the sea before it hit home. Not very much time at all.

He let go of the railing with one hand and leaned over an open hatch to yell down to the boat's signals rating. "Break radio silence. Inform Fleet Command and all units that we are under air attack and that we believe the enemy convoy is on a course east of Tsushima Island."

Sohn didn't wait for a reply but turned away, trying to spot the Harpoons streaking toward him. There. Twin shadows racing over the water almost faster than the eye could see. One was climbing, arcing into the sky as it popped up before plunging down onto the *Revolution*.

Both the fore and aft 30-millimeter guns cut loose with a chattering roar, throwing tracers toward the missile climbing higher above the sea. Sohn's hands gripped the railing as he willed himself to remain motionless. Yes! A 30mm round shattered the American missile, turning it into a tumbling ball of flame that struck the water two hundred meters short of the *Revolution*.

Sohn caught a split-second glance of the other Harpoon's long, white shape as it flashed overhead and was gone. He spun round and staggered as a tremendous shock wave rocked the boat. There, less than a mile off, debris spiraled away from the center of an explosion. When the smoke and spray cleared, the *Retaliation*, his middle boat, had vanished—blown to pieces by the missile's 227-kilogram warhead.

He broke away from the boiling sea left by the explosion and sought out the enemy plane. It seemed to hang in midair, arrogantly loitering to see the results of its attack. "Hard left rudder! Bring us to one eight zero degrees. I want to close the range to that bastard!" He looked wildly around. "Comrade Lee!"

The boat's portly weapons officer hauled himself to his feet. "Yes, Comrade Captain!"

"Prepare your SAM team! I want that plane down!"

The *Revolution* and its surviving consort, the *Avenger*, surged south, speeding toward the P-3 and closer to the rocky beaches of Tsushima Island.

USS *O'BRIEN*

"I'm sorry, Captain. The island's blocking our fire. We just can't hit those Osas from here."

Levi nodded his understanding. His tactical action officer was right. The two remaining North Korean missile boats were sheltered from his Harpoons by the Japanese island's hills. The geometry just wasn't quite right. For a second he wondered if the NK commander had planned it that way. Then he dismissed the thought. It didn't matter. What did matter was finding a way to get a shot at those fast attack boats before they could launch on him.

Levi ran his eye over the plot, half-listening to the constant stream of reports flowing in from the P-3 twenty miles ahead. There really was only one practical maneuver. He stepped to the intercom. "Mr. Keegan, alter course to zero three zero degrees and increase speed to twenty knots. Signal the *Duncan* to take station astern and order the convoy to alter course to zero nine zero degrees."

"Aye, aye, Captain."

Levi stepped back to the plot to speak to the tactical action office. "That'll help us get a clear field of fire faster. And it'll keep the merchies behind us if missiles start flying."

The other man smiled, but Levi's ASW officer didn't look so pleased.

"Problems, Bill?"

"If there's a sub out there, Captain, we're in a world of hurt. At this speed, our sonars aren't going to be worth a damn."

Levi nodded gravely. "I'm aware of that. But that's a risk we'll have to take. Our helos will have to shield us while we take out those NK boats." He stopped, hoping he wouldn't have to eat those words at the court-martial that would follow any defeat.

SIERRA FIVE

"They're still closing, Skipper. Now less than seven miles away."

The P-3's pilot smiled. "Maybe they think we're gonna let 'em get close enough to use those machine guns on us. Keep your eyes on them, though. The boys on the *O'Brien* and *Duncan* can use any info we pick up."

Sierra Five continued its lazy orbit, watching as the two North Korean missile boats charged in. Navy intelligence reports said the NK Osas didn't carry any significant antiaircraft weapons.

DPRK *REVOLUTION*

Sohn kept his eyes moving, swiveling back and forth from the American plane to the SA-7 SAM team crouching low beside the aft 30 mm gun turret. They were almost in range— just a few hundred meters more. Closer. Closer. He brought his hand up, ready to signal the attack. Almost . . .

SIERRA FIVE

"Range is now five miles, Skipper."

The P-3's pilot heard the questioning note in his radar operator's voice and let it feed the small uncertainty growing in his own mind. The North Korean missile boats were now clearly visible to the naked eye. "Yeah. That's close enough.

Let's put some airspace between us and get that sonobuoy line laid."

His hands were already busy banking the aircraft in a shallow turn away from the NK craft.

DPRK *REVOLUTION*

"It's turning away!"

Sohn saw the massive four-engined aircraft changing shape as it changed course, pulling out of the slow figure-eight orbit it had been following. He leapt for the rear bridge railing. "On your feet! Fire! Fire!"

"But Comrade Captain . . ." The boat's weapons officer tried to stop him, babbling something about the angles and ranges. It was too late.

The sailor clutching the SA-7 Grail SAM launcher rose from beside the aft gun turret and lifted it to his shoulder, letting the missile's seeker head find the heat emanating from the P-3's engines. It locked on and he fired, braced against the pitching deck as the missle ignited and flashed into the sky.

SIERRA FIVE

"Shit!" The P-3's pilot saw the smoke trail curving after him and jammed the throttles all the way forward. A fuckin' missile, he thought, they've got SAMs on those goddamned things. Who would've thought it? You should have, cried a voice inside his skull. He watched the airspeed indicator climb, agonizingly slowly, as the SAM gained on them, streaking in at close to a thousand knots.

Sierra Five got lucky.

The SA-7 closed rapidly on the P-3, veering toward the heat thrown off by its two port wing engines. Then, just two hundred yards or so behind its target, the North Korean missile—its propellant exhausted and momentum gone—tipped over and fell away into the sea. The P-3's turn and burst of speed had carried it out of range.

The pilot breathed out, a little more shakily than he would have liked. That had been too close. He looked into the mirror.

Now far behind him, the two surviving North Korean boats were curving away, heading southeast.

"Tell the *O'Brien* that she's gonna have company in a few minutes. Those NKs look like they plan to go head-to-head." Then he clicked the intercom to speak to the whole crew. "Okay, guys, that was fun. But now let's get back to doing what they pay us for—killing subs."

A faint cheer echoed his words. Submarines didn't shoot back.

USS *O'BRIEN*

Levi wheeled toward his tactical action officer. "Light 'em up. Signal *Duncan* weapons free!"

The response was immediate. "Two small surface contacts! Bearing three five one. Range eighteen point four miles!"

At the same time, Levi could hear one of his ratings yelling, "ESM report! Strong Square Tie radar emissions, bearing three five one!"

"Fire four Harpoons! Two at each contact."

Four missiles roared away from one of the ship's two Mark 141 launchers.

DPRK *REVOLUTION*

"Five radar contacts, Comrade Captain. Two medium-sized, bearing one seven one, range twenty-nine point five kilometers. Two large and one medium-sized, bearing one six nine, range thirty-five kilometers."

Sohn smiled. He'd been right. He'd found the American convoy. "Inform all units of the position, course, and speed of the enemy."

"Missile alert! Four missiles fired at us from the lead group of enemy vessels!"

Sohn slapped a hand on the bridge railing, making his officers jump. "Very well! Those must be the enemy escorts. If we sink them, our submariner comrades will find it easy to deal with the merchant tubs left afloat." He looked at the chubby weapons officer. The man's face was wet—though whether from salt spray or fear-induced perspiration was beyond Sohn's ability to guess. "Fire our own missiles at the lead enemy vessel. *Avenger* will fire at the other."

The man turned to obey, and Sohn and all the rest ducked away as the *Revolution*'s four SS-N-2C Styx missiles thundered out of their enclosed launchers and sped toward the as-yet-unseen American ships, trailing tongues of fire and choking thick white clouds of missile exhaust.

USS *O'BRIEN*

The radar operator's voice squeaked into a falsetto that would have been comical under other circumstances. "Missiles inbound! I count . . . seven, eight small, high-speed contacts!"

Levi stayed calm. He'd already calculated the odds. "Warn *Duncan*. We'll engage when the inbounds are within range."

The situation he and his ships confronted showed the need for close teamwork. As a Perry-class frigate, the *Duncan* didn't carry the destroyer's big five-inch guns or an ASROC launcher. On the other hand, its Standard SAM missiles far outranged the Sea Sparrows on the *O'Brien*. Essentially, Levi knew, his destroyer was the escort's sword. And the *Duncan* was his shield.

He stood watching the CIC's display screens, listening to the chatter from the men around him as the opposing missiles sped toward their respective targets. For the moment he was as much a bystander as if he'd never taken a Navy commission. This battle was in the hands of the computers and the men who served them.

He watched as six Standards raced out from the *Duncan* toward the first group of four North Korean missiles. The rival groups merged in just thirty seconds, and three of the Styx missiles disappeared—blown out of the sky. The fourth kept coming. Two more Standards reached out and intercepted it while it was still more than ten miles from the *O'Brien*. Four others met the second wave of Styx missiles and drowned two of them. The two survivors made it to within seven miles before they were shot down by the destroyer's own Sea Sparrows.

At the same time, the *O'Brien*'s four Harpoons skimmed the waves on their way toward the NK Osas. Aware of the threat, the two North Korean boats turned and fled north, jinking wildly from side to side in a vain attempt to shake off the pair of American missiles pursuing each of them. Their close defense weapons missed, and Levi kept his eyes on the radar plot as the Harpoons struck, annihilating their targets in a series of blinding explosions. All the screen showed was a sudden absence of any blips. But sixty North Korean sailors were dead.

Levi heard the collective sigh of relief from his CIC crew and felt the tension draining away from all around him. Some of that was good, but too much relaxation on their part would be bad. He brought them back on guard with a rapid series of orders. "Signal the convoy to resume normal steaming positions, course, and speed. Mr. Keegan?"

"Yes, Captain?"

"Slow to twelve knots and take us back to the front of the convoy."

"Aye, aye, sir."

Satisfied that his men were back in hand and paying attention to their duties, Levi allowed himself his own slight smile of relief.

The action had taken just over two minutes.

ABOARD THE DPRK *ADMIRAL YI*, EAST OF TSUSHIMA

"Sonar reports multiple explosions bearing three four three, Comrade Captain."

The North Korean captain's pockmarked face looked up at the interruption. He'd been jotting down notes for his next political lecture. The captain had never been a particularly agile public orator, and he found it difficult to speak coherently, especially when using the standard Party jargon. As a result, he often found himself trying to cram additional preparation time in whenever he could—even while his submarine was busy hunting an enemy convoy.

"Explosions? Any other noise—propellers, sonars, that sort of thing?"

"No, Comrade Captain. Just the explosions."

The captain grunted, unsurprised that his sonar operators hadn't heard anything more. In these confined waters the

Romeo-class submarine's Feniks passive sonar was lucky to pick up any kind of sound within five kilometers.

"Very well. I'll come forward."

With a stifled groan he stood up from his narrow writing desk and waddled forward to the Control Room. His chief officers were all there waiting for him. He fixed his eyes on the senior lieutenant. "Anything more to report?"

"No, Comrade Captain. There have been no further explosions or other sonar contacts."

"I see. Well, let's take a look at what's going on. Raise the periscope."

The captain waited for the scope to come all the way up out of its housing before stooping to stare through the eye-pieces. Something in the *Admiral Yi*'s plain fare had given him a severe case of indigestion—indigestion that made sharp movement painful. "Nothing there."

He started to spin the scope through a full circle. After all, he might as well check the whole horizon while he was at it. . . .

ABOARD HOTEL THREE

"So I said, 'Sorry, babe, I'm fresh out of quarters.' Man, you should have seen the look in that bimbo's eyes. Talk about pissed off . . ." Hotel Three's pilot broke off as he saw something strange off the helicopter's port side. "Holy God! That's a mothafuckin' periscope!"

The SH-2F Sea Sprite dipped and spun round to face the long, thin cylindrical object sticking six inches above the sea. Sunlight sparkled off the lens. There couldn't be any doubt that it was a periscope.

"Want an active buoy?" the helo's copilot asked, still stunned by the suddenness of it all. Not one of their passive buoys had picked the submarine up. Not one.

"Hell, no! Drop a torp! Left search pattern," the pilot snapped as he brought the Sea Sprite into hover right over the spot where the rest of the enemy submarine had to be.

"Weapon away!" The helicopter lurched upward, freed from the weight of the Mark 46 as it plunged into the sea. It acquired the enemy submarine within seconds and dove straight for it.

The captain and crew of the DPRK submarine *Admiral Yi* died without ever knowing they were under attack or even how close they'd come to finding the American convoy.

ABOARD THE DPRK *GREAT LEADER* NEAR THE NORTHWEST TIP OF TSUSHIMA

Chun sat rigid, holding the *Revolution*'s last contact report crumpled in his hand. His plans had failed. His forces had attacked piecemeal and they'd been defeated piecemeal. Worse yet, the Americans were ahead of him—a fact that would make it difficult, if not completely impossible, to successfully intercept them.

"Do you have any change to make in our orders, sir?" His first officer sounded solicitous. Chun's lips thinned. The man was right to worry about him. A failure now would erase any memory of Chun's earlier successes and would probably result in his being stripped of command, rank, and all their accompanying privileges.

He shook his head. "No. Carry on with your duties, comrade." He tried to smile and partially succeeded. "We'll catch them yet."

The first officer smiled back and nodded. "Of course, Comrade Captain." He started to turn away and then stopped. "Would you care for some tea, Captain?"

This time Chun's smile was more genuine. Tea would be just the thing to help settle his nerves and occupy his mind during the long quiet run ahead. "Indeed, comrade. And have the cook prepare enough for all of us. After all, you know I hate to drink alone."

Polite laughter greeted his small jest.

SIERRA FIVE

"Hear anything?"

The sonarman sat straighter in his chair and stretched weary muscles. His back was killing him. "Nope, Skipper. Not a peep on any of the buoys. Maybe we got 'em all."

"Maybe." The P-3's pilot didn't sound convinced. "Anyway, this is why Uncle Sam sends us such big monthly checks. So stay sharp, guys. Only four more hours till we have to land and refuel."

The expected groans met his announcement. They'd already been airborne for eight hours.

DPRK *GREAT LEADER*

The chief cook grumbled to himself as he bustled about in the *Great Leader*'s tiny galley. Officers! First do this. Then do that. And none of them appreciated the difficult conditions under which he worked. They wanted tea prepared—tea for all of them to guzzle. Well, he'd be willing to bet that not a single one of them realized his tiny electric burners could only boil two kettles of water at a time. Yes, he'd wager a month's ration books on that.

He rummaged through storage cabinets, looking for the special tea leaves the sub's officers insisted on using and cursing under his breath all the while. Behind him, one of the kettles started to whistle thinly. Too soon, damn it! The cook spun round to turn the burner down.

Disaster struck. As he turned, his elbow knocked a stack of metal pots off the shelf. Instead of simply falling quietly onto the *Great Leader*'s rubber-coated deck, they tumbled and clattered against each other all the way down. Startled by the sudden noise, the cook slipped and his hand landed palm-first on the boiling kettle. The man's scream echoed throughout the submarine.

Chun reacted instantly. "Slow to five knots! Rig for silent running! And tell that fool to shut up!"

SIERRA FIVE

"Transient! I have a metallic transient and other noise on number forty!" The sonar operator's shout brought the Orion around in a tight turn, orbiting around the plotted position of sonobuoy number forty.

"Anything?"

The sonarman shook his head unconsciously before realizing that his commander couldn't see him. "Negative, Skipper. Whatever's down there just went real quiet. And I mean quiet. Like, they're doing a pretty good impression of being a plain, old, harmless water molecule."

Forward in the cockpit, the P-3's pilot considered that. Any sub that could stay that silent was a damned big threat to the convoy, and it would probably be impossible to localize with passive sensors alone. On the other hand, staying that quiet also meant it couldn't be moving very fast. Which meant it was still close at hand. He clicked his mike, "Frank?"

"Yeah, Skipper?" the Orion's tactical coordinator answered.

"Drop a DICASS. I think we can ping on this guy."

"You got it."

The active sonobuoy splashed down noiselessly into the water and unreeled its hydrophone.

"Activate."

Sound waves pulsed out through the water in widening circles, seeking something solid to bounce off. They found it.

"Bingo! Sonar contact bearing one four five. Range fifteen hundred yards!"

DPRK *GREAT LEADER*

Piinng!

"They have us, Captain."

Chun nodded. The noise was too loud for any other possible conclusion. "Take us to periscope depth, comrade. We'll scratch this flea off our back." He hoped his voice conveyed his confidence.

Although detected by some kind of American ASW aircraft, they still had a chance. Its Soviet builders had equipped the *Great Leader* to deal with such a contingency. The submarine's periscope mast carried an SA-N-8 SAM system. Now Chun and his crew would learn whether or not the system was worth the added expense.

Piinng!

"Up periscope!"

vived the ejection process relatively intact, but he knew it had taken a lot out of him. He felt a little light-headed and had to

SIERRA FIVE

"Contact bearing steady, range one thousand yards."

The P-3's pilot eased his throttle back, settling the plane into its attack run.

"Look! Dead ahead!"

He followed his copilot's pointing finger. Their target had raised its periscope well above the water. It made a good aiming mark. But what was that box attached to the scope?

"Jesus!" His startled shout was echoed by the other man in the cockpit as a finger of orange-red flame suddenly erupted from the box.

The missile flew straight into the Orion's outer starboard engine and exploded—throwing red-hot fragments into the turboprop's fuel lines and fans. It seized up and fireballed. The P-3 dropped toward the water with its starboard wing trailing flame.

"Feather number four and activate extinguishers!" He held the Orion on course while the copilot and flight engineer worked frantically to put the fire out.

"Range five hundred yards." The sonar crew was still on duty.

"Dump that torpedo!"

The pilot felt the Orion lift momentarily as the Mark 46 released. He pulled back on the control, trying to gain altitude.

"Skipper, the fire's out of control. It's gonna—"

Sierra Five exploded in midair.

DPRK *GREAT LEADER*

Chun watched pieces of the American plane fall into the sea and grinned. "We got him! We killed the American bastard!"

"Captain! High-speed screws bearing three two five! Range close!"

Chun pulled his head away from the periscope and whispered, "And he has killed us . . ."

Then he recovered and roared, "Left full rudder! Flank speed!"

He had to try to save his boat—not just for himself and for

his crew, but for his country as well. The *Great Leader* was North Korea's most modern, most effective submarine. Without it, the North's already uphill battle to interdict the South's sea lines of communication would become completely unwinnable. American reinforcements and materiel would flow virtually unchallenged into the South's teeming harbors.

Chun felt the *Great Leader*'s deck cant as it turned, slowly at first, but faster as the submarine's speed picked up.

It was still too slow. When the American torpedo reached its target area, the *Great Leader* was moving at just nine knots. That wasn't fast enough for Chun's abruptly ordered turn to form the "knuckle" of disturbed water needed to confuse the torpedo's onboard sonar.

Instead, the torpedo steered right through the patch of mild turbulence, corrected its course slightly, and then drove straight into the *Great Leader*, striking just aft of its conning tower.

The Mark 46 exploded and ripped open a gaping hole in the *Great Leader*'s pressure hull. The submarine flooded in seconds and settled to the bottom on its side, trailing a stream of bubbling air, debris, and fuel oil.

North Korea's prewar naval strategy sank with it.

ABOARD THE USS *O'BRIEN*, IN PUSAN HARBOR

Captain Richard Levi swept his eyes over the rows of merchant ships riding at anchor in Pusan harbor and then looked back at the three moored closest to the *O'Brien*. The *Andrew T. Thomas*, *Polar Sea*, and the *Thorvaldsen*. He'd done it. He and his crews had brought their ungainly charges to safety. Now gangs of South Korean longshoremen swarmed over the three, unloading their precious cargos for immediate shipment to the front. Levi permitted his shoulders to sag ever so slightly. Now he could rest.

"Captain?"

He turned to find a signals rating waiting. "Yes?"

"Message from Seventh Fleet, sir. Marked urgent."

Levi took the message and scanned it. Almost imperceptibly he straightened. Relaxation would have to wait.

"New orders, Captain?" his executive officer asked.

"Yes, Mr. Keegan." He looked out across the crowded harbor again, focusing on a group of gray-painted Navy ships anchored together near Pusan's largest dock. "We've been assigned to the amphibious group assembling here. We'll join the escort when it sails north."

For a moment he stared at the massive amphibious transports and helicopter carriers riding uneasily at anchor. It was time to strike back. Time to cut the North Koreans off at the knees. Then Levi turned away from the sight. He and his officers had a lot of work to do before the *O'Brien* would be ready to get under way again, and not enough hours to do it in. He didn't have time to waste.

C H A P T E R
39
High Tide

JANUARY 7—UN FORCES HEADQUARTERS, SOUTH OF CH'ONAN

McLaren stood motionless for a moment, listening to the wind howling outside the command tent. His breath misted in the chill air before vanishing. It was so cold outside that not even the headquarters' most powerful oil-fired heaters could do more than make things inside the tent barely livable. He snorted, reminding himself that conditions were infinitely worse for the fighting troops on the front lines. They existed in a kind of frozen hell, unable to stay warm unless they moved and liable to be killed by enemy fire if they moved. He shook his head wearily. Christ, if either side in this war were really civilized they'd have long since called the fighting off on account of weather. With things as they were, both sides might even be taking more casualties from frostbite than from enemy action.

The Combined Forces J-3, Major General Barret Smith, moved up beside him, tamping tobacco into his pipe.

"How much longer, Barney?"

Smith lit a match and puffed his pipe into life. "The Met boys say this latest cold snap should lift by morning. Their satellites show another warm front moving through by then, and that could raise temperatures by up to forty degrees."

"Still be below freezing, then?"

The dour-faced New Englander nodded.

"More snow expected?"

"Yes."

McLaren frowned. Now that the UN forces had achieved almost complete air superiority, he begrudged every snowstorm. They limited his air support to the available all-weather attack squadrons—several of which had been worn down to uselessness by cumulative losses. He wanted clear skies so his fighter-bombers could hammer the NK columns from the air and see the SAMs reaching up for them from the ground. Every hour of limited visibility gave the North Koreans time to recover from previous aerial poundings, and McLaren didn't want to give them a minute's rest.

Smith interrupted his thoughts. "Staff's ready for the briefing, Jack."

"Coming." He turned on his heel and strode back to the main table—now covered with charts showing the rugged hills around Ch'onan. McLaren's eyes narrowed as he saw the markings of planned defensive positions scattered across the maps, but he stayed silent. Instead, he looked around the table at the shadowed faces of his senior staff. They looked tired, but not as exhausted as they had in the first days following North Korea's surprise attack. War, like all other human occupations, had its own rhythms, and his officers were beginning to adjust to them. "Okay, gentlemen, let's get down to it."

Smith stepped further into the light. "Certainly, General." He bent over the map table. "Now, as you can see, we've laid out a proposed—"

"Hold it, Barney." McLaren shook his head. "Let's start at the top first. I want an overall brief before we get into the small-scale stuff."

The J-3 took the pipe out of his mouth, surprised. But he recovered fast enough. "Of course, Jack, whatever you say. Colonel Logan?"

Logan took Smith's place under the light and launched into a detailed evaluation of the military situation across the whole Korean peninsula. The J-2 spoke plainly, only occasionally referring to his notes when McLaren asked an unexpected question. Of all the headquarters staff, the colonel had been the most changed by the war. His old, lazy, "get along, go along" attitude toward the job had sloughed off—replaced by a hard-driving determination to get the facts, no matter what the cost in sleepless hours or even lives. It was as if Logan were burning himself up from within to make up for his failure to predict North Korea's invasion.

The picture he painted was mixed.

First, Seoul had not been seriously attacked, despite being surrounded on all sides. Instead, the five second-line North Korean infantry divisions besieging the South Korean capital had contented themselves with heavy artillery bombardments directed at suspected UN defensive positions and with half-hearted thrusts aimed at the city's water and power supplies. All had been repulsed. On the other hand, civilian casualties in Seoul were growing, and all attempts at air resupply had failed miserably. Even so, the South Korean garrison commander estimated he could hold out for several weeks under the present conditions. And the raids launched by his Special Forces units were tying down a large number of NK troops needed at the front.

Conditions were similar along the rugged eastern half of the DMZ. The ROK units there had thrown back every North Korean attack on their positions and saw no difficulty in holding their ground indefinitely. At the same time, their commanders saw little prospect of being able to go over onto the offensive. Neither side could hope to make significant gains in an area so crisscrossed by natural and man-made defenses.

The news in the air war was less ambiguous. After fourteen days of unpleasant surprises and heavy losses, the UN edge in equipment and air combat training was beginning to pay off. North Korea's most modern fighter and ground-attack squadrons had been decimated, and its small force of surviving pilots and planes had been almost completely withdrawn from combat—pulled back to defend Pyongyang and the North's other cities. Kim Jong-Il and his marshals clearly expected the Americans to repeat the devastating strategic bombing campaigns that had been so successful during the first Korean War. McLaren's U.S. Air Force liaison officer smiled sourly at that. He'd just gotten off the phone with the USAF Chief of Staff. Growing tension with the Soviet Union had forced the President to cancel the planned transfer of an F-111 bomber wing from Europe. So there wouldn't be any bombing of North Korean cities—not for the foreseeable future. This air war would be waged solely on the tactical level.

The war at sea was also being won. The carrier air wings operating off the *Constellation* and *Nimitz* were back up to strength, and the Navy's escort forces could now guarantee an uninterrupted flow of seaborne supplies into Pusan and Pohang. Confronted by superior technology, training, and numbers, North Korea's navy had virtually ceased to exist as a viable fighting force.

All of which brought Logan to the most important theater of the war—the land battle along South Korea's western coast. Everything else hinged on the outcome there. Victory against North Korea's armored spearheads would ratify the UN Command's hard-won successes in the air and at sea. Defeat would render them meaningless.

Logan's verdict was short and painfully blunt. "That's where we're getting our ass kicked, General. The troops we've committed to this area are just plain fought out. They've been in action for two weeks now and they need help. Oh, sure, supplies are getting through for once, that doesn't change the fact that our boys are outnumbered, outgunned, and out of luck."

Several of his South Korean staff officers murmured at Logan's lack of tact, but McLaren simply smiled. The colonel was absolutely right. He looked at Smith. "Recommendation, Barney?"

The tall New Englander came back to the map table. "Simply this, General. We've been surrendering eight to ten kilometers of ground every day, just to keep from being surrounded and crushed. That's got to stop, and we"—he gestured at the assembled staff officers—"believe this is the place to do it.'' His pipe rested on the map showing the ridges and hills around Ch'onan.

"Oh?"

"Yes, sir. We've made the calculations and believe that, by using the divisions held out thus far as reserves, we could hold these positions indefinitely.'' Smith's hand traced the line of ridges. He stepped back a pace and stood waiting.

McLaren shook his head decisively. "No."

Several officers moved forward in protest. "But General, if you'd just . . ."

"We could stop 'em cold on . . ."

"Sir, we've got to do someth . . ."

He held up a hand. "Gentlemen." They shut up. "I'm not interested in just holding our ground. That's how we got into this mess the first war around, back in '52 and '53. I don't want a replay of that stalemate. I want victory."

His eyes settled on a figure waiting quietly off to the side. "Doug, go ahead and start setting up my dog-and-pony show."

As his aide moved forward to the table, McLaren continued, "Gentlemen, what I'm about to tell you must not go outside this tent. The maps Captain Hansen is laying out contain the bare-bones outlines of an operation I've code-named Thunderbolt. And if I hear any one of you so much as whisper that name anywhere but here, I'll personally kick your ass. Is that clear?"

Heads nodded.

Hansen finished and stepped back, clearing the way for the others to study his handiwork. McLaren heard gasps from around the table.

He grinned. "I'm gonna start by telling you that the trouble isn't that our troops have been giving up too much ground. The trouble is they've been giving up too little ground. Now, here's what I mean by that . . ."

McLaren spoke for nearly half an hour, without notes and with complete conviction, stabbing the maps with an unlit cigar to emphasize particular points. While speaking, he kept his eyes fixed on the faces of all around him, ready to pounce on the faintest sign of doubt or disagreement. He knew that he had to win these men over. For security reasons he'd kept his staff largely in the dark while formulating Thunderbolt, but now he needed their wholehearted support to make the plan work. He'd have enough trouble selling the plan to the Joint Chiefs and the two presidents without worrying about dissension among his own subordinates.

He closed with a single admonition. "Taejon is the key, gentlemen. That's where we're going to make Uncle Kim's bastards think they've hit a solid, brick wall." He slapped a hand onto the map, all five fingers covering the outlines of the city of Taejon. "Right there. We're going to hold the NKs by the nose, while we kick 'em in the ass."

McLaren smiled at the chorus of approving growls that greeted his statement. They were with him, just as he'd hoped they would be. The urge to hit back, to counterpunch, had been growing with every kilometer they'd retreated. Even his South Korean officers seemed willing to gamble with more of their territory in return for the payoff Thunderbolt promised. "All right. Let's break this up for now. You each know what needs to be done. So let's get it done. Our next meeting is set for oh five hundred hours, tomorrow, and I want to see some preliminary logistics schedules, extra deception plans, and proposed assembly points by then. Any questions?"

Hansen caught his eye and pointed toward the satellite communications gear banked along one wall of the tent. McLaren nodded and looked back at his staff. "None? Good. Dismissed then, gentlemen. And I'll see you all dark and early in the morning."

Several men chuckled, but most simply saluted gravely and dispersed to their desks in the main tent or in the other command trailers.

McLaren turned to Hansen. "What's up?"

"Washington's on the horn, sir. The Chairman wants to speak with you, pronto. The NSC wants a full briefing from the Joint Chiefs on things over here at its next evening meeting. And the Chiefs want to include your views."

For a second McLaren's temper threatened to flare at the unwanted interruption. Then his irritation faded. Phil Simpson had actually been damn good about keeping the D.C. bureaucrats off his back. And so had the President. Both men had bent over backward to avoid trying to micromanage the war from ten thousand miles away. But it was about time that he let the good admiral and the Commander in Chief in on his plans. High time in fact.

He picked up the phone.

JANUARY 8—FIRST SHOCK ARMY HQ, NORTH OF SONGT'AN

Colonel General Cho Hyun-Jae clambered down out of his camouflaged command trailer and smiled appreciatively up into the white, snowflake-filled sky. His II Corps commander stood waiting for him at the bottom of the steps. "Ah, Chyong. I see you've brought me a gift of good weather."

Lieutenant General Chyong smiled back dutifully. His superior usually left all attempts at humor to him. And with good reason, he judged.

Abruptly Cho's smile faded. "Walk with me, Chyong. What news from the front?"

"The news is good, sir. My spearheads advanced more than eleven kilometers yesterday, and they report even lighter opposition this morning. The enemy's resistance on the ground seems to be crumbling."

Cho stopped walking and eyed his subordinate closely. "Are they retreating in order or in panic?"

"Not in panic," Chyong was forced to admit. "But they have been abandoning very strong natural defensive positions without putting up any real fight." He paused and then went on, "Their behavior is hard to characterize. It is not really a fighting withdrawal, and yet they show no signs of collapsing morale."

Cho shrugged. "Fortunately we are not being called upon to characterize the enemy's behavior. The Dear Leader is content so long as our armies move forward." He looked uneasy. "But I admit, I would feel more comfortable if I knew what this Yankee, McLaren"—he mangled the name—"had up his sleeve. There are disturbing intelligence reports of troops being held in reserve."

"What about our air reconnaissance?"

Cho laughed and allowed a touch of bitterness to creep into his voice. "Our Air Force comrades have refused my latest request. Apparently their last camera-equipped MiG-21R was shot down over Pusan three days ago. Naturally they assure me that our Russian friends will soon deliver more modern reconnaissance aircraft. Supposedly they will then be in a position to consider the Army's needs."

He shook his head. "So, Chyong, we are forced to rely on the Research Department and its spies for any information from Pusan. And who knows if any of them have managed to avoid the puppet government's counterspies?"

The two men walked on for several minutes in silence, circling the carefully hidden headquarters complex under a steady rain of softly falling flakes. Artillery thundered momentarily, somewhere off to the south. At last Cho turned back toward his command trailer. He stopped at the foot of its snow-covered steps and straightened his back. "Is there anything I can get for you, Chyong? Or for your men?"

Chyong studied his commander carefully. "My staff is drawing up a formal series of requests for your consideration, sir."

"Spare me the paperwork, Chyong. Just give me the gist for now. Let the bureaucrats worry about the details later."

The lieutenant general bobbed his head in gratitude. He'd always appreciated Cho's prejudice for action. It matched his own temperament. "Very well, then. Most important of all, I need more supplies delivered more consistently. At the moment my infantry battalions and tank crews are subsisting on captured enemy stores, and my artillery units have less than a day's worth of ready ammunition available."

Cho frowned. He hadn't known that things were as bad as that. Some supply problems had been foreseen during the planning for Red Phoenix. In fact, they'd been judged to be inevitable given the enemy's anticipated destruction of bridges, roads, and rail lines. But prewar staff assessments had all assumed that the difficulties could be overcome by a rapid, unrelenting advance and by the careful management of resources.

The First Shock Army's commander almost smiled. He should have known better than to rely on estimates rather than on reality. His logistics staffers must have been shading the truth to conceal their own failures. If Chyong's figures were accurate, the enemy's air strikes were slowly strangling the ability of the People's Army to continue its offensive. And going on the defensive to build up new forward stockpiles of food, ammunition, and spare parts was unthinkable. Losing the initiative would mean losing the war.

Fortunately there was a solution. One that had worked well during the North's first try to liberate the South. It was cumbersome, yes, and overly manpower-intensive. But it would work.

He looked at Chyong, still waiting motionless as snow coated the stars on his shoulder tabs. "You were quite correct to bring this situation to my attention, comrade. I'll take immediate steps to get you the supplies you need."

Seeing the other man's raised eyebrow, Cho explained. "From now on, supplies will move only by night or on days like this. And the convoys will avoid routes the enemy has already targeted. We'll build new bridges and use porters through otherwise impassable terrain if need be. Finally, I shall see to it that our air defenses are strengthened."

Chyong nodded his understanding. Such measures had enabled the Chinese to supply large armies in the South from 1951 to 1953, despite the overwhelming air superiority enjoyed by the imperialists. As a young officer he'd studied the system thoroughly and come away impressed both by its effectiveness and its extravagant use of raw manpower. And that last element raised a question that needed to be asked.

Cho seemed to read his mind. "You want to know where all the men for this will come from? Not from your command, I assure you. The high command has placed two more rifle divisions—the Twelfth and the Thirty-first—under my authority. We'll use them as human pack animals instead of combat soldiers. Better that they should serve the Liberation with their backs than add to our other burdens, eh?"

Chyong's eyes showed his amusement and agreement.

Cho didn't allow himself to feel any trace of doubt about his decision until after his subordinate was gone. He'd planned to use the two new divisions to strengthen his advancing army's flanks. Was it wise to sacrifice the additional security they could have provided? He stood uncertainly in the doorway to his trailer, torn by indecision. Perhaps he should cancel those plans and simply rely on improving the army's existing supply systems.

Then reason returned. There would be no extra security

involved in placing additional troops on the line if he couldn't supply them. He needed combat power, not useless mouths. Cho turned his back on the gloomy skies and entered his trailer. The morning's first briefing was already long overdue.

JANUARY 9—ECHO COMPANY, NORTH OF CHOCH'IWON

The dull, coughing sound of twin explosions rolled across the flatlands and echoed off the steep, rocky hill above the highway.

"Good shooting, Private Park!" Kevin laid an approving hand on the shoulder of the South Korean reservist manning 3rd Platoon's Dragon launcher.

The man smiled shyly and bowed his head in thanks at the compliment.

A thousand meters away, two North Korean T-62 tanks burned in fiery testimony to Park's skill. His missile had slammed squarely into one and exploded, catching the second T-62 inside the resulting fireball. On either side of the dead tanks, other enemy vehicles hastily dispersed, some behind the dense white puffs thrown by onboard smoke dischargers. APCs disgorged their infantry, who promptly sought cover in roadside ditches.

Kevin studied the apparent confusion in satisfaction. His ambush, as expected, had forced the North Koreans to deploy for battle—a maneuver that wasted precious time and fuel. He watched for a couple of minutes more, making sure, and then let the binoculars fall back onto his chest. It was time to head out.

"Lieutenant Rhee!" Rhee's head popped up from beside a boulder. "Move your people back to the next position. We've done enough here."

The Korean nodded and started bellowing orders. Kevin stood aside as the files of white-camouflaged soldiers began slipping past him, down the slope toward the valley spreading out below this last hill. He glanced toward the road. Were the North Koreans reacting any faster this time?

Nope, the NK column was still trying to shake itself out into attack order. From the look of things, it would be at least another ten minutes before they could advance against what they assumed was an enemy-held hill. Kevin would have liked to have met their expectations. The terrain was perfect, too steep for tanks and with too little cover for attacking infantry. Even a small number of defenders wouldn't have had much trouble bloodying a much larger assaulting force.

He sighed. Orders were orders.

Even when they didn't make any sense.

For the last seven days, they'd been retreating virtually nonstop—halting just long enough to delay the North Koreans, inflict a few casualties, and then hustle on. At first he and his men hadn't minded. They took fewer casualties in that kind of running fight. But as the retreat went on and on, they'd started to question the sanity of the higher-ups. The UN forces had been abandoning defensive positions that could have been held. Why? And where were the reinforcements promised from the States and from South Korea's enormous pool of trained reserves?

This latest withdrawal made even less sense than all the others. Once past this range of rugged hills, the North Korean spearheads would again enter flat, open ground—ground perfect for tanks and other armored vehicles. And the next really defensible position lay along the Paekma River, thirty kilometers south and just a few kilometers north of the city of Taejon. Christ, how far did the generals plan to let the NKs go before they did something?

Kevin rubbed a weary hand over his face, glad that the weather had warmed up enough to let him dispense with the makeshift scarf he'd had to wear over his mouth and nose when the last Siberian cold front had roared through—plunging temperatures well below zero. One of his men had frozen to death on guard duty that last hellish night. What was his name? Costello. Try as he might, he couldn't remember the man's face. But he'd never forget that pathetic corpse, huddled stiff and blue at the bottom of a one-man foxhole. Not in a million years.

He followed his men down the hill.

JAUNUARY 10—HIGHWAY 1, NEAR TAEGU

The long convoys of green-painted trucks filled every south-bound lane, moving at high speed past groups of refugees forced to the side of the road. Each had its canvas covers tightly closed, for protection against both the weather and prying eyes, but several still bore markings that identified them as belonging to the U.S. 3rd Marine Division.

One of the refugees, a wizened, old farmer, shrugged his pack onto the pavement and stood straight as the trucks roared by. As a young man he had served beside the Marines in the battle for the Pusan perimeter. Mustering the English he'd picked up then, he called out, "Hey, Mac! Where're you heading?"

A youthful Marine corporal stuck his head out the window of one of the passing trucks and yelled back, "To kick some communist ass!"

Cheers followed the trucks on their way down the road toward Pusan.

JANUARY 11—NEAR THE EMBARKATION AREA, PUSAN, SOUTH KOREA

Shin Dal-Kon was a realistic man. And as a realistic man, he understood that the odds were greatly against his living to see another day. But Shin was also a dedicated man, and he had a duty to perform. A duty that would surely kill him.

He moistened his lips and stared out again through the window, counting ships and vehicles. Shin's small gift shop was perfectly placed, within easy walking distance of the Pusan railway station and less than five hundred meters from the harbor's main docks. During the summer months the store was usually clogged with foreign visitors buying trinkets or postcards—a condition that made other, less ordinary exchanges ludicrously easy.

In fact, his masters in Pyongyang now considered Shin Dal-Kon their top agent in Pusan. Or so they'd always told him, he thought wryly. Certainly he was one of the longest-lived. The short, bald, ordinary-looking man had served the North continuously since 1963.

But now that service was about to come to a sudden end. And all because of Pyongyang's desperate need for information about what the Americans were up to. His control's last signal had ordered him to report any significant findings by radio—and without delay.

He wondered, did the desk-sitters up North know they'd ordered his death in the same signal? Shin had survived for more than twenty-five years for a single, good reason—he was always careful. No dispatch ever followed the same route or ever went through fewer than three cut-outs before it started north. And Shin had never, never used any of the radios which he'd been issued. South Korea's radio-direction-finding units were too skilled to toy with. They could pinpoint an illicit radio transmitter in minutes. That was a lesson Shin had learned secondhand and never forgotten. But now he had to ignore it.

Despite tight security, the American effort was too obvious to be missed. Seemingly endless convoys of trucks crowding the dockyard's roads; warships moored offshore while transports anchored alongside massive cargo cranes; stern-faced security detachments on every street corner, and perhaps most significantly, the complete disappearance of the rowdy American sailors who'd once thronged Pusan's bars and brothels. They all spelled one thing to the North Korean agent: amphibious invasion. Soon the American armada would depart, and Pyongyang had to be ready for its reappearance at some point along the coast.

And so Shin had to sound the warning. And so Shin would die, as soon as South Korea's security forces broke down his shop's door.

He put down the notepad containing his coded signal and went down the stairs and out into his small garden. Carefully he levered frozen soil away at one corner of the garden, knelt, and gingerly lifted a heavy earthenware pot of the kind used to ferment kimchee. Shin hefted the pot and brought it back inside before lifting its top to reveal the ultramodern shortwave radio concealed inside.

Working quickly, partly from fear and partly from an impatient desire to see the thing done, he raised the whip-thin aerial, made sure the frequency setting was correct, and began transmitting.

NSP MOBILE MONITORING UNIT 67, NEAR THE EMBARKATION AREA

The traffic-battered minivan looked like any of the thousands of similar vehicles scattered across South Korea's city streets. But instead of dried fish, cooking oil, or sacks of rice, it contained an array of highly sophisticated radio listening devices.

The senior duty agent for the National Security Planning Agency's Pusan Station leaned over the operator's shoulder. "Anything yet?"

The man nodded abruptly as faint beeps emerged from his equipment. "Yes, he's just started transmitting."

The agent smiled and keyed his own transmitter. "All units report in and stand by for my signal."

Acknowledgments flooded through his headphones. Satisfied, the NSP agent moved back to the other man. "Well?"

"He's still transmitting, sir. This one is either very slow or very unpracticed."

"The latter, I believe," the NSP man said. "This man is no ordinary spy. He's a big fish, and like all big fish he's swum in the depths for years. I suspect he's not happy at being this close to the surface." He stopped, conscious of having been too talkative.

But the equipment operator hadn't even really been listening. "He's stopped!"

"You're certain?"

An emphatic nod.

The NSP agent keyed his transmitter again. "Take him."

THE GIFT SHOP

The Special Forces captain finished attaching the short-fused plastic explosive, triggered it, and ducked back as the gift shop's front door blew in. Two men in gas masks and carrying submachine guns rolled in through the opening, right behind the explosion. Others waited outside, covering every other possible exit.

Seconds passed. Then the captain heard a stun grenade go off and followed his men in. A stretcher team came close behind.

Rapid impressions filtered through his mind as he took the stairs to the second floor two at a time. Swirling smoke. Scorched wall hangings. And then a small room crowded with his troopers, a radio, and a body.

The captain lifted his gas mask and caught the faint whiff of almond still lingering in the air. "Report."

"He's dead, sir. Took a cyanide capsule before we tossed the stunner in."

Undoubtedly true. These men were very competent. And completely trustworthy. "Never mind. We've got what we wanted."

THE MINISTRY OF DEFENSE, PYONGYANG, NORTH KOREA

The heaters in the underground command bunker worked far too well, unlike most products of the North Korean workers' state. And so Kim Jong-Il and the other Military Commission members sweltered in summerlike heat while above them Pyongyang's streets lay buried under several feet of snow and ice. The sweat streaming down his face did not improve Kim's temper.

"So, Colonel General Cho reports that his troops have crossed the Paekma River in no fewer than three places. Surely that is good news enough for you."

"Indeed it is, Dear Leader. But . . ."

Kim frowned. He'd long suspected the speaker, the secretary of communications, of being a covert member of the party's Chinese faction. He'd never been able to prove it, though. Not to his father's satisfaction. Well, the old man was faltering. It wouldn't be long before all the reins of power were firmly gathered in his hands. "But what? Come, come, Comrade Secretary, don't be coy with us. What troubles you now?"

"Cho also reports that he has taken heavy casualties from imperialist air strikes, and that his supply lines are stretched to the limit. I question his ability to continue the advance until air superiority can be regained—"

"That would be extraordinarily foolish!" Kim snapped. "Obviously, as a civilian, you cannot be expected to remember the vital role momentum plays in achieving victory, but I have not forgotten it." He watched the communications secretary flush at the unjustified gibe. As a teenager the man had fought in the first Fatherland Liberation War—winning several medals for his heroic devotion to duty.

"In any event," Kim continued, "I have directed our ambassador in Moscow to press our Russian friends for additional combat aircraft and pilots. With them in hand we shall sweep the skies clear of imperialist aircraft."

Several of the old men around the table looked openly skeptical, and Kim made a mental note to have each of them watched more carefully.

An aide entered and bent low to whisper something in the ear of the Research Department's director. The director signaled for Kim's attention. "Dear Leader, I have urgent news from our agent in Pusan. His findings confirm preliminary conclusions our best analysts had already drawn from Soviet satellite photographs. The Americans are preparing an amphibious force for a descent somewhere along our coast. They have assembled enough ships to carry at least thirty-five thousand men."

Murmurs swept around the table. Many present remembered the catastrophe of Inchon and the subsequent UN drive deep into North Korea. They wanted no repetition of that nightmare.

Kim Jong-Il sat and glared. The panicky old fools! They wavered and fretted at the first sign of difficulty. He turned to the admiral in charge of the Naval Command. "There should be no difficulty in any of this. Assemble your submarines and ambush the Yankees as they steam north. We'll send their bandit Marines to a watery grave!"

A sudden silence greeted his words, broken at last only by the half-whispered words of the admiral. "I have no submarines left to send, Dear Leader. All the ones in the northern Yellow Sea have been sunk."

Sunk? Every one of them? Kim grasped for words. "Why wasn't I informed of this? What didn't you report it?"

"I have, Dear Leader." The older man's face was unreadable. "My reports on the current naval situation have been delivered to your headquarters daily."

And probably held there by some underling fearful of his

wrath, Kim knew. For the first time in months he felt unsure of his course. Events could be slipping out of his hands and that could be fatal. Most of these men bore him little love. With an effort he regained his composure. "I see. The road we must take is clear. We must acquire the naval forces we need from the Russians. They, at least, have plenty of submarines to spare."

The oldest man at the table, a wizened old survivor of the guerrilla war against the Japanese, coughed delicately into a fragile, blue-veined hand. "First aircraft, and now ships as well. What will the Soviets demand of us in return for all these things? Do we risk handing over our Revolution and sovereignty for these pretty toys?"

"These 'toys,' Comrade Choi, are necessary to win this war." Kim controlled his temper, though with great difficulty. Choi was close to his father. "And once we have won this war, we shall rule Korea. Not the Russians. Not the Chinese. Only the Party and its Great Leader!"

No one debated his assertion, but Kim sensed their continued fear and indecision. He closed his folder abruptly. Very well, then. Enough was enough. They wouldn't accomplish any more this day. "This meeting is adjourned, comrades. We will reconvene tomorrow to review the measures necessary to deal with this seaborne enemy threat."

He left the room without waiting for their reaction. There were urgent signals to be sent to Moscow.

THE MINISTRY OF DEFENSE—MOSCOW, R.S.F.S.R.

The two men sat close together in the vastness of the high-ceilinged office. Oil paintings depicting various triumphs of Russian arms—Borodino, Stalingrad, Kursk, and others—covered the walls in martial splendor. Thick curtains blocked any view of Moscow's empty nighttime streets.

An opened bottle of vodka and a half-eaten loaf of black bread sat on a silver tray next to the two men. Both liked to pretend that they were of simple peasant stock. In reality, both had risen to rank through the intertwined workings of favoritism and seniority, carried higher and higher within the Party—the Soviet Union's version of the Czarist aristocracy.

"Then we are in agreement, comrade?" the minister of defense asked.

The head of the KGB locked his gaze on the other man. "Indeed, my friend, Kim Jong-Il's requests must be met. The war is too evenly balanced for any other decision."

"But the Politburo will vacillate. It may take days to make our 'colleagues' see reason on this matter. And such a delay could be fatal to our cause."

The defense minister's assertion hung unchallenged in the air. At last the KGB director nodded his agreement.

The minister smiled and directed his colleague's attention to a single sheet of paper resting on the low table between them. "I am glad you see the need for swift action, Viktor Ivanovitch. I have prepared an order that should satisfy the most urgent of friend Kim's needs. Read it."

The other man did so and sat back in his chair, a faintly troubled look on his face. "You're quite sure, comrade, that this order can be kept, ah, confidential?"

The defense minister laced his fingers across his stomach and nodded solemnly. "Without a doubt." He reached across the table and tapped the piece of paper. "Should matters go awry, this can be denied. Whatever happens can be explained away as a tragic accident of positioning."

"And the planes?"

"Unfortunately, we cannot hope to handle that so . . . discreetly. The movement of whole squadrons of our finest combat aircraft will be a much more, ah, public, matter. No, I fear the decision will have to be left in the full Politburo's hands."

"And this?" The KGB director's beefy forefinger touched the sheet of paper.

"It will be transmitted to Fleet Headquarters in Vladivostok within the hour."

Each man raised his glass to the other and then downed it with a single gulp.

THE WHITE HOUSE SITUATION ROOM, WASHINGTON, D.C.

Only the slide projector's whirring fan cut through the silence. The two photographs shown side by side were remarkably sharp and full of detail, especially when one remembered that they had been taken by a satellite more than two hundred miles above the earth and moving at more than seventeen thousand miles an hour.

"All right, Blake. What's your interpretation of these pictures?" The President's voice sounded loud in the darkness.

"Hell, I'll admit that they just look like a couple of trains to me."

Blake Fowler shook his head and then remembered that nobody could see the gesture. "Not a couple of trains, Mr. President. One train."

"Explain."

"The first slide, the one on the left, shows a loaded Chinese munitions train sitting in the railyards at Pyongyang. And the second slide, the one on the right shows that same train, still fully loaded, heading back across the border into Manchuria."

"So what?" Putnam didn't bother trying to hide the contempt in his voice. Blake's growing intimacy with the President had rubbed his ego raw. "One lousy train goes back to China. Why bother showing us that?"

"Because, sir, that train crossed the border seven days ago. And we haven't spotted a single shipment of Chinese arms or ammunition in North Korea since. My analysts and I believe that what we are seeing is a de facto withdrawal of the PRC's covert support for the North Korean invasion." Blake drew a breath. "And we believe that could offer us a chance to dramatically shift the balance of forces against the North Koreans." He stopped.

The President's voice showed more interest. "Go on, Blake."

"If the Chinese have stopped their support, there must have been a falling out between them and the North Koreans, maybe temporary, maybe permanent. If the Chinese don't regard Kim as their friend anymore, we may be able to move in."

"What've you got in mind?"

"An overture to the Chinese, sir. An appeal for their aid in bringing this war to a close on acceptable terms."

Putnam snorted derisively. "Jesus Christ, Fowler! You expect us to go begging hat in hand to the PRC? And then you expect them to just see the light and join the side of the angels?"

Blake felt himself flushing with anger. "No, I don't. But I do expect the Chinese government to act in what it perceives as its own best interest. And I believe that we can convince them that lies in our corner."

"How?"

"By offering them a free-trade agreement, loans, credits, and the kind of defensive military technologies they need— sophisticated surface-to-air missiles and antitank guided missiles."

Several of the men and women in the darkened Situation Room tried to speak at the same time, but the President's voice overrode the others. "Have you approached the South Koreans about this proposal?"

"Only at the staff level, Mr. President. Nothing higher than that."

"I see." Blake could see the outline of the President's face in the ghostly glow given off by the slide projector, but he couldn't read the Chief Executive's expression. "What about the timing on this thing? We can't go to Beijing while we're still losing. George is right on that. It would look like we're begging."

"Agreed, sir. That's why we're suggesting that State, Treasury, Commerce, and Defense all develop the specifics necessary while we await results from Thunderbolt. If General McLaren's plan succeeds, we've got the base we need to approach the Chinese."

The President nodded and shifted slightly in his seat, turning to face the secretary of state. "Okay, Paul. What's your reading on Blake's idea? Go or no go?"

Bannerman looked carefully from one man to the other, ignoring Putnam's insistent tug on his sleeve. He'd seen the signs of the shifting power base in the White House long ago. The secretary of state cleared his throat and spoke. "I fully concur with Dr. Fowler's plan, Mr. President. I think it offers the best chance we're going to get to keep this war from escalating beyond our control."

The President nodded abruptly. "Okay, then. Blake, put your proposal in writing and have it on my desk by tomorrow morning. Then we can kick it around a little while we wait to see whether or not this Thunderbolt works." He looked at his watch. "Now, you'll have to forgive me, ladies and gentlemen, but I've go to run. Got a photo opportunity with the Boy Scout of the Year to take care of." He paused, a cynical grin twisted on his face. "As you know, the business of government never ends."

The NSC Crisis Team rose with him and remained standing while he left the room.

JANUARY 12—ECHO COMPANY, NEAR THE CENTER OF TAEJON

Kevin coughed and felt the thick, acrid smoke eddying through the room burn deep into his lungs. He rubbed his watering eyes and cursed softly. There wasn't anywhere you could go to escape the smoke—not when the whole damned city was on fire. He scuttled over to where Montoya squatted, keeping low to avoid showing himself through the sandbagged window.

"India One Two, this is Echo Five Six, India One Two, this is Echo Five Six. Over." The RTO took his finger off the transmit button and shrugged helplessly. "Nothing. I can't get nothing, L-T. Probably too many buildings in the way."

Kevin nodded his understanding. Snarled communications were the rule when fighting in a city. Or so the manual said. The low-powered FM tactical sets issued for battalion, company, and platoon use needed good lines of sight to work, and good lines of sight were impossible to come by in Taejon's concrete jungle of apartment complexes, department stores, and other high-rise buildings.

He spread the tourist map of the city he'd picked up at Battalion HQ only hours before and started reviewing his company's defensive positions. He had minutes at most to make sure there wasn't anything he'd overlooked—some fatal weakness that the North Koreans could exploit. The last word from Major Donaldson had been that the South Korean Reserve units holding on Taejon's outskirts had been overrun. The NKs were on their way and could be expected at any moment. Kevin concentrated on the symbols sketched on the map.

Echo Company held a cluster of buildings on the southern side of Chungang-ro—Chungang Street—Taejon's main east-west boulevard. Corporal McIntyre and 1st Platoon anchored the company's right flank from a three-story apartment building with a view north along Inhyo Street. Kevin had put his CP there since it offered the best view. The three half-strength squads of Sergeant Geary's 2nd Platoon were stationed in small shops along the center of the position. And Rhee's 3rd Platoon, the KATUSAs, occupied buildings looking northwest—out over an open plaza built across the frozen Taejonchon River. Kevin frowned. He'd hoped to occupy the Chungang Department Store, right across the street from Rhee's position, but he hadn't had enough troops. Now it stood empty, available as a fire base for the first North Korean infantry to come along. In the limited time available, his men had only been able to liberally scatter a selection of explosive booby traps throughout the department store. That would slow the NKs, but it sure wouldn't stop them.

Two of the battalion's remaining companies were also on the line. Matuchek's Alpha Company held the left flank, dug in from the river to past some place called the Dabinchi Night Club. Bravo Company held the right, in a position centered on the Taejon Railway Station. The other provisional unit, Foxtrot Company, was stationed to the rear as the battalion reserve and quick-reaction force.

Other infantry battalions stretched to either side across the city—a grab bag of assorted American and South Korean units, all worn down by weeks of near-continuous fighting. Kevin shook his head wearily. The scattergun briefing he'd gotten before moving Echo up to the line had shown the better part of three North Korean divisions moving toward Taejon—two infantry and one tank. So they'd be outnumbered by at least four or five to one. He wasn't sure they could hold against those kind of odds, no matter how many times the rear-area brass said that Taejon would never be surrendered. Slogans like "They shall not pass" might sound inspiring to civilian ears, but the front-line combat soldier knew who paid the price for such fine phrases.

"Hey, L-T," Montoya whispered, "OP Seven reports NK tanks and infantry moving down the street. Company strength." He paused, listening, and then went on. "Six has movement, too. Another NK company at least. They wanna know what they should do."

Kevin moved toward the window. "Tell 'em both to hang tight and stay out of sight." He rose slowly to his knees, bringing his eyes just above the windowsill. "Contact the platoons and make sure they know not to fire until I give the word, understood?"

"Gotcha, L-T." Montoya started whispering softly into his handset, relaying his instructions.

Kevin stared out the window, watching for the oncoming North Korean columns. He heard them first. A low, persistent rumbling that expanded suddenly into squealing tank treads, the roar of diesel engines, and the tramp of marching feet. Shapes appeared at the edge of his vision.

ASSAULT GROUP 2, 1ST BATTALION, 27TH INFANTRY REGIMENT

Captain Kang Chae-Jin swore as he slipped on a patch of ice left unmelted in the road. He recovered and kept moving, angling slightly to stay right behind the third of the three T-55 tanks assigned to his company.

He looked up at the buildings rising to either side and frowned. Urban fighting doctrine said that tank platoons should advance in a triangular formation, with one tank moving down the middle of the street, while the other two stayed behind and to the flanks, covering the leader. But doctrine didn't say what to do when the street was too narrow for such a formation, so Kang had been forced to adopt an untested compromise. One of his three infantry platoons led the way, assault rifles held at the ready. They were followed by the three T-55s, trundling along in column, and then by the Assault Group's two remaining infantry platoons.

"Comrade Captain?" Lieutenant Sohn, the commander of his 1st Platoon, had dropped back from the lead column.

"Yes?"

Sohn tilted his helmet back a bit and pointed forward. "We're coming to a major cross-street. What are your ord—"

The lieutenant's question was drowned out by a sudden, echoing crash of small-arms fire, grenades, and tank cannon from off to the left.

Kang threw himself face forward onto the pavement and screamed, "Take cover!"

ECHO COMPANY

"Goddamnit!" Kevin slammed a fist into the wall beside the window as he watched North Korean foot soldiers scatter out of the street into houses and buildings. In another thirty seconds his men would have been able to catch the NKs in the open and slaughter them. But other enemy units had run head-on into Bravo Company first—spoiling what would have been a letter-perfect ambush.

"L-T, Rhee says he's got people moving into the department store across from him. He wants permission to fire."

"Granted. But Third Platoon only."

Montoya repeated that into his handset and machine guns chattered off to the right as Rhee's men opened up. The sound of more shooting rose from beyond the river, near Alpha Company's positions. Maybe. He was starting to lose track of sounds as they bounced around in Taejon's streets and as the discordant mix of artillery, small-arms, and support weapons reached mind-numbing proportions.

He risked another glance out the window and then ducked back. The North Korean footsloggers he'd seen had gone to ground in buildings or sheltered doorways, but their three tanks still sat arrogantly in the middle of a north-south street intersecting Chungang-ro, turrets whining as they swiveled back and forth, searching for targets. Those three tanks had to go. His troops could handle NK infantry, but those T-55s could use point-blank fire to smash every defensive position he had. So they had to be destroyed. But how?

Kevin mentally estimated ranges. The NK tanks were within sixty to a hundred meters. Too close for Dragon missiles— they needed to fly at least twice that distance before they could really be guided. But the LAWs carried by his men were a different story. LAWs were ordinarily useless against heavily armored main battle tanks. When fired from an upper-story window or roof, though, they could easily penetrate a tank's thin top armor.

He got to his feet and ran up the apartment building's central staircase to the third floor.

Several men in the 1st Platoon were equipped with LAWs, and every one of them professed an eagerness to be the first to "bag" his own tank. Kevin picked three of them and deployed them in separate rooms—one to a window.

He took a deep breath and then yelled, "Now! Now! Now! Fire 'em up!"

The 1st Platoon's machine gun teams and riflemen cut loose with a wild, clattering roar, sweeping the windows and doorways of the buildings across the street, trying to suppress any North Koreans who'd already gotten into position to fire back. At the same moment the three troopers carrying LAWs stood up, aimed, and fired.

Two of the three rockets found their targets. One hit the lead T-55 squarely atop its turret, tore through, and exploded inside the crew compartment. The other pierced the second T-55's fuel tank and turned it into a flaming wreck. The third LAW missed. Fired high, it clipped the T-55's radio antenna and slammed into a doorway, mangling two North Korean infantrymen crouching there.

The surviving tank's main gun fired back, and Kevin caught a split-second glimpse of an eerie orange sunburst emerging from the flames enveloping the second T-55.

CRACK. KARUMMPP! He felt the building rock back as the shell hit and exploded. Bricks cascaded out into the street, dust choked the air, and agonized screams drifted up from below.

Kevin grabbed the nearest soldier with another LAW and pulled him over to the window. "Get that son of a bitch before he shoots again!"

The man braced and aimed, but he didn't fire. "It's gone, L-T. It beat feet!"

Kevin looked for himself. The T-55 wasn't where it had been. Oily, black smoke pouring out of the two dead tanks made it difficult to see, but he could hear treads squealing on the pavement. They were growing fainter.

ASSAULT GROUP 2

Huddled in a bullet-pocked doorway, Lieutenant Sohn stared in shock at the thin wash of bloodred flesh and crushed bone that had been his company commander. The retreating T-55 had backed right over Kang without even pausing, and Sohn could still hear the captain's last faint, gurgling scream as he'd gone under the tank tread.

He retched, then winced as another stream of American bullets stitched across the edge of the doorway, spraying tiny slivers of concrete into his cheek. The sudden, stinging pain helped clear his brain and reminded him of one of war's cardinal lessons: First you survive. You can mourn the dead later.

The lieutenant pushed himself farther back into cover and deliberately looked away from what was left of Kang. He was in command now, and it was up to him to bring some order out of the mess he could hear and see around him.

Some of his men had gotten into buildings facing the American positions and were firing back. But others were acting as uselessly as he was himself—pinned down behind the first available cover. That would have to be changed, and quickly. Sohn wiped the vomit off his chin and ignored the blood dripping from his cheek. Then he rose and dashed forward into the smoke to rally his troops.

JANUARY 13—ECHO COMPANY, NEAR THE CENTER OF TAEJON

Rhee's voice was calm and came across the static-laden radio channel clearly. "We're taking heavy fire now from the department store and from houses across the street."

Kevin closed his eyes involuntarily as another flare burst high overhead. Its harsh, white light threw strange shadows racing across shattered buildings and rubble-strewn streets. Rifle and machine gun fire crackled nearby.

"Casualties?"

"Very heavy." There was a muffled, crashing sound, and Rhee stopped talking momentarily. When he came back on, Kevin could hear moaning in the background. "They're using RPGs against our firing slits. These communists are not being very sportsmanlike."

"Can you hold?"

Rhee sounded confident. "As long as we have ammunition. It would help, though, if we could get an artillery mission against the department store."

Kevin sighed and pressed the transmit button. "I've tried, Rhee, but Battalion says no way. There're too many civies still left in the city." The rules of engagement were firm. American artillery would not be used where friendly civilians were at risk.

"My countrymen would understand. This is total war. We must use every weapon."

"Drop it, Rhee!" Kevin snapped. "It's not your decision. It's not my decision. And there isn't anything either one of us can do about it. Got it?" He instantly regretted the anger he'd shown. The South Korean lieutenant was only trying to do his best to protect his men.

"Message understood." Rhee signed off, apparently unruffled by his outburst, and Kevin was thankful for that. He had more than enough on his hands without unnecessarily pissing off his best platoon leader.

The wind shifted slightly to the west and Kevin gagged at the smell it carried—a searing mix of charred wood, charred human flesh, and jellied gasoline. The North Koreans had used a flamethrower in a last daylight attack on his 2nd Platoon's positions. Their wild-eyed charge had been crushed, but not before the burning fuel sprayed by the flamethrower set a whole city block afire. The 2nd Platoon had been forced to flee the flames, retreating to fallback positions in the houses behind Chungang-ro. Several men were still missing, and Kevin hoped with all his heart that they'd been shot to death and not trapped inside the fires.

The flare overhead guttered out and another burst immediately to take its place. Moving slowly in the dangerous light, he handed the radio back to Montoya and followed the RTO downstairs to the CP they'd set up in a windowless, one-room apartment. The previous tenant's delicate silk wall hangings were gone, replaced by hand-drawn maps of the surrounding area showing kill zones and blind spots. Crumpled ration bags and stacked ammo boxes littered the room's polished hardwood floor. Rust-brown stains marked where a wounded man had died before the medics could get to him.

Kevin shuffled through the debris and unshouldered his M16. He laid the rifle carefully against the wall and stretched, feeling knotted muscles unwind ever so slightly. It felt so good that, for a moment, he stood motionless that way, with his arms spread wide and his back arched. His eyes closed and he felt the room melting away. . . .

"You okay, L-T?"

His eyes snapped open and he saw Montoya standing close to him, a worried look on his face. Christ, he'd heard of people falling asleep on their feet, but he'd never expected to be one of them. "Yeah, I'm fine. Just a little tired, that's all."

The RTO guided him over to a thin mattress and helped him sit down. "Hell, L-T. Why don't you take a rest? Nothing major's going down right now."

Kevin resisted the thought. "Can't. Rhee's men are in a firefight, and—"

"Shit!" Montoya sounded disgusted. "Everybody's been in a frigging firefight all day long. Come on, L-T, you've gotta sleep sometime."

Kevin knew that was true as he leaned back against the wall. Fatigue was turning him into a stumbling, shambling, fuzzy-thinking robot. Into exactly the kind of leader who could make too many mistakes and get his men killed wholesale instead of retail. He kept his eyes open for a moment longer and looked at Montoya. "Okay, I'll take a short nap. But get a radio watch set up and make sure everybody knows to wake me if anything big happens. All right?"

The RTO nodded happily and went away.

Kevin let his eyes close again and tried to let his mind drift away from images of the bloody day. Echo had been engaged at some point along its line throughout the day and now for most of the night. Counting the flamethrower attack, they'd repulsed at least five full-scale NK attacks and God only knew how many smaller probes. The streets showed the results.

They were heaped with North Korean bodies and shattered masonry. And the company's own losses had been equally appalling. He had scarcely sixty men left standing of the ninety or so he'd started the battle with.

The rest of the battalion wasn't in much better shape. Bravo Company was still hanging on to what was left of the railway station by its fingernails—pummeled by North Korean mortar barrages that had killed Bravo's CO and two of its three platoon leaders. On the other side of the Taejonchon River, Alpha had been pushed back about a hundred meters or so by a series of fanatical human-wave attacks, but it still held the burned-out remains of the Dabinchi Night Club. Casualties both there and at the station had been so heavy that Major Donaldson had been forced to feed two of Foxtrot's platoons into the line as reinforcements—leaving the battalion with a single, understrength platoon as its sole reserve.

Not a very good situation, however you looked at it, Kevin thought. Still, they'd inflicted tremendous losses on the NKs. Maybe they'd fought them to a standstill. There'd certainly been no serious effort lately to pry his company out of its buildings and cellars. Maybe the NKs were just as worn out as he was.

He fell asleep on that thought.

ASSAULT GROUP 2

Sohn's hand brushed a still-smoldering ember and he bit his lip to stop from crying out in pain. He yanked his hand aside and then froze, fearful that his sudden movement might have alerted American sentries in the darkened building just ahead. He waited for the yell and the shattering burst of machine gun fire that would signal such a disaster. But nothing happened.

The North Korean let his breath out slowly and scanned the ground to either side. From where he lay, the other men of his hand-picked infiltration team seemed scarcely more than shadows. Black camouflage paint covered their hands and faces. They had dulled every shiny surface on their weapons and wrapped the weapons themselves in cloth to help muffle any noise made as the team inched past American outposts and firing positions.

Sohn and his men had started moving shortly after sundown, cloaked by one last diversionary attack and smoke screen. The team's quick, soundless dash across Chungang-ro had been followed by an agonizingly slow crawl through still-smoking ruins left in the wake of the flamethrower assault. They'd made it safely, though singed and scorched, and now were almost within sight of their goal. Only a single, American-held building blocked their path. If they could slip past it without raising the alarm, making it the rest of the way to the objective—a solidly built apartment building squarely blocking the American lines of communication and resupply—would be easy.

Sohn started crawling again, moving with such infinite patience that an unwary eye might easily pass over him and rove on, unaware that it had missed anything. His men crept behind him, weighed down by packs of extra ammunition.

Five meters to safety.

A sound from the building, murmuring voices. He froze again, this time for several minutes. The voices faded.

Two meters left to go. Slowly, slowly, he told himself. Don't rush it. This is your chance for revenge on the Yankees, don't waste it.

Sohn rounded the last corner on his belly, put his back to the wall, and levered himself into a low crouch, stifling a groan as he put more strain on already weary muscles. One by one his soldiers crawled past him and assembled on the pavement. He grinned to himself. They'd done the hard part. All that remained now was to occupy the apartment building he'd chosen and prepare it for an all-around defense.

When the morning came, he'd let the Americans know where he was—and with a vengeance. Then the imperialists would face a difficult choice: to either retreat past his waiting guns or try to dig him out. Either choice would cost many of them their lives. Sohn had few illusions about the odds of his own survival, but he'd seen too many deaths in the past several weeks to let the prospect of his own end deter him from his duty. The stalemate along Chungang-ro had to be broken, and he and his men were the anvil upon which the Americans and their puppets would break.

The North Korean lieutenant stood and used hand signals

to gather his troops. They formed on him and the whole column moved off down the street at a fast walk.

ECHO COMPANY

"L-T?"

Kevin looked up from his half-eaten breakfast. "Yeah?"

"India One Two's on the horn, sir. He wants to talk to you direct."

"Coming." Kevin shoved the ration bag off his lap and took the stairs two at a time. Montoya had finally rigged an antenna from the third floor up onto the roof itself so that no one had to risk getting shot just to talk on the radio. He took the handset offered by the RTO. "Echo Five Six here."

"What's your situation, Kev?" Donaldson sounded exhausted and a lot older.

Kevin listened carefully to the sounds around him before answering. Desultory firing from the left, over by Rhee's position. Complete silence in the center. A single rifle cracked nearby, from one of the second-story rooms, answered at once by a heavier-sounding AK burst from across the street. "It's quiet, Major. Skirmishing only. I think we bloodied 'em pretty bad yesterday and last night."

"That's great. Look, Kev, I've sent some ammo resupply up to your position, and I want to make sure the guys humping it don't get shot up by mistake. Can you see down Inhyo Street from there?"

Kevin moved to a rear window near the staircase. Somebody had knocked out the glass, leaving an unobstructed opening with a view south along the street. "Affirmative, Major."

"Well, that's the way they're coming, so have somebody keep an eye out for 'em. And no poaching to make up your losses. Those boys are all I have to run errands for me. Got it?"

"Yes, sir." Kevin felt himself smiling and wondered that he still could. "Hell, if they've got ammo for me, I'll even send them back to you in a Rolls-Royce."

"On foot is good enough, Kev. India One Two out," Donaldson signed off.

Kevin decided to handle the job of watching for the ammo carriers himself. His troops were either needed on guard or busy trying to get some badly needed sleep. He leaned against the wall and eyed the street outside.

The Inhyo-ro was a study in desolation. The cars and people who would normally have filled it were gone. In their place were ragged-edged shell craters visible now and again through the gray smoke pall left by the hundreds of fires burning out of control across Taejon. The street looked utterly abandoned and alien.

He shivered slightly and blamed the chill he felt on the bad weather.

Men appeared at the edge of his vision, coming closer. Kevin raised his binoculars to get a better look. Several pairs of soldiers, each pair carting a box of precious ammo. Sweat-streaked faces. Young faces, pale and tight-lipped. Scared by this close approach to the real war.

"Jesus!" Kevin heard machine guns open up and watched in horror as the ammo carriers were mowed down, thrown dead en masse onto the pavement. He swiveled the binoculars and saw flashes winking in windows several buildings down. The guns fired for a moment longer, making sure of their victims, and then fell silent.

He spun round and saw Montoya standing openmouthed beside him. "Get Donaldson for me! Now! And tell all the platoon leaders I want them here yesterday! Go!"

He turned back to the window and stared at the tangle of bodies heaped on the street. Things had just gotten a whole lot more complicated.

ASSAULT GROUP 2

Sohn spotted the wounded young American crawling and aimed carefully, bracing his assault rifle on the windowsill. Satisfied with his aim, he squeezed the AK's trigger lightly and smiled as the man jerked once and lay still in a pool of spreading blood.

"An excellent shot, Comrade Lieutenant."

Sohn turned to face the speaker. Sergeant Yi was an

ass-kisser, but at least he was a competent ass-kisser. "Is everything ready?"

"Yes, Comrade Lieutenant. We've barricaded all the first-floor entrances and windows. Every possible approach is covered by cross fires. It will take a battalion to force us out of this place."

Sohn favored the sergeant with an approving nod. "Splendid, Yi. Take your post. The Americans know we're here now, so we can expect them to test your arrangements at any moment."

Yi saluted sharply and left the room.

Sohn settled down to wait. He felt sure the enemy's response wouldn't be long in coming.

ECHO COMPANY

Kevin jabbed the street map with his grease pencil. "That's the target, guys. Unless we can take that building back from the NKs, the whole battalion is well and truly fucked." He looked closely at his platoon leaders to make sure they were following along.

Rhee nodded his understanding, but both Geary and McIntyre looked unconvinced. The burly 2nd Platoon leader spoke first. "Hell, Lieutenant, why try to take it away from 'em at all? Let the NKs sit there. We can resupply up one of these other streets here." His stubby finger traced an imaginary line to the west of the enemy-held building.

Kevin shook his head impatiently. "It's not that easy, Sarge. They've almost certainly got MGs sited to fire down that cross-street. Anybody lugging stuff across is gonna get spotted and hit." He paused. "But even if we can get resupplied, Bravo Company can't. Inhyo's their lifeline to the rear. Every other path out of that train station is under enemy observation and fire. So either we clear that apartment building or Bravo eats it. And Major Donaldson doesn't view that as an acceptable alternative."

McIntyre looked angry. "Christ, screw the major, L-T. Why doesn't he use those guys from Foxtrot to do this? Why should we get all the shit jobs?"

"Because we're all that's left, Mac." Kevin rocked back on his heels. "Brigade took that last Foxtrot platoon away earlier this morning. They needed it to plug a gap somewhere west of here.''

There were deep frowns on every face in the command group. Things were really getting bad when nobody had any reserves held out of line. Plus, anybody with half a brain could see that NK-occupied building was going to be a tough nut to crack. Damned tough. They fell silent looking at the map.

Rhee broke the silence. "When do you want me to attack, Lieutenant?"

Kevin grimaced. He'd known it was going to come down to this, but he hadn't wanted it to. Rhee was a friend—a last link to the past, to days before the war had turned everything upside down. Hell, Rhee was more than that. The dapper, ever cheerful South Korean had saved his life. Was this how he had to repay his friend? By sending him into the NK meat grinder any fool could see waiting for the assault force?

But Rhee was also his best platoon leader. He had the tactical sense and, more importantly, the sheer guts needed to pull this stunt off. Maybe there wasn't really much choice after all. The mission had to come first, ahead of any considerations of friendship or risk.

"You'll attack in fifteen minutes, Lieutenant," Kevin heard himself saying. "Take one of your squads and one of McIntyre's. Battalion's promised us priority on a smoke mission, so you'll have that at least."

The South Korean grinned. "Very good, sir." He stood. "With your permission, I'll leave now to get my force ready to go in. There's no sense in making the communists a gift of time."

Kevin forced himself to match Rhee's smile. "Right. Good luck, Lieutenant. We'll watch your back for you."

Rhee nodded and then looked squarely into Kevin's eyes. He held out a hand and spoke more softly. "I would like you to know, Lieutenant Little, that it has been an honor serving with you."

Numbly, Kevin shook hands and watched as the South Korean bounded down the stairs to assemble his troops.

ECHO COMPANY, WEST OF INHYO STREET, TAEJON

Kevin thumbed the transmit button. "Kilo November Seven Two, this is Echo Five Six. I have a priority smoke mission. Coordinates Yankee Delta three eight seven one nine zero. Over."

The artillery officer's voice crackled back over the speaker. "Understood, Echo Five Six."

There was a five-second pause, and the voice came back on the radio. "Shot, out."

Kevin craned his neck to get a better angle on the silent apartment building less than thirty meters away. He felt naked, completely exposed to any NK sniper watching for a target. Seconds ticked away. C'mon, c'mon, where's the arty?

A single shell screamed down out of the sky and burst on the street, spewing gray smoke in all directions. Kevin yanked his head back around the corner. "November Seven Two! On target! Fire for effect!"

More shells rained down around the North Korean–held building, and he watched the smoke screen rising, billowing above the rooftops.

"Go! Go! Go! Move out!" Rhee's shouted commands brought the men of the assault force to their feet. With the South Korean in the lead, they ran forward and disappeared into the gray mist.

Suddenly the lower edge of the mist winked red in a dozen places as the North Koreans fired. Hundreds of bullets cracked down the street at supersonic speed, shattering brick, chewing up concrete, and puncturing flesh. High-pitched screams echoed above the chattering machine guns and assault rifles.

Kevin sat motionless, instantly aware that the attack had failed. The smoke screen hadn't been worth a damn. The NKs were too well sited. They'd positioned their weapons to cover every possible approach. The bastards didn't need to actually see anyone coming. All they had to do was pull their triggers, confident that every bullet fired was going into a carefully calculated kill zone. The zone Rhee and his men had just entered.

Damn it. He couldn't stand just hearing it. He had to see it. Kevin rolled out onto the street, flat on his stomach below the stream of bullets snapping past low overhead. The screams were dwindling now, fading into low sobs and moans. The North Korean fusillade fell away as well, shrinking to a spattering of single shots and small bursts.

Something scraped on the pavement ahead of him, and Kevin lifted his head to look. Two men came out of the smoke, crawling, dragging a third man behind them. A fourth staggered blindly after them, weaponless, his hands clutching at a spreading red stain on his stomach. The first two crept past him and Kevin's stomach lurched. The man being dragged was Rhee. He waited for other survivors to follow, but there weren't any.

He inched back into cover and sat up, staring deliberately away from the already blood-soaked patch of pavement where Echo's medics were working frantically on the wounded. On Rhee. He closed his eyes, not wanting to think or feel anything. Not anything. This wasn't his fault.

But it was his fault and he knew it. Twelve men had gone down that street. In the blink of an eye, eight had been killed or mortally wounded. He should have anticipated the disaster. Planned for it. Avoided it. Instead he'd hoped for a miracle and it hadn't come. Well, Rhee had paid the price for his mistake.

"Hey, L-T?" It was Montoya. "Kilo November wants to know if they should keep firing. What should I tell them?"

"Tell them . . ." Kevin gagged, fighting not to throw up. "Tell them to knock it off. It's over."

"No." A hoarse, pain-filled voice protested.

He opened his eyes. Rhee had pushed himself up off the pavement despite the medic's best efforts to make him lie still. The South Korean was a horrifying sight, shot at least twice in the chest. Kevin could see blood still welling from one of his wounds.

"You must not . . . abandon . . . the attack," Rhee gasped out, struggling for breath. One of his lungs must have collapsed. "Take them, Lieutenant . . . kill the bastards for us." He fell back, completely spent.

Kevin crawled over to where the South Korean lay sprawled. His friend's eyes were closed, but he was still breathing, if only in short, panting gasps. The medic pulled a syringe out of his kit and jabbed it into Rhee's arm. Kevin grabbed the man's arm. "Will he make it?"

"Jeez, L-T, I don't know." The medic winced as Kevin's

fingers tightened involuntarily. "He needs evac right away, though. All I can do is try to keep him breathing for a while."

"Oh, Christ." They couldn't evacuate any of the wounded, not while North Korean fire blocked every route to the rear. Either he took that building or Rhee would die, almost certainly with most of Bravo Company and a lot more of his own men. But that damned apartment building was too heavily defended. It couldn't be taken, not without more firepower than Echo Company had. He'd need a tank to blast the place open.

A tank. Kevin felt the seeds of a plan growing in his mind. It was what he should have done the first time out. He couldn't get a tank, but maybe he already had the next-best thing. He pushed himself upright and gripped his M16. They weren't finished. Not by a long shot. "Montoya!"

"Yes, L-T?"

"Tell McIntyre I want a fire team in one of those houses next to the objective. They're to lay down a suppressive fire on my order. Then get Geary on the horn and tell him I want Reese and his squad here ASAP. And have 'em bring a LAW for every man in the squad. Clear?"

Montoya nodded vigorously and started whispering into his set.

Kevin turned away and went back to sit by Rhee.

ASSAULT GROUP 2

Sohn rubbed his watering eyes, thankful that the American smoke screen had at last drifted away. He smiled at the carnage visible on the street outside. The smoke had been an inconvenience, but it hadn't prevented his troops from cutting the imperialist assault to pieces. He counted the bodies and laughed out loud in triumph. At least eight enemy dead! And not a man of his even sightly wounded. These Americans might know how to defend, but they were pathetic on the attack.

A nearby explosion wiped the smile off his face. Another attack so soon? He heard more shells bursting in rapid succession.

"Comrade Lieutenant!" Sergeant Yi skidded into the room. "Another smoke screen. This time to the north!"

A machine gun chattered nearby, followed by the softer

rattle of American M16s. The Yankees had shifted their axis of attack.

Sohn brushed past Yi on his way out the door. "Pull half the men to the north! And join me there!"

He ran down the hall, unslinging his AK as he ran.

ECHO COMPANY

Kevin heard the firing from McIntyre's diversionary attack, took a deep breath, and released it in a yell: "Now! Hit the fuckers!"

Half a dozen LAWs flashed from concealed positions on both sides of the street, reaching for the barricaded windows of the North Korean–held apartment building. They exploded on target, bursting in brief showers of orange flame.

Now. Kevin lunged outside onto the street and raced toward the apartment building. He heard men running behind him and heard them yelling. A wild rebel yell rising in pitch and volume, bouncing off the high, concrete walls all around. He fired from the hip, felt the M16 bounce in his hands, and saw sparks fly around one of the shattered, smoking windows.

Suddenly he realized that he was yelling with all the rest.

In! He hurled himself headfirst through the empty window and rolled to a stop in a tangle of gear. A North Korean writhed in agony in one corner of the small room, bleeding from half a dozen splinter wounds. One hand clutched a rifle. Kevin shot him and reloaded.

Reese crashed in through the same window and sprawled, covering the open door.

"Take your squad and clear this side! Move!"

The black corporal nodded and got to his feet. He risked one glance through the doorway and then bolted through it.

Kevin followed him into the hallway and turned the other way, moving toward a bend. He heard running footsteps from up ahead and ran faster. He had to make it around the bend first.

He did it and turned the corner ahead of the North Koreans. There were four or five of them just meters away. Kevin saw soot-blackened faces, waving assault rifles, and eyes widening in shock at his sudden appearance.

"Eat this!" He clicked the M16 to full automatic and held the trigger down, pumping a whole twenty-round magazine into the NKs. They were thrown against the wall in a spray of blood. An AK cracked once and Kevin felt something tug at his sleeve. A bullet. His rifle clicked empty and he ducked back around the corner, hearing only moans from his victims. He pulled the pin on a grenade and tossed it.

WHUMMP! The corridor shook and dust swirled. Silence, followed by more muffled explosions from behind him as his men cleared the lower floor room by room.

He risked a quick peek around the corner. No signs of other NKs moving to the attack. They'd have to be dug out one at a time. Kevin settled back to wait for reinforcements and snapped a new magazine into his M16.

ASSAULT GROUP 2

Sohn couldn't understand it. The wheel had turned so quickly. How could the Americans have broken in? How could he have let that happen?

He shook his head in dismay and turned to Yi. The sergeant looked like a wreck, with his uniform ripped in a dozen places and a jagged cut across his forehead. He still seemed stunned by the rocket explosion that had so nearly killed him. Sohn frowned. The man was useless in that state.

More shots sounded from down the corridor, closer this time. They were followed by another explosion. The Americans were advancing steadily, eliminating his troops as they lay pinned by fire from the outside. They held the initiative on this floor.

Sohn made a quick decision and wheeled to face Yi squarely. "Get every man who can walk to the second floor. We'll murder them on the staircases!" He forced himself to sound calm and confident and was pleased to see the sergeant seem to take heart from his orders.

They could still win this battle.

ECHO COMPANY

"Grenade!" Reese screamed, and threw himself away from the staircase. Kevin flattened and heard fragments whine overhead as the NK grenade exploded. He crawled to where Reese lay patting himself to check for wounds.

"You hit?"

The big corporal smiled thinly. "Nope, L-T. Guess they just wasted some more ammo."

"Maybe." Kevin coughed in the dust-choked air. "What're your casualties?"

The smile disappeared. "Two dead. Watkins and Lonnie Smith. A couple more wounded. None bad, though."

Kevin frowned. Four gone out of the men he'd brought in. That left only five men, plus him. Not enough. He ducked as a new burst of AK fire from above tore up the bottom of the staircase. He looked at Reese. "Any chance of a rush up those stairs, Corporal?"

The man considered it for a second and then spat onto the dust-coated hardwood floor. "Not a chance in hell, L-T. They got it covered too well."

"Grenades, then?"

Reese shook his head slowly. "They'd just toss 'em back down at us. That's how Lonnie bought it."

Kevin took another grenade off his combat webbing and stood, careful to stay flattened up against the wall. "Get your boys together, Reese, and I'll show you a little ol' trick I once heard about from a sergeant I knew." He felt himself starting to sweat.

With the squad backing him up, Kevin edged closer to the staircase. He stopped, inches away from the opening, and listened. Footsteps and whispering voices wafted down the splintered stairs. Then he lifted the grenade and pulled the pin, counting the passing seconds silently. One thousand one. One thousand two. One thousand three.

"For Christ's sake, L-T. Throw it!" Reese sounded shaken.

Kevin shook his head while counting. One thousand five. Now. He stepped to the opening and lobbed the grenade up the stairs.

ASSAULT GROUP 2

Sohn saw the grenade bounce off the bannister and roll toward him. He reached for it. Another weapon to hurl back in the imperialists' faces. The thought brought a thin-lipped smile to his face as his fingers closed around the grenade.

It exploded.

ECHO COMPANY

Kevin used the tip of his boot to roll the dead North Korean officer over and winced at the sight. The man must have taken the full force of the explosion at point-blank range.

"L-T?"

He looked up. Reese was standing nearby, breathing hard. "We got 'em all, sir. The building's cleared."

Kevin nodded and felt the fatigue he'd held at bay starting to rush in. "We lose anybody else?"

The corporal shook his head. "Not a one, L-T, thank God."

"Yeah. And a sergeant named Pierce." Kevin sank to his knees.

"You all right, L-T?" Reese sounded worried. "You ain't hit, are you?"

It took an effort to answer. "No, just used up." He straightened his back. "Look, go find Montoya and tell him to contact Battalion and let 'em know it's done."

Reese stood still for a second and then saluted. Kevin nodded wearily and closed his eyes, listening as the corporal's boots clattered downstairs. They'd won.

JANUARY 14—HILL 435, JUST SOUTH OF TAEJON

McLaren glanced at his watch. Just after midnight. He picked up his binoculars and focused them on the scene to the north.

Taejon lay burning, eerily illuminated by flares. Shells burst brightly in the center of the city, and he could hear the clatter of automatic weapons clearly—even at this distance. Tracers floated lazily through the air, reaching for unseen targets.

He turned to the South Korean major general standing next to him in the foot-deep snow. "Well, General, can you hold?"

The other man didn't move, staring intently at the ruined city. "Yes, we can. My troops have already shattered three of the communists' best divisions. Their dead are stacked like cordwood in Taejon's streets."

A helicopter roared low overhead, carrying wounded to the field hospital at the foot of the hill.

"And your own casualties?"

The major general shrugged. "They are very heavy, too. Around fifty percent." He paused. "We could use reinforcements, General. These men have fought hard. They deserve a short rest."

McLaren nodded. "You'll get them. But only a brigade. I need every other man elsewhere."

"A brigade is sufficient. We will hold them here."

"Excellent, General." McLaren turned back to watch the fires burning their way through Taejon. More flares popped above the city, and the sound of gunfire rose higher. Another North Korean attack going in, more men dying, he thought. "Doug!"

Hansen came out of the shadows. "Yes, sir?"

"Signal all commands. Let's get Thunderbolt ready to go."

The sacrifices made at Taejon would not be in vain.

ALONG HIGHWAY 38, IN THE MOUNTAINS AROUND CH'UNGJU

The long convoy rumbled slowly along the winding road, moving at a walking pace through the darkness. MPs stationed beside the road with shielded flashlights guided the intermingled, kilometers-long column of tanks, trucks, and self-propelled guns. Whenever a vehicle broke down, teams of engineers, mechanics, and combat soldiers were quickly mustered to shove it out of the way and into cover. The column could not let anything delay it. It had to be dispersed and under camouflage before the next Soviet spy satellite swung high overhead.

There were other convoys on the road that night. All were moving west, trundling down toward the flatlands near the sea.

The preparations for Thunderbolt were under way.

CHAPTER
40
The Tango
Incident

Admiral Thomas Aldrige Brown looked at a display screen
filled with symbols. To the trained eye it showed a carrier, a
battleship, over fifteen Navy amphibious ships, ten merchant
ships, and thirty escort vessels. Of course, Brown thought, you
had to know what you were looking at. For instance, a small
blue circle with the letters "ANCH" next to it represented the
amphibious landing ship *Anchorage*. He could even tell its
course and speed by checking the direction and length of the
line emerging from the center of the tiny circle.

Brown smiled thinly as the luminous computer display
flickered slightly, updating the information it showed. He
remembered the visiting congressman who'd complained that
the *Constellation*'s plot screen looked like "the world's most
expensive video game."

The admiral agreed. It was expensive. It was also invaluable. At a glance it allowed him to see the location and status of
every ship under his command and every identified threat they
confronted. And that was precisely the kind of data he needed
to make decisions in battle.

Right now, though, the screen showed a mass of ships
steaming placidly north along the South Korean coast. The
Constellation, the battleship *Wisconsin*, the amphibious ships,

and the merchantmen were all in the center, ringed by missile cruisers and destroyers for close-in protection. They in turn were surrounded by destroyers and frigates assigned to hunt down and destroy any submarines trying to get in among the more valuable vessels.

Brown eyed the ships of his ASW screen carefully, looking for weaknesses in their patrol patterns even though he hoped that their job on this trip would be comparatively easy. Intelligence rated the current North Korean subsurface threat as low, basing its assessment on a careful calculation of all reported and confirmed sub kills by U.S. and South Korean forces. Some of his officers even argued that the entire NK submarine force had been wiped out. Brown wasn't willing to be so optimistic. Preparedness never hurt. Never.

The plot showed the overall formation making a steady ten knots as it traveled northward. Individual frigates and destroyers in the ASW screen showed more variation—with some sprinting ahead at twenty or twenty-five knots, pinging with active sonar, while others drifted slowly at five knots, listening with passive systems. The slowly moving array of dots and lines was almost hypnotic.

Brown switched his gaze to a larger-scale display, one that showed the seas and land around his task force out to a distance of more than two hundred nautical miles. Blips marked the Soviet and Chinese patrol planes hovering near the edge of the declared exclusion zone. And a blinking notation near the corner indicated that the next scheduled Soviet RORSAT ocean surveillance satellite could be expected overhead within minutes.

The admiral grinned to himself, noting the surprised looks among his officers as he continued to stand quietly. Everybody knew that the Soviets were feeding every piece of data they got back to the North Koreans. And every staff officer in the Flag Plot had been prepared for another of his tirades about the damned Russian snoopers.

After all, how could the task force he commanded possibly hope to make a successful landing under constant observation? If the North Koreans and their Soviet backers could track them constantly, the Marines would find NK reinforcements waiting for them on whatever beach Brown picked. And that could spell disaster—no matter how many airstrikes the *Constellation* launched or how many Volkswagon-sized shells *Wisconsin*'s 16-inch guns fired. The staff couldn't see any way around that, not short of downing the supposedly neutral recon craft.

"Admiral?"

Brown turned. Captain Sam Ross, the commander of his threat team, stood waiting with a message flimsy in hand. Ross looked as animated as the admiral had ever seen him.

"Admiral, we just got the latest report from our satellites and recon aircraft. The NKs are definitely on to us. One evaluation is that we've got the better part of at least two NK divisions moving to block any possible landing site."

Brown grinned wider. "Outstanding, Sam. Uncle Kim seems worried by our presence." Then his grin disappeared. "Okay, I'd like a more comprehensive threat evaluation from your people within the hour. We may just be out here to wriggle, but I'm damned if I want to come away with any teeth marks." He turned back to his study of the display.

ABOARD *KONSTANTIN DRIBINOV*, IN THE YELLOW SEA

Captain Nikolai Mikhailovich Markov lay shoeless in his bunk, reading a tactical manual. He looked up without surprise when the *Dribinov*'s chief radioman knocked and entered his cramped stateroom.

He'd been expecting this visit from the *michman* in charge of signals for the past several minutes. The *Dribinov* had just finished a communications period, receiving the daily broadcast while it loitered at periscope depth with its antenna exposed. Petrov always brought the message traffic to the captain as soon as it had been processed.

Today, though, Petrov was not wholly his normal, stolid, unexcitable self. His hands actually shook as he handed Markov a thin sheaf of papers. "Comrade Captain, one of the messages is in Special Code!"

Markov kept his own excitement in check as he looked up from his manual. "Excellent, Petrov. Ask Lieutenant Commander Koloskov to come here at once."

The radioman left hastily, knowing better than to run, but hurrying all the same.

Markov swung out of his bunk and started relacing his shoes, all his prior torpor gone without trace. He'd thought that he and the *Dribinov* had been condemned to endlessly patrol the Yellow Sea's muddy waters—condemned as punishment for last month's failed attempt to embarrass the American carrier force. This latest message might signal a relief from the mind-numbing monotony of counting Chinese coastal steamers. Special Code was used only for extremely sensitive messages, matters of wartime urgency.

He would have to wait to find what the admirals in Vladivostok wanted, though. Regulations required that both the captain and his second-in-command, the *zampolit* or political officer, be present when all Special Code messages were broken. The two-man rule was designed not only to catch errors in decoding, but also to witness the receipt of what were always important instructions. Markov finished tying his shoes and stood up, stooping to avoid smashing his head against the low ceiling.

He turned at a soft rap on his cabin door. "Come."

It was Koloskov, his political officer. "You asked to see me, Comrade Captain?"

"Yes, Andrei Nikolayev, it seems we have a message to decode."

"Certainly, Comrade Captain." Without blinking an eye Koloskov sat down next to his captain and took the blank piece of paper he offered.

Using a lead-lined code book placed between them, the two men worked in silence, translating the jumble of letters and nonsense phrases into a readable message.

The message was short:

PACFLT 4457-1096QR. Begins: U.S. amphibious task force operating in Yellow Sea. Location at 1400 Moscow time grid 261-651. Course 025, speed 10 knots. Submarine Konstantin Dribinov *is ordered to attack, repeat, attack. Priority targets are aircraft carriers and amphibious ships. Nuclear weapons are not authorized. Under no circumstances may* Drivinov's *identity be compromised. Message ends. PACFLT 5423-0998XV.*

Markov drew a sudden breath and double-checked the message's authentication codes. They were absolutely correct. Then he compared the main body of the signal with the *zampolit*'s copy. They were identical.

The contents were electrifying. He'd seen orders like that before, dozens of times, in fact—but only during fleet exercises. Never in peacetime. He read it again, checking the decoding to be sure he hadn't left out a crucial phrase. No, he'd been right the first time through. The Fleet's signal did not say "simulate attack." It demanded the real thing.

Koloskov seemed even more shocked. "Comrade Captain, are we at war?"

Markov paused before answering, "I do not think so, Andrei Nikolayev." He rubbed his chin thoughtfully and then ticked off his reasoning on his fingers. "First, there has been no general war message. And second, the Fleet has not instructed us to attack just any American ship. Only those in this amphibious task force of theirs. So I would guess that we have just been volunteered for limited service with the North Korean Navy."

He paused again. "But whether the motherland itself is truly at war or not is unimportant, eh? We must behave as if we were. If the Americans find us sniffing around their carriers again, they will do their best to kill us. So we must kill them first, agreed?"

Koloskov nodded his agreement. Or was it merely his understanding? Markov wasn't sure.

For the present he decided he didn't care. He read through the message again. Real combat, considered and ordered, unbelievable. He'd prepared for this moment for years, ever since his first days as a snot-nosed cadet, but he'd never really thought it would ever happen. Why, the *Konstantin Dribinov* would be the first submarine to make an attack since the Great Patriotic War, the first Soviet submarine ever to attack an American vessel. It was heady stuff.

And dangerous as well. Someone in Moscow was obviously willing to risk escalating this conflict to the superpower level. Markov hoped his superiors had correctly judged the risks they were running, but knew he couldn't allow himself to second-guess them. He had his orders and they would have to be carried out.

Both he and Koloskov knew why he had been chosen. His experience, his past performance, had all been exemplary. Then, chosen to make that damned simulated attack based on his merits, he had failed. Now he was being given a second chance, a real chance.

He wouldn't fail.

ABOARD USS *CONSTELLATION*

Brown studied the assembled faces of his staff for a moment before continuing. They still looked alert, despite the hour-long briefing, and now he saw eager anticipation as they absorbed its implications. He cleared his throat and put both hands on the lectern. "Gentlemen, you've just heard the details of what will undoubtedly be the single most crucial operation of this war. And though we may not be in line this time for the best actor award, I'll be darned if I'm going to see anyone else walk away with the Oscar for best supporting role."

There were chuckles at that, and Brown smiled. He half-suspected that, when the time came to haul down his admiral's flag, he'd find that his power to move junior officers so easily to laughter would vanish along with his authority. In the meantime, however, he relished it.

He waited for the light laughter to fade and then continued, "Now, if we do our job right, we're going to be attracting a lot of attention. A lot of hostile attention." That sobered them up. "We're going to get one chance at this, gentlemen. One chance. If we screw it up, we're dead. A lot of our fellow sailors and Marines are dead. And a lot of U.S. and South Korean infantrymen and tankers are dead."

Brown leaned forward on the lectern, towering over it. "So stay alert. Be ready for instant action. Remember that we're at war and there aren't any prizes for second place in this thing."

He stepped back. "That's all, gentlemen. Good luck and good hunting."

JANUARY 15—ABOARD *KONSTANTIN DRIBINOV*

Markov knew his officers thought he was behaving in a most ususual manner. They couldn't understand why he'd had his tracking party working for nearly twenty-four hours—more than twice as long as needed for a normal approach. The *Dribinov*'s approach, however, was anything but normal. The normal way of doing things, he wanted to remind them, had nearly gotten them all killed the last time they'd closed with an American force. This time it would be different. Much different.

The submarine's track on the chart looked like a series of loops, approaching the formation from the side, slowing as it closed and letting it steam past. Then as soon as the American ships vanished over the horizon, Markov would angle away and increase speed to run parallel with them again.

Koloskov, the political officer, looked the most worried of all. As the sub's *zampolit*, his duties included ensuring the political awareness and reliability of every crew member, including the captain. And Markov knew that his caution might look like cowardice to the inexperienced political officer. It might also look like foolishness to a professional naval officer.

Every officer aboard seemed sure that their captain was taking a terrible risk. They thought these constant sprints were consuming too much of the *Dribinov*'s available battery power. They were certainly contrary to the Red Navy's standard diesel boat doctrines.

Three weeks ago, Markov would never even have considered ignoring doctrine. After all, his standard approaches during exercises had always been models of classic technique. The pattern was simple—position the *Dribinov* in front of its prey and ghost through the water at one or two knots, just enough speed to control depth and direction. Use any available layer of colder water, a thermocline, to help block enemy sonar. And when the enemy vessels come within point-blank range, fire a spread of homing torpedoes and escape in the ensuing confusion. The classic approach had a single significant edge over other ways of doing the same thing—it used scarcely any battery power, leaving plenty of charge available for high-speed evasive maneuvering.

This time, though, Markov was using all his energy in ten- and twelve-knot bursts. He glanced at the charge indicator. It showed fifty-eight percent, and they were pulling away from the American task force again.

Out of the corner of his eye Markov saw the political officer following his gaze. "Don't worry, comrade, our power is being well spent. That was our last sensor run. Next time we will attack. Look here." He tapped the chart, enticing the man over.

Besides the looping line showing the sub's track, the chart was covered with hundreds of other lines radiating out from the task force. Markov regarded the sheet with admiration, almost with love. The information it contained showed both a sleepless night's work and the key to victory.

"We've been tracking the American formation for almost a full day now, and we've taken hundreds of sonar bearings to his ships, his helicopters, his sonobuoys. Our task has been simplified because he must use active sonar to find us, while we can remain passive and plot the direction of his pinging." Markov smiled at his political officer. "So you see, Koloskov, I now know his formation, his patrol patterns, even where his patrol aircraft lay their sonobuoy lines."

Markov pulled out a clean sheet of paper with an array of different-sized dots drawn on it. "Here is what we think his formation looks like. Valuable units in the center, escorts surrounding them. Here is a Spruance-class destroyer, here is a Knox-class frigate, and so on. I have our tactical team up plotting the exact sonar performance of each class, based on the water conditions."

He smiled wider. "More importantly, I have found a hole in his screen. See this Knox-class frigate? It is not moving randomly. It always moves in the same pattern within its zone. Never become predictable, Comrade Koloskov."

Almost smashing his fist on the plotting table, Markov said, "That's where we will penetrate their screen. Once inside it, they'll never find us, not until it is too late."

ABOARD USS *CONSTELLATION*

The admiral checked the plot with the ASW coordinator. "Anything shaking out there, Tim?"

"No sir, nothing right now. Not even a trace."

Brown wished that was reassuring. "That doesn't mean there's nobody out there." He raised his voice, addressing the whole room. "Let's stay sharp, people. I doubt the NKs are going to let us have anything for free."

ABOARD *KONSTANTIN DRIBINOV*

The boat had been at battle stations for three hours now. The abysmal air circulation had become even worse with all the fans turned off. Water vapor from the thickening air condensed on the *Dribinov*'s ice-cold hull and dribbled down bulkheads.

The strictest silent routine was in effect. Every piece of nonessential equipment had been turned off, both to reduce noise and to conserve electricity. Every crew member not actively manning a post was in his bunk.

Quieter than a school of fish, quieter than the water around it, the *Dribinov* swam to intercept a moving spot in the ocean. Gliding just above the ocean bottom, the sub kept its bow toward the enemy ships, reducing the area available for sound impulses to bounce off.

Above it, the American task force was steaming northward toward its objective at about eight knots. At this distance the thrashing propellors of its nearly sixty ships could be heard clearly through the sub's hull as a dull, rumbling roar.

Markov ignored the faint noise and kept his eyes focused on the plot. It showed each of the amphibious group's escorts patrolling within its own moving box. He'd timed the Knox-class frigate's cycle and was heading for a time and a place when the American ship would turn toward the inside of its zone. That single turn to starboard would expose a blind zone in its sonar coverage for a few minutes. And the *Dribinov* would be there, ready to slip in and follow that blind zone around.

Only long preparation allowed the tracking officer to stay calm. "Contact is two minutes ahead of its projected position, Comrade Captain. We do not recommend a speed change."

Markov was really only concerned about the three nearest American escorts. The others were too far out of position to pose much of a danger to his submarine. Ahead and to the *Dribinov*'s left was a Spruance-class destroyer—normally a serious threat. But its powerful low-frequency sonar and towed array were close to useless in these shallow waters.

The Knox-class directly ahead also had a low-frequency sonar and towed array, but not as effective as the Spruance's equipment. And its predictable movements were what made this approach feasible.

Behind and to the right of the Knox was a newer Perry-class frigate. That was the American ship that most worried Markov. It mounted a medium-frequency sonar that was more effective in shallow water, and its commander was driving it in an extremely aggressive, unpredictable manner. If the Perry moved too far forward in its zone, there was a chance its sonar would pick up the *Dribinov*'s hull, which had to be broadside to that American ship while the sub crept in and was thus easier to detect.

That unpredictable frigate had already cost Markov two precious hours and even more precious battery charge. He'd made a last loop past the task force hoping to find a pattern or at least some system behind the American frigate's movements. He had failed. The Soviet captain smiled wryly to himself. The American captain's constantly changing helm orders must be driving the ship's crew half-mad. He studied the Perry's jagged track and smiled again. The American ship's size and behavior reminded him of a small dog, snarling and prowling in its owner's yard to warn off intruders.

Well, little dog, Markov thought, this intruder has teeth of its own. If it looked as if the *Dribinov* had been detected, he intended to fire a pair of torpedoes at each nearby escort— relying on the ensuing confusion to help him break in toward the more valuable ships inside the ASW screen. He would prefer to save all his weapons for use on his primary targets, but preferences were often meaningless in battle. At any rate, they all saluted the same flag.

The tracking officer measured their progress. "Approaching extreme detection range for Contact Two's active sonar." Contact Two was the Knox-class frigate in front of them.

One of the plotters listened to his headphones for a minute and made a new mark. "Contact Three may be changing course."

Markov resisted the urge to pace. Contact Three was that damned Perry. "How long until Contact Two turns?"

"Four minutes, sir."

The Knox was moving generally north. According to the pattern they'd observed, it would turn east, and then south. The *Dribinov* was moving east now, just outside hostile sonar range. When the Knox turned east, the gap they'd been waiting for would appear.

"Comrade Captain, the bearing rate on Contact Two is changing, slowing down."

Markov was ready. "They've started their turn! Increase speed to fifteen knots." They would move this fast just long enough to penetrate the screen, then slow to a more reasonable pace.

The plotter made another report. "Comrade Captain! Contact Three's sonar strength is increasing."

"Is he in detection range yet?"

The plotter talked into his microphone briefly. "No sir, but sonar estimates a speed of twelve knots." The man fell silent again as another report came through his headphones. "Three is now at extreme detection range, but there is no indication that they've found us yet."

"Plot, is Contact Two still on course?"

"Yes sir, we should be in position north of her in seven more minutes."

Not enough time, Markov thought. If he could get close to and behind the Knox, there was a good chance his sub's echoes would merge with those bouncing off the hull of the enemy ship. And even if that didn't work, the *Dribinov* could be through the screen and gone long before the Americans sorted out just what had happened.

But the blasted Perry frigate was coming up too fast, closing the sonar gap he'd needed to slip through. Markov made a quick decision. The game that had been so leisurely for so long was now accelerating into one that could be won or lost in seconds. "Open outer doors. Fire control party. We will launch tubes one and six at Contact Three, two and five at Contact One, and three and four at Contact Two."

Markov felt a shiver of anticipation. He was about to make his first real attack on enemies of the Soviet Union. His first real attack in over twenty years of service. Every man in the Control Room watched with wide eyes as the settings for the three targets were entered. The ranges were so close that there would be little warning time. With luck, one or two ships would be crippled or sunk, and the *Dribinov* would get the break it needed.

"Make sure the doors are closed as soon as each torpedo is launched." Each open torpedo tube door slowed them slightly, and they would need that speed.

"Three minutes until we are north of Contact Two," reported the plotter. "Sonar reports Contact Three's sonar strength is approaching a twenty-five percent chance of detection."

Markov looked at all the information on their position. That Perry-class frigate was just too close. He was about to fire the opening shots in what could be World War III. The thought terrified him until he suppressed it. He had his duty. "Stand by."

"Captain, Contact Three's bearing rate is changing again. She may be turning!" The plotter's voice went up a half-octave before dropping back to its normal even pitch.

"Fire control party, check fire! Menchikov, ask Sonar if that frigate could be changing course toward us."

The plotter asked, listened carefully, and answered, "No sir. Three has already turned past us."

Markov exhaled heavily. "Close the tube doors. Continue with the original approach." They had done it.

They were inside the screen.

ABOARD USS *CONSTELLATION*

"Sir, one of our helicopters has just reported a MAD contact!"

Brown looked up from the pile of messages he was reviewing. "Where's their contact?"

"In the inner zone, sir."

"What?" The messages were dumped and Brown was on his feet.

He moved to the close-range plot. The ASW officer pointed to one half-circle shape showing the call sign Bravo Four. "This bird was coming in to the carrier after finishing his patrol, sir. He's critical on fuel."

Brown felt an icy sensation down his back. How could anything have gotten in so close without being picked up? "Tell the helo to hold contact for as long as he can. How solid is it?"

"Bravo Four got two good passes in before he called us, Admiral. I'm vectoring other birds from *Connie* and the *O'Brien* at top speed to localize the bastard." The ASW officer looked personally affronted by the idea that anything could have slipped past his screen.

"We don't have time." Brown shook his head. "Okay, have Bravo Four lay one DICASS sonobuoy and then head home. "Who's in ASROC range?"

"*O'Brien*, sir."

"Order her to pair up with *Duncan* and attack immediately. Keep the helos ready to assist." He turned to his chief of staff. "Jim, put the entire formation at general quarters. Increase speed to maximum and turn the heavies away from the MAD contact. And keep the rest of the screen clear so *O'Brien* and *Duncan* can engage. Got it?"

"Aye, aye, sir."

Brown hardly heard the alarms on the *Constellation*. He was too busy trying to make sure the sneaky bastard out there didn't get a shot off. Whoever it was, he was too damn close right now.

ABOARD *KONSTANTIN DRIBINOV*

"Sir, the fire control party is tracking the main body of the formation."

Markov shook his head. "Keep the plot simple. Pick out the three strongest signals and concentrate on them. They are either the closest or the biggest. Either way we want them."

The group around the table got busy.

Markov looked at *Dribinov*'s charge meters. They showed forty-four percent of his battery power left. All of his training screamed at him that this was wrong, that he was in trouble.

He was inside the screen, though. And in any event, the *Dribinov* couldn't back out now, even if he wanted it to. Markov forced himself to relax. There would be plenty of power available for the rest of his approach.

He laid a hand on his first officer's shoulder. "Dimitri, tell the torpedo room I want a new record for reloading. We will probably have to shoot our way out of here." The shorter man nodded his understanding and reached for the intercom. Markov turned to the others. "Tracking party, how long until—"

"Sir, sonar reports heavy screw noises. It sounds like the formation is speeding up." Menchikov paused to listen and then continued. "Bearing rates are changing." Another pause. "Bearing rates on two warships, Contacts One and Three, are constant, increasing signal strength."

"*Govno!*" If a contact was neither going to the left or right of him and its sound signal was getting stronger, then it must be headed straight for him. One enemy ship doing that might be coincidence, but two could not be. Somehow the *Dribinov* had been found.

Markov gripped the plot table and ripped out a string of orders. "Release a decoy. Fire Control party, prepare for a snapshot. We will fire a spread into the mass of the American formation. Make turns for emergency speed."

ABOARD USS *CONSTELLATION*

The ASW officer looked sick. "Admiral, *O'Brien* and *Duncan* are cold. They're still too far away to pick anything up on sonar."

Brown bit down the urge to swear. "Tell them to launch blind. We've got to put the pressure on this guy."

The ASW officer relayed his order, then listened for a minute to a new report coming in through his headset. "Bravo Six is picking up something from the DICASS Bravo Four dropped."

Brown nodded in satisfaction. That was something at least. "When will Six be on top?"

The ASW officer made a rapid calculation. "Three minutes, Admiral."

Brown felt his short-lived relief die. "That son of a bitch will be able to launch in three minutes."

ABOARD *KONSTANTIN DRIBINOV*

"Torpedo in the water! Aft and to port!"

Markov whirled to his first officer. "Release another decoy. And fire tubes one through six! Stand by for evasive action."

It took an infinity of ten seconds to launch all six weapons. Every man aboard the *Dribinov* could hear the *clunk* as high-pressure air valves opened and closed. Each time they cycled, they sent a blast of compressed air into a torpedo tube, literally throwing the torpedo out into the water. Spent air was vented into the boat's hull, and Markov and his crew yawned and swallowed as the pressure built.

"Sonar reports that the weapon is active, but it is drawing left."

Markov felt his heartbeat slowing slightly. A bearing change that quickly signaled that the American torpedo had not acquired his submarine. And that meant it would probably miss. Confident that his prediction would be confirmed in a matter of seconds, he used the time to organize his thoughts, to plan his escape.

Menchikov broke into his thoughts with more bad news. "Sonar reports another torpedo in the water. They think it is distant, but it is directly ahead of us."

Markov watched carefully as a young lieutenant marked the new threat on the plot with shaking hands. There wasn't anything he could do. Not yet.

Clunk. The last torpedo left its tube and whined away toward the fleeting enemy formation. Now! Markov spun to the helmsman. "Right full rudder. Slow to ten knots." Reflexively he looked at the battery gauges. Thirty-two percent.

"Captain, Sonar reports the second torpedo's seeker is locked onto something, perhaps the seabed." A soft boom sounded from ahead as the American Mark 46 exploded on the muddy floor of the Yellow Sea. Markov smiled and relaxed, but not too much.

If they were dropping on him, it was time to get out. But not quietly. Markov had already decided to fight his way clear. The Americans might have detected the *Dribinov* too soon, but they would soon find they'd grasped a tiger by its tail.

He leaned over the plot, mentally calculating angles and

ranges. "Steady on course two three zero. Tracking party, set up a solution on those two warships closing on us."

ABOARD USS *CONSTELLATION*

"She's fired, sir! Torpedoes inbound for the heavies."

Brown saw new lines appear on the display screen, closing on the center of his force. The ASROC-launched torpedoes from the *O'Brien* had almost certainly forced the enemy skipper to fire earlier than he would have liked. But the admiral knew his ships could still be in danger. Most of the amphibious ships and merchantmen couldn't make much over twenty knots— not fast enough in a race with homing torpedoes moving at thirty-plus knots. He turned to his chief of staff. "Jim, order another course change. Bring the formation to zero three zero, and order all ships to maneuver individually to avoid torpedoes."

ABOARD LST-1189 *SAN BERNADINO*

The Newsport News–class LST *San Bernadino* was in trouble.

Originally stationed near the middle of the formation, she'd fallen farther and farther behind as faster ships raced by—intent on saving themselves. As an amphibious transport, she'd been designed for a sustained speed of twenty knots. Real speed and designed speed were proving two very different things, however. Since leaving Pusan, engine troubles had shaved four knots off the *San Bernadino*'s capabilities.

"Jesus!" Captain Frank Talbot, USN, flinched as a gray-painted Navy helicopter roared low over the ship's bow ramp and flashed by the bridge windows at top speed. He pulled himself upright and grabbed the intercom. "Any luck, Mike?"

"Negative, skipper. We've still got that godawful vibration in the starboard shaft. It could seize up on us anytime now." The chief engineer's voice came tinny over the loudspeaker.

He was wondering how long he could push the plant when he felt himself flung hard against the rear bulkhead by a massive, thundering explosion.

As he lay stunned and bleeding on the deck, Talbot felt the bridge tilting downward, toward the sea, and saw the ship's pointed bow rising sharply toward the sky. That was odd, he thought hazily. And then the answer came to him. The torpedo must have exploded directly under the *San Bernadino*'s keel, breaking her back and ripping her in half.

Talbot felt tears for his ship and crew dripping down his face and tried to get to his feet on the sloping deck. Then the pain hit. It drove him down into unconsciousness moments before the ship's stern section plunged below the cold surface of the sea.

ABOARD USS *CONSTELLATION*

News of the *San Bernadino*'s fate swept quickly through the Flag Plot, leaving only a stunned silence.

Brown felt his jaw tighten. First blood to the enemy. He turned to his chief of staff. "I want a full-scale search and rescue op for survivors. I don't want a single, goddamned man left out there in the water. Clear?" He didn't wait for the man's reply before swinging to face the ASW officer. "What about the other torps?"

"No hits, sir. Sonar shows they've all run out of gas."

That was something. The bastard out there had been forced to fire too soon. If they hadn't spoiled his attack, he probably would have caught more than the slowpoking *San Bernadino*.

"Bravo Six is reporting, Admiral. That boat's running at high speed, but the signal's fading."

Brown refocused on the hunt at hand. What was done was done. His job now was to make sure no more enemy torpedoes sought out his ships. "All right, *O'Brien* and *Duncan* have had a chance. Let's give the helos their turn."

The ASW officer nodded his understanding and ordered a circle of sonobuoys placed around the sub's last position, allowing for its reported speed and the time elapsed since it had last been detected. One was hot almost immediately.

"He's still moving, Admiral. Speed estimated at . . ." The ASW officer paused, then grew two shades paler. "Bravo Six has a classification, sir. It's a Tango-class diesel boat."

The admiral felt like an idiot for asking, but he went ahead anyway. "Get a confirmation on that."

The officer spoke into his headset, then listened. "No doubt about it, sir. Six has a very strong signal."

Brown felt the hair lift off the back of his neck. There were no Tango-class submarines in the North Korean Navy, or in the Chinese Navy for that matter. The only Tangos in the world belonged to the Soviet Union. The Russians had just put their oar in the water. "Jim, get me CINCPAC on the secure net. Tell them I have FLASH traffic for Admiral Simons himself."

He looked at the ASW controller. "Get those helos on top of that Russian s.o.b., and get some reliefs spooled up. I want everything we've got aloft. We're up against the first team here."

"CINCPAC is coming on line, sir." The chief of staff handed him the red secure phone and continued, "We've also got a preliminary count on survivors from the *San Bernadino*. Rescue helos have picked up fifty-two men so far, and *Bagley* is still quartering the area where she went down."

Brown nodded grimly. The LST had carried a crew of 290 men, and most of them were probably dead. Well, if he had his way, they'd soon be avenged tenfold. The only thing he could be thankful for was that the *Bernadino* hadn't been carrying any troops. But that was small consolation.

ABOARD *KONSTANTIN DRIBINOV*

Markov was not happy. "One explosion, that's all?"

"Yes, Comrade Captain. But sonar reports hearing the target breaking up."

Markov wasn't consoled by the report. One hit out of six torpedoes. A miserable performance. The *Dribinov* would have to do better than that in this next attack. He tapped the two closest dots on the plot reflectively. The submarine's next targets would be the two American escorts charging toward it. Missing either of them could prove fatal, not just embarrassing.

He looked up from the chart at his first lieutenant. "Dimitri, how are they coming?"

The man put down his phone. "Three tubes reloaded, the fourth in half a minute. And we have good firing solutions on both contacts."

"Three will have to do. We don't have half a minute. Shoot!"

The *Dribinov* shuddered again as three more torpedoes were flung out into the water. Markov moved to the helmsman. "Left ten degrees rudder. Steady on three one zero. Slow to five knots."

His battery was now down to twenty-eight percent charge. He would have to conserve what was left and try to sneak out.

ABOARD USS *O'BRIEN*

"Torpedo inbound! Bearing zero four three."

The sonar operator's report galvanized the Bridge and Combat Information Center into immediate action. Levi's first order called for flank speed, and the gas-turbine-powered warship responded like a sports car, slicing through the sea as its speed climbed over thirty knots.

The *O'Brien*'s CIC crew cursed silently as they tried to keep track of their own ship's evasive maneuvers while keeping tabs on the Soviet sub's last reported position.

Levi stood braced against the tilting deck as his ship turned, hoping he'd made the right decision. Instead of turning away from the oncoming torpedo, he'd ordered a turn toward the enemy. The idea was not to be where the launching unit had predicted and to get away from the torpedo's seeker.

"Bridge, this is Sonar. No change in torpedo bearing. The signal may be splitting into two or more weapons."

Well, that didn't work, Levi thought. He ordered another rapid course change. Screw closing on the sub. Coming right, he steadied perpendicular to the torpedoes' approach. Maybe giving them a rapidly changing angle would throw them off.

The sonar room reported again. "We now have three weapons in the water. Bearing rate on one is changing. It may be going for *Duncan*. Rate is still steady on the other two."

Levi clenched his fists. There was nothing more he could do. "Pass the word, all hands brace for impact." He looked out to starboard and saw another ship heeling sharply. The *Duncan* was also maneuvering.

IN THE YELLOW SEA

Soviet SET-65 torpedoes use passive sonar to home in on the sounds made by a ship's engines and propellers. And so, as the two torpedoes fired by the *Dribinov* at the *O'Brien* closed on their target, their robot brains brought them in behind the American destroyer—with one a hundred yards back.

Both tiny onboard computers evaluated the closest noise source as the rapidly turning screws of an American Spruance-class destroyer. Both were wrong.

They were homing on a Nixie, a torpedo decoy towed behind most U.S. Navy warships. No bigger than a garbage can, the Nixie was designed to make noise on the same frequencies as the ship towing it, but so loud that any attacking torpedoes would be spoofed into attacking the decoy instead.

It worked.

The *Dribinov*'s first torpedo closed on the Nixie and detonated when its proximity fuze sensed the target's position changing rapidly.

The explosion of its six-hundred-pound warhead threw a hundred-foot-tall geyser of icy water into the air, drenching sailors watching from the *O'Brien*'s fantail. At the same moment the shock wave rippling out from the explosion lifted the destroyer's fantail almost clear of the water, and for a moment the *O'Brien*'s propellers raced as they neared the air.

The second torpedo, intent on the same target, raced through the roiled water left by the explosion and suddenly found itself without a noise source to home in on. The SET-65's forward-looking seeker didn't have the intelligence to realize that its original target was now to its left and behind. And the control logic preprogrammed into the torpedo's tiny brain was simple, direct, and mistaken: If a target is lost, circle right and look for another.

Meanwhile, the *O'Brien*'s captain had not been idle. As soon as the first weapon exploded, destroying his Nixie, he'd ordered a hard left turn. Not only was he now closing on the Soviet sub's estimated position, but he and the second torpedo were heading in opposite directions with a combined speed of eighty knots—over ninety miles per hour.

It took roughly thirty seconds for the Russian torpedo to circle completely around to face *O'Brien*'s stern. By that time the destroyer had covered thirteen hundred yards, over half a nautical mile. The torpedo's small size meant a small, short-range seeker, with a maximum range of a thousand yards. So it never heard the *O'Brien* again and simply continued its turn. Left behind by its prey, the torpedo circled mindlessly for about five more minutes, then ran out of gas and sank quietly to the bottom.

ABOARD USS *O'BRIEN*

Levi's heartbeat was starting to slow toward normal when he heard a tremendous, rolling explosion from the right and felt the *O'Brien* rock for an instant. His head snapped right in time to see another towering column of water like the one that had appeared behind his ship. This one, though, wasn't made up of only white, foaming water. It was stained a dirty black and gray and located directly under the *Duncan*'s stern.

The column sagged and then collapsed back into the sea, leaving the frigate hidden for half a minute under a dense cloud of mist and smoke. When it emerged, the *Duncan* was visibly listing to port and down by the stern.

Levi stood rigid with anger. The Russians had struck again. He wheeled to his bridge crew and snapped out a new string of orders. "Indicate turns for twenty knots. Right full rudder. Boatswain, call away the repair and assistance party."

ABOARD *KONSTANTIN DRIBINOV*

The first explosion's rumbling *Crrrummmpp* came through the hull exactly when the tracking party predicted *Dribinov*'s first torpedo would reach its target. There were excited, quickly muffled exclamations from the Control Room crew, followed shortly by disappointed mutters when the time for their second torpedo attack came and went. But the second explosion was right on schedule, and again the control room crew had to stifle its cheers.

Markov hid his excitement well. Three American ships sunk or damaged in a single quick series of attacks. It was easy to be calm when things were going as he had planned. Now to exploit the situation by escaping through the gap he'd just blown clear through the American ASW screen. "We will steer toward the two targets. Steady on course two six five."

The sub changed course slowly at low speed. Normally he would have increased speed to hasten its turn, but the *Dribinov*'s battery was now too low to risk the unnecessary drain.

Markov smiled. He'd only sunk one of his priority targets— probably an amphibious ship—but once past the screen, he could clear the area and snorkel, recharging his batteries. He still had plenty of weapons, and with a full charge he could make another attack.

He moved back to the plot table and started to estimate the maneuvers he would need to make. Assuming about six hours to motor clear at three knots, while the task force continued to the north...

ABOARD *BRAVO SIX*

The SH-3H Sea King hovered low, its rotor wash churning the sea into a bubbling cauldron. A cable hung from under the helicopter, stretching down into the water.

In the Sea King's cockpit, the pilot clicked his mike. "All right, Tommy. Activate the pinger. Let's see what we've got here."

The petty officer in charge of Bravo Six's sonar gear reached out and flipped a single switch—activating the dipping sonar dangling thirty meters under the water.

ABOARD *KONSTANTIN DRIBINOV*

"Comrade Captain! Active sonar on the port bow. Very strong." The plotter's voice climbed in pitch.

"Damn it! Release a decoy! Right full rudder." Markov looked at the charge meter and tried to make a fast calculation. How much battery power could he spare? Not much. He sighed and issued the order. "Increase speed to ten knots."

WHANNNG! A sharp explosion rocked the sub's hull from side to side. Markov felt the shock and automatically adjusted for it, flexing his knees. The lights flickered and fragments of the compartment's insulation drifted down onto the plot table.

It was a depth-charge attack, close by. No warnings this time. "All compartments report damage."

He was just starting to receive reports when the second salvo came in, with a third seconds behind. This time the Control Room lights went out and did not come on again. In the darkness he could hear men shouting orders and he spoke to those nearby, calming them.

His first lieutenant's voice cut through the confusion. "Maneuvering room reports one of the shafts refuses to turn. Also, there is flooding in the crew's quarters."

Shit. Markov couldn't see the plot in this blackness, but his head held the known elements of the situation the *Dribinov* faced. "Right full rudder. Release another decoy. Put all power into the remaining screw. Turn off all but emergency equipment." He coughed in the dust-choked air. "And get the damned emergency lights rigged in here."

ABOARD USS *CONSTELLATION*

"We got good hits on those attacks, sir. It's hard for him to dodge in this shallow water." The ASW officer was cool even at the climax of the prosecution. His earlier case of nerves hadn't prevented him from vectoring in several helicopters to attack the Soviet sub in rapid succession, and Brown was making a mental note about a medal.

"What's he doing now?" Brown wasn't confident that depth charges alone could kill the sub. It was almost impossible to get a direct hit with them. So instead of the simple deadly impact of a torpedo warhead, the Tango out there was being hammered by a series of shock waves from near misses. Or so they hoped. It was difficult to get good damage assessment amid all the roiled water left by the depth-charge explosions.

The ASW officer listened on his radio circuit and made some minor adjustments to his display. "Bravo Three and Five both have good contact with the Sov boat. He's turning right, moving at about ten knots." The officer paused. "That's kind of slow for a Tango trying to evade attack, Admiral. We may have hurt him pretty bad."

"All right, hit him again. Don't give that asshole an inch." Confident that the attack on the sub was in good hands,

Brown turned his attention to the gravely damaged *Duncan*. He wasn't going to lose another ship. Not if he could help it, at any rate.

ABOARD *KONSTANTIN DRIBINOV*

The battery meter was unreadable in the dim red light thrown by the emergency lamps, but Markov knew what it must show. With less than ten percent of his charge and one shaft gone, there were few options left. He hoped to merge with the sounds made by the damaged American ship and then break away to the west. The *Dribinov*'s flooding was contained in the crew's quarters, and if the engineers could find some way to repair the shaft . . .

WHANNNG! WHANNGGG! Two more explosions, both to port. Markov felt the shock, and again the hull rocked to starboard and then back to port. More ominously, the boat took on a forward list. The *Dribinov* was angling downward toward the muddy bottom of the Yellow Sea.

"Sir, the torpedo room doesn't answer!

Markov closed his eyes. That last depth-charge attack must have ruptured the pressure hull right over the torpedo room. He closed his eyes, trying to shut away images of the men now drowning amid their weapons. "Blow the forward ballast tank. We have to compensate for the flooding."

The hissing release of supercompressed air brought the *Dribinov*'s bow up, but only halfway.

WHANNG! Another explosion. Not as violent, but still jarring. Markov knew it was over. The Americans had plenty of depth charges, and he was out of everything—time, power, and most importantly, luck.

He stumbled forward to where his first lieutenant stood braced against the deck's tilt. "Blow all ballast tanks, Dimitri. We will surface." He raised his voice, addressing every man in the Control Room. "Prepare to implement the destruction bill. We won't give the Americans any prizes."

Koloskov grabbed Markov's arm, the fear evident on his face. "Captain! Remember our orders from Moscow. We must not allow the Americans to learn of our involvement. We must escape."

Markov shoved the man away, unworried about any reports he might file. The odds were against either of them surviving long enough for Koloskov to retaliate.

"Listen to that, you idiot!" He jerked a thumb toward the hull. The deep *thrum* made by an approaching destroyer's screws was clearly audible above them. "The only way we'll escape capture is to let them kill us. Is that what you want? Do you want to suffocate inside an iron coffin on the bottom of the sea?"

Koloskov stared at his captain, struck speechless with fear. Then he turned away and retched, fouling the *Dribinov*'s littered deck.

Markov ignored him and wheeled to the rest of the Control Room crew. "You heard my order. Surface!"

ABOARD USS *O'BRIEN*

"Sir, after lookout reports a submarine surfacing!" Keegan's bellow rang across the bridge. Levi had just ordered the whaleboat launched and had been thinking about what should go in the second load for the *Duncan*. Now those thoughts vanished.

He ran across to the *O'Brien*'s port side and grimaced as he saw the Soviet submarine's battered sail and hull lurch up out of the water. The son of a bitch was surrendering.

Another destroyer was already racing toward the enemy boat at flank speed, its guns trained on the crippled vessel. The onrushing destroyer's five-inch barked, throwing a shell across the Tango's bows to let it know that the slightest misstep would end in its destruction.

Men started to appear on the submarine's sail and inflatable boats were thrown on the water. Levi suddenly realized what had happened and started grinning. With survivors and photographs, the Russians were going to have some explaining to do.

ABOARD USS *CONSTELLATION*

Admiral Brown was speaking into the scrambler phone again. "No, George, they scuttled as soon as their people were off.

Explosive charges. We've marked the spot, but we'll have to wait awhile to try to raise it. It's the middle of winter and the middle of a war zone."

The gravelly voice of Admiral George Simons, CINCPAC, rasped in his ear. "I understand, Tom. Now what about your own losses? Can you still carry out the mission?"

Brown didn't hesitate. "Absolutely, sir. *Duncan* is out of action, but I'm having her towed home by another frigate. We lost a lot of people aboard the *San Bernadino*, but that's just made my crews eager to take some scalps of their own."

Simons sounded relieved. "That's good news, Tom. I'll relay your report to the Joint Chiefs for their consideration. In the meantime, I'm authorizing you to take whatever measures you deem necessary to safeguard your command—up to, but not including, nuclear release. Is that clear?"

"Perfectly clear, sir."

"All right then, Admiral. I'll get out of your hair. Good luck."

"Thank you, sir." Brown listened as the transmission from PacFleet HQ in Hawaii ended in a series of clicks and a low hum.

He hung up the phone and called to his chief of staff. "Jim. Effective immediately, extend surface and air surveillance out to three hundred miles.

Turning to the *Constellation*'s air group commander, he asked, "CAG, do you still have Tomcats bird-dogging the Russian AWACS plane?"

The CAG looked puzzled. "Of course, Admiral."

"Shoot him out of the sky."

"Aye, aye, sir." The CAG picked up a phone and started issuing orders to the fighters now lazily orbiting with the Russian radar plane.

He paused, listening to the murmurs sweeping through the Flag Plot. "Admiral Simons has put the Pacific Fleet on war alert. Let me be very clear about this, gentlemen. One more incident like this last one, and we'll begin unrestricted offensive operations against the Red Navy and Air Force. We'll start hitting the Soviets where they live."

The Second Korean War had just escalated.

CHAPTER
41
Thunderbolt

JANUARY 15—OFF THE SOVIET NORTH PACIFIC COAST

The port of Petropavlovsk sits on the eastern coast of the Kamchatka Peninsula. Over thirty-six hundred miles from Moscow, it is so remote that all communication with the area is by air or sea. The region is unpopulated and barren and is located in the same arctic latitude as the Aleutian Islands. On the Siberian coast, good harbors are hard to find.

Petropavlovsk is also the Soviet Pacific Fleet's main submarine base. Almost all of its ballistic missile submarines, many of its nuclear attack submarines, their support vessels, and numerous other naval units are based there.

One of the few Soviet ports that open directly onto a major ocean, it allows ships to sortie without having to go through a landlocked passage or hostile strait. And that gives the Soviets a good reason for putting up with the remote location, high cost, and terrible weather.

ABOARD USS *DRUM*—OFF PETROPAVLOVSK

Captain Donald Manriquez tried to remember how important the base was as he fought the weather to maneuver his Sturgeon-class nuclear submarine, USS *Drum*, into a new surveillance position. His orders were explicit and simple. He and *Drum* were to monitor traffic in and out of this major Soviet naval base. If it exceeded normal levels, he was to notify Commander Submarines Pacific, COMSUBPAC, immediately.

So far, they had been loitering off Petropavlovsk for almost a week, and they'd met with a fair amount of success. In this case, success was a combination of not being seen, being in the right spot to count passing traffic, and hopefully, not seeing the massive surge of Soviet ships and subs that might signal World War Three.

"In position, Captain." His executive officer, "Boomer" Adams, was navigating while they looked for a spot where the currents would not be quite so unpredictable.

"Very well, slow to three knots." By maintaining just enough speed to control its course, the *Drum* minimized its noise signature, and that reduced the chance of its being detected.

The storm overhead was both a help and a hindrance. Its ten-foot waves and twenty-knot winds generated noise—noise that would interfere with any Soviet passive sonars listening for the submarine. Looking for the *Drum* that way would be sort of like trying to hear a cat burglar in a boiler factory.

The problem was that *Drum*'s own passive sonars were also degraded. Luckily, he thought, most of the Russian stuff was noisier than they were. Even so, the bad acoustical conditions meant that Manriquez and his crew had to get in close to hear anything. They were outside the twelve-mile limit, but just barely.

Manriquez could feel the sweat building on his forehead as they crept close to the Soviet coastline.

It was clear from the most recent condensed news broadcasts sent by the Pacific Fleet that things weren't going well in Korea. And that was bad news for the *Drum*. Her "gatekeeper" role was clear, and he was sure that sooner or later the U.S. and Russia were going to go at it hammer and tongs. Well, when they did, he would sound the warning, then get first crack at the units pouring out. The American sub captain was a realist. If a general war broke out, his chances of survival weren't too good, but at least he'd do some damage.

SOVIET FAR EASTERN HEADQUARTERS, KHABAROVSK, R.S.F.S.R.

Commander in Chief Anatoli Sergiev heard the alert bell ring and looked at the clock. Just after fourteen hundred hours. No test was scheduled.

The intercom in his office came to life. "Comrade Commander, this is Major Grozny in communications. The submarine *Konstantin Dribinov* reports that it has been attacked by the American Navy in the Yellow Sea. They are abandoning ship."

"Have the heads of all departments meet me in the command center!" Sergiev was already grabbing his hat and on his way out the door.

The situation map held no obvious surprises. The *Dribinov*'s last reported position was well west of any American units. What were the imperialists up to?

His staff came running in from behind him and from other entrances. Sergiev spotted Admiral Yakubovich, his naval liaison, and motioned him over as Grozny ran up with several copies of the message. After the boyish-looking major handed one to General Sergiev, the rest were snatched from his hands.

Sergiev read the entire message, but it contained nothing more than the hasty summary Grozny had already given him over the phone. Specifically, there was no information on why the *Dribinov* had been attacked. The most logical explanation was a case of mistaken identity, that the Americans had thought it was a North Korean boat. But *Dribinov*, like all over Soviet naval forces in the Pacific, had been ordered to keep well clear of the Americans. And that meant the U.S. Navy had gone to a lot of effort to deliberately hunt it down. Just what the hell was going on?

"Does anybody have any suggestions on possible motives for this attack?" He looked at his staff, but the muttered negatives showed their puzzlement matched his own.

Sergiev frowned. "I see. Well, then, I want answers and I want them fast. Contact Military Intelligence, the North Koreans, anybody who might shed some light on this. We need more information before we can act.

"Grozny." He looked over at the short officer. "Have there been any other transmissions from *Dribinov*?"

"No, sir, and they haven't answered..."

The alert bell rang again. The speaker in the command center announced, "The Il-76 radar plane over the Yellow Sea has reported that aircraft are closing on it at high speed."

There was a pause. "We have lost communication with the aircraft and its escorts."

"That's it! The Americans have lost their fucking minds! They're deliberately attacking us," Sergiev declared. He looked at General Yasov, his operations officer. "General, order all Far East forces to full alert, then notify Moscow. Order the ballistic missile submarines to sea, and I want all air defense forces on a wartime footing."

Yasov looked uncertain. "Comrade Commander, can we take such strong action? Shouldn't we get more information before we react?"

Sergiev opened his mouth to shout at him, but he wanted to keep the atmosphere calm. He took a deep breath and looked at Yasov. "Nikolai, we cannot afford to wait. One attack might be a mistake. Two cannot, and this may only be the beginning. All the measures we are taking are defensive in nature. And I will always choose to err on the side of caution."

Raising his voice slightly, he said, "Now let's get busy. We have much to do, and we may be at war in minutes."

ABOARD THE USS *DRUM*

"Captain, sonar reports active pinging, bearing two nine zero."

Manriquez looked at the chart, but he already knew that bearing was toward the harbor mouth. The tracking party started a plot, ready to add this new contact to the list of others they had recorded.

There was an open line from the control room to the sonar room. Lieutenant Ed Baum headed up the tracking party. "Sonar, do you have a classification yet?"

A tinny voice answered him, "Contact is a surface ship, probably a newer unit. Pinging is low frequency, now bears two nine three."

In such lousy acoustic conditions, their chance of hearing the actual vessel was slim. Instead, they would have to use clues such as the type of sonar pinging to help narrow down the possibilities. The bearing had also changed slightly. By measuring the rate of change, the tracking party could make educated guesses about the contact's course, speed, and position. Of course, they needed a lot more than just two bearings.

Another minute or two passed. "Contact's bearing now two nine five. New contact, designate first contact Alfa, second as Bravo. Second contact also pinging, probably a surface ship. Bearing is two eight seven."

Manriquez sat up a little straighter. So far on their patrol, they hadn't seen a pair of destroyers coming out in team like this. Maybe a large ship was going to sortie? The tracking party got a little busier, labeling and plotting two possible tracks instead of one.

"Contact Alfa now bears two nine six, Bravo two eight eight . . ." There was a pause and then, in a rush, "New contacts Charlie and Delta bearing two nine one and two nine two. New contact Echo, bearing two eight five. . . . Captain to Sonar please."

When Manriquez came into the small space, the chief sonarman was looking over the operator's shoulder. The captain took one look and whistled softly in surprise. Normally an active sonar appears on a scope as a line radiating from the center to the edge, brightening and then fading as each ping is received. But the *Drum*'s scope didn't show that kind of normality at all. Instead, a wedge ten degrees across was filled with pulsating brightness, and the audio signal sounded like a chorus of monstrous bullfrogs.

Sonar Chief Kelsey straightened and turned to face Manriquez. "Skipper, I count at least ten pingers out there, with more appearing all the time. We're receiving low- and medium-frequency signals, and it's impossible in that mess out there to tell what classes or even if they're only surface ships."

The captain didn't wait. Turning to the "squawk box" on the bulkhead, he called the control room. "Control, this is the captain. Sound general quarters. I'll stay here."

The klaxon filled the cramped spaces with sound, and Manriquez squeezed into a corner as the rest of the sonar gang arrived and made the compartment even smaller. There was a quiet bustle, punctuated with exclamations, as the new arrivals saw the sonar display and were briefed on their current situation.

Manriquez looked at the chief. "Concentrate on the low-frequency pingers. They're the biggest threats."

He looked at the scope, trying to pull information out of the lines and patterns. Big exercise? Nothing had been announced. Some sort of snap drill, then? He desperately wanted to find some other explanation than a general Red Fleet deployment.

There were other, more immediate questions as well. Just how many subs were hiding in that mess?

Adams's voice came over the squawk box. "Captain, all stations manned and ready, quiet routine in effect throughout the boat. Four Mark 48 torpedoes loaded and ready."

"Very well. Boomer, ensure we are clear of that mob, but I want to stay here as long as possible. We've got to see if they're sending the ballistic missile subs out."

"Aye, aye, sir." Adams would try to conn the boat away from the group of Soviet ships emerging from Petropavlovsk, but their movements were unpredictable. The simplest thing would have been to work their way to sea and report, but the report would be incomplete. Manriquez needed to see exactly how many units were leaving port.

The sonar operator looked over his shoulder at the captain. "Sir, I've found heavy screw beats, bearing three zero one."

Chief Kelsey looked at the display. "Right in the middle of that mess. If we can hear them at this range, those must be serious screws." He glanced quickly at the captain. "Kiev-class, Skipper?"

"Probably. Let's just sit tight and watch the show."

Over the next hour, they watched the gaggle of Soviet surface ships pass, creeping at slow speed and zigging often to confuse anyone trying to track them.

Once the formation was well on its way to sea, Manriquez walked back to control. Speaking softly, almost whispering, he ordered, "Move us in closer, Boomer. We won't hear any submarines out here."

They started easing their way in. They had to do it quickly, before any subs hiding behind the surface task force slipped past, but movement created noise. And Manriquez was sure that if they made too much noise, the Red Navy's entire Pacific Fleet would come crashing in around their ears.

They closed on what appeared to be empty water, but the chart showed the channel that submerged submarines would have to use to sortie.

The speaker was secured during silent routine. Instead a talker with a mike and earphones spoke softly. "Sir, sonar reports a passive sonar contact off the port bow. Machinery noises, screw beats, classified as a Delta II ballistic missile submarine."

An odd feeling of mixed triumph and anxiety filled Manriquez. He had his answer. The Soviets were sending out their boomers. It wasn't the answer he wanted. "Right. Let's get out of here."

They turned slowly, easing their way out. "Captain, Sonar reports more active sonars. They think it's a line of sonobuoys, bearing southeast. Not too close, though."

Manriquez looked at the plot. The buoy line wasn't close to their intended track so it wasn't a threat to them, but it meant that there were ASW aircraft up screening the Russian subs as they sortied.

"Sonar reports two more buoy lines, to the north and northeast. Neither is close."

Manriquez still wasn't too worried. The Soviets didn't seem to be actively looking for them and they had plenty of sea room. Adams was already steering *Drum* toward one of the gaps in the sonobuoy lines. The question was, were there more fields coming? And what else was out here? In this acoustic murk, active sonar was a good way to see things, but *Drum* couldn't use hers. Not without announcing her unwanted presence to the world at large.

Suddenly, the talker announced, "Sonar reports active pinging close aboard to port!" His tone was the closest thing to a shout quiet routine would allow.

Adams started to turn the sub away from the source, while also changing depth.

Manriquez listened to the exec's hastily snapped orders with one ear and leaned over the plot. "Is it another buoy field?"

The talker spoke into his microphone, then listened. "No, sir, it isn't a multiple source. They think it's a dipping sonar, signal strength moderate."

Dipping sonars were used by ASW helicopters, which could hover while lowering their sonar transducers on long cables into the water. They always operated in pairs, and this close to a major port, there might be many such pairs. Manriquez made a decision. They had to get clear before the Soviets got lucky and landed a helo right on top of them. "Boomer, increase our speed. If they detect us actively, being quiet won't help."

ABOARD THE *ALEKSANDR OGARKOV*

"Comrade Captain, we have a passive sonar contact. Faint screw beats bearing three five one."

Captain Kulakov was also staring at a sonar display. The new contact's postion did not correlate with the location of any of the Soviet attack subs fanning out from Petropavlovsk. It had to be an intruder, an American.

And with sonar conditions this poor, the American submarine had to be close. Too close. The American might already have one of the Red Navy's precious ballistic missile subs in his sights. "Fire control party, prepare to fire a spread on my order."

Kulakov didn't plan to wait for a full fire control solution, intending instead to launch several torpedoes centered on the American sub's location as soon as his tracking party had a rough idea of its heading.

He smiled grimly. The American subs were excellent. And that was why only the newest and best submarines, like his Akula-class boat, were assigned to this work. The *Ogarkov* and its counterparts had sortied with the surface ships, then taken up positions to screen the ballistic missile submarines as they left port.

For once, Kulakov's orders from Fleet Command made sense. He was to protect the deploying subs from sneak attacks, like the kind the Americans had made on the *Dribinov*. His orders made it clear that there would be no more surprises. This intruder would be stopped.

"Sir, screw beats now bear three five three."

"Very well." Kulakov tensed. They had their bearing rate. "Stand by to fire."

ABOARD USS *DRUM*

The talker had a new report. "Skipper, passive sonar contact bearing one seven two. Screw beats."

Manriquez called softly to Ed Baum. "Stop everything you're doing and start a plot on this contact."

"Sonar evaluates contact as possible submarine at creep speed, high bearing rate."

That last bit of information galvanized the control room crew. A rapidly changing bearing at slow speed meant the new contact was very close.

Manriquez took a shallow breath and released it. "Boomer, come right. Put the contact on our beam. As soon as we can determine his course, we'll head for his baffles and try to slip away—"

"Sonar reports transients! Torpedoes inbound!"

Shit. "Launch a decoy! Right hard rudder, all ahead flank! Take her deep!" Manriquez paused for one microsecond, then said, "Fire one and two with a four-degree spread, and make them active homers."

He felt the boat start to heel over as she built up speed and started to turn. He regretted having to fire, but his mission was to survive and report. Shooting at the other side was a good way to start a war, but he suspected that one was already under way.

ABOARD THE *ALEKSANDR OGARKOV*

"Captain, the American has returned fire! Two torpedoes inbound."

Kulakov felt his heart flutter and then pump faster. "Emergency speed! Turn on the active sonar and track the American. Release a decoy!"

ABOARD USS *DRUM*

"Captain, the Russian's gone active. Two of the torpedoes have a high bearing rate, the other two are still closing."

Manriquez swore under his breath and started snapping out

maneuvering orders. This was going to be a damned tight squeeze. They'd dodged two of the incoming torps, but the others were going to be tougher.

OFF THE SOVIET NORTH PACIFIC COAST

The two combatants maneuvered, dodging and turning at high speed as each tried to evade the weapons heading toward them. The Mark 48 torpedoes were faster than their Soviet counterparts, so that even though they were fired later, they reached the Soviet sub first.

Fired without correction for the target's course and speed, *Drum*'s shots depended on the small active homer built into the nose of each torpedo to find and attack the target.

One Mark 48 had been fired to either side of the *Ogarkov*'s estimated position, so that whichever direction it turned, at least one would be in a position to see the Soviet sub.

In the end, both saw him and attacked. Detection range in the noisy water conditions off Petropavlovsk was so short that both torpedoes' powerful sonars illuminated the Akula-class sub at point-blank range.

One struck amidships, the other aft—in the engine compartment. The *Ogarkov*'s double-hull construction could not survive two hits. In addition to the salt water pouring through the two tears in the hull, the double shock wrecked equipment throughout the ship and threw men across compartments into steel walls. With so much flooding there was no hope of saving the boat. Powerless, without any control at all, *Ogarkov* tumbled downward on its long journey toward the ocean floor.

ABOARD USS *DRUM*

Drum's sonar operator heard the explosion, but he was too busy tracking the weapons headed toward them to report it. "Captain, those two torps have locked onto us!"

Manriquez glanced quickly at the scope over his shoulder; the strobes were getting wider and stronger. Jesus.

Ten seconds passed. Wait for it. Fifteen seconds. Now. "Launch two more decoys."

Shot out of the sub's signal ejector, the decoys hovered in

the water and emitted sonar signals designed to confuse the guidance systems of the Soviet torpedoes. One was seduced by the decoys, turned toward them, and exploded. The other was too close and it hit the American submarine forward, just under the sail.

Manriquez, Adams, Baum, and everyone else in the control room were thrown to the deck and plunged into darkness, while one deck below, water shot in through a two-foot tear in *Drum*'s hull.

"Blow everything!" Manriquez shouted, trying desperately to counter the tons of weight being added to the hull as compartments flooded. It wasn't enough.

Too heavy to maintain even neutral buoyancy, air bubbling from its vents and from the gash in its hull, the American sub followed its Soviet opponent down to the bottom.

KING'S BAY, GEORGIA

Rear Admiral John Fogarty focused his night-vision glasses and watched as the long, dark shapes glided silently past his station and out to sea. Two Ohio-class ballistic missile submarines were under way—each nearly twice the length of a football field and larger than a World War II–era heavy cruiser. White foam churned by their massive propellers glistened momentarily in the moonlight and then vanished as if it had never been.

He tracked the SSBNs until they could no longer be seen and then heaved a small sigh of relief. The most dangerous moments for any ballistic missile sub were always in port. Anchored beside a supporting sub tender, the Ohios were nothing more than sitting ducks. But once they were at sea, the huge boats were so quiet that the Soviets could never seriously hope to find them. A significant percentage of America's nuclear deterrent was now effectively invulnerable.

Fogarty turned to the lieutenant waiting with him. "Dave, get a signal off to COMSUBLANT immediately. Tell him the boomers are away." Then he walked back to his office, past an empty anchorage.

WHITE HOUSE SITUATION ROOM, WASHINGTON, D.C.

The display map glowed with color-coded lights and symbols marking the position and alert status of every major Soviet military unit around the world. The symbols along the Soviet Pacific coast glowed bright red.

The President looked grim, an expression matched by every other man and woman around the table. "Are we sure that *Drum* was attacked, Admiral?"

"Very sure, sir. Our long-range acoustic sensors were tracking a large number of ships leaving Petropavlovsk, along with every other port on the Pacific coast. During the deployment, they detected two explosions, which they plotted inside *Drum*'s patrol area."

Admiral Simpson frowned. "Since then she's missed two communications periods and does not acknowledge her call. She was certainly attacked by the Russians, and barring a miracle, was sunk."

"Does that tell us anything about Soviet intentions?"

Simpson shook his head. "No, sir." He moved to the display map. "They've put every interceptor and SAM battery in the Far East on full alert. All surface ships and submarines in port are sortieing..."

"Toward our forces?"

"No, Mr. President. At least not yet. They're deploying into what might be defensive positions." White lines appeared on the map as he spoke.

"That's good news at any rate."

Simpson looked troubled. "I wish I could agree, sir. But the fact is, all of these are the very same actions the Soviets would take if they were contemplating additional attacks. Their exact plans are still unclear."

"Damn." The President closed his eyes and started rubbing his temples, trying to massage away the tension headache building there. No one spoke until he opened his eyes again. "What about your end of things, Fran?"

The head of the National Security Agency shrugged her shoulders. "Again, nothing conclusive, Mr. President. We're

picking up a lot of traffic from Vladivostok to Moscow and
back again. All high-priority FLASH-type stuff, naturally. There's
also been a marked increase in signals to the other major
military commands—Soviet Forces, East Germany, the Northern Fleet, the Black Sea Fleet, and so on.''

''But no change in their alert status?''

''Not yet, sir.'' The NSA boss toyed with her pen. ''At
least not as far as we can tell. We're scheduling some additional satellite passes throughout the rest of today and tomorrow to
try and pick up more data.''

''Christ!'' The President's irritation was clear and easy to
understand. It was also somewhat unfair. Tens of billions of
dollars had been invested in America's electronic intelligence-
gathering capabilities, but no photo-recon or SIGINT satellite
could pry into the minds of enemy leaders or divine their
hidden intentions.

''Have you talked to the General Secretary yet, Mr.
President?''

The President's angry snort could be heard across the
room. ''Hell, no. I tried calling the man direct when this whole
thing first blew up. The General Secretary is, quote, unavailable
for the time being, end quote.''

Simpson frowned. ''So either they're as confused over
there as we are, or they're all busy scurrying for the fallout
shelters.''

''Yeah.'' The President shoved his chair back and stood
up, feeling a sudden desire to pace. He stalked to the front of
the room and stood facing the display map. Europe caught his
eye. ''Maybe we should start shipping troops and equipment to
NATO now—while we've still got time. At least we'd be
ready if the Russians decide to escalate this thing further.''

''I'm afraid that activating Reforger is impossible at the
moment, Mr. President.'' General Carpenter, the Air Force
Chief of Staff, looked embarrassed. Reforger was a plan for
moving American troops and equipment to Europe. By us
rapidly reenforcing NATO, the Soviets would hopefully be
deterred from attacking. ''We don't have the sea- or airlift
available.''

Blake Fowler nodded to himself. The Military Airlift
Command and Military Sealift Command were already stretched

to the limit just supporting McLaren's troops in South Korea. Three weeks of almost nonstop operations were taking a dangerous toll on the flight crews and their planes. Three C-141s and a C-5 had already been lost because of inadequate maintenance or crew fatigue—the Starlifters somewhere over the Pacific and the Galaxy in a fiery crash in California. There were enough planes to keep the war in Korea going or to reinforce Germany. But not to do both.

The President just stared at the map without speaking. Then he turned. "If the Soviets do escalate, can NATO hold without the Reforger forces?"

"Probably not, sir." Simpson shook his head slowly. "Not with just conventional weapons."

The men and women crowding the Situation Room fell silent. Without enough conventional forces, NATO would have to use tactical nuclear weapons to stop a Soviet armored onslaught across the West German border. And nobody in the room really believed it was possible to step halfway across the nuclear threshold. Five-kiloton bombs dropped on armored columns would inevitably be answered by five-hundred kiloton ICBM warheads landing on cities.

Fowler saw the President's shoulders sag. None of the options were particularly palatable. Either push McLaren's planned offensive forward and risk leaving Europe defenseless, or rush reinforcements to NATO while accepting a bloody stalemate in South Korea.

At last the President spoke. "Well, I'll be damned if I'm going to pull the rug out from under our boys in South Korea. We'll have to gamble that the Soviets aren't ready to expand this thing." He turned to Simpson. "In the meantime, Admiral, I'd like to give them something to think about. Now, we've already deployed our missile submarines. What're my other choices?"

The admiral had come prepared for that question, but his answers weren't very reassuring. Nobody felt comfortable playing with nuclear fire.

UN FORCES HEADQUARTERS, SOUTH OF TAEJON

The stars were out, crystalline against the infinitely black night sky.

McLaren stood quietly, waiting and watching. The burning tip of his cigar glowed brighter momentarily and then faded as he breathed out.

"General?"

He turned. Hansen had come outside, backlit by the lamps inside the command tent.

"We've just gotten the final signals, General. All units are in position and ready for your orders."

"Any word from Washington?"

"Yes, sir." Hansen held his notepad up to the light. "It's from the President. Just this: 'Proceed as planned. Our prayers go with you. Good luck and Godspeed." The captain grinned.

McLaren nodded and took the cigar out of his mouth. "Right." He checked his watch. "Okay, Doug. Signal all commands to execute Thunderbolt at oh five hundred hours."

Hansen saluted and reentered the tent.

McLaren drew on his cigar again and stayed where he was. Unseen in the darkness, he crossed his fingers.

THE KREMLIN, R.S.F.S.R.

The General Secretary had never seen his military aide show such a troubled face before. It seemed an odd look for a man named a Hero of the Soviet Union for gallantry in combat against Afghan bandits. "More trouble, Ivan Antonivich?"

The colonel nodded. "I'm afraid so, Comrade General Secretary. With your permission?" He held up a thick leather satchel.

"Please." The General Secretary sipped his tea carefully, almost ostentatiously. Like so many of the reforms he'd sponsored, his efforts to curb rampant alcoholism among Soviet citizens were being resisted. As a result, he never missed the chance to show that he practiced what he preached.

"I've assembled this collection out of our latest satellite

and human intelligence reports concerning the submarine incident and the American reaction to it." The colonel fanned a sheaf of papers and image-enhanced photos across the Party chief's desk.

The General Secretary put his glass down abruptly, slopping tea out onto a bone china saucer. He frowned. "Their reaction, Colonel? What of our reaction to this wanton attack on our submarine in international waters? Surely that is more to the point." He looked at his watch, annoyed. "I asked the defense minister for his recommendations on possible retaliatory moves several hours ago. I've heard nothing since. So perhaps your time would be better spent in making sure my desires are carried out, eh?"

The colonel said nothing, although his face reddened. He simply sat motionless holding out the first satellite photo.

The General Secretary sighed, more to himself than anyone else, and took the photo. His aide was a good man, loyal, intelligent, and a committed Party activist, but he was just too stubborn. He scanned the photo and dropped it negligently onto his desk. "So? I see an empty harbor. What is so important about that?"

"That is the main American missile submarine base on the Atlantic, Comrade General Secretary." The colonel held out another. "And this is their Pacific base at Bangor, Washington. Also completely empty. There are similar reports from the NATO base at Holy Loch in Scotland. Essentially, every seaworthy American SSBN is now at sea—an unprecedented mobilization."

The General Secretary began to see why his aide looked so concerned. "Go on."

"Reconnaissance also shows that major elements of the American Strategic Air Command have also been raised to an even higher alert status and dispersed from their normal operating fields. All leaves for their bomber crews have been canceled—even those awarded for urgent family crises."

The General Secretary felt cold. Had the Americans gone mad? First an unprovoked attack and now this nuclear saber rattling. What were they up to? "You were right to bring this news to my immediate attention, Ivan Antonivich. It should have been done before this by others in this government." He picked up the special secure phone kept permanently beside his desk. "Get me Admiral Marenkov."

Marenkov, commander of the Red Navy, came on the line in moments. The automatic scrambling made his voice sound hollow. "Yes, Comrade General Secretary?"

"As chairman of the Defense Council and Commander in Chief, I am ordering you to institute Plan Sanctuary immediately." Under Sanctuary, all of the Soviet Union's own SSBNs would be deployed behind a screen of minefields, attack subs, and ASW hunter-killer groups. Once safe in their bastions, the missile submarines would stand ready to strike back should the Americans attack.

"I understand. Sanctuary will be under way within the hour."

"Excellent, Yuri. I'll confirm this order by teletype before then." The General Secretary hung up and reached for a sheet of paper. He began writing with quick, forceful strokes of the pen. "Ivan Antonivich, you will carry this to the Communications Office personally. Under no circumstances will you allow its transmission to be delayed. Understand?"

His aide nodded and took the written order in hand. He still looked uncertain.

"Was there something else, Colonel?"

"Yes, sir. There have been certain, ah, rumors, about the attack on our submarine and its mission in those waters. Perhaps they are nothing more than idle gossip, but if true . . ." The colonel's voice trailed away.

The General Secretary sat up straighter. He'd learned early in his career never to discount rumors. They were often the best possible source of information. "Very well. Repeat these whispers to me."

When the colonel finished speaking, the General Secretary's face was set in hard lines. He suddenly looked older than his sixty years. "Thank you for your candor, Colonel. I shall take what you have said under advisement. You are dismissed for the moment."

After his aide had gone, he picked up the secure phone again and placed another call.

JANUARY 16—ABOARD THE USS *WISCONSIN*, OFF THE KOREAN COAST

The lowlight TV picture was perfect. So perfect that the officers clustered around the monitors in *Wisconsin*'s Combat Engagement Center could easily make out individual foxholes and camouflaged heavy weapons. The view shifted slightly as the Israeli-made reconnaissance drone began another orbit.

"Well, well, well. Look what we have here, Skipper." Lieutenant Commander Jason Matthews, the battleship's gunnery officer, poked the monitor's screen gently.

Captain Edward Diaz followed his subordinate's stubby finger and smiled. The screen showed a collection of tents liberally festooned with radio antennas. "That's a pretty nice looking command post, Jas. Any bets on just what kind?"

Matthews matched his commander's smile. "Oh, I'd say a regimental HQ at least. Maybe a division."

"Fantastic. Make that the first target."

Matthews nodded and moved to the ship's ballistic computer. The ratings manning it nodded as he spoke, fingers flashing over keyboards. After just a few seconds the gunnery officer looked up at Diaz. "Guns locked in, Skipper. Ready to fire at your signal."

Diaz glanced at the clock: 0359. A minute left to go. He shook his head regretfully. "Hell, I never was very good at waiting. You may fire when ready, Jas."

Matthews's finger stabbed the fire control button and the *Wisconsin* rocked back—surging against the recoil as her nine 16-inch guns roared, hurling shells toward the Korean coast at 2,500 feet per second.

The men aboard the battleship watched their screens, waiting for the recon drone to show them where their shells landed. It took forty-eight seconds for the nine high-explosive-filled shells to fly the twenty nautical miles separating the *Wisconsin* from her targets.

"Holy God!" Matthews couldn't hold in his exultation as the screens showed dirt and smoke bursting skyward all around the North Korean headquarters complex. When the smoke cleared, all that could be seen were a series of overlapping craters. Every tree within two hundred meters of the impact point had been blown down. "Scratch one collection of NK brass!"

Diaz was awed by the destruction his ship had unleashed. This was the real thing, not just target practice. He shook himself. "Gunnery Officer! Shift your fire to the other preplanned targets. Fire at will."

"Aye, aye, Skipper."

The *Wisconsin*'s captain stood watching as his guns began systematically obliterating North Korean beach defenses, supply dumps, and artillery positions. He grinned. It really was too bad that there weren't any U.S. Marines within a hundred miles to take advantage of the holes they were tearing in the NK coastal defense.

The North Koreans might think they were going to get hit from the west, but they were wrong. McLaren's knockout blow was coming from the east—from out of Korea's rugged mountains. The NKs were about to get sucker-punched.

4TH REGIMENT, 3RD MARINE DIVISION, OUTSIDE MASAN, SOUTH KOREA

Colonel Tad Lassky, USMC, was a happy man. His three battalions had already advanced more than ten kilometers in the seven hours since the attack began—moving against light and sometimes even nonexistent opposition. And from what he heard over the command net, similar progress was being reported by each of the other nine American and South Korean divisions involved in the counterattack. For once the intelligence boys had got it right. Most of the best North Korean units were tied up in the bloody fighting around Taejon or along the coast. Those left guarding the eastern flank were spread too thinly to put up an effective resistance.

"Colonel, Second Battalion's on the line."

Lassky grabbed the handset. "Papa Fox Four Six to Fox Four Five. Go ahead, Bill."

Lieutenant Colonel William Kruger's bass tones crackled back through the receiver. "We're coming up on a little village here, Tad. Recon reported some movement around it earlier this morning. Do you want us to bypass it or steamroller right through?"

Lassky checked the map before answering. "Clear it, Fox Four Five. We're gonna need that road for supplies."

"Aye, aye, Fox Four Six. Consider it done."

Lassky smiled at the confidence he heard in Kruger's voice. It was a confidence he shared. The 3rd Marine Division had been on the ground in South Korea for more than two weeks, pent up in secluded camps, waiting for just this moment. And now that McLaren had slipped the leash, Major General Pittman and his regimental commanders intended to make the most of their opportunities.

2ND BATTALION, 4TH MARINES

Kruger waved his three lead rifle companies into action. The white-smocked Marines spread out into a skirmish line across the frozen rice paddies and advanced, closing on the small cluster of houses several hundred meters ahead. He and his command group followed them off the road, stepping carefully onto the snow-coated ice. The 2nd Battalion's CO believed in front-line leadership.

Everything stayed quiet until the Marines came within two hundred meters of the village. Then the North Korean defenders cut loose.

Kruger dove for the ground as NK machine guns and automatic rifles opened fire from concealed positions among the houses, raking the fields and toppling Americans whose reflexes weren't fast enough. Kruger raised his head to see what was going on. Most of his men were in cover behind rice-paddy dikes, but several were sprawled unmoving out in the open.

KARUMMPHH. The ground trembled slightly as a small explosion blasted dirt and snow into the air behind the crouching Marines. *KARUMMPHH.* Another burst, this one closer. The North Koreans were walking light mortar rounds in on top of his pinned-down troops. Kruger swore vilely and crawled over to the Marine aviator assigned to his battalion as its FAC— forward air controller. He tapped the younger man on the shoulder and asked, "Well, Lieutenant, think you can rustle up some air support on that fancy radio of yours?"

The lieutenant looked up and spat out a mouthful of snow. "I sure can try, Colonel."

"Then you do that, son. We ain't getting out of this field any other way."

Both men flattened as a mortar round burst nearby, spattering them with dirt. Others were less lucky. Kruger saw one of his staff sergeants splayed up against a paddy dike. The man's right leg was missing.

"Top Dog One, this is Papa Fox Three One, over. Top Dog One, this is Papa Fox Three One, over."

Kruger bellycrawled back to his radioman. "Fox Four Five to Alpha Five Two. I have a fire mission, over."

The officer commanding 2nd Battalion's eight 81-millimeter mortars responded immediately. "Ready to shoot, Fox Four Five."

"Okay." Kruger flinched as NK machine gun fire cracked over his head. "I need an incendiary smoke mission. Coordinates YD eight four five one two two. Fire that in"—he glanced toward the FAC and saw him holding up two fingers— "two minutes."

He crawled back to the small cluster of men around the air controller. Marines on either side were starting to return the enemy fire. One minute left. He took a deep breath and then bellowed, "Okay, boys. We've got fast movers coming in! Mark your positions! Use purple smoke!"

Seconds later, canisters tossed by men in each of the battalion's platoons started spewing bright purple tendrils of smoke. They rose and mingled in the wind to form a single line of purple clearly marking the battalion's location from the air.

With a sudden roar, four snub-winged Harriers flashed overhead toward the North Korean positions, flying in pairs. As each jet pulled up sharply and to the right, it threw sixteen small, finned objects tumbling into the village: five-hundred-pound Mark 82 general purpose bombs. They went off in an endless, teeth-rattling series of sun-white explosions.

Other explosions flashed amid the shattered houses. The battalion's mortars were joining in—tossing white phosphorus rounds that had a dual purpose. Burn and maim the enemy while building a blinding curtain of smoke.

"Marines!" Kruger bounced to his feet, M16 in hand. Helmeted heads all across the field turned to watch him. He climbed high onto a paddy dike and waved his hand toward the gray-cloaked, burning village. "Advance!"

"*UURRAH!*" Guttural voices rose in the rhythmic battle cry as the marines surged forward toward the North Korean positions, firing on the move. Kruger ran among them.

It took fifteen minutes of bloody, close-in fighting to clear the town. But at the end of it the road lay open and undefended.

17TH RIFLE DIVISION HQ, NORTH OF ANSONG

Major Park Dae-Hwan stared approvingly at the carnage around him. The attack had been sudden, unexpected, and savage—perfect in fact. Bodies littered the camouflaged camp, some in full uniform, others entangled in sleeping bags or naked in the snow. Most of the North Koreans had been cut down in the first minute. Few had even had time to grab their personal weapons.

He smiled thinly. The communists had concealed their headquarters well, hiding its tents, armored vehicles, and radio gear in among the towering trees of a small pine forest. It would have been almost impossible to spot from the air. Of course, that same abundant cover had made it possible for this South Korean Special Forces team to sneak right up to the camp perimeter without being spotted.

Park snapped a new magazine into his CAR-15 carbine and slung it across his shoulder. Then he whistled sharply, summoning his Black Berets to the rally point. They'd idled here long enough. He and his team had been inserted by helicopter behind enemy lines two days before and held in readiness for just such a mission. Now they had other work to do. The communists had a whole network of supply dumps, communications facilities, and security detachments posted along this highway. Park intended to destroy them.

"Sir!" Sergeant Kwon came toward him with something clutched in his hand. Park remembered seeing the burly sergeant sawing away at the uniform of one of the North Korean officers.

Kwon stopped in front of him, saluted, and held out a strip of cloth. "A trophy for your collection, Major." The sergeant grinned broadly at his own joke.

Park took the rigid piece of cloth and stared at it. A shoulder board with a single star. The insignia of a People's Army major general. He nodded in satisfaction. One of the six North Korean divisions trying to stem General McLaren's attack had just lost its commander and its entire staff.

He slipped the dead general's shoulder board into his tunic and turned to leave. His men followed in single file. They had a long march ahead to reach the next objective.

1ST BRIGADE, 10TH INFANTRY DIVISION HIGHWAY 4, SOUTH OF UCH'ON

"Gunner! Sabot! Tank at ten o'clock!" The South Korean captain felt his M-48's turret swing left and waited.

"Up!"

"Fire!" The tank bucked as its 105-millimeter main gun went off with a loud roar. Acrid fumes filled the turret as it recoiled and spit out a used shell casing. The gunner hurriedly loaded another armor-piercing shell. It wasn't necessary.

Their target, a T-55, sat burning on the raised shoulder of the highway. Fifteen others were scattered across the iced-over rice paddies, wrecked and on fire. It was over. The counterattacking North Korean armored battalion had been slaughtered—caught charging across open ground by twenty South Korean tanks waiting hull-down behind the highway embankment. A single M-48 sat mangled, its turret ripped open by a communist shell.

The captain undogged his hatch and stood high in the turret, gulping down deep breaths of fresh air. Although the entire engagement had taken just five frantic minutes, he was exhausted, worn ragged by the extraordinary combination of extreme physical exertion, fear, and intense concentration needed in battle.

The brigade commander's voice crackled through his headphones. "All units. Continue the advance in echelon. Division objective is now Uch'on."

The M-48's commander squinted into the setting sun and nodded to himself. The village of Uch'on lay eleven kilometers ahead. They just might be able to make it before nightfall. And that would put the division's lead elements more than thirty kilometers past what had once been the thinly held North Korean main line of resistance.

Thunderbolt had broken through.

II CORPS HQ, NORTH OF TAEJON

The two generals stood together in the shadow thrown by a tall tree. Both were bundled against the cold.

Off to the south Taejon's battered skyline glowed faintly with the light of a hundred fires, and smoke rising from the city stained the sky a dull, barren black. At this distance the sounds of the fighting were muted, reduced to little more than the quiet crackling of small-arms fire interspersed with the heavier thumping noises made by artillery and mortar rounds.

Colonel General Cho Hyun-Jae grimaced. "I fear, Chyong, that we stand on the edge of disaster. You've heard the reports?"

Lieutenant General Chyong nodded. They'd begun picking up the scattered transmissions earlier in the morning. First, news of a possible amphibious invasion on the coast near Seoul. Then, fragmentary reports of a massive assault force rolling out of the eastern mountains. Every signal had been garbled—a victim of imperialist radio jamming. Nothing was certain.

Chyong studied his commander carefully. The older man looked inexpressibly weary. "Is there more news?"

Cho shrugged, barely lifting his shoulders. "Nothing. I've dispatched couriers to each of the division headquarters with word to send me more details. I've heard nothing from them." He shook his head. "Since my security troops report that the countryside behind us is crawling with puppet government assassins, I suspect that my messengers have been intercepted." He drew a hand across his throat.

"Perhaps."

Cho looked down at his hands. "In any event, our course is clear. We must shift forces northward to meet this enemy thrust. The imperialists cannot be allowed to sever our line of communications. We must counterattack."

He turned away from the sight of Taejon. "I shall need two of your best divisions, Chyong, and two more from the Fourth Corps. I'll also need two of the three armored regiments supporting your attack."

Chyong frowned. Cho's requisitions would leave his corps a toothless tiger, incapable of capturing the city. And there were other problems that could not be ignored. "My forces are at your disposal, comrade. But my casualties have been very heavy. Even my best units are barely at half-strength." He moved closer. "Worse yet, our supplies are extremely low—food, ammunition, fuel, everything. There may not be enough fuel to move my tanks far enough north to attack the imperialists."

Cho's lips thinned in anger. "I am aware of your supply problems, comrade. Intimately aware!" He took a breath, trying to relax. "Pyongyang has assured me that resupply columns are moving south at this moment. Your tanks will have their fuel. That I promise you."

Chyong wished his leader sounded more confident that Pyongyang's promises would be fulfilled.

PHOENIX FLIGHT, OVER HIGHWAY 23, NORTH OF SOKSONG

Major Chon looked at the dark, undulating landscape flowing by five hundred feet beneath his plane. The moon had risen an hour ago, and it now threw just enough light to keep him out of trouble. He glanced quickly back over his shoulder and then forward again. The three other A-10s of his flight were still in position, following him at three hundred knots.

He smiled beneath his oxygen mask. Technically, A-10s weren't night-capable aircraft, but the high command was throwing everything it had into this counteroffensive. Their orders were clear—to keep the pressure on the North Koreans around the clock. And if that meant that he and his men had to take unexpected risks, then Chon would see to it that those risks brought results on every mission.

Their prey this time was a North Korean supply convoy that had been spotted late in the afternoon by an RF-5A photoreconnaissance aircraft. Even though the NK trucks had been carefully camouflaged and concealed among some trees, their still-warm engines had shown up clearly on the recon plane's infrared film. Intelligence believed the communists were moving only at night to try to avoid detection.

Chon's flight had been readied immediately as part of the

ongoing effort to interdict all supplies heading for the Taejon area.

"Phoenix Flight, this is Voodoo, over." A quiet voice came through his headphones. There was his signal. Voodoo was an observation plane, an OV-10D Bronco. It had the low-light and thermal-imaging sensors that Chon's attack aircraft lacked, and the slow-moving spotter had been launched at dusk, an hour before Chon's jets. The radio contact meant his A-10s were approaching the most likely area now.

"Phoenix Flight, location Alpha X-ray four seven three seven, over."

There wasn't any need for the spotter plane to say what was at that location. Chon looked at the map taped to his knee and made some rapid calculations. The A-10's avionics weren't all that sophisticated, and a lot of the navigating was still done by the pilot.

"Roger, Voodoo, ETA three minutes." Chon flashed his navigation lights twice to alert his subordinates and banked a little to the left. Once on course he stole a quick glance behind. The other A-10s were still with him.

He checked his armament panel, then glanced at the map. The terrain stayed hilly, with a highway winding around the highest elevations. The best approach route was across the road, moving from east to west, but they would have to do some fancy flying to avoid slamming into a hill at three hundred knots.

He clicked his mike. "Phoenix Flight, this is Lead. Standard attack from the east. Voodoo, our ETA is one minute."

The spotter plane pilot came back on the air immediately. "Roger, Phoenix. Prepped for illumination on your call."

Chon answered with two clicks and flashed his lights again. He broke hard left, knowing that his wingman, Captain Lee, would follow him. He looked right and saw the other pair moving away, off to the north.

There was the highway, a thin black line against an irregular gray-and-white landscape. "Voodoo, this is Phoenix Lead. Now, now, NOW!"

Chon kept his eyes on the surface of the road. Even so, the sudden bright, white light cast by the OV-10-dropped string of flares ruined his night vision. Their harsh, flickering illumination wasn't easy to see by. He blinked, looking for patterns, regular shadows, or shapes along the road.

There.

A row of boxy shadows, still moving in column down the road.

Chon's thumb reached for the cannon trigger as his A-10 dropped lower toward the road.

ON HIGHWAY 23

The flares swaying down out of the sky could mean only one thing. Disaster.

"Get off the road! Disperse!" Major Roh In-Hak screamed into his radio, then leaned out of the truck cab. He waved his arms frantically, motioning the drivers behind him off to either side of the road. Most stared uncomprehendingly back.

It was too late. Roh heard a howling whine and looked back and up. Two dark, cruciform shapes were roaring down out of the sky—heading directly for him. Death on the wing.

The major panicked and threw himself out of the truck cab. He pinwheeled down a steep embankment and landed hard against the frozen earth of a rice-paddy dike. He lay motionless, gasping for air.

Roh looked up at his still-moving truck just as the first attacking aircraft fired. Its bulbous nose was illuminated by a blaze of light even brighter than the flares drifting overhead, and a stream of fire reached out and ripped into the earth near his truck. Then it leaped toward the vehicle as the pilot corrected his aim.

The North Korean major buried his face in the ground as the truck exploded, sending a searing sheet of orange-and-red flame just over his head. It had been carrying artillery ammunition destined for the heavy guns bombarding Taejon. He knew his driver was dead.

More explosions rocked the earth, lighting up the hills on either side of the narrow valley they were in. Roh stayed down as fragments whined all around, trying to shut out the awful sounds as screams blended with the roar of jet engines and the rippling thunder of high-velocity aircraft cannons.

The noise faded and then died away entirely. The enemy planes had finished their strafing runs.

Roh raised his head cautiously and then scrambled to his feet. He ran back toward the rest of the column to check the damage and was relieved by what he found. Only the first three trucks had been hit—all carrying ammunition or food. The supply convoy's precious fuel tankers were still intact.

But they were trapped on this road. His vehicles couldn't possibly escape over the rough countryside. And Roh knew the enemy pilots would be back to finish what they'd started. He went from truck to truck, banging on cab doors and screaming, "Deploy! Deploy! Troops take up positions in the trees! Get the antiaircraft vehicles operational!"

The column's air defenses were pitiful. Every one of the People's Army's remaining mobile antiaircraft guns were stationed up at the front. As a result, all Roh had to defend his trucks with were a few locally manufactured guns, clumsy 37-millimeter weapons mounted precariously on flatbed trucks, and a sprinkling of shoulder-launched SA-7 SAMs carried by the convoy's small infantry detachment. He knew it wouldn't be enough.

Roh heard the jets thundering back and started running away from the road.

PHOENIX FLIGHT

As he banked hard right to come around again, Chon armed his cluster bombs. They would drop all their ordnance in one pass, and there would be no second chance.

"Phoenix Flight, this is Lead. Attack in echelon."

Clicks acknowledged his order, and Chon started concentrating on his flying. More flares went off ahead, lighting up the rugged countryside, and he pulled the A-10's nose higher to clear a hill just ahead.

As he popped over the tree-lined hill's jagged summit, Chon saw what looked like a cloud of fireflies and streaks of light zipping past his canopy. Tracers. He tried to avoid flinching. The A-10 was armored, but no sane pilot trusted in armor to keep his airplane flyable. He'd already been shot down once by enemy flak and he wasn't about to let it happen again.

Chon punched his flare dispenser to automatic and set his HUD for a cluster bomb drop directly over the center of the road now coming up fast.

One concentration of tracers attracted his attention. His eyes narrowed. They were coming from some sort of flak vehicle, and he was tempted to give it a quick cannon burst after he'd made his pass. Chon fought the temptation. Attacking alerted defenses wasn't wise. The mission was to destroy what they were trying to defend.

He reached for the bomb release.

ON HIGHWAY 23

Roh told the men near him to fire, and purely for effect, he emptied his own pistol at the dark shapes streaking overhead. He could see their undersides clearly in the light cast by his burning vehicles.

As his pistol clicked empty, the North Korean swore to himself. He'd identified the attackers. They were American A-10s and pistol bullets wouldn't bother them any more than they would a tank. Each spewed a trail of incandescent flares as it roared past.

His motionless truck column disappeared in a blinding series of rippling detonations. Hundreds of flashes tore up and down the line of now-abandoned vehicles and blossomed across the frozen paddies on either side of the road. A cluster of furnace-white fireballs rising in the air told him that the fuel tankers needed at Taejon were gone.

Temporarily blinded, Roh blinked and looked away from the flames, trying to spot the American-made aircraft as they fled the scene of their victory. He was gratified to see that some of his men were still firing at them.

A shoulder-launched SAM flashed up into the night sky, darting after one of the fleeing jets. Roh urged it on silently, hoping that his troops might achieve some small success by at least downing an enemy plane. But then the SAM veered away, tracking a decoy flare instead of the vanishing A-10. He cursed and threw his pistol into the snow.

Two hundred meters away, the inferno along the highway became visible as the dust and smoke cleared. Almost every truck had been lacerated by fragments or by actual bomblet explosions. And at least half were on fire. Roh stared hard at them, trying to remember which ones carried ammunition.

One of the vehicles exploded, aiding his memory.

The First Shock Army would have to make do without its supplies.

JANUARY 17—NAVAL AVIATION BASE, VLADIVOSTOK, R.S.F.S.R.

The rising sun cast long, sharp-edged shadows across the base and gleamed brightly off snow piled beside its runways. One by one the arc lights that had illuminated the airfield winked off, no longer needed to turn night into day.

The Soviet armaments officer yawned and stretched, trying to work a painful crick out of his neck. He stopped to stare in wonder at the sight before his eyes. It had been dark when the last regiment of bombers flying in from the Northern Fleet had landed, and he'd been so busy that he hadn't really paid much attention.

But now it was impossible not to. He'd never seen his base so crowded before. Nearly sixty twin-engined Backfire bombers were parked across the field—some wingtip to wingtip, others in protective revetments. Every technician he had surrounded the bombers, manhandling AS-4 Kitchen antiship missiles into place under each wing.

He glanced at his watch. Excellent. His men would finish rearming and refueling the Backfires well ahead of the general's deadline. And then the American carriers steaming arrogantly off South Korea would have something new to worry about.

SEA OF JAPAN

The Red Navy's Surface Action Group One steamed southwest at twenty knots, slicing through moderate seas under clear skies. The massive Kirov-class battle cruiser *Frunze* occupied the center, accompanied by two older missile cruisers and two modern Sovremenny-class destroyers. Other cruisers, destroyers, and frigates surrounded the surface strike force as part of a thick ASW and air defense screen.

Three fighter squadrons—two of MiG-23s and one of MiG-29s—orbited endlessly overhead, constantly relieved by new squadrons dispatched from bases near Vladivostok or on the island of Etorofu. All waited eagerly for the word to pounce on any incoming American airstrike.

Surface Action Group One was just twenty hours away from the vital Tsushima Strait.

ABOARD USS *CONSTELLATION*, OFF THE KOREAN COAST

Brown stared hard at the enhanced satellite photos. "When were these taken?"

Captain Ross, his threat team commander, checked his watch. "About an hour ago, Admiral."

"Jesus, Sam, we've got big-time trouble here."

Ross nodded his agreement. Between them, the Soviet bomber force and the oncoming surface action group could catch the *Constellation* and the *Nimitz* in one hell of a bear hug.

Brown handed the photos to his chief of staff and clasped his hands behind his back. "Any political intelligence on their intentions?"

"Negative, Admiral. Still no word out of Moscow on what they're up to."

Brown swore and started pacing the length of the Flag Plot. Ross and the chief of staff kept pace with him. "Okay, guys. Here's the way I see it. The Soviets might just be trying to put some extra pressure on us. Maybe they're hoping to force us to reduce our close-air support sorties for the footsloggers. Maybe . . ." The admiral turned and walked back the way he'd come. "But we can't take that chance. We've got to assume their intentions are hostile."

"Agreed, sir."

Brown stopped by the large-scale map display. "All right, then, gentlemen. Here's how we'll play this thing." He paused and then went on, "Effective immediately, we'll alter course to close the Tsushima Strait ourselves—ahead of that damned Russian task force. In the meantime I want all ground-support missions halted. Tell CAG I want his strike crews to stand down for a mandatory eight-hour rest. After that, I want a full-scale antiship strike spotted on deck and ready to go when I give the word."

Brown looked closer at the plot. "How long before those

bastards cross the line into our three-hundred-mile exclusion zone?''

''Twenty-four hours, Admiral.''

Brown grimaced. ''Then I suspect those are going to be the longest goddamn twenty-four hours of our lives, gentlemen. Let's stay sharp.''

The admiral stayed where he was as the other two men hurried away to carry out his orders. Beneath his feet, he felt the *Constellation* heeling over onto her new course—headed south. South toward the Tsushima Strait. South toward a rendezvous with the Red Navy.

UN FORCES MOBILE HEADQUARTERS, NEAR ANSONG

The M-577 command vehicle swayed as it rounded a corner at high speed. McLaren stood high in the commander's hatch, braced against the personnel carrier's kidney-rattling ride. From where he stood, he could see the whole headquarters column as it wound its way west along the highway. Tanks and troop carriers were thrown out ahead and behind for security, trucks and command carriers intermingled in the middle, and a flight of helicopter gunships orbited overhead, covering the entire mile-long convoy.

The column slowed as it passed through the smoldering, bombed-out ruins of a small town. Corpses and wrecked vehicles dotted the flat, snow-covered fields outside the village. Most were North Korean. Some were not.

The M-577 bucked sharply as its treads ground over a partially filled-in shell crater, and it turned another corner, slowing still more as it passed a column of men marching east on foot—grinning South Korean MPs guarding dazed-looking prisoners. The MPs saluted as McLaren's command vehicle roared by, and he returned their salutes with a grin of his own.

The prisoners they were guarding were a clear-cut indication of just how successful Thunderbolt had been so far. Up to this point in the war the NKs had always fought fanatically—often to the last man. Now that was changing. They were beginning to surrender—often en masse. McLaren could feel the tide turning in his favor.

There were other indications of success. Intelligence estimated that his troops had crushed four North Korean infantry divisions in the thirty-six hours since that attack began. Several others had been hammered so heavily that they were now judged completely combat ineffective.

Better still, his armored spearheads had already penetrated up to fifty kilometers, and the NKs still showed no signs of being able to mount a coordinated counterattack. Most of their best divisions remained locked in combat around Taejon, seemingly unable, or unwilling, to break free and march north. Without them the North Koreans couldn't possibly stop his forces before they reached the sea. And given another forty-eight hours of uninterrupted, broken-field running like this, McLaren knew he could bring victory within reach.

Then he saw a Soviet-made T-62 sitting abandoned off on the shoulder of the road and felt his smile fading. The Russians were the imponderable—the five-hundred-pound gorilla who could jump in at the last minute and wreck everything.

He'd seen the reports. The Soviets had powerful task forces at sea. Their bomber forces were on full alert. And now Category I tank and motorized rifle divisions had been spotted massing at North Korean border crossing points. McLaren shook his head. Were the Soviets really prepared to risk going to war for their North Korean clients?

Jesus, he hoped not. This war was bad enough.

The column sped onward, moving west toward the Yellow Sea, and McLaren moved with it, silently pondering his options if the Cold War suddenly burst into bright-red flame.

C H A P T E R
42
Decision

JANUARY 18—BEIJING, PEOPLE'S REPUBLIC OF CHINA

The Premier of the People's Republic of China studied his colleagues closely, careful to hide his amusement as he watched the Politburo debate settle into its usual patterns. Late middle age had given him a perspective on human nature unclouded by sentiment or optimism, but it still amazed him that China's wisest and most experienced leaders could disagree so vehemently and so predictably about so many different issues.

In fairness, however, the Premier had to admit that the matter now before the Politburo was a momentous one, worthy of considered and careful discussion. Still, time pressed on while these men threw the same tired phrases back and forth. The American and Soviet flotillas were within hours of shooting at each other. A war begun in the Sea of Japan could engulf the whole world within minutes. And still these men talked.

The hard-liners, the archconservative communists, were the most predictable of all—the most vocal. Their leader, Do Zhenping, the Party's general secretary, was the elder statesman of Chinese ideology, the last veteran of the Long March. His words carried weight. "Why even consider this imperialist intrigue? If we act as the Americans suggest, we will help end the war—but it will end in their favor! How do we gain by that?"

"Surely, the answer to that is obvious, Comrade General Secretary?" Liu Gendong was quick to answer. As the minister of trade and one of the youngest men on the Politburo, he led its progressive faction. His oldest son was an exchange student in America now, studying nuclear physics at the California Institute of Technology. Since its early-morning arrival in Beijing, Liu had emerged as the strongest supporter of the American proposal.

He steepled his hands. "The economic and technological concessions the Americans have offered us will be of tremendous benefit to every sector of our economy. And the proposed trade agreements with South Korea are only a start. Japan cannot sit idly by while its archrival trades freely with us. Nor can Hong Kong or Singapore. They will bid against each other for our favor. The Four Tigers will bow to the Dragon!" He smiled, clearly imagining the negotiations he could conduct should such an event occur.

The Premier saw Liu's words cause a stir among the undecideds who held the balance of power on the Politburo. He nodded slightly to himself. The minister of trade was a persuasive, if overly enthusiastic, young man. He opted to display cautious support for Liu's position. "The minister's words are well taken, Comrade General Secretary. China is a poor country. We need markets for our raw materials, and we desperately need foreign exchange to buy technology."

Do Zhenping was unconvinced, his tone unrepentant and uncompromising. "Our merchants have been whoring for the West for years. I see no need to allow them to spread their legs wider." There were grins at the old revolutionary's coarse language. It was his most conspicuous resistance to the smoother, more sophisticated face of New China. The old man continued, enunciating every word. "If change must come, let it be slow and not sudden. Let us emulate the tortoise and not the hare. That is the best course for our Revolution."

"Is it, comrade?" Liu spoke quietly. "Do we have the time? The rest of the world leaps forward while we crawl."

"Let them leap," the older man answered petulantly. "Their mad consumerism is not an example worthy of imitation."

He spoke earnestly, directing his words to everyone at the table, especially the Premier. "We owe the West no favors. They sucked our life's blood for centuries before the people rose up in righteous anger." Do stood up unsteadily. All eyes were on him. Age was still revered in China, and this survivor of the Revolution was the voice of history. "Listen to me. Despite its successes, America can still lose this war. The Russians stand ready to help swing the balance back. If we help the imperialists win, we will be seen as the nation that turned its back on its socialist brothers."

He waved a hand, dispelling arguments not yet voiced. "I have no love for Kim and his gang. His 'dynastic communism' is a perversion, a personality cult reduced to absurdity. But what will the world see? China, aspiring to be the world's third superpower, rescuing capitalist America from a situation that her own weakness and indecision created. I suggest that would not exactly endear us to our fellow communists."

The old man coughed, a reminder of his bout with pneumonia earlier in the winter. He wiped his lips and continued, "And there is risk. The only way we could force Kim to end his war would be to threaten him with our own troops. The Koreans are already firmly in the Soviet camp. Can we afford to back them further into the arms of the Kremlin?"

The Premier looked around the table. Heads were nodding. Do's impassioned words were hitting home with some of the Politburo's swing voters. But not with enough to be decisive. The conservatives and the progressives were too closely matched on this issue for either to prevail openly.

He smiled. The situation was perfect.

China wanted to act on the world stage, but she did not want to be seen as the puppet of another superpower. China wanted foreign trade, but she did not want the foreign influence that must inevitably follow. China wanted to be America's friend, but she did not want to be North Korea's enemy. In short, China wanted it all—the sun, the sea, the moon, and the stars.

And the Premier knew how to get it.

The time had come to intervene—both in the debate and in the war. He leaned forward and rapped sharply on the table. "Comrades! The time grows short. We must make a decision soon, before events move beyond our ability to control them."

His colleagues nodded, somewhat impatiently. That much was obvious.

He looked first at Do and then at Liu. "Comrade General Secretary and Comrade Minister, I do not believe that our respective positions on this matter are necessarily opposed to each other." He saw the skepticism on both men's faces and smiled politely. "Let me show you what I mean."

The Premier took five minutes to outline his proposal and knew that he had won them over before he finished. China would lay its cards on the table of global politics in its own way.

3RD AIRBORNE DIVISION HQ, BEIJING, P.R.C.

The general rubbed a hand absentmindedly through the close-cropped thatch of gray bristles he called a haircut and squinted into the early-morning light pouring through his office window. The courtyard outside, normally utterly quiet and empty at this hour, looked like an anthill stirred by some mischievous child. Soldiers in full combat gear ran everywhere, loading bags of rice, machine guns, light mortars, and ammunition boxes onto a ragtag assembly of flatbed trucks. Others were being marshaled in platoon formations and then marched away toward the airfield. The general knew that similar scenes were taking place at barracks areas all across the capital.

He turned at a quick rap on his door. "Come in."

It was the division's deputy commander, a short, bandy-legged colonel whose flat-featured face showed Mongol blood. "You wanted to see me, Comrade General?"

"Yes, Colonel." The general waved a hand toward the window. "I'd like a progress report."

The shorter man nodded and relaxed slightly. The general's voice was uncharacteristically friendly. "The division's assembly is proceeding precisely on schedule, sir. The First Parachute Regiment and Major Lin's Reconnaissance Company are already at the airfield. The Second Regiment is enroute from its barracks area, and the Third will follow shortly."

"Excellent. So I can tell the high command that we shall be ready for movement later this afternoon?"

"Certainly, Comrade General." The colonel hesitated, apparently unsure about whether to say anything more.

"Yes? Is there something else, Colonel?"

The other nodded and tugged his tunic straight. "Simply

this, Comrade General. I only wanted to ask if this mobilization was merely some kind of surprise drill."

The general frowned and paused, considering his answer carefully. He wasn't in the habit of telling his subordinates more than they needed to know. Still, this was an unusual situation, and his deputy had always been discreet. He opted for candor. "No. I spoke with the Premier himself, late last night. The alert is genuine and concerns possible service outside the People's Republic."

"Indeed, Comrade General?"

"Something puzzles you, Kua?" The general was curious. The colonel's skepticism had been obvious.

The shorter man nodded. "Yes, sir. Before reporting to you, I spoke with General Chen of the Air Force. His transport aircraft have not been alerted. That leaves a question in my mind, Comrade General. If we are being sent to foreign lands, how are we supposed to get there?"

"An excellent question, Colonel." The general shrugged. "And one I am unable to answer. No doubt the Premier has his plans, although he hasn't yet made me a full party to them."

He turned to the window to watch yet another battalion march out the main gate, arms swinging high and rifles slung. He turned back to the colonel. "In the meantime, my friend, we have our orders to carry out. See to it that they are carried out expeditiously. The Premier has stressed the need for haste in this matter."

"Of course, Comrade General." The colonel saluted and left to hurry things along. Assembling an airborne division of more than nine thousand men took constant attention.

THE MINISTRY OF COMMUNICATIONS PYONGYANG, NORTH KOREA

Choi Ki-Wan, a survivor of more than forty years of deadly intrigue, was as cautious in his choice of words as he was in his basic nature. "You have some further word from our mutual, ah, 'friend'?"

Tai Han-Gi, the minister of communications, smiled indulgently at his older colleague on North Korea's Politburo. The man was right to fear eavesdropping by Kim Jong-Il's security forces, but there were, after all, certain advantages to commanding all communications facilities throughout the whole People's Republic. And they included access to the latest Japanese antibugging equipment. Tai had no fear of Kim Jong-Il spies within the confines of his own office.

He folded his hands. "Indeed, Comrade Choi. I have heard much from our 'friends' within these past few hours."

"Do they offer a solution to our common problem?"

Tai nodded and said flatly, "Yes." Then he learned closer to the older man. "Actions are being taken now that should give us the opening we need. But there can be no hesitation, no wavering when the time comes for us to act. We are playing a high stakes game—a game with infinite rewards for the victors and infinite torments for the losers. You understand?"

He read the momentary indecision on Choi's face and wondered if it might prove necessary to arrange a speedy accident for his old comrade in arms. He hoped not. It would be both personally painful and dangerous. Kim's agents were everywhere.

To his relief Choi's uncertain resolve hardened.

"Yes, I understand. Well, we must bear those risks. There is no other way to preserve our Revolution."

Or to preserve our own positions and privileges, Tai thought cynically. No matter, he had Choi's commitment, and with it the collaboration of all the older man's supporters. His patrons outside Pyongyang would be pleased.

THE WHITE HOUSE, WASHINGTON, D.C.

The five men crowding the Oval Office could not conceal their restlessness. The President paced ceaselessly, his face haggard from too many sleepless nights. Paul Bannerman, the secretary of state, paced beside him, looking equally worn and rumpled. South Korea's ambassador, Kang Ki-baek, sat motionless by the fireplace, gazing intently into the dancing flames. Blake Fowler sat beside him, all too conscious of his own bleary, red-rimmed eyes, crumpled suit jacket, and notepad filled with nervous doodlings. Only Admiral Simpson seemed outwardly calm as he stood beside the President's desk, staring out the window at his own reflection.

"Phil, what's the latest word from Brown's task force?"

Blake looked up. The President had stopped pacing and now stood shoulder to shoulder with the admiral.

Simpson glanced at the taller man. "The Soviet strike group is still closing, sir. Tom estimates they'll cross into his declared exclusion zone within five hours. After that he'll have just over an hour before the Russians get within missile range of his carriers." The admiral squared his shoulders. "He'll have to have permission to hit them before that happens, Mr. President."

The President nodded absentmindedly and crossed the room back to Bannerman. "Well, where the hell is he, Paul? What are those folks in Beijing playing at? First their ambassador asks for an immediate meeting and now he's late getting here."

Bannerman looked to Blake for rescue. "Any ideas, Dr. Fowler? After all, you're the China expert here."

"I'm sure it's not an intentional delay, Mr. President," Blake said, hoping he was right. Too many lives depended on this meeting to contemplate being wrong. "The NSA says the signals traffic between the ambassador and Beijing has been extremely heavy all day. I suspect their embassy staff has had problems keeping up with the high-level decoding required."

The President stared at him for a moment without speaking and then resumed his pacing.

His phone buzzed softly and he reached across the desk to get it. "Yes? Okay, June, send him right in." The President hung up and turned to face the others. "The ambassador's car just pulled up. He'll be up shortly."

Shortly was something of an understatement. The Chinese ambassador was ushered into the room two minutes later. And despite his evident hurry, he'd obviously taken great care in dressing. His perfectly pressed charcoal-gray suit, white shirt, and red tie made the small, prim man look more like a prosperous Hong Kong banker than the emissary of the world's most populous communist nation. It also made Blake feel scruffy in comparison.

"Mr. President, I am deeply honored that you have agreed to receive me at this late hour." The ambassador bowed slightly and straightened. "I hope you will forgive me for this inexcusable delay."

The President donned his warmest "campaign" smile and stepped forward with his hand outstretched. "There's nothing to forgive, Mr. Ambassador. As always, I'm delighted to see you."

The two men shook hands and moved to a pair of chairs closer to the fire. South Korea's ambassador settled himself beside them.

The Chinese ambassador wasted little time with the usual diplomatic pleasantries. He reached into the leather briefcase he'd brought with him and pulled out a sheaf of papers bearing the official seal of the People's Republic. "I have my government's response to your request that we aid you in bringing this unfortunate war to an end."

He handed a copy to both the President and the South Korean ambassador.

As the two men scanned the documents, Blake felt his heart speeding up and pressed a hand hard onto his right knee to keep it from trembling visibly in nervous anticipation. He watched the President's face closely and felt his hopes sink as he saw the Chief Executive arch an eyebrow. Had the Chinese refused them or set impossible conditions on their help?

At last the President looked up from his reading and stared hard at the ambassador. "Your government's answer seems" —he searched visibly for the right word—"somewhat tentative, Mr. Ambassador. Much seems to depend on events over which we have little control."

He handed the papers to Bannerman and turned to South Korea's ambassador. "Wouldn't you agree, Mr. Kang?"

The South Korean nodded somberly.

The Chinese emissary sat farther forward in his chair, an earnest and amiable smile on his lips. "Mr. President, Mr. Ambassador, please. It is true that there are certain, ah, conditional aspects to our reply to your proposal." He glanced at his watch. "However, I have been personally assured by my Premier that, even as we speak, actions are being taken that will ensure that those conditions are met."

Bannerman gave the Chinese reply to Blake, who scanned it quickly—astounded by the grand political design it described in such short, simple words. He stared for a moment at the papers, with his mind half a world away as he tried to assess the diplomatic and military pressures now set in motion. Would they be enough?

He felt the President's eyes on him, looked up to meet them, and nodded. What the Chinese intended just might work. Hell, it had to work. There wasn't time to try anything else.

The President nodded back. Blake's unspoken assessment matched his own instinctive reaction. They'd have to hope that the Chinese knew what they were doing. He sat back in his high-backed Georgian chair. "Very well, Mr. Ambassador. We'll wait with you for these 'conditions' to materialize." He forced a smile. "In the meantime, can we offer you something to drink? Tea, or perhaps something stronger?"

The ambassador smiled back. "Thank you, Mr. President. Tea would be most welcome."

"Splendid." The President looked at his watch and frowned. He reached into an inner pocket, pulled out a pen and small notepad, and scribbled a quick note. He motioned to the admiral still standing by the window. "Phil, could you arrange for this to be sent immediately? I don't want any unfortunate accidents while there's still hope that this thing can be settled."

Simpson crossed the room and read the note. It was addressed to Admiral Thomas Aldrige Brown. He nodded abruptly and left the Oval Office at a fast walk. Time was running out in the Yellow Sea.

ABOARD USS *CONSTELLATION*, NEAR THE TSUSHIMA STRAIT

Brown read the signal from Washington one more time. "You're sure this has been authenticated, Jim?"

His chief of staff nodded. "It's genuine, Admiral."

"Shit." Brown stared at the Flag Plot's strategic display. It showed the position of all known Soviet naval and air units in the region. All were closing on his task force. They would be within range in four or five hours at most. He balled his hands into fists and kept them rigid at his sides. The President's order went against all his instincts to hit before being hit.

Slowly, very slowly, Brown forced his hands to relax. An order was an order. He turned to his chief of staff and said, "Okay, Jim. Signal Washington that we're complying. And tell

CAG to keep his pilots in the ready room. Takeoff time has been postponed for at least three hours."

Brown turned back to the display as his chief of staff hurried away. He could see it happening again—the same kind of political indecision and drift that had gotten so many good men killed in the air over North Vietnam. The Soviets were going to get within missile range while Washington diddled around. And there wasn't anything he could do about it. Not a damned thing.

THE KREMLIN, MOSCOW, R.S.F.S.R.

The General Secretary stared slowly around the elegantly furnished room at the other members of the ruling Politburo. Many were his creatures, men he had plucked from lesser positions and promoted to serve his own interests. But if his years in power had taught him anything, it was that loyalty within the Party was a fair-weather commodity. It was there when things went right and gone the instant things went wrong.

And things had been going wrong.

His gaze settled on the defense minister and he scowled. The man sat quiet and unmoving in his chair, his dark brown eyes deeply shadowed and his shoulders slumped. The General Secretary gritted his teeth. The bastard. The foolish bastard.

He rapped gently on the table, ending the low hum of a half-dozen whispered conversations. "Comrades, we face a grave crisis—one with enormous implications for the safety of our motherland."

Heads around the table nodded. They'd all been briefed on the growing military confrontation between the Soviet Union and the United States. All had been shocked by the speed with which it had developed, and most were unsure of the causes.

The General Secretary continued without pause. "Most of us had assumed that American attack on our surveillance aircraft and submarine was unprovoked. Naturally we felt compelled to respond to this aggression—and to respond with overwhelming force. Hence our preparations for a massive retaliatory strike on the murderous American warships."

Murmured agreement swept around the table. Although the Defense Council had made its decisions without consulting the full Politburo, all present had seen the necessity of matching the Americans blow for blow. Any other course would only invite continued imperialist aggression.

The General Secretary held up a hand for quiet and shook his head sadly. "Comrades, it is with deep regret that I must tell you that we were misinformed, or perhaps I should say 'misled,' by one of our most trusted colleagues."

He turned to face the defense minister. "Have I misstated the facts in any way, Andrei Ivanovich?"

A shocked silence spread throughout the room. Only the foreign minister was unsurprised. He'd been briefed by the General Secretary more than an hour before.

The defense minister, seeming strangely smaller despite his height, unwrinkled uniform, and multiple rows of medals, sighed and sat upright. "No, Comrade General Secretary."

The defense minister pulled a handwritten document lying before him on the table closer and began reading in a flat, emotionless voice. "Comrades, on January eleventh of this year, on my own authority, I ordered the submarine *Konstantin Dribinov* to attack a group of American warships. I made this decision unilaterally, without consulting any other member of this body."

He raised his eyes briefly and the General Secretary could read the hate directed toward the end of the table—toward the director of the KGB. The General Secretary could understand that. When he'd confronted the KGB chieftain with his suspicions, the man had buckled and sold his fellow conspirator down the river without a qualm, interested only in preserving his own position—however temporarily.

"Go on, Comrade Minister. Continue your confession," the General Secretary prodded, anxious lest the delay raise further, unanswerable questions in the minds of other Politburo members.

The defense minister dropped his eyes to the paper before him. "I made this unilateral decision in response to an urgent request from our allies in Pyongyang. They needed our assistance to help repel an American amphibious attack apparently aimed at their western coast. They had no way of stopping this attack themselves—"

The foreign minister interrupted, no longer able to contain

his anger or his contempt. "An attack that later proved to be nothing more than a ploy!"

"Yes, that is true." The defense minister's voice shrank to a hollow whisper. He was silent for a second and then looked up from his notes. He'd been reading them verbatim, but as he continued, he spoke from memory. The General Secretary watched closely, ready to break in should the man stray from the agreed-upon version of the facts. "The momentum of the North Korean attack was slowing, and our materiel assistance no longer seemed enough to ensure victory. I believed that a limited, covert intervention by Soviet forces could restore the situation."

The foreign minister snorted. "Your so-called 'covert' assistance is now spread all over the Western media, comrade." He raised an eyebrow. "Why, I believe I saw your Captain Markov giving an interview to one of the American television networks." There were uncomfortable chuckles from the others.

The defense minister flushed red at the gibe. "His orders were explicit. He was not to reveal his identity."

"Then he failed in his orders. And you have brought us to the brink of an unnecessary and unwinnable war with the West." The foreign minister spoke flatly, stating facts.

"That is also true, comrade." The defense minister lowered his head to hide his anger at this public humiliation and then slowly, deliberately read the last paragraph of his prepared statement. "Because of my unilateral actions, Soviet citizens have lost their lives, and our country has been placed in a dangerous confrontation with the imperialist powers. Therefore, I hereby resign my position as minister of defense, my membership on the Central Committee, and my active membership in our beloved Party. Further, I request that I be allowed to retire immediately."

The General Secretary looked slowly around the table, moving his eyes from man to man, seeking their decision. One by one, each shook his head. The defense minister's error was too great. Lives had been lost, Soviet prestige reduced, and the chain of command usurped. He would not be allowed to fade away comfortably. A public trial would only further erode the authority of the State, but the Minister's demise for "reasons of ill health" would soon follow.

Satisfied that he had his answer, the General Secretary cleared his throat and said harshly, "Very well, comrade, you have your answer. You may go. We have work to do."

The defense minister inclined his head, rose stiffly without speaking, and left the room.

The General Secretary watched him go and then turned to face his colleagues. "Now, comrades, we face the difficult task of extricating ourselves from this mess without igniting a global conflict. Some of the actions we must take are obvious, others less so."

He crooked a finger at the director of the KGB. "What is the latest news from the war zone, Comrade Director? How are our gallant slant-eyed allies faring?" He let the sarcasm drip from every word to show the Politburo just how he felt about the North Koreans.

"Disastrously, Comrade General Secretary." The director shook his head. "The imperialist counteroffensive has been astoundingly successful. Our most recent satellite photos show their columns nearing the sea. The Americans and their South Korean puppets are within a day or two of completely surrounding most of the North's remaining combat formations."

"Can they be stopped?"

"No." The KGB director's words were sure and certain. "The armies of the North are increasingly incapable of undertaking any coordinated offensive or defensive action south of the former demilitarized zone. Their tanks have no fuel, their artillery has no ammunition, and their men have no food. They have been beaten."

The General Secretary saw anger and dismay flit across the faces around the table. Previous Ministry of Defense briefings on the battlefield situation had painted a much more favorable picture. Naturally.

During the silence that followed the KGB chieftain's gloomy appraisal, he saw one of the foreign minister's aides slip into the room with some kind of telex. More good news, no doubt. No matter, it was time to show his colleagues how recent events could still be turned to their advantage. He shifted his eyes and broke the silence. "I think it is clear, comrades, that we must persuade Kim Jong-Il to save what he can of his forces in the South. The survivors can regroup behind their fortifications along the Demilitarized Zone. They will of course need to be rearmed and reequipped. And we shall supply those needs.''

He saw the puzzlement on their faces and smiled. ''Think, comrades. Every piece of our equipment the younger Kim accepts puts him further in our debt and in our power. With the Americans and their puppets pounding at his gates, he will have no choice but to accede to our every demand. We shall be the de facto rulers of North Korea. And once that is accomplished, an armistice can easily be arranged. We may not have conquered South Korea, but certainly half a loaf is better than none.'' He smiled at his own plan.

''Forgive me, Comrade General Secretary, but that may not be as easy to achieve as you imagine.'' The foreign minister held out a telex. ''I've just received this communique from Beijing. It seems that the People's Republic of China has just announced that it will support an immediate cease-fire on the Korean peninsula.''

He laid the first telex aside and picked up another. ''And this is a message specifically directed to us. In it, the Chinese announce their intention to oppose continued support or arms shipments from any country not now a belligerent. They go on to say that such interference will be met with any and all appropriate means, up to and including the use of military force.'' The foreign minister folded the telex and sent it down the table toward the General Secretary.

''They're bluffing!'' The KGB director's face had turned bright red. He'd always loathed the Chinese. ''They haven't got enough military power to frighten a small child.''

''Perhaps not by themselves, Viktor Mikhailovich. But what about when they are joined by the Americans? Their message also indicates that they have offered the use of an airborne division to act as a peacekeeping force while the cease-fire is implemented. And that they are asking the Americans to provide the air transport for those troops!''

Silence greeted the foreign minister's words. The news was worse than any of the members of the Politburo could have imagined.

At last the General Secretary spoke through stiff lips. Long-held plans were collapsing around his ears. ''The signal the Chinese are sending is easy to read. They are on the verge of wholeheartedly allying with the Americans."

It was unthinkable. Unimaginable just a few short months before. How could he have guessed that the insane gamble of one North Korean megalomaniac could destroy years of hard diplomatic work and cautious maneuvering? He had come to power as General Secretary determined to reweave the Soviet hegemony over the Far East—to bring China back into its proper orbit around Moscow, to bend the emerging economic powers of Asia to the Kremlin's will. And now all that was falling apart.

He stirred himself into action. He'd fought enough battles in his time to know when to cut his losses. "Comrades, this latest Chinese betrayal changes everything. The new correlation of forces is clear. And our own course is equally clear. We must now act swiftly to save what we can."

He quickly outlined what he had in mind. There wasn't much discussion. There really were no realistic alternatives.

SURFACE ACTION GROUP ONE, NEAR THE TSUSHIMA STRAIT

Admiral Valentin Zakorov read the urgent signal from the Kremlin with great relief. Sanity had evidently prevailed somewhere within those red brick walls.

He looked up at the *Frunze*'s captain, who stood impatiently waiting for new orders. "Captain Nikolayev?"

"Sir?"

Zakorov stuffed the message in his uniform pocket. "Signal the formation to immediately alter course to zero three zero degrees. We've been ordered back to Vladivostok."

"At once, Admiral." Nikolayev left on his errand.

The admiral looked at the chart showing two American carrier battle groups within four hundred miles of his force and sent a mental prayer to the nonexistent God for sparing his ships the test of battle. Beneath his feet he felt the deck surge as his battle cruiser turned and picked up speed—steaming home for safe harbor.

OVER NORTH KOREA

Colonel Sergiev Ivanovitch Borodin blinked his navigation lights three times and then threw his MiG-29 into a tight, rolling turn to the northeast. He looked to either side and saw the planes belonging to the eight other surviving pilots of his erstwhile training squadron settling into formation. Good, the political officer's covert message had reached all of them.

His radio suddenly squawked. "Fulcrum Flight, what are you doing? That turn was not on your flight plan. On your present course you will leave your designated patrol area in three minutes. Acknowledge. Over."

Borodin smiled wryly. At least one of the North Korean ground-based air controllers had been awake. He ignored the voice and opened his MiG-29's throttle, watching in satisfaction as the fighter accelerated smoothly past six hundred knots.

"Fulcrum Flight, you are now out of your patrol area. What the hell are you playing at? Over."

Borodin smiled more broadly. He recognized this new voice. It belonged to the arrogant bastard in charge of the North Korean capital's air defense network—a network he and his squadron were leaving behind at an increasingly fast clip.

He clicked his mike. "Good afternoon, General. This is Fulcrum Lead. We're not playing at anything. We're simply obeying our orders." He glanced out the cockpit. They were crossing into North Korean's rugged Taeback Mountains. Snowfields sparkled in the sunlight.

"Orders? Who gave you orders that override mine?"

Borodin laughed for the first time in weeks. "Moscow, my dear, slant-eyed General. And my orders from Moscow are very simple. We're going home."

He clicked off and switched frequencies to pick up the Vladivostok Air Defense Network. They were less than thirty minutes away from entering Soviet airspace. The North Koreans would have to fly their own planes from now on.

JANUARY 19—THE MINISTRY OF DEFENSE, PYONGYANG, NORTH KOREA

Kim Jong-Il listened to the increasing flow of reports with a sinking heart. There couldn't be any doubt left. The Soviets were abandoning him—pulling every last adviser, combat pilot, and technical expert they had out of the country as fast as they could. Even the munitions trains from Vladivostok had stopped, some within a few kilometers of the border.

"Well, Dear Leader? Now what shall we do? What miracle do you offer?" an insolent voice asked.

He looked up at the speaker, Tai Han-Gi, and felt his despair transformed into a towering rage. How dare any man, even one on the Defense Council, address him in that manner? He was the son of the Great Leader—and a great leader in his own right.

Kim slammed his fist into the table. "Coward! Chinese puppet!" He pointed a pudgy finger at the unmoved face of the minister of communications. "Your time is coming, old man. I advise you not to hasten your own end."

He saw the other old men around the table frowning at his words and forced himself to calm down. With the crisis upon them, rage was an unproductive emotion, and his revenge for Tai's slights would have to wait. He lowered his voice to a more reasonable level. "Comrades, we need no miracles here. Certainly the situation we face is a difficult one. But it is not insoluble. It is true that the Russians and their weapons were useful, but we can live and fight without them."

Kim levered himself up out of his chair and moved to the situation map hung on one of the underground bunker's reinforced concrete walls. He tapped the area around Taejon. "Our First Shock Army is still fighting gallantly, and I have no doubt it will soon crush this temporary enemy incursion into our liberated zone." He saw the sneer on Tai's face and chose to ignore it.

"Even more important, comrades, we still possess vast, untapped resources. Our Red Guard militia alone musters more than two million fighting men and women. With them fully mobilized, we shall be able to sweep down from the north and crush the fascists once and for all. This war is not lost! The final victory is within sight. We have only to reach out with both hands and seize it."

Silence greeted his words. A silence broken only by a single, dry cough.

"Yes, Choi?" Kim couldn't keep the disdain he felt from showing.

"A simple question, Dear Leader." Choi coughed again, covering his mouth with a withered, wrinkled hand. "Do you propose to repeal the laws of mathematics during this final drive for victory?"

"What do you mean?" Kim's uneasiness multiplied. These men were beginning to openly defy his judgment. Perhaps they were even mocking him.

"Only this, Kim Jong-Il." Choi paused to let the insult sink in. "You say that we have two million men and women in our Red Guards. And that is true. But does not the South have twice that number of its own militia?"

Kim dismissed Choi's question with an abrupt wave. "The oppressed masses of the South will not fight their liberators! America's bandit mercenaries will be left to face our people on their own."

Tai laughed harshly. "You seem to forget, comrade, that the 'oppressed masses of the South' have already been more than willing to fight our armies. Read the reports from your own commanders if you doubt my word." The others nodded their agreement. "The truth, comrade, is that you are living in some kind of fantasy world, while the rest of us must live with the reality of the wreckage you are creating."

Kim goggled at him, struck dumb by the man's audacity. Tai must have a death wish, he thought wildly. So be it, I shall oblige him.

The minister of communications continued without letup, "This war is lost. China now stands ready to join forces with our adversaries. The truth is that we cannot afford your ruinous rule any longer."

"Traitor!" Kim screamed, and saw spittle from his mouth spray out. He lunged back to his chair and stabbed a finger onto the security buzzer installed there. Then he straightened and smiled grimly, eyeing the rest of the men around the table.

"Who else stands with this Chinese lackey? I assure you that there are unmarked graves enough for all of you!"

He heard the door open behind his back and heard footsteps. He spoke without turning around. "Captain Lew, you will arrest those two immediately." He pointed to Tai and Choi, both of whom still sat calmly in their chairs. "Then you will stand ready by me. There may be more arrests to follow."

Tai smiled easily. "Comrade Kim, I don't think I've ever seen you so tired before. I think you've been working too hard. In fact, I believe that you deserve a long rest, a very long rest. Don't you agree, Comrade Choi?"

Choi nodded. "Undoubtedly, Comrade Tai." He looked behind Kim. "Don't you think so, too, Colonel Lew?"

Kim felt ice-cold fear stab clear up his spine as he heard a familiar voice say, "Certainly, Comrade General Secretary."

He turned slowly and saw Lew standing there with his pistol drawn. It was aimed precisely at Kim's face.

Tai's smug, triumphant voice came from over his shoulder. "Take him away, Colonel. You know what to do."

Lew nodded without lowering his pistol an inch. "Yes, comrade. I know what to do."

Other uniformed men entered the bunker and seized the man once known as the Dear Leader by both arms. Without waiting for further orders, they dragged him silent and unprotesting toward the door. An unconnected thought raced through Kim's frozen mind. Now he knew why rabbits sat motionless when trapped by the cold, glittering eyes of a snake. And it was knowledge he would never have the chance to use.

Behind him, he heard Choi speaking urgently to the others still in the room. "Come, comrades. There is no time to lose. We must signal Beijing immediately. We must tell them that their conditions for a cease-fire have been met. This foolish war must be ended while there is still time left to us."

C H A P T E R
43
End Game

None of those gathered in the Oval Office for early-morning coffee had slept save in brief, unconnected snatches. They'd been kept busy all night by a continuous stream of ever more urgent developments—trooping back and forth between the basement-level Situation Room and the more comfortable trappings of the Oval Office itself.

First had come fragmentary reports that the Soviets were reducing the alert status of their forces throughout the world. Those reports had been confirmed by a late-night hotline conversation between the President and the General Secretary— their first direct contact in weeks. The Russian had seemed strangely apologetic, and both men had agreed to treat the series of clashes between their armed forces as a series of regrettable accidents. Tensions were still high, but they seemed more manageable now.

Next, NSA, Japanese, and South Korean monitoring stations had all reported a sudden cessation of Radio Pyongyang's normal mix of boastful propaganda and martial music. It had been replaced by a somber and uninterrupted medley of funeral dirges.

Finally, satellite photos and communications intercepts all showed unmistakable signs of a massive Soviet exodus from North Korea.

It all pointed to one thing, and Blake Fowler shook his head in rueful admiration as he glanced through the Chinese government's proposal for what seemed the thousandth time. China was getting everything it had bargained for and more. Much more. He wondered how the Russians had ever come to believe that they were the world's greatest chess masters.

Blake looked up as the President's desk phone buzzed.

"Yes?" The President sounded awake, though he didn't look it. "Go on."

Blake and the others watched as the President listened quietly for several minutes without speaking. At last he hung up with a simple, "Thank you, Mike. Now go home and get some rest."

Then he bowed his head for almost a minute, still silent. At last he looked up at Bannerman, Simpson, Blake, and the others waiting anxiously. His face was absolutely expressionless. "Admiral Simpson?"

"Yes, Mr. President?"

"I want you to contact General Carpenter immediately." Blake caught the faint glimmering of a suppressed smile on the President's face. He looked years younger. "Tell him I want those Military Airlift Command planes on their way to Beijing within the hour."

Blake understood and grinned, but the others still hadn't caught on.

The President saw their uncomprehending stares and care-lined faces and took pity on them. "Ladies and gentlemen, that was the communications room. Radio Pyongyang is reporting that Kim Jong-Il is dead. Kim Il-Sung is still alive but he's an invalid. And Beijing has just announced that the new North Korean government has agreed unconditionally to the PRC's cease-fire proposals. All hostilities on land, in the air, and at sea are scheduled to end in six hours. The Chinese have relayed a North Korean request that we end our radio jamming so that they can inform their forces trapped in the south."

He smiled openly. "In other words, ladies and gentlemen, the war is over. The killing is over."

Blake knew that wasn't quite accurate, but it was close enough. The balance of power in the Pacific had shifted. The eternal seesaw between China and Russia in North Korea had ended, with the Chinese turning the north into a puppet state. Russia's Pacific strategy lay in the same grave as Kim Jong-Il.

The Chinese wanted South Korea as a trading partner. To keep the trade flowing, they would have to lower the tensions, open the North's borders, and stop the terrorism. It was a little early to talk about reunification, but there would be a lot less heat and a lot more light in that corner of the world.

Now he could rest. Now they could all rest.

JANUARY 20—UN FORCES MOBILE HEADQUARTERS, OUTSIDE SONGT'AN, SOUTH KOREA

McLaren stood outside his camouflaged command vehicle, listening to the distant sounds of war. Heavy artillery rumbled far off, a concussive, rolling series of muffled *whump*'s that he could feel as well as hear—something like a cross between the sound of a fireworks display and a thunder-filled summer storm.

He glanced at his watch: 1359 hours, local time. And as he listened, the noise faded and then fell away entirely—leaving behind a strange, empty silence. With a sudden shock McLaren realized that it was the first real, waking quiet he had known since the war began. His days and nights had been filled with the background drumbeat of war—artillery barrages, clanking tank treads, roaring truck engines, static-filled bursts of frantic radio voices, and the distant crackle of small-arms fire.

And now it was over.

Hansen swung down out of the converted armored personnel carrier. He grinned. "All units are checking in, General. As far as we can tell, the cease-fire is in place."

McLaren bowed his head, genuinely praying for the first time in years. He hadn't felt able to do so with conviction since his wife's funeral. But now the words came freely. He thanked God for granting his soldiers a victorious peace, and he prayed for all the dead and wounded, for all those who had suffered so terribly to win that peace. And when he had finished, he raised his head, surprised to find his eyes wet.

McLaren wiped them roughly and blew his nose. "Goddamned winter colds. Always get 'em."

He looked away across the snow-covered fields, then straightened his shoulders. "Okay, Doug. Let's get back to it.

We've got a hell of a lot of work to do before those Chinese paratroopers arrive to make sure this thing stays over.''

Hansen saluted and followed his general in out of the cold winter air.

JANUARY 22—FIRST SHOCK ARMY HQ, NORTH OF TAEJON

A cold wind whipped the tent flap and Colonel General Cho Hyun-Jae shivered, despite the feeble warmth emitted by a charcoal burner standing in one corner. The chill he felt had its origins in his despair and not the weather.

They had been defeated. Defeated and disgraced. The ugly words rang endlessly and uselessly in his mind. He had been able to think of nothing else in the three days since the communique arrived from Pyongyang—the first real signal he'd received from the high command since shortly after the imperialist counterattack began.

The tersely worded message still lay open atop a desk crowded with crumpled maps, radio gear, and his personal weapons. He stared at it unseeing, the cold phrases burned into his mind:

Cease all offensive operations immediately. Cease-fire with opposing forces effective 1400 hours, 20 January. The People's Army will stack all arms, destroy or render useless all heavy weapons and equipment, and move north. List of approved withdrawal routes follows. Troops from the People's Republic of China will serve as escorts and observers of withdrawal process.

Pyongyang's orders and the reported death of his patron, Kim Jong-Il, had caught Cho like a thunderclap. In all his years of service, nothing had ever prepared him for the possibility of defeat and still less for abject surrender. It was literally unthinkable. The Korean People's Army had never known defeat in battle.

Or so its propaganda said, Cho thought.

Reality taught a different lesson. The imperialist counterattack had proved impossible to resist. The enemy moved too fast, supplies were nonexistent, and worst of all, the fascists had complete control of the air. Cho hadn't seen a friendly aircraft in days.

And now this. His eyes focused again on the message. He had failed—failed his men, failed his country, and failed his Great Leader.

Outside, those few staff officers he had left alive were working diligently to carry out his last orders. Under the eyes of Chinese "peacekeepers," they were overseeing the destruction of every tank, armored personnel carrier, and artillery piece left to the First Shock Army. Others marshaled the pitiful remnants of his once-proud divisions in temporary holding camps, awaiting the word to march north weaponless.

Cho clenched his fists. That was the final humiliation—to be shepherded home under the eyes of the Chinese like prisoners. And home to what fate? He had no illusions about his own destiny, but what of the thousands of men he commanded? What would happen to them? What would happen to his country?

Even now he found himself unable to imagine a nation led by anyone other than the two Kims. For forty years the Democratic People's Republic of Korea had been governed by their will and their will alone. Every aspect of public and private life had been regulated by their desires. Now all that was gone—vanished as if it had never been. The Dear Leader was dead, a heroic martyr to the Revolution, they said, and the Great Leader had retired from active government, too ill and sick at heart to carry on. Cho's whole world had changed in the blink of an eye.

"Comrade General?" The voice of his aide, Captain Sung, startled him. He'd lost track of time. It must be nearly sundown.

"Come in." Cho stood and straightened his uniform. Appearances must be preserved at all costs.

The tent flap opened, admitting a gust of frigid air, Lieutenant General Chyong, and an officer he didn't recognize, a tall, gaunt-faced man in a crisp, unwrinkled uniform.

Under layers of fatigue and dirt, Chyong's face looked as if it had been carved from stone. "I'm sorry to intrude, Comrade. But Senior Colonel Yun"—he pointed to the newcomer—"has just arrived from Pyongyang with important dispatches."

Cho couldn't hide his surprise. "From Pyongyang? How is that possible?"

Yun clicked his heels sharply and bowed. "The Chinese People's Liberation Army was kind enough to arrange my safe passage through enemy lines."

"Then your mission must be urgent indeed." Cho felt colder still. The Chinese bore him little love.

"Indeed it is, Comrade General." Yun reached into his tunic and pulled out a folded piece of paper. "I have special orders for this headquarters from the Korean Workers' Party."

There was a deadly formalism behind the man's polite words, and Cho suddenly realized that the colonel's uniform bore the insignia of the Political Security Bureau—the secret police organization responsible for ensuring the ideological purity of the armed forces. With trembling fingers Cho reached out and took the paper from Yun's hand.

It was what he had expected since that first message from Pyongyang arrived.

Cho looked up. "This arrest order applies to General Chyong as well?"

Yun nodded. "Yes, Comrade General. I am commanded to take both of you back to Pyongyang to stand trial before a Workers' Court."

Chyong interrupted for the first time and demanded, "On what charge?"

The colonel eyed him coldly for a moment before replying, "On charges of high treason, of conniving with the enemy, and of deliberately engineering defeat."

Chyong's anger overrode any other consideration. "What fools have put together that tissue of lies?"

"The new General Secretary of the Party and his new minister of public security. And you would do well to remember to show them the proper respect." Yun's hand dropped to his holstered pistol.

Cho laid a hand on his subordinate's shoulder, restraining him as Chyong bit back a bitter curse. "And why have they chosen us for this singular treatment?"

The colonel chose his words carefully. "It is felt in Pyongyang that the 'masterful' strategic plan of our departed Dear Leader was"—he paused—"poorly executed."

Yun spread his hands and stared into Cho's eyes. "You and Lieutenant General Chyong commanded the main elements of this offensive. Its success or failure hinged on your actions, your skills."

"We did everything possible to ensure success," Chyong answered heatedly. "We were defeated by a combination of superior air and naval power. Our ground forces performed superbly. Nothing more could have been asked of them. Look at our rates of advance, at the casualties we inflicted on the enemy. If you want scapegoats, find them in Pyongyang. By every objective standard, General Cho and I have—"

"Comrade General, please." Yun's voice was ice cold. "The issue is not what was done, but what was not done. The liberation failed, and that is enough to convict you a thousand times over."

He looked back at Cho, who still stood motionless. "In any event, that is unimportant here. For the moment you are both relieved of command. Your respective deputies should be able to supervise the withdrawal of our troops." His last words were spat out as if they carried a foul taste.

"I see." Cho stepped back and sat clumsily in his camp chair. He lifted his eyes to Yun and in a flat, emotionless voice asked, "These are the most serious charges I can imagine the State bringing against any person. What penalty will the State exact if we are found guilty?"

"Death." Yun didn't try to soften it in any way.

Cho nodded. He knew the kind of trial he and Chyong would be given. It would be public, humiliating, and absolutely merciless. Their guilt or innocence would not be a factor. They would serve as the State's whipping boys, as the men who failed their people. No, he thought, remembering Yun's words, as the men who had deliberately sabotaged the now-dead Dear Leader's strategy.

And at the end? Nothing to look forward to except a public execution. He nodded slowly to himself, calm now that the decision had been made for him.

Chyong paid him little attention. He stood eye to eye with Yun, raging. "These charges are absurd! Our only crime is that we failed to win."

"That, Comrade General, is the only crime that matters," Yun replied.

Cho stood again, outwardly composed. "Colonel Yun, I submit to your arrest." He looked meaningfully at the man. "But I would like your permission to be alone for a few minutes. I have some personal business to attend to."

Yun studied him carefully and at length nodded. "Certainly, Comrade General. You will have all the time you need."

"Thank you, Colonel. I appreciate your kindness." Cho turned to his subordinate. "You must excuse me, Chyong, but I must ask you to leave as well. I wish you good fortune."

"Of course, sir." Chyong's understanding showed in his eyes. He saluted and stalked out of the tent, followed closely by the colonel.

Slowly Cho's shoulders sagged and he sank back into his chair. For a moment he considered writing a letter to his wife, but then decided against it. He had brought her enough pain already. His hand reached for the pistol atop his desk.

The muffled sound of the shot from inside the tent startled Chyong, even though he had known it would come. He stood rigid facing the closed tent flap.

Yun's voice came from behind him. "So, General Cho has chosen the easier path. Well, he looked like a wise man to me."

Chyong didn't turn around. His voice dripped with contempt. "General Cho was an older man, worn down by this war. I have no intention of making things so easy for you and your Chinese cronies. Go ahead. Put me on trial. I'll fight your lies and falsehoods at every turn."

Chyong heard Yun unsnap his pistol holster and sigh. "You soldiers ... you are so blind at times."

Chyong started to turn, but the bullet caught him first.

JANUARY 25—THE WHITE HOUSE, WASHINGTON, D.C.

Blake Fowler scanned the draft press release quickly, not at all surprised by its contents.

"See any problems?" the President asked blandly.

He shook his head and handed it back to the White House communications director, who sat beside him in front of the President's desk.

The phone buzzed. Blake saw the President pick it up, listen, and smile. "Sure, June, send him right on in."

The President hung up and grinned at his two subordinates. "Gentlemen, it seems that my esteemed national security adviser seeks an audience. I've always said he had perfect timing."

The door to the antechamber opened and Putnam came in, stuffed uncomfortably into a brand-new, double-breasted suit and silk tie that looked one size too small. His hair was now more gray than red, and he wore a grim, determined expression.

"Now, George, what can I do for you this morning?" The President's voice was genial, but his eyes were cold.

"I've come to submit my resignation, Mr. President." Putnam handed him a single-spaced, single-page letter. His hands shook. "I waited until this terrible crisis was over so that both you and the nation wouldn't be deprived of my services when they were most needed. But now, I feel compelled to withdraw from this administration."

"You're leaving your post?" the President asked, seemingly thunderstruck. Blake hid a grin. The critics who said the nation's chief executive couldn't act had obviously never seen him perform in private.

"Yes, Mr. President." Putnam's voice rose higher and quavered. "I've had all I can take. You've systematically cut me out of any substantive policy role over these past few weeks. Instead, you've chosen to rely on political neophytes and hapless academics." He scowled at Blake and then went on. "Well, I won't stand still for it."

"I see. Well, then . . . ." The President took Putnam's letter of resignation, pretended to study it for a moment, and then tore it in half.

Putnam stared at the pieces, utterly surprised. "You're not accepting my resignation?"

The President shook his head slowly. "No, I'm not, Mr. Putnam." He turned to the director of communications. "Rick, show him what you've got there."

Putnam took the draft press release and started reading it. Halfway through he turned sheet-white and stopped. "You're firing me?"

The President nodded somberly. "Absolutely, Mr. Putnam.

And publicly, too. You lied to me, and your lies helped cause a war that cost tens of thousands of lives." He paused. "All things considered, I think you're getting off damned easily."

Putnam didn't seem to hear him. "But my career, what will I d—"

"Get out." The President didn't bother to conceal his disdain. "Any personal effects you've left in your office will be shipped to your home. But get out of my sight right now."

Blake watched his former boss leave, unable to suppress a momentary twinge of guilt at the joy he'd felt in seeing the man torn down. But it passed. The President was right. Putnam was getting off easy. Disgrace only mattered if you had a conscience, and that was something the former national security adviser seemed to lack.

He suddenly realized that the President was watching him closely. "Not a pretty sight, was it, Blake?"

"No, sir. It wasn't."

The President nodded. "Necessary, though." He picked up a file folder from his desk. "Now, that brings me to my next problem. Having rid myself of the son of a bitch, I need to find a replacement for him. Got any ideas?"

Blake thought carefully. "Well, Mr. President. There are any number of qualified people I'd recommend. There's—"

"Yes, I know there are," the President interrupted him. "But there's one man I've heard some very good things about. People tell me he'd make a top-notch adviser. I'm inclined to nominate him, but I'd like to know what you think first." He hefted the folder and passed it to Blake. "Here's his personnel file."

Blake looked at the name stenciled across the top of the folder—DR. BLAKE FOWLER—and blinked. He sat still, thinking hard. It would mean more work and more hours away from his family. But it was also work he could do and do well. And Mandy would back him. Hell, she'd kill him if he turned this down.

He looked up at the President and smiled. "I think he'd be very honored, Mr. President."

FEBRUARY 4—THE DRAGON WATER MOUNTAIN RESTAURANT, SEOUL

Seoul, though battered, was unbowed.

With rubble still blocking key streets and armed soldiers standing guard on every corner, Seoul's merchants and restaurateurs were bringing their city back to life as fast as they could. Their guts and native drive were a constant reminder that South Korea's identification with the phoenix was apt indeed.

Tony Christopher had picked the restaurant tonight with great care. The Yongsuan was one of the best. Not cheap, but money wasn't very important right now—and certainly not tonight.

This place was perfect for his purpose. They served authentic Korean royal court dishes in private rooms. They'd also been lucky enough to escape any war damage. One of his other favorite hangouts wasn't much more than a hole in the ground and a few charred timbers.

Tony admired Anne in the candlelight. The rich decor of the room complemented both her dress and her red hair. She'd been talking about her work rebuilding the Army's battered logistics system, and Tony had been half-listening in a mode known to men the world over. He wasn't bored, but there were other matters on his mind.

Tonight they were celebrating the second week of peace since the official armistice. At least that was the reason he'd given her when he'd made the date. He smiled suddenly. She'd probably even believed him.

Anne stopped talking momentarily to smile back and then went on. "So anyway, everything was so scrambled, they're really letting us start from scratch. I just finished blocking out a completely new system. New computers, new software, new procedures."

Tony made an enthusiastic sound somewhere down in his throat and then started his approach. "Anne, can I change the subject for just a second?"

"Of course, darling." She smiled brilliantly and then deepened her voice, trying out a thick French accent. "Ah, my darleeing, let us, how you say, talk about us."

He chuckled softly, then looked closer at her. "No, really, Anne. I have some important news." His serious expression erased her smile.

There was no easy way to say it. "I received new orders this morning—posting me back to the States. They want me to do some intelligence work at Nellis, then I take over as the ops officer of the Aggressor Squadron."

Anne could hear the mixture of pride and sorrow in his voice and wondered which was stronger.

She sat silent for a moment or two, and then in a quiet, even voice she asked him, "Where is Nellis?"

"Just outside Las Vegas."

Five thousand miles away. "When do you have to leave?"

Tony looked down at his hands. "In nine days. I'm turning my ops duties over to 'Otto' Sanchez. He's a good man. And Hooter's going to be the new leader for First Flight."

He reached out and took her hand. "Look, Anne, this wasn't supposed to happen so suddenly. Technically my tour wasn't supposed to be up for another two and a half months. The Air Force just wants to get its combat veterans into the training system as quickly as possible. Also, I think the combat losses we suffered have screwed up the normal rotation . . ."

Tony stopped talking and looked closely at Anne. In the soft candlelight it was hard to see that she was weeping softly. "Honey?"

She spoke quietly. "I was so happy. Everything was going so well. This messes up everything."

"No, it doesn't." He took a small, felt-covered box out of his pocket and opened it. Moving carefully, almost tenderly, he set it on the table in front of Anne.

He took a deep breath and whispered, "Will you marry me?"

Anne just looked at it. Her expression changed, from sorrow to surprise to joy to shock and then to confusion. Inside the box was a beautiful diamond ring.

She started to reach out for it, but suddenly she pulled her hand back. "I don't know, Tony. It's too quick. Is this wise?"

He felt his heart racing in panic. Christ, this was a lot worse than flying combat. "Anne, I love you, and you love me. I want us to have a future together."

Her eyes closed and Tony saw the tears glistening in her long lashes. "I love you, too, but I wasn't ready to think about marriage."

He reached out and took her other hand, feeling her pulse jump against his fingers. "We might have had two more months before I rotated out at the end of my one-year tour, but this is forcing our hand. The war shocked me into understanding how I felt about you—"

"Me, too," she added quietly.

"—and now the aftermath is forcing my hand again."

"Our hands," she said.

Tony leaned closer. "Anne, I can't think of any other way to say this. I really love you and I want to spend the rest of my life with you. I want to marry you because, scary as the thought of marriage is, the thought of being apart is even more scary."

Her eyes opened and the hint of a smile appeared on her lips. "Keep talking, I love the things you say."

He felt himself turning red. "C'mon, Anne, I'm dead serious."

She smiled again, more gently this time. "And so am I. I love you, and I do love what you're saying. I also want to marry you, but really, sweetheart, is this wise?"

"Look, Anne, I'm not talking about getting married tomorrow, but when I thought of me being in the States and you being here, I couldn't stand it. We might have arrived at the same decision in a month or two. My orders just gave us a nudge." He smiled tentatively. "And in the right direction, too, I hope."

Anne sat, considering. She pretended to frown. "This really isn't fair. You've had all day to decide to ask me, and now I have to decide yes or no right now."

Tony grinned. "You don't have to decide right now. Of course, I'll be in turmoil until you do."

"I have decided." She kissed him, disengaged her hands, and picked up the ring. "Do you think we can get all the arrangements made in less than nine days?"

FEBRUARY 6—PUSAN ARMY MEDICAL CENTER, PUSAN, SOUTH KOREA

Kevin Little walked quietly down the long row of hospital beds, looking for a familiar face. He found it near the end.

Rhee lay half-propped up against a pillow, reading a newspaper. He glanced up at Kevin's footsteps and quickly laid the newspaper aside. Bandages still covered the upper part of his chest, and he looked much thinner than Kevin remembered him. But his eyes were clear, and the South Korean's smile was still as jaunty as ever.

"This is an honor, Lieutenant . . . ," Rhee started to say, and then stopped, staring at the twin silver bars on Kevin's uniform jacket. "I mean, this is an honor, Captain Little. Please allow me to congratulate you on your promotion, sir."

Taken aback by the South Korean's earnest formality, Kevin forced a shamefaced grin. "Yeah, it surprised the hell out of me, too. The brass'll probably take it back once they've had the chance to sober up."

Rhee smiled again. "I don't think so, Captain. The rank suits you." He gestured to a chair beside his bed. "Please, sit down, sir."

Kevin sat and felt more at ease. Now that he and Rhee were on the same level, their conversation flowed more naturally. It soon turned to current events.

"Well, we're being kept pretty busy as I guess you could expect. Resettling refugees. Dealing with would-be NK defectors. Clearing rubble. You name it and we're up to our necks in it." Kevin shook his head. "Hell, sometimes I think winning the war was the easy part. It's winning the peace that's hard."

Rhee grinned lazily. "Ah, Captain, how I regret being unable to lend you a helping hand." He waved toward the pretty, white-frocked nurses working at the other end of the ward. "Alas, my prison guards there have assured me that I'll be kept chained here for another few weeks."

Kevin shook his head in admiration. "Jesus Christ, Rhee, only you could think of a way to get wounded just to dodge all the real work."

The South Korean's grin grew wider still, reminding

Kevin of a certain fabled cat. Then Rhee's expression grew more sober and he asked a serious question. "What has happened to the company?"

"It's gone." Kevin couldn't keep the hurt out of his voice, even though he'd known it had to happen. He'd grown to love the men of Echo Company. "Echo was just a provisional force. Strictly for the duration only. Once active hostilities ceased, Battalion wanted its clerks, typists, and quartermasters back. So they broke us up."

Rhee shook his head sadly.

"Well"—Kevin glanced at his watch—"I've got to head out for now. The major's called a conference for later this afternoon and I've got to catch my train." He stood up and rebuttoned his jacket.

Then he turned. "Look, they've given me Bravo Company in place of Echo. It's got some pretty good guys in it, but I'm short an executive officer." He looked down at the South Korean and said more softly, "I could use you there. You've done a pretty good job so far of keeping me alive and on track."

Rhee stared at him silently for a moment and then slowly shook his head. "No, Captain, you don't need me anymore for that. You've become a soldier on your own."

Kevin thought about that for a second and nodded abruptly. "Maybe so." Then, suddenly, he smiled and asked, "But who the hell do you expect me to play poker with if you're not there?"

For once the South Korean was the one caught at a loss for words.

Kevin grinned wider himself and tossed Rhee the pack of cards he'd brought along. "So you'd better get well fast, Lieutenant. And you'd better practice up while doing it. I don't play with amateurs."

He looked down at his friend. "I'll see you up at the Z in a few weeks. You'll like it up there. It's a pretty quiet place these days."

And with that, he turned and walked out of the ward, whistling.

GLOSSARY

A-6E Intruder: A twin-engine attack plane, the Intruder is one of the few planes that can strike a target in any weather. It is launched from carriers and has a prodigious payload. The crew of two sits side by side, and although the copilot has no flight controls, he can fly the plane by telling the plane's computer what to do.

A-7E Corsair: A single-engine, single-seat attack jet, this plane first appeared during the Vietnam War. It is classed as a "light attack" jet and lacks the sophisticated sensors and massive payload of the A-6 Intruder. It is a popular aircraft with its pilots.

AA-2 Atoll: The first Soviet heat-seeking air-to-air missile, it is a direct copy of the 1950s-vintage AIM-9B Sidewinder. Like the early model of this missile, it can attack targets only from the rear. It has a range of about two miles.

AA-7 Apex: A Soviet radar-guided missile of mediocre performance. It has a range of about twenty miles.

AA-11 Archer: A Soviet short-range, heat-seeking missile. It has a range of about four miles, and most importantly, the ability to engage enemy aircraft from the front.

AIM-54C Phoenix: A U.S. radar-guided missile, it is linked to the F-14 Tomcat's AWG-9 weapons system. This huge weapon has a range of over one hundred miles and a speed over five times the speed of sound.

AIM-7M Sparrow: The standard U.S. radar-guided missile, its 25-mile range is shorter than that of the AIM-54C Phoenix, but much longer than that of the Sidewinder or any other heat-seeking missile. It has gone through many improvements. Although the initial versions used in Vietnam were poor performers, the later makes are considered very effective.

AIM-9L Sidewinder: One of the most effective and successful missiles ever made. After launch, it homes in on the heat given off by an aircraft and explodes. Unlike earlier models, or other similar missiles of other countries, it does not need to see the hot tailpipe of a jet aircraft but can even lock onto an aircraft from the front. It has a range of about ten miles.

AK-47: A Russian-designed assault rifle, this simple, effective weapon has been exported widely and copied by many nations. It is a 7.62-caliber rifle that can be fired either in semi or full automatic. It weighs about nine and a half pounds.

AKM: A newer and slightly lighter version of the Soviet AK-47 rifle.

An-2 Colt: A Soviet biplane first designed in the late 1940s. In spite of its ancient appearance, it is an excellent performer, is cheap, and has good short-field characteristics. Popular as a light transport and utility craft, over 18,000 have been built.

APC—Armored Personnel Carrier: A general term used to describe vehicles designed to ferry infantry across the battlefield. Their light armor provides protection against artillery fragments and small-arms fire.

APS-115: A U.S. radar carried in the nose of the P-3C Orion. Called a "surface search" radar, it is used to look for ships and especially periscopes.

AS-4 Kitchen: A Soviet cruise missile, the "AS" stands for "air to surface." "Kitchen" is the NATO code name assigned to the weapon. Supersonic, it is launched from large aircraft like the Backfire. It has a range of 280 miles and a one-ton warhead. The warhead can be either high explosive or a nuclear bomb.

ASROC—Antisubmarine Rocket: Fired from Navy ships, it is used to attack submarines. A solid-fuel rocket quickly boosts a Mark 46 homing torpedo several miles to the presumed location of an enemy submarine. Once it arrives in the target area, the homing torpedo is lowered into the water by parachute. In place of the torpedo, ASROC can carry a nuclear depth charge.

ASW—Antisubmarine Warfare: The art and science of killing enemy submarines.

AWG-9 radar: The radar mounted in the nose of the F-14 Tomcat fighter. A very powerful and sophisticated unit, it allows the aircraft to track and fire AIM-54C Phoenix missiles at up to six air targets simultaneously.

BDU—Battle Dress, Uniform: The Army's new name for cam-ouflaged uniforms.

BLU-109 bomb: A type of 2,000-pound bomb. It has a special-ly hardened case that allows it to penetrate many feet of reinforced concrete before detonating.

BMP—*Bronevaya Maschina Piekhota*: A Russian armored per-sonnel carrier, it carries seven troops and has a crew of two. A modern design, it has a small turret that mounts a 73mm gun or 30mm autocannon, an antitank missile launcher, and a machine gun. It is tracked, and amphibious.

BOQ—Bachelor Officers' Quarters: A cross between an apart-ment house, a dormitory, and a zoo, it is a place for unmarried officers to live on base rent-free. Each room has a combined bedroom and living room and a small bath. There are no kitchen or cooking facilities, although there is usually a refrigerator.

BTR—*Bronetransportr:* A Russian term for a series of eight-wheeled armored personnel carriers.

BTR-60: An eight-wheeled armored personnel carrier, it first appeared in the early 1960s. The first of a long series of similar designs, it has a boat-shaped hull and can carry fourteen men. One flaw in this design is its two gasoline engines, located behind thin armor. This was corrected in later versions.

C-141 Starlifter: This four-engined transport is the stardard cargo plane for the U.S. Air Force. It can carry over 200 troops or 35 tons of cargo.

C-5 Galaxy: The largest aircraft in the U.S. inventory, this monster can carry 110 tons of cargo. It rarely carries troops but instead is used to carry items too bulky or heavy for the C-141 Starlifter.

C4: The designation for a type of plastic explosive used by the U.S. Army and others. It can be worked like modeling clay, burned, or dropped, but it will not detonate without an igniter.

CAR-15: A South Korean–built version of the U.S. M16 rifle.

CEV: The M728 Combat Engineering Vehicle looks like a cross between a bulldozer and a tank. It has a built-in crane, a bulldozer blade, and a large, low-velocity "demolition gun." It is used by the Army to clear obstacles and build entrenchments.

CH-53: A twin-engined cargo helicopter, the CH-53 was also used in Vietnam as a combat rescue helicopter, with machine guns, armor, and a hoist for recovering downed pilots from inside enemy territory. This was so successful that the idea was expanded to the present MH-53E Pave Low, an ultrasophisticated machine loaded with sensors and weapons.

CIA—Central Intelligence Agency: One of many U.S. intelligence agencies and the one most widely known. Headquartered in Langley, Virginia, across the Potomac from Washington, D.C.

CIC—Combat Information Center: The compartment of a Navy warship where displays showing information from the ship's radars, sonars, lookouts, and any other sensors are located. The ship's captain will normally "fight his ship" from here, where he can see what is going on around his vessel. It was first developed during World War II, when sea battles moved out beyond visual range.

CINCPAC—Commander in Chief Pacific: A U.S. officer in command of all American forces in the Pacific area. The post is usually occupied by an admiral, but he also controls Army, Air Force, and Marine units in his jurisdiction. Also referred to as a "unified commander."

CINCPACFLT—Commander in Chief, Pacific Fleet: The admiral in charge of all U.S. naval forces in the Pacific Ocean. He reports to CINCPAC.

Claymore mine: Most land mines are buried in the ground and are tripped when a vehicle or soldier passes over them. The Claymore is different. Spikes hold it upright on the surface of the ground. It is tripped electrically, on command, and sends out a fan-shaped pattern of steel balls that shred anything in their path. It is called a "directional" mine.

COMSUBPAC—Commander Submarines Pacific: The admiral in charge of all submarines in the Pacific Ocean. There are corresponding commanders for surface and air forces, COMSURFPAC and COMAIRPAC. All report to CINCPACFLT.

CP—Command Post: The term used to designate the location of an army unit's headquarters.

DEFCON—Defense Condition: A series of formalized levels describing the status of U.S. armed forces. DEFCON V is peacetime, IV is heightened readiness, III is crisis, DEFCON II indicates a conventional war is in progress, DEFCON I indicates a nuclear war is under way.

DICASS—Directional Command-Activated Sonobuoy: Dropped from aircraft, this device is used to help search for submarines. Once in the water, on command, it will send out sonar pings into the water.

DMZ—Demilitarized Zone: A four-kilometer-wide area between the two Koreas where no military forces are allowed. While the Zone itself is not militarized, the areas just north and south of it are very militarized. Troops stationed along it commonly refer to the Zone as the Z.

Dragon: A medium-range, wire-guided antitank missile that is fired by an infantryman. It has a thermal sight, a range of about 1,000 meters, and will penetrate all but the heaviest armor.

DSC—Defense Security Command: Part of the South Korean Army specifically tasked with watching the officer corps for signs of disloyalty or an impending coup. Their authority is absolute.

E-2C Hawkeye: A twin-engine turboprop, this plane is instantly recognizable by the massive radar saucer that sits on top of the fuselage. Carrying a crew of radar operators and fighter controllers, the E-2C can see air and surface contacts hundreds of miles out and control the defense of a task force. It carries no weapons and is relatively slow.

E-3 Sentry: An ultrasophisticated AWACS—airborne early warning and control system—built into a Boeing 707 fuselage. Like the E-2C Hawkeye, the E-3 is characterized by a massive radar saucer and by its ability to monitor and control air battles within a several-hundred-mile radius.

EA-6B Prowler: A heavily modified A-6 Intruder, this twin-jet aircraft carries powerful jamming equipment in the fuselage and in pods under the wings. The A-6's normal crew of two is doubled to four, three of whom operate the Prowler's electronics. It can interfere with enemy weapons, radars, and radio communications at long ranges.

ELINT—Electronic Intelligence: Aircraft equipped with sensitive receivers patrol off enemy coasts or near enemy ships, recording the radar and communications signals they detect. The information is then taken back to base and analyzed.

EMCON—Emission Control: Radars and radio send out active signals, emissions, that can be detected (see *ESM*). Emission Control is used to restrict such transmissions and reduce a task force's chance of being detected.

ESM—Electronic Support Measures: This meaningless term is the name for a type of sensor carried on warships and some aircraft. It is used to detect the radar transmissions of other ships and aircraft, and to determine their nature and direction.

ETR: Estimated Time of Repair.

F-14A Tomcat: A huge, carrier-launched fighter, it is designed exclusively to engage enemy aircraft at long range with Phoenix and Sparrow radar-guided missiles. It is also fairly maneuverable and carries Sidewinders and a 20mm cannon for close-in work. It has two engines and a crew of two.

F-16 Falcon: A single-engine, single-seat fighter used by the U.S. Air Force. An excellent "dogfighter," at present it lacks the capability to fire long-range, radar-guided missiles.

F-15 Eagle: A twin-engine, single-seat fighter used by the U.S. Air Force. Almost as maneuverable as the F-16 Falcon, it is much larger and can fire long-range, radar-guided missiles.

F-18A Hornet: A twin-engine, single-seat jet designed to re-place the A-7 Corsair II. The F-18A is a multirole aircraft intended to be equally adept as either an attack aircraft or an air-superiority fighter. It is very maneuverable and is designed to be launched from carriers.

F-4 Phantom II: A twin-engine, two-seat fighter, it was designed by the U.S. and exported widely. In terms of the number produced and different roles it has performed, the F-4 is probably one of the most successful aircraft of all time. It can carry radar-guided missiles, but is used by the South Korean Air Force for ground attack, at which it is most effective.

FAC—Forward Air Controller: Fast-moving jet aircraft have trouble picking out small, camouflaged ground targets. Forward Air Controllers fly in slow-flying aircraft at low altitude and act as "spotters" for the attack jet. They find enemy targets, sometimes mark them with smoke rockets or a laser designator, and steer the incoming air strike right in on top of the enemy.

FEBA—Forward Edge of the Battle Area: An Army term meaning the point where U.S. and enemy troops are in contact.

Feniks sonar: A Russian sonar carried by Romeo-class submarines. It is a forty-year-old design and has extremely short range.

GAO—Government Accounting Office: The fiscal watchdog of the federal government.

GAU-8/A gun: A 30mm Gatling gun mounted in the nose of the A-10 Warthog. Designed specifically for tank killing, the gun has a rate of fire of 4,200 rounds per minute. It fires a special round made of fantastically heavy depleted uranium.

GRU—*Glavnoye Razvedyvatelnoye Upravleniye:* Chief Intelligence Directorate, Soviet General Staff. Soviet military intelligence, responsible for collecting information on the military forces of opposing countries.

GSP—*Gusenichnii Samokhodnii Porom:* The Russian name for a tracked amphibious ferry used to carry tanks and other heavy equipment across a river.

HARM—High Speed Antiradiation Missile: An air-launched missile designed to home in on enemy surveillance and guidance radars and destroy them.

Harpoon: The American-made Harpoon missile can be fired from ships, from aircraft, and even from submarines. This versatile antiship missile can carry its 500-pound warhead to targets up to 60 nautical miles away.

HARTs—Hardened Artillery Site: A type of fortification used by the North Koreans to protect artillery from attack.

HQ: Headquarters.

HUD—Heads Up Display: Projects important information onto the windscreen directly in front of the pilot's eyes, making it possible to avoid going "heads down" to look at cockpit instruments. The HUD is a vital aid during a fast-moving air combat. The data displayed on the windscreen includes speed, altitude, weapons status, g forces, target data, and fuel status.

IFF—Identification Friend or Foe: An airplane or ship sends a coded electronic signal out to an unknown contact. A black box on an aircraft, if it receives the proper code, responds with a signal of its own, telling the observer that the aircraft is friendly. Aircraft without the proper codes are the enemy. The codes are changed daily.

Il-18 Coot: An elderly Russian four-engine airliner. Versions are used by the military and by Aeroflot, the Soviet Union's civilian airline.

Il-76 Mainstay: Based on a large, four-engine jet transport, this radar plane has a large saucer radome on top of the fuselage. It can monitor air and sea movements up to several hundred miles away. It is the rough equivalent of the American E-3 Sentry.

INS—Inertial Navigation System: This device keeps track of the user's position by measuring his movements in three dimensions. The result is most often displayed on a small map or as a latitude and longitude readout. When started, an INS must always be "told" where it is.

IP—Initial Point: A U.S. Air Force term that refers to the geographic location used as the start point for an approach to a target.

ITV—Improved TOW vehicle: This converted M113 armored personnel carrier mounts a two-tube launcher on top to fire TOW antitank missiles. The launcher and its attached sight can be extended several feet into the air, allowing the vehicle to stay hidden while searching for targets.

Jian-7: The Chinese designation for their copy of the Soviet MiG-21 fighter.

KA-6D tanker: A modified version of the A-6 Intruder, this plane is fitted with a hose and reel. It is launched from carriers and is used to refuel the other planes in flight after they have been launched.

KATUSA—Korean Attached to U.S. Army: Term for a South Korean soldier serving as part of an American Army unit.

KGB—*Komitet Gosudatstvennoy Sigurnost:* Committee for State Security. The Soviet organization responsible for the security of the Soviet state inside and outside its own borders. It deals with subversion, espionage, intelligence gathering, and other matters.

LAMPS—Light Airborne Multipurpose System: See *SH-2F Sea Sprite*.

LAW—Light Antitank Weapon: A 66mm rocket in a fiberglass tube, this one-shot, throwaway weapon weighs about five pounds. It has a short range and limited penetrating power, but it gives the individual soldier a powerful one-time "punch" against lightly armored vehicles, bunkers, or buildings.

LOFAR—Low Frequency Analysis: The sound signature of each submarine is subtly different, and by analyzing the sounds they make a subhunter may be able to determine the nature of his opponent. The term is also used to refer to a class of relatively inexpensive passive sonobuoys dropped from ASW aircraft to listen for enemy submarines.

LRRPs—Long Range Reconnaissance Patrols: During the Vietnam War, small detachments of soldiers were inserted deep in enemy territory, where they operated alone for extended periods of time. Specially trained, they gathered intelligence and conducted ambushes, sabotage, or assassinations.

M16: The standard U.S. Army infantry weapon, it is much lighter and smaller than its predecessor, the M14 rifle. The M16 weighs eight and a half pounds. It can be fired on semi or full automatic.

M-48 tank: This vehicle was first designed in the early 1950s. Mounting a 90mm gun and with a gasoline engine, it was used by American armored units and exported widely. Obsolete since the 1960s, many have been reworked with larger 105mm guns, diesel engines, and improved fire-control systems.

M-60 tank: The M-60 tank mounts a 105mm gun and served as the U.S. military's main battle tank for nearly two decades. It is still in service, but is being gradually replaced in front-line units by the M-1 Abrams.

M60 machine gun: The standard U.S. Army machine gun, it is actually derived from a World War II German design, the MG 42. It weighs 23 pounds and is normally fired from a bipod.

M61 Vulcan: This revolutionary 20mm cannon revived the "Gatling gun" principle for use as an aircraft weapon. It has a rate of fire of over 3,000 rounds per minute. First appearing in the 1950s, this principle has since been applied to other calibers (see *GAU-8*).

M-113: An armored personnel carrier first deployed in 1960, it is little more than a thinly armored box on treads. Armed only with a .50-caliber machine gun, it remains popular and cheap—despite its inadequate protection. It is being replaced in the U.S. Army by the M-2 Bradley Infantry Fighting Vehicle.

M-577: A heavily modified version of the M113 armored personnel carrier, it is equipped to serve as a mobile command post.

MAC—Military Airlift Command: Part of the U.S. Air Force, it operates their fleet of transport aircraft and is responsible for ensuring the rapid air movement of U.S. troops and equipment to trouble spots around the globe.

MAD—Magnetic Anomaly Detector: A sensor carried on Navy subhunting aircraft. It detects the distortions in the earth's magnetic field caused by the presence of several thousand tons of steel making up a submarine's hull.

Mark 82: One of a series of low-drag bombs used by the United States and other countries. The Mark 82 weighs 250 pounds, the Mark 83 1,000 pounds, and the Mark 84 2,000 pounds.

MiGs: "MiG" stands for "Mikoyan and Gureyivich," whose aircraft designs have been produced since World War II. Other design bureaus have also produced fighter designs, but the MiG series has been the most famous and the most successful. All Russian aircraft have been assigned code names by NATO, since they do not give their aircraft names like "Falcon" or "Eagle." Fighter code names always begin with *F*, bombers with *B*, and special-purpose aircraft with *M*.

MiG-19 UTI: A twin-engine, single-seat fighter that appeared after the Korean War, the MiG-19 Farmer is an older design that is still fairly maneuverable and has shown that it can take some punishment and still survive. The "UTI" is the Soviet abbreviation for the two-seat training version.

MiG-21 "Fishbed": The MiG-21 is a single-engine, single-seat fighter designed by the Soviets but widely distributed to their allies. Though an older design, it is still a fairly maneuverable aircraft and a dangerous opponent in a close-in dogfight. It carries a primitive radar and radar-guided missiles in addition to heat-seekers and a cannon.

MiG-23 "Flogger": The MiG-23 is a single-engine, single-seat fighter also distributed by the Soviets. Very fast, it is a notoriously poor dogfighter. It does have a fairly effective radar and radar-guided missiles to take advantage of that fact.

MiG-29 "Fulcrum": A brand-new Soviet fighter that has been heavily exported to their allies. While not quite as good as current U.S. designs, the twin-engined MiG-29 is too close for comfort. It is equipped with a good radar and missile armament.

MLR—Main Line of Resistance: Term for a line defining the forward edge of a military unit's main defensive position.

MRE—Meals Ready to Eat: The modern replacement for the legendary "C" rations, an MRE is a series of plastic pouches filled with freeze-dried foods. While individual opinions vary, on the whole they are seen as a vast improvement over their predecessors.

NSP—National Security Planning Agency: The new name for the KCIA, or Korean Central Intelligence Agency. This organization is responsible for stopping espionage and subversion threatening the Republic of Korea.

OP—Observation Post: A small, often concealed, position occupied by one or two men whose mission is to provide early warning of enemy movement.

OV-10D Bronco: A twin-turboprop observation plane, it was designed during Vietnam to serve as a forward air controller. It has a crew of two and carries a small weapons load of its own.

P-3C Orion: A four-engine turboprop, this successful design is based on the Lockheed Electra airliner. Instead of passengers, the fuselage carries many different sensors, computers, and a bomb bay full of sonobuoys and homing torpedoes.

PFC: Private First Class.

PMP—*Pontonno-Mostovoi Park:* The name for a type of Russian pontoon bridge.

Radar-Guided Missiles: All air-to-air missiles have some sort of guidance mechanism to help them find the target. The two most common types are infrared, or heat-seeking, systems, such as the AIM-9L Sidewinder, and radar-guided systems, such as the AIM-7M Sparrow. Essentially, radar-guided missiles home in on a target "painted" by a friendly radar. They are longer-ranged than heat-seeking missiles and can usually attack a target from any angle. They are also more complex and cost more to build.

RF-5A: A reconnaissance variant of the F-5A Freedom Fighter. It is a small, simple, twin-engine fighter with the armament removed and cameras installed in the nose. Its only defense is speed.

RIO—Radar Intercept Officer: The U.S. Navy term for the flight officer in the backseat of a two-seat fighter, such as the F-14 Tomcat or F-4 Phantom II. While the pilot flies the aircraft, the RIO operates the plane's complex weapons systems.

ROK—Republic of Korea: South Korea.

RORSAT—Radar Ocean Reconnaissance Satellite: A Russian radar satellite that searches for ships. It can transmit information back to naval headquarters in the Soviet Union or even provide targeting data directly to surface ships or subs with long-range weapons.

RPG—Rocket-Propelled Grenade: Russian designation for a series of simple antitank weapons. The most common is the RPG-7, which is a shoulder-fired weapon with a short range.

RPK: A Russian designation for a light machine gun of mediocre performance, especially when compared to the U.S. M60 machine gun. It weighs a little over 12 pounds.

R.S.F.S.R.—Russian Soviet Federated Socialist Republic: The largest of the fifteen republics making up the Soviet Union. The R.S.F.S.R. contains more than half the Soviet population and three-quarters of the nation's territory. It stretches from the Baltic Sea in the west to the shores of the Pacific Ocean in the east—including all of Siberia.

RTO—Radio Telephone Operator: Any soldier assigned to carry and operate a unit's radio. He is usually found near the officers.

S-60: The designation for a Russian-designed twin 57mm antiaircraft gun. They are normally deployed in batteries of six or regiments of twenty-four. The guns are radar-guided.

SA-2 Guideline: An elderly Soviet antiaircraft missile. The "SA" stands for "surface to air." It is designed to engage high-altitude targets.

SA-7 Grail: A small, shoulder-fired missile with a heat-seeker. It can engage low-altitude targets at close range. A later version, the SA-14 Gremlin, has improved performance.

SA-8 Gecko: A newer, mobile antiaircraft missile, it can engage aircraft at low and medium altitude. It is completely self-sufficient, with the radar and missiles mounted on an amphibious wheeled vehicle.

SA-N-8: A naval version of the shoulder-fired SA-14 Gremlin, it is a short-range, heat-seeking antiaircraft missile.

Sabot: Technically the French word for "shoe," it is also the name for an armor-piercing tank shell. A small superheavy tungsten alloy or depleted-uranium penetrator is fixed to a larger boot, the sabot, which is the same size as the tank's main gun barrel. When the round is fired, the boot falls away as it leaves the barrel, freeing the penetrator for its fight to the target.

SACEUR—Supreme Allied Commander in Europe: A NATO command, the billet is occupied by a four-star general who would command all NATO forces in Europe in wartime.

SAM—Surface-to-Air Missile: A general term applied to any missile used to shoot at aircraft.

SAR—Search and Rescue: The use of aircraft and specialized rescue teams to search for and recover aircrews downed behind enemy lines.

SH-2F Sea Sprite: A small twin-engine helicopter with a crew of three. It can land and take off from the fantail of a small warship and search for ships or chase down sonar contacts. It can carry torpedoes or depth charges for use against enemy subs. It is also called the LAMPS Mark I, for "Light Airborne Multipurpose System."

SH-60B Seahawk: A twin-engine helicopter designed to replace the SH-2F Sea Sprite. Equipped with powerful engines and advanced electronics, the Seahawk is also called the LAMPS Mark III. It can search for surface ships or submarines and attack both types of targets.

SIGINT—Signals Intelligence: Similar to ELINT, it encompasses both the collection of enemy electronic emissions and the later analysis of those emissions.

SMG: Submachine gun.

Sonobuoys: Small, air-droppable sonar devices used to detect submarines. They may be either active pinging sonars or passive listening devices. ASW aircraft and helicopters usually carry large numbers of sonobuoys.

SOP—Standard Operating Procedure: Standardized instructions covering the optimum procedures for many different types of operations—for everything from forming a convoy to attacking a bunker. Because it is supposed to be "standard" Army-wide, it allows different units to cooperate more efficiently.

Soviet submarine designations: The Soviets do not reveal their names or designations for their submarines. NATO has thus designated each class of Soviet subs with a letter of the phonetic alphabet—Alfa, Bravo, Charlie, and so on. They are not designated in sequence, so that the Kilo-class diesel-electric submarines actually appeared after the Tango-class.

SQS-56 sonar: A medium-frequency sonar carried on the U.S. O.H. Perry-class frigate. While not as powerful as other American sonar designs, it is more effective in shallow water.

SS-N-2C Styx: A Soviet-designed surface-to-surface missile. With a range of roughly 46 miles, the Styx is intended to give even small naval vessels a powerful punch. The missile has been fired in anger in a number of conflicts around the world, and it has sunk a number of warships and merchantmen.

However, the Styx has proven ineffective against newer, more sophisticated missile defenses.

Su-7 Fitter: Produced by the Sukhoi design bureau, this thirty-year-old design is a single-engine, single-seat attack aircraft. It has poor range and can carry only a mediocre payload.

Su-27 Flanker: A new twin-engine, single-seat Soviet fighter. Roughly equal to the U.S. F-15 in performance, it carries a large number of radar-guided missiles.

T-55: An older Soviet tank with a relatively weak 100mm gun and many design flaws. Among other things, the ammunition is poorly protected, so that any solid hit on the tank is likely to detonate the shells.

T-62A: The successor to the T-55 tank, the T-62A first appeared in the 1960s. It mounts a 115mm gun and improved fire-control system. It has thicker armor but compares poorly with its U.S. equivalent, the M60 tank.

T-72 tank: A modern Russian design, the T-72 mounts a 125mm gun and improved armor. It has several flaws, notably its fire-control system and a cranky automatic loader. Nevertheless, the T-72's heavy armor is still hard to penetrate, especially from the front.

TACCO—Tactical Coordinator: A Navy term for the officer on an ASW plane who controls the attack. He must coordinate the use of his plane's weapons and sensors, and possibly those of other units as well.

TOW—Tube-launched, Optical Wire-guided missile: A large, long-range antitank missile that first saw service in Vietnam and was a spectacular success. Since then it has been improved and is now the standard U.S. heavy antitank weapon. It has a range of 3,750 meters.

Tu-16 Badger F: The Tu-16 Badger is a 1950s-vintage twin-jet bomber. It has been used in many different roles since its introduction. The "F" model is loaded with electronic sensors designed to record information on enemy transmissions.

Voyska PVO: The Soviet name for their air defense forces, which are organized into a separate military service. The PVO consists of an array of early warning radars, surface-to-air missiles, and interceptors.

XO—Executive Officer: A Navy term for the officer who is second-in-command of a naval vessel. He is responsible for the day-to-day administration of the ship, while the captain keeps track of the big picture.

Z: Slang for DMZ or Demilitarized Zone.

ZSU-23-4 Shilka: A Soviet tracked antiaircraft vehicle, it carries four 23mm antiaircraft cannon. It has an onboard radar and is considered a dangerous opponent.

ZU-23: A Russian twin 23mm cannon on a ground mounting, it has a limited effect but the advantage of being cheap and numerous.